HAWAI'I

ALSO BY MARK PANEK

Big Happiness

Gaijin Yokozuna

Acclaim for Mark Panek

Big Happiness

"Panek's *Big Happiness* proves to be one of the most socially important and poignant books to come out of Hawai'i in recent memory."

—*Ka Palapala Po'okela Award Judge's Statement*

"[Panek's] account of Kipapa's death, including the arrest and trial of his accused killer, is a as compelling as any mystery novel…his eloquence as a writer, diligence as a researcher and insight as a longtime observer of the Hawaiian scene makes *Big Happiness* a larger, more important book than its subject suggests."

—*The Japan Times*

"This skillfully written book is not about one man or even one loving and close family. It is about all of us who love Hawai'i. It is about people who kept their heads in the sand too long."

—*The Honolulu Star-Advertiser*

"Panek's perceptive piece of investigative journalism is carefully researched and expertly written, causing the reader to feel the author was present at every event."

—*Honolulu Weekly*

"[*Big Happiness*] is a deeply researched, insightful look at the many problems facing Hawai'i's poor and rural neighborhoods, and a fitting tribute to a man who passed too soon."

—*Honolulu Magazine*

"This smartly written tale mixes the personal with the political to create a portrait of the Hawaii tourists never see."

—*New York*

Gaijin Yokozuna

"Few books in English or Japanese can match [Panek's *Gaijin Yokozuna*] in bringing sumo—and one sumotori—to vivid, compulsively readable life."

—*The Japan Times*

"Panek tells this story masterfully."

—*The Honolulu Advertiser*

HAWAI'I

a novel

MARK PANEK

LŌ'IHI PRESS
HONOLULU

This is a work of fiction. The thoughts and opinions depicted herein are those of the characters in a made-up story, and not of the writer. Further, while this is a "realistic" novel set in real places, locations such as the State Capitol, the Hawai'i Convention Center, Pauahi Tower, Aloha Stadium, and many others are used fictitiously. And while the story contains "real" characters such as football players and state senators and waiters and gangsters and power brokers and activists, every one of them has been invented, and none have been "based on" any real person.

Copyright © 2013 by Mark Panek

All rights reserved. No part of this book may be reproduced in any form or by any means, except for review purposes, without permission in writing from the publisher. This is a work of fiction. All names, places, characters, and situations are products of the author's imagination or are used fictitiously.

FIRST EDITION

ISBN-13: 978-0-9822535-3-3

Titles in *Franchise* and *League Gothic* fonts
Text in *Adobe Garamond Pro*

Printing provided by Penmar Hawai'i

Cover Design by Anyah Albert
Cover Art:
   Kahiko Hula Dancer © by Ann Cecil
   Waikiki Beach © Michael Sweet
   Dice © Robert Barclay

Lō'ihi Press
733 Bishop Street
Suite 2302
Honolulu, Hawai'i 96813
www.loihipress.com

For everyone born here who has had to move away

Contents

Acknowledgments xi

Prologue: Owned 1

Part One

A Few Remarks 13
The Rules 36
Front Page 54
The Top of the Volcano 70
Sustainable Development 80
Kapiʻolani Theater 106
Man of the House 117
Finding the Cracks 132
Obligation 152

Part Two

The Tap on the Shoulder 173
Aloha Tower Views 186
A Special Occasion 197
Executive Privilege 209
Blood on the Table 224
All In 229
Enemy Territory 248
Nearer My God to Thee 255

Part Three

Invisible Waiter..271
Opening Day..287
The Bottom Feeder...314
Exhaustion...329
Sunday Fellowship...355
Team Captain...380
Hello, Kitty!...397
Native Intelligence...406
Hawaiian at Heart...426

Part Four

God's Country..453
A Hawaiian Sense of Place..................................470
A Done Deal..494
Our Own True Sons..507

Epilogue: Game Day...537

Acknowledgments

The writer is indebted to the work of that great chronicler of late 20th century America, Tom Wolfe, whose fans will recognize the genre, and particularly its reliance on point-of-view, as one Wolfe himself borrowed from Dickens, Thackeray, and Zola. They will no doubt recognize several other nods to Wolfe as well, including the homage to his essay "Radical Chic" in chapter 26.

Further thanks to the many people who generously sat for the interviews that allowed for this Wolfe-ian brand of realism, including lobbyists, developers, journalists, activists, people who have worked in various capacities in the state capitol (including a former governor), and many others. Much of this research was funded by a grant from the UHH Research Relations Committee.

Early drafts received important feedback from Sara Collins, Nicholas Conway, Kevin A. Dineen, Apollo Harris, Anthony Holzman-Escareno, Craig Howes, Bennet Hymer, Thomas McGann, Alexei Melnick, Jerilee Negrillo, Maria O'Rourke, Michael Schuffler, and Andrew Wagner. Although these readers all appreciated the book's realism, they also understood that it is a work of fiction—that such actual locations as the State Capitol, the Hawai'i Convention Center, Pauahi Tower, Aloha Stadium, and many others are used fictitiously, and that none of the story's football players or political leaders or waiters or UH administrators or gangsters or power brokers or activists, and so on, have been based on any real person. Thanks also to Anyah Albert for her incredible design work.

Finally, none of the pages that follow could have been written or revised (and revised) without the tremendous continuous help of the novelists Chris McKinney and Robert Barclay, who provided invaluable assistance at every stage from handwritten draft to final page proof.

Prologue

OWNED

"Coach Brock, you scrub!" came the shout, its last syllable elongated so as to cut through the pouring rain across eighty rows of seats and hit its target: the angry fat man way down there on the sidelines pacing back and forth on the flood-lit and rain-soaked FieldTurf. *Scru-u-u-u-u-ub!*

They kept coming, too, these shouts from the local boyz, a whole army of them packed under the overhang in Section LL, boisterous and happy, like UH was *winning:* "You da man, Coach!"

"Automatic!"

"Ho, top shape, Coach!"

"Top *shape!*"

HEE-hee-hee-hee-hee-hee-hee-heeee!

On and on and on.

Even with the rain pounding down, the drunken shouts ricocheted all around the orange-and-yellow canyon of Aloha Stadium's fifty thousand empty seats:

"Two frikkin' minutes to go and you get your firs' touchdown!"

"Now you earning that paycheck, Coach!"

Whoo-hoo-hoo-hoo-hoooo! HEEE-hee-hee-hee-hee-hee-hee!

The boyz went right on whooping it up, even though their team was down by eighteen points to a lowly rival like UNLV—a team that, in the program's brighter days, UH used to *pound.* Anybody watching would blame the giddy mood on the alcohol, or on the strength-in-numbers camaraderie that had turned the whole day into a party, win or lose, rain or shine. Or maybe it was just more fun to take it out on that fat *haole* coach the haole-Japanee booster club had brought in. From Frikkin' *Texas.* To "restore the program." For $1.1 million.

$1.1 million!

Not that the object of all this taunting could hear any of it. Way down there, Coach Brock was busy trying to protect his already-soaked coif with the clipboard held over his head while he barked something into the helmet of Ufi Tapusoa, his lightning-quick 280-pound linebacker, the anchor of his defense, and the only one of his players with any hope of getting picked in next year's NFL draft.

Coach Brock. Stacy Brachman. A big, fat, red-faced fresh-off-the-boat Texas ball of dough dressed from head to toe in Warrior black, his drenched polo shirt now pasted to every Michelin Man fold of fat and hanging skin. The un-tucked shirt hung down, too, almost halfway to the knees, to hide that mountainous belly of his. It looked like some kind of fat man's mini-skirt.

For tradition's sake someone had also draped a couple of leafy vines of *maile* all the way around those snowman shoulders of his—a good-luck gesture that was supposed to mark him as the blessed and confident leader in this battle, but wound up making him look about as comfortable as some supersize-it Bubba tourist who gets dragged onto the hotel lūʻau stage to do some…faggot dance…in front of God and everyone.

Coach Brock.

Shoots, even if they were winning, Coach Brock would have been a target.

"News flash, Coach: It's OVA!"

Whoo-hoo-hoo-hoo-hoo! Hee-hee-hee-hee-hee!

And indeed it was *ova*. Though the clock promised to prolong the agony for another two minutes and seven seconds, way back in the third quarter, well before the rain had even begun to fall, some forty thousand weary UH fans had begun heading for the exits—no *way* Coach Brock could rally the troops back from such a hole on the last game of another dismal season. As usual, two mainland teams would fight it out on Christmas Eve in the Hawaiʻi Bowl right here at Aloha Stadium, where right now only the odd pocket of die-hards remained scattered around. Like that group across the field protected from the rain by their own upper-deck overhang. Or those drunk and painted Warrior green frat boys leaning over the rail way down in the student section. Or those weekend-in-paradise UNLV fans over by the visiting bench.

Anyone else bothering to stick around had to have some money on the game.

"Don't fuck up now, Coach Brock! You finally cova the spread!" *Hee-hee-hee-hee!* "Eh Kekoa, da bastid finally wen' cova, firs' time all season, jus' like you tell us! Now we *rolling*, cuz!"

Which was also true. Section LL remained as packed as it had been at the opening kickoff, packed full of bangers, full of playas, full of boyz dat was *rolling*, a diamond stud in every ear for ten seats over and three rows up and down. This one wore an 808 logo cap, the round gold emblem still stuck to the bill just the way B-Dolla T did it, the California rapper whose jams he was constantly downloading onto his phone. That one had on a vintage Emmitt Smith Cowboys jersey. Another wore a gold rope around his neck thick enough to tow the Ford F-350 he'd had parked out by the main entrance in some VIP section manned by his cousin from Nanakuli. And all of them—except one—every available space of their brown skin was covered with tattoos: names written in elaborate calligraphy, life-like depictions of their moms' or grandmas' faces, Chinese characters for "strength" and "death" and "mercenary," and the inevitable triangular pattern of the Hawaiian warrior—the real Warrior, not some hired Texas butterball coach. Alladeese bangers, the *real* Hawaiian warriors. *Rolling.*

"You know I neva going steer my own cousin wrong, ah Nalu," the one named Kekoa said. Kekoa was also the one whose skin was free of tattoos, who in fact displayed no visible marks of the local-boy gangsta thug. He even wore a black UH logo polo shirt over his wiry frame—the same model Coach Brock had on—as if to say he was *so* tough, *so* fearless, that his confident scowl was all he needed.

"Rodja that," Nalu said, a smile plastered from diamond stud to diamond stud beneath that acne scarred nose of his, right foot madly pumping up and down. One fat blala, Nalu, he was…basking…in the attention of…*Me*, Kekoa thought. Kekoa Meyer. The *man*. Organized this whole afternoon with a couple phone calls: an entire section at the UH game, more than forty guys, the whole stack of tickets handed, at the window, to one of his boyz for free. Plus then Kekoa has everyone bet on UH, guarantee they going cova, and they *do*, firs' time all year. They only losing by eighteen wit' almost no time left, the spread was 24½. On toppa alladat, the seats is *covered*, like Kekoa could even predict the weather, grab one of the few sections under the overhang in the whole stadium.

Aloha Stadium! As a kid Kekoa had always heard it from his dad, a bull of a proud man who'd driven a refuse truck for the City and County: this stadium is putting Hawai'i on the map! State of the art! Can move entire *sections* big as twenty-story buildings—one barn-sized diesel engine pushes them along a set of giant rails into *different configurations* for football or baseball or soccer! First of its kind, not just in the Pacific Basin, but in the world! They built it back in the New Hawai'i boom years, right next to the new freeway that was supposed to lead Honolulu development out past Pearl Harbor to the "Second City" named after it. An *announcement*: Look at us! New Hawai'i! Come Super Bowls! Come Olympics! Come Major League All Star Games! World Cup soccer! Come one and all to the Crossroads of the Pacific!

Except the big rust bucket had started corroding away the moment they erected all this naked steel right in the middle of the only crevice of south-west facing O'ahu that caught much rain at all. Every ten-twelve years, had to fleece the taxpayers for twenty million dollar scrape-and-paint jobs even though the designers had claimed the exposed I-beams and cables and girders were *supposed* to rust, that the rust would create a *protective coating*. They did get the NFL Pro Bowl. Michael Jackson. The Rolling Stones. A single MLB series. But the Olympics never made it here. One day the NFL bolted. Now the top money stream flowed from the frikken Swap Meet held under all those tents in the dusty parking lot on Saturdays. At least Kekoa's dad had passed away before the rust had frozen the movable sections into…permanent football configuration.

But right now? Dad would have been proud! If there was any one point in all these forty years that this pile of scrap metal had ever come close to fulfilling the lofty promises that had greeted its opening, it was tonight. Put Hawai'i on the map? Rodja that. Kekoa Meyer had just put Hawai'i on the frikken map all right. Just *owned* that fat fuck of a Texas coach, the state's highest paid public employee, memberships at O'ahu Country Club and the Pacific Club thrown in, house in Portlock, you fat fuckin' fifty-year-old has-been NFL benchwarmer getting *seven* figures to lead a field full of dream-big Hawaiians and Samoans and mainland junior college rejects to one sorry record after the next. I *own* you, brah. Put Hawai'i on the map? Not you. Not Coach Wagner. Von Appen. Not Greg McMackin. Not June frikken Jones. Me! Kekoa Meyer!

He turned to Javen, his cousin in the seat next to him. A narrow (relatively) gold chain hung out over Javen's official Colt Brennan jersey, his black hair jelled and cut so short you could see more brown skin than hair. Aside from Nalu, Javen was the only one in on the secret of what Kekoa had just managed to pull off, and so Kekoa was able to compress the entire sentiment that had just passed through his head into a single word:

"Owned."

Javen nodded and narrowed his eyes and said it right back, like an answer, to indicate that he'd caught the word's full poetic meaning: "Owned." And then he said, "Watch. They just going hand off to that big *solé*, Sagapolu. Every time UNLV runs out the clock, they give it to him. Mandatory."

Like a lot of Kekoa's boyz who'd pulled time, Javen, who'd been forced to serve two years in Hālawa for some "petty-anny" assault on some friend of a friend who was "acting stupid" at his cousin's sister's wedding, now punctuated many of his sentences with *mandatory*.

Sure enough, that's what was happening down under the bright lights at around the fifty yard line: the UNLV line was huddled up tight under the pouring rain in protective run formation, their lanky second string quarterback grabbing the snap and burying the ball deep in the gut of Sagapolu, who squeezed it into his stomach with both hands and lumbered forward in classic clock-eating fumble-prevention style. Two or three more shots at Hawai'i's exhausted line and he'd get a first down, allowing the remaining seconds to tick away and, in so doing, complete the masterpiece of Kekoa Meyer.

"Show your tits, Coach! Show your tits!" Nalu was shouting. *HEE-hee-hee-hee-hee-hee-hee!* And the taunts started raining down again, the entire…army…whooping it up some more. "Automatic!"

Yeah, automatic. If Kekoa had known how easy it was going to be, he'd have tried it years ago. All you needed was one or two solid local boys from the next generation down, boys who *looked up to you*, who could call you "Uncle" without making you feel old at 42 because they'd been calling you that for fifteen years now. And Kekoa had one: Kyle Ching, the son of his cousin Boy, who'd had to move to Vegas back in the '90s to find work. When Kyle wound up covering receivers in the UNLV defensive backfield last year, Kekoa's plan pretty much presented itself all on its own. All he'd had to do was pull out his phone say three words: "Keep it close." And the kid *knew*: no questions about the 24½ point spread, no discussion of strategy. Kyle had just slipped into the pidgin-English tone he liked to use to show his Uncle Kekoa how *local* he was even though he grew up in Vegas and said, "No worry, Uncle—we get 'um for you." All that remained, as the events of the game had dictated, was for Kyle to tangle legs with the safety on UH's last possession, leaving the sure-handed Leshawn Walker wide open for the score that had cut UNLV's lead to...eighteen points.

The torrential rains had helped Kyle Ching pull it off so smoothly that no one could have noticed—though it occurred to Kekoa, just as that fat *solé* Sagapolu was smothering another handoff, that he'd maybe like to see the whole play dissected on SportsCenter, all the way back to Boy's decision to move to Vegas. And not like he wanted to *take credit* for what had just happened. It was just that people needed to *know* that this Hawaiian had just...owned!...not just the $1.1 million imported haole coach, but the whole docta-lawyer booster club Honolulu *elite*, all the local Chinese and Japanese and haoles who'd all trodded off to their Beemers and Lexus LX 670 SUVs in the third quarter to drive back to Portlock and Mariner's Ridge and Niu Valley. This *Hawaiian*: just *owned* all you motherfuckers.

That right there is what Dad would have been proud of.

He turned to Javen again...except...the thought was so deep, no way you could share it with Javen without coming off as...gay. Even though both cousins had wives who were still smoking hot after three kids each, fuck, hadda man up. Man up like Javen himself, every one of his fat fingers cut by one skull-shaped ring biting into it as he grabs that tub of Heineken. Maybe Kekoa could wear the same frikken shirt as Coach Brock, maybe he'd always been so NOT-gay that he could even do well in school, had the raw courage to walk straight up to some thug outside some Keʻeaumoku strip bar and *send him home* even though he packing heat—but he was...petrified...for even *looking* anything *close* to one fag. So he just tried to convey the whole thing with a silent nod.

All the same thoughts must have been bouncing around in Javen's head, because he shot back a narrow-eyed smile and said, "Dis going send one *loud* message, cuz." Then he drained the rest of his Heineken and said it again: "Loud."

Except Javen wasn't talking about the Honolulu elite, or even Coach Brock. He was talking about the *solés*, the Samoans. SportsCenter or not, the *solés* would find out what had really just gone down. And once they knew that Kekoa Meyer could *fix a UH game*, they would all stand in line, and for the first time in almost 25 years, the *power* would be consolidated in one man.

After that, keep building, and who knows? Look around: maybe you have Aloha Stadium surrounded by Pearl Harbor, Hickam Air Force Base, Fort Shafter and Red Hill military housing. But look north, *mauka*: Hālawa State Correctional Facility, the place bursting with just-scrap tough-as-nails young and energetic *Hawaiians*. Build a big enough army of us and maybe you could start to…push back…carve something out of that…elite…all of it starting from right here in Section LL, now rocking with drunken laughter, right here from Aloha Stadium, here in the pouring rain right at the Crossroads of the Pa—

"*No!*" The word exploded out of forty mouths at once, the whole section on its feet roaring it out again and again: "No! No! No!" Roaring! Because—*No!*—Fia Sagapolu had somehow broken through the line and straight into the arms of the only first-team All-WAC player on Coach Brock's sorry team, into the arms of Ufi Tapusoa, and—No!—*bounced off*, spinning his big beefy body around to his right and then churning his stumpy legs into a full sprint down the sideline, 50, 40, 30…this not *happening*! Not *here*! And then a full swan dive into the end zone that smothered the angry shouts.

All at once a heavy silence hung over Section LL, which was suddenly quieter than even the surrounding rows upon rows of empty seats, quieter for the fact that more than forty testosterone-soaked Hawaiian playas who only seconds earlier had been lost in a happily drunken boisterous victory party now sat seething and pouting in the worst possible kind of down-to-the-intestines this-shit-ain't-*right* kind of anger: six long rows of empty blank stares from one end to the other.

"T'row da flag, ref!" Nalu's voice finally rang out. "T'row da fuckin' FLAG! Holding! Personal foul!"

But it was no use. UNLV's kicker easily sent the ball through the uprights for the extra point to put his team up by…25 points, sending everyone within earshot ten, twenty, maybe even fifty grand into the hole. Sure, there may have been 42 seconds left on the clock, but even

Coach Brock admitted it a lost cause, having his quarterback take a knee on the first play after the kickoff.

Kekoa could see Kyle Ching down on the field, his helmet in hand, filing towards the tunnel opening up behind the south end zone just below a scoreboard that read like an obituary: UNLV 41, Hawaiʻi 16. Gone. Just like that. All UNLV had had to do was run out the clock. And then out of nowhere this lumbering fat *solé*—the perfect guy for simply running out the clock—runs into Ufi Tapusoa—the perfect first-team All-WAC future-NFL-draft-pick for wrapping up some clock-eating fullback—and he *breaks free*. For the first time in his long career as a ball carrier, all the way back to Pop Warner time, Sagapolu sees daylight, so he starts running as fast as he can to *take it to the house*—never mind that there's less than a minute to play, never mind that he's running up the score, never mind that the whole UH defense is going to want to *t'row blows* and swing helmets and crutches and whatever for such a humiliating gesture, never mind that—

Hold on. That's exactly what should be happening on the field right now after such a pile-it-on last-minute score. But look: the rain stopped, all the coaches and players from both teams mixing together walking to the tunnels as…orderly…as the six-seven hundred fans walking to the exits. Scrap? Fuck, the fuckas all look like old friends! Even Sagapolu and Tapusoa right down on the sideline walking side by side. Not talking. Tapusoa get his head down…cannot really tell from all the way up here…shouldn't Tapusoa at least been jawing something at him? Just letting him know *you don't do that in our house*! Fuck, what the fuck going *on* here?

"Eh Kekoa, you hear that singing cuz?" Nalu. His ugly round face all *blank*, like he just watched somebody shoot his dog right in front of him. "Try look across there, way up in da blues, unda the Firs' Hawaiian Bank sign."

Directly across the field, the whole section of blue seats under the opposite overhang: all full. Plus now you could see it bubbling and waving, all wound up like one World Cup soccer match just ended. Not one of the fuckas dressed in UNLV red. And that song—that sing-songy melody, those whistles and high-pitched hoots blaring out—no doubt, cuz: the whole frikken section, maybe a hundred and twenty-somet'ing guys, alla them fuckin *solés*. The Samoan mafia. And they *singing*.

Now Kekoa, he holding it in, holding in the fucken shame, he ready for start dry heaving right here in fronta all his boyz, all *sick*, head pounding, sick all the way to the *na'au*, like Sagapolu wen' bury his fucken helmet right in Kekoa's stomach, he so full of shame, so scared for even turn his head and face his boyz cause yeah, they all know… once you tell fucken Nalu, he just going start running the frikken mout' cuz. They know they been punked—and more worse than just the ten-twenty-fifty grand. Fucken *shame*. Fucken *solés* make him look *stupid*. And forget about sharing *this* with Javen.

But Kekoa swallowed another dry heave and turned to his cousin anyway, and saw…humiliation…like somebody wen' kick him in the stomach too, look at him working for keep the Heinekens down. An' look the other way: six-seven rows, da boyz, forty-somet'ing guys, every one a them already making *hard*, already their eyes stay burning, burning with…loyalty…aching for revenge. Good.

He turned back to Javen and said it: "Front page, cuz. Front page."

Javen looked up at him for a long minute. He didn't say anything, but you could tell he was thinking the same thing.

He gave Kekoa a nod.

"I no care, All-WAC, All-American, NFL draft, whateva. Tomorrow morning dat fucka front page."

Part One

A Few Remarks

Eight miles away a *savage* face, tattooed in black tiger-like stripes, eyes wide, tongue sticking out in a primitive angry warrior cry—this face glared out across the river of rented Jeep Wranglers and Dodge Calibers and tour trolleys crawling through the shadowy canyons of the world's most famous resort destination. Eyes like manhole-covers, it spread ten feet wide from wrinkled brow to pointed chin across the towering rear panel of a sixty-foot Grumman Luxury Liner now ferrying its sunburned herd back from the PCC, the Mormon-owned Polynesian Cultural Center. And when the traffic ground to a halt, just before the entrance to the Hilton Hawaiian Village's 22-acre urban campus, the giant native began to draw stares, astonished looks, frantic pointing, and even laughter from the parade of Japanese and Chinese (Chinese?) and mainland tourists meandering up and down the sidewalk.

Like the ten-year-old sun-crisped haole kid decked out in the same faux-surfer gear as his father, and his older sister, and his mother, who stuck his own tongue out and started hopping around clapping his palm on his open mouth like a whooping High Plains Indian. Or his sister, who stuck out her tongue and launched into a hip-swaying gyration that owed more to hip-hop than hula. Or Mom, who joined in with thrusts of her own, catching the whole thing on her phone camera to post it on Facebook. All Dad could do was stare at the face and say, "C'mon! That's an authentic Hawaiian doing the traditional *ring of fire* dance we saw on the Discovery Channel!"

Although it wasn't. The face belonged not to a Hawaiian, but to a Samoan student from the Hawai'i outpost of Brigham Young University, which occupied a couple of hundred acres of former sugarcane land right next to the PCC up on the North Shore.

No, the only actual authentic Hawaiian within a hundred yards was a man named Russell Lee, who just wanted to curse the face through the tinted windows of his Lexus LX 670—not for the typical culturally insensitive reaction it was drawing from the sidewalk tourist parade, but because it was blocking his way.

His way.

Him! The kingpin of the State Senate, convener of the Joint Task Force on Meth Addiction, blocking *his* way, just a matter of ten or twenty more feet to the Hilton's entrance! Russell Lee! President! Of the State Senate!

Even worse than not knowing who Russell Lee was, the face was calling him out: Eh Russ! You're *late*! Where you been? Been *chasing*? They waiting for you Russ! Whatchoo going tell them? You was betting on *football*? Again? Russ!

Worse still: it was right. On both counts. Senator Lee had indeed been glued to a seat downtown at the Extra Pint all the way to the end of a meaningless UH game that had been decided in the third quarter.

Just *had* to see it through, ah Russ? Even though you knew your committee clerk long ago booked you to speak at the Hokulani Drug Treatment Center's annual fundraiser. You know, the one that started half hour ago? Even though you *knew* the game's end would put you into the thickest hour of the Saturday evening rush, you sat right there to watch, all because you'd bet… *fifty thousand dollars*. On a *college football game*. A *UH* game. Russ!

Fifty thousand dollars!

That right there confirmed that being late wasn't even the half of it. Maybe *being on time* lay at the root of how Russell Lee liked to conceive of himself as a leader who *got things done*, different from his colleagues who just came to show face at these sorts of events before being whisked away for more important things.

And yeah, *being on time* also meant he wasn't *lazy*—a word that contained every one of the teenage-pregnancy, high-unemployment, high-incarceration-rate, domestic-violence, drug-addiction, alcoholism stereotypes that always brought Russ nothing but a painful sense of shame for his people. And sure, the bus hadn't moved an inch through two complete cycles of the traffic light ahead—a real Hawaiʻi Five-0-Elvis-Adam-Sandler-ed-up crowd out there on the sidewalk now all doing their Indian dances, phone cameras in hand. But Russ would take that any day. *Late?* He'd take late any day over . . .

Shit, had he really just lost *fifty grand?*

Had Russell Lee, whose eternal candidacy was still based upon the caché he'd earned nearly thirty years ago starring on that same eternally-trying University of Hawaiʻi football team—had he really just gotten sucked into putting nearly a year's pay into the hands of...Coach Brock?

Listen to that face again: Nice, your car, ah Russ? Still get that new-car smell ($800 payments!), the cool blast of a.c. ($300 a month on gas! and don't forget insurance! full coverage!), the how-you-put-'um, *richly appointed interior*, all leather and soft polished wood. Hadda get it fully loaded, ah Russ? Hadda get *surround sound*. A video monitor. Eh Russ, where the fuck you gonna find *fifty thousand dollars* to pay off that thug of a *solé* banger, Lave Salanoa? Whatchoo going do, refinance the house? Again? Whatchoo going tell Cathy? You gonna *chase* it? Put another fifty on the NFL games tomorrow? Again?

"I'll figure it out," Russ said aloud. And was he really *talking* to the back of a PCC tour bus? Okay, why not: What about *you*, boy, and your authentic Maori-not-Hawaiian pose? The Mormons put you up to that? They pick you off some island in Samoa and give you a "scholarship" to BYU-Hawaiʻi and make you a ten-dolla whore so they could shake these tourists down, tap into their mysterious-natives-in-*paradise* prejudices and sell them on the *adventure* of crawling through Waikiki traffic? You pulling off that pose in an *ironic* way, knowing full well these haoles and Chinese are going to jump around like Indians? Are they going to send you to the Utah campus so you can play—

Football! Fifty thousand dollars! On a college football game!

"I said I'd figure it out." And he would, too. Just last month he'd gotten in ten grand deep and, well, hadda do some maneuvering until Alan Ho floated him some "consulting" work for Pacific Properties to cover it. Then there was the NBA finals before that, which he'd covered with a shot in the dark on the major league all-star game. March Madness. The Super Bowl.

But Russ! Fifty *thousand?*

"I'm telling you, I'll figure it out."

Mercifully the bus finally roared through the intersection, freeing Russ to turn onto the Hilton's Village Lane, where things hardly sped up, just your typical Saturday-at-dusk speedometer-on-zero halt that he should have remembered from his last visit to Waikiki what, a year ago? It had been someone's wedding...no...the Legal Aid fundraiser at the Lehua hotel, the very same hotel where Russ had worked rolling stacks of eight-foot round tables through dim back-of-the-house corridors as a banquet porter. Back in the '80s. The good union job had helped feed him through UH's Richardson's School of Law after he'd exhausted his football scholarship. Even back then there was always some kind of water main breaking, or a parade closing down Kalākaua Avenue. Why hadn't he thought of that back at the Extra Pint? Shit, why hadn't he looked at the football schedule when Cliff Yoshida, his committee-clerk-slash-perpetual-campaign-manager, had signed him up to speak at the fundraiser?

To top things off Russ hadn't considered that to park in this monstrosity of a "self-contained resort complex," you either had to snake your way up a seven-story parking garage and take an elevator all the way back down, or drive a quarter mile through cliffs of sky-scraping time-share towers and more shops designed in the fashion of...an Austrian ski village?...to find a valet, all the while fighting the crowds of walrus-shaped haoles and Chinese tour groups wandering across the flagstone crosswalks that cut the lane every fifty feet.

If only someone could just drop him off right here, he'd at least have a shot at taking a seat before the main course was served. And let's just be honest: shouldn't a public figure of such importance have a chauffeured SUV, a security detail to clear a path and escort him right upstairs?

Creeping, creeping, creeping, and now the belfry clock tower of a... Japanese steak house...adorned with an old-fashioned wooden water wheel. Now the *clock* was shouting at Russ too: Late! Late! Late! Catch the end of the game, Russ? Any *action?*

"Listen, I'll figure it out!"

By the time the Lexus had crawled all the way up to the porte-cochere, thick with cars and crowded with let-me-explain haoles telling the understaffed valets how to do their jobs, by the time Russ finally stepped out and walked back past the Tapa Bar, a couple of fake waterfalls, a New England-style white country *church* someone had thought to erect right there in the middle of the lobby and surround it with Christmas trees for the holidays, through a double bank of elevators big enough to serve a New York City office building, then up a two-story escalator long enough to allow the surf of crowded lobby noise to recede—that is, when he finally reached the Aliʻi Ballroom, all was silent except for the occasional muffled clatter of a dessert plate being cleared to one of the bussing stations on the room's opposite side, and the solitary amplified voice of the blonde middle-aged haole man pacing back and forth across the stage to his left, cordless microphone in hand: "…when I woke up four days later, on the floor of a *crack house*, in the middle of Chicago's *worst neighborhood.*"

The keynote speaker. And from the sound of it, the guy was already well into some kind of I-hit-rock-bottom-and-finally-went-to-rehab anecdote, this one involving his loving and supportive wife and kids, and his need to re-visit the scene where that particular life-changing moment had occurred.

Russ began scanning the crowd for anyone he could expect to pepper him with "good natured" Hawaiian Time barbs about his lateness. And there they all were, too, scattered at power tables all around the room, with Alan Ho at what must have been the VIP table. Right there in the front of…three rows of dinner rounds, all full…nearly 150 people if you counted those women at the two skirted twelve-footers in the back all dressed in identical flower-printed green muʻumuʻus…and who in the world were *they?*…UWP President Stan Medieros, more godfather than "president," *waiting*…Fred Nesmith, Hawaiʻi Electric Power Authority CEO, *waiting.* House Speaker Charles Uchida. The Honolulu Mayor. HVCB Director.

Every one of them, waiting.

"And I said, 'Don't you *remember* me?" the haole guy shouted out. "'I used to buy *crack* from you!'"

A wave of laughter washed across all fifteen tables, its volume enhanced by the image up there on stage: the most clean-cut all-American boy-of-a-married-father-of-two, dressed in creased khaki pants, his spindly arms jutting out of the kind of designer aloha shirt that indicated he usually gave this little talk in jacket and tie, but that someone had gotten to him in time to advise him on what casual-formal meant here in Hawai'i. "'Every other day!'" Laughter. "'For five years!'" More laughter. "'How've you *been?*'" Still more laughter, and Russ concluded that the image was meant to underscore what were probably the themes the guy pounded at fundraisers all across the mainland, namely: *Addiction is a disease!*, and, *It can happen to anyone!*

Prisoners. That's who they were, these women lined up along the twelve-footers.

Russ figured they'd been bussed in from the Leeward Women's Correction Center, part of that cultural reclamation outreach project Hokulani had begun doing after Cliff Yoshida had advised him to bundle their grant request into The Joint's proposal last legislative session. From the looks of it, the women hadn't been brought over just to witness the inspiring spectacle of recovery up on stage—although the guy kept giving them "I know you-all in the back row know what I'm talking about!" shout-outs after each of his I-needed-appr*oval* biographical points.

Just then another haole stood up from the center table and low-stepped his way past the stage, making his way towards Russ with an ingratiating smile spreading across his bearded face. Gary Wright, Hokulani's Director. A graying, pony-tailed Berkley Ph.D. who'd gone through the Mayo Clinic himself after getting hooked on cocaine while following the Grateful Dead around back in the '80s, Wright had been evangelical enough about the value of treatment in his testimony to The House-Senate Joint Task Force on Meth Addiction to get Russ and his colleagues—who, behind closed doors, liked to call themselves "The Joint" in a purposefully ironic way—to fund treatment programs. Now he was pumping Russ's hand and going on in a low voice about how happy he was that the Senator had been able to fit the fundraiser into his busy schedule, and would he mind waiting here until Wright brought him up to *deliver his remarks* by way of introducing the women, who were in fact from the prison, to perform a hula.

Russ sent the bright beam of his *charm* down onto Wright, melting the aging hippie further with sincere thanks for saving him the embarrassment of having to do his own low-step to where his empty seat had waited all the way through dinner and dessert, and where, as he could now see from across the room, the Reverend Tom Watada was seated, along with Peter Varner, the (haole) UH President. Steven Foreman, his (haole) Athletic Director. Malia Chung from Kamehameha Schools. Alan Ho. Everyone else had their heads turned toward the stage, so it was hard to tell.

But there was Tom Watada, his wiry frame decked out in formal black button-down shirt and white priest's Roman collar. Tom's church had spent a decade organizing the town-hall meetings that created the political pressure to get the Legislature to finally notice Hawai'i's thirty-year drug problem. His own testimony for The Joint's proposal had been Oscar worthy—for once, Russ had actually agreed with him. Other than that one time, though, the Reverend's uncompromising anti-development stance had pitted him against Russ so often that, right now anyway, he was relieved to put off having to sit under a gaze that would be doing nothing other than passing judgment for his having strolled in just in time to *show face*.

Up on the stage Mr. All American Boy was now talking about how he was genetically predisposed to addiction, pointing to the back of his head and saying, "Somewhere back here, the *wiring* is different for addicts than it is in 90% of all human beings, no matter where they're from, no matter how loving and stable their upbringing was."

As much as Russ had lately learned about addiction, he had to think about that one. Back in the '80s he himself had vacuumed up enough coke to line the field at Aloha Stadium (where someone had just *missed a tackle* that had cost him *fifty grand!*...but anyway). He probably wouldn't have gotten through law school without all that blow to power him through all the tedious memorization, case after case after case. But when he felt it creeping up on him, he simply quit. Cold turkey. You just had to *want to* quit, and if you didn't, you were probably just…lazy.

"And that wiring was telling me I *had to be perfect*," the guy went on. "I had to be *in control*." Heartfelt look and dramatic pause. "I had to *please everyone*." Pause. "I had to *make them like me*."

Around the room people were nodding, especially the group at that half-occupied back corner table—they seemed as out of place here as the women prisoners. You could tell from the placards clipped into the polished silver stands that served as centerpieces at most of the tables—most of the *$5,000 tables*—why Cliff Yoshida had pushed Russ into making an appearance. Honolulu's Punahou-'Iolani-Mid-Pac elite were well-represented: First Hawaiian Bank, Bank of Hawai'i, Central Pacific Bank had all bought tables of their own, as had former Big Fivers like Amfac, and Alexander and Baldwin, and Castle and Cooke. There were the unions: Local 5, UWP, the teacher's union. The land trusts: Kam Schools, Knotting Estate. A couple of mainstay downtown law firms. PR firms. HEPA. Starwood Hotels. Brokeum and Cellit, the commercial real estate firm. All of it added up to clusters of haole and local-Japanese and local-Chinese faces everywhere.

Except…way over back in the corner it looked more like Wai'anae Foodland had bought a table and sent some of its cashiers and shelf stockers: big, thick women, strings of gold Hawaiian bracelets weighing down each of their arms, all dressed like they'd plundered someone's 1980s closet for dress-up clothes better worn by women half their age to wear to the Hilton. Russ wondered how any of them could have afforded a ticket to the event. Then he wondered why on earth they could have been so enraptured by the haole up on stage, nodding along like it was some kind of call-and-response at a Southern Baptist church.

The haole guy must have caught on, because he held a cupped hand up to his ear and punctuated a point about the intersection between his need to *make them like me* and his awkward adolescent years, with: "So I turned to the first drug I could find, and that drug was…?"

Half the room erupted: "Marijuana!" A wave of knowing laughter. And then it hit Russ: the women in the back corner who had led the cheer—they weren't Foodland cashiers. They were *chronics*. Or, as Gary Wright called them, *alumni*. They had *graduated* from Hokulani, and, apparently, gotten their lives back together. They were *living examples* of what Hokulani was doing, of what Russ himself was doing at the Legislature, of what was possible when such *friends of Hokulani* as First Hawaiian Bank and Amfac and others *offered their support*. When you *got together as a community*, when you *faced this problem head on*, you could *save lives*.

In the same moment Russ was mildly surprised that the wave of knowing laughter had washed so vigorously across the tables of The Elite and Concerned, and that so many of them had joined in shouting out "Marijuana!" Perhaps he wasn't the only one who enjoyed the occasional spliff while watching a movie with his wife on a Friday night, or even who turned to his sixteen-year-old son for buds when the urge hit. Had smoking pakalolo become such a tame act when compared to the death spiral of crystal meth that anyone could freely admit, in front of their vice presidents and colleagues here in the Aliʻi Ballroom, that they liked to burn once in a while?

"Cocaine!"

Cocaine!—the shout nearly knocked Russ off his feet! What were they all going to do next? Admit to the whole world that they'd all gone straight through to meth? That the reason Pacific Savings was here was so we could all refinance our houses?

But before the echo died, he began to see that the shouts hadn't at all come from the Pacific Savings table. Interspersed between all of the *elite* he could see tables full of…you had to look…it wasn't just that one table at the back—they were everywhere: *chronics*.

Over there: a guy in his late-forties—maybe even the same age as Russ—with his black hair slicked back, his smile missing at least two teeth, an old Salvation Army aloha shirt hanging over the only long pants he owned. Next to him: sista had dyed her hair light brown and feathered it back like someone Russ himself may have danced with after doing a few lines in the bathroom at *Rumors* back in the '80s. Table after table of middle-aged chronics, each of their faces etched with the weary road map of a life spent sucking on the glass pipe, their heads nodding with complete understanding at the well-educated haole crack head on stage.

Yeah, he may have been talking about crack-cocaine, but if anything meth was supposed to be even more addictive. And Gary Wright must have done it on purpose—put all these chronics right in between all the $5,000 tables—just so the donors could see what all their good work was accomplishing for the…alumni.

Such as they are, Russ thought. This "meth monster" hadn't taken *him* down, even though his own biography matched right up with those of most of Gary Wright's alumni: part Hawaiian. Partied through their club-going twenties when meth was the fashionable drug, just beginning to arrive in Hawaiʻi by the crate load. Likely from the rural Windward side, where, as a socio-economic impact statement he'd had to read as part of The Joint had put it, *the pressures of urbanization* had led to a *disruption of traditional cultural values* that resulted in *increases in violence and substance abuse*.

It had probably been worse for Russ, who spent the first ten years of his life working literally sun-up to sundown farming taro with his father, Samuel Lee, that big bull of a man who used to shake him awake in the cold dark of the early morning. "Dis world is changing fast, Russell," Dad would say, "and you no like get run ova, you gotta *work*." At the time Russ had tried to tune it all out, but unlike the rest of these chronics, at some point he'd simply decided to *grow up*, to work against that dreaded stereotype for which his father showed so much contempt: the Lazy Hawaiian, the one always complaining about—

Russ could *feel* the eyes on him, those eyes right over there boring holes through the frameless glasses of Reverend Tom Watada, who had turned around to look straight at him from all the way across the room. Everyone else was still locked in on the stage, but there was the Reverend, staring as though Russ had been shouting his condescending observations into a cordless mic of his own, looking evenly at Russ like it was just the two of them alone in…a confessional…like Tom was telling him, *You sat on The Joint for a year and a half and studied all of this stuff, Russ—you know that drug addiction isn't a "choice." These people aren't "chronics"—they're heroes, Russ. You know that.*

Before Russ could react, the haole crack head (thankfully) drew Tom's attention by evangelizing into his rousing conclusion: "…three thousand, four hundred and twenty-two days and sixteen hours ago, I walked out of that crack house for the last time." Applause! "And if I never walked back, it was because of the kind of support I see all around this room." More applause. "No one is ever 'cured' of their addiction. The fight goes on, every hour, every day, right into day number three thousand, four hundred and twenty three, and beyond." Dramatic pause. "The alumni all around the room are fighting that fight. Those incredible women there in the back row are fighting that fight. We are, all of us all around the country—we are all fighting that fight. Every single day. Thank you."

The room erupted, everyone rising up into a standing ovation, the haole crack head tearing up now, until he was rescued by a haole woman dressed in some kind of news-actress aqua pants suit get-up, her blonde hair buzzed short on the sides.

Russ recognized her as Susan Brushette, the 1980s KPTV news co-anchor who, once she'd drifted far enough past her Earnest News Hottie stage that the studio's make-up artists could do nothing more to help, had followed the typical route of many local past-their-prime "journalists" who either became the "spokesperson" for some state agency, or started a PR firm—which was what Susan Brushette had done with Trina Hyde, the fifty-ish local-Chinese weather girl who'd retired from KMON a few years earlier. Brushette and Hyde were now apparently doing pro-bono work for Hokulani emceeing their fundraiser.

Susan Brushette leaned forward to give the crack head one of those we're-not-really-hugging pats-on-the-back embraces and took the mic, mock-wiping tears of her own and simply saying "Wow!" And when the applause faded into a few scattered claps she said, "Well, I think we all learned something tonight about what treatment can accomplish." She thanked the speaker "for all of us here in Hawai'i"—she used the exaggerated "proper" Native Hawaiian pronunciation that many local-haoles made sure to use (though incorrectly), which came out like "Ha-vai-ee"—and went on to recycle a few sound bites from his speech.

"And to show how much this really hits home here in Ha-vai-ee," she went on, "we have a special treat for you, Mr. Weber."

The crack head, Weber, made an I'm-Honored face and then smiled.

"And to introduce that special treat, we have a man who has been a bigger friend to the treatment community here in Ha-vai-ee than anyone else in the Legislature, where he convened the House-Senate Joint Task Force on Meth Addiction. Folks, that task force put together a package worth more than $18 million dollars for treatment and prevention programs." She paused to elicit a brief round of applause. "Tonight, the Hokulani 'ohana is honored by the presence of State Senate President Russell Lee."

Russ bounded onto the stage and leaned forward to meet Susan Brushette's we're-not-really-hugging hug before shaking hands with Weber, leaning down to thank him for all he was doing to fight "the monster." As the applause faded he looked out across the room, thinking he might break the ice with a little joke about the poor banquet staff's prospects of making much money from the bar in a roomful of addicts and recovering alcoholics, but decided it would come off in poor taste. All the faces looked at him expectantly, tables full of alumni dotted around the room like a flotilla of brown islands in a sea of white—even Tom Watada, who was still holding him in that same cold judgmental gaze, but really, what did that matter? What did any of it matter? What, even, did *fifty thousand dollars* matter? He would indeed figure it out.

Yes he would.

Because in that instant a familiar feeling came over Russ, a feeling he could only describe as the…buzz…the…charge…the charge of *leadership*…of *getting things done*. And yes, this was why he'd agreed when Cliff Yoshida had suggested he make an appearance tonight. And sure, the applause and the attention had something to do with the feeling, but more important, Russ had done something to *change lives*. Really, would Gary Wright have been able to line up such a list of donors had they not essentially been attaching themselves to Russell Lee's commitment of funding from the Lege? Russ had even managed to get Tom Watada, of all people, to *work with him* on this, on *the possible*. Oh, the things you could do for your people as a leader, as a holder of a real position of power! Me! Give me the *power!* And more!

So Russ turned up the dial on his *charm* and said, "Aloha kākou, ladies and gentlemen! And how about that incredible speech!" Another round of applause, and then: "I want to personally thank Mr. Weber for flying all the way out to our islands to spell out some of the problems we've been facing in such an engaging, honest, and heartfelt way." Applause. "This is truly an issue that touches each and every one of us. Not just the alumni who have the courage to be here tonight, but everyone—from UWP over there helping to protect its members from this deadly disease, to Pacific Properties and everyone else. I've been able to see first-hand, in my role on the Joint House-Senate Task Force on Meth Addiction, that this drug does not care where you work, or how much money you have, and I think Mr. Weber brought that home loud and clear for us." Applause. "He's a hero, just as all of you alumni are heroes, for having *lived* that story." Polite applause from the donors, modest looks down from the alumni. "He also looks pretty good in an aloha shirt." A ripple of knowing laughter, Gary Wright good-naturedly slaps the grinning Weber on the back, and now Russ is *rolling*—he's got this room in the palm of his hand! He's *leading* them!

"Another thing I've been able to learn on The Joint that—The Joint *Task Force*—that Mr. Weber really underlined for us here tonight is that addiction isn't something you're ever cured of." He paused. The Joint! Did they catch it? He plowed on: "It's a monster you have to go on fighting, long after you've quit your daily habit. That is why Hokulani is such a vital part of our community, and why all of the alumni deserve our continued support, because they are our 'ohana." Polite applause. "I can sum up that support in one word: *Imua*!" More applause, and Weber and Wright turned to each other, each of their faces registering an unconsciously irreverent smiling question, "What does this oonga-boonga word *mean*?" which Russ picked up on immediately: "It means, *go forward*."

Around the edges of the stage, Russ could see the prisoners gathering, each crowned with a fresh flower haku lei. It might have looked like the start of the Merrie Monarch hula festival except for how utterly shaken the women all were at the prospect of performing in front of so many people. They exchanged nervous glances, a few of them trying to reassure each other with a thumbs-up and, with obvious effort, a smile. There was something so *endearing* about it that Russ became wrapped up in the moment enough to allow himself to be…proud…proud of himself, sure, for the help he'd been able to provide in leading The Joint, but just as proud of these chronics who'd been in bone-shaking, sweat-inducing, full-blown withdrawal only a matter of weeks ago. Here they were all set to dance a hula in the Ali'i Ballroom. They were indeed *turning their lives around*.

"This evening we are blessed to be in the company of so many walking examples of *imua*," he went on. "One of the most powerful of those examples has come to us from the Leeward Women's Prison, where a grant appropriated by The Joint *Task* Force has funded a pilot program called *Na Pua Kapono o Ka 'Aina*, 'The righteous flowers of our land.' Our strongest weapon in his battle is our *local values*—values rooted in the tradition of our host culture, values that are uniquely *Hawaiian*." Spirited applause. "So without further ado…" And then Russ looked around, as if for help for having said something so cheesy. "Did I just *say* that?" He smiled his best self-deprecating smile, earning more polite laughter. "Here, let me try out my Kimo Kahoano impersonation." Even more knowing laughter—Senator Russell Lee was going to channel the silky baritone of the very host of the Merrie Monarch hula competition! "Ladies and gentlemen!" he boomed out, leaning down into the microphone. "Under the direction of kumu hula Darlene Wright, Nā Wahine o Leeward Women's Prison!"

Still buzzing—no, *on a high* now—Russ stepped down and took his seat at the VIP table, and not for the first time the thought flashed through his mind: *this* was what was possible when the right man had *power*. And then: what if Russ had *more* power? What could he accomplish *then*?—but this last thought he worked to stifle, yet again, because, well, it was difficult to explain…you had to be more *humble* than ambitious to win political support in Ha-vai-ee. Had to wait your turn. Plus, well, you don't just throw away a twenty-year career in the senate, which was what Hawai'i's resign-to-run law expected you to do if you ran for…higher office.

In any case the women now gingerly took their places in formation, working to hold their nervous smiles in place. Russ could make out the hibiscus print on their dresses, and, just as clearly now under the spotlight, the deep lines cut into each of their faces. Their bodies ranged in size from the rotund tita on the right, to the emaciated chronic in the back row looking out in terror through those bulging round eyes. They all appeared to be in their forties, but with what meth could do to the face of a twenty-year user, who could really tell? That mother-daughter pair on the end could just as easily have been sisters. A swirl of calligraphy covered nearly every inch of exposed skin: names, along with the odd star or sunshine design, some of it obviously professionally done, but much of it almost handwritten in the kind of jailhouse tat script you only used to find on some thug-of-an-ex-con truck driver. Though here and there you'd see a clumsy attempt at that series of triangular shapes that made up the kind of traditional Polynesian warrior design popular among UH professors, mainly it all came together as a sad, sloppy collection of black ink.

And the skin.

There was no getting around how dark these women were, even after months in prison. And when the piped in music began to fill the room, the distinctive high three-part harmony of the Sons of Hilo launching into their haunting hymn-like anthem, *Kanilehua*, it became clear—and why hadn't it registered earlier?—that every one of these chronics now stepping into the first swaying motions of their hula—indeed, every member of that flotilla of brown-skinned tables set out in high relief against the mostly-haole and local-Japanese executives and the office hotties they'd brought along—was Hawaiian.

And these women on stage, these *prisoners*—all the way up and down both lines of dancers now reaching a hand and a nervous smile up toward the Aliʻi Ballroom's plastic chandeliers, you had to notice that distinctive round nose, those masculine high cheek bones, that thick barely-tamable hair. You had to wonder if more than a few of these women were among those rarest of all post-millennial creatures: some of those *faces* up there—they could only be pure Hawaiian.

Yet within the first few steps it was plain to see that up until the prison program's self-esteem-building class where they had all lined up a couple of times a week in their drab brown uniforms to take instruction from some retired Kam School music teacher, if any of them had ever known a thing about the rich traditions of their ancestors, it hadn't included hula. Though no one could expect the precision of the Merrie Monarch, where huge troops of young men and women were drilled relentlessly for months into fiercely unified move-as-one ensembles, these dark tattooed prisoners, a step off here, a step off there, didn't even look ready for the dinner performance some tourist hula class stumbles through aboard the *Star of Honolulu*.

The third woman from the end on the left—the real skinny one with the bulging eyes—spins in the opposite direction from her partners, and then endearingly puts her hand over her shame-smile as if to acknowledge and atone for the gaffe before moving on. Another woman rushes to complete a missed hand motion, awkwardly catching up with the rest of the line and then smiling like a schoolgirl caught not paying attention in class.

Though you couldn't help but be moved at the sight of them all up there trying so hard, just then a word began to creep into Russ's mind: *lazy*. A bunch of chronics who had all at some point *made that choice*, in some senses their vivid missteps reflected the kind of haphazard living that had led to *that choice* in the first place: why couldn't they just *get it right*?

On the other hand, the unsteady dance also reflected what they had all gone through to simply set foot on that stage in the first place. It was beautiful in a way the Merrie Monarch competition could never be, Russ decided. Its amateurish quality lent it even more poignancy, in the sense that if these women—these *Hawaiian* women—could not dance in lock-step like a Merrie Monarch *halau*, it was because their lives, and their cultural traditions, had been robbed by The Monster. Thanks to Russ's leadership on The Joint, they were *reclaiming* that cultural identity, right before his eyes.

They were becoming Hawaiian.

Again: *the buzz!*

Russ could actually feel his chest well with the next thought: you could *do* it! You could accomplish things in the Legislature! Even as a mere state senator. You could *help your own people!* And how lucky was Russ? That he could have channeled his own ambitions—to go into politics, to rise to a respected position of *leadership*—in such a nakedly altruistic direction? Helping his people! Right here! Tonight!

Even Tom Watada looked moved, his steady gaze following every step, every wave of the hand. And why wouldn't he be? The behind-the-scenes hand that had made the first push against Hawaiʻi's drug problem, as Russ was always happy to admit, had belonged to the man sitting right across the table: Reverend Tom Watada. Though you'd never see Tom marching with the protest sign or taking the mic for his turn to rant at the public hearing, whenever a group of Windward Hawaiians started waving signs about water rights, or restoring some ancient fish pond, you just knew Tom Watada was involved somehow. And at least this time, the Reverend would have to congratulate Russ for *getting things done.*

All around, people were locked in. *Reclaim* really was what these women had done, too. In some other life any one of them might have set her bare feet onto the hallowed plywood of the Edith Kanakaʻole Stadium stage over in Hilo, where the actual Merrie Monarch was held. And that was the most moving part of the whole performance, wasn't it—that you could go back into any one of their lives and find the tragic wrong turn that had led them to take that first hit from the glass pipe. The abusive boyfriend, the uncaring teacher, the father or husband who had walked out. And just like that, twenty years disappear. Or even if simple laziness *had* led them all to smoke away a good half of their lives—look at them now! Up on stage! Taking on the Monster!

Everyone could see it. Look at Stan Medieros: he's got that white linen napkin held up to his watering eyes. Look at Varner. Look at… is that…Ikaika Nāʻimipono? Over at the KEY Project table? Russ had heard his old high school football brother sat on the youth center's board, a Hawaiian face, a role model for the kids, a taro farmer himself and one of the state's most vocal Native Hawaiian rights activists. Look at him: wiping away a tear. Even Ikaika, always the first to publicly call Russ on *making compromises*—even he would have to congratulate Russ for his success *working within the system*. Look at him! Look at Malia Chung. Look at Alan Ho too, the back of his left hand up to his nose to quiet a sniffle. Everyone, *wiping away tears*. Even the banquet waiters had stopped what they were doing to stare at this remarkable group of middle-aged Hawaiian women up there on stage taking hold of—

Wait a minute! What was this? This little local-Japanese cupcake over there at the Brokeum and Cellit table, the one with her silky black geisha hair spilling over those tan lines plunging down into that shoulderless black dress? Who was she? She looked like one of those twenty-something pieces of 'Iolani-UH-Communications-grad eye candy you always saw walking around Bishop Square at lunchtime in heels *just high enough* and a skirt *just short enough* to let you know she'd been thinking about more than the workday when she'd dressed for the office that morning. And now here she was, this still-living-with-Mom-and-Dad-in-Niu-Valley, pinkish-rastini-at-Indigo-after-work, *Honolulu Sentinel* Downtown First Friday Party Pics model, here she was at the Hokulani fundraiser with that look on her face.

With that *look* on her face. That look—she wasn't *moved* or *touched* like everyone else. No, hers was a look of…approval. She *approved* of these women, like a first grade teacher at a school assembly pleased at the way her students are behaving. She, who had been handed every possible advantage along a rigidly planned path toward eventually marrying either a doctor or a dentist and then having her mother and a hired Filipino nanny raise her own two babies while she chatted away her afternoons with her "best friend" at the Honolulu Club or a trendy lunch spot like Ballena's, she *approved* of what these women nearly twice her age were doing. *Approved!*

And if Russ could get a little deeper into that Hello Kitty head of hers, he decided, he would find that this brainless little sheltered office geisha *approved* because she'd been raised to never have any expectations for Hawaiians in the first place. She was 'Iolani (or Punahou, or St. Francis, or Mid-Pac), and they were Kalaheo, Castle, Farrington, Wai'anae, or any one of a number of other ghetto public schools. The

'Iolani teachers may have taught her about the overthrow of the Hawaiian monarchy, and some "kumu" may have come in to walk her fifth grade class through the steps of this very same hula for some May Day assembly. And she certainly had a couple of "super-nice" Hawaiian friends—light-skinned Kam School toenail-Hawaiians she'd met at a downtown "wine bar" after work one evening. But she'd been programmed to *look down* since all the way back in high school, if not before, when her mother had given her a list of acceptable *ethnicities* for boyfriends, in order: local-Japanese, Japanese, local-Chinese (4th generation or higher), and, if it turned out to be otherwise unavoidable, haole.

Absent from the list were Filipinos, Micros, and, most especially, Hawaiians.

Hawaiians were lazy, violent, inarticulate, and ignorant. They complained endlessly about lack of educational opportunities, but they were happy to drink beer after beer in the carport instead of reading to their kids. They whined about their disproportionate rates of incarceration, but were happy to go around assaulting the deliverers of even the slightest apparent insult, even their own wives and children. They wondered why they were always at such an economic disadvantage, and then had more and more and more children they couldn't possibly afford to raise, and/or bought chrome rims for the $30,000 SUVs they were financing with welfare checks and money that, thanks to public housing and EBT cards and other entitlements, didn't have to be spent on rent or food. The drug problem targeted them unfairly, yet they were happy to sell meth to their own cousins. You'd *never* catch a local-Japanese doing such things, her mother had always reasoned.

But these Hawaiians up here on stage—well, it looked like being in prison had taught them a lesson. Maybe now they would finally make something of themselves.

When the last strum of the twelve-string sounded, each prisoner stood with one hand outstretched and another reaching skyward, and the room erupted in cheers, a prolonged standing ovation even louder than the one they'd given Weber, their *whoops* and whistles and shouts ringing out all around. The women, all breathing heavily, were draped in looks of relief that they'd gotten through this thing in one piece.

And as Russ stood there clapping, it began to dawn upon him why he was getting so angry over one ignorant young local-Japanese girl's look of approval. The truth was that the deeper he got into the girl's head, the more he found himself *agreeing with her*. That's right—it was pretty clear that all of her nonsense about the chrome rims and reading to your kids fit right in there with what his dad had predicted long ago. And the girl's mom's little ethnic status chart? A simple look around the room confirmed that little piece of folk wisdom as sound advice for anyone's daughter—or anyone's son, for that matter, especially if your eyes happened to fall upon that hopeless collection of tattered lives now exiting the stage.

Look at Reverend Tom Watada: he sees it even deeper. Susan Brushette's up there gushing over "that wonderful hula," urging everyone to dig for their loose change and put it into one of the envelopes someone had put under each table's centerpiece, but none of that matters to Tom Watada, who's staring at Russ again.

This time the Reverend flashes a polite smile and turns to watch Susan Brushette wrap things up, but Russ can tell exactly what he was thinking. Tom would not even have attended if Gary Wright hadn't told him that the money from the fundraiser could help him get upwards of 100 more addicts back on their feet. But when he looks at these centerpiece signs dotting the room, the HEPA and the Castle and Cooke Homes and the Starwood Hotels signs, the Reverend doesn't see $5,000 donations to a good cause.

He sees *tourism*, and encroaching development financed by big banks. He sees the very "social forces" that caused the drug problem in the first place sitting there in a lame and transparent effort to *come off* as being *friends of the community* who were *helping*, when in fact no one was more responsible than they were for the chain of events that had led to twelve spent and tattooed Hawaiian women learning their first steps of hula at age forty in some prison "reclamation" project. He sees it just like Ikaika over there, leaning down to whisper the same observation into the ear of the haole woman next to him.

Russ wanted to tell himself the usual—that though Ikaika Nāʻimipono and Tom Watada may have had *principles*, what they really did was hold up the inevitable and prevent their people from getting anything at all in return. Russ wanted to tell himself, again, that when you swallowed a little bit of pride, when you did the *possible*, every now and then you got the better of the other side and did some good.

But shit, that simple look of *approval* from that brainless office geisha had told him otherwise. That look—it had *spoken* to him: Eh Russ! Here's what alla your behind-the-scenes within-the-system state-senator nickel-and-dime bullshit made *possible*: made it possible for everyone in this room to stand on their feet and wipe away more tears and applaud *themselves*, while all the time they just thinking: *See what happens? See what happens when you make that choice? See what happens when you don't bother to raise your own children? Fuckin' chronics! Druggies! Lazy Hawaiians!*

And here Russ had thought he was *helping his people*, when suddenly it hit him—and why hadn't he *seen* it until this very moment?—that compared to the scope of the problem that had taken a proud people down, $18 million was chump change. Little better than a five grand donation. A couple of hundred bucks into that envelope Susan Brushette was talking about, the one—

Russ felt a tap on the shoulder. Peter Varner, the newly-imported haole UH President brought in to raise money for a decades-old plan to finish building a leeward UH campus. Varner was giving him that gracious ear-to-ear grin of his that had impressed the university's Board of Regents into awarding him half a million taxpayer dollars annually, plus the keys to the President's Mansion on College Hill and a new Lexus. He handed over Susan Brushette's envelope.

Loose change, all of it. Vanity checks. Look-at-me-I'm-helping *guilt money*.

And come on: you had to be able to do *more*. More than five frikken grand, more than pass around an envelope, more than even $18 million dollars in treatment funding.

Much more.

Ikaika Nā'imipono and Reverend Tom Watada—they were right to think tonight was all bullshit.

And yet...

You didn't just give up. You had to work within the system. Do what was possible.

The possible.

Only now was Russ really *seeing* that the *possible* didn't have to be limited to such table scraps. No, it was entirely *possible* to get... more...to get enough to actually solve the problem instead of allowing a roomful of trust-fund haole wealth to *tell themselves* they were helping. Enough to finally fix things right. Show-face charity bullshit wouldn't do it. Half-measures from the Lege wouldn't do it. Twenty years of seniority or not, *president* or not, a seat in the state senate wasn't going to do it either.

You had to go *all in*. Now.

As Russ reached for his wallet he saw that Tom Watada was handing Gary Wright another envelope, one he'd brought along himself.

"I wanted to pay for my own ticket," Tom said.

"No, Tom, you were invited!" Wright said, his face turning red even though he was half-reaching for the prize anyway. "You're already doing far more than your share to fight this problem, right in the streets, where it's happening."

"It was a wonderful evening," Tom said with a smile. "And the food was great! Just let me pay for my meal." Wright didn't put up too much of a fight, grabbing the envelope with a bit of good-natured mock disappointment in Tom's inability to accept his hospitality. The whole thing was so purely righteous Tom Watada—not a sliver of self-importance—that Russ almost had to laugh, thinking, what were the rest of the invited VIPs supposed to do now? You couldn't very well promise to send in a check later on, could you?

That question was answered when Russ looked in the envelope, which was thick with hundred dollar bills, a stack of them half an inch wide. He opened his own wallet and found…a five and two ones. And he would need the five to get his car back from the valet.

The sight was enough to rekindle the thought of Russ's hours-old fifty thousand dollar debt. But only briefly, because yeah, he had indeed figured it out. All of it. The fifty grand. The way to really show people like Ikaika Nāʻimipono and Reverend Tom Watada what was indeed possible to *help his people*. Even the parking. All of it. You had to do it from the very top of the volcano. The fifth floor of the State Capitol.

The *Executive* floor.

Sure, he'd have to talk it over with Cathy. The hard part would be getting the ever-practical Cliff Yoshida to finally see that at long last, the *moment* had arrived, whether it was his "turn" or not, and that putting your senate seat on the table—resigning to run—was worth the risk.

But Russ would figure that out too.

And though there was the matter of raising money—and far more than a piddling fifty grand—well, look at Alan Ho over there chatting away with Sidney Rogers, the old retired (haole) CEO of Pacific Savings.

Just the other day Alan had asked Russ along to provide back-up at one of his little shakedown meetings what, day after tomorrow, where he planned to "facilitate" a deal involving some Chinese investor, as far as Russ recalled it.

Who knew that Russ would be able to cash in on the favor so soon? And that was just for starters. Just look around: throw in this our-son-paddles-for-Lanikai-Canoe-Club, designer-aloha-wear, front-row-at-the-Ha-vai-ee-Theater-for-the-Sons-of-Hilo crowd now roaring into their conversational goodbyes at all these five thousand dollar tables—folks who *wanted* to care about Hawaiians, wanted to *be Hawaiian themselves* in that pathetic "Hawaiian-at-Heart" sense—and it all added up to a pretty well-funded campaign for Russell Lee, their *bootstraps* Hawaiian, a man who had spent an entire career exploiting himself as the candidate voters could use to obscure from themselves their deeply rooted prejudices about Lazy Hawaiians.

A Hawaiian who met their…approval.

Deep in such thoughts, Russ barely noticed that two HPD officers had entered the Aliʻi Ballroom—a short, stocky local-Japanese, and a beefy Kam School grad part-Hawaiian. Hats in their hands, drop-dead-serious looks on their faces, they made straight for the VIP table. The shorter one leaned to speak something into Varner's ear, while the other one spoke softly to Foreman, the AD.

Under other circumstances Russ would have been filled with curiosity. But now he took it as his chance to grab the two ones out of his wallet, stuff them into the middle of all those hundreds, and hand the whole thing off to Gary Wright without anyone noticing.

Varner stood with quick and general goodbyes and departed with Foreman and the two cops, sending the rest of the table into I-wonder-what-*that*-was-abouts, and why-do-you-think-Foreman-ran-off-with-hims, and did-he-say-*Ufi-Tapusoa?*

Someone threw in a joke about Coach Brock maybe falling asleep at the wheel on his way home, and before long people took Varner's departure as a signal to get up, everyone milling around the room and falling into brief how've-you-*been* conversational clusters or slowly streaming out the doors.

"And Senator," Gary Wright was saying, "we have to thank you for that wonderful speech. *Imua!*" He gave a little power-fist salute.

"Yes," Tom Watada said. "You got here just in time, Russ."

Got here just in time! Russ had to smile, because this time Tom was dead wrong. This time it wasn't just another show-face charity event on Russ's schedule, to deliver a few remarks. This one, Russ already knew, would turn out to be a game changer.

"Don't worry Reverend," he said. "I'm just getting started."

THE RULES

Bishop and King. If ever there was a point on the map that thought it was fulfilling the statehood-era promise that Hawai'i would become a nexus of international commerce on par with Beijing and Singapore and Los Angeles and New York, a place right up there with sixteenth-century Venice—once the very center of the *known world*—it wasn't the rusting hulk of Aloha Stadium.

It was right here, at the corner of Bishop and King.

So obvious was the symbolism in the geographic middle of downtown Honolulu, roughly as equidistant from the technical marvels of Japan and the bright lights of Hollywood as it was from the frontiers of Australia and the mountains of South America, that sometimes you had to say it out loud. Even today, with most of the surrounding glass-and-steel towers now owned and controlled by publicly traded foreign and mainland firms that did most of their business elsewhere, you had to say it: *the Crossroads of the Pacific.*

Certainly that's what the *de facto* planners of downtown had had in mind—people like Charles Bishop himself, a missionary who'd married one of the last Hawaiian princesses, heir to the vast land holdings of the Great King Kamehameha which today amounted to nearly a fifth of Hawai'i. Or Samuel Alexander and Henry Baldwin, missionary sons whose former sugar land stretched across a further ten percent. Or Walter Dillingham, the missionary son whose partnerships in Washington had led, eventually, to the current U.S. military occupation of yet another twenty percent, and whose own estate's holdings covered ten percent more.

If you stood at the corner of Bishop and King, you could still see the massive footprint of these four men whose hands had once been wrapped up in more than half the state's land. There down toward Honolulu Harbor: the distinctive beige sandstone façade of Dillingham's Hawaii Railroad Company Building, a technical marvel of its day built on the backs of Japanese sugar slaves, yards and yards of sandstone reaching up ten stories and finished in intricately carved patterns, *all of it* shipped across thousands of miles of open ocean in ships owned by...Matson Navigation, the only Pacific highway that exited onto the *Crossroads*—a monopoly that today explained why struggling island residents paid upwards of nine dollars for a box of Honey Nut Cheerios. Then back in the '60s, Matson had been bought out by Alexander & Baldwin, and their marquee building sat right there across Bishop Street from Dillingham's.

But the crown jewel of *The Crossroads*, everyone knew—even after the First Hawaiian Center had risen to eclipse it in height back in the '90s—was the shining black monolith of Pauahi Tower. Buffered from the bustle of King Street by a little stretch of mall-like manicured greenery, it rose up from a three-tiered reflecting pool—itself meant to represent the hillside steps of a traditional Hawaiian life-giving taro patch—like some kind of monument, though not to the Hawaiian princess for whom it was named. The tower was more like a declaration of Honolulu's *presence on the world stage* not as a mere sugar merchant, not as a some backwater hawker of pineapples, but as a *leader in international finance*.

Built on the backs of Japanese sugar slaves? Not this one. The sleek modernistic building had risen in 1983 at the hands of a mainland insurance company, a proud symbol of Hawai'i's ability to *attract outside capital*, to *diversify its economy* beyond tourism and agribusiness, to *build a bridge to the future*.

That was exactly what a thirty-four-year-old aspiring real estate developer named Sean Hayashi was thinking this very morning, Monday morning, gazing out from a soft-tinted twenty-first floor conference room window right here in Pauahi Tower overlooking the whole thing: Bishop Square, the great battleship hull of the First Hawaiian Center,

Honolulu Harbor beyond, the small white dot of an airliner heading east over the bright blue ocean. *A bridge to the future!* Yes, it was one of those hokey phrases his professors at UH's School of Business might have spouted out back when he was trying to credential himself up with what turned out to be an utterly useless business degree. But what else could you call this meeting between some Euro-bank, CreditFranc, and a Chinese multi-national, TsengUSA?

Up to now the closest Sean Hayashi had come to such a power meeting had been the phone call with a broker friend who'd passed along that one-bedroom Makiki foreclosure he'd added to the five-unit empire he'd had spread around town—that, and maybe the meeting that had first put him in contact with Alan Ho. But today they were talking about a 300-room oceanfront hotel way up on the North Shore. And maybe *nervous* wasn't the right word—right now Sean Hayashi was *terrified* just to think about the details: CreditFranc had gotten stuck with the Dolphin Bay golf resort after a mainland firm defaulted on a loan worth nearly $400 million.

$400 million!

It seemed like all the money in the world, and a far, far bigger deal than anything Sean had any right to be involved in observing, let alone helping to facilitate. For Chrissakes, he was still supplementing his real estate kingpin dreams with the safety net of a job—and god, he sure hoped Alan Ho never found out about it—a job *waiting tables* (three hundred a night easy, but still) at the Lehua hotel. And now this? When was somebody going to tap him on the shoulder to let him know some kind of mistake had been made?

Sean's fear, thankfully, was mixed with a sense of giddiness, because damn, here he was, somehow pulling off this plan of his, hatched so long ago: to avoid the fate of pretty much every one of those little bodies far down below scurrying across the little park on the way to their cubicles and computer terminals, their little existences as corporate care-taker lawyers and time-serving accountants and affluent-husband finders. Here on the verge of the biggest moment of his career, the whole improbable climb flashed through Sean's brain: somehow a couple of blind investments from what was left of the forty-grand trust his grandma had left him for college, plus a real estate license earned along the way, had led to…a meeting at Pauahi Tower.

$400 million! His mouth was parched dry at the mere thought of it. A tap on the shoulder.

Sean whirled and looked up into the understanding face of Alan Ho, the long-time behind-the-scenes power broker upon whose career he'd long dreamed of modeling his own. *Hero* may have sounded hokey, too, but what else would you call the very orchestrator of local development throughout the yen-crazed 1980s and beyond? And to think: here was Alan Ho himself, greeting Sean Hayashi as though he *belonged* on the 21st floor, the two of them here early to go over their strategy one last time. Alan Ho! Could you even begin to believe it? Pulling it off!

The great man—at just over six feet, he stood a full head taller than Sean—Ho looked out at the First Hawaiian Center and said, "That whole thing is one giant thirty-story shakedown."

Leave it to Alan. Sure, the guy was older now, his hair peppered with gray, but that only added to the aura that he held enough sway to send state legislators cowering out of his office with a threatening look, even though he still wore one of those moustaches a lot of local-Chinese and local-Japanese men had sprouted back in the '80s as a way to make themselves look more manly.

Sean's father had even sported a 'stache back in the day but wound up shaving it off a few years after they'd gone out of fashion. His father... his father... Yet again the thought crossed his mind: how different was Alan Ho from inept little Milton Hayashi, DDS!

"All '80s money," Alan went on. "*Yakuza.*" He kept staring wistfully at that steel-and-glass wall across King Street like he was remembering a scene from a favorite movie.

Yakuza! That was the most important distinction between Alan Ho and Dr. Milton Hayashi, too: the real all-encompassing *power* Alan wielded, stretching from his money and connections down to the unshakable confidence that had kept him from getting anywhere near the kind of safe treadmill career Sean's father had aspired toward.

His thick shoulders, too, exuded power, physical power, even now that he was in his sixties, sculpted by a life of racing outrigger canoes with the Waikiki Beach Boys, a club for which he still paddled four times a week. And the graying moustache still worked on Alan, too, as did his Reyn's orchid-outline-print aloha shirt, about three shades darker blue than the one Sean himself had on, tucked into pleated wool slacks reaching down to polished bench-made black leather shoes that as much as said, "I'm a man who gets what he wants."

"I thought they built it twenty years ago," Sean said. He wondered if Alan could detect any of the trepidation he was feeling about what they were going to do this morning , which the word "yakuza" hadn't really helped.

While he may have spent the past three weeks powering down on every Dolphin-Bay-related document he could get his hands on down at the Department of Land and Natural Resources—he'd even looked at *microfilm*—all Sean really knew about the First Hawaiian Center was that Charles K. Bishop had founded First Hawaiian Bank over a hundred years ago. That, and back around the time Sean had begun plotting more effective ways of using grandma's money than dumping it all at UH, people had started complaining so loudly about another shadow-casting downtown skyscraper that the FHC developers were forced to include a "park" on a three thousand square foot corner of the project's property, which they then trumpeted as "open space."

"They did, but that was all '80s money," Alan went on. "Back then, those guys were *flush*. And not just the money from meth and prostitution and all the rest of their illegal stuff, either. Japanese bubble time, the Japanese banks were extending these guys lines of credit up into the hundreds of millions of dollars. They wanted to run rampant over the whole state." He smiled. "But we wouldn't let them."

A young haole banquet waiter offered them each a cup of coffee, but they declined, waiting instead for the rest of the meeting's players to arrive. The view of the FHC, Sean was beginning to see, was yet another carefully placed prop in what was about to unfold. The nice Diamond Head view from Alan's own offices over in the Hawaiian Electric Building lacked the sky-scraping urban grandeur that now faced them, so the man had put in a phone call to a client who did investments for Pacific Properties, one of several corporations through which he conducted his "consulting" business, and the whole thing had been set up here on the 21st floor, right down to the catered continental breakfast.

Sean wasn't sure how to steer the conversation next—not without appearing helpless and…needy…like an utterly uninformed and inept…fraud. So he just said, "I thought they wound up buying everything in sight."

"Oh, that they did, that they did," Ho said. "All the hotels in Waikiki. Maui. Big Island. Kauaʻi. Every golf course on Oʻahu except for the Oʻahu Country Club. Many of the residential properties."

"I heard about guys pulling up in limousines and walking up to houses in Kailua with suitcases full of cash and just buying out the owner right on the spot."

"That's true," Alan said. "And we couldn't really control that. But the rest of it, the big money—it had to come through us, and a lot of those resort properties changed hands two and three times before the bubble burst. They wanted to build eight new golf courses on the North Shore. They wanted to build three golf courses in Waikāne. Another guy—but this guy wasn't Japanese, he was a haole guy, European—he wanted to build a billion-dollar resort on the Big Island, and an airport to service it, too. But he didn't follow the rules."

The Rules. That was what today's meeting was all about, after all. And now Sean could look across the thick crawl of King Street morning traffic and see the FHC, see the whole thing, exactly along the lines of how Alan Ho had been preparing him for the past three weeks. The Tropic Seas hotel, just for one of the hundreds of possible examples, had been sold back in 1989 for more than $70 million—a deal that would not have been possible without…facilitation…from someone as connected as Alan was. If you stopped to do the math on all the rest of the deals that were…facilitated…in the same way, and considered how much of that money got scraped off and stayed right here in this *center of international finance*, you would see that the $175 million that had paid the stevedores who shipped all that steel and glass and granite, that had fed the construction workers who stacked it all up thirty stories high, was really just a piddling amount compared to the sum total of all the money made during the '80s, that riotous decade of *the shakedown*.

Best of all, it was totally legal, at least as Alan had explained it. Back in Japanese bubble time enough state agencies and county permitting officers had stood in the way of Dolphin Bay's initial expansion plans that all Alan had had to do was "lawyer" the Japanese owners—essentially just pick up the phone and make a few vague references to "water testing" or "zoning approval" and then explain that they needed to hire a representative from Pacific Properties LLC to help address such issues—and they'd simply complied.

That one sentence—"You'll need a lawyer"—somehow captured the entire list of "technicalities" upon which any approval they were after, including a simple sales transaction, could be "hung up." (A completely incredulous Sean had later googled an interview with that frustrated European investor Alan had mentioned and learned that yes, the process had actually been that simple: he'd been "lawyered.") Along the way Alan had been able to squeeze the Dolphin Bay owners into setting up a charitable trust that provided scholarships for Kahuku High School kids that included an annual "donation" pledge appended to Dolphin Bay's deed. And while Alan had been happy with what the trust did for the community, more important was the fact that as long as he chaired its board, he would have a seat at the table whenever the property changed hands. Just so he could facilitate things.

When the bubble burst, it wasn't exactly like downtown deals stopped all together—Alan himself had kept busy enough turning former sugar plantations into suburban housing, converting hotels into timeshares and so on—but today, this very morning, it was like the sun was rising for the first time in over twenty years. This morning, things were…different. The Chinese were here. Which meant that for the first time in decades, there was some real money on the table. *$400 million.* And that was only the beginning. "Over the long term," Alan had told him, "we're talking *billions.*"

Yes, he must have sensed that Sean had finally gotten it, because Alan never got to the reiteration of this morning's strategy. "I think you're ready," was all he said.

All Sean could do was take a deep breath. That, and try to stop waiting for that tap on the shoulder.

Twenty minutes later everyone was seated around the conference table waiting for Russell Lee, the president of the State Senate, and Cliff Yoshida, the clerk who followed him everywhere. Sean had taken a moment to introduce the CreditFranc senior loan officer—one of those caricatures of a pretentious tennis-player-looking Euro-businessman, a guy named Emile Richard (Ri*shard*), with whom he'd been speaking on the phone and texting—to a beaming Qihong Liu, the dainty looking pale-yellow human computer in the rimless glasses who served as the vice president for TsengUSA. But there was only so much glad-handing and halting half-English small talk you could do within the group's language barrier limits—even with that British barrister-type the Chinese had brought along to interpret for them, a fellow named Michael Prescott, with whom Sean had also been communicating. So they'd all filled their little white porcelain plates with fruit and pastries and settled at either end of a slab of finely polished koa so long a fishing canoe might've been carved from the rest of the tree that had produced it.

The French bank officers, as it oh-so-poetically turned out, were all fanned around the table's west end, while the Chinese sat to the east. The remaining seats were occupied by…facilitators…and a relatively streamlined collection of them than what you usually had around such a table, Alan had told Sean, since, thankfully, none of the large land trusts had any interest in this particular deal.

Sean himself sat about midway with his back to the floor-to-ceiling windows, as planned, to make it appear initially as though he were the one leading the meeting. Then Alan, and to his left, Charles Uchida, the Speaker of the House. Across from the Speaker, his stubby finger jabbing into his touch screen on the table, was Uchida's legislative aide, a perpetually amped-up 28-year-old Pearl City Japanese kid named Grant Nishikawa.

Bits of small talk in French and Chinese filled their respective sides of the room, the occasional sound of a laugh being exchanged. A couple of suits on either side—even the women were dressed in tailored suits that hung on their shoulders like a second silk skin—were dragging their fingers across their own touch screens, no doubt scrolling through the morning news. In short, Sean picked up a light-heartedness—and Alan had told him to expect this—that suggested no one had any idea what was about to hit them: just look at that piece of Euro-eye candy over there, her bright blue eyes just shining out of that angular model's face, a face already tanned to a deep chestnut perfection, a tan that reached all…the…way…down…to…*there!*—her white blouse was unbuttoned to show off as much cleavage as her bikini must have all day yesterday beside the Halekulani pool.

And it wasn't just her.

Every one of these Euro-frogs looked like they'd been lounging around the pool for a week. Tan! They were treating this whole trip to Hawai'i like some kind of…junket! Sean didn't know whether to feel under-gunned in the face of their well-healed money-bolstered *confidence*, or to laugh at how naïve they all were about…The Rules.

Though the other end of the table wasn't quite as tanned—most of them still had the skin tone of those middle-aged women who always carried umbrellas around Chinatown on bright sunny days like this one—their mood wasn't any less jovial.

The little Vice President, flanked by Prescott on one side, and his own piece of office dim sum on the other, was laughing loudly at something Prescott had just told him, laughing just like…well…Sean hated to think of it, but the laugh belonged to some caricature of a Chinese laundry owner. The guy hardly fit the profile of one of the builders of the 21st-century Shanghai skyline or whatever it was. And was Liu always this relaxed, or was he, too, thinking of this little meeting as some kind of…afterthought?

In any case, Sean decided to let it put him at ease, this light-hearted atmosphere—could it really actually be this easy?—and he was beginning to see how Alan Ho, a man who'd grown up in public housing, could have gone on to become such a confident figure: you sit in a room such as this one enough times, and it's going to rub off, particularly when you *know* that knowing *how things work around here* will trump a ten-thousand-dollar custom tailored suit every time.

Even that "lawyering" thing: half the time it had to be bullshit, all the references to "water testing" and so on. The very vague nature of it all, including Alan's own position ("Vice president" of what, exactly? What sort of company *was* Pacific Properties LLC?) all added up to an aura of *power* that had caused all these investors over the years to simply give in and pay up. Just look at Alan chatting away with Charles Uchida: the guy just doesn't give a fuck.

That little quality, more than the lats and the beefy shoulders, was what Sean himself was always working hardest to emulate—even before he'd met Alan. An attempt to muscle up at 24-Hour Fitness had lasted just long enough for his spindly arms to draw outright chuckles from the tattooed ex-high school football star crowd grunting away in the gym's free-weight section, yet again causing Sean to curse his father for both his weakling Hayashi genes, and for always having been too busy waxing his rented Beemer to push him towards the God of Football that might have long ago thickened him up past his current 145.

But Sean had walked out of the gym that day with something far more valuable than python arms. Maybe it was that he'd had enough of getting treated *like one punk* since high school, but whatever the reason, right then he had simply *decided* to pattern his life after someone who just *did not give a fuck*. Alan Ho had in fact told Sean that his *confidence* was what had separated him from the stable of much more qualified Punahou-Stanford grads he could have chosen from when he'd decided to take on an understudy, and—

"Nah!" It was Grant Nishikawa, shouting out, just a *bit* too loud even considering the hum of the French and Chinese side talk, shouting out *in pidgin*, here on the 21st floor of Pauahi Tower.

Sean couldn't stand Grant Nishikawa, always madly pumping his leg up and down like some little kid who needed to use the rest room. One of those wannabe-Hawaiian-thug local Japanese, Nishikawa walked with his arms sticking out away from his body as though his lats and his triceps were *so huge* he had to make room for them. He insisted on speaking pidgin, even though he'd gone on to Yale after 'Iolani (how such an impulsive airhead ever made it through an ivy league remained a mystery to Sean) before some uncle hooked him into the job with Uchida's office. Pidgin. Even in settings like this one, even now that, outside of places like Waimānalo and the Wai'anae coast, pidgin had become a dead language spoken only by retired state workers over their spam-and-egg breakfasts in the Ala Wai Municipal Golf Course club house. His eyes were always bulging, too, as though the whole world turned on whatever inane thought it was he had to share.

But the main reason Sean couldn't stand Grant Nishikawa—and Sean had no trouble admitting this to himself—was because it was abundantly clear that Grant could *kick his ass*. Of course it would never come down to it, but this unspoken fact was what caused the foot-pumping assistant to always *put his hand* on Sean's shoulder whenever they met, to give him that *death grip* handshake, to treat him with… impertinence.

Right now Nishikawa had those bulging eyes fixed on his touch screen tablet, waiting for someone to show interest in that *Nah!* teaser he'd just thrown out. When no one did, he looked up anyway, wholly amazed, and said, "Tapusoa is *dead!*"

Sean had no idea what he was talking about.

But Alan Ho, equally amazed, spoke right up: "You mean the football player? Ufi Tapusoa?"

"It's right here on the front page of the *Sentinel*," Grant said, his eyes back down on the touch screen. "Single car accident…H-3…vehicle crashed head-on into the wall beside the east-bound entrance to the Hirano Tunnels…death likely upon impact…body tested negative for drugs and alcohol." He looked up again: "It happened on Saturday night, right after the UNLV game. Ho, I was *at* that game!"

Typical of Grant Nishikawa, Sean thought, to take such shocking news and immediately turn it toward himself, as though he and Tapusoa had been *boyz* since *hana-butta-dayz*. Typical of the *Honolulu Sentinel*, too, to drape their front page with the story of some juiced up hired thug from the perennially losing football team with, as even Sean knew, the $1.1 million coach. The most earth-shattering and consequential events could be happening all over the state, but if it wasn't something straight off HPD's police log about another brawl in Waikiki or somewhere, or another report of a Big Island brush fire, or a multi-page spread about football, you weren't going to find it in the *Sentinel*.

"Dat boy was headed for the NFL," Alan Ho said.

Jesus, listen to Alan. And with his own whiff of pidgin, no less.

"UH career sacks leader," Charles Uchida chimed in, shaking his head sadly.

No one even paid any attention when Russell Lee and Cliff Yoshida finally arrived, with Yoshida of all people, the Senator's clerk, he of the Stanford economics degree—this slight little balding walking encyclopedia of a spindly-armed, pot-bellied policy wonk who would have made a better legislator himself had he not been such an un-electable wet blanket—it was Yoshida apologizing for the two of them being late and saying, "Did you hear about Tapusoa?"

This little query gave Grant Nishikawa the chance to romp off on a display of all the details with smug satisfaction. "I was *at* that game," he concluded again. *Me and Tapusoa, we was BOYZ!* "Left early, but. UH was getting blown out again."

Sean began to wonder if they'd all forgotten the room was full of billion-dollar international players here at *the Crossroads of the Pacific*. Alan and Yoshida were off on a side conversation about the ineffectiveness of Stacy Brachman, the UH coach, thankful that another dismal season had finally ended. Uchida and Nishikawa were into their own life-cut-short speculation into how Tapusoa would have done in the NFL. And Russell Lee was…well…Russell Lee was just staring off out towards the distant ocean, silent.

"Did you know him, Senator?" Sean asked. "Senator?"

Lee turned with a start, suddenly back on the 21st floor. "No, no," he finally said, signaling for one of the waiters to fill the white porcelain coffee cup in front of him. "It's just such…sad news." He stirred in some cream, put down his silver spoon, and ran both hands through his thinning brown hair. Then the senator resumed staring out the window.

Strange.

By now Sean was irritated enough by the way Grant Nishikawa had hijacked the most important meeting of his young career—even some of the French bankers were getting in on it now, comparing it to the premature death of a promising young alpine skier—that he was no longer the least bit nervous. So he began gently ringing his spoon against his crystal glass of guava juice, bringing the room to a polite silence. (Although, true to form, Nishikawa continued to whisper three or four more sentences about Tapusoa's draft hopes across the table to Uchida before he, too, finally shut up.)

"Good morning everyone," Sean said. "Mr. Ri*sh*ard, I believe you know Mr. Liu. And this is Mr. Prescott, Mr. Liu's attorney."

"How do you do," Prescott said, in a kind of Euro-Brit way that must have grated on Alan Ho. Everything about that thick pale haole in the gray worsted suit—at least that's what Sean thought they called those things Prescott was wearing—must have grated on Alan, not least of which being what sounded like the guy's total fluency in Mandarin Chinese. But Alan was managing to keep it hidden, no doubt waiting for the pure adrenaline rush, as he'd put it to Sean, that was sure to follow.

Prescott introduced the others at his end of the table—a real exotic looker (even to someone like Sean who'd gone to Kaimuki High, a place with no shortage of hot local-Chinese girls), and another reedy looking man who didn't look a day over fifteen—as "Mr. Liu's assistants." Richard answered by naming his underlings from the bank—the bank's secretary, who looked like a World Cup soccer player dressed for his big contract signing, and the tanned hottie, Marlise Deveaux (to Sean it sounded like some stripper's stage name), who turned out to be the head of the bank's real property division.

And then it was up to Sean: "This is Russell Lee, president of the State Senate. House Speaker Charles Uchida."

Faces at either end of the table were trying to register warmth over mild surprise—the same struggling reaction Alan had told Sean to expect. He went on to introduce Nishikawa and Cliff Yoshida before saying, "and this is Alan Ho, vice president of Pacific Properties LLC here in town." Now the looks registered confusion, with rounds of whispers both east and west, in Mandarin and French. This, too, Alan Ho had predicted: everyone trying to figure out why you had basically the entire legislature represented at such a meeting. So Sean gave the unspoken question his answer, prepared well in advance, which was this: "We're all here to help you."

Although what this really meant never sank in immediately, Alan Ho had told him, you knew that at some point when the haole or the Japanese developers (or in this case the Chinese) looked back on the whole thing, the first mention of the word "help" turned out to be the meeting's key moment: the *rules* captured in a single word.

So while they all sat there looking across Hawai'i from China to France and from France to China, Sean softened them up for the next blow by reviewing a deal whose particulars were already well-known by everyone there. 892 acres of the only virgin ocean-front land left on O'ahu still zoned for urban and resort development currently sat in the reluctant hands of CreditFranc—the bank had foreclosed on the Dolphin Bay Hotel, its two golf courses, and the surrounding land after plans to build five more hotel towers had fallen through due to delays caused by local environmental groups suing on the basis of the project's thirty-year-old Environmental Impact Statement, and an economic downturn that had been dragging on for nearly ten years. TsengUSA was ready to purchase the property and immediately follow through on an even larger five-tower expansion.

That, in a nutshell, was it. Sean reached the end of his summary almost surprised to find that it had all gone...perfectly. Easy. Nothing to it.

"And as Sean pointed out earlier," Alan Ho said, "We're here to help."

Backdropped by the sweeping view of his…domain…the Pacific Tower, the Bank of Hawaiʻi Building, the FHC, if not the harbor and the ocean beyond, Alan made one of those open-palm gestures and let the word hang in the air: *help*.

Prescott interpreted the whole thing for Liu, clearly a sharp man who was already picking up quite a bit of what was going on based on body language alone—if in fact he really *couldn't* understand English.

Liu stared straight ahead as he listened intently. He then spoke quietly to Prescott in a tone of a different man than the one who'd been laughing loudly over his breakfast only minutes earlier.

"Excuse me, Mr… Ho?" Prescott said. "Mr. Liu is very grateful for your assistance, but he explains that TsengUSA is ready to proceed with the purchase."

Alan Ho looked taken aback. Back in the '80s, as he'd explained it to Sean, the Japanese had come into these meetings and basically done what they were told, perhaps not wishing to offend their hosts. Even that European guy who'd tried to invest in the Big Island had followed along for a while before imploding in a typical display of haole emotion. But this was different.

"Yes, I believe the terms are favorable to both parties," Richard said, and Alan swung his head towards the other end of the table in…could it be? Sean wondered. In dis*belief*?

Alan Ho remained silent for a moment, and then said, "You probably don't want to rush something of this…magnitude. Our…concern here…our…*concern*…is for the long-term interests of TsengUSA."

Another exchange in Chinese. And then Prescott: "We understand your concerns. But we're ready to bring over thirty six hundred new jobs to this island. That's not even counting the initial construction work. Permanent jobs. Thousands of them. Right now."

Alan clearly couldn't believe what he was hearing. It usually took a good twenty minutes before anyone figured out what kind of "help" he was offering, if they managed to figure it out at all. But not this time. There wasn't going to be any "looking back" on this meeting to figure things out—they were onto him right from the get go. Both sides!

Alan gathered himself and went on: "What we're saying is that if we proceed too quickly here," *we proceed*, "there could be plenty of… problems."

"Problems?" Richard said.

"Yes, problems."

Prescott: "Such as?"

And for the first time this little idea about the seating arrangements—designed so it wouldn't *at first* look like Alan was presiding over the whole affair, so that he could *spring it on them all* that he was the one in charge—it didn't seem like such a great idea: in the next series of brief exchanges about environmental groups, and a potential widening of the highway servicing the property, and so on and so forth, Alan's head kept swinging back and forth from China to France and from France to China like he was at some kind of Olympic tennis match, because *none of it was working.*

On it went, back and forth, until at last Sean heard…*his own voice?*…speaking up: "Does that development have SHPD approval yet?"

Silence.

Just like that, all eyes were pinned on him.

The moment stretched, a cloud of *awkward* hanging now over the 21st-floor conference room in the Pauahi Tower, while Sean Hayashi sat wondering what it was he had just done. You could hear the hum of the air conditioner, punctuated by the soft clatter and clink of one of the waiters clearing a breakfast plate onto a tray at the room's edge. Had he actually spoken up, here in the thick of the meeting? State Senate President Russell Lee, House Speaker Charles Uchida, a Chinese multi-national's vice president, a senior loan officer from one of the biggest financial institutions in the world, not to mention Alan Ho, his mentor, who was looking mildly annoyed at this departure from the script—they were all *looking at him.* Even Grant Nishikawa had looked up from his touch screen, a smirk beginning to make its way onto that round face of his, no doubt in anticipation of someone putting Sean Hayashi in his place.

At last it occurred to Sean that if ever there was a time to *not give a fuck* (and early on he'd learned that simply *deciding* did not always make it so), it was right now. This was his *chance*. This was *it*. The whole reason why you didn't wind up heading down some safe caretaker-lawyer career path, some tooth mechanic graveyard, some lifer state job prison.

This! Now!

He forged on: "I mean, that costal region, with its relatively sandy soil…you've still got to conduct the Supplementary EIS, and the SHPD is going to require some kind of subsurface testing, and that place has to be littered with bones."

All eyes on him.

The air conditioner clicked off. And God, he hoped he hadn't fucked it up, because Alan Ho? If he was known for anything, it was that he never, ever gave anyone a *second chance*. Sean had heard so many stories he could imagine the man's wake littered with thirty years' worth of discarded office staff, consultants, and every commercial enterprise from shoddy hired caterers to the poor idiot who'd been stupid enough to do a rush job detailing his car that time.

But just then then the edges of Alan's moustache began to turn up into…a smile—the smile of a proud father, if Sean knew anything about it. Suddenly Sean could feel his own chest beginning to well with pride, really physically *feel* it. Rising! He'd *done* it! Clearly Alan hadn't even considered the SHPD, which Sean had only discovered after eight straight hours one day down at the DLNR—all along the man had indeed been counting on nothing more than his props, his aura of power, his reputation.

"What Sean is talking about," Alan said, "is the State Historic Preservation Division."

"Historic preservation?" Prescott said in that choppy accent of his. "Aside from the golf courses, this is virgin land, and the one existing hotel tower is hardly of historic value. It was built in 1972, and it looks like some kind of…I don't know…*spaceship*."

This drew a laugh from Alan, who was beginning to enjoy himself again now that he saw how irritated Prescott was becoming. "Spaceship!" he repeated. "No, Mr. Prescott, you can assure Mr. Liu that once all the proper state permitting requirements are met," here he deliberately paused, and turned his head to look squarely at Richard, and then turned it back to face Prescott, "and the proper utilities infrastructure has been built to adequately power everything," the same deliberate motion: pause, turn, turn, "and so on," pause, "once all of those important…concerns…have been addressed, he can pretty much do whatever he wants with the property's existing structure. He can build it thirty stories high if he wants. Even higher! The sky's the limit!" Big ingratiating smile. "What the SHPD would be interested in is the rest of the land—the part where he wants to build the five additional towers. I can't say for sure at the moment, but as Sean here points out, geologically speaking that entire stretch of coast would have been the perfect place for a Native Hawaiian cemetery. You wouldn't be allowed to plant a shovel there without SHPD approval, and even then, the process of exhuming and reburying all of those bones would be, well... complicated."

At this point Alan Ho did something the likes of Prescott and Richard, and certainly Liu had likely never seen before in any context, let alone that of a corporate conference room at a Monday morning breakfast meeting. He leaned back completely in his chair, and folded his hands behind his head in a way that brought out the full...*power*...of his thick, paddle-sculpted shoulders, and arms, and chest, and lats, and he fixed Prescott in a calm stare whose meaning was unambiguous: *I don't give a fuck.*

Now the silence was music to Sean's ears.

Let this moment stretch! The Chinese vice president: speechless. His arrogant haole interpreter: speechless. Marlise Deveaux, madly scrolling through the touch screen on the table in front of her, as if in search of some bit of overlooked information that would make this pesky hurdle of a back-country third-world state agency disappear. Emile Richard, now rubbing both hands the length of his face, wondering how he'll ever explain that December suntan to his superiors if he has to drag that $400 million albatross all the way back across two oceans to the bank. Russell Lee—he'd been through enough of these things to know that even with the results a foregone conclusion, the moment of victory was always a sweet one. Ditto, Charles Uchida.

Even Grant Nishikawa gave Sean a nod, as if, now that Sean had played such an important role in stomping these rich and powerful outsiders, Grant wanted to make sure he knew they were *boyz*, right? Since way back, ah? *Hanna-butta-dayz, brah!*

At last another volley of French took over this end of the room, and another round of Chinese took over that end of the room. The little Chinese suit was now a different man—not the gregarious laundromat owner, not the seething deliberator. His eyes opened wide, his forehead a range of deep crevices, he was firing angry bullets at Prescott and trying not to nod towards Alan, who had leaned forward, his ropey muscled forearms now on the table in front of him, his expression having shifted to a look of it's-out-of-our-hands empathy that would have been comical had it not been etched into his face with such deep sincerity.

Finally Prescott spoke up: "What exactly is it you want, Mr. Ho?"

Alan Ho leaned towards him, palms open. "As Sean here explained"—and even as they were spilling out, those words echoed in Sean's own head and confirmed it loudly: that the tap on the shoulder wasn't going to come, because he was indeed, beyond any doubt, pulling it off!

"As Sean here explained," Alan was saying, "We want to help you."

Front Page

It was only because the place had valet parking that Kekoa Meyer and Javen Campbell agreed to wait at frikken *Ballena's* while the wives "got their shop on"—plus, any man who *ran his own shit in his own house* wasn't going to be tagging along on some oh-yes-dear-that-$90-scarf-would-look-great-on-your-madda hunt through a place like Ala Moana Center, tagging along like one puppy dog.

Like one haole. Like one a those Okay Honey haole husbands you always saw at Kailua Beach or Lanikai. Or here. At Neiman fucking Marcus. On a Monday morning.

So here they were on a third-floor lanai overlooking a parking lot paved on top of the taro farm that had once fed King Kamehameha, overlooking a blue-tarp homeless colony beyond in Ala Moana Beach Park: two sullen men not just passing the time sipping…cappuccinos… but trying for figure some shit out and plan for the fallout.

On toppa alla that, as if the fucken *situation* hadn't been enough for set Kekoa off, maybe the gods were against him somehow too, throwing alladese things in his face just for fucking irritate him more: the Disney-fied wonderland of fake waterfalls and koi ponds lined with palm trees that had led them to this place.

Christmas lights. On frikken *palm* trees.
Poinsettias.
Store windows clogged with thousand-dollar handbags and *designer* this and *designer* that, designer frikken *cookware* and makeup and fucking *coffee*, the same kind of fag coffee they was drinking right now.

The gay wicker chairs with *throw pillows*.
A *table for two*.

Worse: couple bangers like him and Javen not sucking back green bottles at 10:30 in the morning—they sipping that…fag coffee…from little white China cups ringed with…pansies.

More worse: the reason for drinking coffee instead of sucking back green bottles in celebration. Fuck, celebrating was the last thing anyone felt like fucking doing now.

Kekoa could tell the pansies and the peach linen napkins and all the rest of it had Javen locked in fear that he might actually catch that highly contagious disease, *homosexuality* (even though he had two gay cousins, real strapping three-hundred-pound lipstick-and-mascara *mahus* both), that if Javen spent another minute in a place like Ballena's he himself might *turn gay*. Look at his leg: bouncing up and down so fast under the table he might wear a hole in the polished flagstone floor. Look at his head swiveling this way and that, scanning to make sure no one he knows spots him in such a fag place.

Usually Kekoa—fuck, he was so NOT-gay he could wear the same shirt to Aloha Stadium as that fat pink fuck of a football coach, Coach Brock. He could drink something other than a Heineken once in a while, a *cappuccino*, even a glass of wine like he did that time he took Dawn here for her birthday—fifty bucks for the kind of fish his father used to spear for free out in Waimānalo Bay, on a white porcelain plate the size of a pizza pan and stacked around a mound of purple mashed potatoes like some third grade science project. He could talk like one haole (at least when he wasn't so fucking irritated). He could go to college, *finish* college. That's how man-up NOT-gay Kekoa Meyer was. No more even any tattoos. No airbrushed likeness of his kids' faces. Warrior triangle patterns. Chinese characters. AK-47s. No I-shalt-smote-thee quotes from the Bible. Nothing. Man enough already cuz.

Except now all of it was irritating him, the white China cappuccino cup, the way their little California waiter "Michael" not "Mike" kept walking by with *no shame* for that thinning blonde hair or that *paunch* or those girly wrists sticking out of his white button-down shirt, or that baby-blue hibiscus relief necktie—irritating him, because when you put it all together it washed over like some kind of grim reminder that Kekoa Meyer's…grip…his hold on things…his man-up fucking *sway* had just…taken cracks. Dirty lickens. He was losing control. And there was the evidence, right there on the table.

"No worry cuz," Javen said. "Someone going call and take credit. Mandatory. Somebody going tex you. Watch." But they both knew nobody was going call, or text. Anyone going call, wouldda called right away. Fuck, one a da boyz wouldda been *proud* for take the credit, impress Kekoa Meyer. Proud.

And look now, right next to that fucking *gay* peach colored linen napkin: the all-out *front page* announcement that may as well have been spelled out in headline bold: *Kekoa Meyer Punked! Again!* An actual copy of the *Honolulu Sentinel*. They'd both read the headline on their phones—"H-3 Claims Tapusoa"—but Javen had spotted a real newspaper that someone had left on a table outside Starbuck's and grabbed it, like he and Kekoa could go and find a frame shop in here someplace preserve it forever behind glass as a symbol of their power. It was only once they'd ditched the wives that Kekoa could tell his cousin that there was just one problem: "Wasn't me, cuz. Wasn't me." Javen's eyes had bulged out at this revelation. That was when the leg had started pumping too.

Javen took a sip from his cappuccino, the dainty white cup contrasting violently with the silver skull rings biting into each one of his thick fingers. Both of them stared out past the blue tarps into the deep blue ocean and sky. And fuck, that ocean deepening in shades of blue all the way out towards Diamond Head way over on the left—its frikken post-card picture perfect outright beauty just irritated Kekoa even more. Shouldda been happy at the news, and the moment he'd seen it, he'd felt that *rush*. It had set everything right, punked the fucken *solés* right back to San Francisco or Samoa or wherever the fuck they was from, even if it was just Kalihi, sent one frikken message, put some *blood on the table*. Make *me* look stupid? Kekoa Meyer? Brah!

That rush—it was the same one he'd felt at Aloha Stadium when the whole thing was going down, like he'd done something *big*. Not his usual penny-ante protection taxman bullshit—but something up there with the way his dad had believed in that stadium, believed in this whole place. His dad. George Meyer. A man who had done all the right things and worked hard to support his family, who had *one good job* he performed with pride, only to wind up with some rare form of cancer, eaten up within a span of weeks and dead before his fiftieth birthday. Kekoa, all of fourteen at the time, had watched the big man die in a Castle Hospital ICU room whose tangle of tubes and wires hooked to all kinds of computers could do nothing to keep his father from becoming yet another statistic in the sad mortality figures Hawaiians kept chalking up, watched as a ring of his aunties held hands and offered up their equally useless prayers. And in the very moment the line on the screen went flat, he vowed to make things right somehow.

For my dad.

At first it had been school. From that moment on every time Kekoa entered a classroom he could hear his dad's voice: *Don't end up like me, Kekoa—you gotta do good, boy, you gotta study hard—you neva want to look back an' say you only wen' mess up because you neva really try.*

Kekoa's scholarship to UH—it hadn't been for football. He'd actually gotten kicked off the Kaiser football team halfway through freshman year for snapping at fucken Kalani "Too Tall" Anderson, the fat fucken senior lineman who'd been dogging him, dogging him, hazing the "rookie D-back" all season long until one day in the locker room Kekoa, all of 5' 9", like 175 at the time, he just walked over, took two steps and a jump, and bit down. Almost ripped half that fucka's cheek off right in front of everybody. Would have, too, would have spat it right out on the floor, blood gushing everywhere, warm in his own mouth, fucken Kalani screaming out like one bitch—and that too, in a much different way, had been for his dad, because ever since the man had been robbed from their lives Kekoa had learned how to tap into a well of anger and resentment known only to those confined to watching others spend their lives taking their own living fathers for granted.

Sometimes Kekoa dove deep into that well—usually he took small sips, like when he mixed the resentment with the memory of Dad's *gotta-make-good* advice to push him through a free ride at UH as a Chancellor's Scholar. By junior year he was vice president of the UH student senate. History degree, *suma cum laude*. He'd had all the tools. A bright future, everybody said. A leader.

But after graduation? Nothing. Weeks scouring the ads had netted offers like Assistant Manager at DFS Hawai'i. Long's. ABC Stores. His adviser started telling him to move to the mainland. Guys that worked with his dad started telling him to try City and County. Somebody knew the valet manager at the Hilton, the boys made good tips parking cars. Ten-dolla whores, every one of them, was all Kekoa could see.

That was when Javen had called. Again. Javen had been calling all though school, telling Kekoa he already was "one legend." Kekoa snapping on Kalani "Too Tall" may have cemented it with all its blood and gore, plus not once in that fat fuck's whole life had anyone had the balls to even think about calling out Kalani Anderson.

But Kekoa had been *down* ever since elementary, and the legend had taken root because he'd never actually "called out" anyone—it had always been more like a reflex: they all working themselves up fo' scrap, maybe they give you The Bump like one signal they like challenge you, like they tapping gloves in the ring, j'like they get frikken *rules*, one way for conduct one *fair fight*. Fair fight! What, you going drop the sixty-eighty-hundred pounds you get on me before we go? You going reel those arms in so you no more that ten-inch reach advantage cuz? Right! So we make 'um fair: while you getting all work-up, I just going drop you before you know what hit you, an' I going use whateva get in reach: glass bottle, keys for my truck, fork on the table, fucken waiter's fucken ball point pen brah, gouge your fucken eyes out. *Dat's* your fucken rules. *Dat's* your fucken fair fight.

Except Javen's call after graduation—there had been more to it: "We going need you cuz, need somebody wit brains, somebody understand how for organize, how for lead. We could do 'um together, cuz, you the brains, I the muscle." Javen's dad had been the bull of Maui back in the day, and when Javen had taken over Uncle Freddy's trucking company, the chicken fights and the clubs had come along with it. Even Uncle Freddy had called: "My son, he one good boy, Kekoa, an' people respect him, and you know I love my boy, but he's jus' not a leader, an plus you—you went *college*, boy, we need you."

Kekoa knew his own dad never would have allowed it back when he was alive, except that after weeks of getting turned away even for the ten-dolla-whore jobs that these frikken mainland community college drop-outs seemed to walk straight into, he'd worked it out that the old man would have understood that nowadays Javen's offer was all you had left, the only way to equal Dad's tremendous pride for Hawai'i, the only chance Hawaiians had anymore to take charge on their own land, put this place on the map, a map that was looking more and more like a map of California. Those few brief moments the other night when Aloha Stadium had become Kekoa's *domain*, when he'd *owned* that fat haole coach and everyone else—it wasn't just that he'd won. The whole thing had confirmed at last that in throwing in with Javen all those years back, Kekoa had taken a path that would have made his father proud.

And then the fucken *solés* make him look fucken stupid. Plus now the headline: *H-3 Claims Tapusoa*. One whole day had passed and nobody had let him know about the "accident." Not his boyz. Not one-a-the young kids. Not even one of his cop friends from high school, the ones he hired in their off hours to work for the private security company he ran with Javen.

Nobody.

"I say we come out blazing," Javen said, and right there you could picture it: Uzis and assault rifles lighting up Hotel Street, its concrete surface littered with shattered glass and splintered wood and moaning brown bodies, even the cops at the corner Mauna Kea Street station hiding like bitches in their own basement. Five-ten years ago that would have been the first option, too: go on offense, start smashing, bullets flying and even more blood on the table before anyone finds out the ugly truth that he wen' get punked not just once but twice, that someone *else* wen' take out Tapusoa.

"That's what I like do right fucking now," he said.

Except…he couldn't put words to it, but something was telling him main t'ing cool head, going get your chance, watch. Gotta be one nodda way. But what? Some kind of "summit" meeting? You going walk in there an' play like you *was* the one wen' waste Tapusoa when you neva? Fuck, not even Kekoa Meyer NOT-gay enough for pull that off. You talking about *loyalty*. You talking about respect from this gang of frikken *solés* wen' grow up jus' like you, walking fearless into schoolyard fights where the point was never to *win* but to *do damage*, even if was six a them an' they wen' lick me but I wen' get plenny cracks in too so. You going walk into that an' *make* like you wen' take out Tapusoa? Fuck, I give you credit. Cause it going come out later thatchoo neva. An' then the whole t'ing going fall apart. Watch. Or what? You going just walk in there with your palms open and say, "Look, you know, I really *wanted* to do it, but it wasn't me, see, let me *explain*." Brah! I give you credit!

"Everybody going t'ink it's you anyway, cuz," Javen said.

Kekoa shook his head. "They all already think it was me, even these fuckas wen' cova the whole thing up. If you read what they wrote, it sounds exactly like that's what wen' happen: 'unfortunate accident.'"

"Yeah, then everybody start talking: 'Ho, you seen the game the odda night? You seen how Tapusoa wen' miss the tackle! Mus' be somebody wen' take 'im out. Gotta be!' But they cannot put that kine stuff in the paper—they gotta protect the 'Warrior program'! Everyone in the booster club going pull all their ads, you start speculating about a UH player fixing one game. Warrior pride—that shit runs *deep*. They going cova this shit up j'like they wen' cova up the coach that knocked up the volleyball playa, when what they should do is try fo' find out who really did 'um. Mandatory."

Javen was right. Forget about the paper—people knew anyway. The *Sentinel* had even turned off the online comment section, and not just for that story, either, and not just for all the other football stories. Kekoa had been checking the website every day for years and never seen them block every comment section for the whole paper. He said so to Javen.

"Right away they going talk about t'rowing the point spread, about gambling, this an' that," Javen said. "They going leave links to the play on YouTube. They going talk about 'rival factions' and 'underworld gambling activity.' But the way they putting 'um now, when the *solés* read 'um, an' when anybody who bet on the game read 'um, they going know it's you. Who you t'ink did 'um, anyway?"

Kekoa looked back out past Ala Moana Beach Park again. A nice left was breaking off the edge of Magic Island, a little dot of a surfer making cutbacks on the wave's shoulder. "That's the thing," he said. "I don't fucken know." They went over again how they'd all waited in the stadium parking lot, how Vic Maehara and Steven Lum, both former UH linebackers from the winless fucken Von Appen years, knew exactly where the players exited. Just in case, they'd stationed boyz all the way back toward Kahuku along the Windward side, too—Tapusoa was Mormon, so he wasn't going party after the game, he was just going go straight home. But H-3, especially by the tunnels up there, had *cameras* all over H-3, so you couldn't just pull off on the side and wait. And maybe it was the rain. Maybe the *solés* had disguised Tapusoa's exit.

Either way, Kekoa had been made to look...stupid. Again—a thought that suddenly got amplified—you couldn't explain it, it was just that it was so frikken *irritating*, on *sight*, especially when you added it to the peach colored linen napkins and the fag waiter and the rest of it—amplified by this pair of haole ladies walking right past their table.

Both of them in their fifties maybe, hard to tell with these haoles, they spent so much time frying their skin in the sun like they wanted everyone for know they *lived here*. The taller one had on this tight-fitting hibiscus-print muʻumuʻu that showed off the thick rolls of fat gathered in her upper back, the shorter one in tan shorts and a pink polo shirt—her hair spilled out of a U.S. Open Shinnecock Hills visor like straw, like one fucken scarecrow, an' look at her throw that sideways glance at Kekoa and his baggy black jeans stuffed into his black-and-red high-top Jordans, his white long-sleeved warm-up jersey tagged at the neck with a tiny black Nike swoosh. Look at her eyeing Javen up and down: his gold chain. Authentic yellow Kobe Bryant jersey over a white T-shirt. Nevermind it's "authentic" cause Kobe himself wore it during an actual NBA game. You could hear what she thinking: my goodness, they let these...*mokes*...into a place like Ballena's...and don't they even know what "Island Casual" means?

That was what the frikken menu said. Island fucking Casual. Kekoa was about to say something too, except right then his phone started buzzing on the table, lighting up with a picture of...you could see it from here, that ex-con-hustler's look of *We boyz, ah cuz?* flattery on the ghetto-serious man-up face of fucken Nolan fucken Kahaiue. As if Kekoa already wasn't in a foul enough mood.

Nolan Kahaiue. Dis fucka. He been dogging me for what, two-three weeks now behind on his tax: no worry Kekoa, no worry, I going take care. Like he *playing* me, trying for see how far he can push, even he get the money the whole frikken time, he think he one king pin just cause he get his own six-acre compound back of Kahaluʻu, one $50,000 Cigarette speed boat he never took out. One huge second-floor lanai he never used because he drank with his boyz under the florescent lights in the garage instead. All from slanging clear all up and down the Windward side. Ice. Meth. He banking, too, cause he smart enough for stay off the stuff himself, not like alla the little playas like man up, soon as they see they not going light up Aloha Stadium they turn straight to trying for be bangers, dealers, trying for slang clear, and soon they hooked on the shit themselves and then lock-up. Not Nolan.

Maybe Nolan would have done well in school too, except right now he *calling*, too—he neva text. He neva text cause he cannot *see*, cannot see the screen on his phone, he all squinting, holding it up far away like one old man trying for read the newspaper. But he too proud for go and get glasses, too scared somebody going call him one fag, one frikken poindexta widdiz fucken glasses. Fuck, maybe he think he smarter than me, but today of all days fucken Nolan betta *have something*.

Kekoa picked up his phone to catch the message, and good: instead of the usual bullshit flattery, another excuse, he heard a…request…a request to come by *whereva you stay* and pay the tax *today*. Frikken Nolan almost sounded like one of the regular clients Kekoa "protected" in the legal way through the legitimate security company he ran with Javen, Aloha Protectors of Honolulu. Good. Kekoa returned the call right away, and got more of the same with the real live Nolan Kahaiue too: more flattery. Even better: when Nolan went on with his "You know we love you, brah," Kekoa could detect none of the guy's usual I-going-flatta-you-but-I-going-put-one-*edge*-on-it tone.

Just to test things, he decided to give Nolan an opening: "You know the Neiman Marcus?" Kekoa told him. "Third floor, the restaurant, it's called Ballena. We stay out on the lanai."

Right there you could see Javen start looking this way and that and trying to pull his toughest faces, like he was practicing to show Nolan Kahaiue that he himself neva would've picked a place like this. Kekoa waited for Nolan to make some kind of *What, you guys on one date?* comment. Instead Nolan just promised to show up in fifteen minutes and hung up.

"That fucken punk say one fucken thing about we sitting out here, I going choke his frikken neck," Javen said, his foot pumping away.

"No worry cuz," Kekoa said. "Fucka scared."

They both thought about that. Scared. Scared of if Kekoa Meyer wen' take out the UH star linebacker and get away with it, what he going do wit' some frikken bottom-feeder drug dealer like Nolan Kahaiue. You could hear the fear over the phone.

Then Javen said, "Eh, what if the *solés* wen' do 'um themselves?"

Kekoa smiled. The *solés* had been on his own initial list of potential…*suspects*. Now that Javen had thought of the same thing, it didn't seem so… Machiavellian.

Machiavellian!

It was one of Kekoa's favorite terms from all of the classes he'd taken at UH. Machiavellian himself was some French philosopher or something—that part was kind of vague in Kekoa's head—who'd talked about how men had used behind-the-scenes-type maneuvering and lying and shit to gain power. As his example the professor used post-statehood-era governor John Burns, how all five State Supreme Court justices he himself had appointed chose whoever he "suggested" to run the world's richest land trust.

And people call *me* a fucken gangster…

"It sounds stupid, but," Javen said, almost embarrassed.

"Then why was I thinking the same thing?" Kekoa said. "You calling me stupid, cuz?"

"Nah, nah, nah!"

And then they went on: the *solés* act like they following this guy home for protect him. Somebody starts a race, on the H-3, in the pouring rain, good fun-kine, blow off steam after the game-kine, everybody laughing. Not too hard then for run him off the road, right into the frikken' *wall*. But wouldn't that show up on the cameras? Maybe it did, but look how they wen' cova everyt'ing up. An' forget about the gambling—the booster club wouldn't want it getting out that the fucka die racing either. So now he dead, an' the *solés* know that everyone jus' going t'ink it was Kekoa-guys wen' do 'um. But *why?* Well, that's where they get all Machiavellian on everyone.

"See, they *like* everyone t'ink it was us, cause then they get one reason for *come afta* us, for *come out blazing*. They get the same idea as us." Kekoa lifted his white porcelain cup to take a sip. And it hit him, the true nature of the little power struggle that had unfolded in rainy Aloha Stadium. Even putting aside the far-fetched idea that the *solés* had killed Tapusoa themselves: "It wasn't just a football game for them either," he said. "They like be the next Sonny Bulger too."

Sonny Bulger. No one needed to elaborate—the name, a magical name from way back when people from Hawaiʻi still *ran things*, was enough. Right up until the early '90s, the *power*: still right here, just like before Captain Cook, with King Kamehameha, with Kalākaua. Even when the haoles took over they at least kept their power concentrated here. But Sonny Bulger…along with that ancient U.S. senator who'd just died in office, Sonny Bulger was the last man with *local control.* Right when Hawai'i started putting itself on the map, and here come the Japanese *yakuza* on one side, and the American mafia on the other—Sonny Bulger was standing in the way. The man used to have his driver take him from one end of his empire to the other in a long black Cadillac. True, Kekoa heard he gave up Waikiki to the *yakuza,* but that hadda be one minor concession, one exchange for "protecting" the ice trade, which, back in the mid-'80s, was all Japanese.

Sonny Bulger! *Nobody* fucked with Sonny Bulger. Small guy, too, small just like Kekoa, but the fucka was *off!* Had one story about how he "allegedly" killed these two informants and cut them into little pieces and buried them in a shallow grave up in Waikāne Valley. Even he got caught, he *still* managed to get acquitted after allegedly bribing a judge, a judge with all the signs of a gambling addiction. A few years later they found the frikken judge dead in the parking lot outside his Vegas hotel. Acquitted! It took the Feds until 1992 to take Bulger down—that, and a Kentucky prison cell—*the man,* dead at the age of 53.

Since then nobody had stepped up. A couple of guys had tried, but in over twenty years, still nothing. And in all those years, what had Kekoa been doing?

Marching up is what.

Recruiting one army, one that could fill one whole section at Aloha Stadium. Building one empire, piece by game-room-strip-club-massage-parlor-tax-paying-drug-dealer fucken piece. Ten years. Finally getting into that…position…where not only you can pull off fixing one UH game, but thatchoo fixing it for one *reason,* fixing it to make one *statement,* to finally fill that power void. After twenty-plus years. Until…

Fuck. He'd been fucking 43 seconds away. Fuck.

Now here came the gay haole waiter, Michael-not-Mike, with that little smile of his. The little elf turned back to face the inside of the restaurant, and made this sweeping open-palmed motion toward their table, his tanned face beaming in pure delight, his knee bending into a slight bow, like some Price is Right game show hostess displaying the winning washer-dryer set.

If the guy was fucking with them, it was working: Kekoa felt like lighting the little faggot up right here. Javen's heel-bouncing tripled in speed, him fumbling for his phone like he trying for look busy, like he wish there was some trap door next to his seat so he could escape all of this…*gayness*.

The two gangstas looked up to see Nolan Kahaiue slowly walking their way and looking around like he was more afraid of this place than even Javen, forget that he was built like a fire hydrant, baggy denim pants reaching down into these blinding white high-tops, his still-thick neck bulging out of a black tent-of-a-shirt two sizes too big that shouted out the word *Ainokea*. His Popeye forearms were covered in tattoos, a stiffened black UH Warriors "H" cap perched slightly sideways on his head in that banger way.

"Will the gentleman be joining you?" Michael asked, raising his eyebrows in a way that made all three of their stomachs turn.

Kekoa and Javen both stared bullets into Nolan, Javen clearly thinking the same thing Kekoa was, which was: go ahead, you fucken cliché bottom-feeder mothafucka, go ahead and *say something*. An' get ready, you fucken tax delinquent, I going tell you about all the juice still running on that nut you neva pay me until now, I going ream your fucken ass you dumb fuck.

"Nah nah nah nah," was what Nolan said instead, waving a hand in front of him—and it was a neutral sort of nah-nah-nah, with no hint of irony or sarcasm. "I no like interrupt," he said, also without managing to insinuate anything. "I jus' like drop somet'ing off, and den I gotta run." He was already rocking back and forth on his heels, likely praying for the waiter to disappear before he too got infected with homosexuality.

"Are either of you gentlemen ready for another cappuccino?" Michael asked.

Javen didn't answer. He just kept fixing Nolan in that death stare that as much as shouted, "It's not whatchoo *think*, brah. We not *gay!*"

"No, we're good for now," Kekoa said. And with that the little elf was gone.

Kekoa turned to Nolan and said, "The girls stay inside doing their Christmas shopping. You sure you no like join us?" he asked, further daring Nolan to even think about drawing any conclusions.

At the same time he could tell how everyone else in the place had turned to stare at Nolan, at the rumply *Ainokea*-shirted figure of a middle-aged man nervously rocking back and forth. Those three older local-Japanese banker-lawyer-kine guys at the table over near the wall, that gaggle of girls-day-out 'Iolani-Mid-Pac Island Casual housewives near the bar—everyone had stopped talking and started staring, and now they were all echoing the thoughts of those two sun-dried haole ladies: You never knew how people were going to dress nowadays, but this was *Ballena!* And these men, these…*mokes* (like it was perfectly okay to use the local equivalent of the n-word) these mokes are polluting our *club*, was what they wanted this place to be. And while you might get away with a new white Nike warm-up shirt, or even a basketball Jersey as long as it marked you as…of a certain means…an *Ainokea* shirt was pure ghetto. *Ainokea*, they were telling themselves: someone had proudly invented a word for throwing your spent styrofoam plate-lunch box out of the window of your lifted Toyota Tacoma after picking up your six kids from Hawai'i's taxpayer-funded after school daycare program. A Hawaiianization of "I no care," it meant that you wanted to blame everyone else for all of your troubles, that you wanted everything handed to you while you drank your life away hoping that one of these weeks all of your football picks would come through.

"Nah nah," Nolan said again, this time with a smile. "I'm all good, cuz. Me, I'll stick to Pepsi and green bottles. I jus' wanted fo' drop this off for you." He reached into a side pocket and pulled out a crumpled dirty white envelope, smudged with engine grease and too thick to close. "I jus' like thank you, bradda Kekoa," he said, slapping Kekoa's hand and hanging on with a local-boy handshake and staring into his eyes with deep sincerity—sincerity that for the first time felt…genuine. "An' I gotta apologize too. I know dis long time coming, an' I not been dat good about paying my tax, an' even, yeah," he looked off for a second, searching for a way to put it, "even, I gotta admit, I shame about the way I been acting. You know I always look up to you, Kekoa."

As he went on stammering out the apology—a real one, too, not one of those if-you-was-offended kind—Kekoa could see that Nolan was…uncomfortable…and that his discomfort had less to do with the gay surroundings than with his need to make things right with Kekoa Meyer. *Scared.*

"We all like thank you," Nolan was saying, "me, Freddy, Johnny-boy—das' from alla us guys. Thank you fo' taking care us guys. You da *man*, cuz. You know the Windward side, das the only place lef' in the whole state not getting ova run. From Kahalu'u all the way up to Hau'ula, jus' get me, an' Freddy, and Johnny-boy, an' then alla da guys running offa us guys, and dassit. Once in a while you get one young punk from Wai'anae or someplace. But as soon as we bring up bradda Kekoa? Whoo, da fucka *split*. Gone! An' no more Mexicans. Wetback mothafuckas stay *invading*, Kona side, Kaua'i—all ova. But not Windward. We no more problems Windward. Everyt'ing smooth. We love you, cuz."

Kekoa put the envelope down on the table. He didn't have to look to know that it was stuffed with hundreds, at least twenty grand worth, and good, you fucka. Neva mind the money starts rolling in, going… embolden…embolden a guy like Nolan Kahaiue, grew up thinking one EBT card was how you got food, returning cans an' bottles, neva graduated Castle fucken High. Good now you scared. Good you feeling obligated. Good you stay rocking back and forth like that.

Just to fuck with him Kekoa said, "So what, you an' Freddy-them been dropping my name up there?"

Nolan's eyes bulged open and he started backpeddling: "Not like *that*, bradda Kekoa, not like we chirping. You know we love you brah."

So Kekoa narrowed his eyes and said, "So you mean you *not* dropping my name then Nolan?"

More backpeddling, now in the opposite direction: "Nah, nah—we dropping 'um, cuz, we dropping your name so everybody know you the king bull, brah, you know, we all looking up to you Kekoa. Just that nobody talking shit. No bullshit, cuz, you-know-what-I-mean." Nolan lifted his arm to wipe the sweat off his brow, breathing heavier now too.

Kekoa let him rock back and forth a little more. At last he said, "You sure you no like join us? They get beer too you know." But it wasn't an invitation.

"Nah nah," Nolan said. "I gotta go pick up Marla, she stay doing her own Christmas shopping. Nordstrom's." Javen looked relieved. Nordstrom's! How gay was *that?* Nordstrom's. "Aloha, my braddas," Nolan said, and then he beat it out of this froufy place…*scared*…right back in fucken line, too, from now on he neva going be late again.

And look at that thick dirty envelope: that was how the whole thing was supposed to work, the whole tax collecting enterprise: they gotta be *happy* to pay, cause when they paid one single tax to you, they not paying three-four-five taxes to all these otha fuckas standing there wit' their hands out: the liquor inspector, the cops, the four-five other wannabe-gangsta thugs that stay shaking them down right now. That's how Sonny Bulger did. That's how he controlled the drugs, and how he was in on the gambling. Plus they gotta think you *off*, like you frikken going jus' pull outchoa nine an' start pumping rounds right here.

Which was suddenly exactly what Kekoa felt like doing: pumping fucking rounds at alladese *cosmopolitan* motherfuckers watching the *Ainokea* ghetto country *island nigger* exiting their precious club, hopefully going back to that Kahalu'u shack of his, the one with the two rusting VW bugs up on blocks in the front yard. *Hawaiian hedge.* Because bottom-feeder or not, Nolan Kahaiue slangin' his fucken clear, his fucken ice—he was better than all these fucking Island Casual motherfuckers put together.

Listen to these people, even local people—townie locals, yeah, Kam school lawyer-kine, accountant-kine, real estate-kine, faded hundred-dollar-aloha-shirt kine, still yet, they local—listen: someone get that *moke* to quit contaminating our presence, and oh, praise and thanks to Neiman Marcus for blessing Honolulu as a real place, a worthy place, and not some grass-shack pineapple outpost where we're all confined to buying our clothes from…Sears…McInerney's…Liberty House.

Look at them snapping pictures of their popovers with their phone cameras. Kekoa had read about their type *lining up outside overnight* when the store first opened, with a traditional Hawaiian blessing, kicking off another huge expansion of the rest of the 2,000-acre mall: Macy's, Nordstrom's, Coach, Louis Vuitton, Disney, Victoria fucking Secret. Enough *fanfare* to push the biggest corruption scandal ever to hit Hawai'i right off the front page. Reports that the Legislature was so deep in the pockets of a $10 billion land trust that they ousted the Attorney General to stop her from taking everyone down—that news had taken a backseat to that little popover they gave you instead of a bread roll here at Ballena—named not after some local fusion chef, but the fucking Spanish word for *whale.* Because the Honolulu elite didn't want *local.* They wanted fashionable. *State of the art.* Neiman fucking Marcus. Not Long's or Foodland or the Crack Seed Center. *Fashionable* looked down on *local* like a mid-level Punahou bank manager looked down on a 42-year-old Hawaiian dressed in an *Ainokea* shirt…on another

42-year-old Hawaiian dressed in a pressed white Nike warm-up shirt. It looked *down*.
Because local was *lazy*. Local was stupid. *Stupid*.
An' okay alla you Island Casual motherfuckers. Watch. Go on thinking Kekoa Meyer just one F-150-driving Hawaiian thug—I going Machiavellian every one a you. I going *own* you. An' maybe just had one little minor…setback. But we going regroup. Come back stronger. Outsmart alla you, an' we'll see who's lazy. We'll fucking *see*. Starting with the fucking *solés* that fucking set us back in the first place. Watch.
He turned to Javen: "Okay here's what we do," he said. "For now, we going wait. Salanoa-them not going do anything until afta the funeral, guarantee."
"Ho, that's a long time cuz. You eva been to one Samoan funeral? They call alla da relatives from everywhere—outer island, mainland, Samoa, all ova. Going take weeks for set the thing up."
"That's the point. If they really the ones that did it, they probably expecting us fo' do somet'ing right away. Even if they not the ones. But no worry. You gotta be calm, cool, collec', but right afta one funeral, everybody stay all emotional. Everybody *react*. And that's when they fuck up. Everybody all worked up fo' scrap, you *reacting*. So I tell you what we going do. We going *show up* at that fucken funeral. We going stand in line, look right into the eyes of the madda-fadda-them, right there in front of everybody. That right there going set them off. They going go *off*, cuz. An' that's when we waste allathem fucken *solés*: we wait for them for fuck up—an' they *going* fuck up—that's when we jus' start *blazing*."
He turned and shouted out: "Eh Mike!" His voice startled the two sun-dried haole ladies, and caused the gaggle of girls-day-out housewives to look up, and turned the head of some hotel GM over at the table over there with the smoking-hot dark-haired hapa girl half his age.
The little balding California waiter came running like it was some kind of emergency. Good.
"Two Heinekens," Kekoa said. "In the bottle."

THE TOP OF THE VOLCANO

Rumrum rumrum rumrum! Clackclackclackclackclackclackclack! Rumrum rumrum rumrum! Clackclackclackclackclackclackclack! Rumrum rumrum rumrum! Clackclackclackclackclackclackclack! The roar from that Board of Water Supply diesel generator just kept *exploding* up from the Capitol's rotunda floor all the way down there, punctuated by a machine-gun blast of a couple of jackhammers. And it sounded just like the inside of Russ's *head*, which was clacking and roaring away with the scatter of its own frantic thoughts.

Like these: Now it's *public*, Russ! Right there on the front page! *H-3 Claims Tapusoa!* It's spreading like wildfire across an entire state! Sure, Uchida's aide said the paper had painted the whole thing as an accident, but anyone who'd seen the last two minutes of the game had to at least wonder! Because how on earth could Ufi Tapusoa, All-WAC, All-American, headed for a high pick in the NFL draft, fail to wrap up a clock-eating fullback like Fia Sagapolu? With less than a minute left? Allowing UNLV to cover the spread? When the fix was supposed to have been in in the other direction?

That's right—Russ had heard about the fix, too, which was why he'd called Lave Salanoa in the first place to place his bet…seven would cover the day's losses…no, why not ten…shoots, if the fix is in, why not *fifty*? And before you knew it, Leshawn Walker was streaking through the pouring rain to cut the UNLV lead to 18 points. It had all seemed so simple until…until…until…

Rumrumrumrumrumrum ROAR! Clackclackclackclackclackclackclack!
There was still only one way out that Russ could see, and that was to

pay Lave as quickly as possible and turn around and run before anyone down at the *Honolulu Sentinel* did enough digging: Senator Lee! Who *you* been hanging around with? Been *chasing*?

And paying off Lave—that was going to depend on a lot of things, not least of which was whether or not Russ could get Cliff Yoshida here to go along with his idea of going *all in*, of cashing in on the twenty-year career in the Lege to finally run for governor, forget that he was third in line at best.

Clackclackclackclackclackclackclack! Rumrum rumrum! Clackclackclackclackclackclack! Jesus, at the same time all that racket sounded like some kind of high-powered version of the old desk-top computer Russ used to have in his office that rattled away whenever you had to wait it out while it was "thinking," because that was exactly what Russ was doing now, too, with Cliff: waiting him out while he sat there, *thinking*.

Not that the act itself was unusual—if nothing else, little Clifford was the king of all deliberators—or even the location: a stone bench on the Capitol's fifth-floor terrace overlooking the forest of gleaming downtown towers and the ocean beyond. After any big meeting, Russ always made it a point to come all the way up here to sort things out with Cliff. Whether it was the view from the building's sweeping open-air upper level, Russ couldn't say. Maybe it was because this was the *Executive* floor, where you could at least dream of someday walking through one of those two pairs of beautifully grained coffee-colored fifteen-foot hardwood doors facing each other up here on opposite balconies to your *own office*, the Governor's office.

Either way, the bench up here was always preferable to Russ's own cramped third-floor cell—especially now, even with that roar and clatter down there in the pit of the volcano, even with most of the cracked and buckling terrace area in front of them roped off by that orange construction fencing running in front of them.

For one thing, up here you were practically right on top of 'Iolani Palace, which rose up right there in front of the capitol. A real *state house*—not some statehood-era cartoonish Hawaiian-sense-of-place monstrosity, was what the State Capitol was, loaded down with symbolism so cheap and obvious that even a former linebacker like Russ could figure it out: a lattice-like box (a grass shack?) supported by long rows of column-like "palm trees" and perched atop two ground floor chambers sculpted round like the sides of…a volcano…springing from an "ocean" of stagnant algae-thickened reflecting pools, rising on four sides of the football-field-sized rotunda and narrowing at the top like a real volcano does. A volcano! Then they'd crowned the whole thing together up here at the top by what looked like a circle of canoe outriggers sweeping skyward?

More important than the view, though, Russ could be sure that back down in his office one person after the next would be rushing in to discuss the big news of the day. The *front page* news. And damned if he wanted any further reminders about how close his whole fifty grand debt was to *going public*. Just the thought of it—

Rumrumrumrumrumrum ROAR!Clackclackclackclackclackclackclack!

At least the ever-pragmatic Cliff Yoshida was *pondering* it this time, was all Russ could tell himself. He looked out at those turrets and arched windows of the palace in front of him, the Hawaiian flag proudly flapping in the trade winds. And even in the thick of his…waiting…it occurred to him that now more than ever, that majestic building evoked a *bygone era*—and not of the years when it had in fact served as the state capitol, but of the Hawaiian monarchy, officially well over a century behind them.

Only officially, though.

And therein lie even a practical argument why Cliff here, of all people, might believe it was indeed *time*. For the past sixty years Hawai'i had been *de facto* ruled by its senior U.S. Senator, an octogenarian World War II veteran who'd built up so much seniority in Washington that he could annually send upwards of $10 billion in federal military pork into the state's economy. Although "monarch" was hardly the term (political "godfather" was more like it), just as the man's endorsement could win you any race from county council on up to the U.S. Congress, a mere ruffle of his feathers could sink you for good. Four years ago it had taken Cliff's calm advice to basically save Russ's own political career, when he'd first considered doing the unthinkable by refusing to wait his turn and run against a sitting Lieutenant Governor that Senator had already anointed.

Russ could only hope that this time his clerk was mulling over the fact that Senator had at last *died in office*, creating a free-for-all within the Democratic party which had left "waiting your turn" by the wayside. Or that although the current governor, Donald Nakayama, had exhausted his two allotted terms, everyone else would be fighting for the U.S. congressional seats, whose occupants would vacate to vie for the seat now symbolically held by Senator's 85-year-old widow—everyone except the current LG, James Hendrick, a haole transplant who had once made enough of a name for himself as a champion of local water rights to get elected to the house, and then later as LG.

Now that you thought about it, Cliff was always the one pointing out how Hendrick had taken the "do-nothing" part of a do-nothing office to new heights, counting on Senator's endorsement to carry him through.

Russ's clerk indeed must have been mulling over all these things, because at last he looked up and, raising his voice above the roar, said, "Are you sure about this, Russell?"

Russ had to wonder if he'd heard it right through all the noise. Mr. Risk Assessment himself—was he actually…taking it seriously?

Speechless, Russ just nodded his head.

"Clearly you've given it a lot of thought," Cliff said loudly. "But I know you Russell, and frankly, your optimism doesn't always serve you well. Are you really sure about this?" And on he went about how this wasn't a simple state senate campaign you could take with thirty thousand votes—this was the big leagues, they're going to come after you, both in the primary and in the general, millions of dollars in outside donations, all lining up to dig and smear, and smear some more. But however *practical* it all sounded, you couldn't help but hear it in the little man's voice: *possibility!*

Russ's heart rate jumped, a cascade of thoughts following in a single breath: if you could get *Cliff* to go along with it, then it was because the little man knew you were a shoe-in, so you were as good as elected already. You, Russell Lee, only the second Hawaiian governor in the state's history, right at the top of the volcano!

Think of what you really finally *could* accomplish for your people! You do it right! You could be another Kalākaua, the 19th-century king who built that majestic palace rising up right over there to support that Hawaiian flag, a man once more powerful than even the dead U.S. Senator, a man who'd held so much sway over the haole sugar barons that he could build a *real* state house with their money. 'Iolani Palace even had a telephone long before the White House did. Because Kalākaua had done *the possible*, had recognized the power of the sugar money and worked with it. What would someone like Ikaika Nāʻimipono or Tom Watada say to *that?*

"So given the fundraising climate," Cliff was saying, "along with how you would be competing with Hendrick for money, not to mention how much a dogfight against him in the primary would wind up costing, along with the fact that he'd have Nakayama's endorsement, plus the name recognition of his two terms as LG, well, I hate to be the one to break it to you, Russ, but I just don't see it happening."

Huh?

Russ was crushed. Here was Cliff Yoshida, for the first time in history, actually *considering* the goal that had propelled former All-Wac Defensive Team linebacker Russell Lee on his path from—let's admit it—from the football field and into law school and all along his climb up the state senate food chain (because if you don't have your sights set on the *top*, on the *fifth floor*, there's no sense in playing in the first place), and right here when it's finally *in his grasp*, after years and years of building relationships, making connections, figuring out *how things work*, honing the natural leadership skills he'd first built captaining the UH defense—after all that, it's *I just don't see it happening?* Just like that?

What the fuck was Russ supposed to do now? Not to mention…he hated to think it…but, fuck, the guy wasn't going away…what about Lave Salanoa? What about *fifty thousand dollars?*

"Look, Cliff," he said, raising his own voice above the noise, "you were right about this last time, and I value your judgment above anyone else I know. Even Cathy. I've probably spent more hours with you than with her over the past twenty years. In fact I know I have, if you added it up. But sometimes you've got to take some risks, or big chances can pass you right by."

Cliff was listening intently—but that's what Cliff always did whenever Russ went off on one of his emotional lines of argument. So who knew.

He plowed on: "The fundraiser. The one for Hokulani?"

All at once, the clacking jackhammers stopped, and the generator wound down to a low hum, low enough that you could now hear the sound of the breeze, even. It was startling, the silence.

"What do we *do* here, Cliff?" Russ went on. "This is supposed to be the *Crossroads of the Pacific*, and it just keeps looking more and more like some third-world banana republic. That fundraiser—it brought in like, a hundred thousand dollars."

"That sounds about right." Cliff said. "That's fifty outpatients Gary Wright can now help. And then there's the exposure an event like that brings to his mission. Total cost was low. The Hilton probably donated the space and staff time and the food as a write-off."

"That's chump change," Russ said. "Guilt money. It does almost nothing to get at the root causes of the problem, to really help the Hawaiian people." And then he laid out the whole thing and how it had hit him the other night: the poignancy in the missteps of the amateur hula dancers, how any one of them, in some alternate life, might have even wound up a ruling aliʻi right over there in ʻIolani palace. And then the office geisha and her look of *approval*. And was Cliff…getting it? Still hard to tell.

"Look, you're right about my optimism," Russ went on, "and how I still tend to want to go make the big play instead of looking long-term. But this time it's different, Cliff. This time I'm ready to put it on the line. Right now."

No machine-gun clacking from below, but there was Cliff again, *thinking*.

"Resign to run," Cliff finally said.

"It's time, Cliff. It's *time*."

More thinking. Again, Cliff was *considering* it.

"Maybe…" the little man said at last.

"Maybe?"

Cliff shook his head and said, "No, it would never work."

"What would never work?"

"I was thinking maybe you wouldn't have to resign just yet—you could sort of test the waters, even up to the end of the next legislative session, and then make a more informed choice later. But it would never work with this project."

As usual, Cliff was four steps ahead of him, so Russ had to ask for clarification. "You mean Alan Ho's project? With these Chinese people?"

"Yeah, I was thinking maybe you could *Vili* it, but with the Dolphin Bay thing, it would just send too many people Hendrick's way."

Vili. The term referred to how years ago the former Honolulu mayor, Vili Harmington, had used his support for a doomed public infrastructure project to propel a failed run for governor, scooping hundreds of thousands of dollars' worth of free PR along the way.

And right there it hit Russ: *$400 million.* This TsengUSA expansion thing they'd sat in on this morning was going to have to navigate all kinds of opposition stirred up by far more than Tom Watada and Ikaika Nāʻimipono. That meant television ads, internet pop-ups, and even a print campaign. Russ's little cameo at Alan Ho's shakedown meeting may have been just that—a show-face appearance meant to send the message that Alan had *power* behind him. Russ had hoped to cash in on the favor by getting Alan to help fund his campaign, but this? What an opportunity! You could attach smiling Russell Lee images to all of it.

Talk about *cashing in!*

"Cliff, they just dropped *four hundred million dollars,*" he said. "You think Alan Ho would have any trouble getting them to *Vili* it as part of the deal? And look at all the jobs it's going to create. What did the guy say? Thousands of them." Then he explained how they could spin it to look like the project would generally lift the boat in the area so drugs and domestic violence and other symptoms of poverty simply began to disappear—the whole point of his idea to finally run in the first place: to *help his people.*

"I wouldn't be so sure about the jobs," Cliff told him. "The potential for massive construction work is there, but that's only temporary. And if the Chinese company follows current trends, those aren't going to be hotel towers. That's the windiest place on the island. How are they going to maintain occupancy? It must be around four thousand rooms. They're probably already planning to sell all those units out as timeshares, and that cuts out housekeeping and bell service and all the rest of it—all the same sort of jobs Waikiki has been losing for the past ten years. You'll have a hard time balancing that with the argument about the project's social impacts."

Social impacts. Russ figured Cliff could even give you a well-informed estimate on the number of hotel jobs that were lost when the Princess Kaiulani hotel went condo, with a plus-or-minus four jobs as his margin of error. But he also knew you had to be able to do more than "create" the kind of "jobs" they did back in the '80s with the Japanese money. One of his former aides had called it "leakage," meaning that a Japanese visitor could come here and stay at a Japanese-owned hotel and shop in Japanese-owned stores staffed mainly by Japanese nationals and so on and spend five or even ten thousand dollars, and nothing but the tips, minimum wage allotments, and the hotel room tax would "leak" into Hawai'i out of the Japanese economy.

"So what if we change the odds?" he asked.

Cliff just sat there with those skinny arms resting on that paunch of his, his eyebrows raised.

"It has to do with 'leakage,'" Russ said.

"Leakage?"

"Yeah, it's like when a Japanese guest stays at a Japanese hotel—"

"No, no, no," Cliff said, lifting a hand. "I'm aware of the term. You know it's actually supposed to refer to the money that leaks *out* of the tourist destination?" Cliff shook his head with a laugh.

"I'm talking about…it's more like a *partnership* with TsengUSA, like the state retains some control over what goes on up there. I can't say what it would look like, but what if you could ensure somehow that local people were hired first, even into management positions, and that the place had some kind of training program for area residents, and maybe even some kind of revenue sharing agreement. You'd stop the leakage."

Again Cliff was silent, staring out across the skyline toward the ocean. And Russ wondered if Cliff's gaze wound up settling on it, too, settling on 'Iolani palace, and whether for Cliff the majestic sight, crowned with its Hawaiian flag, had opened a light into a prior era…of local control…Kalākaua, shaking down the sugar barons.

"It's only going to work if Alan Ho agrees to it in the way you've just laid it out," Cliff said.

And did he just *say* that? Because of course Alan Ho would agree to it. For once, Alan Ho *owed* him! Cliff knew it as well as anyone, which meant—was it actually happening?—had Russ somehow managed to get *Clifford Yoshida*, a man so risk-averse he'd never even put five bucks down on an office pool on the NCAA tournament, to *throw in* on one of the biggest gambles of either man's career? Just the thought of it— Russ could *feel* the adrenaline surge through his body, feel his very *brain* soaked in *dopamine*, and did Cliff just *say* that?

"That, and if you can find some way to talk Nakayama into giving you an endorsement in the primary," his little clerk went on, and sure enough, Cliff had indeed *thrown in*, like he himself had finally reached that...point...that point in his career where you can see the end, five ten years away, that point where you see that chances like these, well— this might even be the last one. "You'll need Alan Ho to set up an exploratory committee right away." Cliff thought for a moment, and then: "If the election were held next week, Hendrick would destroy you on name recognition alone. Then there's the general, with all that outside Republican money coming in. Like I said, they're going to come after you."

And then with a smile Cliff asked, "You don't have any skeletons in your closet I'm not aware of, do you Russ?"

Skeletons, skeletons. How about *fifty fucking thousand dollars?* Yeah, Russ had better hurry up and figure out some way to pay that one off quick—and would a thug like Lave Salanoa understand how *complex* it was going to be to funnel a pile of *Vili* money that huge into the hands of an *illegal gambling house?*—pay it off before anyone blew the lid off of who'd actually "claimed" Tapusoa—and you could bet Russ wasn't the only one thinking that it hadn't been a mere "accident" on the H-3 freeway.

Who you been hanging around with, Senator Lee?

But Cliff didn't need to know about any of that.

"Let's see," Russ said. "Other than that running tab I have down at Susie's Penthouse in Keʻeaumoku?"

Cliff's eyes widened. Keʻeaumoku: that six-block stretch behind Ala Moana Center dotted with strip clubs and hostess bars, Club Bye Me and Club New Club D'Amour, Evergreen Lounge and Club New Office, all right there on Kapiʻolani Boulevard. High-backed vinyl booth seating. A "private room" back by the restrooms where a middle-aged state worker work-a-daddy could go for a rub-and-tug after filling the nineteen-year-old Inchon immigrant in the prom dress on his lap with four hundred bucks worth of twenty dollar hostess drinks. Even *Cliff* had heard about such places.

"Kidding! Kidding!" Russ said.

His clerk went on thinking aloud about how tight the race would be, how much it would depend on Nakayama's endorsement, all the words again blending in with the renewed roar of the diesel and the jackhammers pounding up from the rotunda floor, all such concerns dissolving in...the buzz...the buzz...the buzz brought on by, yes, the thought of, at long last, Russ's own security detail, of his fifth-floor office, of the...benefits...of *executive privilege*...of raising his right hand and swearing to uphold his duties as governor of the state of Hawai'i.

"You should get in touch with Alan Ho right away."

SUSTAINABLE DEVELOPMENT

"Don't take the cheese! Don't take the cheese!"

Though the big man said it under his breath, his words carried the same weight as those thick shoulders protruding from his white tanktop, the brown tree-trunk arms folded across that solid belly. Just one man in a crowd of over two hundred concerned citizens now filling row upon row of cafeteria tables in the darkened Kahuku High School Cafetorium to listen to the representatives from TsengUSA "talk story," he radiated with energy and charisma, with *mana*, just sitting there, his graying black hair smothered by that faded red bandana, with that *look* on his face, that seen-it-all-before look.

Some haole PR woman was walking them through a slick powerpoint presentation aimed at defining the Chinese company's scheme to build *five* new North Shore hotel towers as *sustainable development*. The slide up on the screen—it looked like somebody had waited for a rare day when the wind wasn't howling to go up in a helicopter and take the soft-tinted shot of Dolphin Bay, which for once looked…tranquil…a beautiful "gem" of a spot for which the development was going to "enhance public access," including parking so that "local families" can once again be able to "enjoy one of Hawai'i's most *spiritual* beaches," where you could "relax in the presence of your ancestors" on the edges of "an ancient Hawaiian burial ground."

"Don't take the cheese!"

To hear him you had to be sitting right next to this tremendous presence of a man—Ikaika Nāʻimipono was his name—and thankfully

Makana Irving-Kekumu was, because Makana had been just about to, well, *say something!* Anyone could see that there were all kinds of things wrong with actually *marketing* the remains of the ancestors of everyone seated in the immediate vicinity, starting with the fact that TsengUSA had thought to hire out their "community outreach" efforts to Brushette and Hyde instead of having the respect to show up themselves to try to snow everyone on the "benefits" of upwards of 4,000 new hotel units on the North Shore. Talk story! Like this was just some backyard *local* event, that a multi-billion-dollar Chinese company coming in to swoop up nearly a thousand acres of sacred land just wanted to get all bradda-bradda with their new neighbors.

Typical, was all Makana could think.

A good ten years younger than Ikaika but already well along the tenure track as a Windward Community College professor, Makana had to wonder why the haoles didn't even *bother* to get it right what, more than twenty years after a band of Hawaiian activists had succeeded in taking an entire island back from the United States military, more than twenty years after the fruits of the Hawaiian Renaissance had blossomed into a flotilla of DOE Hawaiian language immersion schools dotted around the state, where your children could be taught everything from art to zoology in the language of their ancestors. More than twenty years after the UH Hawaiian Studies Department had sprung out of a taro patch on the edge of the Mānoa campus and charged straight into the public consciousness with competing narratives of everything from the 1893 overthrow of the Hawaiian monarchy to the construction of the H-3 freeway. More than ten years after UH Hilo began offering a *PhD* in Hawaiian language, after so many years of scholarship by committed and educated Natives such as... *himself*.

After all this, the best that Susan *Brushette* and Trina *Hyde*, who both had in fact witnessed and even "reported" on many of the controversial events contributing to an overall deepening of public sensitivity regarding Hawaiian issues over the past twenty years before they'd gone into PR— *Relax in the presence of your ancestors!* Was that the best they could do?

Just the thought of it all made him want to *say something* all over again. Barely fifteen minutes into this whole power-point thing, and he'd already had it... up... to... *here* with the *win-win* and the *jobs for the community* and the *sustainable growth* and the *economic boost* and, most of all, with the *'ohana* and *Ha-vai-ee* nonsense. But instead he listened to Ikaika and welded his mouth shut. It wasn't easy.

And Makana could tell he wasn't the only one. When the blinding fluorescent lights flooded the crowded room they sent a wave of murr-murr-murmuring from wall to wall. Just look at Susan Brushette up there, leaning so casually against that long table in one of those news-hottie aqua pants-suit get-ups, look at her clutching that cordless mic with such an…earnest!...look painted on her face that made you want to *throw* something at her, never mind say something. Everyone had to be thinking the same thing, thinking they wanted to shout at the equally…earnest!...Trina Hyde, wanted to scream at that sniveling smug-looking local Japanee-lawyer-type fixer guy seated up there at the table with her. And it wasn't just the wall-to-wall enviro-haoles—every one of Ikaika's core group of activists looked ready to *pounce*.

Especially Aunty Maile, the group's silver-haired matriarch, a woman who had rooted herself to the 'āina way back in the 1970s when they were trying to turn her father's Waiāhole Valley papaya farm into a gated subdivision.

Look at her, *holding back* down at the end of the row there next to Ray Boy Thomas, Makana's classmate from the UH Hawaiian Studies program what, ten, twelve years ago now, his goatee'd face drawn into a silent growl, his long skinny arms folded in front of him and covered with a long-sleeved Gabbyfest 2012 T-shirt, his knee madly bouncing up and down. Ray Boy had once jumped right in front of a bulldozer on Maui that had just plowed up his own great-aunty—bursting into tears, he'd been! Das' my *aunty*, my great aunty, her bones sticking *outta the ground!*—and now they're talking about…bones?

There in the seat just behind Ikaika and having a harder time holding back than even Ray Boy—sucking her teeth, harumphing and sighing, turning her head this way and that, and of course, rolling her eyes—was Kanoe Silva, Ikaika's niece, now 28 and enrolled in the UH Richardson School of Law. When Trina Hyde took the mic and started pacing the stage like some middle-aged former beauty pageant contestant and going on about "mana" and "respect for our host culture" and all the rest of it, you could tell what Kanoe was thinking: Talk story! Who you folks kidding? You staged this whole thing so TsengUSA can say they "consulted with community leaders"—which you're legally obligated to do anyway for the Supplementary Environmental Impact Statement the courts ordered before you can even plant a shovel at Dolphin Bay. Bullshit!

Ikaika had to shoot his niece another look.

That was all it took, too: a look. The man had eyes like a cobra, hypnotic eyes, eyes that *spoke*.

Ikaika. Makana knew the roots of Ikaika's legend about as well as he knew the creation myths he taught in his Hawaiian Chant class. If he'd had half the charisma of his…well, admit it: Ikaika was his hero… Makana would never have taken the safe path into academia, where your cruise nine-month, nine-hour per week taxpayer financed "job" (which, though he never admitted it, ultimately meant "tourism and U.S. military financed job"), which was guaranteed for life, eventually paid you close to six figures a year. He would have gone into law, where the stakes were higher (or, where there were, in fact, "stakes"). He would have gone down into the trenches and been able to draw people to his cause with no more than a word or two, the way Ikaika did it.

The man had dropped—*everything!* Back when he was only sixteen Ikaika had been observant enough to know that when the billion-dollar H-3 freeway plowed straight over a stack of environmental and cultural protection laws, right through a sacred valley, only to connect two military bases, you couldn't just stand on the sidelines and let it all happen. When Ikaika had come home from football practice one evening his junior year at St. Martin's—he *loved* the game, used to get a *rush* from just putting a hit on someone—his mother told him to jump in the car, had to go to bail Aunty Maile out of jail.

Up until that point, the story went, Ikaika had never cared one way or another about "development," but when he'd learned that Aunty had been arrested along with six other women for camping out in the path of the nine- and fifteen-ton bulldozers that were clearing Hālawa Valley for H-3, he quit football on the spot. No amount of hounding from his teammates or coaches could change his mind. Not even the UH coaches, so impressed with his game that they could overlook the fact that he'd skipped his senior year, could get him back on the field.

Some wondered how Ikaika could have traded a free UH degree for the backbreaking life of a taro farmer, standing up to his knees in mud day after day on the Waiāhole *kuleana* parcel passed down from his great aunty, struggling to keep his two sons fed and ready and relying on his wife's job to take care of their medical. But the football crowd had taken it a step further, shaking their heads at the thought of someone giving up what was widely considered a sure shot at the NFL to…wave signs? To march? To sit in at the UH astronomy building in protest of plans to build a telescope atop Mauna Kea? To paddle a surfboard out in front of that monstrosity of a whale-killing battleship, the SeaHighway Ferry? Ikaika had possibly sacrificed *millions of dollars* to devote his life to…this?

As devoted as Makana himself admittedly was to UH football (and hadn't Ufi Tapusoa gone to Kahuku High and eaten in this very room?…and what a tragedy that had been…the great UH linebacker struck down only a couple of weeks ago…even now dotted throughout the crowd you could see two or three Warrior jerseys bearing his number 58…all over some gambling thing, was what everyone had been whispering at the booster club luncheon the week after UH's final game), anyway, as devoted a Warrior fan as Makana was proud to call himself, if you wanted a real hero all you had to do was look up at Ikaika Nā'imipono here under the fluorescent glare, and you'd just *know* that whatever he'd given up, it had been worth it, that every inch of movement was done with purpose, and that he intended to win. And most of all, if he told you to keep your mouth shut, particularly in a setting such as this one, you kept quiet.

Not so, the haoles. That wave of murr-murr-murmuring—the one that fell just short of the two TV cameras pointing out at the angry mob from either side of the stage—it had been pure haole. They'd covered the walls with huge placards and banners—some of them professionally printed by some graphics studio with all the usual slogans: "Environment Yes! Development No!" and "Save Our Beaches!" and "Real Dolphins, Not Dolphin Bay!" among many others, including, of course, "Keep the Country Country." Every last one of them wore a faded green T-shirt in an iron-clad show of unity dating back at least ten years, to when they'd successfully challenged the validity of the 1980s-era EIS that had first accommodated for the construction of the five towers—a victory that had sent the property's then-owner into bankruptcy, and brought about the need for the supplemental EIS TsengUSA was currently conducting.

On top of all that, they had the Reverend Tom Watada on their side—the aging figure dressed in black way over there in the back corner who was arguably the only reason why any part at all of the Windward side from Kāneʻohe north remained green to this day. But above all else, the haoles were *loud*, and they *wouldn't shut up*.

The murmuring in fact had only been stopped by...more noise... this time the sound of a single member of the audience way in the back row somewhere clapping his hands in a slow and sarcastic rhythm meant to announce what was already clear to everyone who'd just sat through thirty minutes of Susan Brushette's pie graphs and "artist's renderings" and soft-tinted postcard shots: "That was the biggest load of bullshit I've ever heard in my life."

The clapping might have been effective on its own, everyone in the room turning to look towards its source, but then the man stood—a little wiry guy with his white hair buzzed short above his ears, deep into his sixties it looked like, but fit enough that you might find him on the starting line of the Honolulu Marathon—he stood and cupped his hands around his mouth to shout it across a good hundred feet of crowded tables: "Thatwasthebiggestloadofbullshit."

His words ran together until four or five other haoles up near the front shouted back at him, all California life-long-surfer-types and retired-real-estate-agent-types and Pupukea-doctor's-wives and first-wave post-war trust fund babies with nothing better to do on a Wednesday evening than *band together as a community to preserve the ʻāina*, not one of them, it seemed at a glance, a day under fifty: "We can't hear you!" someone shouted, and "No one can understand!" and then back and forth among themselves: "Someone should tell him to use the microphone" and "He should use the microphone," and then the shouting again: "You have to use the microphone!" "Yeah, he needs to use the microphone!" "Someone tell him to use the microphone!"

In the end, the poor guy just sank back down into his seat, tapping the guy next to him on the shoulder and making a self-deprecating smile, probably trying to make a joke out of the whole humiliating episode and hoping they would just move on with things.

Again: *typical haole*. And though he wouldn't admit as much with a gun to his head, Makana Irving-Kekumu spoke with some authority on the subject because he too, well, *was* haole. More than ninety-five percent. Pale as any of the surrounding aging ex-pat California boys and their sun-wrinkled wives (he didn't even *tan* well). Haole!

It had come to sicken him so much that he'd made a career out of fighting it, mostly by reclaiming a proud past through his scholarship translating vast archives of Hawaiian language newspapers, or passing the lessons of history along to his students, many of whom were Hawaiian themselves, and most of all, out of his vocal presence in such public struggles against further colonization as the one in which he and Ikaika and the rest of them now found themselves.

So mainly Makana Irving-Kekumu knew better than most that these haoles *wouldn't shut up* because he'd grown up in the house of Bennett Irving, a man who'd built his own six-figure-profiting recycling business within a decade of arriving in Honolulu from Utah on a Mormon mission, but always a perennial contender for the title, "King of the Haoles." Had he been here tonight, Bennett would have stepped right into the middle of this back-and-forth over the microphone like some kind of self-appointed referee.

Susan Brushette made for a more than credible stand-in, taking the little flare-up as an opportunity to go over the logistics of what was to happen next, going on for a bit about how two microphones had indeed been set up in each aisle about five rows back, how concerned citizens were to line up and take their time to air their concerns, about how everyone could also address any questions they cared to ask to the local-Japanese guy at the table. Brushette introduced him—a young looking little guy in a soft red-print banker's designer aloha shirt—as Sean Hayashi, who was representing TsengUSA "here in Ha-vai-ee."

"Basically what we came here for tonight is to just listen to you folks," Hayashi said.

This sent the room into a spasm of hissing and sarcastic laughter that only quieted once the faded green-shirted woman already standing at the mic began tapping on it, the string of Hawaiian bracelets on her tanned arm rattling away towards a bony elbow. She reminded Makana of his days as a Waikiki bar-back—a job he'd taken (though again, he'd never admit it) to try to mask the fact that he was the only one of his UH classmates whose (haole) father was paying for everything. Every Sunday a gaggle of middle-aged leather skinned straw-blondish haole women would gather in front of the stage to swoon like teenagers over a

Hawaiian icon named Henry Kapono, singing right along to prove that they *lived here*, that they weren't…tourists. Look at me, Henry! Pick me!

This particular woman confused Susan Brushette by identifying herself as Charlene…Matsuda? While her face was cut with two line-like wrinkles so deep it looked like she wore one of those 1920s fu-manchu moustaches, she couldn't have looked any less like a Matsuda—though if anyone in the room was aware that that must have been the point, it was Makana Irving-Kekumu.

These haoles were always trying to out-UN-haole each other: hula lessons, peppering their speech with Hawaiian words like "puka" and "akamai" and "pono," always singing along to the *ha'ina* of every Hawaiian song. Once they'd lived here long enough to figure out that it was such an important local code word, they tried to insert "respect" into every possible sentence—indeed, they always had to tell you *how long* they'd lived here, as in, "I'm from Seattle, but I've lived here for 22 years now—I'm *kama'āina*"—a word they used like a proper name. But this woman's having married a local-Japanese doctor or whatever, along with the name change, must have given her a level of *local* caché that was the envy of every woman in the room except the ones who'd married actual Hawaiians, or adopted Hawaiian foster babies and given them names like Kai and Malia and Makua.

So Charlene Matsuda, she dug in and let this other local-Japanese, the little local-Japanese *sell-out* up there on the stage—she let him have it: "I see that TsengUSA doesn't even have the respect to come down and share our *mana'o* directly," she began evenly. That was another word the haoles liked to use: *mana'o*—in this case likely to mark the haoles as "native" and Brushette and even this skinny Japanee guy, Hayashi, as outsiders. (Because if there was one thing that really grated on haoles—haoles like Makana's father—it was that local-Japanese, local-Chinese, and even fresh-off-the-boat Filipinos always came off as more "local" than any haole, even if the haole in question was third-generation.) "I see that they had to employ a PR firm," she went on, "and then send along some lackey from downtown."

This drew a collective *Oooh!* from the crowd, and even a little chuckle from Ikaika, whose face was fixed in a smirk.

"So I guess what I'm saying is that if this little 'Talk-Story' was supposed to make some kind of inroad into gaining the trust of the community," Charlene said, "the fact that no one from TsengUSA is even here tonight means that you've done the opposite." Then she paused, and wound up with a rousing, "We don't trust you!" that won her a smattering of applause.

Susan Brushette just kept things moving right along, saying, "Well, thank you for sharing those concerns with us! And let me remind everybody that what we're doing here tonight is just a *first step* in developing a relationship with the people who stand to benefit most from TsengUSA's partnership with the community." Then she pointed to the microphone set up in the opposite aisle, its own line of six, seven, eight! faded green T-shirts strung out behind it, and said, "Who's next on this side?"

Tap tap tap tap tap! Tap tap tap tap tap! Everyone turned to see Charlene Matsuda tapping away on her own microphone. Her face was drawn into such a scowl that two additional deep pits had formed above the bridge of her nose. "I wasn't finished yet."

"Thank you Ms....?" Susan Brushette searched for the name.

"Matsuda."

Susan Brushette struggled to push another confused look from her face, and then said, "Ms. Matsuda!" as though they were long lost sorority sisters. "Please allow me to remind everyone that we'd like to be able to hear from as many of you as possible. It's not that we want to limit what anyone has to say, but we do want to make sure everyone has a chance!"

"Let her talk!" someone shouted.

"She didn't get to ask her question yet!" came another voice.

"Let her talk!"

Makana was, needless to say, disgusted. He tried to tell himself that, yeah, he'd been warned. And not just by the memory of Bennett Irving, either. Ikaika himself had used the very same words out in the parking lot during the pre-game meeting, going on to tell everyone, "What they're trying to do is *help*"—advice that had immediately reminded Makana of his Uncle Mike, who'd once even *explained* that you have to "insert the key into the ignition and then turn it *clockwise*" in order to start the car. "To us it may come off as disrespectful," Ikaika had told everyone. "But we can't forget that it's coming from a place of concern." They'd all listened intently even though it wasn't the first time any of them had heard Ikaika deliver this little cultural insight, because everyone understood that the reason Ikaika knew all about haoles was that he was married to one.

She was sitting right next to him now, on the other side, Meg Ross (Makana had no idea why anyone would pass on adopting a great Hawaiian name like "Nāʻimipono," but nevertheless…). Meg was recognized all over Waiāhole and among her fellow Castle High football player parents as *one good haole*. Ikaika had met her nearly twenty years ago, a Wisconsin environmental studies major on exchange at UH. Six months later she was pregnant, a year after that they were married, and then a year later their second son was born.

Meg had always talked about finishing her degree and maybe getting a job with DLNR. But after H-3 it was the bones at the Keʻeaumoku Wal-Mart, the Army's land-grab for the Stryker Brigade. The telescopes. Makua Valley. The SeaHighway Ferry. Meg had done enough research related to these issues, Makana guessed, to have accumulated two or three law degrees, but she wound up with little beyond the satisfaction of the occasional victory against the Powers that Be. Her own major source of income amounted to bartending in a Temple Valley karaoke bar for…ten years now. So if Ikaika had learned much about the type of faded-green-shirted haoles now surrounding them, it had to have been from the many trips he'd taken back to Wisconsin over the years to visit—

"C'mon! Let her talk!"

"Yeah, let her ask her question!"

Susan Brushette, a big smile plastered to her face, had no choice but to motion for Charlene Matsuda to continue.

"Thank you," a self-satisfied Charlene Matsuda said. "My question is for Mr…Hayashi is it? Mr. Hayashi. Mr. Hayashi, what were you doing ten years ago?"

The Japanee guy's eyes widened. He only looked to be in his midthirties. Makana imagined that ten years ago the guy had probably been at home in mommy and daddy's house in Pearl City locked in his room watching internet porn for hours on end.

"I was studying for my real estate license," came the answer, "and completing my degree at UH. Why do you ask?"

"I ask because you're young enough to be my son, and my son was away at college in California, at Stanford," she said, unable to resist slipping that little status marker in, "and even though he's my son, he had no idea what was going on up here ten years ago. Can you tell me what was going on up here ten years ago?" This, too, brought a little chuckle from Ikaika.

"Ten years ago, the company that owned this property tried to ram a twenty-year-old plan down your throats based on an outdated EIS," Hayashi said, and now it was the haole woman's turn to be surprised. "TsengUSA is aware of the concerns that arose," he went on. "That's why we are openly and comprehensively conducting the Supplementary EIS you folks were calling for back then." He said it as though he were doing everybody a favor, gesturing with his palms spread open in front of him. "As I said, basically we're just here to listen to you folks." He then pointed to the opposite mic and said, "Who's next on this side?"

Charlene Matsuda opened her mouth, but nothing came out this time, so she beat a retreat back to her seat, deep-creviced scowl firmly back in place.

There could be no doubt about why the man standing in the direction Sean Hayashi was pointing would be opposed to 4,000 new hotel rooms practically within walking distance of Sunset Beach, and only minutes away by car from all the rest of the North Shore's fabled surfing grounds. From the looks of his own deeply lined face and that neatly trimmed mop of graying hair, along with the graying of what had once been a carpet of blond hair on forearms still ropey with muscle, the guy had to be in his fifties, at least. But Makana couldn't help but be impressed that he still had the body of a twenty-year-old athlete, which was on full display inside a faded green T-shirt about three sizes too small for him, and in faded camo-print board shorts that covered the thin wiry legs of a waterman who spent more time paddling than he apparently did walking.

Whether it was the typical trust fund, or some lucky dot-com-era investment, or whether he'd been able to flip enough properties during the housing boom, or even if he'd actually been of use to the world in this lifetime—a star surgeon perhaps, or the inventor of Prozac—he'd somehow been able to live out his dream of moving to the Mecca for anyone who'd ever paddled into a wave—even people from places like Australia and parts of Indonesia, where comparable if not better waves could be found without having to deal with what were already staggering crowds of people. (That the North Shore had been far less crowded before people like Mr. Life Long Surfer had ever stepped off the plane had doubtlessly never occurred to the guy.) Several years back some idiot had made the whole thing even worse by shooting some stupid teen girl fantasy chick flick about surfing the North Shore called *Blue Crush*, and overnight the crowds out in the lineup had doubled. Imagine: now you had to fight *women* for waves, too! And now this! 4,000 rooms! Herds of people coming to ruin *his* waves!

But rather than openly come out and admit to such a selfish position, the man—an environmental lawyer, as it turned out, who did live in California most of the year, but who "owned property here" and had "been coming to the North Shore every winter for the past twenty five years" and wasn't alone in his "disgust and sadness" at how the "character" of the place had "already begun to change" and become "more commercial"—he framed his argument around the question of...traffic.

"Aloha Mr. Hayashi, Ms. Brushette, Ms. Hyde," he began. "I want to begin by thanking you all for giving us the chance to voice our concerns tonight." The PR team up on stage nodded their heads. "As you can see, we're very passionate about what goes on in our community here in the country. This is a special place, a sacred place, a place for which we all hold a tremendous amount of deep respect. And when we say that we're interested in preserving it, we don't just mean for the people who live here."

Right! Typical draw-bridger: now that *I'm* here, lift the bridge and let no one else enter.

"We want to preserve it for our children, our grandchildren, so they can experience the beauty we've been able to experience. We want to preserve it for the rest of the world, too. There comes a point where a fragile place like this one can no longer sustain growth and development. That point for the North Shore has already passed." He went on and on about "gridlock" during surf season and "bottlenecks" at Laniakea, where tour busses always stopped so people could get pictures with the turtles.

"And if that isn't enough, I'll direct you to the Revised Traffic Impact Analysis that was conducted as part of the Dolphin Bay Resort Master Plan six years ago," he said. "You can read it yourselves, but basically it anticipates, ten years from now, a traffic rate of around 1,200 vehicles per hour. That's an increase of nearly 200 vehicles *per hour*, and that's *without* your five new hotels." Murmur-murmur. "Now if you build your towers, they anticipate a rate of nearly *two thousand* vehicles *per hour!*" *Oohs* and *Aaahs*, all around. "And those aren't my numbers. Check them out yourselves."

He folded his arms, stuffing a fist behind the bicep on each arm and then pushing outward. It occurred to Makana that while years of surfing had sculpted the guy's forearms and his bulbous triceps, and had also formed a nice V-shape to his lats, his biceps—generally useless muscles for paddling a surfboard, but oh-so-important as props in a manly stand-off such as this one—had been left out of most of the action. The guy had stuffed his fists behind them to make them look *bigger*.

"I'm glad you raised the issue of traffic," Hayashi began, leaning into his mic, "because that was one of TsengUSA's main concerns before they even considered purchasing the property out of foreclosure. Look, we're all the way up on the North Shore, a good distance from the airport, and there's just this two-lane country road going in and out, and it's got to pass through your community. If I'm not mistaken, traffic was also the major issue that came up ten years ago. Am I correct on that Ms. Matsuda?" he asked, scanning the crowd, out of which eventually came a reluctant "Yes." "Well, I can assure you folks that we are in the process of addressing that issue."

"How?" someone shouted.

"Be specific!"

Hayashi took a breath and said, "As I said, we're working on that plan. Look, we wouldn't come all the way out here to just go and do the same thing the developer tried to do ten years ago. We're here to address your concerns." Another low murmur swept the room. "The traffic thing, as you can imagine, is pretty complex."

"You can say that again!" someone interrupted.

"Otherwise," Hayashi forged on over more murmuring, "otherwise, the prior owner would not have been asked to conduct a supplementary EIS. I can't give you details beyond that because it's still at the speculative stage, and we'd prefer to deliver you a more concrete scenario later. I do know that they're looking into low-cost housing so that a portion of the workforce will be able to live on site, and they're looking into other things, like bussing guests directly from the airport, running a shuttle for shopping in Haleiwa similar to the one between Kaʻanapali and Lahaina on Maui. Offering a limited number of rental cars on site has been discussed, renting cars by the hour as a way to allow guests to go on excursions, but discourage them from driving too much. Look, isn't it in the interest of TsengUSA to have the guests remain on property and spend their money there? We're really on the same page here. We're also in discussions with the Department of Transportation to widen the road in the vicinity of the entrance, so there won't be a bottleneck—"

"Whosgoingtopickaab?" came a muffled shout from the back of the room.

And then it started up again: "We can't hear you!" "Speak up!" "Use the microphone!" "Somebody tell him to use the microphone!"

And then, "He has to wait his turn!" "Yeah, he has to wait his turn! Everyone else is standing in line!" "Go get at the end of the line!"

Tap tap tap tap tap! This time it was the California lawyer, Mr. Life Long Surfer. "I think he said, 'Who's going to pick up the tab?' You know, for the road widening project. It's a legitimate question. Is your road widening going to be funded by the taxpayers?" A fold of the arms, a push of the biceps. It was like a teenage girl trying to show how she had cleavage if you just pushed them together.

"While such a public works project—" Hayashi was interrupted by a loud groan on that one, so he paused for it to dissipate, and then picked up his pace as if to avoid further interruption. "Such projects have in the past been dumped on the taxpayers. Sewerage lines to the Princeville on Kauai, those floating docks for the SeaHighway Ferry—Hawaiʻi has a sad history of funding infrastructure for outside investors. We know that, which is why it's already part of TsengUSA's construction budget—the cost of the road widening. Legally, that project falls under the purview of the DOT, but, to answer your question, TsengUSA will be picking up the tab."

All around the room, mouths opened, but nothing came out.

"Next?"

There in front of the other mic stood, surprise surprise, a *local guy*—a dark-skinned Hawaiian at that, with those thick arms and that big stomach that would have made a haole look fat, but that made this guy look like a bull of a power lifter. He was wearing jeans stuffed into half-open construction boots. His long-sleeved T-shirt was not the faded green everyone else had on, but a bright fluorescent green, the better to be seen by the drivers of big dump trucks and cement mixers and bulldozers beeping in reverse. It was the uniform of the calling of the 21st-century local male, who had been failed by generations of worthless public schools that had conspired against his success in other areas, failed by a statewide obsession with football (which Makana admittedly shared) that had planted his head with unlikely dreams of a pro career, failed by a local-male-sub-cultural conviction that to perform any sort of work that did not involve pouring cement or swinging a hammer was…gay.

"Aloha," he began, clearly nervous. The room answered with a soft collective "aloha" of its own, as if it were a response in church, as if people were in awe to be spoken to by *a real Hawaiian*. A silence came over the crowd that seemed…out of place…considering the raucous and angry back-and-forth that had dominated the atmosphere up to now.

The guy collected himself and then said, "I'm not too good at dis kine, dis *public speaking*. Or with grammar in general." He said this with a smile that brought a ripple of sympathetic laughter from the crowd. "But I get somet'ing for say tonight, somet'ing from the *na'au*, from deep inside." He put a hand on his stomach and paused again, looking for the next sentence.

"You geev 'im, brah!" one of the old-man haoles said, and another ripple of soft laughter crossed the room.

And for Chrissakes, what a *fucktard*. Of all the out-UN-haole-ing these people engaged in, nothing was worse than when they tried to speak pidgin. You were *embarrassed* for them. All you ever thought was, *hasn't anyone TOLD him?* And there was never anything you could say to a haole pidgin speaker, either, so convinced were they all that *their* pidgin wasn't like the haole pidgin everyone *else* spoke—*theirs* was pitch-perfect James Grant Benton pidgin, Roland Cazimero pidgin. Trying to explain otherwise was like informing a co-worker she had a breath problem. And then to bray out like that at a time like *this*?

To his credit the construction guy let the gaffe melt into the sound of the two big electric fans swirling air around in the back of the room. And then he coughed into his hand before continuing: "My name is Bud Souza. I get t'ree kids," he said. "My wife, she works cashier, Lā'ie Foodland. We live homestead, Hau'ula, wit' my madda, my fadda, my sista, her four kids—her husband, he lock-up, Arizona, fucka was dealing—oh, excuse me!" Bud Souza put his hand up to his mouth, feigning surprise that the word had slipped out. "Sorry, ah? Like I tol' you—me and public speaking…" He gave a shrug, and together with his sensitivity about the naughty language, it drew another murmur of church laughter.

"Anyway, all of us stay in my fadda's four-bedroom, homestead. An' me…let's see…how you put 'um? Me, I gotta admit, I get *pride*." He paused. "I try for stay humble, ah? But I get pride inside me. An' every morning, every morning for *six years* now, I get up, I make breakfast for everybody, I dress my kids. Or really, I *used to* dress my kids—by now they all dressing themselves. Anyway. An' then I drive my kids to school. An' then I drive my wife to Foodland. An' you know what I do nex'? Nott'ing. All day."

Makana figured that more than a couple of Bud Souza's haole listeners were wondering why he didn't at least walk across the street and catch some fish for his family, not bothering to fathom that Souza probably had never been taught the first thing about what to do with a rod and reel, and was now too deeply ashamed of such a cultural anomaly that he was afraid to ask anyone for help.

"All day," he said again. "Sometimes I clean yahd, dis an' dat. An' I wait. I wait until it's time for pick up my kids from school, because they all stay waiting for their dad, and they know their dad *no work*—my youngest, he *neva even seen me work*, I been on the bench for *six years*, he probably t'ink his own fadda jus' one *lazy Hawaiian*."

The whole room was now locked in on Bud Souza. Makana could see a woman at the end of the row behind them, her straw-blonde hair spilling out from a U.S. Open Shinnecock Hills golf visor, shaking her head in…pity.

"An' not like we starving or anything like that," he went on. "Maybe we get on each odda's nerves all crowded in that one little house, but at leas' we *get* one nice house. Plenny guys, my friends from way back, they not so lucky. They homeless. Divorce. They chronics, sucking on dat pipe up the valley. Some-a-dem pulling time too—das' what they turn to, they get desperate enough. How you t'ink *their* kids feel?" Now he clenched his hand in a fist and held it to his heart and said, "But all of us, all of us been sitting on the bench alladeese years, we not *lazy*. We like work. We like set one example for our kids. We get *pride*." He let that hang for a few seconds and then said, "Thank you folks. Aloha."

A long silent moment, all these people trying to reconcile their reverence for the Hawaiian and their respect for his touching predicament with how at-odds it all was with what they knew was *right*. Makana could have sworn he'd heard a couple of those sarcastic claps from the back of the room, but someone must have had the sense to grab the old man's hands, to know how…inappropriate…it would be to introduce the possibility that this poor gentle giant had been planted here by the carpenters union.

Sean Hayashi didn't even take advantage of the moment to offer some spiel about job creation or anything like that. He didn't have to. Neither did Susan Brushette or Trina Hyde bother to link current economic conditions to the very social problems now plaguing all of O'ahu, namely the conjoined twins, drug addiction and petty theft. Bud Souza, Mr. Can't Handle Public Speaking, had nailed it all in four or five sentences.

Now no one was moving.

The guy at the mic on the left—a lanky trustafarian affluent hippie-type, white hair down to his shoulders and a traditional Hawaiian bone hook necklace hanging over the faded green of his T-shirt—he was trying to defer his turn to the woman at the mic on the right—some retired bond trader's forty-year-old second wife, a woman with girlish short brown hair who, if Makana could take a guess, began her mornings with a five-mile leg-shaping jog before settling in on her ocean-front lanai with a cup of Orange Blossom tea and a good book. Against all odds, she wasn't ready to speak either.

That left it up to Susan Brushette to steer things forward. "Thank you so much for your honesty, Mr. Souza," she said. This drew a brief round of subdued and respectful clapping. And then she turned to the trustafarian: "I believe you're next, Mr.…?"

"My name is Matt but everyone calls me Pono," the guy said, "my Hawaiian name."

Makana caught Ikaika stifling another chuckle at this. Ikaika, in fact, seemed to be the only one in the room who was back in the moment. He was all eyes and ears as he analyzed each of these exchanges, while everyone else was still mired in the emotional soup Bud Souza had just served up. Ikaika just sat there watching as Call-Me-Pono paused and looked down for a place to start.

"I don't mean any disrespect to Brudda Bud over here," he began. "I mean, obviously times are hard, and people are looking for work and all. But I guess what I have to say comes from the *na'au*, too." Pause. "This place called to me over thirty-five years ago now. I literally *heard* the spirits calling me here. I could get into how, but I don't want you all to think I'm nuts." Another brief murmur of church laughter. "What I mean is, this place—there's nowhere else like it left on earth. It's a *spiritual* place. And when I got here,"—now "Pono" began to choke up—"I. Was... *Accepted*. They...accepted...me...here, with...*aloha*. These braddas, they treated me like *one of their own*. I learned their ways. I learned about *respect* and *aloha*. I became...Hawaiian at heart. I remember one time..."

He couldn't go on. Now Matt was holding his own fist up to his chest, pausing again to collect himself as he wiped away a tear with his other hand.

"There's just no other place in the world like this," he finally said, "no other place that has *the aloha spirit*. And the aloha spirit comes from Hawaiians, real Hawaiians, people whose ancestors are buried right here. People like Brudda Bud. And like, there's gotta be some other way we can get Brudda Bud back off the bench, right?" He looked over at Bud Souza like they were indeed "bruddas," which sickened Makana almost as much as this business about "Hawaiian at heart" did. Bud gave the guy a nod—another little act of "acceptance" that, even though it was probably feigned in order to avoid embarrassing the guy in front of everyone, had the effect of sending another tear down the wide-eyed stubbled face of "Pono," who at last choked out the words, "Thank you. Aloha."

Makana was about ready to start in with some sarcastic rhythmic clapping of his own, but then he reminded himself that he and "Pono" were on the same side of this particular argument. Either way, in an instant he'd already missed his chance.

Ms. I Can Still Wear These Short Denim Cut-offs And Tie My Green T-Shirt In The Back Like A Teenager Even Though I'm Forty, now safely distant from the emotional bomb Bud Souza had dropped, was already launching into whatever it was she'd had prepared to say in the first place—and look out: she was carrying a clipboard. Makana caught Ikaika stealing a look at his watch.

"…and Pono brings up the most important point," she was saying, "the most obvious point, but one we seem to be overlooking when we focus on details like traffic surveys and jobs data—and that point is that the North Shore is *heaven on Earth*. The North Shore is *God's Country*, whether your god is Madame Pele or Jesus or Allah or whoever. The North Shore is a *refuge of sacred beauty*." On and on she went, offering her own examples of the kind of "spiritual attraction" Call-Me-Pono had tried to convey.

Then she said the word *iwi*, and Makana's ears perked up. "I'm talking about bones," she said.

True, enough Hawaiian remains had been unearthed in the past three decades that nearly every development project had become a Hawaiian rights issue. And the Dolphin Bay Resort sat on the exact sort of sandy coastline the U.S. military had paved over at Mokapu peninsula, where they boasted that their *golf course*—Makana's father had shown him one of those glossy pamphlets they give you to keep your score—their golf course sat atop the remains of thousands of "Native Hawaiian royalty."

Still, even Makana could have told this woman the bones argument was a non-starter: all the Dolphin Bay expansion's necessary zoning requests and building permits had been approved way back in the 1980s when the property's owners had thrown just enough money around to pave the way.

None of that stopped Ms. Denim Shorts—she just kept reading from her clipboard: "Almost *ten years ago* now, the State Historic Preservation Division concluded that the land you want to develop, and I quote, 'is located in an area where numerous subsurface burials are located.'" Then she looked up and said, "That was almost ten years ago. The SHPD was talking about *human remains*, remains of *Hawaiians*. Those remains are still there, and presumably," and she cut a glance towards Ikaika's group, "the Native Hawaiians would like them to *stay* there, that's why they *buried them in the ground there* in the first place. So when you talk about 'respect for the host culture,' does that mean running a bulldozer across the graves of thousands of Native Hawaiians so that rich Chinese people can go on vacation?"

Makana turned to see Ikaika wince, likely thinking that the woman had been on the right path, but then she had to ruin the whole thing by *being right*, by *winning the argument* with that "rich Chinese" crack instead of being *reasonable*.

"I believe you're quoting from the 2007 letter from the SHPD Director to the firm that conducted the archeological study for the prior owners of the property?" Sean Hayashi said, immediately wiping the smug look off of Ms. Trophy Wife's face. Oh-so-slowly and reluctantly, she nodded. "If I remember correctly," Hayashi went on, "that letter recommends a modification of the development plans?" Another slow nod, like that of a child being lectured. "I think it recommends a shoreline setback of at least 120 meters, is that correct?"

This time she just stared at him, angry that this little…well, not that the word would form so fully in her head—she wasn't, like, *racist*—that this little *Jap* would have the temerity to, you know, to know how to *read*, know in detail the history of this particular civic battle. Damned if she was going to stand there and nod a third time.

"Beyond the 120-meter setback," he went on, "there are no sites of cultural significance. TsengUSA intends to fully comply with those recommendations for the setback. We believe the SHPD performs a valuable function in protecting our cultural resources, and while we admittedly want to use those same resources as a selling point in many of our marketing materials, we intend to do so with sensitivity and respect. So I guess what I'm saying is that we're in total agreement with your concerns." He waited, but the woman said nothing. She instead retreated back to her seat, tail between her…*legs!*…as Hayashi turned toward the other mic.

"Next?"

Makana turned to see the woman with the U.S. Open Shinnecock Hills visor trying to angle her mic down so she could reach it. She was built like one of those gym-teacher-golfers, too—wide around the hips, wide at the shoulders, wide everywhere else.

The irony must have been lost on everyone in the room but Makana and the rest of Ikaika's group: this sudden native rights activist had apparently enjoyed a U.S. Open played upon land stolen from the only indigenous people still living on Long Island, New York—the Shinnecock tribe. But there was more to come once she opened her mouth, and a voice came out whose gravely sound suggested plenty of time sucking on Marlboro Lights and vodka gimlets at the nineteenth hole—perhaps even after a round on one of the Dolphin Bay property's existing two golf courses, which had been paved and planted years before the SHPD had even been formed.

"Has anyone even *asked* the *Hawaiians* what they think of all this?" is what she said. And off she went on an impassioned but decidedly *amateurish* excursion across "Hawaiian history," from Captain Cook on up through the overthrow and the way Hawaiian language had been "outlawed"—a myth that even Makana always worked to correct, mostly because it made his side of the argument look hysterical, since everyone knew the language had only been banned at one time *as a means of instruction*.

For some reason it began to grate on him, though, the fact that she was *speaking for the Hawaiians*—and not even that it was in such an ill-informed way, but that it contained, in all its gravely-ness, that unmistakable hint of…again, no one would want to call it *racism*, that would have been so P.C., so 1990s.

But when you put it in the context of a hundred years of white anthropologists and biographers and historians and novelists *telling our story* because deep down they think *we can't do it ourselves*, what else were you supposed to call it? Here we all are trying not to *take the cheese*, and this woman thinks we're not up there at the mic *saying something* because we *don't know how*.

"If you're talking about 'respect for the host culture,'" she said again, "then you need to consult with the Hawaiians. And I'm not just talking about trotting out some token Native you may have paid off. I'm talking about unconditional broad-based support from…from *these* people," and with that she waved a hand in the direction of Ikaika's group.

Makana could almost hear the words telepathically now: *Don't take the cheese.* Here was this woman baiting him and all the rest of the Hawaiians without even knowing that was what she was doing. And those words of Ikaika's—they may have been all that kept him rooted to his seat. God, it was hard.

"We're very early in the process here," Hayashi said. "But I can assure you that by the time we begin construction, TsengUSA will have satisfied the concerns of any Native Hawaiian group that might now be opposed to this project for cultural reasons. We know we're a long way from having done so, but once we've had the chance to sit down and talk story with these groups, we're confident that we'll be able to find a solution everyone can live with."

The woman smirked and went back to her seat, just as Ikaika was shooting looks in every direction to keep his troops in line—the sighing and the harrumphing and the nodding and the eye-rolling was now emanating out from Kanoe to everyone short of Ikaika himself.

Luckily everyone else in the room had turned towards the other mic, where another green-shirted sixties-ish haole man—and weren't they all green-shirted sixties-ish haole men and women? Except maybe those three second-wife late-thirties former bikini models over there, and that woman with the incredible legs, weren't they all won't-get-out-of-the-way baby boomers with far too much time on their hands, representatives of the very generation that had damaged these islands the most?

This one had his shirt tucked over a growing paunch and into belted brown shorts that gave way, well above the bony knees, to the palest of white legs covered with little wires of curly black hair and a pair of ratty off-white gym socks. Not an old-man surfer, not a retired California baby boomer, not a trust fundie looking to take advantage of his last chance to eke out some meaning in a life filled with yachting and golf and traveling to exotic places for no good reason. No: this was a classic UH Professor, Dr. Serial Protester, the kind who bullied their students into marching for this, that, and whatever. Makana had seen the type all over campus back when he was attending UH Mānoa.

Hands on hips, Dr. Protester spread his feet into a comfortable stance, arched his back a bit, and let go, slowly arching forward as he did: "YOU PEOPLE HAVE NO IDEA WHAT KIND OF PERMANENT AND UNALTERABLE DESTRUCTION YOUR FILTHY CAPITALIST PLANS ARE ABOUT TO WREAK ON AN INNOCENT PEOPLE AND ON A VALUABLE NATURAL RESOURCE!"

The trajectory of his lean had brought him so far forward that his face was now buried in the mic, so he had to pause, take a deep breath, and arch backwards again to wind up his spring. Again he let 'er rip: "WHAT WE ARE TALKING ABOUT HERE IS NOT 'LISTEN-

ING' OR 'COMMUNITY BUILDING,' BUT *EXPLOITATION* IN ALL SENSES OF THE WORD!" Again he took a deep breath and began arching back.

Makana turned to see the widest of smiles spread across Ikaika's face, and now that he thought about it, how could you miss the comedy in this little display? But just as quickly the answer formed in the image of the Reverend Tom Watada, seated way in the back corner.

The Reverend was now shaking his head as Dr. Know-It-All put his entire being into making his own side of the argument, and Tom's too, look ridiculous. On he went, red faced: DISTRIBUTION OF WEALTH this, and DISPLACEMENT OF NATIVE PEOPLES that, and MENIAL WAGE LABOR the other thing. He probably would have kept on going if he hadn't completely exhausted himself after three interminable minutes.

"Thank you professor," Susan Brushette said when he was through. "We hear you loud and clear."

This brought a smile to Sean Hayashi's face, and to Trina Hyde's. Ikaika's whole contingent was working to stifle giggles. But the rest of the room was silent, proud that one of their own had laid it all down so forcefully, had *won the argument*, had told them to *stick it where the sun don't shine!*

"Over here?" Brushette pointed to the opposite mic.

When another bourgeois-hippie Henry Kapono groupie started in about her "journey to this spiritual place," Ikaika looked at his watch again, and then looked to see that both lines were now seven or eight (haole) people long. The news camera crews were now beginning to pack up, so he turned to Makana and said, "We go."

They all filed out towards the parking lot, where a glare of floodlights blazed down on a long row of SUVs and pickups. Makana caught sight of a UH Warriors booster club sticker on the bumper of someone's Camry, the flag flying at half-staff here at Ufi Tapusoa's alma matter, which again together evoked the memory of his favorite UH Warrior, recently...*murdered.*

The rest of the vehicles were all tagged, of course, with *Keep the Country Country* stickers and various versions of *Save the Whale*s and *Act Locally* and *Eddie Would Go* and *Stop Domestic Violence* and so on. *Namaste* was popular. Just as they were all adorned with bike racks, stand-up paddle board racks, one-man outrigger canoe cradles, and of course surfboard racks. Even the Prius over there (Makana had expected to see the parking lot packed with Priuses or Leafs, but could find only the one), wedged between the taxi-cab yellow Nissan X-Terra and the royal blue Nissan X-Terra—it had some kind of carbon-fiber contraption welded to its bumpers and sticking up like two black laundry line poles to accommodate what must have been a two-man sea kayak or some other trendy sea toy.

Once everyone had circled up, Ikaika exchanged a look with Aunty Maile as if to ask permission to begin, and then spoke: "I think it's pretty clear what that was all about," he said. "They were after two things, and they got one of them. When you turn on the ten o'clock news tonight, you're going to see a three-minute report that glosses over the context of this whole thing, with a couple of money quotes from the haoles—especially that professor guy," he said, shaking his head with a smile, "he goes all the way back to H-3, that guy. So they'll get a quote from him, and maybe one from that guy who was crying, and one from Brudda Bud Souza. And since the only print reporter there was that twenty-three-year-old Japanee girl, that's all you're going to get. The hotel itself is almost secondary now—they've turned the whole thing into a 'haole versus local' issue, because all those frikken' haoles in there, every single one of them—they *took the cheese*."

This drew a laugh, and then Aunty Maile said, "They wen' take the *cheese*, the mouse trap, the stuffs scattered *around* the trap—they wen' take everything!"

More laughter, and then John: "Butchoo cannot blame *them* you know! They cannot help it, they always take, take, take!"

Makana cut a look at Ikaika's wife Meg, who, long used to such analyses, was smiling along with everyone else.

"That brings me to how they *didn't* succeed," Ikaika went on. "And I have to say, I'm very proud of you all—especially you, Kanoe." A knowing laugh spread around the circle.

"I know, Uncle, I know," she said, looking up at the big man. "I wanted to *stand up*—especially when that stupid little Japanee punk started in 'no sites of cultural significance.'"

Now Paul spoke up: "Ho, right there, cuz. I was like, 'Don't piss off Kanoe!'" Again everyone laughed.

Ray Boy: "An' that lady start talking about the *iwi*, she had *no idea!* I was ready for jump up an' jus' *tell* everyone!"

"But you didn't take the cheese," Ikaika said. "That's what I'm talking about. The haoles, they just made themselves look like the loud, know-it-all, more-Hawaiian-than-the-Hawaiians haole, the one everybody can't stand." This, too, drew a laugh, but Ikaika was serious. "You seen Tom Watada sitting there in the back shaking his head? He knows that when the local guy turns on his TV tonight, he jus' going say, 'See—there they go again, da fuckin' *haoles*.' But what he *not* going be able for do is go, 'Look the Angry Hawaiian!'" Ikaika paused again, his head tilted up so you could see the whites of his eyes as they passed over everyone in the circle. He towered over everyone, even, it seemed, Ray Boy, who may have matched him in height, but whose lanky frame failed to exude nearly the same aura.

"See," Ikaika went on, "the other thing they wanted tonight was the Angry Hawaiian. That fucka Hayashi, those PR people, they were baiting us the whole time. They want to marginalize the cultural concerns, make them look as stupid as they're making the environmental concerns look—they want us to be the 'stupid sovereignty Hawaiians' to all the rest of the Hawaiians, the don't-live-in-the-real-world Hawaiians against the we-need-jobs Hawaiians. Butchoo neva take the cheese."

Ikaika's gaze spread around the circle again. Although Makana had seen enough of these post-game re-caps over the years, yet again he was amazed at how someone who'd never gone to college, who worked day in and day out on a taro farm in the back of Waiāhole Valley, could always nail it so succinctly, seeing every thin layer of unspoken argument in any verbal exchange, from a public meeting on down to a simple handshake. At first it seemed like it was just part of Ikaika's genetic hardwiring. But Makana had come to see that Ikaika was so good at figuring this stuff out because he *never stopped thinking about it.* Even tonight, he'd be lying in bed rehashing the whole thing with Meg late into the night, and together they'd come up with five possible scenarios as to where it was headed.

"And there's another kine cheese, too" Ikaika went on. "Did you all hear what Hayashi said about 'satisfy the concerns of Native Hawaiian groups,' and 'find a solution everyone can live with'? A loud collective groan. "These people are going to try to buy you off. Split from the rest of us." His eyes narrowed now in intensity, and he held a fist up to his chest. "You gotta *listen to me*: I seen it happen. H-3. The telescope on Mauna Kea. Even small-kine development projects—I *seen* 'um. They going approach you individually. At work. At your house. On your way outta the store. And they going offer you *money*. Big money. You heard what the guy was saying about the road expansion, ah? They going *willingly pay* for that, that's *millions of dollars* they get in their budget already, jus' for that. So how much you t'ink dey get fo' jus' t'row around for smooth things over wit' us? They going approach you wit' twenty-thirty-fifty *grand* kine money, 'cause they know they getchoo alone, and they know you struggling…I telling you: *don't take the cheese*. We going win, but if we going win, it's going be because we taking the high road. Because we not going demonize the other side. Because we're the ones who offer the only reasonable alternative. 'No development' has to be the *reasonable* choice." He looked around at all the faces. "You don't take the cheese, then our hands stay clean. And that's the only weapon we got. Clean hands." He paused again and then said, "Anyone else have anything they like share?"

Heads turned, but no one spoke.

"Kay, den. Let's *pule*." They all held hands and bowed their heads, and Ikaika began: "We thank you *ke akua* for the wisdom and the strength, and the patience to endure in this struggle. We ask that you continue to protect us and our families as we walk this dangerous and challenging path, which we would not be able to do without your blessing. *Amene*."

"*Amene*," came the collective response.

Ikaika then cut a glance at Makana, who took a deep breath and began his chant, a deep guttural sound of *Eiii homai ke ii ke maai…*, from deep inside, from the *na'au*.

KAPI'OLANI THEATER

Pulling it off? Forget about "pulling it off." Sean Hayashi was *killing it*. All by himself, too. Even though Alan Ho had been a no-show, a no-text, a no-call, Sean had just managed to bait a roomful of enviro-haoles into looking like shrill knee-jerk NIMBY obstacles to much needed job creation for locals. It was enough to make him want to pop open a Bud Light and gaze out over the breathtaking sight from his twentieth floor lanai, a quarter moon rising way out past the darkened Ala Wai golf course over the iconic silhouette of Diamond Head.

Killing it!

Except...that one haole woman tonight could have smoked him on the biography of the Dolphin Bay land if she'd only tried a little harder. And that lawyer-guy with his traffic stats—Sean had barely managed to pull a response to that one *straight out of his ass*. And worse than either of those near misses, beyond that single SHPD letter he'd stumbled across online the other day, Sean had no clue whatsoever about any of the *specifics* regarding this concern with Native Hawaiian remains, which to him already seemed like a potential show-stopper. So while yeah, he'd treat himself to that beer, he also had his laptop out: gotta study up, study up, study up....

Which was tough to do with all that *noise*. You could be all the way *up here* and hear it, like you yourself were right next door in one of the other sorry two-floor walk-ups crowded onto those four blocks *down there*, instead of safely ensconced in Kapi'olani Gardens, one of the seven concrete-glass-and-steel high-rises that ringed the area like some kind of Greek amphitheater to create such wonderful acoustics. Sometimes it was little kids being called for dinner, or a guy singing away in the shower like he was auditioning for American Idol, no shame. Once in a while you were awakened in the middle of the night by a living porn soundtrack, right down to the *Oh baby, oh baby, YES! FUCK ME! Oh yeah!* People thought nothing of screaming such stuff out and then passing each other on the stairs the next morning as if no one had heard every last pant and squish of your…personal life.

Tonight the latest episode in a recurring drama here at Kapiʻolani Theater, one entitled Public Male Humiliation—it was blaring out loud and clear, with the usual *You always* and *You never*, along with all of the other why-do-I-even-have-to-*bring-it-up*-again markers of working poor domestic strife.

"Why don't you jus' get one *real job*, you lazy fucka!" the woman's voice went on. Though she'd been at it for a while, from her tone it sounded like she was *just getting started*. "You t'ink you one *playa*, you t'ink you one *banga*, butchoo *NOT*, you cannot do *notting*!"

Sean wondered if maybe the woman never spoke pidgin in her daily life, but wound it up for the benefit of her considerable audience, the better to humiliate her target like a tough tita girlfriend would.

As for the guy, well, once in a while you'd get a drunken fool off on some this-is-*my*-house chair-throwing tirade, and then he'd start *t'rowin' hands*, a big tough *man* inflicting violence on his own wife and sometimes his own kids, and pretty soon the stage would be lit with flashing blue lights. But usually the guy getting castrated down there would just sit and take it. In the first act you'd hear him answer with a bunch of "Okay!"s and a few "ShhhSH"s so loud that they, too, would reach the twentieth floor—all the signs of a diamond-studs-in-both-ears guy trying to head off the impending announcement to upwards of seven thousand people with prime tower seats of how he had *completely fucked it up THIS time*.

"An' now you come in an' tell me you los' *TWENTY GRAND?*" she brayed. "On one *FOOTBALL GAME?*"

Sean spat out a whole mouthful of Bud Light and started laughing. That UH game! Grant Nishikawa's little breakfast nugget at the CreditFranc meeting! Though the official news reports had never gone further than "unfortunate accident," so many people had been passing around YouTube clips and running it through the rumor mill that by now even Sean knew all the details. He had to laugh again when it occurred to him that the scene below must have been playing out, in various versions, all over the state. Public Male Humiliation times, like, fifty frikken thousand!

And the sad truth of it was that while from way up here it all looked like pathetic ghetto hopelessness—during the day you could see that the lanais down there, designed with the idea of creating an airy outside space where a couple could enjoy their breakfast in the cool morning air, were instead all stuffed with boxes overflowing with clothes, yellowing unused surfboards, exercise equipment whose primary function had become a place to hang laundry, and plastic children's toys that never made it to the Ala Wai Park only a block away—while it indeed *looked* like a sad poetic description of all the trappings of multi-generational welfare poverty, most of the people struggling away down below had decent jobs, likely somewhere in the service industry.

"Shaddap!" Now the chorus was ringing out from somewhere else. That was the trouble down there, too—there was no way anyone could afford air conditioning, so pretty much every one of the banks of dusty jalousie windows had to be open at all times. So when the play went on too long, the chorus started letting everyone in on the obvious: that the *whole world* can hear *every word*, and we've all *had enough*.

Sean took a sip of his beer, proud of himself, again, for having had the drive, and the brain, and the—yes—the *balls* to have avoided such a fate. Right after high school he'd gotten his job at the Lehua, where he still put in a twenty-hour shift alongside all these just-scraping-by-on-fifty-grand-a-year hotel lifers. (Back then fifty grand had seemed like *plenty*—except when close to half of it got chopped off by your landlord, and except that it amounted to a *dead end* on the service industry salary scale, any future raises *for the rest of your life* lucky to keep pace with that ever-quickening cost-of-living rabbit.)

The difference between Sean and the lifers was that before and after work, he'd locked down on the books—and still did. On his way to an MBA at UH he found himself surrounded by a bunch of loafers who spent four years searching for the line marking the *least possible amount of work* one needed to simply pass, and a bunch of profs who…let's be honest: if you knew anything at all about investments, why would you be *teaching*, and at such a third-rate state school? He figured there was nothing he couldn't learn on his own for free with a library card, a real estate license, and the rest of grandma's college money. So instead of flushing all the money down the UH toilet, Sean cut his losses and put what remained down on his first condo in Makiki. Within months he'd leveraged that asset into five more units spread all around town, including the one in which he now sat listening in on the latest sordid drama to unfold in Kapiʻolani Theater.

"Cannot even support your own fucking *kids*, you t'ink this whole t'ing one frikken *game*!"

"Shaddap!"

All Sean could think was, *Not me!*

With five of his six rental properties producing income and appreciating—you could charge *two grand* for a one-bedroom in Makiki these days—Sean hardly needed the waiter gig anymore. But the union job (with benefits) allowed him to plow all that money back into building the empire.

Face it: you could get the check on a table of four up over four hundred easy at a place like the Hibiscus House—the Lehua's signature restaurant. How do you walk away from a job that basically hands you two and three hundred dollars *in cash* for around five hours' work? As long as nobody found out about it, well…three hundred bucks…it paid for a lot of books. Christ, half this history shit he needed still wasn't available electronically…*Land and Power in Hawai'i*: click on that… *How the Land was Lost*: click…*Broken Trust*: click. *Know thy enemy*, was how Alan had put it to him once.

Alan. Shit, carrying tray had also led to Sean's first meeting with Alan Ho. The great man's table had already ordered by the time Sean had been able to confirm it was him. When he learned through their conversation that Ho would attend the upcoming Honolulu Realtors Association Convention, Sean then made it a point to show up. In the lingering touch-base moments afterwards when everyone was filing out of the Sheraton Waikiki ballroom, he made his pitch: I'll work for you for free, I'll do whatever you want, I just want to learn.

Alan had fixed him in his gaze, and though there wasn't even a flicker of recognition—waiters were *invisible* to people like Alan Ho—Sean would never forget that tense moment waiting for that moustache to rise into a response of some sort. The man asked for his card before turning to some glad-hander from the legislature, and to Sean's surprise, a call had come from Ho's secretary the following morning, a woman named Joyce Yamashita, who even over the phone sounded like one of those pineapple-shaped moon-faced middle-aged women with short brushy permed hair who bring two dozen malasadas to the office so they can eat four of them themselves without guilt.

A meeting was set up whose first lesson, as Ho had told him, was that you never work for free. Soon the two of them were walking across the street to the Department of Commerce and Consumer Affairs, and then signing the papers for a new limited liability corporation called Island Sustainability LLC, with Sean himself listed as "President" and Alan Ho as a mere "Officer."

As it was all happening, Sean kept waiting for someone to shake him awake and tell him some mistake had been made—sure, he'd developed a talent for getting the most out of the comparatively nickel-and-dime deals he'd been making up to that point, and had even begun low-balling contractors for routine renovations and squeezing front-line loan officers for better financing, all in classic Don't Give A Fuck fashion.

But this was *Alan Ho.*

Only after several months of shadowing the man at even the most routine lunch meetings did Sean finally find out why Ho had taken him on with such enthusiasm. According to Joyce Yamashita, several years earlier Ho had lost his only daughter, who was the same age as Sean. She'd been visiting from USC over Christmas vacation when she was found dead in her car at Waiāhole Beach Park. Her body, as it had said right there in the news, had tested positive for crystal meth. That was all anyone ever knew about it, but Alan Ho had never been the same. It had "softened him up," was how Joyce had put it.

Sean hated to think of such a tragedy as…an opportunity…but as things turned out, that one little chain of events was what had constituted his unbelievable break.

Unbelievable!

Especially considering that tonight, well, when Susan Brushette had asked if Alan had just sent Sean in his place, Sean had basically… stepped up! He'd seen Alan evade and deflect and redirect and all that in enough instances that he figured he could pull it off himself, and well, pull it off? It would have been nice to have elicited some kind of hissy fit from the Hawaiians, true. But the haoles had more than done their part. That ranting haole professor? Perfect! Then along comes Bud Souza—in uniform, no less, as if Susan Brushette had planted him solely to turn the issue into one pitting locals against clearly affluent haoles. Ah, if only Alan had been there to see it.

"Shaddap!"

"Eh, you like tell me fo' 'shaddap,' den you need to come down here and tell me dat to my face! Betta yet, why don'tchoo jus' go back to dying in front of your TV old man, an' mind your own fuckin' business!"

"Shaddap!"

And on it went. "Shaddap!" "Shaddap!" "Shaddap!"

If anything it was heating up down there, the woman going into exaggerated sarcasm now about how they could pay off the twenty grand by selling their "piece of shit boro-boro ten-year-old Honda civic that you and your friends lowered to the ground over one of those coffee-can-looking race car mufflers and then painted black with spray cans from City Mill!"

Ouch!

Right at the point where things usually began petering out, they were getting interesting enough for Sean to fold up the laptop and go grab another beer for more reveling in the fact that he'd managed to put himself so far above such a sorry existence. Think about it: a gang-banger connected enough to know about *the fix* ahead of time, connected enough to be *rolling*—at least up until now…

Now that someone had apparently come to collect. Twenty grand on a football game! Was he going to finally answer back? Was she going to start in about how they'd have to sell the flat-screen TV? Take out a loan from her hotel's credit union? Oh, they were all in for a good night at Kapiʻolani Theater!

Sean located center stage, and again he had to laugh out loud. If he was correct—and you could never really tell, the way the sound bounced around down there—the loving couple lived in the building way over there at the edge of Walk-upville, right across the street from where, every morning, a stream of luxury hybrid SUVs—each worth about four times poor Kimo's sudden crushing debt—came to drop off little MacKenzie and Ashley and Parker and Jayden at…ʻIolani School.

Even now, not two football fields away from the unraveling of another young marriage, a foursome of middle-aged alumni mommies were out there whacking the ball around ʻIolani's flood-lit tennis courts. Sisters forever from the class of '94: playing *tennis*, oblivious to the whole predicament the young couple now found themselves in! *Making Rent* was a foreign country in which they would never set foot. Sure, they must have *thought* they worked hard for the chance to bat a ball around with an $800 composite racquet in a multi-million-dollar "athletic complex" paved over land worth untold millions more.

And sure, they *thought* they lived concerned and engaged lives, especially when they attended $500-per-plate charity fundraisers for homeless shelters or battered wives or drug addicts. But look what was happening *right across the street!*

Ah, that view—it never let you down. Back when Sean had bought the Kapiʻolani Gardens penthouse unit out of foreclosure a couple of years ago for just $200,000, he'd planned on turning around and renting the place right away. Though "penthouse" in this case had meant nothing more than a regular box of a two-bedroom that happened to sit on the squat building's top floor, and "Gardens" referred to the three-foot-wide swath of grass separating the building from the traffic rushing by on Kapiʻolani Boulevard, given the location and the parking, he could have made a killing. But he just hadn't been able to resist that ongoing, never-ending oh-so-rich-in-irony carnival that was the view of ʻIolani School.

Marisa always got on him about that—she teased him that it was an obsession of his, an *inferiority complex*, and Sean had to admit there was some truth to her diagnosis. Little Milton Hayashi—even with a profitable career as a dentist he had nothing beyond the Kaimuki four-bedroom, close enough to the edge of that ghetto district so he could always tell people he "lived in Kahala," and so staggeringly mortgaged to the hilt that there had been no way to send his son to Mid-Pac, let alone Punahou or ʻIolani.

That had left Sean with a worthless DOE "education" *right across the street* from ʻIolani, at Kaimuki High School, where he routinely had to pay "protection" to tattooed gang-banger thugs who lived with their aunties in some two-bedroom walk-up, their fathers and mothers undoubtedly in prison.

In that sense, Marisa had a point.

Kaimuki had helped nurture in Sean both a strong resentment for his weakling of a father and the man's cheap attempts at displaying status he couldn't really afford, and a burning need to one day *own*, in all senses of the word—especially the Alan Ho *power* sense—*own* them all.

Inferiority complex. Sean always smiled at that, before jokingly deferring to Marisa's far superior expertise in a subject like psychology, which they'd taught her right alongside math and reading at 'Iolani as, well likely as a *fourth grader* or something. 'Iolani! And it was *so much better* than that hated rival school, Punahou! (And you only ever compared 'Iolani to Punahou—certainly never ghetto public schools like Kaimuki.) 'Iolani made you so much more *well-rounded* than Punahou! Where else could you take both clinical psychology *and* glass blowing? And it was so *rigorous*, and *disciplined!* The class sizes made it so *intimate* and *personal*, and your teachers, who all had advanced degrees in their subjects and were even given release time to conduct scholarship, they *really cared!*

Just last night at dinner Marisa had told him how her parents had sat her down on the sofa of her Niu Valley living room with the kindergarten acceptance letters to both Punahou and 'Iolani and asked her to choose which one she liked best.

Kindergarten.

Back then her father, Glenn Horiguchi, had been a DOE Assistant Superintendent of Curriculum who took down $135,000 a year doing time in an air conditioned Pearl City office. And her mother, a part-time nurse at Queens Medical Center, could also certainly have made a more informed choice than a five-year-old. But to them, at least in the pre-Barack Obama days, Punahou and 'Iolani were one and the same.

Just tonight, Marisa had told Sean that 'Iolani had been "the best choice I've ever made in my life! Look at how it prepared me to…" and off she went on all that *well rounded* nonsense, and then on to what great connections she would have all around town as she worked her way up the food chain at Brokeum and Cellit, the commercial real estate firm for which she'd been working since UH handed her a Communications degree five years ago—UH, because even though she'd gotten into Stanford, Marisa had never wanted to leave the Hello Kitty comforts of her own bedroom.

Indeed, Marisa Horiguchi was *hooked in* downtown—a fact that had been as attractive to Sean as the tan lines her shoulder-less black dress had exposed the morning he'd met her at that "coffee hour" that James Hendrick, the Lieutenant Governor himself, held for the local real estate community in the atrium of the State Capitol building. Those tan lines—they all but begged you to imagine what the rest of that petite little body of hers looked like decorating the sand at Kaimana Beach in a micro bikini. Once he'd found out she'd gone to 'Iolani, well…think of what her connections would be able to do for *his* career, too! Think of how they could do it together!

Right there he'd tapped into *not giving a fuck*, talked himself up not as Sean the Waiter (she still didn't know about his job at the Lehua), but as Sean the Dealer, and somehow he managed to get her number. From that moment he'd been well on the way to presenting Marisa with that little blue box, the one with the six karat diamond ring inside.

He had it all planned out, too. He'd be a gentleman about it, just as he'd been such a gentleman the whole time—I mean, you didn't want to *rush* things with a girl like Marisa Horiguchi, a good girl, a proper girl who still lived with her parents, nothing like the skank-hoes he'd gone to school with at Kaimuki and later at UH, girls who could turn a routine collaborative homework assignment into an hour of grunting and rutting with someone they'd never laid eyes on before. No, not Marisa Horiguchi.

My god, Sean hadn't even…*made love* to her yet. And just to prove what a perfect gentleman he was, he would wait until after he'd sealed his true commitment with their marriage vows, which couldn't have been very far off now that everything he'd spent his life working towards was finally *coming together*. Oh, happily ever after!

"You TOUCH ME, I'll call the fuckin' cops, watch!"

"Call 'em already, I no care, call the fuckin' cops, you fuckin' *cunt!*"

Ooooh! You could almost hear all five thousand surrounding voices at once: *Oooooh!* This was even better than that brawl a couple of months ago, that full-scale, hadda be twenty-on-twenty baby gang-banger 2:00am *brawl* in the Ala Wai Park that had gone on for over an hour before the cops finally showed up. From here, Sean knew, it was a short step to a slammed door and the peeling wheels of a lowered black boro-boro coffee-can-mufflered Honda Civic roaring off into the night.

The "C" word! Right out loud! And then: *slam!* went the door, *roar!* went the starting car, *screech!* went the tires, and there sped the little black dot, zooming right past the sacred gates of 'Iolani School, past a gaggle of attorneys' wives babbling away on Court 6 down there under the beaming floodlights, oblivious to the whole thing.

Oblivious. And not only to the plight of the working poor living directly across the street, but to the whole…*context*…of what anyone could clearly see from up here on the twentieth floor, beginning with a multi-million-dollar sports complex built so a select few school children could play games or swim in a pool named after Walter Dillingham, and ending with the Nangaku Building, standing just over there in the shadows beyond the tennis court, yet another *shakedown* from back in the '80's, when a "Japanese businessman and philanthropist" bought a thousand acres from 'Iolani School and then sank $100 million into it to build the Koʻolau Golf and Country Club.

The facilitator for that deal, as Alan Ho had explained it, had managed to extract a $2 million "donation" for the building as a way to smooth over the…concerns. And just like that, this paver of pristine rain forest, dumper of thousands of gallons of herbicide and pesticide annually into the Oʻahu aquifer, all for the benefit of a handful of Japanese millionaire golfers, this Masao Nangaku—he was a *philanthropist!*

And of course.

That was how you smoothed over this Hawaiian burial thing. Not with Susan Brushette's "job creation" argument, even with the word "billion" attached to it, as in, "Over the next five years alone we'll be pumping over $8 *billion* dollars into Hawaiʻi's struggling economy." Not by trying to *reason* with them and get them to outright *agree* to the development—I mean, some of them had turned down what Alan Ho had called a "bottomless pit" of Department of Defense shakedown money to oppose a stadium-sized telescope on the Big Island.

No, you had to box them in. Make it look like you were *addressing their concerns*. Marginalize their opposition *in these challenging economic times*. You had to make a very public offer that would paint them as *immoral* if they stood against it. In the image of the now-moonlit Nangaku building, Sean could see the solution staring him right in the face. He could close his eyes and picture it, too: the TsengUSA Center for Hawaiian Studies.

Just then his phone started vibrating away on the table inside. *Joyce Yamashita.* Joyce Yamashita? Alan Ho's secretary? At…10:15 at night? And calling instead of texting? He picked it up.

"It's Alan," she told him. "I've been calling everyone I thought he'd want me to call just to let them know."

"What."

"He's had a heart attack."

Sean was stunned. His immediate reaction was to wonder what he was supposed to do about TsengUSA, about the Hawaiians, about the enviro-haoles, to mention nothing of the six karat diamond for Marisa.

But of course, he reminded himself, the main concern was Alan's health, right? In his sixties or not, the man kept himself in better shape than Sean did, or anyone else Sean knew, for that matter. Heart attack? Alan Ho? I guess you never knew.

"Is he okay?" Sean asked. "I mean, what happened?"

"I don't know the details. Carol was pretty shaken when I talked to her." Joyce sounded pretty shaken herself. "He was out paddling, and then suddenly he slumped over."

Sean's mind drifted as Joyce went on about how Alan was in the ICU at Queen's in critical condition, something about how someone in his crew carried a waterproof phone, and good thing, because if the ambulance hadn't been waiting when they pulled in at the Ala Wai, he wouldn't have made it, and on and on and on, all of it melding together, because despite how much Sean really wanted to be concerned for his mentor's health, how much he really wanted to *care*, well, just for starters…

How the fuck were you supposed to go about naming a *building* after someone anyway?

Man of the House

At that very moment, at 10:15 on a Wednesday night, Russell Lee was piloting his Lexus LX 670 homeward along Kalaniʻanaʻole Highway, his mind a racing hurricane of numbers: fifty thousand minus two thousand minus eight hundred minus another thousand plus five thousand minus *another* fifty thousand, and what had he gotten himself into *now*, and how on earth was he supposed to explain it all to Cathy? Even after all these years of marriage, no one ever *told him what to do*, but a hundred grand, well…fuck.

And now the SUV's interior was *shouting* at him, its marks of obvious frivolous consumption taking on the voice of Russ's father: *nice your power windows, ah boy, butchoo really need that automatic rear door? Rain-sensing wipers that go on by themselves? Rotating headlights? Form-fitting power bucket seats, j'like thousand-dollar living room recliners? You need that refrigerated "cool box" built into the center console? A* monitor *and* cameras *for keep you from ramming into one fire hydrant when you parking? You* need *alla that boy?*

All in, the car had cost Russ nearly a hundred thousand dollars, but he still owed more than seventy five grand on it ($800 monthly payments!), so if he sold it now he'd barely put a dent into what he owed the increasingly persistent Lave Salanoa, not to mention whomever it was that had approved his line of credit at the Pearl City game room where he'd just dropped *another* fifty grand.

That's right. Another fifty grand. Though he never would have gone as far as giving the thought actual words, the hole had doubled in size, because Russ had gotten…desperate. It wasn't just that Lave Salanoa was almost four hundred pounds of sumo muscle, one of those the-bigger-they-get-the-higher-the-voice Samoans. Or that he headed a football operation so complex (he had tried to explain it to Russ once) that not even Cliff Yoshida would have been able to unravel the way the guy was able to cover bets placed by who knew how many gamblers in both directions on a hundred college games, some of them at the very last minute while the game was already well underway. Or that he was part of some larger Samoan…gang?…and, now that he thought about it, the big *solé* had indeed been right at Aloha Stadium when Russ had called, sitting in the rain watching an entire quarter of garbage time.

No, on top of everything was the lingering fear, despite how the story of Tapusoa's death had simply vanished from the news, that all of this might *go public* and sink the already-elaborate campaign plan Alan Ho had been constructing.

At first, Lave had respectfully waited, not even call or a text until the following Tuesday, and even then he'd been polite about it, that sweet high voice of his saying "I know you good, Boss, I know you good." He'd waited another week before calling again: "I know it's a lot of money for come up with one time, Boss, you no need pay the whole thing now, we could set somet'ing up."

Russ had simply fed Lave some excuses about trying to scrape together the money without his wife knowing about it, and some assurances about maneuvering into his retirement account, and then hung up and did his best to pretend it would all *just go away*. But then this morning his phone had started vibrating in the darkness, its buzzing sound sending an electric jolt that caused him to fumble around to stop the racket before it woke Cathy up. It would have awakened Russ, too, but his eyes had been wide open since 3:14 am, when another anxious dream of cascading numbers had shaken him from a deep slumber. When he'd checked the message a few seconds later, he found that Lave's voice had dropped at least an octave: "Eh Russ! We gotta *do somet'ing* 'bout dis kine, dis *situation!*"

Tonight it seemed like the solution to wipe out Russ's debt—now more than three weeks old—had simply…presented itself. State Senate President Russell Lee, friend to public education, had been invited to deliver a few remarks at Pearl City High School's Senior Project Night. He couldn't very well pass it up, not with Cliff defining it as "good strategy," especially since Pearl City lay so far outside his own district. So Russ had endured an hour of westbound evening traffic just so he could stroll around some DOE High School library *ooohing* and *ahhing* over a collection of poster board displays that 17 local-Japanese girls and one Filipino boy had made depicting their "Service Learning" *experiences* volunteering in "at-risk" elementary schools out on the Waiʻanae coast, a giant collage of eager and smiling pale Asian faces hard at work with striving-to-please little brown Hawaiian and Samoan faces.

Though the photographs immediately lodged in Russell's brain the vivid image of a Niu Valley office geisha gazing with approval upon a stage full of middle-aged Hawaiian recovering ice addicts, the *charm* kicked in. Soon he was talking all about "giving back" and "hands-on learning" and the "quality education" our public schools were providing.

Afterwards he'd found himself on Kam Highway driving right past an old corrugated steel furniture warehouse that, to Russ's gambling-savvy eyes, may as well have been bathed in a thousand flashing lights and adorned with a marble Roman fountain five stories high. He figured a couple of hands of Texas Hold 'em wouldn't hurt, and maybe he'd get on a roll and come away with a few hundred or even a thousand to make things look good for Lave.

Within minutes he'd more than tripled the hundred and twenty bucks in his pocket. And then one of the boyz working the floor—Russ knew him as Nalu, a big ugly local gangsta-type with an infectious high-pitched laugh—Nalu had come by and told him, "Eh, Seneta, we know you good. No worry—you can jus' sign for 'um." Russ took one look at the piddling little pile of chips in front of him, and another look around the table, where he saw nothing but easy marks: two twenty-ish local-Chinese computer-geeks with stiffened black "808" baseball caps pulled down over their eyes, three drunken haole jarheads from Fort Shafter or Hickam or Red Hill or somewhere, and two fat retired-DOE-principal-types with graying moustaches and bloodshot eyes, chasing. "I'll take fifty," he'd said. (*Stupid stupid stupid stupid!*) Nalu's eyes had widened to the size of a couple of chips themselves, but he walked off and reappeared anyway with five thick stacks of five-hundreds.

The next twenty minutes had flown by in a blur. And even now as Russ turned the LX 670 ($800 payments!) up Portlock Road (*Portlock?*), he could still feel the understanding hand on his shoulder, still hear the sound that had awakened him from his stupor: "It's okay, Seneta, we know you good."

So *figuring it out* had just shot up to a level Russ hadn't encountered since, what, back in high school that time when he'd gotten so deep in at the chicken fights back of Waiāhole Valley these frikken thought-they-were-syndicate guys—serious, too, Hernandez-them—were going to break his *football legs*. It was only because Ikaika Nāʻimipono had stepped in that Russ had been allowed to even walk onto the field for the all-state senior year.

Russ could still recall it clearly: Ikaika—he'd started out by trying to tell Hernandez that Russ would pay him back, he one good bradda, he *my* bradda from way back. And when that hadn't worked, Ikaika had offered to put up his *own truck*, the gleaming F-150 his dad had bought for him off a friend he drove dump truck with, for collateral. Long after he'd quit the team too—that's how deep Ikaika's loyalty ran.

Even now. Even if the…issues…put the two men in constant conflict. Whenever they did run into each other it was a big-slap handshake and a hug, let's put those issues aside and reminisce, and yeah, *hard* these days for raise a young boy, not like when we was coming up. Now that Russ thought about it, Ikaika had never even brought up the fact that had he *not* stepped up like he had so long ago, well…it was no secret that Russ's whole I'm-your-man political career had only grown (or been able to grow) because he'd once been given the seed of a UH football scholarship.

With that thought Ikaika's usual hectoring began—the same hectoring that always seemed to fill Russ's head whenever he found himself driving up this golden road to some of the most desirable homes in all of Hawaiʻi—all pre-McMansion-era open-air beach spreads spilling down the back slope of Hanauma Crater to take full advantage of the sunset ocean view and the glistening lights of town. Yes, whenever the Lexus rumbled past the suburban sprawl of Hawaiʻi Kai (once the largest traditional fishpond in all of Polynesia) and through this corridor of ferns and palms hiding all these six- and ten- and fifty-million-dollar tropical palaces from the prying eyes of the unwashed, there was his old football brother, talking right into his ear with the usual string of… gentle reminders…like about how Russ had claimed residency at the Kahaluʻu farm his dad passed down to his sister so he could "represent"

Windward Oʻahu's District 23 instead of solidly Republican Hawaiʻi Kai/Portlock, choked with haoles and retired *yakuza* and vacation rental tenants willing to fork over ten grand a month to avoid Waikiki. Or how Russell Lee was the only Hawaiian on all this leasehold land dating back to Kamehameha the Great, all of it owned by a ten-billion-dollar land trust that was supposed to educate Native Hawaiian children but that ignored 90% of them so it could focus on being a PR front for mainland developers. On and on.

Except tonight Ikaika's hectoring—and right away, too—it turned straight toward Russ's sudden crushing debt: Eh Russ, gonna what, *make some compromises*? Put yourself under some kind of obligation to Alan Ho or Darryl Kawamoto or somebody? And do those downtown players really just throw those "personal services" contracts all around the Lege right out in the open? How *would* a "gift" of a hundred thousand dollars in cash look on the financial disclosure form of a guy running for governor, Russ? You *figure it out* yet?

Normally Russ would have gone back and forth a bit with Ikaika, telling him that if you *really* wanted to change the way the affluent and the powerful treat Hawaiians, you didn't do it with a protest sign and an upside down flag—you did it by living and working together with them. Except that the closer he got to home, the more Ikaika's voice… *make some compromises?*… it started melding…melding…melding into the hysterical shouting and sobbing from Cathy, and the rest of her reaction to the impending news…because *figuring it out* was exactly what had just doubled the size of the anchor dragging Russ to the bottom of Moanalua Bay out there…and I'm sorry honey, but we might have to *move out* of our beloved *Portlock home*.

How on earth was he supposed to tell her? The question had been mildly pestering him since the UH game what, three weeks back—it seemed like a lifetime ago now, those good ol' days when he'd been so concerned about having to come up with a mere $50,000.

Now it pounded in his head, its volume compounded by the sight that confronted him when the LX 670's big tires crunched upon his Caribbean-style crushed-shell driveway into a manicured yard bordered with so many ferns and fruit trees and tropical flowers you thought you were in the middle of the country: there was Cathy's Lexus SC 10 convertible ($72,000!) with the 18-inch machine tourmaline alloy rims

($2,600!) and even a rear spoiler ($440!), parked right next to the rig they'd bought Joel as a reward for getting off of academic probation at 'Iolani: a black Toyota Tacoma X-Runner V-6 ($32,000!) lowered over 22-inch chrome rims ($2,800!), which itself was parked in front of a trailered Yamaha Waverunner SuperJet ($8,499!)—Joel's reward for getting himself off of academic probation last year.

These vehicles alone were bleeding Russ nearly $2,500 a month, not to mention the insurance, which really wasn't that much if you held it up against what they had to scramble together for the mortgage payments on a *house in Portlock!* A yard landscaped like the garden behind the Royal Hawaiian Hotel ($200 a month! Plus another $200 to keep it all watered!). 2,000 square feet of living space (cleaning: $200 a month!). Sure, it had been an incredible deal—Alan Ho had steered Russell toward first crack at a foreclosure ten years ago, and Cathy had fallen in love with the place on sight, and Joel, all of six years old at the time, was thrilled he'd get his *own house*, the little one-bedroom cottage on the property's edge.

Cathy had had no trouble cashing in the $300,000 equity her parents had left her to put towards the down payment. But when the dust had settled, they were still left with a $3,700 dollar monthly nut. Not bad for a one-point-two-million dollar house in Portlock. And yet…

What sort of engine did they have to propel them against the endless current of…37 plus 25 plus 1 plus 2 plus 2, plus plus plus…nearly *seven grand a month?* Even more if you threw in cable and electricity and outrageous Honolulu property taxes and, well, *food?* You had only this: the meager salary of a part-time public servant ($52,706), plus the retainer fee for the "legal work" Russ conducted for Alan Ho's banker friends ($120,000). Though it seemed like a lot, after what got washed away by the waves of state and federal taxes, plus the $21,600 annual chunk that was eaten up by 'Iolani, well, the $55,780 Cathy earned (before taxes) at the top of the seniority scale as a Northwest flight attendant…money they once thought of as a kind of slush fund for vacations and dabbling in investments…it had become *vital*…and were they really living paycheck to paycheck? In *Portlock?*

Cathy. In all of their twenty-two years of marriage, he'd never had to keep anything from her (other than what had happened that night on the junket to Vegas eight years ago, and then two years later when the

Tourism Committee went on that mission to Japan and the JTB hosts had arranged to provide Russ's whole contingent with private...*massages* is really what they were, and what was the harm, anyway, when no one would ever find out about it...). Never. Not once in twenty-two years.

But now Cathy really had no idea about this financial bottomless pit she was suddenly living in, this low-slung, tastefully appointed, Spanish-tile-roofed stucco dwelling of theirs bathed in its soft lights. Whether it was a measure of her faith in Russ as a breadwinner, or in her own artist's delusions that everything would always have a way of working itself out, Russ couldn't say. But Cathy seemed to think they were...*rich*. She was, after all, married to the president of the State Senate, but while the Lege had a long history of guys on the take from one special interest or another, Russ, perhaps acting upon the influence of his father, had stayed completely clean. (As for the arrangement with Pacific Properties LLC, well, when anything involving Pacific Properties ever came before him in the Lege, Russ made sure to take off his Pacific Properties Attorney hat and put on his State Senator hat and treat the matter with the utmost impartiality.)

No, the Lees were far from rich, but there was no explaining this to Cathy, a quality of hers which had been among the first arrows Cupid had shot when Russ had fallen in love with her in the first place: she didn't *care* about such details, or, better put: she was *carefree*, a *free spirit*, a wonder.

She'd only taken the sky waitress job after earning an art history degree because she'd *wanted to travel!* She'd hardly ever been out of Maine, spending her summers on a lake outside a little ghost of a mill town called Farrington—the same place, in fact, where Hawai'i's most prominent missionaries, the very haoles who had *built this place*, had originated.

When she finally visited Hawai'i, she immediately *fell in love with the place* and made arrangements to move here. Soon after, Russ met her at a Super Bowl party at Players downtown, where he saw her sitting at the bar, a throw-back Roger Staubach jersey hanging off her sun-tanned shoulder. She had this exotic kind of blue-eyed, well, *haole* beauty, like nothing Russ had ever seen before. They started making dollar bets on whether the next play would be a run or a pass, or whether someone would make the sign of the cross after a good catch. Their first "date" came a week later when Russ took her to the VIP section of the Pro Bowl.

The final arrow had been shot not by Cupid, but by Cliff Yoshida, who pointed out that, given the political unrest over the 100th anniversary of the overthrow of the Hawaiian monarchy, and the rumblings about sovereignty from militant Hawaiian rights groups, a haole wife would help paint Russell Lee as a more moderate Hawaiian of the sort with which most non-Hawaiian residents liked to identify themselves. Russell had agreed, and within months he and Cathy were married.

When Russell finally opened the front door he was immediately hit by a wave of sweet-smelling marijuana smoke that nearly knocked him off his feet. Under other circumstances, he might have gotten upset—not that someone was smoking, but that they were being *so obvious* about it right here under the roof of one of the most prominent members of The Joint. But tonight that wonderful smell was sweeter than freshly baked chocolate chip cookies after school. To Russ, it was the smell of *relief,* for it meant that Cathy had gotten stoned with Joel, and the two of them were watching some Hawaii 5-0 re-run, leaving Russ completely free to put off telling anyone anything about their current financial situation.

There they were on the sofa in front of the 80-inch LED TV ($5,280!), his fifty-year-old wife and his sixteen-year-old son, with some kind of high-tech bong on the coffee table in front of them. Cathy's hips had widened considerably since that night at the Super Bowl party, but Russ was always happy to note how those wonderful full breasts allowed her to get away with it, even at this very moment as they swelled out from the aqua one-piece swimsuit she wore under a pair of khaki shorts. She and Joel—who, as usual, was wearing nothing but a pair of black board shorts that more than likely hung down halfway over the crack of his ass when he stood, the better to put as much of that lithe *youthful* body of his, especially those cut abdominal *bricks,* on full display at all times—they had apparently just taken a swim out in the pool (pool man: $200 a month!) overlooking Moanalua Bay.

Now they were bonding over a couple of hits of Joel's kush, their wet brownish hair combed back and reaching about the same length down each of their necks. That's what Cathy liked to call it, anyway: *bonding*—though Russ was never too sure about this open acceptance of drug use or, for that matter, anything at all to do with parenting in this day and age—an uncertainty that had created a kind of…distance… between himself and his son that caused him to envy Cathy's relationship with Joel.

Russ didn't want to come off as his own father had, with all the preaching about hard work and getting ahead and all that—he vividly recalled how such pestering had pushed him straight into his cocaine days back in the '80's. Sure, Russ had been able to quit coke cold turkey, but this meth thing—it could *take you down*. You'd have to be a total idiot nowadays to even try the stuff, what with what everyone knew about how a *single hit* could lead to addiction. And what was a sixteen-year-old boy but a *total idiot*?

When Russ and Cathy had caught Joel a year ago one night coming home reeking like some Puna hippie, Cathy had made a convincing argument that "at least it's just pot," which, she also reasoned, was "harmless" even when compared to having a few beers, "especially when all these kids are driving everywhere" and with all these late-night "brawls" you were always reading about in the news. She'd gotten her medical marijuana card a week later.

Part of the deal whose gravity Joel had understood even better than his mom was that every possible precaution had to be taken to be…discreet about the whole operation. And within months Joel had shocked Russ by becoming some kind of horticultural expert. The kid may have been just barely keeping his head above water at ʻIolani, but he knew all there was to know about cross-pollination and hybridization and average sunlight hours and all the rest of it. Joel grew *kush*. On *purpose*.

Not like Russ would have ever shared such sentiments with Joel, though, so when they both looked up at him, his fifty-year-old wife and his sixteen-year-old son, he just gestured towards the TV and said, "Any good?"

"You mean this stuff?" Cathy asked, pointing to the bong and drawing a laugh from Joel.

"Yeah, that too," Russ said with a smile.

"It's another Haolewood masterpiece," Joel said, his face suddenly mock-focused on the screen. They turned out to be watching not Hawaii 5-0, but what looked like some low-budget coming-of-age movie set in Hawaiʻi. "The haole transplant goes from being ostracized by a group of local thugs, and then he slowly earns their respect by driving them around in his new Tacoma, and then they all scrap with some rival gang, and finally he's *in wit' da boyz.*" Joel punctuated his irony-laden description by punching his open hand with a *slap!* Irony, in fact, was the only tone the boy seemed to speak in lately, every verbal exchange yet another attempt to display his newly found skills of wit and repartee. Still, Russ was happy to have the kid talking to them at all, recalling clearly his own teen years when he avoided his own father at all costs. And he had to admit, Joel could be funny.

"Don't forget the part about the exotic young beauty," Cathy said.

"Yeah, yeah, but that's secondary. The haole boy fantasy is really more about getting *in wit' da boyz*, getting *accepted*. Even the ones that are born here. You should see all these idiots at 'Iolani mooning over the football linemen when they walk down the hall—it's like the first time they ever even *talked* to a real Hawaiian, these guys are cel*ebrit*ies. Football players!"

"Eh, your dad was one dumb football playa too you know," Russ said, laying on the pidgin and happy to draw some good old fashioned stoned laughter out of his family.

"Speaking of celebrities, how did your little address go tonight?" Cathy asked.

"It was pretty routine. Parents, DOE people, school kids."

"Oohh!" Joel said, "The *future!* Pearl City! So you're wrapping up the union-protected local-Japanese state-worker-lifer vote, ah Dad."

And damn, what do you say to *that?* Though Joel had nailed exactly what he *had* been doing, Russ could never have brought himself to describe the act with such irreverence—with the irreverence of…a sixteen-year-old 'Iolani student with his own $8,500 jet ski. It was what you had to *do* if you wanted to become governor.

And just then it occurred to Russ that right from the start his son had treated the news of his run for governor as yet another topic for amusement. A launching pad for the next glib witty comment. Just as Cathy had treated it, in her own free-spirited way, as a kind of that's-really-*nice*-dear matter of course rather than a calculated political risk.

"That's about the size of it," Russ finally said.

And then he made a stab at some irony of his own: "It's amazing how a few empty words from a podium in some public school library can convince people that you're capable of administering an entire state government."

"Yeah, that and standing next to the road with a *sign*, standing there and *grinning* and *waving shakas* at everyone, like *that* proves you'll make a good governor!"

"Eh, don't underestimate the Willful Ignorance vote, brah."

"What are you talking about?" Joel asked.

"You know, the voters out there who can't locate Hawaiʻi on a map of Hawaiʻi—the ones who think the guy with the best smile, or the best looking wife, or who wen' grad wit' my bradda-sista-them will make the best governor. Sign waving catches the Willful Ignorance vote."

"Yeah, the *Ainokea* vote!" Joel said, and then he turned to his mother and repeated it, dissolving into a fit of giggles: "The *Ainokea* vote!"

Not for the first time, Russ was surprised he'd dug himself into such a cynical hole simply by trying to one-up his son in a game of Irony, a game the kid lived by. Here he was, on the verge of attaining the highest office in the state, an office from which he could *do something*, something *long lasting*, something that would *change this place* for Hawaiians, for *his people*, and yet to listen to himself, well, it sounded as if he'd already given up on the world.

"Maybe you should sing!" Now Cathy was joining in. "Seriously—do a commercial where you're singing. Remember years ago when that girl from Kaimuki was on American Idol? Jasmine Trias? I think it was something like twice the voter turnout for any Hawaiʻi election—they were all calling in to vote for her, *paying money* to call in and vote for her for some stupid contest. That would *never* happen in Maine."

"Oh God, there she goes again, my haole mother," Joel said, and then he slipped into an exaggerated pidgin voice: "Well dis not Maine, sista, an' dis not the *Maine lanʻ*, dis *Ha-va-ee!*"

There he went again, Russ thought, his local son giving his mother a hard time, more *local* than she was despite the fact that she'd lived in Hawaiʻi five years longer than he had, if you did the math. Russ always enjoyed watching these little exchanges, too, mostly because they tended to bring out the *haole* in his wife, which reminded him of the days back when they'd first met. Sure, she'd mellowed a bit over the years, and she'd certainly educated herself about the historical complexities of "paradise," growing, unlike many haoles who pack up and go home after a couple of disappointing years, to love Hawai'i all the more for the sense of *hope* that it clung to despite all its warts.

She'd found her place here, too—although her "place" was rather *haole* if you stopped to think about it—a little art gallery in the Aloha Tower Market Place she ran with a friend from work, a woman named Marsha Damon who was married to a commercial real estate broker. The guy had somehow gotten them the space on a flat percentage-of-gross basis, meaning they only had to pay rent if they sold a few of those fake Wyland cartoons of half-underwater whales they were always bringing back when they took Northwest's runs to Vietnam. After a couple of years it had come to serve mainly as a means for Cathy and her friend to define themselves as "Art Dealers doing business in East Asia" instead of the mundane "Flight Attendants."

"Don't worry, Mr. Local Boy," Cathy said. "You'll see how it is in a couple of years when you step off this Third World rock and go out into the real world."

"Oooooh!" Joel said, cupping both hands over his stomach as though someone had just punched him. "Third World rock! What says the Governor?" he asked, to which Russ just gave a patient smile. "The 'real world.' You mean when I go off to live among all the Andover and Choate and Pingry kids who got rejected from Harvard and Yale and Dartmouth? When I go away to *Colby College?*" He gave an evil-looking grin, and then bounced into the back of the leather sofa in another fit of giggles.

"Yeah, when you go to Colby," Cathy said, "*if* they're willing to accept you. And that reminds me," she said, turning to Russ. "It's my turn to host the Colby Club party this year—I just wanted to let you know." The Hawai'i Colby Club. Cathy had graduated decades ago from the little in-the-woods New England college and (who knew why) she still felt obligated to it.

Into Russ's brain flashed the image of a collection of the five or six ancient Colby alumni dotted around town, plus a handful of the more recent grads of the sort Joel had just nailed—in this case Punahou and 'Iolani grads who hadn't been good enough for the Ivies, all of them watching the sunset from the terrace of the Outrigger Canoe Club and trading stories about their orientation trip camping in the Maine woods, or about the time they'd rescued their roommate from being drawn on in indelible magic marker after he passed out from drinking too much champagne on the library steps before graduation. Just as quickly another image appeared, which was what the phrase "it's my turn to host" meant in its entirety: not only would Russell have to attend the sorry event; he'd have to *pay for it all* as part of the annual alumni gift that kept Cathy in the President's Council category of Colby donors—that is, upwards of *five thousand dollars.*

Now. Now was the time. Stoned or not, there it was on the table for everyone to see: the topic of their *financial situation*. If ever there was a moment to bring the entire matter out into the harsh light of day, it was right now. *No, Cathy*, he would say, we just can't do it this year, and while we're on the subject, there's something else I've been meaning to tell you, it has to do with—

But right at that moment the impulse to just *tell* her, to *get it over with* and *move on* and *see what we can do* about this...situation...that impulse was met at the line of scrimmage with his need to...*be a man*... for there was his own sixteen-year-old son, right next to her on the sofa, leaning back so his *bricks* stood out in high definition, his young forearms, which looked like someone had wrapped them in *cables* of muscle, folded just below those rock-hard pecs, the kid could paddle a surfboard *all day*. Though Russ still stood a couple of inches taller than Joel and outweighed the boy by a good fifty pounds, his son looked as quick and solid as a young pit bull, *young* being the operative word, a young *man.*

In the heat of his little internal struggle it occurred to Russ that he should start hitting the gym again, that he couldn't just let his body *go* just because he was over fifty, that he still had a good five years or so of the responsibility of providing the kid with a *solid physical example of manhood.*

Manhood! So what was he supposed to tell Joel? That he'd gotten *punked* on a football bet, and then *punked again* in a Pearl City game room by some fat retired Japanee elementary school principal, and that he could no longer afford to support them in *the lifestyle to which they'd become accustomed*?

"When is it?" he asked Cathy. "I'll clear the date."

Cathy started talking about "the first Friday in January" and how she'd already booked the ocean-front banquet room, but the words were all mixing together into an incomprehensible sound Russ could no longer hear, because the moment he'd agreed to plunk down another five thousand dollars on such a stupid and vainglorious event as an "alumni dinner" to benefit a whitebread learning institution servicing over-the-top wealthy white people some seven thousand miles away, he realized that even putting aside his concerns about being *the man* in front of his irreverent young son, he didn't have it in him to disappoint Cathy. Even if Joel had been outside burning in his cottage, Russ doubted he would have been able to refuse the $5,000 request, let alone broach the subject of...*putting their Portlock home on the market*. What, were they supposed to move into some little three-bedroom spec home pushed out to the edges of a 6,000 square foot lot in Ahuimanu? Cathy would be heartbroken.

She'd be right, too! At least Ahuimanu was in his district, but come on. For starters, where would they park their cars? Right out there on the street? Only blocks away from all the chronics congregating around the Kahaluʻu banyan tree? Right. Nearly $200,000 worth of vehicles right out there in plain sight. Great idea. That was before you even brought up Joel's jet ski, not to mention his kush—Thieving Chronic magnets both. Would Joel have a collection of pots right out there on the driveway? And would he smoke up with his mother within five feet of his loud and noisy neighbors on both sides, so close you could hear the toilet flush right next door? And was Joel supposed to live in a bedroom not fifteen feet from their own, separated by nothing but a few quarter-inch-thick slabs of drywall and a box-of-a 200 square foot room that doubled as Russ's office and Cathy's art studio? How were they supposed to *make love* with their sixteen-year-old son right there within earshot every night? And what about the pool?

It sounded silly to put it into words, but once you lived within a few steps of your own pool overlooking Moanalua Bay, let's face it: there really wasn't any turning back.

So Russ went back to the bedroom to change into a pair of board shorts and tried to comfort himself with the fact that at the very least, Alan Ho had agreed to chair his exploratory committee—that if all else failed, Alan would somehow figure out a way to work around this one. These were the thoughts that ran through his head as he made his way out to the pool, and looked out across that magnificent view at the distant twinkling lights and the back of Diamond Head: that although he may have been in deeper than Cathy or Joel or even Cliff Yoshida would ever know (*Skeletons?*), starting tomorrow he would double down, showing his face at every baby luau from Waimānalo to Wai'anae, from Lihue to Hilo. He'd make an appearance at every charity fundraiser, DOE "awards" dinner, and local TV talk show that Cliff could schedule him for. Ribbon cuttings, building dedications, sporting events, graduation parties, weddings—you name it.

And Alan would take care of the rest.

FINDING THE CRACKS

Sean Hayashi had *Don't Give a Fuck* revved up about as high as it could go right here in Hale 'Ākoakoa, the sparkling Taco Bell hacienda that centered the otherwise *typically UH* Windward Community College campus. The rest of the place was so dilapidated-but-trying that some of its offices and classrooms were still housed in old buildings abandoned by the neighboring State Mental Hospital, unfit for the mentally challenged but perfectly fine for "educating" the parade of probably-ought-to-major-in-*business* willfully ignorant know-nothings that rotated in and out of its former cells for a couple of months each semester before dropping out.

Hale 'Ākoakoa, built, no doubt, with some kind of multi-million-dollar legislative appropriation aimed at "rebranding" WCC, still emitted that chemically-sealed-stain-resistant-commercial-carpet/hint-of-institutional-interior-paint fragrance that spelled New State Building. Its tens of thousands of square feet boasted a cafeteria, a "bookstore," and just two classrooms—a little room off in a corner somewhere where a dead art called "journalism" was taught, and the multi-function retractable-divider-walled lecture hall in which Sean and the rest of the meeting's principals were now seated around a make-shift conference table, surrounded by so many onlookers that a few had to sit on a new gray carpet that was already pocked all over with blotches of spilled coffee and soda and what-not.

"So it's not really that big a deal to sign the Memorandum of Agreement," Sean was saying. He liked the way he sounded in here, too, here in this roomful of Windward Hawaiian rights activists, and their students, and their official representatives from the Office of Hawaiian Affairs, and from Hui o Ka 'Āina—Aunty Maile Chang's resistance group. To himself, Sean sounded like he was *in charge*, like it was *his deal*. He sounded like Alan Ho would have sounded.

Alan Ho. Alan was supposed to have been the one running this meeting, too, but, under doctor's orders, he'd had to send Sean. The heart attack had been pretty severe—if Alan hadn't been in such great physical condition, they'd told him, he wouldn't have survived. That a man so fit could even have a heart attack was one of those mysteries of DNA, and, if everyone was being honest, of diet, Alan having used his rigorous paddling routine as an excuse to shovel untold amounts of butter-coated escargot and foi-gras down his throat over the years. So from here on out, Alan could only promise his behind-the-scenes support and advice, along with the clout of his connections. "It's going to have to be up to you," was what he'd said. Sean would not have been happier if even Marisa Horiguchi had gotten down on *her* knee and presented *him* with a six-karat diamond ring. *Up to you!* It was his *chance*!

And here he was! Running with it!

"'Agreement' doesn't mean necessarily that you 'agree' to the project," he went on. "What it does is basically clarify that you understand the terms of our project, it allows you to set up an advisory committee that has a say in how the project is carried out. It actually gives *you* the right to sue *us* if *we* violate the terms of the agreement."

That this statement was initially met with stone faces on the other side of the table did not bother Sean in the least. Eventually they'd come around. Basically you were talking about a group of public school morons, frankly, who in this case had managed to *victim* their way into the UH Hawaiian Studies program and then get drilled with its anti-American, anti-capitalist, anti-everything angry rhetoric—a taxpayer-funded act financed in its entirety, as Sean loved to point out, by the capitalist tourist industry and the U.S. military.

Just look at their leader over on the other side of the table, Ikaika Nāʻimipono, his tree-trunk arms folded across that big stomach of his, a layer of fat covering the broad, thick shoulders sticking out from his white tank top, like one of those City and County Hawaiians you always saw sucking down Heinekens as they stood around the back of someone's F-150 at a beach park somewhere trying to see who could get diabetes first. The guy was practically mute, and may actually have *been* mute.

Then there was the guy's Aunty Maile Chang down there at the end of the table in that tent-of-a pink polo shirt, a plumeria she'd picked off the ground outside stuck in the slot between her left ear and her stiffened silvery hair. Unbelievable that they hadn't been able to get Aunty Maile to go off on one of her unintelligible what-you-folks-need-to-know-is-thatchoo-all-wen'-take-our-*land* angry rants a couple of weeks ago at the Talk Story in Kahuku. Now she was sitting next to Andy Kalehua, the lanky OHA trustee. A few of Ikaika Nāʻimipono's other lackeys Sean recognized: the skinny guy with the goatee, the young-ish looking heavy-set woman always pulling around that rolling backpack of hers, the darker young Hawaiian with the red bandana over his head, Josh Gibson or something, Sean recalled, down at the end with his laptop open and taking the meeting's minutes. That haole professor, Makana Irving-Kekumu, the one with the light brown hair who kept on insisting he was Hawaiian.

It wasn't even a fair fight.

Next to Sean was Michael Prescott, the swollen former rugby-player-looking Englishman, the blue-print sleeves of his designer Aloha shirt reaching halfway down his thick biceps, both pale as a sheet and covered with a rug of black hair. Yi Quian, that human computer of a slender fifteen-year-old boy genius Qihong Liu had brought along to the Pauahi Tower meeting (the guy, Sean had found out, was really 33). A couple of WCC administrators Alan Ho had recommended Sean invite in order to pound home the offer of WCC scholarships for Hawaiian students, thus putting the Hawaiians in the position where they would have no moral choice but to sign the memorandum that would void their right to bring a construction-delaying lawsuit under the National Historic Preservation Act.

And Mae Ling Chen, over there to Quian's left—she may have been dressed like some kind of office cookie in that red silk blouse pulled down tight over the lines of that push-up bra, but Sean had a feeling—though it was just that: a *feeling*—that she was, far and above, the smartest person in the room.

"We're not signing anything," Ikaika Nāʻimipono finally said, his arms still folded.

Sean was a bit taken aback—not by the initial negative response *per se*, but simply with the revelation that Nāʻimipono could *speak*. He turned to Prescott: "They don't want to sign the Memo."

"I'm sure we can work something out so we can all get ourselves on the same page here," Prescott said. As irritated as he'd been back at the Pauahi Tower meeting, Prescott had eventually realized that the local shakedown contingent was indeed proving to be of help. No doubt someone had drawn up some kind of color-coded flowchart depicting the bureaucratic path through which TsengUSA's plans would have to travel before they could even start clearing their land, a chart that had to look like the entangled vines of the banyan tree now bathed in the floodlight outside.

So now whenever he and Sean spoke, Prescott was *interested*—in personal things, too, like, could Sean recommend a good neighborhood for him to rent a house or a condo for the next few months, and what was this music all about, this "slack key" guitar thing?

Sean turned back to the Hawaiians: "He's talking about helping the community," he said.

Now they *all* had their arms folded in front of them. Andy Kalehua had that scowl on his face, the one Sean had seen whenever the guy was on public access TV talking about how OHA was supposed to have been compensated for former Hawaiian kingdom lands—places like the Honolulu Airport and UH. The guy was always asking for two and three and four hundred million dollars in retroactive compensation, as if the state had some huge stash of money buried in a lava tube somewhere. He was actually kind of skinny—but he'd perfected that look that made you think he was ready to rip you in half.

No matter, though: Sean would soften them all up. "It's not like TsengUSA just wants to ram this thing through," he went on. "They want to make sure everyone's happy."

Ikaika Nāʻimipono nodded to Makana Irving-Kekumu, who then said, "Look, we appreciate that you've come all the way up here tonight to hear our *manaʻo*, our concerns. We know the memorandum looks harmless, and that it appears to be in our interest to sign it because of what it holds *you* folks to, but until we have more details, especially regarding the burial sites, we don't want to document any involvement whatsoever in your project, which is what signing this thing would do."

Sean turned to Prescott again: "They're concerned about the archeological review." He and Prescott had been over this part. At first Prescott had been incredulous, wondering aloud that if you wanted to, you could define the whole of Hawai'i as a potential burial site. If that had been the case in a place like New York, he'd said, most of one of the world's most densely developed cities would look like Central Park still does. It wasn't very developer-friendly.

"I think we can make some kind of deal with regard to cultural preservation, and to education, that will make everyone happy," Prescott said.

"He's talking about scholarships," Sean said with a smile. "Scholarships for Hawaiian students." He looked around the room to see if any of the students themselves had brightened up at this. But the dutifully angry looks remained. Here they were, willing to sacrifice their own futures over some mystical nonsense like *bones*. Well, they'd come around eventually.

Even if this "scholarship" thing didn't work and they had to throw a few dollars on the table, was how Alan Ho had explained it to him from his hospital bed. When Sean had brought up his idea of offering them a building, a Hawaiian "cultural center" of some kind, Alan Ho had simply laughed, saying, "I like the way you think, but let's see if we can get them to come around for a few trinkets first." As Alan explained it, you could look all the way back to the *mahele*, that coup that had brought the wonderful concept of private land ownership, of *fluid capital assets*, to these islands back in the mid-19th century. Or the opening ceremony for the H-3 freeway, when a Hawaiian group had been "persuaded" to perform a chant to "make peace" with a development many Hawaiian sovereignty advocates, including Ikaika Nā'imipono here, had risked their lives opposing.

Decades later that group could be held up as the blanket Native Hawaiian "acceptance" of the freeway, simply because someone had realized you were dealing with people who likely lived two and three generations to a three-bedroom spec home, were unemployed (or at least underemployed), likely without health insurance, their kids brainwashed by TV into thinking they deserved to wear a $200 pair of sneakers—here they were, standing behind something with *no practical value*: their cultural convictions. All you had to do was...find the cracks...strike the right...

deal...one that gives them a...a *way out*, that lets them *hold onto their principles* somehow.

"We're talking about real educational opportunities that can change lives," Sean said.

Ikaika Nāʻimipono then turned to the young heavy-set woman on his right, the one in the maroon polo shirt, and said, "Okay Kanoe."

Though Kanoe looked to be only in her mid-twenties, you couldn't detect a whiff of nervousness. Sean was sure she'd start peppering them with a list of historical tid-bits delineating how this piece of land was "stolen" and these water rights were "grabbed from the Hawaiian people" and so on and so forth. But to his surprise, she let the moment stretch *just a bit* in a way that began to worry him, although he couldn't have explained why. This silence of hers, it was a *composed* and *confident* silence, one that said, "Just give me a moment while I think of a way to put what I'm about to say into terms an idiot like you would be able to understand."

Finally she looked Prescott in the eye, and in a very even tone, she said, "Let me try to explain why we might have a problem with this Memorandum of Agreement, and with the idea of an 'advisory committee,' and particularly with this notion of scholarships." She paused again, like a concerned parent reasoning with a headstrong teenager, and then went on: "Getting us to sign this memo, it's going to make you look like you *are* just pushing this thing through, that you did some back-room deal with just *one* small group of Hawaiians and got some sort of buy-in. What you've got to do is hold hearings on this stuff and let people know what you're trying to push through, and do it in a way that doesn't look rushed, because honestly it looks like you're trying to get away with something."

No way! In three sentences she had nailed Sean's entire strategy—a tried-and-true strategy that had worked on project after project for *decades*. He had to redirect. Fast! "I'm glad you brought up this thing about the scholarships," he said. "We're talking about full scholarships to WCC for up to fifty Native Hawaiian students. Vice Chancellor Barnes," he said, turning to the UH contingent seated over to the left of Mae Ling Chen, "could you explain for us what that means?"

Mitch Barnes, the graying former frat boy who served as WCC's Vice Chancellor for Student Success, was leaning way back on his chair down at the end of the table next to Owen Funai, his Interim Associate Vice Chancellor (and who on earth made up these *titles*, anyway?), the two of them flanked by their "personal assistants"—a silken-haired petite hottie at the tail end of her Ocean's 808 Mid-Pac reunion club days named Marsha Yoshikawa, and a real let-me-just-give-up-and-cut-my-hair-short stumpy matron named Aileen Fujiuchi, who had long since slid into those pull-the-sweater-over-each-roll-of-fat years, the tube of lard around her waist matching in girth the one around her upper chest, adorned as it was by two little lumps of man-boobs—a body shape which, as it sadly occurred to Sean, Marsha here would evolve into before too long.

Barnes sat like he was lounging on the sofa in someone's living room, his hands folded in front of him on his prosperous lap. This guy was *haole*, with double italics and maybe a capital H, and for a moment Sean wondered why so many of these UH administrators were imported F-O-B haoles with absolutely no concept of the *context* of the place they'd just moved to, and at what point along the career path at some mainland university had things gone *wrong enough* for you to wind up at a place like Windward Community College?

All of this flew through Sean's head in an instant, because Barnes himself was happy to join in the conversation right away, saying, "Aloha everybody!" with a big grin. "I'd be happy to talk about what this means, at least for the Windward Community College 'ohana." This was the first time Sean had heard a Hawaiian word spoken in a lilting southern accent. "But since this is all still at the speculative stage," Barnes went on, "and since I've only been here in Hawai'i for a bit over two weeks, at this point I can only offer the mildest form of opinion."

Sean hoped no one else noticed how obviously the guy was trying to use *charm* and a couple of long and empty sentences to try to think of something useful to say. At least Josh Gibson over there had to have noticed—he'd just had to type all this meaningless drivel into the meeting's record.

Barnes then went off on a long tangent on the "mission" of community colleges in general, and spoke about how WCC faced particular "challenges" in light of "the current budget situation" and so forth. Three minutes in and he'd yet to say anything of substance, which was just fine by Sean: if nothing else, the subject had been successfully changed. "But in the end I think you people are going to be happy with the opportunities these scholarships provide."

You people!

Redirect! *You people?* How the fuck could he have said *you people?* Hadn't Aileen Fujiuchi at least taught him *that* much? That *you people* would be taken as code for a general overall typically *haole* affliction of ingrained and unacknowledged racism? She could teach him about *'ohana*, but then let him go around spouting *you people?* Redirect! Redirect!

"Thank you so much, Dr. Barnes," Sean said. He didn't have to look to the other side of the table—he could feel the glares shooting out at him, at Barnes, at Prescott, just as he could hear the muffled murmuring and sighing from around the room. "And Associate Vice Chancellor Funai,"—and was that how you were supposed to address the guy? Should he have said *Interim?*—"earlier you were sharing with me some deep concerns about enrollment next academic year."

To Sean's relief, Funai jumped right in with the enthusiasm of a game show host: "What we're talking about here is a potential increase of *seven-to-twelve percent!* I don't have the capacity to handle that kind of increase, and our financial aid office doesn't have the resources to provide for any more than we're already providing for."

A skinny Japanese-American guy (from Baltimore?) with a 100-watt smile that competed with the blinding white WCC golf shirt covering his bony weekend tennis player's frame, Funai waved his arms around excitedly as he spoke, going on about the college budget, and salary allotments, and the dry-up of "overload pay" and "lecturer money" inhibiting "my ability to schedule extra sessions" and so on, and how the extra tuition these scholarships provided would help him "bridge the gap" to help him "graduate students on time," which to Sean sounded like code for *shovel people through in huge classrooms regardless of what they learn,* a translation Funai confirmed by saying, "so they can get their degrees."

He went on: "The money TsengUSA is willing to provide for the college, above and beyond these fifty scholarships, is going to help me provide more classes and more opportunities for WCC students." Here he was introducing another carrot Sean hadn't even mentioned yet—a blanket endowment for WCC. "And even when we're not talking about the fifty scholarships, it's important to consider that my enrollment here is over thirty percent Native Hawaiian. We are the major educational opportunity for all these Hawaiian communities—Waimānalo, Kahaluʻu, all the way up to the North Shore. And let's face it: the days of asking for that kind of appropriation from the Legislature are over. They're over." The guy sat back in his seat, his knees spread wide, and folded his long spindly arms.

Now these Hawaiians had to choose between educating not just fifty, but *hundreds* of their community's children—they had to choose between *that*, and *the possibility* of a bunch of bones someone may have buried in the ground hundreds of years ago. Education for your people, or…bones!

Perfect!

And it had come directly from the Interim Associate Vice Chancellor for Student Success! The man with his *ear to the ground*, the man with his *finger on the pulse!*

No one said anything for a long time, until finally the young woman, Kanoe, looked into Prescott's eyes. "You offered them money, yeah?" she said.

"Like we explained, Kanoe," the Englishman said, full of patience, "you and I are probably not as far apart as it appears. You see, TsengUSA is also interested in cultural preservation, and in providing tangible benefits to the Native Hawaiian people."

"Good," Kanoe said. "You *should* give money if you have money to give to underprivileged communities, because it's the *pono* thing to do."

"*Pono* means 'righteous,'" Sean said to Prescott. He said it calmly, but inside he was jumping up and down: It had *worked!* They were going to take the scholarships! Help their people! Sign the memo!

He turned to Kanoe: "So you see that this is an actual tangible and direct effort to help the Hawaiian people, right?" Oh, this was beautiful! He couldn't wait for the answer!

Kanoe thought for a moment, clearly angry at how they'd painted her into such a corner. And then she said: "I can't answer your question, because your question is not right. You're trying to get me to say something that I cannot say. You're giving me one of these false options, you know? You're putting me in the position of having to choose between my culture, and educating Hawaiian children, and that's it. But those aren't the only options, and you *know* those aren't the only options."

Sean tried to redirect, but Kanoe held up a hand that inexplicably stopped him in his tracks. She turned to Prescott and told him, "As I said, giving money to underprivileged communities is the *pono* thing to do. But if you think *for a moment* that that money, even for a moment, somehow sways them against the truth of the situation...*don't* think so."

Her head tilted downward so you could see the whites of her upturned eyes. "Or if you put an obligation on WCC in exchange for doing what they should be doing anyway, which is educating the young people of this community so they can have a chance at pulling themselves out of poverty just like the vice chancellor here explained, then we'll blame *you* for putting an obligation on them." Then Kanoe sat back and said, "How can you burden an underprivileged community more than they've already been burdened? How?"

"Oh, no, no, don't misunderstand!" Prescott said.

Redirect! Redirect! Sean could see Prescott starting to get irritated with this whole business of appeasing a bunch of brown people who believed in ghosts, when he could have been...somewhere else...sipping on a mai tai. The last thing he needed was for Prescott, who would never have any idea of what the stakes *really* were here—I mean, these people had delayed the H-3, a United States *Department of Defense* project, for God's sakes, by *twenty five years!*—the last thing Sean needed was for Prescott to get into it with an obviously well-armed and clearly underestimated and very overeducated opponent like Kanoe Silva here.

"I think what Mr. Prescott means is that there's no need to worry about 'obligations' or constraints and so on," he said, "especially since we're carving out an important space for Native Hawaiian involvement *throughout* the project. Once the advisory committee is formed, well, that's an arena for direct community input. We want to hear from all of the stakeholders as we move forward, and the Native Hawaiian community is one of the biggest stakeholders in that area. We want to listen."

Oh, this was fun! Just like that, you could *change the subject!* Now Prescott could catch his breath—and before anyone could realize that Kanoe Silva had just successfully called Sean on his scholarship dilemma strategy, too. Moving on to this advisory committee thing was the thing, and he'd been able to do so *just like that!*

Kanoe Silva then looked up at Sean, it faintly occurred to him, for the first time all night, and said, "Mr....Hayashi is it?"

"Yes. Sean is fine, though," he said with a smile. "I think we'll come to see that, as Michael here put it, we're really not that far apart here, so you might as well call me Sean."

"Sean." Pronounced *toolbox*. "Okay. Look, Sean. I'm not exactly sure why you're here—it seems clear that this is a conversation between the developer and the people who are asserting a long-standing cultural right of access to this land. But we don't wish to have any advisory committee. We're just—" and on she went about *iwi* and *cultural practitioners* and *land of our ancestors*, though Sean had stopped catching any of it beyond *why you're here*. He was livid! So much that it only faintly occurred to him that this woman was dangerously close to blowing his cover. *Not sure why you're here?* I'd better *say* something before Prescott catches on.

"And in fact," Kanoe was saying, "that's just another way of making Hawaiians second class citizens in their own land."

"Oh, no, no, no!" Sean plunged in. He could feel his whole body—his chest, the muscles in his arms, his legs—all begin to tighten, just as his heart rate shot up to about 180. Not sure why I'm here! Had anyone else caught it? He was here because he was *facilitating* this meeting, because he was *in charge*.

Laboring to keep his tone as even and friendly as possible, he said, "What we're trying to do is give Hawaiians more of a *say* in what happens to the land. As you know, and as you're so adeptly pointing out, it's a very complex issue, one that TsengUSA would not be able to steer through without someone with local knowledge to help negotiate these things with the area's long-term stakeholders."

Now the haole professor, Makana Irving-"Kekumu," spoke up: "We're the *right* holders of public land, not *stake*holders," he said. It wasn't lost on Sean how the guy liked to say *we*, as though he were Hawaiian himself. "There's a difference. Stakeholders are those who need to take all the resources. But the *right* holders are the ones who give consent, who decide if it's okay to take that resource. And that means both Native Hawaiians and the general public. If you don't include the general pub—"

"I see your point about the access rights," Sean said, jumping in just in time. He had to keep them from putting into words the other primary component of his strategy, which was to create as much division as possible, both between the Hawaiians and the "general population," and among the Hawaiians themselves. Doling out a few scholarships to some Hawaiians and not others was one prong of that strategy, while providing limited access to TsengUSA's property for "cultural practitioners" and no one else was another.

This time Sean decided to just steer the subject around a bit: "I think we can assure you," he said, gesturing to the reasonable folks on his own side of the table, "that full access will be given to any and all cultural practitioners. The development will actually enhance access, with parking and paths and roads and so forth, especially for kupuna." Pivot, twist, spin. Pivot, twist, spin. Oh, what fun! How about a handoff? The Chinese hottie hasn't said anything yet—how about a *distracting* handoff? Sean turned to Mae Ling Chen and nodded for her to pick up the thread.

"You know Kanoe, I work for a developer, but I have feelings," Mae Ling said, leaning forward. Her English had this endearing British lilt to it, like she'd gone to Oxford or the London School of Economics.

"Oh, well we didn't hurt your feelings, did we?" Kanoe said with genuine warmth. It was working already, Sean could tell, this shift away from potential gender war grounds. Kanoe was suddenly a different person altogether.

"No," Mae Ling said with a laugh. "I mean I have *feelings* about things."

"Okay, good," Kanoe said with an endearing laugh of her own. "I didn't want to offend you, you know."

"Oh, no no no, it's not that! What I mean is, several months ago TsengUSA considered doing this project in Saipan. But then when this foreclosure happened, we came to Hawaiʻi. I went to both sites. And I have to be honest with you: Saipan is not like Hawaiʻi."

Saipan? Though Sean wouldn't have been able to explain why, this mention of Saipan immediately seemed like a bad idea.

"Okay…" Kanoe said.

"I put my feet down in Saipan, and I lifted them up and sat back down in the car and said I want to leave. It didn't *feel* good to me."

Kanoe let that sit for a moment. Whether it was out of respect for some cockamamie new-age Oriental superstition, or because she, too, believed in these *feelings*, Sean couldn't tell. And then she said, "Okay, but that feeling you get up on the North Shore is why we want to keep its integrity."

"I know," Mae Ling said, "but I want you to know that we don't want to hurt anybody either."

Pause. "But what you want is to have it both wa—"

Emergency! Now Sean couldn't jump in fast enough! "I think that's kind of why we're here tonight," he said, "to come to some kind of win-win solution. Once the advisory committee is set up, your input as we move forward with this will be guaranteed."

"I've got just one question about this advisory committee, Sean," the haole professor said. Professor! It was almost like calling a chiropractor "Doctor," this business of addressing a WCC babysitter with such an elevated title, when pretty much all of WCC's faculty had gone through watered-down UH Mānoa grad programs where all you had to do was write a couple of papers parroting the faculty's leftist political views to get a Master's, the only requirement for a WCC faculty position. But on the other hand, this first-name thing, *Sean*—it was a step in the right direction.

Maybe this guy could calm the rest of these lock-myself-to-the-gates-of-ʻIolani-Palace sovereignty fanatics into making some *sense*. Maybe this was one of those *reasonable* Hawaiians, like Russell Lee or Duke Aiona or somebody.

"When you say 'advisory,'" Makana began his question, "are we going to have power?"

"Well yeah, Makana"—my pal Makana from *hana-butta-DAYZ!*—"Sure you'll have power. Of course." When no one immediately jumped in to question what he'd just offered, Sean congratulated himself for another successful redirection. And not only that, he seemed to be making some progress with this professor, this learned man, the one voice of *reason* over *emotion*. Now maybe they could get somewhere on this memorandum of agreemen—

"What you're saying is not true."

Not true? Sean swung his head around to see Mae Ling Chen, her arms folded on the table in front of her, on *his own side* of the table, no less…contradicting him? And he'd thought *this* was the smartest person in the room? This was a dingbat if he'd ever seen one! London School of Economics or not, she was just plain stupid!

"At least not technically," she went on in that ridiculous My-Fair-Lady accent of hers. "We're going to make this advisory committee, but they're not going to have any power over the development plans. It's mainly about access to the property once the development is complete."

Redirect! Again! Sean had to say something before Kanoe Silva or even Ikaika Nāʻimipono himself jumped in. He looked at his watch. "Enhancing access is the major benefit of this project," Sean said. "What Mae Ling means is that full access will be given to any and all cultural practitioners."

Then he heard himself say, for the second straight time, "The development will enhance access, especially for kupuna." He tried looking at his watch again. "Look, it's getting kind of late, but what Mae Ling means is that while we see your concerns, we couldn't be more emphatic about this access issue."

But it was no use. Kanoe Silva fixed him in that uneven stare and fired away: "You know Sean"—rhymed with *dumb-ass*—"if you're in a hurry, you could speed things up if you just stopped *translating* everything. I think we can understand pretty clearly what Mae Ling just said, and what Mr. Prescott and Dr. Barnes and Dr. Funai over there are saying, and I'm pretty sure that they can understand what we're saying, okay? You know, stop interrupting us, because we're having a substantial and actually *useful* dialogue."

Sean was stunned. Stunned! In that instant he wracked his brain for some kind of response, knowing that the worst one was to let this woman's succinct condemnation of his very *identity* waft around the room and settle into the consciousness of everyone there for all time.

So he ripped a page out of the Vice Chancellor Mitch Barnes playbook and began filling the empty space with *words*: "I think it's very much in the interest of everyone here that we come to some kind of… equitable solution…some kind of…agreement…where there's a sense of…aloha…and everyone is…included in this…in this *thing*…and I know that I don't have to even be here but I think it's important that whatever solution we come to is the correct solution, the *pono* solution."

Whew! That might have done it! That wasn't bad! He may have been waving his hands around a bit too much, but the more words he'd strung out, the better it all seemed, like you could just scrub away all that nonsense about "translating" and so on. Not bad at all! He forged on: "And I think we all agree that the *pono* solution involves protection of, and access to, the precious cultural resources you and Makana"—*Brudda* Makana!—"have identified so well."

Prescott must have picked up on what Sean was doing, this business of redirecting things, because now he jumped in, too: "Don't worry Kanoe—we're going to let the Hawaiians in."

Sean cringed. Thanks a lot, haole boy! Fuck, the guy sounded like her high school vice principal. Well, he'd get his redirection all right, wouldn't he. He should have just kept his fucking mouth shu—

"How *dare* you say such a thing!" Kanoe said. No pauses, no reflection, no attempt at a calm and even delivery—just a rat-tat-tat machine-gun burst at this condescending haole, one that Sean couldn't half blame her for. Fuck, how the fuck was he supposed to deliver the Hawaiians to these people when they kept saying such stupid shit? And did anyone really need any further evidence of the need for a local *facilitator?*

"First of all, *you* do not say 'let,'" Kanoe went on. "That shoreline area is a temple, and the temple doors stay *open*. Second, are you trying to create a situation where the Hawaiians have exclusive rights, and everyone else sucks? It's not gonna fly. And third, what you're saying to me is that I could go, but my mom, who is not Hawaiian, couldn't go. That Makana here could go, but his dad, who is haole, could not go. That Ikaika could go, but not his wife. How's *that* one? Aloha is not a *color*, Mr. Prescott."

"Ho!" came thundering out from around the room, spoken out in a voice sixty strong.

Prescott sat there in shock as a wave of murmuring swept by, leaving nothing but the sound of Josh Gibson over there typing away at the minutes. Yi Quian looked around nervously and then locked his gaze onto the pile of papers in front of him. Mae Ling Chen turned to look straight at Sean, as if for some kind of help. Sean himself wanted to jump in with some more win-win, something else about the scholarships or the advisory committee, but what could you say to *that?*

What, even, would Alan have said? He probably would have wanted to get up and take of his jacket to put his muscular shoulders on display, but what good would that have been with someone like Kanoe Silva?

To Sean's dismay, the silence was broken by an obviously irritated

Michael Prescott, who decided to pour kerosene all over this little fire by saying, "Look, let's all be honest here. How much money is this going to take?"

"Ho!" Around the room sixty voices strong. And then another wave of murmuring, followed by more silence, a different kind of silence, a deafening silence. Somewhere outside you could hear the *zing!* of a Japanese motorcycle whizzing by, but in here, nothing. There it was, right out there on the table, the ugly monster they'd all been trying to talk about and ignore at the same time all night long: *How much money.*

Sean braced himself for another barrage, but it wasn't coming. Not from Ikaika Nāʻimipono, who sat…mute…arms still folded, a face of stone. Not from Makana Irving-"Kekumu," eyes as round as a pair of quarters. Or Aunty Maile, who was sharing can-you-*believe*-this looks with the goateed guy next to her. Or even Kanoe Silva, who could only lean forward on her elbows and hold her face in her hands and give Ikaika a sideways did-they-actually-just-*do*-that glance, and then a sigh, at the fact that Prescott had come right out and *said* that the cultural beliefs they all felt so deeply in their…bones…were right there on the table to be bargained away.

"HOW ABOUT A BILLION DOLLARS!"

The voice of Andy Kalehua, the Chairman of OHA, literally shook the room, startling upwards of seventy people into gasps of surprise. He pounded the table and stood, a surprisingly tall man, and looked all the way down to the opposite side of the table, where Owen Funai happened to be seated. Kalehua took a deep breath to compose himself and then looked the little Interim Associate Vice Chancellor of Student Success in the eye and said, "This is *bullshit.*"

He said it nicely, like he was doing Funai a favor by pointing it out for him. Then he settled on Mitch Barnes: "This is *bullshit.*" He skipped past their "personal assistants" and said, "You!" to get Yi Quian to look up at him, and then calmly said, "This is *bullshit.*"

All the way down the line he went, until he got to Sean, when he said it again: "This is *bullshit.*" And with that he turned and stormed out of the room, marching away to cheers and applause from the fifty-plus onlookers.

Soon the silence returned, a real what's-gonna-happen-*next* anticipatory silence.

But Michael Prescott was more than happy enough to break it by saying, "Look, let's try and be rational about all this."

"Ho!"

My God, Sean thought, didn't these haoles ever *learn*?

"Hey, look." Now it was Kanoe: "Andy Kalehua is the Chair of the Office of Hawaiian Affairs." And then she blasted away, all of it coming out as one word: You'renotentitledtoblowoffthechairofthe-OfficeofHawaiianAffairs. "Okay?"

"Ho, Kanoe," Josh Gibson piped up. "I totally didn't understand what you just said." He was looking up from his computer screen.

"I don't think I quite got that either," Prescott said with a little smile.

To Sean's surprise, Ikaika Nā'imipono spoke up: "Well what you do need to understand is that now you really pissed her off." A murmur of laughter from the onlookers, smiles from around the table.

"Yeah, but at least she talking," the guy next to him with the goatee said with a smile. Ray Boy. "You don't have to worry about Kanoe when she's talking—you have to start worrying when she *stops*, Mr. Prescott. When she stops talking, just smile and move on. If not, you *toast*, brah. We gotchoa numba and you going *down*."

Prescott's little smile quickly melted into a smirk, the sight of which pulled Sean together long enough to jump in again and try to get this thing back on track. "Okay, okay," he said. "Out of respect for the Chair of OHA, if you want to put a response into the record, then let's just say that an offer of a billion dollars was put on the table, and that offer was considered, but that in light of the budget constraints of the project, it could not be met. I know Andy just said all that in the heat of the moment, but if you want to make it official, how about that as the response from TsengUSA to the Chair of OHA?" Yeah, how *about* that? Even in this ridiculously tense moment, Sean was able to *move things forward*. He may have even rescued the meeting entirely.

Then Ikaika Nā'imipono opened his mouth, *again*: "How much would TsengUSA be willing to pay, anyway?"

This was even better! At last they were *getting somewhere*, all in spite of Prescott's completely boneheaded approach! Maybe all of these tense exchanges were just…air…maybe the Hawaiians just needed to get some things…off their chests. You just had to give them a chance to *air their concerns*, and then they'd finally get down to the business of *negotiating!* Hadn't Alan Ho told Sean to expect as much? Why had he ever gotten so worked up over things anyway? It was all working out fine! Sean Hayashi, all the way from Kaimuki High School—here he was again: pulling it off!

Prescott turned to Yi Quian, who looked up and spoke his first words of the entire meeting, also with the hint of an Oxford accent: "We're authorized to offer you $250,000."

This drew a murmur from around the room, but Ikaika Nāʻimipono and the rest of the Hawaiians just sat there. Clearly $250,000 wasn't going to do it, and Sean whispered as much to Prescott.

"$400,000," Prescott said.

But the Hawaiians just sat there.

Considering the stakes involved, and the potential cost of a long drawn-out court battle, not to mention the carrying costs on the land if they delayed construction much further, 400 grand was chump change. They should just get this thing over with—another sentiment Sean whispered to Prescott, who couldn't have been happier with the suggestion—he'd long since had enough of this little pow-wow with the natives—so he had Mae Ling Chen pull out her phone. After a little exchange in Chinese, she hung up and turned to Prescott and gave him a number, presumably, also in Chinese.

"$600,000," he beamed.

Still nothing from the Hawaiians—not even a smirk or a smile or an exchange of looks.

Prescott nodded to Chen, who got back on the phone, had her little exchange in Chinese again, and gave him another number.

"Look, they're willing to go as high as $900,000, no strings attached." Now Prescott was talking like he and the Hawaiians were *on the same team* against whoever that cheap bastard was on the other end of the phone.

Still nothing.

He nodded back to Mae Ling Chen, who hadn't hung up this time, and the process was repeated, with Prescott working to align himself more and more with the people on the other side of the table, to become *Hawaiian at heart*, to be *less haole* than whomever it was feeding the numbers to Mae Ling Chen. Back and forth they went, three more times, with no movement whatsoever from the Hawaiians, until at last Prescott had to say, with complete resignation and even *sadness*, that the best he could get out of those cheap fucks on the other end of the phone was an offer of $2.3 million dollars, and could you work with me on this, Mr. Nāʻimipono? "It's a pretty generous offer," he said.

Ikaika Nāʻimipono remained perfectly calm—even friendly—him and Michael Prescott, just a couple of guys sitting across the table from one another talking story.

At last he told Prescott, "We didn't say we wanted an offer. And we didn't accept or, for that matter, refuse any of these 'offers.' We were just curious as to what you think our culture is worth."

Silence. The big Hawaiian let that hang in the air, keeping his gaze locked not on Prescott, but on Sean, to whom he'd turned the moment he'd put the hammer down on the end of that devastating sentence.

Sean's mind may have been thinking *Redirect!*, but the muscles in his jaw had suddenly been rendered powerless, and he could only sit there…mute. It was a strange feeling, this paralysis, because it didn't really seem to have anything to do with fear—if it had, indeed, Sean would have been quick to fight it away by *not giving a fuck*. Though the big Hawaiian could certainly look intimidating, there was more to his glare than that, more like a kind of…hypnosis…a sweetly sung telepathic message, a message whose meaning in this case was unambiguous: *Eh, Japanee boy, we know all about your bullshit "redirect!" tactics, so just do the right thing and keep that mouth shut this time.* Against every instinct now screaming out that the whole thing would begin to crumble if he didn't *say something*, Sean remained frozen into silence.

"This meeting is adjourned," Ikaika Nāʻimipono said, looking from one end of the table to the other. "You may go now."

Owen Funai was the first to jump out up out of his seat. Mitch Barnes wasn't far behind, and pretty soon everyone on Sean's side of the table, which is to say, the side occupied by the party that had called the meeting in the first place, everyone was getting up as though class had been dismissed by the real party in charge.

Sean was surprised to find himself standing up along with the rest of them, and then following his feet out of the room as they marched on behind the swaying black skirt of Mae Ling Chen, the hurried gait of Yi Quian, the purposeful march of Michael Prescott. Now they were all caught in the shuffle of the exiting mix of students and community activists that had made up the crowd of onlookers, which at first made for an annoying elbow-shoving delay that irritated Sean even further, irritated him until he suddenly became grateful for the bustle and the ambient noise it provided, which was now drowning out what only he among his party could hear: a riotous wave of belly-deep laughter from the only people who remained seated in 'Ākoakoa 101.

OBLIGATION

Right in the middle of Nalu's niece's daughter Kayla's first birthday, a yellow Nissan X-Terra squeezed its way into the last parking space at Waimānalo Beach Park. No one thought anything of it, so caught up were they all in sucking up Heinekens, laughing over this or that funny story, putting down another plate from the table of foil trays inside the pavilion. Over a hundred Waimānalo Hawaiians, musta been, celebrating the baby's passage through that difficult first year and into a life surrounded by a huge extended family who would be with her from here on out in times of trouble and joy, from birthdays to graduations to marriage and beyond, to her wedding-sized sixtieth birthday party, right on to her distant funeral, which, once all the crying was done, would be capped with another party that looked exactly like this one: a *celebration* of *life*.

For weeks the baby's uncles had been diving in the clear aqua bay out there spearing octopus and fish for the occasion, while that five-piece guitar-guitar-bass-keyboard-drums unit of high school kids in black backwards baseball caps had sweated it out in someone's carport to tighten up that bouncy Jawaiian imitation of Ten Feet they were laying down. Yesterday an army of aunties and uncles and cousins had chopped and fried and boiled and steamed, while the baby's father and his tattooed strapping young friends had dragged the red jumping castle out of bradda's truck and staked it to the ground next to the baseball field, and set up table after table after table, all of which were soon packed with neighbors and friends and family who'd received painstakingly handcrafted invitations weeks ago.

Now here comes this frikken' yellow X-Terra. Kekoa Meyer, who had just parked his own king cab Dodge Ram 2500 with the 22-inch chrome rims in the adjoining second-to-last spot, couldn't believe it.

"Oh, shit, she's got a dog!" Nalu said with about a six-Heineken smile plastered to his jowly round face. A Terrell Owens 49-ers jersey draped over his big stomach, he had stopped to greet Kekoa and Dawn and the girls, but his reddening eyes were glued to the impending action. The woman—your typical Kailua haole somewhere in her twenties and dressed in board shorts and one of those I'm-*not*-a-tourist Great Aloha Run T-shirts—she was leashing up a smiling golden retriever next to her typical Kailua haole ride.

"Wait till Uncle Jonah sees this!" Nalu let out that laugh of his: *HEE-hee-hee-hee-hee!* He was talking about Jonah Makanani, the thick-necked bull of a man who basically owned Waimānalo Beach Park. Years ago when the whole place had become infested with chronics and covered in trash, Uncle Jonah had gotten a group of 'Nalo lifers together and booted everyone out within about twenty minutes one afternoon. Soon the whole community was helping re-landscape the entire park. And Uncle Jonah—his goal was accomplished: get the kids back into the water again.

Now there must have been fifty of them out there splashing out in the clear blue of Waimānalo Bay…screeching and laughing…getting their boogie boards pushed up onto the beach by the gentle shore break…digging in the sand…and there were Kekoa's own three girls going off to join the fun. Uncle Jonah. A retired county worker living on homestead land who'd had to fight for every little thing his entire life, and who never backed down—a lot like Kekoa's dad would have turned out, it now occurred to him.

"Excuse me, ma'am!"

"Watch this cuz!" Nalu said with another laugh.

Uncle Jonah's eyes narrowed as he approached without spilling a drop from that tall red plastic cup in his hand. "Do you have some kind of bag in case your dog makes a mess on the beach?" He'd asked it nicely enough, Kekoa thought, even putting some haole tone into his speech.

"Oh, it's okay," the woman said, trying to make her way past this nosey old man. "Leilani's a good girl. She already went before she got in the car." Still walking.

Nalu looked at Kekoa and said, "Here it comes."

"Eh! I talking to you!" Uncle Jonah shouted, freezing the woman in her tracks and drawing a look of…anger? Was she kidding? "You see those little kids all digging in the sand out on the beach? One a dem kids finds one little surprise in the sand 'cause that's where you decided to bury it, I going take that surprise an' smear it all ova your fuckin' windshield!"

"I didn't realize this was a private beach park," the woman said. She hadn't even missed a beat. She had no frikkin' *idea*.

"We *made* this beach," Uncle told her. "We been coming this beach for *generations*, got it? Now hurry up an' walk your frikken' dog and go the fuck home already."

"Are you threatening me?" the woman asked.

"I not *threatening* you," he said calmly. "I jus' telling you that if your dog shet on this beach like you wen' let 'im shet las' weekend, I going smear it all ova your fuckin' windshield."

Now the woman's head kept revolving between her precious gleaming yellow haole ride, that long ribbon of beautiful white sand she'd been thinking about all afternoon, and the face of this belligerent and likely drunken, *certainly* drunken (and why were all of these people alcoholics anyway, and drug addicts too?) *moke* blocking her way. Stuck.

Some way, somehow, Uncle Jonah had silenced the haole. Fuck, no *idea*, this woman, no idea that Uncle Jonah used to *pound* punks who broke into the tourist's cars at his beach.

"Well just forget about the whole thing then," she finally said, turning back to her car. "Sheesh, whatever happened to the 'aloha spirit'?"

"Eh, all you hadda do was bring one *plastic bag*. An' aloha to you too!"

With that she backed her car out into the Sunday afternoon traffic and pointed it back toward Kailua.

"You get 'um, Uncle!" Nalu said.

"Eh! Kekoa! How you!" Uncle's face brightened, like someone had flipped a switch.

Big hugs and a handshake, and a kiss for Dawn, a real get-plenty-beer-inside-the-cooler, go-make-plate greeting, total hospitality and even deference for Kekoa Meyer, who in fact wasn't related to him at all. It was enough that Kekoa was from Waimānalo, and that…that was the thing…no one ever actually said out loud what Kekoa Meyer did for a living…he could walk right into someone's baby luau and command a rock-star kind of respect based on second- and third- and fourth-hand stories that proved he was a *playa*, that he *ran the whole Windward side*, that—lately—after the *solés* wen' punk him, he frikken killed one future NFL draft pick and then *got away with it* even though it was right there on the front page.

"I guess you wen' tell *her*, ah Uncle," Nalu said.

"Ho, I tell you," Uncle Jonah said. "Alladese haoles from Kailua come here wit' their dogs, an' they just burry the doo-doo right in the sand. I tell *you*." Right now the woman was probably making up some bullshit about how she'd been "threatened" and "verbally abused" by some drunken racist *local*, a story she couldn't wait to bust out the next time she and her haole friends got together for lunch to exchange you-should-have-seen-the-stink-eye-the-woman-gave-me-when-I-tried-to-*explain* stories.

Never once would she stop and think that Jonah Makanani lived in one of the last remaining four pockets of Native Hawaiian communities on an entire island once covered with them—a place with so many multi-generational households that Uncle Jonah and his friends had had to rescue the beach park just so their neighbors could get outta their frikken *houses* once in a while, an' here come all these Kailua people, can't walk their dogs on their own beach within walking distance of their own houses.

"But neva mind that stupid bitch," Uncle Jonah said. "Come."

Under the pavilion roof Uncle Jonah let out a loud introduction. A quick scan of the surrounding faces told Kekoa that here on his home ground, he wouldn't have to flex his muscles today. Though his life had become the grown-up high-stakes version of King of the Schoolyard, a game where he was continuously on guard for the next ambitious scrapper with the nerve to challenge him, here in 'Nalo he knew he could always relax, relax just like Boy Ching over there, his cousin from Vegas, home for the Christmas holidays and looking like an ad for some kind of paradise escape with his shirt off, exposing that eternal benchwarmer's physique of his because, why not? I'm in Hawaiʻi!

"Eh, mista security, don't rough me up too bad now," Kekoa said as the two cousins hugged one another. Kekoa always liked to tease Boy about the term "security" in relation to his job at the Mirage, which had more to do with computers and sophisticated surveillance equipment than it did with something as caveman as "working the door" at some secret Chinatown game room. Though Boy may have somehow managed to father a swift and sculpted D-1 UNLV defensive back, he himself was a computer geek who weighed maybe 150 soaking wet, even now into his forties.

"No worry, cuz," Boy said with a smile. "I neva have to rough anyone up yet. People see the guns, they always just turn and *run*." He put on a tough face and held up two spindly forearms you could've snapped like broomsticks, sending Dawn into laughter.

"So that's how you keep all the gamblers in line!" she said. "Shee, I'm glad you stay all the way up there—I don't know how my husband would handle that kind threat in his own backyard!"

"Eh, I like nothing betta than to come home for good," he said. "That way I can back your husband up, ah Kekoa?" He flexed again, drawing more laughter.

"Automatic, cuz. Automatic."

They caught sight of Nalu's grandma and went to greet her with a kiss, going down the line of kupuna seated around the table farthest from the stage. They congratulated the young parents, and Kekoa let them take a picture while he held the baby.

When Dawn ran off to greet a friend she hadn't seen since the last baby luau, Kekoa took a seat across from a shoulders-bobbing-to-the-beat Nalu, just outside on the grass. He wound up facing that steep wall of mountains off beyond the homestead neighborhood, and even after 42 years in 'Nalo you couldn't help but imagine those mountains rising straight from the ocean floor, all the way from Makapu'u Point up to where they began to peter out in their immediate steepness up towards the North Shore, one long psychological barrier.

Just look at the nightly news: some anti-drug rally in Kahalu'u, a car accident in Hau'ula, a bunch of haoles screaming about development at a neighborhood board meeting in Kahuku—those town spokesmodel news anchors talked about anything Windward like it was happening on another planet.

Above all else, what the green mountains walled off was Kekoa Meyer's…domain.

So soon someone handed him a cold Heineken, and someone else put a plate heaped with lau-lau and kalua pig and poi and chicken long rice in front of him.

Then The Parade: a few shouts from dads and uncles, and the kids all stopped what they were doing, a schoolyard-recess full of nieces and nephews now running over to greet Uncle Kekoa. Then the high school wannabe bangers, they calling that Michael Vick jersey "vintage," the Plaxico Burress "throw-back," guys who only just retired, guys six-seven years younger than Kekoa, and had these kids ever even heard of Terrell Owens? Forget about Emmitt Smith.

And here came Boy's son Kyle Ching, also back from Vegas for the holidays, a look of pure loyalty that caused a stab of…guilt…another twinge of…uncertainty? But never mind.

Next, the boyz, some of them twice Kekoa's own size who should have been able to kick his ass but were smart enough to know better, boyz who would jump in front of a bus if he asked them to, they were now coming from all sides with big-*slap*-handshakes, you-know-we-love-*you*-brah/cuz/Hawaiian, thank-you-for-whatchoo-doing-for-us pledges of respect, all the way down the line:

Slap!

"Top shape, Bradda Kekoa!"

Slap!

"Automatic!"

Slap!

"Owe-raaht!"

At one time this little routine had been a real test of the local-boy humility on which Kekoa prided himself. Today he'd been looking forward to The Parade, like it might juice him up for the bloodbath he knew lay ahead, and yeah: this unfinished business with Salanoa-them was eating at him…dragging on as it was…and did these people really wait a *month* before having their funeral?

But now that The Parade was happening, somehow he just wasn't… feeling it…and when it had run its course, leaving the less-fawning inner circle of Nalu, Kimo Hee, Junior Tanouye and his brother Aaron, he found himself watching Boy, who kept looking out at the emerald bay like a tourist, like it was some mystical scene out of a movie, and could you *do* it?

Could you find a way to get Boy home for good someday?

The thought was interrupted when Kimo shouted out a laugh. He kept bouncing that skinny leg of his up and down and taking long sips from his Heineken as he went on with a story about some hot young enlisted haole girl he'd met on the Kāneʻohe marine base, where he still hung onto his civilian job in the metal shop. "I don't know if it's those blue eyes or the way she smile or what," he said, "but I telling you, I like *sample!* Ah, Kekoa!"

Kekoa blessed the little anecdote with the nod of approval Kimo had been looking for.

"Eh, main t'ing you don't get caught!" Junior said.

Kekoa blessed that one, too, with a nod.

Then Rodney jumped in: "Ho, like my fadda always says: dat's the Hawaiian man's downfall, cuz! Blonde hair, blue eyes!"

"Owe-raht!" Kimo said, *all right!*

Rodney didn't tag his comment with any pleas for approval, but Kekoa threw out a smile for him anyway, which obviously pleased the young guy immensely.

"Yeah, you get jungle feva, brah," Aaron added.

And okay, why not join in: "Jungle feva!" Kekoa repeated with a laugh. "Only reverse, ah."

Nalu, that big ugly fuck, he just sat there shaking his head in a way that said, "Nah, Kimo, you get 'um wrong."

"What," Kimo finally said.

"Nah, notting," Nalu said. "I no like say." But he had this I'm-hiding-something smirk on his fat round face.

"Cuz, you cannot be giving us that kine look an' then jus' say 'Nah!'" Kimo said.

"It's jus' that you only get 'um half right."

"Whatchoo mean, *half* right?"

Nalu drained his beer and let out a belch. "You get the jungle feva part right," he said. "Butchoo fuckas stay in the wrong jungle."

All around: "Ho!" And okay, yeah, maybe The Parade hadn't done its job, but having his boyz around was actually proving to be a good… distraction.

"So tell us then, mista…anthropologist," Kekoa said. "What jungle you been exploring?"

Nalu craned his neck this way and that like you do before telling one *solé* joke—looking for his wife was what he was doing—and then he lowered his head and lowered his voice and said "Niu Valley."

"Niu Valley!" Junior shouted, a good eight beers into it, obviously, catching a crack in the back of the head from Aaron.

"Eh, shut the fuck up already," Aaron growled, "he telling us one *secret!*"

"Kay kay kay kay," Junior said, lowering his voice. "Niu Valley. Shoots. Go then."

Kekoa nodded for him to continue.

"Get this little downtown Japanee girl, like the ones you see in the party pitchas in the *Sentinel*."

Kimo spat out a mouthful of beer at that one. "The *Sentinel!*" he said. "What, choo catching up on the news now, cuz? *Sentinel!*"

"Eh, I go for check the scores, prep football, whateva, they jus' asking you for click on that: 'Firs' Friday at Hotel 39,' 'Mardi Gras on Merchant Street.' Whateva."

"I click on that too," Kekoa said. "An' anyway, how about alla you shut up an' let 'im finish his fuckin' story already. Go Nalu. Niu Valley. I have a feeling this going be good."

Everyone leaned in, and Nalu looked around again before going into how he was driving by…Farrington High School? He driving by Farrington one Saturday night an' he seen the jumbo-tron out on the lawn, an' allathese *women* stay flooding into the auditorium, an' leave it to fuckin' Nalu to frikken *pull ova* an' go check it out, that horny bastid—he always get one story about bottom feeding at the supermarket or even the frikken library, except this time it doesn't sound like bottom feeding at all, sounds like he struck it rich: inside musta been thousand-something people, five piece band up on the stage, was like one concert at the Blaisdell, an' fuck, single women everywhere! He finds a seat right next to this Japanee office girl, she *by herself*, and comes this part where you supposed to greet your neighbor, and wit alla this…inspirational music…and whatchoo call, *fellowship*, she hugs him. So he hugs her back, and she's got this…smile…an' next thing you know he following her back to her local-Japanese parents' house in their local-Japanese neighborhood—her parents in Vegas for the weekend—an' then she texting her boyfriend about this church meeting running late.

"Ho, right there in the kitchen cuz, she stay *ripping* off my clothes, I *ripping* off this little dress she wearing. An' I mean *ripping* 'um, *tearing* that t'ing to shreds, cuz." Nalu couldn't go on, like he was getting all wistful at the memory. And then he said, "You look at her, you neva believe it. Get pitchas of her all over her frikken house, daddy's little girl-kine. 'Iolani all the way. Even her name: Marisa. Marisa fucken Horiguchi. But you get 'er all alone someplace? Pa! She turn into one porn star, cuz. Real Faith Chapel. Dat's the place, brah. Automatic."

Everyone was leaning way in, all ready to find Jesus.

"Praise the Lord!" Kekoa said. And all five of his boyz roared with laughter.

Which was fine, but the more it went on—a story here, some witty responses there, everyone looking for the Kekoa Meyer Seal of Approval on everything from the most elaborate anecdote on down to the smallest interjection—the more it went on, the less it felt like a break from the stress of thinking about what lay ahead after this funeral…the stress of…pulling off the biggest hit of his life…or, if they didn't hurry up and do something, the worry that people would start finding out how Tapusoa really died…that Kekoa'd been punked *again*. Whatever it was, this regular talk-story suck-'em-up Saturday afternoon with da boyz, presiding in a way that had always pumped up his ego? It wasn't workin—

"WHOA! WHOA whoa whoa whoa!" the shouts roared out, a hundred of them at once, a pure eruption of sound so loud it drowned out even the band, who all immediately stopped playing and turned to follow everyone's frantic gaze and the gallop of charging feet.

Kekoa sprung from his seat and kicked off his slippers and charged along with them, as did Nalu, and Boy, and even the old uncles, and especially Jonah Makanani, whom Kekoa caught out of the corner of his eye, a seventy-year-old man in full stride throwing his red plastic cup to the ground and rushing towards the gathering crowd out past the bounce house, where a woman's scream pierced the roar, and then another. A ring of people ten deep had formed, growing deeper by the second, fists waving in the air at the sight of…the *fight*…everyone on the outside struggling to push their way up to see who it was, Jonah Makanani shouting at the top of his lungs, "Get the fuck outta my way! Now!"

Kekoa only had to tap a few shoulders to get people to stand aside, until he reached the young and thick and muscled ink-covered shirts-off body of a man half his age who outweighed him by a good fifty pounds, but of course the guy would move once he got him to stop shouting out and waving that fist in the air, an' what, I gotta *push* you outta the way?

"Eh fucka!"

The kid turned and stared at Kekoa—*stared down at him?*—and held the gaze a good long second more than anyone should have. But he did turn aside, and Kekoa would have dropped him right there just on principle if not for what he saw at the center of the circle: another mountain range of sweating rippled muscle covering a bare brown back drenched with black ink in the form of a bleeding open palm pierced by a giant spike, a spike driven right into the center of two lats so thick they looked like wings, the wings of a rock-hard defensive lineman on his knees and straddling whoever that poor bastid was there lying under him, the one getting *punished* in a ground-and-pound flurry of punches, punches thrown in high loping arcs that were now landing left and right on the face of…

Kyle Ching.

Kekoa walked forward into the circle, slow motion, cool head main t'ing, calm, the sounds around him turning to a blur of white noise. Years since he himself had had to throw hands instead of just call out his dogs, yet it was all coming back in an instant, his mind running through a short list of possible moves and counter-moves and an instant evaluation of the strengths and weaknesses of what looked to be a man far faster and more powerful and—did it register? *Younger?*—than any Kekoa had ever had to face.

Then: two loping steps forward, and he planted his left foot firmly into the sandy grass as he swung his right foot back like a field goal kicker before pulling the trigger, sending that foot forward and catching this thinks-he's-in-the-middle-of-the-octagon steroid motherfucker just below the chin, a move that sent the guy's head snapping backwards, and the rest of that sculpted *jacked* MMA body of his tumbling onto the grass. Out cold. *Dropped.*

"Ho!" fifty voices strong.

Dropped, mothafucka. An' let's see who else ready for jump in outta alla your juiced up friends, watch me rip your fuckin face off an' spit it out on the ground right here. Or maybe you smart enough for see you outnumba'd, an' maybe alla you fuckas is the lucky ones, all six a you, cause here comes Uncle Jonah for put one stop to dis thing before I gouge your fucken eyes out wit one broken green bottle, wit somebody's fucken car keys, wit my own fucken teeth brah.

Jonah Makanani: at the center of the circle, eyes ablaze, the old man shouting and pointing and rounding up alladese fuckin' troublemakers, an' if you don't get da fuck outta here *right now* I going drop alla you fuckas myself, nevamind you an' your fuckin' jujitsu bullshit, I going find one *way*, an' you going be sorry you eva set foot in dis park, an' if I eva see anyayou fuckas here again, I going *drop* you j'like Kekoa wen' drop your fuckin' friend. "Now beat it! Now!"

See: you lucky. You fucken surrounded, even you thinking about rushing Uncle here too. Look: Nalu, Aaron, Kimo—alla da boyz surrounding you, these fuckas would die for Kekoa Meyer, you lucky they get so much respect for Uncle Jonah, get twenty-thirty guys jus' holding back, you can *feel* it, they only holding back for Uncle, cause everybody know you no fight in Uncle's beach park.

So whoeva they was—and Kekoa would find out, for sure Nolan Kahaiue would know—they roused their dazed bradda and made for a white Escalade parked next to the road, the victim of Kekoa's field goal kick turning just before he stepped behind the dark tinted windows—was he *serious?*—to shoot Kekoa a glare, right in front of everyone, and then—*not!*—a *smile*, a smile that as much as said "That kick of yours? I hardly even felt it."

Dis fucka, he looking at *me?*

Nevamind: Kekoa turned toward where his nephew had been lying on the ground beneath a pure fighting machine that had to weigh 280 if he weighed an ounce. A feeling of pride drowned the anger, because Kyle was already standing—leaning on his father's shoulder, yes, but standing.

His face was badly swollen, his cousin Noreen wiping a gash above his left eye that was spitting blood, but he was lifting a hand to his mouth to check his teeth and apparently finding them okay. Kekoa knew all along how Kyle could take a hit on the football field. But this!

It took a while, but before too long Uncle Jonah got everyone back to their tables, and the band started in on some Kekai Boyz song, and the buzz of the party returned, now at a higher volume fueled by retellings of the fight and rumors and gossip of who these fuckas was, up from Kalaheo someplace, or Ka'a'awa, and they betta watch out now they wen' piss off Kekoa Meyer!

You see how he wen' step right up: *Poom!* an' kick dat big fucka right inniz frikken jaw! Fucken guy had hundred-somet'ing pounds on Kekoa too, but Kekoa Meyer—he no care, brah. *Poom!*

You seen 'um?

All across the park, and all this talk should have all been making Kekoa feel...*juiced*. Could there have been a better demonstration as to who *runs things*? It should have given him that King of the Schoolyard adrenaline-fueled delirious feeling of *victory*. But no. He was still heaving for breath, and that image, that *feeling*, that perfect and true hit, that sight of the guy's head snapping back like that, and—*tim-ber!*—of him falling to the ground in a lump—it kept slipping from Kekoa's mind, crowded out by another image—"*Eh fucka!*"—of that ink-covered shirts-off front-row spectator turning around and *staring down at him*. And another: that fucking *smile*, the one that said: "That kick of yours? I hardly even felt it."

Maybe it was some kind of premonition, because right then Kyle walked up and hugged him long and hard, because if someone hadn't stepped up soon—and in this case, "soon" meant a matter of seconds—there would have been an ambulance and wired jaws and reconstructive surgery and the rest of it, if not permanent damage or even death.

"What happened?" Kekoa asked.

"Notting, Uncle, just one scrap," Kyle said, but anyone could tell he was lying. He'd said it calmly, too, like the fight had ended an hour ago, while Kekoa's own heavy breathing had yet to slow down.

"Eh, if we going rush these guys later, I gotta know. Dat fucka wen' false you?"

Kyle looked at the ground. "No, Uncle. Was me." He spat out some blood. "I wen' false him."

Kekoa smiled. "You get some allas, ah boy. You wen' false that frikken' LT mothafucka. Why?"

Kyle looked out at the ocean.

"C'mon boy, you gotta tell me," gulping for breath. "How come you wen' false someone get what, one-twenty on you, one-fifty maybe."

"Had to, Uncle. Fucka kept mout'ing off."

"Mout'ing off. About what."

Kyle looked down at the ground again. And then he finally said it: "He was calling you one punk. 'Kekoa Meyer, fuck Kekoa Meyer, dat fucka one *punk*.' Fucka kept going, too." He spat out some more blood. "I heard that, I jus' wen' snap."

That was it. Simple.

That was why The Parade had, for the very first time, failed to remind Kekoa that he *owned* the Windward side, had done nothing to make him feel like a powerful leader who instilled fear and commanded respect. Maybe they all kissing his fucken feet, but they *know*: "The Samoans plus whoever beat you to *sending one message* by wasting Ufi Tapusoa—maybe they wen' embarrass you brah, butchoo da man, Kekoa!" (Except that you one punk!)

And then all these Just Scrap MMA brawlers Kyle just challenged, guys who should have been first in line at The Parade, they not just standing off to the side instead—they *mouthing off* while they at it. This whole frikken shirts-off brawl, right in the middle of Kayla's baby luau—like one *announcement*: Kekoa get cracks. No need fear Kekoa Meyer. Kekoa Meyer *old*. Look how hard he still breathing, he only really jus' throw one single kick, he still all worked up. Look: breathing heavy. Breathing like Uncle Jonah, brah! Fuck, Kekoa's time wen' pass!

Right then Kekoa finally had a word for what The Parade had made him feel like: a fraud. Another: a pussy. Or this: *haole*. He had to admit it: they weren't all wrong. Especially if you compared his current 42-year-old self to the 280-pound rock solid ball of pure energy he'd just managed to drop. With a surprise kick to the jaw. From the blind side. While he in the middle of fighting somebody else.

Kekoa should have rushed the boy's head and grabbed on, blind him with his thumbs or rip his fucken nostrils out, make the fucka cry for mercy, cry like one baby. But a blindside kick? Plus on toppa that Kekoa's foot was starting to frikken throb with pain, swelling now by like a third bigger than normal, meanwhile his opponent probably already started bragging: he wen' *eat* Kekoa Meyer's fucken blindside kick, and then walk away *smiling*.

More worse: somebody else going step up next. Then somebody else.

And there was only one way to head off all the challenges, and that way had a name: Sonny Bulger. Yeah, you could go after this one kid and his five friends and *send one message*, get all *front page* on them. But pretty soon the next amped up young buck would be ready for step up and try. Fuck, all up and down the Windward coast—up and down *Kekoa's* Windward coast—you had young Hawaiians like these guys pounding heavy bags and pumping weights and sparring with each other and studying MMA videos on YouTube and *getting it down*, waiting for their chance. You had alla these LT mothafuckas who weren't even *born* when Lawrence Taylor was lighting up the NFL, and to even cite LT to someone Kyle's age was as good as saying Sam Huff or Bart Starr or someone who wore a frikken leather helmet, LT retired *decades ago*. Doubtful any of them ever heard of Sonny Bulger either.

But no matta. You just did how Sonny Bulger did, because no one challenged Uncle Sonny. Once you reached that level, it was understood. Maybe they scrapped among each other for a piece of this strip bar or that game room or line of clear or chop shop or whatever, but in the end they paid their tax. They paid their frikken *tax*. Getting into some scrap at the beach park? Fuck, Kekoa *was* too old for this shit. Time to put one stop to this shit. You either go up, or you step aside, and no way Kekoa going step aside. So it was go up.

And all right, he'd admit it: that that whole plan about waiting until Tapusoa's funeral? It was just…procrastination…motivated by…fear. And these fuckas could *smell* fear. From Hau'ula to 'Nalo they could smell fear. He should have gone after Salanoa-them right away, come out blazing like Javen wanted to, even if it did mean raining bullets down all over Hotel Street.

"You did good, boy," he said to Kyle. "You did good."

They turned to head back to the party, and Kyle must have heard him wince because he said, "You okay uncle? You need some help?"

"Nah nah nah nah." Help? I *that* old?

His breathing was finally beginning to slow, but as he worked to mask any sort of limp, plus any more winces from the pain shooting up his leg with each step from what had to be a broken bone in his foot, the thought started leaking into Kekoa's brain that maybe the bloodbath he had in mind for after the funeral would solidify his hold on his… domain…plus extend his reach into downtown, which the *solés* had run for years now, along with Kahuku and the North Shore. But beyond that, what if these fuckas today thought Kekoa *had* taken out a future NFL star and gotten away with it, and then challenged him *anyway?* What then?

People were smarter than back in Uncle Sonny's day. The world ran faster. Maybe you needed something…more…more than being King of the Schoolyard at some beach park scrap. More, even, than being able to fix a UH game. More than being able to murder the most well-known man in Hawai'i, a man better known than the governor himself. What it was, Kekoa had a hard time bringing into focus. But there was no doubt you needed *something*.

And—could it be?—the answer began to materialize, way over there across the park where Uncle Jonah was quick-stepping it over to the parking lot and then directing people this way and that to make space for someone's cream-colored Lexus LS 670 luxury SUV. Whoever it was, there could be no doubt that this was someone big, maybe even as big as Kekoa himself. Was it Akebono? That former sumo star who years ago had put 'Nalo on the map handing out *dirty lickins* to the Japanese in their own sport? Or was it one of the Pahinuis? Uncle Martin? Uncle Cyril? Hadda be *some*body, not just…he's kind of tall…definitely part-Hawaiian…some guy in his early fifties, he's got on a faded maroon "Gabbyfest 2010" T-shirt and…that bright beaming smile of…of a *politician.*

And not just any politician, but a Hawaiian politician. And not just any Hawaiian politician, but a Hawaiian politician who owed Kekoa Meyer *fifty thousand dollars.*

Uncle Jonah was now walking alongside State Senator Russell Lee, his face lit up, all get-plenty-beer-inside-the-cooler, go-make-plate hospitality. So full of respect was he for Senator Lee and the man's ability to, well…that was the thing, too—no one ever actually knew for sure what a state senator did for a living, either. Russell Lee could walk right into an event like this one and command a rock-star kind of awe, all of it based on…the abstraction…that he was involved in *politics,* whatever that meant. There was something about his work fighting the drug problem, and he'd supposedly had something to do with ending Furlough Fridays, too. Wherever he went, heads would turn, as they were all over the pavilion this very moment, with there-he-*is* murmurs making their way from table to table. Soon someone would hand him a cold Heineken, and someone else would make a plate for him, and a parade of people of all ages would come up to pay their respects.

Fifty thousand dollars. Kekoa considered this obligation of Senator Lee's. The guy was going to run for governor—the "resign to run" law kept him from announcing it officially, but this wasn't even his district, and here he was glad-handing everyone in sight at a baby luau, likely on his way to Sammy and Brianna's wedding over at the quarry, and then some funeral or whatever that waited up ahead in Kailua or Kāneʻohe. From the looks of how everyone was fawning over the senator, Kekoa liked the man's chances. Russell Lee may have been a fraud, a pussy, a coconut Hawaiian. But he was going to be governor. And he owed Kekoa *fifty grand*. It was almost enough to make him forget about…the pain…the throbbing pain in his swelling foot…and don't let any a your boyz see you wince as you sit down.

Worse than that: don't let them see you *shaking*, don't let them see Kyle go grab some ice from the cooler for Uncle's foot.

Now this big bradda of a Hawaiian, hadda be 350 and looking eye-to-eye at the tall Russell Lee, this big bradda sitting next to his haole wife, he lifting himself up and greeting the senator with a warm smile and a long bradda-bradda hug like you'd expect to see at a high school reunion, an' yeah, maybe the two men had been classmates. Ikaika Nāʻimipono—that's who the big man was—Ikaika Nāʻimipono. You had to respect someone like Ikaika. The man was righteous. Real. The man had principles. No bullshit. He lived for his people. And here he was hugging the likes of Russell Lee right here in front of everyone.

Well, that was just the kind of guy Ikaika was. He wasn't about to go and spoil Kayla's baby luau by getting into some kind of shouting match with Russell Lee for what a sell-out he was, or even just ignore him, which would have been just as rude. So the man had found some kind of common past, some redeeming piece of goodness in the senator's otherwise weak character, and grabbed onto it with a real and sincere embrace and a how-you-my-bradda. That's what Ikaika was *like*.

It didn't take much for Kekoa to admit that, well, that wasn't what he himself was *like* when it came to Russell Lee. No, what he saw in the glad-handing, fifty-grand-owing, vote-begging prospective leader of all of Hawaiʻi was…*a solution*…an answer to the *something more* dilemma.

An answer of what kind, Kekoa still couldn't say. Neither could he tell how or when he would wind up cashing in on—he still couldn't believe it, even as it was unfolding right before his eyes—cashing in on the *governor's* obligation to him, maybe cash in on it right now, except after what just happened, with the pain from that foot shooting up his leg, he didn't trust how it would come out.

For now it was enough to have Russell Lee on the hook, and even if the senator somehow managed to come up with the money, fuck: it was fifty thousand dollars of *illegal gambling money*.

"An' you gotta meet Kekoa Meyer," Uncle Jonah was saying as he brought the senator over. You could tell that Russell Lee had no idea who Uncle was talking about with this Kekoa Meyer character, but that he did detect something familiar. He was beaming that show-face politician's smile of his, trying to place Kekoa's name into some kind of context and not quite nailing it. Outside of the perpetually darkened Pearl City game room, he wouldn't even recognize Nalu, a guy he knew well. Look at him: trying to place it...he knows this guy from somewhere...or he heard the name somewhere...could it have been...

"Don't worry senator," Kekoa said, looking up into Lee's face and shaking his hand. "It'll come to you."

PART TWO

THE TAP ON THE SHOULDER

Only fleetingly did it occur to Sean that the Queen's Medical Center occupied a phenomenally valuable piece of property: directly across Punchbowl Street from the sweeping landscaped entrance to the State Capitol's underground parking garage. But not merely because the pure waves of Public Humiliation he had endured at the hands of Ikaika Nāʻimipono and Kanoe Silva and Aunty Maile and the rest of them had yet to stop crashing now two days later. Public Humiliation wasn't the half of it. Not when Alan Ho, a man who had built a fortune stomping all over the mediocre and incompetent, who had likely chewed up and spat out an army of underperforming ladder-climbers along the way, had just *summoned him to his hospital bed!*

The call had come from Joyce Yamashita an hour ago, late at night on a Sunday, too. She hadn't provided any details other than to warn Sean that Alan "wasn't happy"—that, and a motherly admonition to try not to upset him further, since they hadn't even released him out of the ICU onto the regular med-surge floor. So all Sean could think as he made his way to Queen Emma Tower 4A was whether or not this was where you finally got that tap on the shoulder. Pulling it off, Sean? Nope. Ikaika Nāʻimipono just finally did it: fully exposed you as the perennial waiter-fraud you know you are. And after Alan fires you, you can be sure Marisa won't be far behind in calling a meeting of her own.

Don't Give a Fuck—Sean must have left that in the car, because by the time he pulled the bedside curtain away and saw Alan squinting off into the flickering light of that ancient box-of-a-TV welded into the darkened room's opposite wall, he was ready to spare the great man the long lecture he'd inevitably prepared and simply hand in his resignation.

Shit, the guy would probably have some kind of a stroke a good halfway through such a lecture. A week ago when Sean had come for advice about the WCC meeting, Alan had finally *looked his age* instead of like sixty or even fifty. But now he just looked *old*, wasting away there in front of his television, his once-powerful shoulders deflated of all their muscled youth, an IV tube running out of each arm and into a hanging bag of clear liquid. Two wires emerged from that white sheet-of-a-nightgown he had on, plugging into some kind of EKG touch-screen monitor beside the bed displaying a crawl of green jagged peaks indicating the weary beat of what was left of the old man's heart.

It was a tough sight to stomach.

"Sean!" he said. The edges of his moustache rose, and his face brightened into the expression of…grandpa? "Come! Come sit down!"

So they exchanged a few pleasantries about hospital food and then Sean obeyed, taking a seat just as the nurse entered: a petite thirty-ish-looking Japanese woman with her black hair up in a bun and a stethoscope draped over her shoulders. She was dressed, like everyone else in the hospital, in surgical scrubs—in her case a baggy top with patterns of the cartoon character Scooby-Doo, and form-fitting green pants the color of the Mystery Machine.

"Hi Alan!" she said with a brightness that matched her sunflower expression. She struggled endearingly with the "L" in Alan's name too, which tripped a switch in Sean's head: Japan-Japanese, as of yet uninfected by the daddy's-little-girl the-world-revolves-around-me sense of privilege of, to be totally honest, someone like Marisa.

"I see you have a visitor."

"Yes, this is Sean Hayashi."

"It's nice to meet you," she said. Then she turned to Alan: "You know it's after 10 o'clock, Alan."

"It's okay Yuriko, Sean is family."

Family. It made Sean wonder if he was going to get some kind of kiss of death along with the tap on the shoulder, the way Alan seemed all excited to see him. Family.

"Are you feeling okay then?" she asked.

"Oh, you don't have to worry about me," he said. "10 o'clock, 8 o'clock, 4 o'clock—whatever. All I do is just lie here." He waved weakly towards the TV, where the news seemed to have settled somewhere between its nightly recitation of the police log and the requisite goofy tour of some hole-in-the-wall restaurant out near Sand Island or someplace. The screen was filled by the face of—and wouldn't you know it, too—Ufi Tapusoa, whose funeral, as the anchor explained, had been scheduled for a distant date two weeks from now up in Lāʻie. Some kind of Mormon army was already planning the logistics of setting up giant white tents and thousands of folding metal chairs on the grounds of the BYU-Hawaiʻi campus to accommodate the huge crowds they expected.

"Is that the football player?" the nurse asked, "Tapusoa?"

Oh for Chrissakes! A Queens ICU nurse, named Yuriko, maybe a year or two off the boat from *Japan*—she's wrapped up in all this shit too? Where would it all end? Was someone going to erect a Heisman-like statue of Tapusoa next to Father Damien down at the Capitol?

All Sean could do was shake his head, and yeah, the football small talk was at least distracting Alan from finally lowering the axe, but fuck, let's just get this over with already.

The screen cut to a press conference, the UH AD standing at a podium with a somber look on his face, surrounded by…the UH president, Coach Brock…and was that Sidney Rogers? Those lawyer-types in the suits must have been from the Lam Foundation—the one that had paid for the new million-dollar practice field. Steven Foreman started talking through the camera flashes about the "tragic loss" that is "already impacting our entire state," before getting into how the booster club had raised enough money to cover the expenses of the funeral, including flying in several members of Tapusoa's extended family (hence the long delay in burying the fallen Warrior), and how UH planned to honor Tapusoa on national TV at the USC game that would open next year's season. The guy was choking back tears, as were all the heavyweights standing around him, and for fuck's sake, what did it all *matter* when Sean himself was basically watching his one big dream vanish before his eyes. Football!

Alan must have seen the smirk on Sean's face, because right then he said, "Eh, don't laugh."

"But it's a *football* player," Sean said. "I bet a hundred other people have died in the last three weeks."

Alan smiled. "True," he said. "But you know, you're ignoring a real emotional component to this football thing. Sure, it's just a game. But it's one of the few things that brings this whole state together. Just look at all those guys up there by the podium. Look, there's Tony Abe. His construction firm is going to wind up building the Dolphin Bay hotel towers. And it's not like the UH booster club is some kind of secret enclave where all the deals get made, either—believe me, I've tried to use it that way and I got nowhere. You go to one of their meetings—and anyone can join, it's just fifty bucks to join the thing—and all they want to talk about is football. These guys really *care* about it. Look at them all up there crying. I might be crying myself if I hadn't seen this report three times already."

Alan may have had a point, but Sean didn't hear much of it beyond *Dolphin Bay hotel towers.*

Nurse Yuriko was now leaning over to check Alan's monitor and then click on a touch screen next to it—a scrub-tightening move that gave Sean the opportunity to view a nicely high-cut panty line then revealing itself, even in this light.

"You know they brought Tapusoa here that night," she said, "that night after the UNLV game, the one where Sagapolu broke free when he was supposed to be eating the clock?"

Sean couldn't believe it. Then it occurred to him that right here at Queen's, a block away from the State Capitol, for a nurse surrounded day-in and day-out by co-workers and patients and visiting family who had nothing better to talk about than…The Game…it wouldn't have taken even Yuriko here very long to start talking like John Madden. Even Marisa could name every player back like five years on the UH squad. She said it gave her a leg up at Brokeum and Cellit, which was probably true. But she also *liked* the game, was *hooked* on it even, like it *meant* something.

And well, what the fuck did it matter anyway? Soon, Sean could imagine the whole thing as clearly as a movie, the moment he broke the news to her that Island Sustainability LLC had been dissolved, and that he had "struck out on his own" without Alan Ho. Marisa would feign concern, and then offer "support." Within a week she'd be calling him up to "rethink" where "things are going," and maybe we should "take some time" to "figure out where we are."

"Did you see the game?" Alan asked the nurse, and for fuck's sake would he just get *on* with it?

"I was there," she said. "The ICU nurses always buy two season tickets, and it was my turn to go. But we had to leave early. The Warriors were getting pounded! And so much rain!" She adjusted a pillow under Alan's feet.

"So what do you think happened with Tapusoa?" Alan asked her, and finally Sean had to wonder whether Alan was trying to put off the inevitable uncomfortable moment too, or if it was nothing more than that he wanted to keep the nurse around a little while longer because these brief little visits had become all *grandpa* had to look forward to. "You hear all of these rumors around town, you know?" Alan said.

Nurse Yuriko looked at him and bit her lip. "Well, I'm probably not supposed to say anything," she finally said. "But anyway I wasn't working that night, and I guess you could say it was only part of the rumor. But I heard that downstairs they said it was GSW."

GSW? Sean had no idea what she was talking about.

"Downstairs," Alan said. "In the ER?" Apparently Alan did, though, like he'd already done enough time in here to nail all these hospital acronyms.

"Do you need anything else Alan?" she said. "Can I get you some juice or some more water or anything? You hardly even ate anything tonight, you know."

"No, that's all right Yuriko. Wait—on second thought, why don't you bring us a bottle of cabernet and some warmed French brie? Or maybe some haupia pie? Something to nibble on."

She smiled and then lifted a finger: "Maybe I'll get you some carrot sticks and celery!"

Alan gave her a mock wince of pain, and then she left the two men alone. At last.

"She's the best," Alan said with a smile. "A real professional. They really take care of you at Queens, you know. Although I never thought I'd even make it here. Trust me, Sean, you never want to see the inside of an ambulance. It's like a rolling death chamber," and on he went, just as he had last week, about this ailment and that soreness, and when were they going to just let him out of here, and only a week ago he'd been *fit as a fiddle* and now he was an *old man*, and on and on and on. It was pitiful how Sean's *hero* had turned into this completely self-absorbed complainer, going on and on until at last he couldn't take it anymore.

"Alan?" he interrupted. "Alan? Look, I know you called me in here tonight for a reason, and I just have to say that, well, I understand."

Alan looked up at him, almost offended at the interruption. He fixed Sean in his gaze as if he were trying to figure out exactly how to put things. And then he said, "Yes, of course. Right. You're talking about the meeting." It was like Alan was doing him a favor here, finally getting to the point. "We were contacted by their people in China, you know." And then he paused, again thinking of how to go on. "How do you think it went, Sean?"

"You sure you're up for this?" Actually Sean was less concerned with Alan's health than he was irritated that the old man was going to make him re-live the entire humiliating episode and *then* send him walking.

"So the Hawaiians are digging in," was what Alan said. "I suppose they're a bit more organized, and certainly more educated than they were back in the '80s." He let out a little chuckle. "We can thank UH for that—all of our tax dollars headed up there to fund a bunch of Marxists so they can get their foot soldiers to cripple the economy, and then they collect their checks anyway, for what amounts to part-time work hours."

"They were tougher than I'd expected," Sean said, and okay, Alan *had* given him his first big break—he did at least owe the guy an explanation. "This one woman was like some kind of lawyer. She could see straight through to the bottom of everything we were trying to pull. But that wasn't the whole problem." He went on about how the Hawaiians had baited and hooked Mae Ling Chen into pretty much arguing against her own position, and how easily flustered Michael Prescott had gotten, and then how the fiasco had ended. "It felt like I was working both sides, trying to keep Prescott in check. So the whole thing collapsed." He watched Alan's face for signs that he might be getting angry. The tap on the shoulder—it couldn't have been far off now.

But then Alan said, "I wouldn't let any of that discourage you, Sean. I can see how that might have happened."

Huh?

For a second you had to wonder if dementia had begun to set in along with the rest of Alan's old-man ailments.

"I guess we should have anticipated Prescott's reaction a little better," Alan went on, "and then done something to keep it from happening."

Sean could do nothing but watch the jagged green peaks on the EKG screen scroll by and think: there it was. For the first time in history, Alan Ho was offering somebody a *second chance*.

And just like that, it all started flooding back: Sean Hayashi, *facilitator* (and not waiter), Sean Hayashi, future husband of Marisa Horiguchi. It was all he could do to stop himself from jumping around the room and punching fist-holes into the air.

Tap on the shoulder? Come on! Sean was still…pulling it off!

"It's not at all like working with the Japanese," Alan was saying, "and I should have expected that." He let out a sigh.

Pulling it off! Yes! And, yeah, not like the Japanese, and let's just try to regroup and get back in the conversation, and what was Alan talking about? Fuck it, just repeat what he said and go from there.

"Not at all like the Japanese," Sean said. "But the guy Prescott's been pounding my phone ever since he got here, and not about work stuff either. It's more of that Paradise Syndrome thing you see with a lot of haole guys that move here—I see it…" and he caught himself just in time—in all the excitement he was about to go into an anecdote about the waiter mafia and how all the transient haoles he worked with were trying to get *in with the locals*. Just when he was given new life, he'd again nearly exposed himself as a fraud still clinging to his job *waiting tables*, and fuck, three hundred a night or not, Invisible Waiter intelligence gathering or not, just as soon as this deal got off the ground he'd quit for good. I mean, what if Alan ever did find out? Or Prescott?

What if Marisa found out she was marrying a *waiter*?

He plowed ahead: "Suddenly these haoles all want to *live here*, they want to know the *good* beaches to go to, the good restaurants, the ones where all the *locals* hang out. I gave Prescott more credit for at least trying to figure out how things work before that meeting. But he couldn't keep his mouth shut."

Alan chuckled again. "I'm sure he knew better. He probably couldn't help it." Then they traded a few stories about the haole meltdowns they'd seen over the years, the this-would-never-happen-on-the-mainland, what-kind-of-third-world-country-is-this, and the typical you-should-do-it-*this*-way rants that always preceded a haole's eventual move home.

Up on the TV screen now a weather hottie named Holly Chu was taking a good twenty percent of the newscast's allotted time to explain what anyone could have told you with a look out the window: after some morning windward and mauka showers, tomorrow would be a beautiful sunny day in the lower 80s. She had to be at least 35, no more than a year or two away from the career switch to PR—a thought that caused Sean's mind to drift to how much better things had gone back at that first meeting with the help of Brushette and Hyde. Then he quickly concluded that Kanoe Silva could have eaten Susan Brushette like a light snack if she'd only wanted to.

"What do you think we should do?" Sean asked.

"I don't think things are as bad as you think," Alan said.

Sean thought about sharing with Alan the fact that he'd walked in here tonight expecting to be fired, but well, that wouldn't have happened anyway, he decided—even if that had been Alan's plan, Sean would have found some way to convince the old man that he was still brimming with confidence and thus still the man for the job.

"It's just going to take a little more maneuvering now," Alan said. "Some sort of blanket settlement achieved publicly is clearly no longer an option. Even if it was a good deal, the Hawaiians wouldn't be able to accept it and still save face. Not now that they've pointed out to everyone that you're just trying to buy them off anyway. But that isn't the only option."

"You mean pick them off?" Sean asked.

Alan paused for what seemed like a long time. At first Sean thought he may have been trying to make a dramatic point with the pause, but then he realized the guy was just plain *tired*, and trying to wind up his spring for another bit of pointed analysis. "That's exactly what I mean," he finally said. "And I think you'll find that even Prescott will be able to help. It sounds like if you get him one-on-one, especially with this in-with-the-locals thing you're talking about, he's not the big blustery haole he is in front of a roomful of people. He might be able to connect with some of their lower rankers, get them alone and then make the right offer. I'd send the Oxford woman after this Kanoe Silva. The haole professor—don't even try with him. But if you start eroding this thing from around the edges, then you're going to make it harder for Ikaika Nāʻimipono to keep standing in the way."

Ikaika Nāʻimipono. The mere mention of the name brought back the residual trauma of being paralyzed by the big man's hypnotic death stare. If Sean had learned anything from the whole horrible experience aside from how *haole* Prescott could be or how *reasonable* Kanoe Silva came off, it was that Ikaika Nāʻimipono was no mute thug moke. The guy had this, well, *aura* around him, a presence…okay: he had *mana*. So much of it that no matter how many of his followers they picked off, all by himself the guy could probably stop this whole thing in its tracks. How Alan thought he could get somebody like that out of the way, a guy who had basically given up everything in the name of his principles, Sean had no idea.

So all he said was, "Ikaika Nāʻimipono?"

Alan looked up at him with a smile. "You don't believe me, do you. Well it's never easy, but I've seen it happen. H-3. Back in the '70s on Kauaʻi. I don't care how strong the leader is. It's almost *easier* if he's strong—that's why I don't think you should waste your time with the haole professor. He has a secure position all mapped out with that tenure thing he's got going. He wouldn't have the *balls* to take a payoff. But I've seen it happen with these leaders. You just have to find the cracks. And then you have to give him some kind of way out after he's gotten his check or whatever it is."

Another long pause. A deep breath. And then: "I think it's time you brought in Russell Lee."

"The senator," Sean said, the word coming out in a hopeless tone. At that moment it also occurred to him that the man lying before him hooked up to all manner of tubes and wires was also ostensibly chairing the exploratory committee for Senator Lee's run for governor.

"You still don't believe me," Alan said with another smile. "Russell Lee, he *knows* Ikaika Nāʻimipono. They played football together at St. Martin's."

There it was again. Football. Stupid as it sounded, that one word really was enough to link the two Hawaiians, who otherwise could not have been further apart in every conceivable way, into some kind of lifelong brotherhood. No one who hadn't grown up in Hawaiʻi would ever believe it, but even Sean knew it was true.

"Russell was a linebacker, and Ikaika played on the line," Alan said. "Russell Lee even went on to star at UH, as you know."

And of course. Only in that moment could Sean see how well-choreographed the whole meeting way back at Pauahi Tower had actually been: Alan had invited Lee not because of his position as State Senate President—he'd invited him because even then he'd foreseen a man Russ *had played football with* as the main obstacle to TsengUSA's development.

"That'll give anyone a leg up on a political career in Hawai'i," Alan went on. "I think you need to sit down with Russ."

"Why wouldn't you just call him yourself?"

The muted blare of a TV commercial hung in the air while the old man wound up his spring again. It was one of those Bank of Honolulu ads depicting a happy professional couple out on their stand-up paddle boards. "That's the question, isn't it," Alan finally said. "I suppose I could call him, but maybe the bigger point is that I haven't called him yet. You know, ten years ago, or even two weeks ago, I would have been dying for this chance to *get back in the game*, to do it all again like we did it in the '80s. And not for the money. Just for the excitement of trying to figure out how to maneuver this person into that position and then watching it all fall right into place—I used to live for that feeling."

He took a few breaths to gather himself. "Now, well, I hate to admit it: I just don't care enough. But you, Sean, you've got the *fire!* I can see myself in you."

Sean didn't quite know what to make of all this, and frankly, the emotional content of it was making him uncomfortable. And then true to form, the old man launched into that whole bootstraps narrative again explaining why he'd picked Sean instead of some Punahou-Yale grad, about how a young struggling Alan Ho had wandered into McCully Chop Suey one day, how this "wheeler-dealer" named Newton Matsuzaka who grew up with his father starts introducing him to "all these guys" he's eating lunch with, the city's managing director, some guy who had all these buildings near UH with his name on them, some bank vice president, "plus this one other young guy around my age, just graduated from USC, went to Punahou." One of them starts passing around this sheet of paper, guys start signing it—yes, a diagram of a little six-story condo project, everyone signing off on an entire floor of condos, four hundred down for each unit. "So I start doing some calculations: let's see, four thousand dollars—and that was a lot of money back then! I didn't know what I was doing, but I figured, eh, why not take a chance?"

He paused again, his sunken chest rising up and down under that nightgown. It was now Sean's turn to humor him, and okay, considering that Alan had basically given him that *second chance*, why not? So he asked: "How'd you come up with the four grand?"

"I never had to. A couple days later, the broker calls me and says, 'You wanna flip a couple?' I said fine. So I go down after work and I sign what he tells me to sign, and then I sign something else that routs part of my profit into my deposit for the ten units. And the guy keeps calling, every couple of days, the broker: 'You wanna flip a couple?' And I keep going down after work and signing these papers, and pretty soon I've made almost ten thousand dollars. Ten thousand dollars! In 1972! That's when I said to myself, 'I gotta learn more about how *this* stuff works!'" A wistful pause. "I've worked on these multi-million-dollar deals since then, but I'll never forget that first one. It was like this money was falling out of the sky. I kept waiting for somebody to tell me some kind of mistake had been made."

And did Alan just say *tap on the shoulder*? For the first time it all gelled in Sean's mind: these guys were *all* afraid of being exposed as frauds, they'd *all* built it on smoke and mirrors, a couple of fortunate small-town connections, a good dose of *not giving a fuck*. That was just how you did it. Even that Maui rancher way back, had his hands in even legitimate Japanese land deals, everyone called him a *godfather*, when all he really was, was a cop who happened to be friends with…the governor…the guy had stoked and traded on his frightening godfather image, too, but if he really had been *linked up*, then where was the *next* godfather? Smoke and mirrors. There was no *next* all-powerful Maui rancher godfather-type because there was no ex-cop who was friends with the current governor—just a bunch of wannabe-banger-*playa* thugs more interested in bling and rims than actual *power*. Was it really as simple as…knowing the governor?

"All that, just because I forgot my lunch that day," Alan said. "And that's really what I mean when I say that I see myself in you, Sean. That Punahou guy? He neva signed the paper. He had something to lose. Me, the deal falls through? I'm right back where I started. This Punahou guy, he grew up with some kind of built-in expectation to be coddled in a position of security. He's already got something to lose. And that can be dangerous. But you, Sean—you would have signed that paper. I could see that, and I'm sure Russell Lee could see that when you took over that meeting at Pauahi Tower. So go and talk to Russell. It's your turn."

Alan aimed his remote at the TV and turned it off, but even in the darkness Sean could see the old man was exhausted. Only three or four months earlier he'd completed a marathon outrigger canoe race from Moloka'i to O'ahu, and here he was looking like death warmed over after twenty minutes of talking.

"And you probably want to talk to him about that, too."

"About what."

"His campaign. He's running for governor. I'm supposed to be chairing his exploratory committee. You'll have to let him know that I'm stepping away from that too." Another long pause. "He'll probably ask Darryl Kawamoto to chair it, but you've got to be at the table."

Sean was stunned. First the tap on the shoulder doesn't come, and now he's supposed to help pull together all of Alan's connections to get Russell Lee elected governor? Where the fuck was he supposed to start?

"Don't worry," Alan said, as if reading his thoughts. "I'll be here working behind the scenes. But you can *do* this, Sean—and really, the two projects are one and the same: publicizing the development deal, and the election. You just have to *Vili* it. You have the confidence, and people can see that. Even Russell, although he might take some convincing at first."

"What am I supposed to tell him?"

"Russell Lee?" Alan coughed out a chuckle. "Give him some story about how you sympathize with the working man, how this project and his candidacy are both going to create jobs for local people, blah blah blah." A pause. "He's a sucker for that sort of thing, and in fact that's how he framed it when he asked me to head the committee. The guy actually *cares*."

Sean began to visualize how they could plaster Lee's face to all of the Dolphin Bay PR Brushette and Hyde were already setting in motion, and there you had it: an unofficial official run for governor. The Hawaiians would take some doing, but with Russell Lee's...football connection—Sean still couldn't believe that such a decades-old association between what looked on the surface like two sworn enemies would actually be enough to get someone like Ikaika Nā'imipono out of the way...and yet, Alan had been right about the emotional content. For

Chrissakes, it was more like the state religion, the way UH football could bring grown men and women to tears. So yeah, he'd have to meet with Russell Lee right away.

And if anything went wrong—though in truth Sean was now having a hard time imagining the need for help from such a withering old and spent near-corpse as Alan Ho—his mentor wasn't exactly going to be hard to track down. Who really knew how long Alan would remain in the care of his favorite nurse, Japan's number one Warrior fan.

Right there Sean had to smile at the image of nurse Yuriko out there heckling Coach Brock, or screaming for the scalp of an opposing player. And what had she meant, anyway, GSW?

"I'm kind of confused with all these acronyms they use around here," he told Alan as they were saying their goodbyes. "ICU, ER, EKG—it's worse than some kind of state bureaucracy alphabet soup."

Alan managed a tired smile. "Beyond ER and ICU, I don't think anyone knows," he said. "The acronym becomes the thing they're referring to."

"But your nurse, she said it like it was so important: 'GSW!'" Sean said, trying to imitate her accent.

Alan smiled and said, "Either you're not watching enough TV, or I'm sitting here all day watching too much. I thought everyone knew that one."

Sean gave him a quizzical look.

"It means 'gunshot wound.'"

ALOHA TOWER VIEWS

Now it was a clock tower ten stories tall, screaming it out how very late, how twenty minutes late Russell Lee was, and why hadn't anyone thought of parking? You'd think whoever had gotten the bright idea to "revitalize" the downtown waterfront thirty years ago with a "Marketplace" of tiny niche retail outlets that served mainly as hobbies for the bored corporate-lawyer housewives who owned them—you'd think that the designers had *planned* for the whole complex to sit empty, that the three semi-popular restaurants responsible for its faint pulse had been some kind of...mistake.

Four trips around that little postage stamp of a "parking lot" out front and Russ had given up and surrendered to the valet (a ridiculous expense at this point), and here he was, quick-stepping it towards the tower on his way to a microbrewery called Gordon Biersch, two peripherals passing by: a ten-foot neon sign announcing RESTROOMS, and one of those faux-casual half-open-air foodie places packed with the product-drenched heads of look-at-me downtown professional *diners* congratulating themselves on their pizza-pan-sized white porcelain dishes sculpted with layers of shrimp and lemon grass while the Sons of Hilo themselves played *background music*.

On through the palm-lined promenade of barren shops, the music fading quickly behind him, The Sunglasses Hut, the UH logo gear shop, the magnet store, Paradise Ukuleles, Kona Coffee Outlet, Cathy's art gallery, its neighboring stretch of used-to-be-Don-Ho's under-construction space tagged with a roll-out sign reading "Coming Soon: Ruby Tuesdays," and once again, Russ, yeah—he'd take late. He'd take it over the ever-present reminders of his…financial situation…if it wasn't Lave Salanoa pounding his phone, or the concern, particularly after that cryptic greeting the other day from what's-his-name, that banger from Waimānalo, Kekoa Myer?—it was the lingering worry that somehow the news of Russell Lee's double debt to known local mafia figures was just going to…explode…onto the front pages and sink everything.

And that wasn't even the half of it. No, far worse than *late*, far worse than the rolling avalanche of numbers denoting his crushing *debt*, was this: the entire TsengUSA development project now lay in the hands of…Sean Hayashi?

When Cliff Yoshida heard, he'd almost jumped ship, going on about, *who in the world* was this Sean Hayashi anyway but some money chaser who'd ass-kissed Alan Ho enough to tag along at Pauahi Tower (to Russ's complete astonishment Cliff had even used those words: *ass-kissed*), and hadn't that meeting itself been enough to show that the most powerful man in town was named not Uchida or Lee or even Glenn Nakayama, but Alan Ho, and without Alan we didn't stand a chance, even with Darryl Kawamoto to chair the exploratory committee, and now Ho wants this Hayashi *on* the committee, and on and on. Any fool could tell that Cliff was *right*. Alan had to be fucking kidding.

Russ found Hayashi outside by the harbor at one of Gordon Biersch's corner bar seats, an empty one between him and a couple of on-vacation make-doers, it looked like, who must've been abandoned in this cavernous retail graveyard by that free trolley from Waikiki. All the surrounding outside tables were packed with more product-drenched hairdos, many of the women in new-looking…jeans shorts… the downtown celebrating-our-co-worker's-28th-birthday crowd at this wish-it-was-Seattle (or Baltimore) waterfront microbrew with its polished concrete floors. Everyone covered in tattoos, the arms of even most of the young ladies completely sleeved in swirling designs fit for Cathy's gallery.

Everyone but Sean Hayashi, whose thumbs were hard at work sending a text. He looked about twenty years old.

"Senator Lee!" he said, not getting up, likely, because he was so short.

Like a reflex the beam of Russ's *charm* ignited itself in call-me-Russ fashion, and he took the seat next to the young man, who thanked him for coming, and congratulated him on his work in the Lege, and what an honor it is to be working with you, etc., and let's get you something to drink. Russ flagged down the bartender—a fortyish local-Chinese with a name tag that read "Josh"—and ordered one of the micro brews.

"I hope I didn't keep you waiting too long," he said. "It's just been real busy lately."

"Not a problem, Senat—I mean, Russ," Hayashi said. "Anyway, all these pretentious assholes put on enough of a show to keep me entertained."

Russ took a sip of his beer—some kind of gourmet "winterfest" thing—and found himself wondering what Dad would have made of beer that tasted like fruit.

"What happened?" he asked.

"At first it was enough to just observe these spiked-hair, black-button-down-shirt-open-at-the-throat-because-my-neck-is-so-huge guys," Hayashi said, "and these plunging-neckline-to-show-off-my-*perky*-cleavage women around here."

Russ found himself letting out a laugh.

"But then some trust-fund son of investment banker California royalty," Hayashi went on, "he comes up to the bar—*this* bar, at Gordon frikken Biersch—and he orders a bottle of Dom Perignon to spread around to his six friends while he's waiting for his table." He explained how the idiot started berating poor Josh here about the vintage, how they had to send one of the servers all the way back inside again for another bottle, how the trust-fundie's making a real scene, the bartender all full of the proper nodding and fawning to a petulant man who looked a good ten or fifteen years younger than himself, they pour the bottle out and the guy starts *explaining* the important *distinctions* between the two years on a two-hundred-dollar bottle of top-shelf Champagne.

"The whole time I'm thinking, pubic hair," Hayashi said, and Russ had to let out another laugh. "The guy's got no idea how much pubic hair he's eaten in his lifetime. Pubic hair, booogers, ass juice. He doesn't even know." He took a sip of his own beer, this tiny little hand gripping his glass, Russ couldn't help but notice. "I just never got that, why anyone would ever fuck with someone who had access to their food."

With that Russ was surprised to find himself, against political instincts honed by years of exposure to *charm*, immediately liking Alan

Ho's boy. The guy was funny—but there was more. Maybe he went to 'Iolani or whatever, his mommy and daddy taking care of him out in some local-Japanese enclave like Pearl City or Moanalua, and maybe he had some kingpin real estate developer dreams. But here he was identifying with the working man, with Josh the Bartender, with the Samuel Lees of 21st-century Honolulu.

"You know years ago I worked as a porter at the Lehua hotel," Russ said. "This one waiter, his name was Jeff Lavern—I'll never forget it. Father of three, wife, real straight-laced guy, Jeff." He took another sip of his beer. "Anyway, one night I'm carrying tables downstairs to do a set-up in the ballroom, I see Jeff in this corner of the basement, he calls me over, he goes, 'I just need someone else to know about this.' He unzips his pants and starts rubbing his balls around in this little bowl of parmesan cheese." This drew a laugh from Hayashi. "He zips up and leads me back upstairs, telling me the whole story of how this guy from LA just *kept running him*. He serves the dinner, and there he is, sprinkling the cheese all over this guy's pasta. *Jeff*, of all people, had been *driven* somehow to do this horrible thing!"

Hayashi just shook his head. "Sometimes that's all the power these poor front-line service people have," he said. They both drank down some more beer, looking out onto the harbor now lit up from every angle. A platoon of tugboats was dragging an aircraft-carrier-of-a-container ship out from the Sand Island piers, whose giant crane-like loaders stood out in a blaze of floodlight towers deeper back in the harbor.

Okay, so Russ *liked* him.

But really, that was just going to make it a tinge more difficult to break the news that, sorry Sean, Darryl's got everything under control, and this campaigning thing may be just a little…over your head…and like, what the fuck was Alan thinking, anyway?

Russ had a hard time figuring out how to put such a thing, so he just fixed his gaze on the little would-be fixer and asked it: "So what's happening with Alan."

Hayashi calmly pointed out that Alan was going to be laid up for a number of weeks, and then painted this sad picture of an old man hooked up to life support, finishing his image with, "I'm afraid he won't be up to getting back in the game for months, if at all." But before Russ could say anything, the kid launched into a summary of where the Dolphin Bay project now stood, detailing a town-hall-ish talk-story meeting thing up in Kahuku. He talked about this guy Prescott, the TsengUSA rep, calling him up for paradise-syndrome-type advice on where to go snorkeling and so on. Prescott had *apologized* for messing up this meeting at WCC, he explained, and asked for advice on how to avoid insulting local people with his brash "outspoken" personality. Another friend seemed to have Hayashi's back at the City and County Planning and Permitting office, a few others in the DLNR. A lawyer friend worked for the Office of Hawaiian Affairs.

The whole time Russ was watching the tugs dragging that container ship right past them, twenty stories tall, it must have been, the different colors of paint that marked the ship's low-water line extending some thirty feet above the harbor's black surface, its stacks of truck-sized containers now empty. And whether it was Hayashi's confident delivery, or Russ's own wish to feel like *everything was okay*, none of it set off Russ's well-oiled bullshit detector.

"Check this out." Hayashi pulled out his phone and did some tapping around with his thumbs and then handed it over: a fluorescent-shirted local guy standing before a background of lush tropical scenery, the words, "Help Russell Lee get him off the bench" flying above like a…campaign ad. A touch of the screen and another image appeared, an old campaign shot of Russ at some groundbreaking ceremony, shovel in hand, the words, "TsengUSA: Creating jobs for Windward Oʻahu."

Hayashi ran through several similar images and then said, "We're clearing it with the lawyers just so we don't cross the line on resign-to-run. But these ads could start running as early as next week. The first thing people see every morning when they click on the *Sentinel*, or *Civil Beat*, or the *Honolulu Weekly*, or the *Hawaii Reporter*, plus all the TV websites—the first thing they're going to see is your face and the word 'jobs'. Every day."

And okay, this indeed was *Vili*-ing on a grand scale—and look at those pictures!—but *Vili*-ing the Dolphin Bay thing had been Russ's own idea in the first place. Susan Brushette and Trina Hyde had probably outsourced most of the work to some tech-whiz in India or whatever. And anyone could *talk* a good game.

So Russ decided to start peppering Hayashi with a few questions— What about OHA and the ceded lands issue? Why do you think that rail transit plan turned into such a disaster? How would you use the TsengUSA project as a way to address the meth problem along the Windward side?—basically anything he knew Alan Ho would have hit out of the park. And here was Hayashi…holding his own? So far anyway. Then Russ drained his beer and said, "So what about this place?" He took a look around. "What went wrong here?"

"What, you mean Aloha Tower?" Hayashi asked.

"Yeah. My wife and her friend have a little gallery here, and they're lucky to have four or five diners come in and browse around before heading off to NomFusion for dinner, and that's it. None of these other stores do much better."

Hayashi drained his own beer. He gave a nod to Josh for another round and said, "First, whoever designed this place got so caught up in their nostalgic little harbor-terminal motif that no one stood up and said anything when it started looking like Honolulu International Airport, including all these perpetually empty retail shops dying their slow deaths while everyone hurries past on their way to someplace else." He pointed out that Ala Moana Center, a city unto itself of name-brand designer shops, was only a mile away, that they should have anchored the place with Duty Free Shops, which fit right in with their harbor-terminal theme, how DFS had instead spent millions to renovate the Waikiki Woolworth's with a three-story indoor façade of a fake cruise ship, when they could have had an unending parade of real ones right here.

When the beers appeared they each took another sip. *Fruity.*

"Then there's the parking." Hayashi went into the lack of the parking structure, the constant need for valets—all entertaining enough in the delivery, but Japanee boy wasn't exactly adding anything new to a conversation that had begun back when the place first opened.

Until he started talking about…flip charts?

"You know, pass out magic markers and 'break into groups' and 'brainstorm' and come up with lists and write them all down on a big flip chart." Hayashi explained how a friend of his was going through the DOE teacher certification program even though she already had an education minor and a Master's in biology. "But that's another story," he said. "Anyway, she says the flip chart is one of the default 'activities' all the teachers use—they call it 'hands-on learning.' There's a lot of cheerleading and clapping when all the charts are combined into one big flip chart and then hung on the wall. And then the students all pretend that they've learned something, and the teachers pretend they've taught something. I went through the same thing time and again at Kaimuki, but back then I'd thought it was because my English teacher had a communications degree, and my science teacher had a Spanish degree. I never realized it was an official DOE teaching method."

Though Russ himself had never had to endure such nonsense at St. Martin's, over the years you'd have these legislators putting a committee through this flip-chart deal. Now that Hayashi was pointing it out, Russ could recall having been his group's 'spokesperson' on a number of occasions, playing along so as not to offend the collaborative spirit of things. Only now did it startle him to consider that what had always seemed a pretty useless exercise had actually been employed to produce actual written-in-stone State of Hawai'i *laws*.

"There's obvious potential here," Hayashi said. "You've just always had a bunch of people running it—well-meaning people, I'm sure—but people who pay themselves two and three hundred thousand dollars a year who have no idea what they're doing."

You could say that about a lot of things, Russ thought. The notoriously top-heavy DOE itself, for one: Assistant Superintendent this, Curriculum Specialist that. And how about Peter Varner, the new half-million-dollar UH System President? As Russ understood it from his time on the Higher Ed committee, it was a wonder any teaching and research got done at all at UH amid the flurry of make-work memos about "strategic planning" that kept burying the overworked and burnt-out faculty, while upwards of sixty percent of the Higher Ed budget went to… administrators…who, rather than do anything so pedestrian as publish or teach, spent their days babbling around a conference table and called it "work." Given what your typical UH grad was capable of doing, it wasn't a stretch to compare that ivory tower of mediocrity with…Aloha Tower.

"It's controlled by a state agency called the Aloha Tower Management Group," Hayashi said. "From what I can tell, they sit around and do a lot of this flip-chart-meeting stuff—'throw out ideas' and come up with lists of 'stakeholders' and 'revitalization goals' about 'stimulating use of waterfront property' and 'enhancing beautification' and 'new beginnings'." He went on about how 'new beginnings' was just a nice way of saying that all the other 'beginnings' were failures—the opening itself in 1994, the renovation in 1999, the openings and closings of some of the signature restaurants.

But all Russ could hear was: *Aloha Tower is controlled by a state agency.*

That was it. The concrete phrase that defined the prior abstraction in Russ's mind…the one where, as governor, he himself would be able to ensure that local people—even Hawaiians who'd been displaced to Vegas—would get the real jobs at Dolphin Bay. Profit sharing. Employee stock options. Everything he'd talked about with Cliff Yoshida. And not just construction jobs, or front-line slave work where the best you could do for pushback would be to sprinkle some pubic hair in a rich tourist's salad, but *real* management positions, all preserved by keeping the place a hotel instead of timeshares. *Controlled by a state agency.*

"And it's never really been adequately funded," Hayashi was saying, of the Aloha Tower Management Group. "Half-measures all over the place: no solid anchor tenant, no room for the valets to maneuver out front. Twenty years into it, and that front road is still covered with orange traffic cones. If you could somehow drop a hundred million dollars on this place, it would thrive. And there'd be so many people lined up to get involved, it would filter all those enhance-beautification flipcharters right out, so you'd finally have some brainpower managing the place. Think of all the jobs *that* would create."

It's never really been adequately funded.

Now those words kept swirling around inside Russ's head, because *controlled by a state agency* wasn't going to do it. You needed more of a *partnership*. One with a deep-pocketed investor.

Yes, someone like…TsengUSA…whose $400 million was only the beginning, a drop in the bucket that would ripple out across the state from Hanalei on Kaua'i all the way to Ka'u on the Big Island, where you could even picture them someday reviving the mega-resort plans that European guy had abandoned back in the '80s.

Adequately funded?

Dolphin Bay?

You had to be talking billions of dollars. An endless flood of Chinese cash to *help the Hawaiian people.*

And with that thought it began to occur to Russ that not only was Hayashi here bright, and capable, and above all *hungry*—he hadn't gone to 'Iolani after all, he'd gone to Kaimuki—as much as any of that, Russ had to admit it: if he was ever going to get the Chinese to agree to such a partnership...controlled from the fifth floor...by Governor Russell Lee...even more than anyone like Darryl Kawamoto or Tony Levine, Russ was going to need a man on whom Michael Prescott of TsengUSA had come to depend.

He was going to need Sean Hayashi on his exploratory committee after all.

"I've got to confess something, Sean," he said, turning on the *charm*. "No offense, but when I heard about what happened to Alan, I wasn't sure we could continue forward—even with Darryl Kawamoto chairing the committee. But with your help I think we might just pull it off." He held up an empty glass to the bartender. And well, why not just lay it on thick: "I don't really even see what you need *me* for," he said with a smile. *Charm!*

"Well, there is one thing," Hayashi said.

"What."

"It's the Hawaiians."

Russ had to stifle a chuckle at that one. He could imagine the hard time Ikaika Nāʻimipono and Aunty Maile Chang and the rest of them were probably giving Hayashi here—and Reverend Tom Watada had to have a hand in the whole thing, too. But he couldn't fathom any of it ever really being a *problem*.

Especially Ikaika.

You had to have respect for the guy, doing what he did, and without an ounce of opportunism—a characteristic Russell envied, because when you could just stand in blanket opposition to everything, there wasn't ever much need to be opportunistic, to build alliances, to make deals. It always just came down to the same simple "no." Ikaika could have...principles. Loyal to the cause, loyal to the end, loyal to a fault: Ikaika Nāʻimipono.

Russ could recall *pleading* with him way back when he quit St. Martin's "to fight for our people," as he'd put it, and even though he did quit, Ikaika had remained fiercely loyal to his teammates, as if to compensate for leaving them behind on the football field. He still never failed to greet even Russ with a how-you-my-bradda hug as sincere as the one he'd given him in Waimānalo the other day, falling straight into a string of glory-days football memories—anything to keep their differences deep beneath the surface unless it was at some kind of actual debate forum. Principles, the guy had.

Except there was just one thing: when all was said and done, as far as Russ could recall, Ikaika had never actually managed to *stop* anything.

"What've they got, anyway?"

"They're talking about bones," Hayashi said. "We've got some contacts in Historic Preservation, and we've checked out what the Hawaiians did to oppose the project last time. It looks like the potential show-stopper for our project could be the Burial Council. But we don't know for sure."

Nothing new, really, as far as Russ could see. He recalled people losing on that stuff back into the '90s, when Keʻeaumoku Wal-Mart had gone up anyway right on top of an ancient cemetery. "And even if they've got nothing," Hayashi said, "and this is the real problem: they know enough about what they're doing that they could really delay this thing."

Russ still didn't see much of a problem with that. It would give Cliff more time to draw up what this new state agency would look like.

"We're working to isolate some of them," Hayashi was saying, "you know, pick them off. But Alan's afraid that unless we can get Ikaika Nāʻimipono out of the way, especially after what they did at WCC, they could just delay it to the point where the Chinese give up and go to Saipan."

Russ raised an eyebrow, thinking, on the one hand, *get Ikaika out of the way?* And on the other, *until the Chinese give up?* Had this whole deal been built on a foundation as flimsy as that?

"You know the agreement they wound up making with that French bank?" Hayashi went on. "After they saw how nervous the French were getting about the prospect of it all falling through, they turned around and got the whole thing on a three-year *option*. They didn't plunk down the whole $400 million—they just put up a million dollars to reserve an option to buy outright. That means that technically they could still just walk away at any time."

There it was.

Russ could only look out past the dark harbor entrance, that huge empty container ship now a dot of white floodlights on the horizon, and think: Ikaika Nāʻimipono has finally made it. For the first time in recorded history, he actually *is* in the position to stop something.

And though Russ knew the rest, yeah, he had to ask it anyway: "Okay. But what do you want me to do about it?"

Hayashi placed his glass on the bar. "Alan says you know him."

A Special Occasion

PARKING, PARKING, PARKING. Though Helen was right—of course it would have been easier to just valet the thing, and NomFusion did validate your parking ticket—Makana Irving-Kekumu just didn't feel right about handing his pride and joy off to some amped-up twenty-year-old dressed in a green-tinted white Aloha Tower Marketplace button-down uniform shirt/shorts ensemble, only to watch him gun it around into the tight confines of the former dock-hanger over there that they squeezed three restaurants' worth of cars into every night. It was like giving your keys to one of your brainless but-you-didn't-*remind*-us-about-the-homework students.

That's what he told himself anyway, because if he really wanted to be honest, Makana would have admitted that despite how big a part of his carefully constructed local-boy identity the towering black diesel F-350 was—more important, even, than his obsession with UH football, or the triangular pattern of tattoos running up under the hunter-green *laua'e*-leaf-print Eve Yuen aloha shirt he had on right now—tonight the truck would make him look like a construction worker. Like Bud Souza from Hau'ula. Tonight he would have been, maybe not *embarrassed*—more like he would have felt obligated to *explain himself* when the valet reappeared after dinner in front of the usual Kam School reunion crowd gathered curbside in front of NomFusion waiting for their own cars: *Well, you see, I bought the F-350 mostly for its symbolic value*, he would have to tell them, *to better align myself with my Hawaiian brothers, brainwashed over generations into the trappings of a consumerist-capitalist-*

globalist society, but rebelling, to the extent that they can, by cloaking their castrated selves in the biggest hunk of metal they can find. It was such a mouthful he wouldn't have been able to get it out before everybody else tipped the college kids and drove off in their own detailed Acura SUVs and Honda Pilots and hybrid Toyota Sequoias.

"Your local-boy special not even going *fit* in one of these spaces, brah!" Helen said with a chuckle, her pidgin a put-on stab of irony aimed at the truck itself. She always tita'd up her speech a bit when she found herself riding around in this thing, especially when she was dressed as she was tonight, about as un-tita as you could get in that plunging backless black dress. She'd done some kind of magic with that gorgeous Hawaiian-Filipino face of hers, too—a couple of black pencil strokes to her eyelids, a brush of foundation, some lipstick, and now it beamed out like the face of a Merrie Monarch dancer.

"Yeah, I should have valeted it like you said," Makana told her. "I'm all for historic preservation, but saving the 'open spaces' designation for some dead haole sugar baron's donated 'park' land instead of building a parking structure…and God, look at *that* thing." He pointed at the ten-story clock tower bathed in soft lights rising up beside the mall.

Though it was now dwarfed by the collection of metallic skyscrapers congregated just behind them around Bishop and King Streets, from 1926 to around statehood Aloha Tower had been the tallest building in town—taller, even, than the Dillingham Transportation building across the street, put up around the same time, he knew, by a white supremacist who had built a fortune filling in and then selling off traditional Hawaiian fishponds with coral blasted from the reefs outside Honolulu Harbor, and who had such a tight relationship with the U.S. military that he could ensure his hand-picked territorial governor would allow a group of alcoholic U.S. Navy enlisted sailors to get away with freely killing Hawaiians.

But anyway.

"If ever there was a symbol denoting a point in history where this place took a big wrong turn," he went on, "it's that tower. Sure, the plantations were up and thriving by the time they built it, and most of the land had already been taken through the *mahele*, and the overthrow had already gone down. But before that thing went up, at least the money and the power was all *here*. But no! They had to go and proclaim themselves the *Crossroads of the Pacific*." He knew he'd made his point—and that Helen was already plenty well versed in Hawai'i's tragic colonial history, too—and yet he couldn't stop: "That tower gave birth to the racist fantasy of a 'tropical vacation,' even if back then only the super-rich could afford passage here on a steamer and a multi-week stay at the Royal Hawaiian. You know they used to throw coins into the harbor so they could watch the little brown kids dive in and fight over them?" He had to laugh.

"And that's funny?" Helen said.

At last he found an open spot parallel to the landscaped curb—two of them, and he'd need them both, plus a three-foot swath of grass for his giant tires.

"What's funny is how lovingly the thing is bathed in those lights, and how we've made it a symbol of a proud past, *our Hawai'i*. Once Aloha Tower went up, all you needed to add to that escape-to-paradise narrative was cheap jet air travel, and just like that, the taro patches of Waikiki become an urban jungle. Add the internet, and you've replaced all the residential neighborhoods with 'vacation rentals.' But no one even cares. They just have some vague nostalgic longing for 'Boat Days' and quaint, simpler times."

Helen just rolled her eyes. "Thank you, Kanoe Silva!"

"All right, all right!" Makana said. It did sound like something Kanoe was always saying—although from her it somehow never came off as complaining. And what were you going to do, anyway? Tear down Aloha Tower?

And for god's sakes, tonight they were *celebrating*. It wasn't every day a UH community college professor and his immersion school teacher wife could have a night out, up to their ears as they were in mortgage payments on their three-bedroom Kahalu'u spec-home—far more than they could afford, but Makana just *had* to live in Kahalu'u, the very birthplace of the legendary Reverend Tom Watada's local land-rights activism back in the '70s. (Technically, their house sat just outside Kahalu'u in one of those cramped local-Japanese/haole Ahuimanu subdivisions, an address that didn't provide much in the way of F-350-local-boy cred, but anyway.) Even after Makana's father had plunked down two hundred and fifty thousand toward their down payment, he and Helen were on the hook for almost three grand a month, plus the stifling Honolulu property taxes. When you added the payments and insurance for the F-350 and Helen's Accord, plus cable and water and electricity (he really should go solar one of these days), you didn't have much left to throw around on a three-hundred-dollar dinner at a *place to be* such as NomFusion.

But once in a while, on a *special occasion*...the passing of his Ph.D. oral exams, securing the WCC professorship, his 30th birthday...and tonight: tonight, *special* just didn't capture it, because tonight they were celebrating the news that, at long last, Helen was pregnant.

"You know, I love you," Makana said, leaning over the vast expanse of the truck's cavernous cab to give her a kiss, and yes, even now, more than ten years into a relationship that seemed to blossom by the day, he still had moments such as these, moments when he just couldn't believe such a woman would have married him in the first place.

"Good," she said. "Now where's my parachute? They're going to give our table away in there already."

"Parachute!"

He made his way back to his own door and climbed down to walk over and help Helen from her perch, Helen *Kekumu*—and that too, even after ten years, sometimes Makana couldn't help it: couldn't help mentally referring to his own wife by her proper name, that *name*, that oh-so-perfect name. Yes, all by itself, *Kekumu* had not just rescued him from a lifetime of shark-bait stink-haole Barney-Rubble schoolyard taunts. It had *advanced his career*, from the moment Helen Kekumu had agreed it wouldn't at all look ridiculous for him to add his name to hers in the same way professional women back in the '80s used to do all the time.

Even though he could sketch out his family tree back to that one branch from his mother's side that accounted for the 3% of his Hawaiian blood—a branch he clung to like a sailor in a hurricane—"Irving" was about as haole as a name could get.

He would have dropped it altogether had he not been banking on his substantial publishing record, much of it tagged with the hateful moniker, to combine with his community service work alongside Aunty Maile and Ikaika Nā'imipono to give him a leg up on the directorship when the new UH West O'ahu Hawaiian Studies Center finally opened out in Kapolei.

But no one named "Irving" was ever going to get even a paid-by-the-class lecturer position in anyone's Hawaiian Studies program, much less a directorship.

"Makana! Happy New Year!" And there he was! Nom Souphanvong himself! Short and stout, his jet-black hair spiked with product, right here beside the podium—and look at that welcoming smile! "I can still say that a week after New Year's, right Makana?" *Makana!* After what, five years? "Helen, you look wonderful!" And okay, maybe it worked that way too, this name thing: having the only hyphenated Hawaiian last name that ever appeared in Nom's reservation book made you that much easier to recall. Nevertheless, it felt *special* indeed: this sturdy young star of the local fusion cuisine scene greeting them *by name*.

After the requisite small talk Nom directed a pretty little Kam school part-Hawaiian hostess to escort them inside towards....weren't those the Sons of Hilo themselves, David, Nate, and Bobby, tuning up on the little stage in the corner? And would they get a table right up front? Or better still—yes!—off to the side of the stage next to the *window*, where people walking by would be able to gaze upon them with envy and even resentment for having attained such a lofty station in life, for being able to celebrate with a glass of fine wine uniquely paired to Nom's original Laotian-Fijian-Indian-accented island dishes—all to the sounds of…the Sons of Hilo! Right there! All to help, according to a *script*, it looked like, to help with a celebration that eclipsed all others in its life-changing importance.

Because the baby—that would be the final piece in a puzzle Makana Irving-Kekumu had been constructing since he'd first entered immersion school himself, back when he'd told all of his classmates he lived in Keolu Hills and not on the estate in neighboring (haole) Lanikai where his parents had raised him before trading it in, just a few years ago, for a compound on a lake somewhere outside of Portland. And while normally a baby might be considered a drag on the ambitions of a professor right in the middle of the publish-or-perish years, how could a man—or more specifically, a married man rather than someone among the culture's highly respected homosexual community—how could such a man consider himself Hawaiian without any kids?

The moment they were seated Makana engaged in the first thing you always did after settling in at Nom's, which was to see who *else* was here, even before taking a sip of your glass from that bottle of Riesling opened, poured, and set next to your table by your articulate and precise waiter dressed all in black (so that he may easily be identified without standing out in a blare of color—Nom had thought of everything!). Look! A mere table away: Del Andrade, the Hawaiian music legend who, as everyone knew, was a good friend of the Sons of Hilo—there he was, enjoying a cocktail with a couple from Japan, perhaps arranging an upcoming tour to the Orient. Over there: that long-time semi-retired news anchor, yucking it up with some former game-show host and their wives.

And what do you know! The UH System president, Peter Varner, right back there, dropping a couple grand from his discretionary fund on that group of potential donors and their spouses, it looked like. (Makana never understood how you could extract a donation in such a setting, where you're basically saying you're going to blow most of the donor's money on…schmoozing other donors…but never mind.) People at other tables took turns turning to wave to Helen—man, this place *was* a Kam School reunion! And wasn't that…now what's *his* name? And look!

"Eh Helen," Makana said, "you're sitting *two seats away* from Bryson Fernandez."

Helen's eyes widened, again in that mock-local-girl way of hers, as if to say it out loud: "The UH quarterback! Right next to *us!* And are those his *parents?*" She loved to tease Makana about his devotion to something so Neanderthal-manly as UH football even more than she ragged him about his Local Boy Special parked half-on-the-grass out front. And though she was restricted to iced tea, with that *glow* of hers it seemed like they were sharing the bottle of wine. "I wonder if they flew out here for the funeral, Fernandez's parents."

"You mean Tapusoa's funeral?"

It hurt to even think about it, the sad scene of that farewell to such a great player—and a good local kid at that. "I don't think it's for another week or so, but may be."

Helen must have sensed how even bringing it up could have put a damper on their evening, because right away she changed the subject, pointing out the window at a tall-ish local man waiting at the valet stand right in front of them: "Isn't that Russell Lee? The senator?"

It was! State Senator Russell Lee, on his way home from drinks at Gordon Biersch. Then again, Makana wouldn't have put it past Lee, a former UH star himself, to catch one of the college bowl games all the way at the bottom of Aloha Tower's socio-economic subdivision of folks able to even *afford* a night out—at Hooters, where a rotating collection of California UH sorority sisters served up heaps of deep-fryer carbs to tourists worn out by three straight nights at the Cheese Cake Factory in Waikiki.

"You know Dolphin Bay's right in the guy's district," Makana said, draining his glass of Riesling. "I bet he's already deep into plenty of TsengUSA money. I bet TsengUSA is spreading money all over the legislature. It's a billion-dollar project, and Lee is always such a pushover sell-out. At least that's what Ikaika always says. He's always standing up for 'Hawaiians this' and 'Hawaiians that,' and then he turns around and plays the game with all these people."

Nom himself appeared with their appetizers, and lots of explaining in that wonderful soft-toned accent of his. Makana wished that somehow Russell Lee would turn and look through the window, but it was enough that a good half the room saw the *owner* acting as their own personal waiter. He even detected some head-turning and who-*is*-that whispering.

"Do they even know Dolphin Bay is a legacy project?" Helen asked, dipping a long battered coconut shrimp into a ramekin of sauce. Legacy project. Why hadn't Makana thought of that himself?

"I doubt it. Russell Lee is probably just looking at it in some foolish 'create jobs' way. Ikaika says he's operating off of this supply-and-demand idea rather than organizing for collective abundance. Like the Hawaiians did, like, if there was a drought, or a famine, the chiefs and the higher advisors were looked upon to sort that out, you know, in the heavens." He chomped down a bite of shrimp and went on, even though yeah, Helen knew all about this stuff, too. "They had an incentive for everyone to prosper, is how Ikaika puts it. But today there's an incentive of making sure everyone feels in the scarcity mode, just scraping by so we'll willingly take these menial jobs at their hotels. And then they dominate the political spectrum by ensuring that Hawaiians never have a place."

"Isn't Russell Lee Hawaiian?" she asked between bites.

"Well, genetically speaking. I think he's almost half"—an empirical fact that pissed Makana off immensely. "But culturally and spiritually?" He smirked. "The guy is Hawaiian only as it suits his ambitions. After that? He'll sign on the dotted line." And…out the window…pulling up to the curb…the valet getting out and holding the door open…a Lexus!

"There's your evidence," Makana said with a laugh. And while he'd just made the observation from a table at NomFusion, well, he and Helen were here for a *special occasion*, after all—that made them far superior not only to Russell Lee, but to…those two late-twenties lawyer-accounting-firm couples at the next table, three local-Japanese and one—the one with her hair cut with a straight line of bangs and sculpted short—Chinese-Hawaiian, each of their freshly-minted JDs and CPAs likely providing them with twice what Makana was paid after eight years as a well-published community college professor. *They* may have chased the money into downtown, Russell *Lee* may be chasing it all over the Windward side, guys like that Hayashi character too. But Makana was *in the trenches*, he was *making a difference*.

"And then there's Japanee boy," Makana said. "Sean Hayashi. He thinks it's the '80s all over again and that the Chinese are the new Japanese. He wants to be one of those players, one of those fixers. You know there was this one couple back in the '80s who scraped millions off of that Japanese developer to 'help' him build the Luana Hills golf course in Kailua? They wound up fleeing to Oklahoma? Tom Watada has all kinds of stories about these people. Anyway, Sean Hayashi thinks he's just like they were, but he has no idea. You should have seen Ikaika crush him at that meeting."

Wonderful, Makana thought, this Riesling, the way it cooled your mouth from the spices of the appetizer.

"Maybe somebody should let them know that this whole thing is probably a legacy project," Helen said again, his beautiful *glowing* wife, his beautiful glowing *Hawaiian* wife with her silky dark hair spilling over those bare chestnut brown shoulders. She could be utterly relaxed and still come up with the most pointed observations. "Like, here's this Chinese multi-billionaire or whatever," she went on, "and he just wants to be the first Chinese to really invest in Hawai'i, and it won't do unless he plants his own buildings with his own name on them just so everyone always remembers him." She took another bite. "An' maybe someone should let the Chinese guy know, too—yeah, you can make a bad legacy too."

As always, Helen was right. And Makana would bring it up at the next strategy meeting that somebody should say something. He was also drafting an article for a top-tier journal called *Pac-Asia*, and this "legacy project" idea of Helen's would provide an interesting conflict to drive the article's thesis arguing how the activist Ikaika Nā'imipono was being marginalized and demonized by a hegemonic power structure and an interlocking series of capitalist institutions. He could historicize the problem with a couple of good quotes from Tom Watada on the land eviction protests that had solidified *local* resistance so long ago, and then send it forward forty years into the present, grounding it as a systemic societal problem rather than an issue of individuals. He could use Ikaika Nā'imipono as an effective stand-in for the plight of *all* Hawaiians. Probably get like, three or four conference presentations out of it to really fill out his CV.

A quick-strum beat filled the room, the Sons of Hilo jumping into their second set, and suddenly Makana Irving-Kekumu felt…lucky. The Sons of Hilo! That seamless three-part harmony, that wall of sound emanating from just three instruments: Nate's thumping bass, David's six-string, and in the middle, the koa tenor Kamaka ukulele resting comfortably on Uncle Bobby's big belly upon which he plucked sweet-sounding lightning-quick single-string licks all the way up and down the neck.

So enraptured were Makana and Helen that they hardly noticed the waiters clearing the appetizer plates, and serving the main course, and however wonderful and boldly cutting-edge *fusion* the cuisine was, you almost didn't even notice it, the music softening now, drifting into the silky soft melody of *Kaleohano*, a classic the Sons of Hilo often covered, written about a man living on Keaukaha homestead not far from where the Sons themselves had grown up just outside sleepy downtown Hilo.

It pleased Makana to no end, too, that he and his Hawaiian wife were the only ones in the room other than the Sons and perhaps Del Andrade who understood not only the words, but all of the hidden meanings as well.

Kaleohano had been written a good thirty years ago now, back when young Hawaiian men were still writing and playing Hawaiian music. Nowadays you'd be hard pressed to find a single Hawaiian kid who could play anything other than that inane pumping reggae beat of the bastardized "Jawaiian" music that had utterly taken over what had once been a vibrant cultural reclamation celebration of re-toolings of old gems like "Hiʻilawe" and "Kawika," and even newly-penned instant classics rooted in the forms of the place-name creation chants Makana taught his students. These days all his students wanted to listen to were dopey songs about plate lunches or crybaby laments about loving my baby "unconditionally" sung in fake Jamaican accents.

And it wasn't as though Makana had anything against reggae either, especially going back past even Bob Marley and Jimmy Cliff—that really *was* roots music—it had pathos and warmth and real poignant emotion that captured the existence of the hopeful struggling man in an oppressive world. It had *soul*, like old American delta blues, like… like *Kaleohano* had soul…Kaleohano coming out live less than ten feet away, the Sons of Hilo, *right there*, so close Makana could stand up and touch them if he wanted, or at least call over a request. *Call over*—forget about *shout*—he'd hardly have to raise his voice.

Just as the song ended he was moved to do just that, only because he *could*, so everyone would see him sitting right here up front—everyone, maybe even (especially?) President Varner—not that the system president would ever wind up on a hiring committee… and yet he *could* unilaterally order a dean to make a salary adjustment, or steer coveted funding in certain directions.

On top of all that, the $500,000 man had been brought in mainly to raise money to finally complete UH West Oʻahu. Sooner or later that manservant he always had following him around would tell him how deeply revered the Sons of Hilo were on the Leeward side, the area of the state that UH West Oahu was planned to serve with a Hawaiian Studies department more tightly woven into the community than even UH Mānoa's. And then President Varner would recall this Professor Makana Irving-Kekumu: Didn't I see you somewhere before? Wasn't it at NomFusion? And weren't you having a *conversation* with Uncle Bobby of the legendary Sons of Hilo?

So when Kaleohano ended and the resulting applause died down, Makana did just that: he called over and said, "Eh Uncle Bobby, could you guys play *Pua ʻIliahi?*"

"Sure my bradda," Bobby said. *My bradda!* Makana couldn't help it: a big smile overtook his face. Braddas! Me and Bobby. My Bradda! And then: "Where you folks visiting from?"

Where you folks visiting from.

The words hit like a kick to the stomach. Hadn't Uncle Bobby seen his Eve Yuen aloha shirt? Hadn't he heard the pidgin Makana had sprinkled into his request? And would a *visitor* have requested a song like *Pua 'Iliahi* in the first place?

Or had Uncle Bobby simply looked up and immediately registered the single word that everyone in the entire world always did the moment they laid eyes on Makana Irving-Kekumu: look at this *haole* in the front row—he must be a real fan to know a song like *Pua 'Iliahi*, and even call it out without messing up the pronunciation somehow. Let me make him feel a bit more at home here in Honolulu.

Haole.

Helen must have sensed what Makana was feeling, because in that inimitably charming way of hers, she was somehow able to both scold Bobby and make a joke at the same time: "We visiting from all the way over the odda side a da mountains! Dis place called Kahalu'u!"

This drew laughter from all around that Makana forced himself to join in good-naturedly. To most of these town Hawaiians, raised as they were on school trips to campy community theater productions that made liberal use of the dialect for no other reason than to get a laugh, pidgin had simply become a marker of attempted humor, something that immediately put an ironic twist on whatever it was you were saying. So when Helen shouted out, it was as though she'd beamed a single thought into nearly every head in the room: Oh, that sounds like a line straight out of a Lisa Matsumoto play!

"Eh, I t'ink I heard a dat place," Nate said, lifting a hand to his chin and looking off into the distance in deep thought. Bobby and David were now broken up in laughter, the whole little exchange turning into one of their famous comic interludes, which only led everyone in the rest of the room to start craning their necks to see who this *haole* in the front row might be. Visiting!

"Okay okay okay," Bobby said, trying to compose himself. "You folks celebrating something tonight then? Or should we just make a dedication to your true love?"

"We're pregnant," Helen announced.

A chorus of *Aww!* swept the surrounding tables, glasses raised all around in congratulations, all three of the wide-eyed Sons reaching over to high-five Makana. The young lawyer-types at the next table reached over with beaming smiles to shake hands. A couple of Helen's old Kam School classmates came bounding over with Oh-my-gods and kisses and congratulations.

"By request," Bobby then said into the mic. "For the impending parents."

"Yeah, enjoy your last date for a while," Nate added, drawing another round of laughter.

And with that they launched into another melodic wall of sound.

But Makana couldn't hear any of it. Not a single note or verse or line. The high-fives had been a nice touch, and everyone had done a good job at turning the whole thing into a good-natured joke and all, but the only sound echoing through Makana Irving-Kekumu's head was, *Where you folks visiting from?*

"Eh Professor Kekumu," Helen said, squeezing his hand under the table. "Tell me again how my baby's fadda going be Director of Hawaiian Studies."

Makana just looked at her, looked into her eyes. *Glowing*, his wife. So he started in on his plan, but just so everyone would know, he did it in Hawaiian. He had to raise his voice way up to compete with the music, and when the last chord was strummed and the resulting applause dissipated, he kept it up there. Just so everyone would know.

Executive Privilege

As if Russ hadn't made it with conviction right from the start—his big decision to run—well, *this* just solidified things: stepping out of a black monstrosity of a hybrid Chevy Tahoe along with Governor Donald Nakayama, Charles Uchida, and two thick jacket-and-tie ear-piece security goons way out here on Lagoon Drive, out on the back edge of Walter Dillingham's vast two-thousand-acre plain of a reclaimed coral gateway to paradise. Far across the asphalt desert he could see the concrete terminals of Honolulu International Airport, a big interconnected block of a building right next to the six-story tombstone of the Federal prison. Indeed the terminal itself looked like a prison, where at this very moment some poor minimum wage TSA agent was directing masses of the unwashed to take off their shoes, and then wanding them through a perpetual fog of jet fumes to sit on a packed gate floor and wait, and wait, and wait to stuff their belongings into an overhead bin and then stuff themselves into a little airline seat where they would fight for elbow space with who knows who. But if you were the governor? You headed straight for this little oasis of buildings out by the aqua blue sea, and then right on through to your…private jet.

Technically speaking, the jet didn't belong to the governor or the state. But enough of these little jaunts were always coming up that it sure must have felt like you had your own private jet. Tokyo. LA. Sydney. Nakayama had once told Russ a story about getting whisked off to the Super Bowl in California. He'd been making a point about the lazy media, who, when they'd found out the governor was out of state, had only asked a single question: "Where is he?" "He's in Santa Barbara."

And no one had ever asked to clarify. The "campaigning" trips to Florida and New York sponsored by the Democratic National Committee. The bank-sponsored "fact-finding" trips to the Caribbean to see how *they* were handling the economic downturn, or to some South Pacific island paradise to see how *they'd* implemented desalinization and "sustainable" agriculture. The "recruiting" trip to Texas to try to land that fat loser of a football coach arranged by the booster club, a couple of whose members had jets of their own parked out next to those of the growing squadron of haole investment bankers here for a weekend at their $60 million fourth homes. If you added it up, the governor was probably out of Hawai'i as much as he was in it.

Today, just like *that*, with just over a week to go before the legislative session's mid-January opening, they were headed for Macau. Macau was this little island off the southern coast of China, was all Cliff Yoshida had been able to tell Russ when the call had come down from the fifth floor requesting that someone clear the senator's schedule for the next three days. Russ figured it was some kind of golf junket—Nakayama was nothing if not a golf addict—and he'd agreed to go along for a list of reasons, beginning with that of putting off his impending meeting with Ikaika Nāʻimipono (he'd figure it out), of avoiding the likes of Lave Salanoa and this Kekoa Meyer character—he of the cryptic *It'll come to you, Senator*, an *ainokea* gangster if you ever saw one, must've had something to do with Russ's Pearl City debt (he'd figure all that out too). So this little China trip made for a good escape—and not just from his growing list of creditors (as if the gangsters weren't enough, a Bank of Hawai'i "loan officer" from somewhere in India had called twice about a missed car payment), but also from a sentence of Death by Small Talk at Cathy's Colby Alumni Dinner (and the Outrigger Canoe Club could wrestle for *their* five grand with everyone else—somehow he'd figure that out as well).

At the top of the list, though, was Nakayama himself, because even with the backing of a Chinese billionaire's company, without the governor's support in what was indeed shaping up to be a slugfest against Hendrick in the primary, Russ wasn't going to be boarding too many private jets in the next four years.

And though he and Cliff had reasoned that an eight-hour plane ride would give Russ his best possible shot at making his pitch to Nakayama, neither of them could imagine how the old man would react to a request that he ignore the custom of strongly endorsing his LG—a tradition that dated back to statehood.

That, too, Russ would figure out, because, *Hello!* Look at this! Three nubile UH-dancer-cheerleader-types in tight shorts and matching lime green polo shirts sauntering out to greet them, *by name*, with smiles and leis and crystal glasses of fresh pineapple juice. Nice touch!

As if that weren't enough, the ladies then escorted them into the cool confines of a climate controlled waiting room like none Russell had ever seen.

Skyway Partners, one of what looked to be four or five corporate jet docking services out here on Lagoon Drive, had thought of everything. First you were greeted by the view of your own jet, that bright gleaming white bird sitting right over there on the tarmac outside that wall of soft-tinted windows. Polished bamboo (and not plastic laminate) floors. Walls adorned with koa framed original Pan Am advertising posters—the woman by the waterfall with the flower in her ear, the clipper pulling into some secluded and mysterious tropical bay, the iconic plane-over-Diamond-Head painting. A glass-topped rattan bar, a glittering stock of bottles shelved behind it. Instead of rows of vinyl seats, the room was dotted with three polished antique four-strand rattan furniture clusters. All this for a room you simply *walked through*.

And right there standing to greet Russ and Charles Uchida and Donald Nakayama like he did this every day—escort the entire leadership of the state of Hawaiʻi onto a Gulfstream G650, a machine worth upwards of seventy million dollars that would get them across the ocean at a hair under the speed of sound—was...Sean Hayashi? Had *Sean Hayashi* set up this little face-to-face with the Chairman and CEO of the Tseng Corporation?

"Nice work, Sean," Russ said, "very nice."

"I just thought you and the governor might want to try teeing it up on one of those exclusive Chinese mountain courses," Hayashi said.

You and the Governor. Those words had Darryl Kawamoto written all over them. The moment Nakayama's flight had come up in one of their exploratory meetings, Russ figured, Darryl had found a way to invite Russ along, immediately seeing a trans-Pacific flight as the ideal place to wedge an endorsement out of Nakayama.

"Isn't this where you guys really do business?" Hayashi went on. "In these secret away-from-the-Lege meetings?"

"Sure," Nakayama said. "It's just like everyone thinks: all the big decisions really do get made on the golf course."

"Eh, if that was really the case I'd be in big trouble," Charles Uchida said. "Me an' golf, we don't mix too good. Lose money!"

"I think I'd be in trouble, too," Russ said, though he honestly would rather have ignored Uchida. "You know the governor here taught me how to shoot a 72 once."

"72!" Uchida said, his eyes widening.

"He said it's easy." Russ let that one sit up there on the tee for the governor himself to drive out into the fairway.

"Just stop playing after twelve holes," Nakayama said with a shrug. "72. Easy." This broke everyone up as they followed one of the smiling tight-shorts dancers out onto the tarmac, a blast of hot wind hitting them when the doors opened. The flight crew was lined up and waiting for them at the foot of the stairs leading up to the G650, a beautiful white bird parked at an angle. From out here it looked like a smaller version of the Fokker F-70s non-union Go! Airlines had used to basically destroy the locally staffed Aloha Airlines years ago, dumping millions into a months-long five-dollar ticket campaign that had sent Aloha into bankruptcy and hundreds of island families moving to Las Vegas.

From then on it was jack up the prices and nickel-and-dime everyone for a checked bag—a policy aimed as much at discouraging bag checking (so as to reduce the need for hourly paid baggage handlers) as at collecting additional funds.

So the size and shape of the bird—that was where all similarity ended with Go! Airlines. Instead of a pair of 23-year-old Arizona flight school grads at the end of a 36-hour shift (who needed the overtime to pump their $32,000 salaries into a range where their paychecks weren't being completely smothered by a six-figure student loan), you got a personal greeting from two forty something fit-and-ready veterans of the Chinese Air Force, it looked like, smartly dressed in Navy-blue uniforms whose shoulders bore the lotus insignia of the Tseng Corporation.

And instead of a mainland community college drop-out eager to parade her thunder thighs up and down the aisle and drone on and on and on about the Fokker F-70's safety features, you got…well!

Flight attendant was hardly the term. You got these two long-legged…*hostesses* was more like it, and not in the proper British sense of the term "Air Hostess," either, even considering their own navy high-shouldered jackets over white silk blouses, unbuttoned at the neck and tucked into navy skirts cut only inches below, well, *there*. They each wore their black hair up in a bun, capped with one of those pillbox hats that Russ used to see the stewardesses wear in 1970s magazine ads for Singapore Airlines. And yes, they too greeted you *by name*.

And the G650's interior? Forget about banging your head on an overhead compartment or trying to squeeze your way down an aisle twenty-or-so seats long. *Rows* of seats? Try double-wide Italian leather recliners, eight of them arranged at comfortable distances from one another on the thick navy carpet, in two clusters around the low glowing circles of two beveled glass tables etched with the Tseng lotus, each lit from above by pin lights recessed into the soft grains of a light colored hardwood that paneled the ceiling and the walls. Russ didn't know if this was some kind of Feng Shui arrangement designed to please the spirits, or just another way of saying, "Sure! We could fit more seats in here, but why *cramp* things when additional guests can be flown in one of our *other* Gulfstream G650s?" Whatever the case, despite even the high expectations he'd brought to his first experience in the mega-wealthy skies, Russ was blown away.

It did occur to him as the men all took their seats around the fore table—Russ and the governor facing aft and diagonally inward towards Uchida and Hayashi—that there were a couple of problems with this "cluster" arrangement.

The first was that Russ couldn't imagine spending eight hours or whatever it was seated in such close proximity to Charles Uchida. Whether it was a symptom of the man's job as House Speaker, or whether he was just an arrogant prick, Russ couldn't really tell. On the one hand, compared to the Senate president, the Speaker had to run a tight top-down ship, what with more than twice as many members to keep on point with whatever it was you were trying to push through. Running the senate was more like herding cats, so things like building relationships, and calling in favors, and not holding grudges, and just plain *getting along despite our differences* were paramount if you were ever to get anywhere. Not so in the opposite chamber. Over there it was *do as I say or get buried somewhere on the Committee on Public Safety, or Military Affairs.*

But that didn't make it any easier to take a seat next to Uchida—even on one of these plush designer recliners—recliners, Russ was happy to notice, that were a bit too big for the speaker's little frame, his legs dangling off the carpet like those of a little kid at the grownups table.

"Eh Russ, I heard you running for governor," Uchida said, thus putting the second problem with the seating arrangement right out there on that etched glass lotus (and leave it to Uchida to fuck things up). Right away the question of Nakayama's endorsement was going to come up, when Russ had hoped to discuss the proposition at least semi-privately.

"Yes, that's big news," Nakayama said with a smile. "And Hendrick is none too happy about it." Nakayama chuckled in that resigned way someone's grandpa chuckles over a misbehaving kid. "He was practically whining to me, on and on and on, 'It's supposed to be *my* turn,' and 'Doesn't he have any *respect*,' and 'He hasn't paid his dues.' A real haole meltdown. I kept waiting for him to burst into tears."

This drew a laugh from Uchida, who was accepting a steaming towel from one of the Chinese hostesses. "Paid his dues!" Uchida said. "What, Russ, I t'ink you gotta sit on the fifth floor an' stare out the window for eight years as lieutenant governor!" Everyone laughed at this. "Paid his dues!"

The other hostess stepped up and suddenly all of them—Hayashi, Nakayama, and Uchida—they were all smiles, schoolboys in the presence of the homecoming queen, each trying not to get caught measuring the distance between the first *two* unbuttoned buttons on her white uniform blouse and imagining what tempting vistas lay beyond the third and fourth. But all Russ could think was, what the fuck am I supposed to do now? I was going to *gently break the news* to Nakayama, and even *apologize for putting him in this awkward position*. How could you do any of that in front of Charles Uchida?

And there was Uchida, bravely endeavoring to hold a fix on the hostess's dark eyes as she suggested a glass of Louis XIII cognac, or Tattinger champagne, or even a beer to drink *during takeoff*. The governor led off with an order for—and why not?—the Louis XIII, which Russ recalled the Lehua selling for $75 a *glass* when he worked there back in the '80s. The rest of the men—and why not?—followed suit.

"Why was the LG so upset?" Hayashi asked as the hostess walked away. "I mean, lieutenant governor and all, I don't know much about it, but he's got to think he has some chance at winning the primary. Russ hasn't even declared his candidacy yet. Haven't enough people been brainwashed into seeing Hendrick's name right up there next to that word *governor* over the last eight years to think he's next in line?"

They waited for Nakayama to address the question, but the old man seemed to be lost in the fantasy of following the hostess to the back galley. His eyes were glued to the swaying bumps of the curves beneath that skirt, to her long legs, terrific smooth legs, exposed all the way… up…to…*there!* And not even shielded by pantyhose! They were *naked*, those legs.

Uchida was more than happy to speak up: "The guy gotta know he no more notting fo' show for eight years." Russ wondered if anyone else was getting annoyed with this chummy we're-just-a-bunch-a-*da-boyz*-on-a-junket way Charles Uchida was suddenly infusing his speech with pidgin. But then Uchida surprised him. Instead of trying to one-up him in some way like he usually did, or offer some I'm-kidding-(but-not-really) jab about how it takes a *real* leader to run the house, he said, "And suddenly he's gotta face somebody with a strong record to run on. Da guy might be one lazy-ass haole, but he not stupid. The whole time he t'inking Seneta going 'anoint' him."

Here Uchida was talking about Hawai'i's recently deceased reigning monarch, the senior U.S. Senator. "He t'ink Seneta's word going be enough, that he only going have to face some Republican Jesus boy in the general. An' then whoa! Seneta dies, an' here comes Russell Lee!"

Russ mined Uchida's pronouncement for the requisite sarcasm, but to his astonishment, it wasn't there. Now both hostesses were back, each taking a subservient knee and offering up a snifter of cognac. Despite everything, Russ almost laughed out loud at the thought of Cathy performing such an act on a Northwest flight. Then he vaguely noticed, if only from some movement outside the window, that they were taxiing, and may have been for some time already.

"Russell Lee not jus' been sitting around the past eight years," Uchida went on. "He running The Joint. He working with the schools. He working with UH. He *working*. James Hendrick? Notting. The guy in deep kim chee, and he knows it."

Russ might have been flattered by the whole thing if he hadn't been able to see the obvious, which was that Charles Uchida liked his chances, and even at this early stage, he was ready to begin creating an obligation centered on his behind-the-scenes support of a Lee candidacy. In fact, now that Russell thought about it, that had probably been Uchida's reason for dropping everything to come along on this meaningless excursion to some obscure Chinese island in the first place.

But what of it, anyway? Uchida did have power over there in the house, and that "obligation" thing went both ways. Russ would be able to use him. Let him be opportunistic. And shoots—right now his kiss-ass opportunism was already helping make the case for Nakayama's endorsement. Maybe it would work, even right here in front of Uchida and Hayashi.

"So watchu going do, governor?"

And there it was, right out there on the table.

The old man offered a tired smile and then took a sip from his cognac and said, "Russell, tell me why it is you want to hold this office."

And there *that* was, too. Russ wasn't exactly sure where to start. His whole heartfelt pitch—the whole time he'd been expecting to deliver it as one selfless committed public servant to another, *alone*, and what would the likes of Uchida and Hayashi even *get* about such a naïvely foreign concept as selflessness?

"Well there was this fundraiser for Hokulani," was what started coming out anyway. "You know, the drug treatment center? It was just some show-face community service thing over at the Hilton to 'spread awareness' about the value of drug treatment and all."

"See that's what I talking about," Uchida interrupted, swirling the cognac around in his snifter. "That's whatchoo got on Hendrick. You go to these things, yeah, butchoo *mean* it, too." He turned to Hayashi. "You eva been to one fundraiser, brah? Usually it's all show. But Russ, he wen' deliver for those people. Like 18 million-somet'ing dollas."

"That might be the one Marisa went to last month," Hayashi said. "She was going on and on about these Hawaiian chronics who'd gotten their lives together who were up there dancing hula. She said the whole thing really 'opened her eyes' about how 'treatment can really help Hawaiians with the choices they make about drugs'—something like that."

"See, that's what I talking about," Uchida said.

Immediately Russ regretted having brought it up at all. This Marisa, Hayashi's girlfriend or whoever she was, had already ruined the picture he'd planned to paint with her glib little observation that wound up doing the exact opposite of what the whole evening had intended, which was to disabuse people of the notion that the words "addiction" and "choice" even belonged in the same sentence.

So he just said, "Right, getting their lives back together." He turned to Nakayama. "But something hit me while I was watching them struggle through their hula up there that night, and that was that if they'd been able to do something so heroic as get off drugs, then I owed them something when they got out—some sense of hope."

He was ready to go on, but you could see Nakayama knew exactly what he was getting at, looking off into some distant memory when his own hopeful ambition had taken root and he'd decided to devote his own life to the people of Hawaiʻi, and so he just left it at that.

"In a sense I'm obligated by the traditions of the office," Nakayama said at last, "which means I'd probably have to come out and support Hendrick."

For an instant Russ was jolted, a kick to the stomach, a cascade of images, of himself calling Hendrick to concede on election night, of scowling Lave Salanoa, weeping Cathy, smirking Joel, headshaking Samuel-Lee, and defeated-chronics-in-prison *images*, one after the next in a flash through his brain until—

Pained. Nakayama's face: clearly it pained the man to make such a frank admission, *come out in support of Hendrick*.

"Jeeze, I'd have hard time doing that." The governor shook his head. "I know it's a do-nothing job—I did it myself for eight years. The 'resign to run' law acknowledges as much. It's the only elected position you don't have to resign from if you want to run for governor. But I've been throwing Hendrick opportunities for eight years: the Film Office. The Economic Revitalization Task Force. The Sustainability Team. The guy is just lazy. He's been good with the photo ops, and he gets his name in the news all the time. But things have changed." Nakayama paused, looking back, no doubt, into an idyllic past from just after statehood straight up through the '90s when the Democrats controlled everything.

"The Republican base has really grown in the last ten years," he went on, "what with all these mainland retirees." He delved into the strength of the religious right, the worthlessness of the kind of union support that had initially propelled the Democrats into power—"I can't understand why people are so anti-union, even people making eight and ten dollars an hour at Home Depot"—into how Hendrick always trots out his Asian wife in all of his campaign materials. "That just doesn't work anymore."

"Didn't tradition die along with the Senator?"

Everyone turned to see Sean Hayashi, swirling his own Louis XIII around in that big snifter in his hand. "What I mean is, now that Senator is gone, can't you just do what you want?"

Uchida was shaking his head in you've-got-a-*lot*-to-learn mode, and Nakayama gave Hayashi his understanding grandpa smile.

Hayashi was only saved from further embarrassment by one of the hostesses, who returned to prepare the men for takeoff, succinctly explaining how the seats occupied by Russ and the governor would rotate around to face forward until the plane reached a cruising altitude of 36,000 feet.

"It's kind of a steep climb," she said, "but it should only take a minute or two. If you'd be kind enough to lift your feet?"

The men did as instructed, but other than a roar from the Rolls Royce turbofan engines, and a noticeable thrust that drew Russ into the back of his thick mattress of a seatback, you could hardly tell you were accelerating up to nearly 750 miles per hour.

If not for the slope of the climb, Hayashi back there could have rested his glass on the table, so easy was the takeoff. And while it may have been almost immediate—the cabin leveling off, the roar of the engines dissipating behind them, the hostess returning to gently inform them that their seats would rotate back into cluster formation, and to apologize for interrupting their conversation as if some alternative had existed that she'd so stupidly forgotten about—though it probably had only taken two or three minutes, to Russ it was an eternity to wait for the answer: *Can't you just do what you want?*

As if to prolong the suspense, the governor just smiled, and again allowed his gaze to follow the hostess's…*legs!*…to the rear of the cabin. Only then did he turn to Hayashi and say, "You know, you do have a point. About this 'tradition' thing. I think a lot of people will see that if I endorsed someone other than the LG, it would come off as an insult to our late Senator. But if that's the case, we've also got to be honest and ask, what is my endorsement really worth anyway?"

"Governor!" Uchida said. And indeed, they all were shocked with the man's candor.

"This state is in a shambles," Nakayama said. "I know it's been steadily deteriorating since the turn of the millennium—four-day school weeks, layoffs, more and more of our young people leaving for opportunities on the mainland, the Hawaiian problem, the tremendous homelessness problem, you name it. Crime. Drugs. We've long since exhausted the hurricane fund and the rainy day fund. But let's face it: I've failed to make it any better."

Now they all sat silent. Russ felt simultaneous stabs of pity and admiration for the old man, who, to his credit, had come right out and said it, said it honestly. Hawai'i was a mess, and whether that mess was an ocean liner too big to be turned, or whether Nakayama had simply lost the energy after working so hard just to get elected in two hotly contested races, Russ couldn't say. But whatever it was, well, the guy did still hold onto a loyal retired local-Japanese/former-union/Mānoa grandma base whose support would turn out to be essential, was how Cliff had put it.

"So here's what we're going to do," Nakayama said at last. "I'm going to 'stand above' and encourage a 'spirited debate' between two 'equally worthy' candidates. That way we can have it both ways: my formal endorsement won't push any swing voters away from Russell Lee, and my base will see that what I'm actually doing is giving you my unspoken blessing by not coming out and endorsing Hendrick. What do you think?"

What do I *think*?

Russ worked to keep himself from slamming back the rest of his cognac and shouting in joy, because what did he *think*? I think you're right! This is *better* than an endorsement! And is Hendrick really that much of a tool that beyond a few silent moments during takeoff, you're not even *pondering* it, Governor? Or have you, too, been thinking about a Russell Lee candidacy all along? What do I *think*?

"Governor, I think you're a wise man."

"Then let's have a toast," Nakayama said. "Me, I had high hopes eight years ago, and honestly, it's a major task. I just wasn't up to it. I'm old enough to admit that. But Russell, if there's anyone who can fix this state, it's you." All four men lifted their glasses. "To Governor Russell Lee!"

Two hours later, Russ and Hayashi were alone, the governor having retired to a recliner in the darkened rear of the cabin right after finishing the German chocolate cake the hostesses had served as a topper to their Kobe steak dinners, which they had washed down with two bottles of 1979 Chateau La Tour Haute-Brion. As for Uchida, after a final shot of port, he'd excused himself to go rotate one of the remaining aft recliners to a position where he could enjoy something from the collection of tens of thousands of digital movies and classic sports events without disturbing Nakayama. Hayashi here looked about ready to test the flat-out recline position of his own comfy chair.

But Russ, still high on the prospect of what Nakayama's non-endorsement-endorsement would do for his candidacy, couldn't resist calling one of the Chinese hotties over for a refill of his own little crystal port aperitif glass. Because if indeed he was finally on some kind of, well, *winning streak* was what it was starting to feel like—if he could convince Cliff about running for governor…if he could talk Nakayama into getting behind him…then why not play out the hand with this TsengUSA chairman?

Except that up until a few minutes ago Russ had never even heard of him. If he was indeed going to push the agenda at this little meeting they were crossing the Pacific for—to go for *more*—then it would help if Hayashi had learned something about…Bradley Zao was his name.

"So Zao wants to discuss this condo-hotel thing," Russ said.

"That's basically it," Hayashi said. "Prescott said he wasn't happy about how things were going."

"How'd you manage to wedge that little bit of information out of him?"

"Yeah, I'm surprised myself at how this guy blabbers everything out. At first he's all business and trying to be secretive, but then he gets this urge to just tell me everything that's on his mind."

"Typical," Russ said.

"Either that, or you know, I don't think he particularly *likes* this guy, Bradley Zao. You know it's his brother-in-law?"

Russ gave him a look that said, "You're kidding!"

"Prescott told me the whole thing. He married into the family fifteen years ago—this was before Zao controlled the company. They'd hired Prescott on as one of their token ethnic outsiders—all of these companies have a few, it turns out—and somehow the guy hit it off with Zao's father. Prescott seriously thinks it was because of his golf game. The old man used to get up at the crack of dawn and play nine holes every morning on this exclusive billionaire course in Hong Kong, and sometimes he'd bring Prescott along. Prescott says he's a scratch golfer."

"And that gets him the boss's daughter?" Russ said with a laugh.

"I'm sure the boss weighed the cost-benefit beyond what it did for his golf game," Hayashi said. "Like I said, all these Chinese multinationals have a few token haoles in relatively important positions. They're trying to make themselves look less Chinese, more worldly. That's also probably why Zao kept Prescott on after his father died and left him in charge."

One of the hostesses appeared with the bottle of port, but Russ waved her off. There was something about this *less Chinese*, this business with the English first name. Maybe you could play the guy's interest in Hawai'i as an exotic place, a non-Chinese place.

"Did he say anything about why his boss would go to the trouble of flying all of us over there instead of coming here himself?" he asked.

"No. I guess he wants to create some kind of impression."

Made sense. Wine and dine the governor of Hawai'i, along with the leaders of both houses in the Lege. Show them your private plane, the reach of your power on your home ground, whatever that amounted to.

"This guy must be somebody over there," he said.

"Somebody?" Sean said. "The guy is a godfather. He runs the place, literally."

"Godfather? Are you saying these guys are mafia?"

"Yeah, but it's not really that simple," Hayashi said. "Not like they go around blowing people away. It's kind of like the *yakuza* in Japan, how connected they are, especially in real estate and development." He went on about how Bradley Zao's father, a guy named Henry Zao, was one of a handful of ambitious men in Southeast Asia who had just enough money and connections to turn World War II into a cash pot that would make someone like Alan Ho blush. First it was ferrying Japanese troops around southern China during the war. Then it was post-war reconstruction contracts. "Remember Ferdinand Marcos in the Philippines?"

Russ vaguely recalled that the Filipino dictator had died in a Hawai'i hospital—plus his wife owned a tremendous amount of shoes.

"After the war it was smuggling steel and oil and even weapons into China during the Korean war embargo," Hayashi went on. "And before you know it, these guys are running almost all of Southeast Asia: Indonesia, Malaysia, of course Singapore, the Philippines, Hong Kong. And almost all the money is going through Macau."

Before today Russ had hardly even heard of Macau, having lumped it together in his mind with burgeoning manufacturing sweat-shop islands like Indonesia or Saipan. He'd even thought it was somewhere near Saipan, way off the coast of Japan, until Cliff Yoshida told him they had ferries going to Hong Kong and the Chinese mainland.

"Why would all the money go through Macau?" he asked. "I thought Hong Kong was the financial center, or Singapore."

"I'm sure much of it goes on to a legitimate Hong Kong bank," Hayashi said. "But they've got to clean it up first."

"Clean it up?"

"They've got to launder it. Macau started off as this Portuguese colony, and they didn't give it back to China until the turn of the millennium, just like the British and Hong Kong. But way back in the 19th century the Portuguese started allowing gambling in Macau. So when all this smuggling started picking up, the place exploded. The few people involved—and Bradley Zao's father was one of them—they made a fortune. Now the place is bigger than Vegas. But most of the casinos are owned by the Tseng Corporation, which holds one of only eight exclusive gaming licenses. And in the rest of China—and who on earth is more obsessed with luck and fortune?—in the rest of China, gambling is illegal. It's only allowed in Macau because Macau is a 'special administrative region' with some control over its own laws."

Somebody. Bradley Zao was indeed somebody. And that wasn't the half of it, Russ thought. He had a hard time going deep enough into his thoughts to really sort out the relationship between this "special administrative region" thing and the interests of the powerful Chinese government that allowed it to happen, but he felt somehow it had to be wrapped up in the absolute power wielded by these "godfather" types Hayashi here had obviously studied up on. These guys could negotiate with even the Chinese government and come out with terms favorable to pretty much whatever they wanted, was what it looked like to Russ.

Hayashi went on some more about percentages of Chinese ownership in Indonesia, and how the U.S. State Department referred to Macau as a "financial cesspool" thanks to how many of the casinos were still used to launder money, these days mainly from the illegal sale of North Korean weapons to terrorists. But his words started to drift right on by, because Russ's mind was now wandering to the warm and delicious thought that he himself would soon have the local equivalent of that…power…from his seat atop the volcano back in Hawai'i. Maybe it wasn't Hong Kong or Singapore, but with the right…leadership…the right…connections…to the right Asian godfathers…you could see the day when Hawai'i finally did fulfill its promise of becoming a financial center of the Pacific.

And what was this? Movement in the darkened rear of the cabin.

Could it be?

It was hard to tell in this light, but if you squinted a little bit and shaded out the glare of those pin lights, you could see it! Not ten feet away! One of the lithe little bare-legged dim-sum eye-candy hostesses, she was on her *knees*, right there in front of old Donald Nakayama, waves of her black hair now spilling down the back of that white blouse, untucked, her head bobbing up and down in that unmistakable way, yes it was, indeed it was. And maybe *that* was really the moment, wasn't it. That was when you just couldn't wait to be governor of the state of Hawai'i.

Blood on the Table

There in the dark next to Dawn, Kekoa alternated between following the blades of his ceiling fan and urging the red lit digits of the bedside clock forward into the biggest day of his life. The soft cast the doctor had put on his foot—it was like some kind of ski boot—its weight kept him from rolling around too much. It kept him from going to check on the girls, too, which he usually did without fail whenever he awoke in the middle of the night. Part of a full walkaround, sometimes two-three in the morning, not because you really *had* to here at the dead-end cul-de-sac of a 'Nalo Hawaiian homestead street where the neighbors had known each other for generations. It was more of a might-as-well thing, as much for the scares their oldest used to give them when she woke up with her choking asthma attacks as it was out of any concern for some business-related…retaliation. Plus whenever Kekoa didn't do his walk-around, he only wound up…pondering…putting himself into the mind of his enemy, thinking, if it was me, if *I* wanted for take out Kekoa Meyer, I going do it when the guy sleeping.

Pondering was what he was doing now, since dragging the boot around the house at this hour would have caused too much of a racket. It wasn't any pain that was keeping him awake, pain from what had turned out to be a fractured metatarsal. More like the scene just kept playing itself out in his brain, a decade-old scene crowding everything else out as it had been for days now: ten years ago, way back, alladese bangers, guys from Wai'anae and Hilo, guys Kekoa looked up to, they'd had it all planned out too, but in the end wound up all lock-up on the mainland someplace.

You had to be a fool not to see the parallels: a funeral. Three cars full of armed men, all worked up fo' scrap, following one another to some kind of high-noon showdown back in the valley. That much matched right up with what Kekoa was about to do, and it matched up on purpose. He'd chosen today because the Waiʻanae boyz had gotten that part right ten years ago, the part about the funeral. Take care of it when everyone stay all emotional. Cool head main t'ing, but hard fo' keep cool head at a funeral for one a your boyz. An' then Kekoa Meyer shows up? Those fuckas going *trip*. Watch.

They going do somet'ing stupid.

But then he could only imagine the rest of it like some kind of bad Hawaiʻi Five-0 episode, how it had all turned out for the Waiʻanae boyz: Hawaiian Memorial, somehow everyone agrees to go meet in the deserted jungle parking lot of the Koʻolau golf course just up the road—years ago the Japanese had carved these narrow fairways into the rainy mountainside, fairways you could only reach by hitting across two-hundred-yard ravines, all for like eighty bucks a round. Fuck, *no one* ever played there. Perfect. Nice and quiet. No witnesses. So everyone piles into their trucks. And then something happens, right at that moment, cause you don't just go and *shoot* someone. I no care how cold you are. You gotta *work up*.

Maybe they surprised the meeting even going happen. But they so *worked up* they miss the turn to Koʻolau. They so *worked up* that even afta they miss it, they say fuck it, let's keep on going, turn into the City and County Pali golf course up the road instead, neva mind it's only 1:00 in the aftanoon, the place packed with old local-Japanee men drinking their Bud Light afta paying five bucks for their round.

The moment where it had all gone wrong. It wasn't when they all started blazing in a crowded municipal golf course parking lot in broad daylight. It was when they *missed the turn*.

The blazing part had been decided right when they all rolled out of Hawaiian Memorial. Because if you started working yourself up weeks before, and you spent the whole night staring at the red digits of a bedside clock while you filled yourself with enough hate, and drew on enough cold and calculated moments of anger and revenge, all the way back to schoolyard brawls in elementary, then how could you blame them? It wouldn't be hard to do either, miss that turn. That turn creeps right up on you after you leave Hawaiian Memorial. And after that, you not going make two U-turns back around the Kam highway median, so whatchoo going do? Call the whole thing off?

That was really it: cool head. You keep cool head, you get everyone for keep cool, calm, collec', an' jus' wait for the right moment, an' you going pull this off. Cool head main t'ing.

That, and the right gun. That was the other thing about the Pali golf course shooting ten years back. You like wipe out some *solés*, you betta bring more than a .22. You betta bring eitha one nine or one .45. "Mandatory" was what Javen said over the phone, and Kekoa had seen Javen blast some Mexican up on Maui point-blank with his nine, the fucka kept slangin' right in the middle of Lahaina trying for squeeze out one a Javen's boyz widdiz Mexican clear, Javen kept saying *You gotta send one message to these frikken WETbacks*, an' stuff like, *Gotta put some blood on the table*, an' *They cannot be thinking they can jus' come right in an' set up shop, cuz*.

So Javen gettim in the alley behind Moose's, he pull out his nine like he pulling out his phone, all calm, cool, collec', he raise the gun an' steady it with both hands, all taking his time. An' then: *PA!* The bullet so big it blew the fucka's face *in half*, took off one whole side of his head, more like he got eaten up by cancer. That's how much powa you had with one nine mil. An Javen jus' walk away, too—frikken Lahaina cops *happy* to see Mexican bangas die. They list it as an "unattended death" or "potential suicide" or something. Javen.

The hardware was already waiting in the cab of Kekoa's Ram: a Beretta Px4 Storm .45 with a quick-detach SWR HEMS 2 silencer for Javen (the .45 was even bigger, by a shade, than the nine mil). A Ruger P95 nine for himself. And just in case, two Glock 34 nines that held seventeen subsonic rounds each, all three equipped with SWR Shadow 9 silencers he'd screwed into place last night. Fuck, just feeling the weight of one of those cold cannons in your hand made you feel fucken twenty feet tall. The bullets themselves were made of brass with a steel core and not lead, because lead ricocheted off course when you shot it through a windshield or a metal car door.

Silencers.

Yeah, that part was pretty close to being…gay. You really like *send one message*, you not going put one frikken eight-inch metal tube on your cannon. Not much *blazing* going be happening wit' one silencer for muffle everything out. An' yeah, ten years ago Kekoa never even would've thought about it. Except now—

An' right then he really wanted to do it, ski boot and all: get up and do his walkaround, go check on the girls—an' not cause he worried somebody going jus' break in an' hurt them in the middle of the night either. And okay, maybe that wasn't always why he wound up doing his walkaround in the first place wheneva he did do the walkaround. Maybe it wasn't really always some paranoid para-military check-the-perimeter security maneuver. Maybe he just liked standing in their bedroom doorway watching his babies, all innocent, all arms and little legs splayed in different directions, or little knees pulled up to little chests, mouths wide open in peaceful dreamland sleep. Maybe he just liked standing there and watching, like his dad used to do with him when he was a kid. *Every night afta you sleep I come in an' kiss you, boy*, was what dad used to tell him.

Dad.

Even all these years later Kekoa could almost hear the old man say those same words whenever he did the same: went in and kissed each of his girls on a sweaty forehead.

So gay or not, *safe* insteadda I-no-care-I-gotta-pull-some-time-in-Hālawa banger or not, Kekoa'd had somebody order the silencers. They going blaze all right. But no way they going get caught for this shit. No way the girls going visit their fucking dad in Hālawa. Or worse: fly to fucking Arizona, talk with their own dad through one sheet of bullet proof glass. More worse: *skype*—an' just the thought of that made him even more mad, even more *ready*.

If anything the fucken silencers made the guns *heavier*. Maybe fat fucken Nalu raise his fucken eyebrow at the sight of the long metal tubes, but nobody say nothing. Not him, not Kimo, not the odda six boyz they was bringing along. Everybody just armed and ready, no questions asked. Time for put up or shut up, eitha you go up or you go out.

Not a word about the next challenge from the next amped up MMA playa. Nothing about what they risking in getting caught for any of this. Nothing about most of them had kids to raise too, about the cost of trying to beat a murder or manslaughter charge if it came to that, or of pulling some time on the mainland if it came to *that*. Kekoa'd just had to pick up the phone, and it was no different than what a young and loyal star-struck foot soldier like Kyle Ching would have said: "No worry cuz, we get 'um."

Could've brought way more guys, too. And Kekoa had thought about it. But he didn't want to risk one of the younger boyz mouthing off, an' then watch: hundred somet'ing *solés* descend, an' the whole thing pau. No, this one was going be quick and dirty, real efficient, like one military mission, bang-bang and we outta there. Had Nolan Kahaiue and some a his boyz stationed around the college and the temple, but that was it other than Nalu-Kimo-them—just one real loyal core of back-in-the-day braddas. Guys not going fuck everything up. Going *do* this. Do 'um right. For da boyz, brah, for da boyz.

Taken together, it was enough to ease the fact that, yeah, all of this was about to go down right in the middle of what Javen called "enemy territory." Just look at the mountains. Lā'ie was the place up north where the Ko'olaus receded from the highway like the crumbling final edges of the frikken great wall of China. You drive up past Hau'ula, you turn a bend and suddenly it's wide open. A shopping center. A tourist theme park. New hotel. A college. Subdivision. The frikken Mormon temple, this big wide street leading up to it like the entrance to some kind of resort, palm trees and all. A ranch. The ocean recedes, too, in the opposite direction, hidden by the rusting hulk of the dead sugar refinery, the shrimp farms, the golf courses, the ironwoods, a stretch of time-share cottages. You couldn't really call it the Windward side anymore, this place, and you couldn't really call it the North Shore either.

And the other thing you couldn't call it was Kekoa Meyer's *domain*, because Lā'ie and Kahuku didn't belong to Kekoa Meyer. Lā'ie and Kahuku belonged to the *solés*.

Until today. Even we do 'um the hard way, we spilling blood.

Punk *me* on the greatest fix in the history of the state? Try make *me* look stupid? You fuckas going *down*. Watch. By the end of today, Lā'ie, Kahuku, North Shore—the whole thing going belong to Kekoa Meyer. If only those red digits would *move*.

All In

BRIGHT LIGHTS! FLASHING! GOLD! All the way up the walls, across the full length of that great dome of a ceiling. Gold! Pings and beeps and whirls of the ringing slot machines, shouts and whistles, all bouncing around and ricocheting off of pure gold!

A roar from the crowd surrounding one of those tables far, far, far across this airplane hangar of a cavernous hall echoed off of pure gold above the festive ambient crowd noise of a thousand people, a collective cheer of victory from somewhere *way over there*, like a golfer four holes ahead of you just sank an incredible putt to climb into contention at the Master's. Ahead of *you*—not some PGA star you were merely *following* around the course—but *you*, because in this room, you could *play* in the Master's. The Super Bowl. The NBA finals, all wrapped up into one drop of the marble: push your mighty stack of chips with both hands onto the roulette table's red square, and everyone stopped to *watch*, your own personal gallery, *behind you all the way*, just like they used to do when you made a big tackle for St. Martin's, or when you sacked the UNLV quarterback at Aloha Stadium, or when they surrounded you on November 4th as the election results poured in and your opponent called to concede. They shouted and cheered as the dealer spun the wheel and the marble bounced and bounced and bounced and bounced, c'mon, c'mon, c'mon, and found its…home!

Eruption! Like you just hit a walk-off home run to win the World Series! Heads at the surrounding tables turned in wonder: who's the big *winner* over there? Your gallery could have told them, because before they started slapping your back and shaking your hand simply because they were happy to see someone *winning*, someone had asked your name. And as the chips piled higher your name spread, spread among this strange mix of Europeans and Australians and wealthy Chinese, some of the men dressed in tuxes, the women in evening dresses like this was Monte Carlo in the sixties, all mixed into a crowd of hundreds of dowdy work-a-day gamblers from the surrounding provinces (but never mind them). So you let it ride: all five stacks of colorful chips there on that red square, red and not black because, hey, we're in China, aren't we, and isn't red the lucky color? And just feel the *rush*! Feel the…*love*… and yeah, being in *love* is what it felt like, that head-in-the-clouds let-me-take-on-the-world because I'm in *love* and I can do *anything* feeling, and listen to them calling out my name: "C'mon, Russell!" and "On ya, Russell!" and "*Ganbare* Russell!" and "Go Russell!" Half of them couldn't even pronounce it, but no matter: "Go Russell!"

In love. That was how Russell Lee felt this very moment. In love and drunk, although he hadn't touched a drop of alcohol since that glass of port on the plane what, six, seven, eight hours ago? So wrapped up was he in the moment that time had lost all meaning, that it never occurred to him that what had in fact happened to him was indeed chemical in nature, but that the chemicals were his own, that the lights and the sounds and the cheers and his growing stack of chips had caused certain channels in his head to open themselves, flooding his brain with… dopamine…a word he would have recognized from the many reports he'd read as a member of The Joint, because dopamine was the very same neurochemical that was triggered in vast quantities by…ice…by crystal meth.

The plane? The plane? The vague flash of someone meeting them at the plane, a car, yes a car, it blipped through Russ's brain, but what difference did it make, how they'd made it to this gleaming tower of light called the Grand Dragon Macau, how the governor and Sean Hayashi and Charles Uchida had been led off to their suites to freshen up for the meeting—*meeting?*—how Russ had just wanted to step into the casino and take a look at the pit, and what a pit it was, more like a *canyon* of pure adrenaline, and suddenly he was suited up in full pads awaiting his introduction in the Aloha Stadium tunnel, and just like that some young woman in a red Chinese dress, it had this diagonal fold across the chest fastened with what looked like four pure gold buttons, she walks up, she's got an earpiece in one ear—female security?—and gives him a handful of chips to play with, a thousand dollars' worth, and—

What was this about a *meeting?* Oh, what did it matter, anyway. Russell Lee was winning! In love! Everything was going to be fine! Look at all these chips! Listen to this crowd! Go, Russell, go!

It was a far cry from some dingy warehouse of a local-thug-run Pearl City game room reeking of stale beer and catering to wannabe high rollers and a sad collection of gambling addicts—that was the thought that suddenly flashed into Russ's can-do-no-wrong head in this very instant. Or one of those sad little California Indian welfare check magnets outside of LA or San Diego, plastered all around as they were with real live images of utter sadness and defeat.

Not this place. *Otherworldly* was more like it, even when compared to the California Hotel or the Freemont, where you went on your fifteenth package tour to Vegas so you could cash in your vouchers in the only dining room in any proximity to the strip that served saimin and oxtail soup and actual *rice* that wasn't haole rice, where you might run into one of your high school classmates, or even a cousin you hadn't seen since the last time you were both seated in front of the very same bank of flashing slot machines, shrug off your losses with a cool Bud Light and a live performance by Willie K or Henry Kapono, here on a detour of his west coast swing through the pockets of displaced Hawaiians hungry for anything that might remind them of home.

No, it wasn't that at all, either, and it wasn't the distinct lack of fat white people you always saw waddling around the Vegas strip. You obviously didn't play at the Grand Dragon Macau in your tank top and shorts and slippers. What you did was play among the highest of the high rollers on the planet, half of them Chinese multi-millionaires.

Meeting?

Forget about the meeting. You've got to concentrate here. You've got to *will* it to happen, you've got to *make* it happen, for all of your fans. You've done it before. A thousand turned into two turned into four, and then you pushed your chips over to black and four turned into eight turned into sixteen and now that you've pushed them back to red and if the dealer over there, man, she doesn't look a day over twenty, black pants and a red Chinese top with the same gold buttons as that security guard's dress, if she just spins that wheel fast enough to generate some reverb and maybe an extra bounce or two out of that little white ball, and if she just puts a little *spin* on the ball itself when she sets it rolling on that inside track, and well, the laws of probability say it's about time for it to land on red again and then you're up over *thirty grand* and you've only just gotten to this magical place, only been on the ground for…an hour? Two? Three? Who knew, anyway, a few ticks of the—

"There he is! Eh Russ, they all looking for you you know!"

She spins the wheel and sets the ball rolling in its track. Silence. A ring of fifty, sixty people, mouths agape, stock still, awaiting the million-dollar putt, the last-second field goal, the 3-2 pitch. Not even the ambient crowd noise behind and the pinging beeping sounds echoing off the pure gold ceiling could penetrate the wall Russ's brain had constructed to block it all out, to filter it into a kind of ringing white noise in his ears, a ringing now pierced with a loud *Clack! Clack!* went the little white marble, *clack, clack, clack clack clack clack clack clack* rhymes with—

A collective groan, fifty people strong, wide right, swing-and-a-miss, it grazes the edge of the cup and runs five feet past the hole. Over. The little Chinese dealer, the little *China doll* of a dealer, she makes the call, placing a dragon-shaped marker over square number 17, which, no matter how hard Russ tries to wish it into being otherwise, is the color of night. Then out comes the rake, carved of some kind of wide-grained finely polished hardwood, it cradles itself around those stacks and stacks of chips, Russell's chips, and pulls them all across the green and black and red colored felt and straight down a chute in front of the dealer. Over.

"Well, you had a good run for a while, Russell," someone says to him. People are patting him on the back and smiling and encouraging him to get back in the game, get back up on the horse, give 'er another go. But it's no use, because someone else has pulled a plug somewhere in his brain, and all of that wonderful dopamine has drained all the way down to somewhere near his shoes, where it can do no good.

As if things couldn't be any worse, he now finds his fans have deserted him to go and cheer on the next hot hand, and he stands alone in the middle of this crowded convention center of a room next to… Charles Uchida.

"Eh brah, we gotta get going!" Charles was saying, grabbing him by the arm and leading him towards the bank of elevators far, far across the room inside the lobby. Two security guards were escorting them—these were men, it faintly registered to Russell down in the depths of yet another crushing blow, and they were dressed in tailored business suits and speaking into air, to the person addressing them through their earpieces.

"They stay waiting for us upstairs, you know," Charles was telling him.

Yes, the meeting.

Something about a meeting. That was why they'd flown all the way to this little…some kind of Mediterranean old-world trading center… jammed with what must have been fifty-sixty lights-a-flashing thousand-plus-room casino hotels, one of them crowned with a white light shaped like the autograph of the Vegas kingpin Steve Wynn, the first outsider to score a gaming license in over a century of failed attempts, was what Hayashi had said. But who knew the whole damned island would look like Vegas. On *steroids*. Or that it would be so choked with humidity and smog that just about everything appeared to revolve around being *inside*. And once you set foot inside a casino, well, whose adrenaline isn't going to grab hold?

Okay, meeting. Well, Russ had been playing with house money the whole time anyway, hadn't he. He'd turned his stack of free chips into sixteen stacks, and now that it was gone, so be it. Live to fight another day. Meeting. Yes. It shouldn't last more than an hour, tops, and then he could come straight back here and make everything right.

Security escorted them to a private elevator guarded by two more men in tailored black suits—these two a bit taller, and as you could plainly see, even draped as they were in their jackets, *jacked* by what must have been an hours-long daily gym routine. The thought crossed Russ's mind that security must have been a complex operation at a place like this, with thousands if not millions of dollars in chips floating around out there in the arena, to say nothing of the multi-billionaire upstairs in need of protection.

The elevator shot up with terrific ear-popping force and then opened into a red-carpeted waiting area marked by two hardwood doors reaching all the way to a fifteen-foot ceiling, each carved with a relief of a dragon in profile so deep it seemed to jump out at you. For a second the image of the state capitol's top-floor foyer flashed through Russ's brain, and vaguely he began to recall why he was actually here, and consider what he could get out of such a meeting, in monetary terms, that could put him in that fifth-floor office.

"Dr. Zao has been waiting for you." The words came from one of two smiling receptionists, both of whom could have passed for sisters to Zao's Miss Universe Taiwan in-flight crew. The second one indicated with a sweep of the hand that they should enter through those giant doors, which then opened automatically.

Wow.

Russ may have been blown away by the sight of the interior of Bradley Zao's Gulfstream G650, but compared to his office suite, that luxury private jet was little more than a rusting city bus. Any comparison to the governor's office was just plain silly. The fifth floor of the capitol? Try the *fiftieth* floor. Your eyes didn't know what to look at first up here, such was the dreamy carnival of lights blasting in from three glass walls fifteen feet high. You could fit like three tennis courts into this vast space perched way up here atop the Grand Dragon Macau.

Far across on the other side Russ could see a two-ton hardwood desk, a stanchion of dark hardwood bisecting the glass wall directly behind it that appeared to be covered with certificates and diplomas of some kind. (And what was this *Dr. Zao* business, anyway?) Over here you had what looked like a king-sized-bed of a red felt English billiards table. Over there, that vast green surface, was that…a practice putting green! Complete with undulating breaks and slopes and little flags marking one, two, three…nine holes…recessed right into the floor, all of it covering a footprint bigger than that of Russ's entire Portlock home.

Up there just to stage right of Bradley Zao's desk sat a living room arrangement of leather furniture spot-lit from above, two sofas and two chairs surrounding a beveled glass table set with a vase of fresh flowers and surrounded by…Sean Hayashi, Donald Nakayama, Qihong Liu— the VP from the Pauahi Tower meeting—and that must've been Bradley Zao, all of them standing and now striding towards Russ and Charles.

Zao—a surprisingly small man in these sleek steel-rimmed glasses—he was dressed in a dark ten thousand dollar custom tailored suit that hugged his shoulders like a second skin. His face beamed, the picture of a welcoming host, his hair buzzed short on the sides like a U.S. Marine.

And here comes Qihong Liu: "Senator Lee! Speaker Uchida! Thank you for flying all the way out here to join us! Allow me to introduce Dr. Bradley Zao, the Chairman and CEO of the Tseng Corporation."

Son of a bitch! The guy could speak perfect English after all! The whole thing blipped through Russ's head along with a memory of that little Pauahi Tower meeting, where Liu had probably been instructed to add some mystery to the proceedings to gain some kind of leverage—he'd feigned that whole little burst of anger at Alan Ho's shakedown attempt for no other reason than to frighten the French bankers into offering him the Dolphin Bay property on option, almost like *he* was the one playing Alan Ho (to shake down the French) and not the other way around. Fucken Liu—that's how Joel would have put it, throwing on his local boy pidgin—gangsta, the guy. O.G.

Just as eagerly, Zao himself shook their hands—Russ was happy to see that the chairman was around Charles Uchida's height, although that jacket of his—Russ kept noticing the jacket—it hung on the thickened shoulders of a man who obviously employed his own personal trainer.

"And may we offer you gentlemen something to drink?" the little man asked.

Russ's brain was whirling around at top speed in search of some kind of advantage in these proceedings…his position in the Lege…his connections with City and County Planning and Permitting, not to mention the connections of Alan Ho and even Sean Hayashi and…his general overall local knowledge. Russ had also bootstrapped his way up from a shack at the back of Kahaluʻu, while Zao here had likely been riding in the latest Gulfstream private jet offering since he was in the womb—that is, Russ knew how to *work*. All formidable advantages, but not much when you held them up to whatever this this *multi*-billionaire had at his disposal—this one hotel probably had more rooms than the entire Waikiki beachfront, and it was only one of how many in this guy's empire?

Okay. Butchoo know what? I'm taller than you, brah. *Way* taller than you.

Right away it occurred to Russ that *getting his way* wasn't going to be a simple matter of laying out *the way things work*. Russ and Hayashi and the rest of them had to keep Zao interested in the deal, because anyone could tell a million dollars was nothing to this guy. He'd dropped more than that decorating this office alone, and that money factory downstairs probably pumped out as much in a matter of hours. Zao would have no problem just walking away from such a miniscule slice of swampland as Dolphin Bay even if it meant forfeiting what he'd paid for the option. And then just forget about the run at governor…the house…he didn't even want to think about the house in Portlock… Cathy…

As all of these thoughts passed through Russ's head, the term *high stakes* appeared right along with them, because on the other hand, Russ wasn't going to be played. For the sake of his people, he had to win permanent state control, to create actual jobs beyond cleaning rooms and parking cars—especially now that Russ was supposed to somehow *reason* with…Ikaika Nāʻimipono. And while Russ still had no idea how he was even going to approach Ikaika, there was no way he was going to bring back that same old condo-hotel story.

"No, no thank you, we're good Dr. Zao," Russell said.

"You'll have to call me Bradley," Zao said, still beaming up at Russ.

Bradley. For a second Russ wondered who'd given Zao a name a Chinese guy wouldn't be able to pronounce in a million years, and yet here he was singing it out with perfect British diction: *Ber-Ad-lee.* The name must have had something to do with what Hayashi had said about the prior generation of Asian godfathers trying to make themselves appear more sophisticated and international: not only did they give their offspring English names, they gave them names with lots of Ls and Rs in them.

"Bradley!" Russ said. "I'm sorry to have kept you waiting, too—I kind of lost track of time down there at the tables. You've got quite a facility here."

"Thank you for your compliment," Zao said. "I hope you came out a winner?"

"I had a good run going," he said, "but then Lady Luck deserted me at the end there. It was fun while it lasted."

"You know you come out even, I say you're winning," Charles Uchida piped in.

Zao let out a little chuckle. "As long as you get to experience the rush of the game," he said. "I think it's one of the greatest forms of entertainment, feeling that rush. Sure, we'd like the tables to be as profitable as possible, but at the same time we don't want our guests to go home unhappy. At the end of the day, what we're providing for them is an entertainment experience. So I'm glad to hear you were entertained!"

Zao invited everyone to join him on the putting green, which was suddenly bathed in light. He'd heard that Nakayama was something of a "golf nut, just like I am," and so after the two of them were handed titanium putters by yet another pair of Miss Universe Taiwan assistants, they started rolling fifteen footers while everyone else looked on, going from hole to hole way up here fifty floors above that exploding carnival of lights down below.

Russ was surprised to find that Nakayama was in fact pretty good at reading the breaks and the speed of—was this *real grass?*—of the grass, sinking a few here and there, and leaving none more than a few inches from the cup. Soon he and Zao were laying dollar bets on each putt, and Russ couldn't resist following suit with Hayashi here next to him.

"So as Michael Prescott probably already told you," Zao said, leaning over another putt, "what we initially had in mind for the project was a high-end luxury condo-hotel." He struck the ball cleanly, if a bit too fast, but then Russ could see that Zao had employed the firm stroke on purpose to cut out the break. It clanked into the back of the hole and landed in the cup with a rattle.

Zao went on to explain how the "product" he'd had in mind could be easily marketed to the growing number of Chinese willing to buy a million-dollar vacation property in the blink of an eye, a property they might not even visit more than once every couple of years. He also knew about the supplementary EIS, and how the self-contained condo-hotel resort he'd had in mind, along with a shuttle from the airport instead of car rentals—perhaps even a helicopter—it would be able to show a more minimal traffic impact than the plan envisioned by the property's prior owners that had been successfully challenged by local environmental groups. "But now I understand that such a product would not be viable under current circumstances. Oooh! That's unfortunate, Governor." Nakayama's putt had just lipped out, leaving him—and Russ, who was betting on the governor—a dollar behind.

So there went a good portion of Russ's *general local knowledge* advantage. Russ had to admit: the guy seemed to know his stuff. Zao had to have more important things to think about, what with this empire to take care of, but he talked as though Dolphin Bay were his only project. Sharp, the guy. But yeah, a short little guy, and young, too. What was he, around *thirty?*

"I'm in favor of the development," Russ said, putting on his best Alan Ho impersonation. "But it's a lot more...complex...than it looks. I'm sure Prescott has explained the cultural issues involved."

Zao struck another putt, but this time it came to a stop just at the edge of the cup. "We haven't discussed it in detail, but I understand there are concerns with some of the archeological aspects of the property, those things Alan Ho was bringing up in your meeting with the bankers."

Russ couldn't believe it. Zao had turned to look him straight in the eye, turned up from the putt he was lining up even, when he said "Alan Ho." Was that some kind of code? That he wasn't going for it, whatever Russ had in mind? Was it some kind of I-know-what-you're-up-to-so-don't-even-*try*-to-shake-me-down *message*? You couldn't tell, the guy was so...relaxed, so...at ease.

Russ went on to explain that there was a Hawaiian rights group that opposed the development, and that they had some power to hold things up, if not stop the show altogether, mainly through a public commission called the Burial Council, and that it would be possible to get some buy-in from the group, but not in the form of a symbolic payoff, and some menial jobs, at best, for Hawaiians.

"That's been the pattern since the 1960s," Russell said. "It's just not going to work nowadays. People have a lot more information at their fingertips, and they're a lot more sophisticated. Regardless of that, I wouldn't be able to support such a scenario anyway. I think we can do better."

"That's also what happened to the developer that got foreclosed on," Sean Hayashi added. "He thought he could just buy the Hawaiians off. Russ is right—I don't think that's going to work anymore." Russ couldn't help but notice that Hayashi looked like he'd found himself a new hero—look at him watching Zao stand over his putt, that smooth backswing, that relaxed stroke, and then of course it goes in the hole. Somewhere near Hayashi's age, and living his dream tenfold, and god, Russ himself had never seen another human being more comfortable in his own skin.

Some witty-but-friendly trash talk began to pass between the two competitors as Nakayama matched him. And then Zao suddenly turned to Russ and said, "So you're running for governor, Russell?"

Nice, was all Russ could think. Nice how you bring that one up, right when you see me staking out my ground on this little deal of yours, bring up how much you've already thrown in to the unannounced campaign, all those pictures of State Senator Russell Lee creating jobs for his district, Russell Lee partnering with TsengUSA, Russell Lee, Russell Lee, Russell Lee. Remind me of my…obligation. Nice, Bradley.

"Well as you know, we have a resign-to-run law in Hawai'i," Russ said, "so I really haven't been able to officially declare my candidacy yet." Nakayama rolled in an eight-footer, oblivious. "But I've been getting all this…exposure lately." He waited for Zao to stand over his next putt and then said, in a this-works-both-ways-too-brah tone: "I'm practically the official spokesperson for your development project."

Zao stepped back from his putt and said nothing.

So Russ plowed on: "And it's working, too."

Still silent, Zao stood back to line up his putt again, and stood over it, and smoothly hammered it home—all as if to prove he could not be rattled.

"My involvement is adding that 'local values' angle to the PR push," Russ continued. Sure, the guy was practically handing him what would amount to a bottomless well of support in the election, which would in turn lead to the end of all the financial woes now plaguing him at home, among many other things. But Russ wasn't just going to roll over. "Of course the exposure is going to help my campaign," he went on, Nakayama again swinging through his next putt, and all Russ could think was: *All in!* Push that pile of chips over onto red and say it: "But that isn't going to be enough."

Nothing. Zao just stood there waiting for Nakayama to retrieve his ball from the hole, and even indicated where the governor should line up his next putt by *pointing*. And while it wasn't like the guy was mad or anything—at least it didn't look that way—he was utterly unruffled in that suit of his, the very picture of *relaxed*—well, had Russ actually gone too far?

Hayashi jumped in: "What Russ means is that no amount of PR or political posturing is going to sway the Hawaiian rights activists currently standing in the way." And then he just came out and said it: "I mean, he said it's complex. That's not some kind of stall tactic, Bradley. We're not just trying to scrape you for a more favorable deal or go fishing for some kind of payoff or whatever. It really *is* complex. I could get into it all if you want but it would take a while. Basically you're standing at the end of a long line of developers, including the United States military and even NASA—many of them perfectly well intentioned—who've basically steamrolled Hawaiians for the past sixty years—even further back if you want to get into agricultural development. What we're saying is, they're hip to all that now."

Again Zao, still as calm and assured as he was the moment he'd first greeted them, again he said nothing. And the silence—it didn't strike Russ as some kind of calculating-my-next-move thing, either. It was more like he was...considering...considering new information.

"You'll have to forgive me," Zao said at last. "To be perfectly honest, I'm just not at all familiar with this sort of challenge. The hotel you're standing in—we built it on land that didn't even exist ten years ago," he said with a smile. "This whole surrounding area is reclaimed land." He thought some more and said, "And even in other cases when we did need to clear existing neighborhoods, the people who had to relocate were always happy with the arrangements. We made sure of that."

Nakayama knelt down to line up another putt, far more absorbed in this little game with his stick and his ball than what was now so obviously taking place, almost as though now that they'd discussed his "endorsement" back on the G650, the weight of it all had slid from his old and tired shoulders. And there was Charles Uchida kneeling down on the other side of the hole acting like he was helping the governor read the break, when really he was just trying to mask the fact that the conversation was...over his head? And what they'd both just missed was the breakthrough moment of these negotiations.

With his little admission about his ignorance relative to Hawaiian cultural issues—and no one was *that* good a liar to be able to fake the tone of concern with which it was delivered—Zao had basically answered Sean Hayashi's call, a call that in so many words had said, "Let's just put the bullshit aside, let's just be a bunch of guys out...out on the golf course...honestly hashing this thing out."

"Then I guess we're basically talking about the same thing," Russ told Zao. "You know—making sure everyone's happy." He went on about how you needed to create *real* jobs, jobs for local people—and mainly Hawaiians—and not just imported haole community college drop-outs eager for the chance to live in "paradise" and willing to do so for ten dollars an hour with no benefits for a couple of years before heading back to Arizona or whatever. He went on about how a condo-hotel wouldn't provide enough permanent jobs, and how it would also further widen the area's income gap, and thus create further resentment towards the visitor industry. "And my people," Russ concluded, "they need something to hope for. Honestly, Bradley, I'm not in this just to become governor. I believe this can be done right, in a better way than it's been done in the past, just stomping all over Hawaiians or simply buying us off. I want to help my people."

All the while Bradley Zao—he may have been lining up the next putt and sinking it, retrieving his ball, lining up his next putt—in fact he could not have been listening more intently or with more respect. Even mid stroke, he'd stop to look up and acknowledge a particular point Russ was making, his face sharing the concern on Russ's own where appropriate, and he'd pause until the point was made before going back to his shot, going back to the game if only so the governor would not be kept waiting.

Finally he said, "You know, we don't want to do anything that will hurt anyone. But if we move away from the condo-hotel plan, it may damage our anticipated profit margin to the point where the project stops making sense from an investment standpoint."

Russ could feel his heart jump. And yet, this time he could tell that Zao wasn't just trying to drop some hammer of his own to regain the upper hand in these negotiations—the guy was just being honest about the prospect of maintaining a decent occupancy rate at a property with so many rooms to fill way out on a part of the island that was so windy they'd built the pool *behind* the existing hotel tower.

"So there must be some other way to make the project viable," Zao said, much to Russ's relief.

"We could sell people on some hybrid use of the property," Russ said. "Maybe your guys could come up with some kind of formula for, say, twenty five percent luxury condos, and the rest hotels, or whatever—this isn't exactly my field, but there must be a way. You do have the two golf courses there, and probably room for a third. And there must be other marketing ideas that would appeal to Chinese guests. A water park. I don't know."

Zao thought this one out for a moment, and then he said—just came out and said it—he said, "What if we gave them an offer they couldn't refuse? The Hawaiians, I mean."

Jesus, Russ thought, the guy *was* a godfather, but come on. He and Hayashi exchanged glances.

Zao laughed. "I know, I know—Don Corleone, right? Here's the Asian godfather sounding like Don Corleone!" He laughed again. "But that's not what I mean. I'm talking about money."

"We're working on that already," Hayashi said. "But that, too, well, I hate to keep using the same word over and over, but it's complex. They won't just take it outright, so we're trying to pick them off one by one, and Russ has a relationship with their leader that goes way back, so we're working on that."

Picking them off. Russ really wished Hayashi wouldn't put it that way. That certainly wasn't what he himself had in mind for Ikaika.

"That's good," Zao said. "But that's not entirely what I mean, either. I'm talking about *money*. I'm talking about billions of dollars. For everyone. And not in the form of payoffs and bribes and backroom deals and so forth. Look out the window, gentlemen."

He turned with a sweeping open-palmed gesture. "This little island covers only eleven square miles, and much of that, as I said, is reclaimed land. Look around. Please. These eleven square miles, they generate fourteen billion dollars US annually. Fourteen billion. You want another marketing angle for a mixed use property that will appeal to the Chinese? You're standing at the top of one!"

Damn! How dim were they all that they hadn't seen through it in the first place: *that's* why he flew us all the way out here. Smooth! This wasn't just some convenient way to have a meeting on your investment property seven thousand miles away—fly everyone up here because you're too busy tending to your empire. Bradley Zao was not an *overseer* or a *caretaker* of what Daddy built for him. He was a *builder*, a builder of his own empire.

Look at the Grand Dragon, for Chrissakes, 2.6 *billion dollars* thrown out there on the table in the middle of a global recession. If anything, the guy was trying to get out from under his father's shadow. And what better way than to expand the family business across an ocean, to plant a stake right at the *Crossroads of the Pacific?*

Russ wondered if the guy had been envisioning the casino since the beginning, if this nonsense about a high-end luxury condo-hotel was indeed just that: nonsense. Why else would you bring *Nakayama* along? Look at the guy over there, just lining up another putt, still oblivious to the bomb that had just been detonated. He'd been a lame duck for three years running. Well, here's why: you needed him to sign off on the bill, the bill introduced and run through the Tourism Committees of both houses, whose chairs were to be handpicked *next week* by…the House Speaker and the President of the State Senate. Zao. The guy *knew*, didn't he, just like he knew all the ins and outs of the property's recent history.

But did he have any idea about the countless attempts over the past three decades to push gambling through the Lege?

"Since 1981 there have been almost 200 attempts to legalize some form of gambling in Hawai'i," Zao said, and fuck, he'd had someone study up on that one, too. He was serious about this, almost like now that the Grand Dragon was up and running, it was *boring* him and he wanted to get back into the game again, and what better place to do it than Hawai'i, where you could be…the first. You could be a pioneer. A missionary.

"You've really done some homework!" Russ said as Zao tapped another putt. "And I think if you took a poll of all the legislators, the overwhelming majority of them believe in supporting some form of gambling. These guys all go to Vegas, you know? But none of those bills ever wind up going anywhere. It's very complicated."

Suddenly Charles Uchida piped up: "Plus then there's the Boyds," he said, almost like he was grateful that the conversation had turned toward a subject on which he could contribute. "They own the California Hotel in Vegas. They've got the local market captured—Hawai'i gamblers going to Vegas. They have a vested interest in not seeing gambling in Hawai'i."

Vested interest? And what happened to the pidgin, boo?

Anyway, Uchida plodded on: "Boyd never came out and said anything or did anything overtly, or specifically, but they were very concerned about that whenever it came up. One of their lobbyists would be in to see us every time. And they had good PR, too, those guys. I don't know if it was them or what, but the idea always began to crash whenever the newspapers started editorializing about it."

"That's true," Russ said. "They always talk about, you know, the social ills. And that's not all. I tell you, whenever we start to talk about gambling in the legislature, law enforcement guys start to come out in droves. And aside from the social ills, they always bring up the moral question: here come the churches."

"It winds up not being worth the fight," Uchida said, "because the churches and the newspapers are against it. So what they did was they passed a law legalizing, so that you could play poker in your own home as long as no 'house' could take any of the money, so that was the compromise. And that was it."

"Charles, you keep mentioning newspapers," Zao said, leaving Russ mildly impressed that he'd remembered the speaker's name, so absent had Uchida been from the proceedings up to now. "I doubt that these days you would have much of that vocal opposition—certainly not from newspapers!"

Now Sean Hayashi jumped in: "Compared to even five or ten years ago, I bet it would be pretty easy to mount a successful PR campaign—other than a handful of bloggers, there's really no one left to call you on all those 'social ills' things. The newspapers, there's only one now, and you could just flood it with a bunch of advertising money and you're good."

Zao's final putt rolled up next to the hole and then tumbled in from the side, whereupon he turned to his guests and said, "I wouldn't be concerned with the public relations aspect of it—that's small potatoes." *Small potatoes.* Fleetingly Russ wondered where Zao had picked up all these little speech affectations. "If we can count on the support of the leadership in the legislature and the governor," he went on, "how can I put this? Let me be honest. I don't mean this in a kind of boastful way—it's really just the facts: at the end of the day, there's really no limit to the resources we can commit to a public relations effort, and to a lobbying effort. I don't know the ins and outs of your legislature as far as personalities go, but given the resources, there has to be some kind of realistic way to get such a thing passed this time."

Now the room was silent. The guy was ready to take on Vegas, the churches, the social police, the actual police, the likes of Lave Salanoa and what's-his-name, Kekoa Meyer, however loosely the local underground gambling scene was in fact organized—he was ready to take them all on like he was making dollar bets on a practice putting green. And the reason he was so relaxed about it was because he knew it was a foregone conclusion. What Russ envisioned as a knock-down, drag-out legislative battle, Bradley here, with his untold billions, seemed to be viewing as a simple procedural matter.

And this money: it wasn't going to just dry up like the Japanese money had. The 1980s Japanese? Snapping up Waikiki hotel properties for tens of millions of dollars? Plowing over Windward valleys with hundred million dollar golf courses? That was nothing compared to this. Bradley Zao's money was going to *grow more money*. You had a *billion* people in China, all set to gamble it all away in some other venue than Macau, a smog-choked garbage island so many of them had already visited upwards of a hundred times. Someone could do the math on the economic impact of the money flooding into Hawai'i that would grind the "social ills" and the "attracting the criminal element" arguments into submission. We can *close* the women's prison, because we'll be able to rehab everyone there and give them well-paying jobs, we can end the hopelessness that leads to a young Hawaiian woman covered in jailhouse ink and badly aged from a life of drug addiction, we can *end* that.

All of this, it flashed through Russ's brain in that silent moment. And so naturally his next thought—and even as he thought it, he knew it was an irrational one, but still, I'm so much *taller* than this kid, a mere *child*, and if I'm judging it right, he actually *does* have some kind of emotional fixation on this project now, one that might cloud his steel-strength disciplined bottom-line at-the-end-of-the-day thinking just enough—naturally Russ's next thought was, *Should I go for more?*

So he said, "It's still not going to be enough."

And there he was: all in.

No one could believe it. You could *hear* the silence. Look at Sean Hayashi—you could hear his thoughts: What the fuck is Russ thinking? Here we all are right at the *center* of the biggest deal...of the most *historic* deal ever to be made in the history of the Islands, and here comes State Senate President Russell Lee to fuck the whole thing up. Is Russ actually thinking he can *shake this guy down?* A relaxed and comfortable multi-billionaire, groomed from day one as a multi-billionaire kingpin's son? A guy who could walk away from a million dollar option without even blinking?

"Like I said, it can't be the same old story, even with the casinos," Russ said. And then he detailed all the ideas he and Cliff Yoshida had discussed about company shares, a management training program for local workers, and yes, that he wanted Zao to *give up control* to the state agency he hoped to create so that the hotel jobs could be protected for local people, an agency ultimately controlled by the governor's office. Yes, now that Zao was proposing to flood the state with casino money instead of simply constructing a mere five-tower development, now that we were talking about *tens of billions of dollars annually*, well, now it made even *more* sense to demand state control. "Let's not just pretend my candidacy for governor is linked to this project," Russ said. "Let's link them officially."

Zao let that one sit. By now everyone may have been able to tell that his pauses were indeed genuine, in the sense that he was taking the time to think all of this through rather than jumping in with a string of empty words while he thought of something appropriate to say, and also genuine in the sense that he was giving Russ's words their proper due, and possibly even *changing his mind* about things as new information came to light.

But who really knew? Russ could only recall the sound of that white marble *clack-clack-clacking* around on the roulette wheel downstairs. He wouldn't have been surprised if Zao simply collected his two dollars from Nakayama to settle the golf bet and then escorted everyone back through those big doors in thank-you-very-much fashion, have fun downstairs at the tables, have a nice flight back to your backwater island outpost. *Clack-clack-clack-clack-clack.*

"I think we can work something out in that regard," Zao finally said. "And again, as you pointed out, Russell, I think it goes back to making sure everyone is happy. I don't want to be some money-hungry developer just shoveling everything through to be in a place I'm not wanted. Honestly, what would I want with more money?" He said this with a chuckle, handing his putter off to his hottie assistant with a look that said, "At the end of the day, how many G650s does one man need?"

All of the words were wafting over Russ like some kind of sweet perfume, and he was having a hard time catching the details, or even believing any of this was happening, because suddenly his brain was again flooded, flooded with…dopamine. Russell Lee was *in love*. He'd done it.

He'd laid it all out there on the table, risked a pile of chips amounting to *billions of dollars*. Billions! And he'd won!

"Now to be perfectly honest," Zao was saying, "I'm not all that crazy about surrendering control of operations, but as I said, I'm sure we can work something out in that regard." He went on a bit about how attractive Hawai'i would be as compared to even Macau, babbling on about a "more favorable effective tax rate on winnings than 39 percent" and regaining business lost to Singapore a few years back, where the effective tax, "including VAT," was twelve percent, and maybe Hawai'i could do better than even that.

And then he turned to Nakayama and said, "Governor, you owe me two dollars US."

The governor good-naturedly went through his pockets and then said, "I'm a bit short of cash, Bradley. How about a signature on your gambling bill instead?"

They all laughed at that one, and then Bradley said, "Okay, but as long as I don't get accused of bribery!"

More laughter. And then Charles Uchida said, "Eh Donald, I think you just got bought off for less than any sitting governor in the history of Hawai'i."

Still more laughter, especially from Russ himself, who was so in love in this moment he would have laughed at pretty much anything. "Two dollars!" he said. "The governor's signature for two dollars!" Easy. Life was just plain easy.

ENEMY TERRITORY

Fucken Nolan betta *have* something. Betta know where Salanoa-them *stay*. Betta know where they sitting, what they driving, where they parked. And while we at it, he betta be waiting right in front of the college with one prime spot for us, no way I going be dragging this frikken ski boot through the streets of Lāʻie. Betta have boyz saving seats right up front—that's the point: everybody gotta *see us* there. Betta have *planned* for it, betta have *expected*, j'like these Mormons expected this monsta crowd—they get the whole highway all the way back past Hauʻula lined with teams of Mormon boys in their white-shirt-black-tie Mormon boy uniforms, plus orange vests, real professional, they directing this long line of traffic creeping…creeping…creeping…creeping past the PCC…creeping…creeping…past the Marriot…Javen turns the Ram 2500 left in towards the college…the whole narrow street lined with parked Escalades and F-250s and Expeditions on both sides…and Nolan Kahaiue waiting. Good. So far.

"You right, cuz," Javen said, "that fucka *scared*. Can smell the fear from here."

Scared. If it hadn't been bad enough back when Nolan paid his tax, all just on the rumor that Kekoa wen' *waste* Tapusoa, just look at him now: his head spinning from side to side like he looking around for snipers on top the roof of the college gym on that side of the street, or inside one of these carport living rooms on the other, all while trying for make like he directing them into this spot on the grass he been saving, right in front of the college, big enough for the Ram and for Nalu-them's Tahoe behind them. Good. So far.

Plus not one frikken comment, not even about Kekoa's ski boot.

And then when they got out: "I tried for getchoo seats inside, but these frikken Mormons, they *linked up*, ba. They get their system. Was hard enough for save the parking, but we do 'um for you, Kekoa. Anything for you, my bradda."

Kekoa turned toward the college: thousand-something people streaming into four huge white circus-sized tents joined together, the whole front lawn, big as two-three football fields, covered with people (an' where the fuck Salanoa-them?), we going to have to *stand in line*. Worse: sit way the fuck in the back—if there even any seats *left*—and how the fuck them *solés* going be fucken *trippin*, they don't even know we even *here*?

Fuck. Deep breath. Cool head main t'ing. Calm, cool, collec'.

And look these two haole women coming up to greet them, coming up to greet Kekoa, Javen, Nalu, Rodney-them all loaded down wit' their nines and .45s under their button-down shirts, untucked, yeah, but *loaded down*. Packing. They ready for start come out *blazing*—these Mormon girls greeting us with...*smiles?* BYU students, probably, both in light blue muʻumuʻu with sleeves reaching halfway down their arms: this corn fed Nebraska blond, her nametag: "Sister Mills," and this China-or-Hong-Kong-Chinese girl, "Sister Wang"—they handing off programs for the funeral, leading everybody over to the tent, an' more smiling pairs of Mormon girls all over the place leading gotta be like *two* thousand-something people into that tent. Or that other tent, everybody milling around holding plastic cups and little plates of...food?... like the Mormons could plan to *feed* this whole monsta crowd—but fucken Nolan: he cannot even mafia one fucken row of seats.

An' where the fuck *is* fucken *Salanoa?*

He shot a glare at Nolan: fucka betta know.

No idea: look at him, trying for think of some way to Kekoa-my-bradda his way out of answering.

"I get guys all up an' down the road, brah," he said. "Maybe they neva show up yet."

Bullshit, neva show up. What, Nolan—not enough now the only chance for everybody see Kekoa Meyer at the funeral for the man he wen' fucken *waste* going be in the reception line, not *enough* going be like, *hours* before they ever make it through that line to the family. Not *enough* Kimo, an' Nalu too, got his hand inside his shirt gripped on his frikken Glock already like any minute now he going do something stupid, and the young boyz, Rodney-Jay-them, fast hands both—they holding back already—and yeah, I like stay calm-cool-collec' too, but that's a long time for wait. No—on toppa all that you cannot do ONE SIMPLE FUCKEN THING like tell me where those fuckas *stay*.

Through the crowd, past a circle of six, seven, eight looked like middle aged potbellied UH Class of '82 state worker paper pushers all taking a knee, every one of them wearing dark "58" Warrior jerseys, two or three with their hands to their eyes, their shoulders bobbing up and down, they sobbing like Tapusoa was their own fucken nephew. These two prison-guard-looking braddas, crying like babies, the whole campus like one sea of dark Warrior green, fans coming up to fans to share one good cry, all hugging even they probably never even met before, an' then all these pairs of Mormon girls patiently waiting, with those *smiles*.

"At least you know what they driving," Kekoa said. "Like, your boyz know what to look for. Right?"

Nolan just gave him this resigned what-can-you-do look Kekoa was ready to open-hand right off his fat fucken face right there and then said, "Hard for tell what one *solé* banger driving anymore, pretty much everyone out there rolling wit' their big boy trucks, their Expeditions and Escalades an' their rims, even moms an' their kids."

Stop.

Kekoa turned, both hands on Nolan's round shoulders, and looked straight into his frightened eyes. Calm. Cool. Collec'. *Cold*. And quiet: "Then you go do me one favor then Nolan. You go find out. Find out all you fucken can. I like know what they driving, what they wearing, where they wen' park, what they fucken *eat for fucken breakfast*, whateva. Mostly I like know *where those fuckas stay*. Got it?"

Nolan frikken *shaking* now. Not a word. With a nod and a hard swallow he turned and beat it, disappearing into the crowd with his phone out. Good.

Now past a ring of UH players with their arms around each other like they in a huddle, the two Mormon sisters led them all into the tent to a numbered and roped off area…all the way at the frikken *back*… ten rows of black folding chairs facing this big flat screen monitor: this painted forest-and-mountain landscape screen saver like some fucken

Disney movie. All around, the same thing: little squares of numbered roped off areas facing monitors, like not bad enough we cannot get in line—we gotta fucken sit through some highlight film of Tapusoa first, an' what the fuck is *this* shit?

Bugles and French horns and doves and shit up on the screen flying past more purple mountains, and now this double-chinned pink haole in one suit and tie letting you know how in love—in love!—he was with…the Mormon fucken temple? How the lucky few "worthy members" could "contemplate their faith" in that "sacred sanctuary"? Looked like the fucken Taj Mahal, or some kind of modern art museum-looking tombstone, this "beautiful building" (was the guy *crying?*), on and on about the history of Mormons, God and Joseph Smith and Maroni and Brigham Young and fucken Mormon himself, and *where the fuck is Salanoa?*

Calm. Look your boyz: every one of them and not just Javen bouncing his frikken knee up and down and looking all over the place like one army—that same army wen' put up these circus tents with their twenty-foot poles and all their intricate ropes and stakes and everything going descend—like one army going descend any minute now just cause we packing heat, just cause we ready for come out smashing. Either that army, or Salanoa's one.

Calm.

They gotta be inside this frikken airplane hangar tent someplace, and okay, fine. Nolan not going fuck up again. He going find out now. An' maybe we stay all the way in the back right now, but look: the frikken Mormons, they *planned* it. Alla these five-six roped-off areas, these video monitors—was all just for control the crowd, make it more efficient, bring small groups up one-by-one instead of have everybody standing in line the whole time.

All quiet in here now that that fucken video ended, just that *solé* girl up there on the stage way up front singing that Mormon hymn, and look how frikken…small…how small everyone is…not like every single Samoan gotta look like one UH lineman—an' some a these fuckas do look like linemen—but the rest of them all squat and round, soft like that boy strumming the guitar up there with the *solé* girl. Good.

Now this Sister Mills, she back *already* with her big Mormon smile: "It's our turn to join everyone in the reception line! But before we do,

I'll have to remind everyone to please gather your thoughts and prayers ahead of time so that we're prepared to view Elder Tapusoa in a way that leaves ample time for others to do so after us!"

Fucken Sista Mills. An' okay Nolan, we letchoo off the hook now. Butchoo still betta find out where those fuckas *stay*.

Everyone in line now, Kekoa's fucken ski boot clacking on this wooden walkway someone had laid out for wheelchairs or whatever. Up ahead, the stage: a wood-toned podium on the right, the *solé* girl and the boy with the guitar, the long white opened casket, and then a line of Tapusoa's family, six, seven…hadda be ten of them up there, all dressed from head to toe in pure…white?

A tap on the shoulder. Javen nodded his head toward the stage.

And there they were. Right fucken there.

Lave Salanoa. Manu Savea. What's-his-name, Tufono, the short fire hydrant one, all making their way through Tapusoa's family, all in black, thick gold chains hanging around each of their necks. Had three younger boyz behind them, but Kekoa didn't know who they were. Each one of their thick forearms covered with ink. The young boyz all around Tapusoa's age, like maybe they being groomed to step up in a few years. All in one place. Could wipe them out in seconds. Easy. Could wipe them out right now, just pull out your nine right here and start blazing and the whole thing pau, and look at that frikken *pussy* up there, Salanoa, he crying like one girl, right there on the stage in front of everybody.

Fuck, I going make you cry, you fucken *solé* faggot, I no care you wearing one baggy black shirt too, all untucked so no one can see you packing. I know you fucking packing, brah, an I *still* going make you cry. You going *see* cuz, you going be crawling on the ground kissing my fucken *feet* brah, I going make alla you fuckas cry more worse than you crying standing there ova your dead bradda, hugging the mom and the dad and the aunty-them, I going make allayou bitches fucken cry more worse than right now.

Watch.

He turned to Javen: a pure and tightly wound mass of *anger*, one cold hard I-going-*kill*-you-mothafucka stare a mirror of his own, and of Kimo's, and of Nalu's.

"Cool head, cuz," he said. "Main t'ing cool head."

Javen just barely gave him a nod. He glued his eyes back to the stage.

"We going pick the right spot, no worry," Kekoa told him.

He turned to the rest of his boyz and told them the same thing with a look: "No ac' stupid." And the line moved ahead, the ski boot clacking on the wooden walkway.

Up on the stage Kekoa was frigid. Numb. He could only feel the eyes on him, hundreds of them, thousands of them, the eyes of Coach Brock himself, that fat fuck sitting right there in the front row, could feel the eyes of the UH football team, every one of them locked onto him with pure hatred, and what, you winless fucken punks, you going be the ones ac' stupid today? I neva even *do* it, but I take alla you fuckas right now, I no care. You *see* me up here? Good you see me up here. Take one good long look and don't forget it. Go on thinking I wen' take your boy out. Go. I *like* be the one take your boy out.

And then the open casket.

Tapusoa. I thought they was going bury you in Warrior black you stupid fuck, but it's all white—the shoes, the pants, even the tie, like you headed for one white light somewhere on the other side, some funny white Mormon fucken chef's hat on your head instead of one Warrior helmet.

See brah? You shouldda used those big hands for wrap up that fat fucken running back at the end of the game, you'd still be alive.

But no.

You gotta ac' fucken stupid, ah? You gotta punk Kekoa Meyer. Send me down. Start people talking: Kekoa, he one punk! He get cracks! He *old*, Kekoa Meyer, his time wen' pass!

Cuz, I had *everything*, I had everything lined up, was going *consolidate*, put Hawai'i on the frikken *map*, even get your *solé* braddas on my side unda me, we couldda worked 'um together. Keep out the Mexicans, *La Familia*. The Crips and Bloods. Aryan Nation. Put fucken Hawai'i on the fucken map, cuz. But no. Look now, *solé*. You dead. An' no. Wasn't me. But you still dead. You wen' piss *somebody* off, you wen' punk more than me, an' now you dead, you fucka. See whatchoo get brah? You dead.

Kekoa turned down the line: the mom, the dad, the aunties, uncles, cousins—

Fucken King *Solé* himself, right off to the side of the stage, standing over there in the ring of his boyz at the edge of the tent, his thick forearms folded and resting on his big stomach, his face locked into… the look…the playground staredown—the look that for years stretching all the way back to King Intermediate or wherever it was, Pop Warner, Kaiser High, that for years constituted…an agreement…that a meeting would take place. Hands would be thrown. Except now it wasn't hands. Now it meant bullets would fly…an' yeah you fat fucken *solé*, it worked just like I said, like I fucken *planned* it, cause look: you *trippin*, ah cuz. You like pull out whateva you get unda that shirt and start blazing right here—an' you betta hope you get more than one .22—you *mad*, ah Lave. Trippin'!

Through the line—he wen' *kiss the mom!* Kekoa Meyer fucken *killed* Tapusoa, an' then he come to the funeral an' wen' *kiss the fucken mom!*—the dad, the cousins-them, and off the stage, Nolan waiting on the side, and not with more *bullshit*—but with one *answer*. Nolan, he all right.

"They like meet witchoo," he said. "Salanoa, he come up to me an' tell me for tell you: they like meet witchoo. Fucka stay parked back up the cane road, he driving one black Tahoe." Nolan coldly explained the whole thing: near the Mormon cemetery not a quarter mile away back past the temple, this old dirt road, used to service the cane fields back of Lā'ie.

And there was Salanoa again over by the edge of the tent, the fucka *seething* now.

Deserted fucken cane road. What: you going ambush me, you fat fucken *solé*, going stake that place out? What, you wen' read my script? You *tripping* already, you even jus' *see* me here, jus' *now*. You that fucken predictable, letting me play you like that. Good you trippin'. Good you fulla anger. Good you all…emotional. Good. Cause we get back in that fucken cane road a yours bradda boo? You going fuck up. An' I going *waste you*.

Watch.

NEARER MY GOD TO THEE

Old Bennett Irving would have had a good time with that one: a VIP section. At a *funeral*. Cordoned off with a red *velvet rope*. A rope that was moved aside for entering and exiting dignitaries by this slender white haired retired Provo bank middle manager or whatever, this haole whose name tag read "Elder Cox." Makana's dad would have gone to town! Look, Makana: thanks to your Tom Watada connection, you don't have to sit with that strange mix of local Japanese state worker drones and the wannabee gangstas, the UH Warrior fan base.

Or—and Makana had to stifle a chuckle—that whole line of make-hard tattooed castrated homophobes up there onstage, or that ring of *boyz* over there on the side with their gold chains and their untucked shirts, and what, you one *banger?* Wichoa fucken *ski boot* on your leg? A ski boot? Talk about castrated!

Makana always wondered why so many local men had to walk around in such abject fear of being mistaken for being…gay…that they had to adopt some LA gangsta persona just to get *respect*.

But then just as quickly he had the answer, which was that the lingering effects of colonization had left all these poor men with no other way to assert their autonomy than to pretend that they wouldn't hesitate to fight back with guns—as if any of the boyz in that circle had ever even seen a real gun, and yeah, okay, I forgive you that constant cliché of a man-up posture, but thank God and Maroni himself I don't have to sit anywhere near you.

Look at me right here next to the Reverend Tom Watada: five seats from Peter Varner, the UH President, and his wife, a *faculty wife* if ever there was one, she'd set to "coordinating" some kind of "outreach" program to "promote literacy" in the elementary schools surrounding the Mānoa campus—already among the few DOE schools anyone would even think to send their kids to nowadays before her "help" ever arrived. There's the AD, Steven Foreman. There's Coach Brock and what's-her-name, gotta be a former "intern" third wife cheerleader from his days at UTEP. Coach Brock himself!

As a meagerly compensated UH professor, Makana knew he was supposed to look upon the 1.1 Million Dollar Man with bitterness and resentment at all times. But swept up as he was in what he also knew was an irrational sense of pride for Warrior football, win or lose, he had a hard time summoning up any ill will towards the program's leader. Aside from Makana's need to support his team during this difficult time, the chance to hear Brachman speak was his main reason for coming to the funeral at all, and here he was, only three...four...five seats away from the man and his herd of "assistants" and "coordinators" and so on, each of whom made far more than any of the WCC faculty. The union rep in Makana's division, an anthropology dinosaur named Curtis Kam, was always going on about how even the running backs coach made $90,000 a year. "Ninety grand!" he would say. "And UH almost never even runs the ball! And they're asking *us* to 'do more with less'?"

Nevertheless here they were, and on time, too, despite the thick line of traffic that had stretched nearly all the way back to Kahalu'u by the time Makana had picked Tom up and pointed the F-350 north towards the country instead of south towards town.

Truth be told, Makana's brain had been at war with itself for days over whether or not to do what he really knew he should have been doing: making important contributions to the breakfast meeting with Lieutenant Governor James Hendrick that was getting underway right about now downtown.

Hendrick was already gearing up his run for governor, taking advantage of the fact that he could openly announce his candidacy right away, and thus appropriate a no-growth stop-the-urban-sprawl anti-development create-jobs fix-public-education *sustainability* platform before Russell Lee got a chance to.

As one of those "Hawaiian at Heart" haoles, Hendrick was going to need the public support of as many prominent Hawaiians as he could find, so he'd contacted Ikaika Nā'imipono and invited him to bring a few of his "folks" along to "talk story" at some restaurant in town. At the last minute Makana had backed out, sending Helen instead—they'd certainly all understand that he was *helping*, helping the team, helping the Tapusoa family.

That had also been the connection that had gained Tom these incredible seats—along with good parking alongside an old cane road at the back of Lāʻie's cramped suburban neighborhood, where a "worthy member" activist friend of Tom's named Roger Ferguson had saved them a spot behind a row of blinged-up SUVs. (And why in the world did even a *family* car need 22-inch chrome rims these days?) Though Tom's call last night asking for a ride to a *Mormon funeral* had surprised Makana, the Reverend later explained the whole thing as they'd sat in traffic.

Mixed in with his usual camel-through-the-eye-of-a-needle socialist references to scripture was the story that Ufi Tapusoa's family was facing eviction—this even after Caleb Tapusoa, Ufi's father, had migrated from Samoa to attend BYU and, of course work at the Mormon-owned PCC, and even after he and the second-generation Samoan Mormon who'd become his wife had worked diligently to put together a down payment for a home and then go on to raise five boys, even after more than twenty years of faithful tithing.

Tom had pointed out the house, too, along the narrow street leading to the old cane road, where someone had even converted the carport into the family's actual living room.

Even as he sat there watching Tapusoa's dad bravely greet even the make-hard wannabe-bangers up there on stage, all Makana could think was: He can't make his mortgage payment, and yet they're still demanding ten percent of his salary for...tithing. Tom had gone on about how the Tapusoas had refinanced their house so they could send two of the boys to college at BYU's main campus in Utah, and how, like many of their neighbors, they'd had to supplement their hourly pay at the PCC, along with the extra money Tapusoa's father earned as a part-time security guard at BYUH, by cramming three of their big boys into one room and the other two into their own room so they could rent out the third to two BYUH students.

Tom had learned that Tapusoa's other two sons worked "security" in Chinatown someplace, which had at first evoked for Makana the same image of the dad as a BYU rent-a-cop—that is, until the sight of the boyz who'd just greeted the family up there—a *ski boot?*—those understanding sorry-for-your-loss looks of theirs melting right back into a comical make-hard scowl the moment they gathered over there off to the left beside the stage—just like that, the word "security" turned into something else entirely in Makana's head, something to do with *actual* bangers and gangstas, with illegal game rooms and even—yes, it was still floating around, even here at the poor boy's funeral: the rumor of fixing college football games.

Could a life of working-poor deprivation, of being crammed into such a little house your whole life with such a huge family, with *tenants*, and then once you finally made it to the ESPN stage, of watching the millions of dollars you almost single-handedly raked in for UH over four years all go towards paying a herd of redundant mediocre administrators, all while you had to buy your own locker room soap to simply take a post-game shower—could it all have led even the sons of such a "worthy member" as Caleb Tapusoa in such a direction?

All because of a squeeze being put upon them by some bank? It all sounded...*evil*.

At first it didn't make sense, the thought of such a...*biblical* word—and one that didn't at all square with how damned *nice* everyone around here had been all day. In the whole two hours right here in the heart of Mormondom, in fact, Makana had yet to see anyone even remotely... irritable. *Nice.* Every one of them. All along the walk from Makana's truck over to the BYUH campus, you'd run into them, all dressed for the funeral, all greeting you with a big sincere "Good Morning!" and a...*smile!*

Then again, maybe that *was* the "evil" part about it, Makana decided, thinking it was a bit like what Ikaika had once told him about *charm*, about guys in banker's aloha shirts who try to make you *like* them, except here it was *everybody*, powered up and so genuine it was like they *meant* it, this level of niceness.

Ikaika. With that thought Makana found himself pulling out his phone to check if anyone had texted or called, pulled it out even though he knew he would have felt it vibrate if someone had, and God he hoped he wasn't missing anything too important down at Hendrick's breakfast meeting.

Of course no one had texted—a fact Makana took as a sign that things were going just fine without him, which didn't necessarily mean his input wasn't, like, *essential*—it probably just meant the "meeting" was more of a get-to-know-you thing where more than likely nothing serious was being discussed, otherwise of course he would have been contacted by now.

Nice. There it was again, etched right into the pink face of the tall white haired Elder What's-His-Name bringing up, at last, the rear of the reception line, maybe around a hundred or so people to go, with that *smile* on his face, and do you work for the Mormon bank during the week, Mr. Worthy Member? You using this whole elaborate celebrity funeral for…PR?

Makana turned to the program in his hands, and though he'd scoured all four pages, he could find no evidence that Ufi Tapusoa had ever played football. The picture on the front looked like it had been taken in a Utah Sears portrait studio, the boy seated in front of a backdrop of painted steep purple mountains and tall pines. They'd dressed him in his white shirt and black tie, combed his hair. But most of all Tapusoa had that…*smile!*…that Mormon smile. And now that Makana thought about it, that smile was starting to creep him out, is what it was, just another part of the evangelical sales pitch.

And how had Makana missed it in the first place?—all these nice people were actually *using* Tapusoa's funeral to *recruit new members*, just as Makana's father had told him they'd wanted to use his wedding. The moment Makana and Tom had walked into this circus tent they'd been forced to sit through some propaganda video that actually claimed, right out loud, that the Mormon colonists were the ones who had first taught the Hawaiians the meaning of "family."

The tent wasn't as bad as their church, where you had that Disney-fied Charlton Heston portrait of Jesus looking plaintively down upon you, the one Makana's father always used to rip on. ("The guy looks more haole than I do! And he's from the Middle East?") But here they were: shamelessly selling their product to a captive audience all under the guise of *helping one of our members during this difficult time.*

On the other hand, how could you blame them? Look around: two, three thousand people here for the taking, a huge crowd among them whose only religion was UH football.

Makana turned to share his brilliant little insight with Tom Watada, concluding with, "Talk about colonization!" As a UH professor, Makana admittedly did throw the term around all the time, but come on: at the turn of the century the Mormons bought up nearly seven thousand acres in what had been in pre-contact times a Hawaiian city of refuge. They'd appropriated the "refuge" story, built a Mormon temple and four churches, and a branch of the Utah university named for the storied leader who'd brought them nearly all the way across the U.S. continent and founded their capitol in Salt Lake City. The Lāʻie "Stake"—as in "tent stake," one of the many "stakes" lending support to the great and mighty tent known as the Church of Jesus Christ of Latter Day Saints—the Lāʻie Stake had gone on to become one of the most fertile religious recruiting grounds in the Pacific basin. Hawaiians, the Mormons claimed, were some "lost tribe of Israel" in need of redemptive conversion. Samoans, same story. As Makana well knew, the first wave of Samoans who migrated to Hawaiʻi were already Mormons, the products of years of missionary work across the Pacific.

You could see the connection right on stage, the whole scene backed by a wall of colorful and elaborately woven mats fit for the Samoan exhibit at the Smithsonian. These mats had been woven, Makana figured, by Tapusoa's relatives, and appeared to be a Lost Tribe tradition the colonizers had made allowances for.

As he recalled it, the more mats you had, and the more elaborate the mats were, the more important you were. From the looks of that stage, Ufi Tapusoa was some kind of Samoan chief.

Tom leaned over and said, "I think 'colony' is actually a very good word when you're describing Lāʻie. Except for a strip of beachfront land the church sold several years back, the entire town consists of LDS Church members. You won't find many non-Mormons working at BYUH or the Polynesian Cultural Center, either."

To Makana the PCC complex was a thatched-roofed embodiment of exploitation, an even worse form of the plantation system than the import-Japanese-slaves-and-work-them-to-death-while-raping-them-at-the-company-store-while-you-rake-in-untold-profits model that had been so successfully employed by the haole sugar barons, including the Mormons themselves, who had financed much of Lāʻie's growth with cane refined in the Kahuku sugar mill now rusting away just up the road. The PCC had their own indentured servants—college kids from Fiji and Tahiti and New Zealand and Samoa, employed for next to nothing in "I-Work" work-study arrangements with BYUH—you had them parading around like cigar store Indians, prostituting their "native cultures" in exchange for a "scholarship" and a meager stipend (minus ten percent for tithing) they spent at…the company store!

Doing a few dances in front of a bunch of fat white tourists had to be far easier work than toiling under the blazing sun in a cane field for twelve hours a day. But look at the *damage* the Mormons were doing to the cultural identities of these kids.

"That place has been the most profitable and popular tourist attraction in Hawai'i for the past fifty years," Tom said. "And they're still able to operate it as a tax-exempt non-profit arm of the church."

"That's almost funny, isn't it," Makana said. "You take the natives out of their homeland and then bring them all here, and the natives themselves become the commodity. And in the meantime you're 'educating' them and 'civilizing' them."

"Turning them into Mormons," Tom said.

"Cultural reproduction. You're colonizing their minds, just as you're exploiting their native cultural practices." Instantly proud of that little insight, Makana filed it away to stick into another conference paper that was suddenly gelling in his mind, this one about Lā'ie as an example of a post-colonial cultural contact zone in an era of mass-tourism and globalization. "You know, you can't even get a bag of ground coffee in the Lā'ie Foodland. And forget about a twelve-pack."

Tom smiled and said, "That may have had less to do with some oppressive church directive inserted into Foodland's lease agreement than with the fact that if they had it on the shelf, no one from around here would buy it."

Makana nodded, thinking, certainly not old Elder What's-His-Name over there ushering the final mourners to greet the Tapusoas (although you could hardly call them "mourners," what with all the smiles), and certainly not—the program named the guy as Bishop Tripp—that meticulously combed and graying banker looking guy now making his way to the podium, his suit and tie set off incongruously by the Samoan funeral mats hung behind him. Tripp was listed just above some state senator Makana had never heard of, a man named Arthur

Tafai, who would precede Coach Brock, and Makana had a pretty good idea what the guy was going to put them through.

His dad had explained it to him once when they were stuck in traffic right in front of the Mormon Tabernacle in town. Basically, it would start with a hymn, and then the Bishop would go on forever talking about "the progression of life" and the "assurance of immortality" for "worthy members" and on and on, more a pitch for becoming worthy yourself than a commemoration of Ufi Tapusoa's life (whoever he was). For a second Makana thought about slipping out to the food tent until Coach Brock took the podium, and he had the feeling he wasn't the only one. But he figured it would be in bad taste, especially with Tom, a man of the cloth himself, sitting right here next to him.

Though Bishop Tripp hardly looked like the type to get up in front of a couple thousand people and just belt one out, the first thing he did after welcoming everyone was direct them all to a hymn in their programs called "What Is This Thing Called Death." You heard a shuffling of paper all around as people dutifully complied. But when the guy held his head high and lit into the first line—and what happened to that silken-voiced Samoan girl who'd sung the earlier hymns, songs like "Nearer My God to Thee" and "Oh Lord My Redeemer" that Makana had recognized from when he was a little kid, back when his dad would knock back a couple of gin and tonics and let loose, with no shortage of irony, in his own deep baritone?

What happened to her?—when the old haole man up there lit into his first line, you would have thought Boise State had just run back the opening kickoff for a touchdown, so full of what-the-fuck's-he-*singing* shock had Warrior Nation become.

"Oh God, touch thou my aching heart, and calm my troubled fears!" Bishop Tripp went on in Battle-Hymn-of-the-Republic cadence. "Let hope and faith, transcendent, pure, give strength and peace beyond my tears!" The soft surf of a couple of hundred game Mormon voices rose up just a little bit, and President Varner and his wife over there were giving it a shot, if only trying to mouth the words. And all Makana could think was that if this was part of the PR, then the Mormons were in trouble.

It all seemed about to go terribly wrong, with people beginning to stifle yawns, guys all over the place taking out their phones and starting to text their friends, people on the edges sliding out for a cigarette or a cup of juice or whatever—anything but *this*.

And just like that another voice began booming out, a strong and surprisingly practiced tenor, rising above even that of Bishop Tripp up there on the stage: "There is no death, but only change, with recompense for vict'ry won!" Heads turned this way and that, looks of exaggerated surprise crossing the long rows of crowded seats. No way! No frikken *way!* How's *that?* Phones were being shut off and pocketed. Makana caught one of the early leavers stopping dead in his tracks and whirling back to his seat. He himself couldn't help but straighten up and rifle through his own program to find the words to the hymn. All around the tent, voices were rising and joining in, joining in with the loud and confident tenor of their leader, of…Coach Stacy Brachman: "The gift of Him who loved all men, the Son of God, the Holy One!"

Coach Brock!

Right then Makana felt the vibration of his own phone. He tried to regain his focus on Bishop Tripp, who followed right on the heels of the rousing hymn, just as Bennett Irving had explained so long ago, by starting off on a detailed account of creation and Adam and Eve. If the Bishop kept up the current pace, Makana figured, it would be minimum half-hour before he got into the on-this-earth part of the "progression." The "celestial" heavenly part lay beyond even that. And then you'd have to sit through whatever this Senator Tafai was going to say. Still, Coach Brock had so succeeded in locking everyone in that there was no way anyone wanted to miss any of it now, Makana included.

The vibration. Again. And again he tried to refocus. Maybe it was important. Maybe it was Kanoe Silva. Or even Ikaika himself. They must have *needed his input* at the meeting with the LG. He should have *been there.* Or what if it was Helen? Had something happened to Helen? He couldn't bear it. Maybe it was a text, and he could just read it right here as Bishop Tripp babbled on about paradise.

A text it was. And from Helen. Good. If something had happened, she would have called instead. But then he read it: MITIGATION REPORT?? Fuck! *Fuck!* He'd almost said it out loud. He'd forgotten to give her the copy of the archeological survey Ikaika had asked for—the one conducted at Dolphin Bay back when the plans for the five hotel towers had first been dusted off ten years ago. There were only a few copies of the mostly forgotten 288-page tome floating around, and Ikaika had probably wanted to share part of it with Hendrick. And frikken Makana—he could hear Helen put on her pidgin voice—frikken Makana wen' leave his copy in his truck.

They *did* need him! And why hadn't he just gone to the damned meeting like he was supposed to? Had it been that important to drive all the way up here to basically *look down* on all these Mormons while you waited for Coach Brock to deliver a speech someone would surely post on YouTube? And what do you do now? Do you just dig out and drive all the way into town, an hour away, and leave the Reverend Tom Watada here hanging in the process?

She'd texted twice, though, and much to Makana's relief, the second message let him off the hook: BURRIAL INVENTORIES? That meant that Helen had texted instead of calling because she knew he was probably already seated at the service, but that something had come up requiring a more specific look at the burial inventories.

Now far from locked in on such a meandering trip through the most familiar story in the entire Bible—the guy hadn't even gotten to the snake yet, for Chrissakes—Makana judged that he had a good forty minutes to get back to his truck to find the report, text Helen the information she needed, and return to his VIP seat in plenty of time to catch Coach Brock's speech. And he'd be *saving the day* downtown, for the hand-picked governor-to-be of the State of Hawai'i, no less. So he leaned over to let Tom know where he was headed, and then managed to excuse-me his way to the aisle before breaking into a low-step rush out the side.

Once out on the lawn Makana kept the pace up, texting Helen along the way—GOT IT—and crossing back over that wide two-lane promenade fronting the blinding white palace of the Mormon temple and thinking, despite his haste: what an incredible waste of space, this majestic boulevard, considering how jammed the little town was with house upon house upon house, but it was the Lord's road, after all, leading up to the Lord's temple, that oh-so-sacred piece of real estate there on the hillside.

And in the next nanosecond as the echoes of Bishop Tripp's amplified voice dissipated behind him, the image flashed through Makana's brain of the stars-in-her-eyes Samoan girl who'd led a tour he'd taken through that temple years ago—another PR stunt, where the Mormons had allowed the unwashed behind their sacred walls in the week following the building's last renovation and prior to its re-consecration—right now he could see her, leading his group to the "baptismal font," a tub built upon the backs of the statues of twelve oxen, where you could be the "proxy," getting baptized on behalf of your ancestors so they would be there *waiting* for you on the other side.

As he quick-stepped it down the narrow road, the memory of Makana's hour in that temple flashed by: the "creation" room, whose walls were covered from ceiling to floor in Biblical images of Eden, where members visited to receive "instruction." The earthly world—the mountains and pines of Utah, was what it had looked like. And finally, way up at the top of that white tower, a little box of a gleaming white room, a sparkling display of cut mirrors where you knelt in silence beneath a crystal chandelier that belonged in the lobby of the Lehua hotel, where you walked on hospital-white carpeting from the furniture section at Sears, and you contemplated…eternity. And that Samoan girl—she'd kept on saying it, even though it was just a tour and not a funeral like today: that death was "merely a part of the progression," that they even celebrated it.

No one involved with the tours could specifically tell Makana what was actually meant by "instruction." But he'd heard somewhere that Mormon rituals had been adapted from sacred Masonic Temple rituals, whatever those were. If you did the etymology you could quickly figure out that the Masons had originally had something to do with stone cutting, an ancient art that must have involved a lot of hammering and chiseling and sparks and sweat, depending on what kind of rock you were using.

Just last week some Tongans had pulled up at the house across the street from Makana's and started hammering and chiseling on a huge pile of volcanic rocks, real life masons, they were, hard at work on a rock wall they were building for his neighbor, hammer into chisel into rock and repeat.

In fact for some reason Makana could hear that same sound just now, that hammer into chisel into rock, like some whole tribe of Tongans out past the cemetery or up that old cane road was hard at work under this blazing sun. They must have been the only ones around, too, the whole place completely deserted, everyone at the funeral, just that sound, that hammer-chisel-rock, hammer-chisel-rock.

Except it also sounded like they were hammering on something else, too, hammering on…metal?

Makana picked up his pace, not wanting the next sound to register, but it did: breaking *glass*, shattering glass, and now someone starting to *yell*, to scream out in *pain*, and good thing he happened to be over here in time, here in time to save his truck from whatever these—

A white Ram 2500 king cab clogged the narrow cane road right *next to* his truck, both doors open and two men with their backs to him, both around his own height but much more solidly built—you could tell even with those baggy black shirts they were wearing, it all registered with a glance, the guy on the left had long black pants, too.

And was that some kind of cast on his foot? A…*ski boot?*

A single thought: *run!*

And then: I've got to fucking call somebody, call the police, and listen to that fucking *screaming!*

But Makana could do neither, his feet frozen to the ground because yes, these were indeed…bangers…indeed *playas*…all of them blazing away right before his eyes, committing an act of multiple murder.

Look at the one with the boot leaning on the open window of his door, leaned over to help support that cannon clicking away in his hands as he shifts his aim, that cannon with that long, long barrel…a silencer?…and *run!*

The empty shells pinging on the hard-pack road, bullets exploding through metal and smashing glass…the guy calmly pumping bullet after bullet after bullet into that big black Tahoe not ten feet farther up the road…pumping bullet after bullet after bullet. Just like the guy leaning on the driver's side door…

Run!…the long tube of another silencer…and is it all going to end right here?…more sounds coming from up the road…will it end right on the cusp of my impending directorship?—yes, even that thought jumped across his brain—end right here while Ikaika Nāʻimipono and the future governor of Hawaiʻi are waiting for me, and I'm just frozen here right when they *need me* downtown, my wife *needs me*, the mother of my unborn child *needs me*…*Please! Not when I have so much to live for!*

Helen!

Silence.

It had taken a matter of seconds. And then the man turned, the one with the cannon in his hand, the ski boot cast on his foot...*I'm begging you!*...he turned to get into his truck. He spun around and... hesitated?...squinted?...*Please!*...it was hard to tell...but mercifully he kept turning...jumped in...a hand reaching out to grab the door and slam it...the other guy jumping in behind the wheel.

The truck roared, and only then could Makana dive to the side of the road, dive and roll off into the tall grass, and there it went, the huge white truck, a blur of letters and numbers on the bumper, a B or an R, definitely a Z, a 7 or a 1, an 8 or maybe a 3, roaring off toward the highway, another shard of glass falling and shattering behind him, and after that the only sound Makana could hear was the heave and blow of his own frantic breathing.

Part Three

Invisible Waiter

The old Georgian mansion of a hotel may have looked like a Model-T in a roomful of Expeditions, surrounded by a forest of concrete in the shadow of the gleaming new Makani Kai Tower, whose stacks of blue-tinted windows rose up more than twenty stories above her shingled roof as part of the same joint-hotel resort property. But everyone still referred to the Lehua reverently as "The Grand Lady of Waikiki," like she was some kind of living being rooted in a romantic past, way back when guests were family, when they stayed for months at a time, having arrived at Aloha Tower by steamship, likely having known one another from years past.

Maybe it was just last season's visit to Waikiki. Or perhaps they summered annually in neighboring homes on Martha's Vineyard. Likely they'd attended the same prestigious New England prep school together before going on to Yale. Family! Vanderbilt-Carnegie-Rockefeller. The kind of (white) people who "traveled" back in that bygone era when the Lehua opened, all the way from the turn of the century on up through statehood. And if you wanted to infiltrate their old money ranks, well then, you'd better be Cecil B. DeMille or Rudolf Valentino. Marilyn Monroe or Joe DiMaggio. Babe Ruth. Bing Crosby. Gary Cooper. Because those were the kinds of people who lodged at the Lehua hotel back in that bygone era. Big people. Important people. Rich people, different from you and me.

But once commercial jet air travel ruined everything by letting the unwashed masses flood into Waikiki, the Grand Lady nearly fell apart. Before long someone had turned the Royal Salon, that incredible jewel of a ballroom fronting the beach, into…a coffee shop. Someone else had smothered her beautiful hardwood floors with garishly printed art-deco carpets, hidden her corniced moldings with asbestos tiles, stationed cigarette machines in her once-majestic open-air lobby.

It took a *yakuza*-connected kingpin named Masaru Ito, who'd bought half of Waikiki's beachfront hotels back in the eighties, to set things right. Ito-USA sent someone to the State office of Historic Preservation. Someone else dug up the original architectural plans. Old photos were solicited from dusty albums in every "good" building on New York's upper east side to help authenticate the decor. And soon everyone was marveling at how the historic landmark had been restored to "her original grandeur." For a mere couple of hundred dollars a night, guests could imagine that they, too, were *special*, were different from you and me.

But then the bubble that was the fabulous 1980s rise of the Japanese economy burst. The first Gulf War hit. The Asian financial crisis. 9/11. The Great Recession. The Japanese earthquake. Each one of them a cataclysmic event for the sort of vacationer who can afford to pay two and three hundred a night for a place to sleep.

On top of that, soon the (fat haole) guests began complaining about the rooms. No longer were they "enjoying a nostalgic trip into a bygone era"—an era that preceded the routine guzzling of 64-ounce tubs of corn syrup and half-gallon ice cream "volcano pies" for dessert—they were paying top dollar for cramped little boxes that lacked personal jacuzzis.

Ito-USA went bankrupt and was acquired, eventually, by a Wall Street sausage factory. Consultants were hired. The Royal Salon was turned into an upscale foodie joint of the sort that announced its pretentiousness with its casual sounding name: The Hibiscus House. The hardwood floors Ito-USA had liberated from those unsightly art-deco carpets were covered with plastic laminate meant to look like…hardwood floors. A glossy PR campaign was launched. And then…nothing happened.

It was decided that the Lehua herself had "matured" as a travel destination—a term that served as the industry's death knell. She was no longer "exciting." No longer "fresh." Today's travelers were looking for "a new experience." They were looking for a "new visitor product." They were looking for…The Makani Kai Tower.

"And I'd also like to congratulate this community for its vision, for its faith in a project that itself is just one more step in the dramatic improvements to Waikiki that began a decade ago in the Lewers and Beachwalk corridor, that continued with the refurbishing of the Royal Hawaiian Shopping Center, and that live and breathe before us today. All of this, taken together, has done more to enhance Waikiki's competitiveness than anything in the past fifty years. Ladies and gentlemen, as a world class visitor destination, Waikiki is back!"

Though it had to have been designed as a mighty bring-down-the-house applause line, no one was even listening. Here was Fred Simmons, the MKT's newly imported (haole) GM, belting it out to the thousand-or-so (haole) VIPs crowding the poolside area and the open lobby and the two surrounding restaurants. They'd even set up a little stage for him over by the ocean edge of the new infinity pool, and a podium flanked by one giant banner that read "Grand Opening" and another that read "Happy 115th Birthday, Lehua!"

The PA may have more than compensated for the roaring surf of reveling look-at-me "conversation" washing all around the infinity pool's sleek edges, not to mention the actual surf slamming into the seawall not ten feet from the pool—on Simmons went, about "innovative service" this, and "unique array of amenities" that, and "reviving the legend of the world's most famous stretch of sand." But while the mere GM—that lowly spec of glorified bellman—while he brayed on with the predictable service industry seminar lines, everyone else was engaged in the latest National Sport of Los Angeles: competing to see who'd come to Hawai'i the greatest number of times, preferably to do things like run a marathon, or see Pearl Jam, or attend a USC game, or watch the Lakers in pre-season practice.

As he caught snatches of the babble, Sean Hayashi recalled a U2 concert that had been scheduled the night before the Honolulu Marathon years ago—Christ, the whole combination was so LA you had white people walking up and down Waikiki sidewalks carrying suitcases and searching for rooms, so many of them had descended on the place all at once.

Tonight it looked like someone had lifted that entire Golden Circle section fronting the U2 stage at Aloha Stadium and dropped it right here on the infinity pool terrace.

So *LA* was it all that not a single local power broker or politician or even one of the few remaining kamaʻāina haole socialites had been invited to what amounted to the Money Party of the Year. You could tell as much with a look around, sure, but Sean's quests around the Capitol and Marisa's search through all of her hooked-in downtown contacts had not only failed to produce an invitation—they'd also confirmed that *no one* local was even attending.

That had left Sean only one option: his place on the Lehua's on-call list as…a waiter…and good thing he hadn't gone and quit for good after the trip to Macau had basically cemented his position as a fixer capable of anything on par with whatever Alan Ho had ever pulled off—and could you believe Sean had gotten the president of the state senate, the house speaker, and the frikken *governor* onto a private jet? At a moment's notice? All through a bunch of fortunate contacts, the right amount of *not giving a fuck*, and a stack of well gathered…intel? The first of it gathered right over there at the Hibiscus House as he waited on the great Alan Ho on that long-ago fortuitous night?

So (especially) once he'd found out *no one* had been invited (because yeah, you didn't exactly want Tony Levine or Darryl Kawamoto or any of the other players on Russell Lee's exploratory committee seeing you wearing a *nametag*), Sean just *had* to put in a call to see if they needed help staffing the great grand opening. He promised himself it would be the last time—my god, he'd already come so far *above* the world of nametags and uniforms—reasoning that money could flow from LA just as easily as it was starting to come from China, so why not see what you can…find out?

And *money* was indeed all you saw around this place: faux-casual faded jeans some designer had sold for a thousand dollars, "thrift shop" throw-over-and-skirt ensembles some other designer had authored for like five grand that would get worn *once*, plus all manner of botox and tucks and lifts on all the still-trying women in their fifties so vigorously competing with the surrounding *youth*. Though it wasn't exactly Bradley Zao kind of money, you could tell everyone in sight had dropped like ten-twenty grand just to be able to say they were here.

Bradley Zao kind of money. Among the Power Group that had traveled to Macau last week, Sean might have been the only one who knew how much more that meant than a ticket to Hawaiʻi for some must-attend party and a boob job for your aging wife. Bradley Zao! The guy was only 36 years old (Sean had looked it up), the same age as Sean himself. He defied everything Alan Ho had had to say about the tentative Punahou rich kid, the trust-fundie afraid to take a risk. Zao's father may have been one of the original Asian kingpins. But long before the old man had left him the reins to his empire—which is to say, when Bradley was still in his twenties—he'd begun purchasing "distressed assets" and building a little empire of his own, including the $2.6 *billion* Grand Dragon. Zao was sharper than anyone Sean had ever heard talk. And above all, there was no *Don't Give A Fuck* about him—that's how confident the guy was.

He didn't even *need* to not give a fuck.

"…this unique mix of the traditions evoked by the Grand Lady of Waikiki," the GM was saying, "with all the amenities of the cutting-edge tower rising into the blue skies next door." Never mind that far more of his audience was texting or snapping phone-photos of each other than listening, and true, now that you looked a little closer, many of them looked more like the knew-someone-who-got-me-on-the-list crowd than *money*. But hey, you never knew.

The best part was that tonight, the only one in the room with the slightest idea as to what to do with any of the blabber some drunken investment banker wound up throwing around to try and get laid for free was…Sean Hayashi. I mean, you'd think people were in their own living rooms, the way they could go on and on in front of you, the Invisible Waiter, about anything from a sensitive personnel matter at their workplace, to some secret strategy to undermine a competitor, to some otherwise embarrassing admission of the most personal nature, all with every relevant name on prominent display right out in the open as you hovered over them filling water glasses and clearing plates and so on.

And if Sean's final night of eavesdropping produced nothing on the level of what the encounter with Alan Ho had? At least there was the three-four hundred in cash he was bound to walk with. And if nothing else, too, there was the entertainment.

Just look at them all: the biggest bunch of trust-fund status-climbers you'd ever seen gathered in one place. If any of these people at all weren't trying to out-Hawai'i each other, it was because they forgot they were even *in* Hawai'i, so busy were they all with the usual task of preening and dropping names and, in this case, dutifully participating in the Grand Opening spirit of the event by trading thumbs-up evaluations of their gleaming new surroundings:

"It's just fabulous!"

"It's so elegant, and yet, at the same time…"

"It's like something out of a movie!"

"I really like the vibe here!"

Vibe! Sean wasn't one of those local guys who particularly hated haoles on sight or anything—even guys like Alan Ho, or Russell Lee, now that he thought about it, seemed to *tolerate* haoles more than anything else, while Sean himself usually didn't really care one way or the other. But *vibe*? The word just grated on him, like the speaker just didn't want to bother to really *explain* what s/he was talking about, but, well, you know what I mean. The vibe!

"I know! Me and my friends have been here for three days now, and it's such a great place to come and just *decompress*."

"Exactly!"

"The pool is so serene."

The pool is so serene. Never mind the tranquil blue ocean of the world's most famous beach, not ten feet away…go swim in the chlorine-soaked pool with hundreds of other sweaty haoles.

"S*oo* re*lax*ing!"

"And don't you just love the atmosphere?"

"Totally! Everything is just so immaculate! It's elegant, but at the same time it's just so…I don't know…laid back!"

"Exactly!"

None of this was dialogue, either—at least not in the usual sense of it being a unique conversation limited to two people. You could be standing on either end of the pool, or in the lobby, or over in the Hibiscus House, or sitting at your VIP table inside Alfred Hudson's Grille over there next to the lobby, or pretty much anywhere, and you'd hear the same exchanges.

"And I just love the vibe!"

On and on they went. Those two twenty-something guys over there in the "formal, but at the same time casual" solid-colored T-shits and black denim pants. Those two strung-out third-tier celebrity blondes aged by too many years on the LA party circuit. That guy with the purposefully messy hair from that reality TV show. That ancient Korean bikini girl from Hawai'i Five-0—what was she, like *fifty?* On and on they went. Exactly! Because, let's face it—it was far more entertaining to be confirming how important it was to *be here* than to be listening to some corporate caretaker who probably went to *UCLA* (rather than USC) try to game-show-host his way through a list of goals for "attentive yet un-obsequious service" and "laid-back sophistication." Really, weren't celebrity chefs enough? Did we really need celebrity hotel managers, too?

Exactly!

Neither did anyone bother to listen when "Aunty" Haunani Daley was trotted out to deliver a brief *Hawaiian Sense of Place* spiel designed to take full advantage of "our host culture" as another selling point for a glass-and-steel tower that could just as easily have been erected in... LA. "Aunty" Haunani was introduced as the "Cultural Liaison" for the Lehua's Makani Kai Tower, and she was Kam Schools, Downtown Marketing Firm, dad-went-to-Stanford all the way. Brushette and Hyde all the way, too—Susan Brushette had like a whole stable of muʻumuʻuʻd haku-lei-crowned Aunty Haunanis for these sorts of things—and sure enough, there she was (and leave it to Susan Brushette among *all* of downtown to score an invite here, even a work-related one), there was Susan herself, standing right up next to the stage with a look of approval plastered across her out-to-pasture-and-then-lifted newscaster face.

For a second Sean was jolted with fear: what if Susan *saw* him here?—but just as quickly he knew she'd be too busy glad-handing the reps from the LA firm that was in fact "handling the publicity" for the Grand Opening/115th Anniversary to even notice him.

On and on Aunty went, about the winds connecting with the sea connecting with the ʻāina—the land of her ancestors! On she went about the "aloha spirit," about *'ohana*, about the Hawaiian tradition of welcoming strangers from faraway places, and about how all of it would always translate into a unique kind of service here at the Makani Kai Tower that was sophisticated, but at the same time relaxing and laid back.

Sean himself may have been too busy to catch it all, except that after fifteen years his waiter gig had become so second-nature that he could pack seven drink orders into his head and weave through a crowd even as thick as this one with a full tray without fear of spilling anything on an aging pop star or someone. It was kind of fun, too, because he didn't at all *have* to be groveling around for tips like the rest of these poor lifers, who all suddenly seemed so far *down there* when compared to Sean Hayashi, facilitator of $400 million deals, one of the *handlers* of…the future governor of Hawaiʻi…and my god, had Russell Lee really known *nothing* of what he'd been headed for in Macau? And was that why he'd been able to basically throw it all on the line up there? Or was he *that* much of a gambler?

And yeah, now that Sean thought about it, Russ had actually gone and laid much of his campaign for governor on…Sean Hayashi. If that wasn't a major gamble (at least at the time), you'd have a hard time naming what was. And speaking of gambling, how on earth was Russell Lee ever going get all his fellow senators to ignore "the churches," as Tony Levine always called the gambling opposition, and vote along with him? And how the fuck—or, more important, *when* the fuck—when the fuck was Russell Lee going to deliver Ikaika Nāʻimipono?

Did he really know what he was doing, or was he gambling it all on that outcome, too?

Ikaika Nāʻimipono. Right after the beating Sean had taken at that disaster of a meeting at WCC, he'd spent several hours traveling through newspaper archives (the two dailies had once provided actual news, rather than syndicated accounts of mining accidents and earthquakes) to try to get a handle on the one man who still had a chance to stop this whole thing. He'd come away with a long list of Nāʻimipono's money quotes from over the years, spoken at neighborhood board meetings, at official UH gatherings, all the way back to when the big man had been nothing more than a boy standing futilely in the way of a bulldozer at work on the H-3 freeway.

What would *Ikaika* think of Aunty Haunani's little Waikiki history lesson to this crowd? A sellout! Or worse: colonization of the mind! It wasn't even Aunty Haunani's fault! She'd been conditioned by an oppressive capitalist system! She'd—

"Excuse me!"

Ah, duty calls!

"Yes, are you folks ready for another drink?"

"Oh my god! This place is fabulous!"

Sean sort of half-recognized this woman. Had she actually done something noteworthy in a film, or was it just some one-off appearance as a patient on *ER* twenty years ago? Either way, she'd already tied one on, her and the two idiots wearing those suit jackets over their white T-shirts—the ones both greeting him, the waiter, with a "Hey, Bro!" They both had their dark hair drowned in product and spiked in a self-consciously dorky way off to the side like some kind of sharp-peaked mountain range.

"You guys are all just so *nice!*" the woman went on. It was a bit of a relief, too—sometimes these rich haoles just forgot themselves and actually did *order* you around, but such behavior had recently come to smack of…insensitivity…towards the plight of the working class, particularly among these Hollywood types, and was being replaced by its opposite: buddying up to the "help." The emergence of thousands of wait help across the country blogging about the tipping practices of celebrity customers may have had something to do with it, but who knew?

As one of the few activities that put these people in contact with a flesh-and-blood wage slave (they would have no idea about the thick stack of twenties Sean would take home tonight), the ordering of a cocktail also doubled as an opportunity for a kind of anthropological adventure.

"I know it's like your job and everything to be nice," she said, "but you've all just got that, I don't know, that *aloha spirit!*"

"Thank you," Sean said. "We try to create that vibe here—you know, efficient and professional, but at the same time, friendly."

"Exactly!" She turned to her mountain head friends: "See! That's just what I was trying to tell you!"

"Right on, Bro!" one of them said, to no one in particular.

"Tell me," she said to Sean, "what's it like to *live* in a place like this?"

Here was a question that Sean had been addressing for years at the Lehua, about ten times a shift. He never knew whether to fuck with the person, or tell them what they wanted to hear, or tell them…the truth…the truth about choked freeways worse than even LA at eleven o'clock in the morning, about homeless meth addicts lining both coasts of Oʻahu, about nearly everyone his age with half a brain having to relocate to the mainland for lack of opportunity here outside of wage slavedom in the service industry or a dicey shot at real estate. The hard facts that Marisa and most of her friends still lived with mommy and daddy, or worse, were renting some retired local-Japanese couple's converted garage in Salt Lake for eighteen hundred a month.

The truth about public schools where kids routinely ordered their teachers around and nothing even approximating "learning" ever got done after about age ten, about how such a reality translated into a ridiculously easily manipulated electorate that could be swayed by a glossy "news" ad campaign into voting against their own interests. The truth that this was a place where, once you figured all this out, and once you made the right connections—even if you were making it up half the time like Sean was—if you had just enough *don't give a fuck*, then you could basically do…whatever you wanted.

"It's paradise," he told her. "What can I say?"

"See!" she said to her friends. "Just like I said: we've got to *move* here!"

"Right on, Bro!"

Under the guise of politely being in a hurry on such a busy night, Sean managed to get their orders and head towards the service bar inside Alfred's before losing his ability to maintain a straight face. He could hear Aunty Haunani going on now about the "Golden Age of Waikiki"—none of it as personal as it was supposed to have sounded coming from the mouth of one of those Waikiki museum pieces: a living, breathing real-life Hawaiian.

It sounded just like what Sean and the other lifers had been fed in the pre-service meeting this afternoon—led not by the banquet manager, but by some thirty-something mountain-range headed haole from the LA PR firm. Tonight they weren't just working, they were *performing*—the whole night would wind up on YouTube as part of a "stealth promo campaign."

They were to dispense with the word "aloha"—not an easy task, considering that the main purpose of the four-day orientation programs they'd all endured before ever being let out on the floor at the Lehua had boiled down to that single word—because the Makani Kai Tower, a marvel of modern architecture, was after a more sophisticated…vibe.

That is, the twenty-four story tower of glimmering glass whose top fourteen floors consisted entirely of über-luxury apartments with "nonstop" ocean views, apartments twice the size of your average suburban three-bedroom home and valued in the *eight* figures, and separated from the über-luxury hotel suites below by a "sky lobby" with its own "sky pool"—it was only "partnering" with the Grand Lady insofar that it could evoke the Golden Age of Waikiki, but in a unique and cutting-edge sort of way.

"This whole thing is a fucking joke."

Sean turned from the task of sorting his empty glasses into the rack in the Alfred's kitchen to see Eric Busey standing there right beside him performing the same task, but with the kind of world-weary look you always saw on working-poor UH grad students who'd recently swallowed some bullshit or other from their Marxist professors about "permanent class structures" and "illusion of social mobility" and on and on and on. A fucking joke—it was exactly the kind of thing you could expect from an Eric Busey, not two years off the boat himself and yet already having adopted the mantle of oppression nurtured by his "host culture"—a term Eric himself couldn't stand, a "corporatization of colonization," he called it.

"What." Sean immediately regretted this invitation the moment he issued it. He braced himself for the onslaught.

Eric surprised him, though, by staring wide-eyed and asking just one question, as though the fate of the world rested upon the answer: "Do you see a single person out there who isn't *white?*"

It had occurred to Sean that this haole-fest was far different from the Kam School/Punahou/'Iolani downtown-corporate-caretaker-lawyer-who-lives-in-Mariner's-Ridge crowd you always saw at NomFusion. And if you were going to put a celebrity chef's name on your new hotel's signature restaurant, wouldn't you call upon someone like Nom? Or Chai Chowarasee, or Roy Yamaguchi or Sam Choy or Alan Wong, before trying to land…Alfred Hudson? A second-generation German with six outlets of his designer Southwestern-Eastern fusion cuisine (*Mexican sushi?*) in the LA area alone, among 32 nationwide, three in Japan, and four in China? And wouldn't you hire someone like the Sons of Hilo to perform at your Grand Opening? Even some Jawaiian band would have been better than a haole DJ with an oxford shirt slung over his t-shirt like a dinner jacket spinning four-year-old West Coast hip-hop.

And of course no one from the Lege had been invited to "deliver a few remarks." Or the same City Council that Ito-USA had bought for a mere fifty grand worth of trash cans, and another fifty grand "donation" to the Waikiki Health Center. The usual heavy-hitters, the banker socialites, the local commercial real estate-ors—they'd all been shut out. Eric was dead-on. Not only was everyone in sight haole, but not one of them was even *from* here except for Susan Brushette, who basically amounted to Aunty Haunani's pimp. Not a single Outrigger Canoe Club or Honolulu Symphony Patron.

Still, Sean could hardly resist taking a good hard swing at the softball Eric had just tossed him, so he said: "Aunty Haunani?"

"Oh for fuck's sake, Sean, you know what I'm talking about! I don't mean her. And I don't mean any of those little twenty-year-old Asian trophy third-wives of those fifty-year-old VIP hedge fund managers. That VIP section—that's a joke, too. The whole PR thing is a joke. What, you invite a few Hollywood Squares-level celebrities to the party, and that's supposed to entice these high rollers out of their fifteen million dollar top-floor condos to *lower themselves* to eat in a *restaurant?*"

Hollywood Squares! Nice! But Eric did have a point about the celebrities—why else would you fly all of these airheads over here, likely at considerable expense, just for a single party? Well, maybe because you were talking about the kind of people—the owners of these places upstairs—who hired Bon Jovi and Aerosmith to play in their yards in their gated beach compounds over on Maui—maybe this celebrity contact had something to do with the status points they were all trying to accumulate now that they all had more money than anyone could possibly know how to spend. I had dinner with Christina Aguilera! She was so *down to earth!*

Eric wasn't finished: "And they're all *hedge fund managers*"—pronounced, *child molesters*—"they don't even *make* anything. I don't mind if Bill Gates or Mark Zuckerman or those Google guys or somebody buys this whole damned building—at least they *made* something, you know? They contributed! Even, like, LeBron James. At least he *entertains* us. But these people? They're all parasites!"

Sean managed to extract himself from this little lecture—ah, duty calls again!—but he knew that for the rest of the night Eric would be hounding him about how if someone could afford a condo in the Makani Kai Towers, that meant they also had a sixty million dollar compound on the Kohala coast, and one in Aspen, too, and probably another somewhere on the Mediterranean, and that they were just *hedge fund managers.*

He'd go on and on about how they'd shaken down the taxpayers for the $2.5 million necessary to replenish the beach fronting the infinity pool so that the structure would meet decades-old shoreline setback requirements, and how the sand had all washed right back out within a matter of months, on and on and on.

So Sean did his best to avoid Eric, which wouldn't be so hard considering how easy it was to avoid even Susan Brushette in this crowd, a good couple-hundred of them around the pool now doing the White Man not quite in time with the lazy cadence of some repetitive hip-hop groove. Plus, Sean himself had studied it all already, how Ito-USA had been able to push this whole thing through—they'd even absorbed a solid shakedown from the hotel workers union, who had vehemently opposed the project until Ito-USA agreed to include the hotel suites, thus preserving a handful of jobs for the union's dues-paying membership. You had to tip your cap. They'd done it! They'd been able to—

Accent? I know that accent.

Sean froze. It wasn't really…fear…I mean, he hadn't exactly been caught yet. But had his little intel-gathering jaunt into his nostalgic wage-slave past perhaps not been the greatest idea? Could it turn into… the card?…the card in the delicately constructed house of cards known as Sean Hayashi's career? Was it going to be the card that got pulled out, taking the whole precarious structure down with it? Because that accent—it had pretty much gotten ingrained in Sean's head over the past several weeks. And no, it didn't belong to some beaming glad-hander of a PR expert so intent on connecting with a whole new client base that she wouldn't have time to recognize…the help.

It belonged to a man much more relaxed at this moment, one who existed on a plane far above a perpetual networker like Susan Brushette. And if the owner of that accent so much as glanced up at this very moment, that might finally be the…card…that might be the moment Sean Hayashi gets exposed as a…waiter? Is that what you really do for a living, Sean? We had no *idea!*

The accent of course belonged to Michael Prescott, and the content of what it was now delivering ignited a little war in Sean's head, one where the prospect of his invisibility locked in battle with that—maybe it was indeed fear: fear of getting caught. Because Michael Prescott did indeed seem to be…networking…so why not just lean in and get some *intel*? You've got Michael Prescott *right here*, and what is it?

Is he really trying to come off as having superior knowledge as to how things were done around here…how things were different here in Hawai'i, there were certain channels you had to go through—at least, that's what you had to make them think!

There he was, Bradley Zao's Honolulu point man, right there in the VIP section at Alfred's, across from some plump fifty-ish haole dressed in a Jazz-age white dinner jacket-straw hat ensemble purchased from the Tropical Threads Boutique out in the lobby. Prescott himself was sporting the sort of Eve Yuen aloha shirt that had long served as the uniform for the kind of Merrie Monarch front-rowers who headed home after the competition's first hour. Under the rapt gaze of the two pieces of Asian eye-candy they'd brought along—third or fourth generation gold digger LA Chinese, if Sean was any judge—the two world-shakers went on exchanging important insights on this "new visitor product" and the "new concept" of such a "21st century" property and the "unique taste of luxury" it offered, and what such a thing portended for the future of Waikiki as a competitive destination for high-end travelers.

And quick! Turn away! He's looking up!

Sean put his head down and set to clearing glasses at the adjoining table, thinking, what the fuck is Michael Prescott even *doing* here, and did that mean he'd bought one of those eight-figure non-stop-view rich boy pads upstairs too? And who the fuck was this guy he was talking to? His new neighbor? Was this Grand Opening thing supposed to double as some kind of housewarming? Or was Prescott engaged in some kind of…meeting…with an investor…an investor with access to enough capital for second and third homes in Jackson Hole, a ranch in Montana, a Makani Kai Tower condo?

Sean had wondered why Prescott hadn't accompanied them all to Macau last week. If this was indeed some kind of meeting, then there was your answer. Bradley Zao, or even just Prescott himself—it didn't matter all that much—one or both of them had their eyes on far more than Dolphin Bay.

The surrounding party roar and that inane lazy hip-hop beat made it next to impossible to catch more than a phrase here and there, so

Lean In again locked in battle with Don't Get Caught, because how would it look to Prescott, to this wannabe-Hemingway here, to Bradley Zao when he found out his prime…facilitator…the man with all of the relevant…connections—that Sean Hayashi actually wore a *nametag* meant to hold him accountable to guests who complained about anything they felt like complaining about, who got you *written up* by some UH Travel Industry Management suit from San Diego interning as an Assistant Food and Beverage Manager?

Then again, here was a billion dollars talking to another billion dollars, talking about Hawai'i, talking about Sean Hayashi's *domain*, about Alan Ho's domain, Russell Lee's. Here was a *hedge fund manager*, and what that undoubtedly meant was Andover-Yale "gentleman's C's" and then a straight line into an I-banking training program on Wall Street in some firm related to the one his daddy had sold bonds for back in the eighties, and grandpa had sold commodities for back in the sixties, and great-grandpa had sold commodities for back in the forties (when he wasn't lodging at the Lehua for weeks at a time in a suite next to Bing Crosby's), and so on, all amassing a family fortune of such (multi-billion-dollar) magnitude that no one for generations on out would ever have to work again.

But of course you did indeed go to work. It was only right and proper. Plus, why not *do* something with all that wealth—Hawai'i seems like an untapped resource…a bit of an outpost, yes, but if enough of the *right* people moved here…well, how different would it be from the Vineyard?

"…as long as you humor them, you can get things done…"

What was that? What was Michael Prescott saying? Dare he lean in further? *Humor* them? What the fuck was he talking about? Humor them! Like he could have gotten *anywhere* so far without Sean Hayashi's help, without State Senate President Russell Lee. Come on, do you even *remember* that meeting at WCC? The one you basically ruined? *Humor* them? Are you kidding?

"…just have to convince them you believe it's a lot of money, is how I look at it…"

Huh? Was he serious? Now Sean couldn't tell. It could have just been some form of rich boy one-upsmanship, one old-money billionaire (and face it, Prescott had to have come from a "good" London family to have had any hope of marrying into the Zao dynasty), one old-money billionaire trying to play another. Could that have been it? Or had Prescott actually made some kind of inroad into a new...club, an East Coast Park Avenue-East-Hampton-Martha's-Vineyard club of the sort where the likes of Alan Ho were not even considered, let alone welcome. Was that it?

Right then the sky lit up with such an explosion of color and light and booming sound that a thousand heads at once swung towards the ocean, a thousand heads including Michael Prescott's, which swung in Sean's direction just as Sean's own gaze turned away and towards the light show—a fortunate reflex that kept his cloak of invisibility intact.

His heart raced, and faster still when he heard the voice behind him call out over the explosions of the Grand Opening fireworks, over the music, over the surrounding shouts, call out in that accent with its *Excuse me!* And once again, duty calls. But these particular very important people were going to have to wait for Eric Busey, or someone else, because this invisible waiter was headed off the floor for the last time.

OPENING DAY

That's what everybody called it, because that's exactly what it felt like: opening day! A pure clean slate that offered nothing but hope! The chance to come out…a winner!

It even sounded like the start of the football season. Every year, year after year, the third Wednesday in January—it gave you something to root for. A chance to dream, dream of…going *undefeated*…reaching a postseason bowl game. It set the clock ticking on four action packed months where you could *get things done*. The very bricks of the Hawaiʻi State Capitol radiated on Opening Day, when all partisan bickering would be cast aside. Everyone would come together in *celebration* of their common goal: to make Hawaiʻi a better place, a more sustainable place, a place where our keiki are educated and our kupuna taken care of, where our sons and daughters return after college to exciting new jobs, and to homes where they can raise families of their own. A place where our unique values thrive, the *spirit of aloha* first and foremost.

For one of the few times all year, both chambers would be packed, with one and all eager to be *where it all happened*, if only to be a part of launching that message of…hope!

This year it *looked* like the start of a football season too, what with all of these UH Warriors and assistant coaches and even Coach Brock himself roaming around and signing autographs for all these eager fans crowding the senate chamber, already as packed as Russ had ever seen it. It *sounded* like a football game, that decades-old up-tempo marching band version of the theme from *Rocky* blasting in from out in the rotunda.

The Warriors themselves were all dressed in sweat pants and their black game jerseys, many of them with their thick black hair tied back in ponytails, sunglasses perched on their foreheads just like their coaches, who all seemed to adopt the Stacy Brachman look: black pants and a long black Warrior polo shirt hanging over their ample stomachs about a quarter of the way to their knees like some kind of fat man skirt.

And the fans! Look at them all up there filling the balcony! Sure, the odd pocket of Christian Coalition Red was already gathering over in that corner, and the odd pocket of Kau Inoa black-and-red-clad Hawaiians were gathering over there in that corner, and some of the green in fact belonged to the Keep the Country Country haole environmentalists now gathering way over there. But you could hardly notice any of them, so flooded was the room with all manner of black and dark green T-shirts and polo shirts and authentic jerseys.

And while some of them clearly fell into the retired-public-servant, football-nerd, middle-aged-alum-skipping-work-for-the-day category, most of the Warrior faithful were here on official business—or, as official as the term "meet and greet" could cover, anyway, which was all the lobbying that ever really got done on Opening Day. (Opening Night, with its catered private parties at rented beachfront estates, was another story.)

Even State Senate President Russell Lee, who himself was wearing a black tie peppered with thumbnail floating icons of the Warrior H—Russ looked out on it all from his seat up next to the podium with the joy of a movie director watching some complicated scene come together just as he'd imagined it. True, Sean Hayashi had been the one to suggest it on the plane ride back from Macau, this business of bringing back Opening Day in its full festive form, and then Charles Uchida and even Nakayama himself had jumped right on board with the idea.

But Russ alone had come up with all the important…details.

First among them was to officially honor Ufi Tapusoa. And while Tapusoa may have personally put Russ in the hole by fifty grand, well, what a piddling sum that now seemed! And come to think of it, Russ had been back from Macau for nearly three weeks now and heard nothing from Lave Salanoa, or, for that matter, from anyone connected to his Pearl City game room tab. And what did any of that matter! It would all get taken care of soon enough! A hundred thousand dollars?

It was nothing! Not when compared to this…this *scene*…this wave of faces rising from the pit of the chamber, from the senators now seated with friends and family beside them on folded metal chairs, all the way up to the amphitheater above, a wall of Warrior black and green sixty yards long and ten rows deep.

Off to Russ's right sat the official draw that had filled the place: the whole UH starting defense, along with Stacy Brachman and his defensive coordinator. Right next to Coach Brock sat Tapusoa's father, it looked like, a small man in a white shirt and black tie, along with his mother and…two brothers?

Russ would find out when he hosted the family in his office following the day's speeches. There was Steve Foreman, the AD. Peter Varner, the UH President. Their wives. Over there within schmoozing distance to the players he could pick out Malia Chung from Kamehameha Schools. The UWP president, Stan Medieros. Fred Nesmith, the Hawaiian Electric CEO. Tammy Lim, the Honolulu mayor. There was Joseph Chinen, the HVCB Director. Lorna Park, the state senator from Makiki, whom Russ had tapped to chair the Tourism committee. Frank Ward, the Finance chair, next to Milton Tanigawa, Judiciary. There was Tom Reed over there, that idiot loudmouth Republican Talking Points haole representing Hawai'i Kai.

There was…*everybody*…even behind Russ, where three long rows of chairs had been set up on risers for Governor Donald Nakayama and the usual collection of visiting dignitaries: high-ranking officers from all four branches of the military, plus the Coast Guard, all in their dress uniforms; two of the three living former governors and their wives (the third, a woman, was now U.S. senator for Nevada); the heads of various state agencies; the Supreme Court justice there to swear in the newly elected members; the priests and the rabbi and the kahuna, and so on, all the way to Governor Nakayama's personally invited guest, a Chinese investor named Bradley Zao, who sat between the old man and Cliff Yoshida in a ten thousand dollar tailored suit that fit him so well it made everyone else in the entire hall look like they'd just rolled out of bed.

All of them were waiting, waiting in anticipation and excitement while must've-been-fifty students from the Kamehameha Schools Concert Glee Club serenaded them with a Hawaiian song Russ couldn't recognize (he'd start taking some Hawaiian classes any day now). And language aside, you had to be some kind of stone-cold cynic not to be moved by the sight of all these Hawaiian children lined up in matching aloha wear singing out at the start of something so…monumental—although you couldn't tell by looking at the mayor over there, or anyone else for that matter, everyone treating what only a few people in the room knew would constitute the (unofficial) launch of Russell Lee's campaign for governor—treating it as some kind of *pro forma* showcase.

Well just wait, ladies and gentleman! Just wait! This year you're not going to *believe* it. You have no *idea*.

The echoes of the choir's final song dissipated around the cavernous hall to spirited applause. The various holy men took turns blessing everyone and asking *ke akua* to grant the senators wisdom as they faced the tasks ahead of them and so on. The new members were sworn in—just two this year: a crotchety looking Republican haole from Maui who called himself "Skip" Warner and who immediately struck Russ as a Tom Reed Talking Points clone; and a legacy local-Japanese Democrat from Hilo named Jayden Kaneshiro.

Russ then introduced his "good friend," the Senate Minority Leader—this year it turned out to be a wet-behind-the-ears Samoan named Arthur Tafai, an Afghanistan war veteran in his early thirties (he looked like a soldier, too: short, thick in the chest, buzz-cut hair, his reddish aloha shirt completely free of wrinkles), and as far as Russ knew, a religious conservative (but weren't they all) who'd gotten elected what, a week ago (or so it seemed—the guy had in fact been around for two years already) whom Russ had buried on the Military Affairs Committee.

The guy went on predictably about making tough choices about this or that social program and calling on the Senate leadership to ease the burden on the state's "small business owners" and "entrepreneurs" and so on, "individual" this and "so taxpayers can hold onto their own hard-earned money" that, and all Russ could think was, no wonder these idiot Republicans never get anywhere in our state. Sure, the guy may have sounded a bit like old Samuel Lee and his pronouncements against laziness, but nowhere in the speech did Russ hear even a hint of a collective us-guys 'ohana, of educating "our" keiki, of caring for "our" kupuna. And, like, let's *get on with it* already.

At last Tafai finished, and Senate President Russell Lee, University of Hawai'i Class of 1986, former UH linebacker—he stepped up to the podium and surveyed the faces of his colleagues, his fellow Hawai'i citizens, his—dare he even think it? And why not!—his supporters in his run for governor!

He was instantly flooded with…the buzz!....and with a sense of pride like none he'd ever experienced. Of course he'd delivered opening day speeches before, but never like this! Here it was, the test run of his first (unofficial) stump speech! It was really happening! And was that Tom Watada over there? Dressed in his formal black with the Roman collar? Yes it was! Next to Ikaika Nā'imipono? Aunty Maile Chang? Yes indeed! As he gazed out upon all of those faces, once again Russell Lee was…in love…yes, *in love*, even with Arthur Tafai over there, because watch, watch what was about to happen!

"Ladies and gentlemen, aloha kākou," he began, and a strong choral response greeted him back. "I have to say, I'm overwhelmed with joy, and with a sense of hope, to see all of you gathered here today." Pause. "And I realize that the main draw today may not have been a speech about our plans for the next legislative session, but…" A round of polite laughter. "Particularly for a few of you up there in the back row," he said, thinking now that it wouldn't hurt to start connecting himself— if not his entire candidacy—to Ufi Tapusoa as soon as possible, and as often. Right on cue someone shouted out "Ufi!" and those around him responded with laughter. Russ acknowledged the little salute with a smile and said, "And I promise you, we, too, are filled with excitement about honoring our Warrior brother."

Some more shouts, and another smile from Russ, who lifted his hand as if to say "I know it's tough to contain such excitement! But give me a moment!"

In fact he said, "But in all seriousness, in these difficult times, in the coming legislative session, we would all do well to draw on the kind of perseverance, strength, and perhaps most importantly, the ability to work cooperatively as a respected teammate that we all saw embodied in someone like Ufi Tapusoa."

He hadn't meant that one as an applause line, but here they were, all around the room, clapping! And Russ had just made it up right on the spot! Susan Brushette hadn't even typed it into the teleprompter! Just look at Stan Medieros over there, clapping wildly! And Lorna Park! (Well, she'd *better* be clapping, given the fact that Russ had assigned her that prime chair appointment to the Tourism committee.) And look at Tapusoa's father over there, and come to think of it, would the father do a taped endorsement at some point? Someone should check into it. Anyway…

"Yes, we will need to draw on this spirit of strength and cooperation as we face the tremendous challenges ahead of us this session." And with that, the hall fell into a dutiful let's-just-politely-sit-through-this-speech silence, and Russ tried his best to affect a somber let-me-level-with-you tone as he began reading from the teleprompter: "The economic crisis facing the rest of the nation and indeed the world has not fallen short of our golden shores. It has been hitting us harder than most everyone else, as the Council of Revenues has again predicted a deficit for the coming biennium that numbers more than two billion dollars. *Billion.*" Dramatic pause. "That is a major hit to our general fund over even last biennium, when revenues fell by more than fifteen percent." Pause. "It is nothing short of an economic crisis." Pause. And that did it, that simple recitation of numbers—the *billion* and the *fifteen percent*—it was like turning some kind of release valve. The jovial atmosphere of a Warrior celebration began to leak out of the senate chamber, because now it was time to get down to business. State Senate President Russell Lee was here to *lay it on the line.*

And it was working, too: a look around the crowded hall was enough to tell Russ he *had* them, they were *locked in.* And *two billion dollars*—who wouldn't be locked in? Even Tom Watada up there seemed to be giving Russ credit for being so honest about the challenges facing the state. So onward he marched, through the usual grim statistics on homelessness, on unemployment this, on businesses closing that, on tuition rising the other, all of them marching along with him, until at last the great hall was completely robbed of any signs of the excited buzz that had been charging it only moments ago.

Perfect.

"Our state agencies have tightened their belts about as much as they can be tightened," Russ went on, the ideal segue into the recycled populist appeal Trina Hyde had so expertly inserted into what was, so far, an entirely recycled speech. "We were lucky, again," he said, "with last fiscal year's budget, to keep all of our keiki in the classrooms for a third straight year. But we're hurting. All across the state. Everyone from the farmer up to his knees in mud on a Kauaʻi taro field, all the way to the bank manager in a boardroom at Pauahi Tower, our dedicated teachers, our law enforcement agents who put their lives on the line every day for our safety—everyone is struggling. And this session the legislature will have to come together like never before. To make the difficult choices. To prioritize. To meet these incredible challenges, and to serve the people of Hawaiʻi!" This was an applause line, but what scattered clapping it generated quickly died into silence. Good.

"And so I stand before you as Senate President and *pledge my word* that you can hold *me*, hold *me* personally accountable for bringing this legislative body together to meet all of these challenges!" More half-hearted clapping, and then silence.

Now. It was perfect. He'd done it. Everyone in the room, all, what? A thousand-plus of them? Everyone thinking the same thing, which was this: here we go again. You could see it on all of their faces: Another bullshit speech from the Senate president. So Russell let it sit for a while, the silence.

He let it sit for a long time, until people started getting visibly uncomfortable, their heads turning this way and that, everyone wondering if something had like, gone wrong with the teleprompter. Malia Chung seemed to be urging him on from way over there. Peter Varner had turned to whisper something into Coach Brock's ear. The only ones among them who did have any idea what was going on were Frank Ward, Milton Tanigawa, and Lorna Park, the newly appointed chair of the Tourism committee. Ward and Tanigawa were even sharing smug smiles, waiting for Russ to drop his bomb. And look at Lorna Park in that red power dress of hers, that red get-the-Chinatown-vote-for-a-Korean-woman dress of hers, her arms folded, a wry smile.

Finally Russ gave them all a smile and said, "You know the rest, don't you." This was met with a collective murmur, a few surprised looks. "You've heard this speech before," Russ went on. "You've been hearing this speech for over twenty five years: 'And Senator Tanigawa is going to spearhead the push to fix our education system,' or 'Senator Ogawa, our chair of the committee on higher education, is going to work with our new UH president to bring a first-class learning institution to Oʻahu's Leeward side,' or 'Senator Park, our chair of the tourism committee, is going to work with the Hawaiʻi Visitor's and Conventions

Bureau on a new and innovative plan to increase visitor arrivals and spending over the next fiscal year,' you've *heard* all of that."

Russ paused again, and the great hall was now quieter than if it had been empty, over a thousand people hushed in rapt attention: Was he really just coming out and *saying* it? Saying it *honestly?* "Sustainability," he went on. It rhymed with *bullshit*. "Protecting agricultural land for future generations." *Bullshit*. "Ceded lands for Hawaiians. Ensuring public confidence. Partnering with the private sector. Energy initiatives. Diversify the economy. Creative budget solutions. Oversight committees." *Bullshit*. All of it, Russ's tone proclaimed, nothing more than the usual Opening Day bullshit.

Looks of disbelief were flying all over the chamber now: What is he *doing?*

"You've heard them all before," he said. "All of them good ideas. But let's step back for a moment and ask ourselves, why have we been hearing the same exact speech for the past twenty five years? Why are we always forced to meet such 'tremendous challenges'? Why are we always in the middle of a 'crisis'? *Always*. Always a *crisis*. For twenty five years. 'Limited funds.' 'Falling revenue.' 'Unmet needs.' Always. Why is that?"

He paused some more, letting the implied word creep into everyone's head before he finally let it drop: "I'll tell you why: money. I'll say it: *money*. We have a multi-billion dollar industry here that leaves next to no money behind." This bold statement was met with a round of murmurs: did he really *say* that? "Look, beyond the crumbs offered by the Transient Accommodations Tax, and the wages and tips for a handful of dedicated service employees—and I used to be one of them, hauling banquet tables around the Lehua back when I was putting myself through law school, so I know how valuable even those few jobs are. But beyond that? Nothing."

The room was silent again, a type of silence that led Russ to believe they all wanted to shout out "Ho!" in disbelief, but were too shocked to do so. Talk about slaying a sacred cow! Did he just *say* that?

"Now, I can't stand up here and tell you we have an immediate solution to this perennial problem," and here he did indeed go into the usual Opening Day shout-outs about how during the coming session, Senator Ogawa would work on this challenge, and Senator Ng would work on that challenge, and Senator Cabral would work to meet the other challenge, and so on, all in the face of *declining revenues*, a term delivered in as sarcastic a here-we-go-again tone as Russ could muster.

"Declining revenues!" Russ said again. "Creative solutions!" pronounced *nonsense*. "Now as I said, over the short term, meaning this next session, there isn't much more we can do beyond the usual 'tightening our belts' and 'doing more with less' and the rest of it. But haven't you had enough of that?"

"Yeah!" someone shouted from up in the balcony, and to Russ's delight, a handful of others joined in.

"I know I have. And over the long-term—and by 'long term,' what I really mean is that by the next legislative session, is when you'll begin seeing results—over the long term, we do have a solution. We have a very creative solution. It's called 'More Money.'" This drew some laughter, and then Russ went on: "I'm talking about the self-contained resort project that's in the works at Dolphin Bay."

Another murmur.

"Sure, you may be thinking, 'Here's the usual trickle-down from an outside development project, the usual construction-jobs-creation thing plus some menial hotel jobs, and the token TAT tax, and then the bulk of the money winds up leaving our shores, and how can something like that possibly be of much help? That's what the Disney resort was supposed to do.'" That little pronouncement almost did bring a "Ho!"—Did he *say* that?—in shock at the honest reference, by name, to the latest "jobs creation" resort project that had indeed fit Russell's cynical description to a T, having hired as many mainland community college dropouts eager for the chance to "live" in "paradise" for ten dollars an hour as the locals whose "community" it had promised to "anchor."

"Well I've seen that movie. I've been watching that movie for forty years. I've had enough of that movie." Russ paused again as the room's rapt silence returned. "What I'm talking about is a much different movie. What I'm talking about is a unique partnership between the State of Hawai'i and TsengUSA." Here he introduced Bradley Zao, seated next to the governor, as a "respected investor from China" who was ready not only to "invest a substantial amount of capital in Hawai'i's future," but also to "share the revenue" equally with the state, and to work directly with the hotel workers union and UH's Travel Industry Management

School to tap local employment resources for *all* positions, including substantial management positions. Then Russ succinctly laid out how a new state agency would be formed to partner with Tseng USA to make such a vision a reality, taking a moment to pointedly look across the crowd at Ikaika Nāʻimipono as he did, and yeah, he'd find Ikaika the moment this was all through and the two of them would finally make arrangements to just sit down like braddas and hash this thing out.

"In other words," he said, "much of the money generated by this development, both as it's built and long into the future, will stay here." This line was met with an energetic line of applause that surprised Russ a bit—was this really working? He plowed on: "And let me try to give you an idea as to how much money we're talking about. Dr. Zao's company currently owns eight properties on a little resort island off the coast of China."

Russ tried his best to paint Macau's smog-choked city of blazing sky scrapers as a tranquil island paradise, and then he dropped the hammer: "Last year those properties alone generated an income of eleven billion dollars. *Eleven billion dollars.*"

He let that hang in the air a good long time, and then said, "Our current revenue projections for Dolphin Bay as TsengUSA has planned it are *four billion dollars*. Annually. Under the proposed revenue sharing plan Dr. Zao is offering the State of Hawaiʻi, that leaves us with a constant revenue stream of two billion dollars—a figure that is equal to the budget deficit we're currently facing. What that means is that this partnership will wipe out the current deficit *all by itself*, and forever guarantee that we never, ever, face another crisis."

Russ let the murmurs make their way around the crowded hall, and then he fit the last part in, in the form of another collegial shout-out: "But for all of this to work, we are counting on the diligence and leadership of Senator Lorna Park, chair of the Tourism committee, who will be taking up the important measures to set up the necessary state agency. Along with Senator Milton Tanigawa, the Judiciary Committee chair, and Frank Ward, the Finance Committee chair, Senator Park will also be working hard to craft legislation that will allow legalized casino gambling at Dolphin Bay."

"Ho!" this time they couldn't help themselves: it rang out all around the room, a thousand strong: "Ho!" And who on earth is this Bradley

Zao character anyway? And how much is Russell Lee getting under the table for all this? Can you frikken *believe* it?

"My fellow senators," Russ said, "invited guests, Governor Nakayama. We've been talking about this for more than thirty years now, and the time for talking is over. The time for legalized gaming in the state of Hawai'i is *now*."

A good roaring surf filled the hall, and under other circumstances Russ may have been concerned that it would drown out his entire speech. But right on cue, almost as quickly as they'd begun, the murmurs, the internal debates, the immediate how-many-times-has-*this*-one-been-tried-before trains of thought—they all receded as though someone had flipped a switch, because, well, someone in fact *had* flipped a switch, and banner the size of a theater curtain, two stories high and covering the entire wall behind Senate President Russell Lee and emblazoned in Warrior black and green, and yes, with the number 58—it began to unfurl before their very eyes.

Susan Brushette and Trina Hyde had nailed it! Right at the very moment when the crowd's natural sense of here-we-go-again cynicism was about to rob the whole speech of its sense of honest hope, here came *the moment we've all been waiting for.*

"As you know, we had two things to accomplish this morning," Russ said, "and now I'm going to get to the important one." All around the great hall, faces were glued to the giant 58. Even Arthur Tafai over there couldn't help himself: look at him flash a go-team smile right at… Tom Watada! It was impossible not to respond in kind—whether you really *were* getting wrapped up in the moment, or just unwilling to stand up to the rising tide of social pressure, you just had to tap into your inner Warrior. Everywhere Russ looked: 58, 58, 58! Ufi Tapusoa! And what was that? Something about a casino? Well, what, did the senator say something about four billion dollars or something? This politics thing, I don't really get it sometimes, but it sure sounded like a good idea, this thing about "partnering" and "sharing" and all that, plus like four billion dollars or whatever.

And look at that! It's Ufi Tapusoa's number!

"Opening the legislative session," Russ went on, "and honoring our fallen Warrior brother—I don't think there's any doubt as to which of the two is more important. So at this time I'd like to invite Caleb and Jacinta Tapusoa and their family, and Coach Stacy Brachman and the rest of our Warrior brothers—I'd like to invite you all to join me up here."

The room erupted into the hard static of a thousand people clapping, a sound punctuated by cheers and hoots and whistles as the Tapusoas and the mighty Warriors made their way up and surrounded Senate President Russell Lee—and did he just say something about gambling?—surrounded him at the podium, ten Warriors in all, the entire starting defense with one glaring exception, ten of them along with Coach Brock and four assistants, well over two million dollars of the state budget right there, and that's not even counting the players. But well, didn't Lee just say something about covering the deficit? About *billions* of dollars? Whatever!

Even as they all stood together it continued on, this incredible wall of sound, and now people were standing, the whole room on their feet, a long and sustained standing ovation. On it went, and now the deep chant began to fill the room, the deep "ooooh!" of the man's name, of Ufi, of *Ooo-fee! Oooo-fee! Oooo-fee!* Russ could see people lifting a finger to their eyes, pulling out tissues, wiping away tears, and four billion dollars? Did he say something about covering the budget deficit? Some Chinese investor? Hey, I wonder if that would translate into more football scholarships….hmm…so we could compete with USC, for a *national championship*. Go Warriors!

At last Russ lifted a hand, and once the cheering finally subsided and everyone took their seats, he began all over again: "Ladies and gentlemen. Fellow senators. Governor Nakayama. President Varner. Distinguished guests. And UH Warrior fans"—with that another sustained cheer filled the hall—"we are here today to honor our brother, the UH career leader in tackles," another cheer, "the UH single-season record holder in tackles," a cheer, "the UH single-season record holder in quarterback sacks," another cheer, "and this, too, unofficially: the UH career leader in *points scored* by a member of the defense," another cheer, and Russ paused to let Tapusoa's prowess as an all-around player sink in. "Three-time All-WAC, two-time All-American, and *my brother* in the fraternity of UH linebackers, Ufi Tapusoa!"

Again the *oooooooooo-feee!* chant, and the crowd stood, and the cheering lifted off, and oh, wasn't this rich! Trina Hyde had nailed it back in that planning meeting last week. Sure, she was married to one of these $90,000 Coach Brock bag carriers—a running back's coach for God's sakes, if Russ remembered correctly, for a team that never ran the ball—but she'd *nailed* it. It had been right after Cliff Yoshida had spelled out all the opposing arguments that would start spinning through everyone's brain the moment Russ dropped his casino bomb on them, all the usual stuff about crime and gambling addiction and families losing their homes to foreclosure because daddy just gambled away the monthly paycheck—all that plus the "unique sense of place" nonsense, that canard that Hawai'i drew the kinds of wholesome tourists who wanted to *get away* from such questionably moral pursuits as gambling.

The opposition from the churches—and Russ would get Hayashi, who right now was over in the house watching Charles Uchida's speech, to look into this church opposition thing. But then Trina Hyde had piped up. She'd explained how Russ would be able to use all this Ufi Tapusoa stuff to whip up the crowd—a crowd no doubt filled with weekend football gamblers at that—he'd be able to whip them up into such a frenzy that their brains would be so filled with delirious joy and pride that there wouldn't be any *room* for the kind of cynicism Cliff was imagining. Casino gambling? Sure! Sounds like a great idea! Go Warriors!

And she'd been right! Just listen to them! *Oooo-fee! Oooo-fee! Oooo-fee!*

Again Russ lifted a hand, and once the delirious cheering subsided, he read out a proclamation—the very same proclamation, he told the crowd, that his good friend House Speaker Charles Uchida was at that moment reading in the opposite chamber:

"Whereas, football Warrior Ufi Tapusoa, number 58, has so upheld the values of strength, fairness, leadership, and honor that constitute the core values of University of Hawai'i athletics, and," here Russ paused to allow for a round of cheers.

"Whereas, Ufi Tapusoa personified the concept of 'student athlete,' remaining academically eligible and on track to graduate on time for the whole of his tenure at the University of Hawai'i, and," another pause and more cheers.

"Whereas, in his conduct on the field, in the classroom, and in his community, Ufi Tapusoa has served as a role model not only for his teammates and the University of Hawai'i Football Program, and not only for our state's youth, but for every citizen of the state of Hawai'i, therefore," still more cheers, and louder now, and Russ gamely plowed on, "therefore, Be it then resolved that from this day forward, no University of Hawai'i player in *any sport* shall be issued the number 58, and further," an eruption of cheers! "And further, and further." Shoots, he just had to stop and wait it out, the cheering. "And further be it resolved that from this day forward, the first Saturday of December, so as to coincide with the final regular season game on the University of Hawai'i Warrior schedule, shall in perpetuity be declared 'Ufi Tapusoa Day.'"

Ooo-fee! Ooo-fee! Oooo-fee!

It all rained down as Russ presented a koa plaque with the proclamation mounted in engraved gold to Coach Brock to be hung in the Warrior football offices, and a duplicate plaque to Tapusoa's parents, whose faces, along with Coach Brock's, were now streaked with tears. Cameras flashed all around for the photo-op shot, Tapusoa's ten teammates looking on proudly in the background, and at last the Warrior contingent filed from the dais, again to a prolonged standing ovation.

"Ladies and gentlemen, I'll have to ask you to allow me to step back for a moment from my speech and just say this: I don't think I've ever been more proud to be a legislator for the state of Hawai'i." Russ hadn't really meant this one as an applause line either, but everyone was so wound up that the applause rained down anyway.

"And yes, we have indeed suffered a tremendous loss, having a young hero of ours, a son of our islands who was shaped by our most precious values, values we hold dear—having such a life of hope taken from us, well, in many ways such a thing challenges us all to come together, to help one another come to terms with this loss, and to move on through mourning and into the celebration of that life, as we have done here today." Russ was aware that he was starting to sound like some kind of preacher at a funeral, but so be it. "Coming together, a spirit of 'ohana, of 'us-guys,' if you will—if there's anything that defines us here in Hawai'i that separates us from other places, places where people have gotten too busy and too wrapped up in their individual pursuits, it is our spirit of *coming together*. It is the unique Hawaiian value of *lokahi*. And let me tell you, in the coming months, this legislative body will need to draw on that spirit of cooperation like never before." This line drew yet more applause, everyone in the room still standing.

"And in that spirit of coming together, we have a little surprise for you today." Everyone looked on expectantly. "Some of you may remember an old Opening Day tradition we used to have in more…prosperous times." A few of the veteran senators and their aides knowingly nodded their heads. To them Opening Day had once been right up there with Honolulu City Lights at Christmas, with the Punahou Carnival, and even the Merrie Monarch. "Back before our state was in permanent economic crisis," Russ went on, "before it started to, well, *look bad* to be having a party down at the Lege when so many of our brothers and sisters were struggling with pay cuts and furloughs and the rest of it, we used to treat Opening Day as a proper celebration, local style." Russ had in fact been among the Opening Day veterans opposed to the idea of…*toning things down* was what they'd called it back in 2008. "And as all of you know, it is impossible to have a local celebration of any kind without food."

A round of appreciative hoots from the top of the gallery, and more laughter. "That's the Hawaiian way, isn't it?" he said with a smile. "Well let me tell you, prosperous times are on the way back!" Applause. "So we invite all of you upstairs to talk story with us about your concerns, about what we have planned for the session, about whatever you want. But most important, go eat!" A round of collective light-hearted laughter, another chorus of hoots from above. "Ladies and gentlemen, this year's legislative session is now officially open. Alo-o-o-ha!"

"Alo-o-o-ha!"

The whole thing, it was working! Russ could *hear* everyone's thoughts as they filed out of the exits: Gambling? Yeah, yeah, yeah. Whatever. Casino on the North Shore? Sounds like a good enough idea. And that Russell Lee—hoo, he's fired up! What'd he say, anyway? Something about revenue. Jobs. Some Chinese guy. Billion dollars. Whatever—lets go make plate!

And the plate? The food? Though the Opening Day tab had never been picked up by the taxpayers, and someone *had* pointed out that Chapter 91 of the Administrative Procedures Act would have something to say about such blatant lobbyist expenditures, Cliff Yoshida had *guaranteed* that because of the complexity of the process, no one would ever wind up being fined or punished in any way if they simply just *didn't bother* reporting it.

And that wasn't even the best part about the food. The best part was this: the festivities had indeed returned, but without catered pupu platters from NomFusion courtesy of Starwood Hotels or Ito-USA. No goody bags from See's Candy courtesy of the United Workers. No flower arrangements courtesy of Hawai'i Reserves Inc. Sure, there'd be Yanagi Sushi in every office upstairs. Hundreds of dollars' worth. The spreads would be unprecedented, catered not only by Nom, but by Sam Choy and Chai Chowarasee and Alan Wong and Roy Yamaguchi and a host of other top chefs, including even Alfred Hudson.

Russ had made sure to have every office stuffed with more flowers than a mafia funeral. But they'd kept the whole thing under wraps, this revival of Opening Day, just so no one else could get in on what amounted to an orgy of outright gastronomical bribery.

No, this time all of it had been paid for by a single company: TsengUSA.

It shouldn't have been that hard to find him up here. Yeah, the Capitol's fourth floor balcony was packed like…Aloha Stadium…with meeters and greeters and glad-handers galore—hungry ones at that—but aside from a few of the football players, a couple of those Kau Inoa sovereignty fanatics, a few of those suit-wearing heavies with the cords stuck into their ears that made up the governor's security detail, a handful of the plainclothes HPD, and Russ himself, there wasn't a Hawaiian among them.

You'd think Ikaika Nā'imipono—big as he was, too—he'd be standing right out in this bubbling swarm. And Russ had to find him before all this Opening Day *possibility* began to dim on what he'd just so effectively sketched out in that incredibly rousing speech.

Really, if ever there was a time when even Ikaika could have been softened up enough to be approached—and that's all Russ had in mind: just *setting up* the real bradda-bradda talk story with the man—it was right now.

And after they set it up? Well, if Russ had managed to get Cliff Yoshida to roll the dice on an unadvisable campaign for governor, if he'd been able to wedge something even *better* than an official endorsement out of Governor Donald L. Nakayama, if he'd gotten an Asian godfather like Bradley Fucking *Zao* to basically surrender *half of his four-billion-dollar enterprise to the State of Hawai'i*, then of course he'd be able to reason with his old football brother.

But Ikaika was nowhere to be found in this sea of...*charm* was indeed what it was, flying around all over the place up here...and briefly Russ wondered if one had to be an expert at turning on his own beaming face, for no particular reason, in order to catch on whenever anyone else was trying to do the same thing—if you needed to be in the Charm Club yourself to be able to tell how Senator Cockburn over there was... smiling!...at that fat DOE lifer in that maroon May Day at Nanakuli Elementary suit-dress-thing.

And look at Senator Ward in that bullet proof suit of his over there, watch him turn to...is that Fred Nesmith? From Hawaiian Electric? Indeed it is! And Nesmith is getting the exact same look of *honest recognition and concern* Ward just gave that the enviro-haole behind him. How's *that*?

"Hello! Welcome, everybody!" And now here it was spilling out of Russ's own mouth for the line forming in front of his office door. "Help yourselves! Go make plate!" And well, maybe it was just that kind of day, where you just naturally coaxed maximum wattage out of your own *smile!*

Just like...Tammy Lim...the Honolulu mayor over there, shaking hands and gazing into the eyes of that round retired Department of Transportation Highways Division secretary, the one wearing the throw-back Devon Bess jersey in the Coach Brock Fat Man Skirt mode. Look at the mayor: rooted to her spot, intent on making the woman feel...important! Listened to! Valued! By the mayor herself! And what *was* the mayor even doing here anyway? What did the City and County have to do with the opening of the State Legislature?

Of course the question answered itself the moment it formed: What politician with half a brain *wouldn't* be over here taking advantage of the I'm-Your-Public-Servant love-fest known as Opening Day? And thank God all the necessary City and County permits for TsengUSA's project had already been obtained by the property's prior owner, because Mayor Lim over there—*listening!*—she of the perpetual clean-up-the-sewerage, protect-the-'āina platform, was just the sort of person who would have come out hard against the Dolphin Bay project.

"Great speech, Senator!"

Russ turned to see…Coach Brock himself! Right here! In the flesh! That hottie Texas cheerleader third wife of his hung on his arm, beaming a Crest-worthy smile of her own right up at Russ. A trail of middle-aged men clutching sharpies and miniature replica Warrior "H" helmets followed in the great man's wake.

"Just trying to rally the troops, Coach!" Russ said. "We've got a real fight ahead of us!"

"Well it looks to me like you've got what it takes to turn this state around!" said the $1.1 Million Dollar Man. "Keep up the good work, Senator!" And with that, Coach Brock and his entourage were carried off down the hall by the ebb and flow of the happily bantering crowd… the crowd…and for fuck's sake, Ikaika had to be in here *somewhere*, because, well, how do you like me *now*, Ikaika? How do you like my *four billion reasons* all stacked up to change your mind? Let me tell you about a stage full of spent Hawaiian drug addicts dancing for the…approval… of the likes of most of these "Hawaiian at Heart" people now roaming the Capitol halls for free food. Let me tell you my plan for being their *bootstraps* Hawaiian, their hardworking Hawaiian, the one they can congratulate themselves for voting for, just so I can turn around … and *help our people*.

Me and you, Ikaika. *For da boyz!*

Hawaiian at Heart! And if it isn't Mista Hawaiian at Heart himself, right over there with that plate piled high, all full of *charm*.

Fucking Hendrick.

The guy was already being treated like some kind of Johnny-on-the-Spot hero, and all after just three days as the acting gov while Nakayama was off in Macau. A couple of haoles get lost hiking in Waikāne (how you could get lost in the mountains was another story—all they had to do to get out was *walk downhill*), and Hendrick calls in the National Guard, committing all kinds of resources and putting a couple of helicopter pilots at tremendous risk. Of course the whole thing is captured on the news like he'd driven the damned choppers himself. Three days, and Hendrick's entire eight-year do-nothing record is forgotten, and with or without Nakayama's (semi)endorsement, and Bradley Zao's backing, the race for the primary remains…a toss-up?

Thankfully that line of thought was drowned out by a *herd* of these trough-feeders elbowing their way out of Russ's office with their loot held shamelessly out in front of them: huge paper plates piled high with Nom's famous India fois gras, two-bite slabs of Yanagi Sushi (for these porkers, maybe *one*-bite), skewers of *sate* chicken, and more pointedly, not even a word of thanks to Senator Lee, gotta get out in the hall, where the real party's happening! Anybody seen Coach Brock?

Handshake, pat, handshake, pat, and another line of revelers on their way *in*, "Nice speech, Senator!" A real crush was forming out here—the crowd now thicker than that outside of any of the other offices.

"Well, what did you expect, Mr. TV star?" Cliff Yoshida said to him, and in a way it was true, what with how the TsengUSA PR had Russ splashed all over ads on all three local stations. "You're the life of the party."

Yes, *party* indeed! More like…baby luau, or graduation. Look at Senator Lorna Park over there *listening* to…was that the president of the football booster club? You can hardly even see that red dress of hers, let alone her face, they've piled so many leis on her shoulders it's like these two narrow eyes are peeking out from a tropical rainforest. They're all snapping away pictures like she's just gotten her diploma, too—and she's not even one of the freshman senators that were sworn in this morning.

Like Jayden Kaneshiro. You'd probably have to send out a search party to find Kaneshiro somewhere beneath that canopy of leis piled way up over his head. The whole building smelled like the arrivals area at Lihue airport, all this plumeria and pikake and ginger wafting around, a fragrance so strong it almost smothered the mouthwatering aromas of…the food.

"Nice speech, Senator!"

The food. Without food there could be no *fest*, and Susan Brushette and Trina Hyde and Russ himself had taken Sean Hayashi's little suggestion to bring back Opening Day and run with it, like Ufi Tapusoa taking an interception *to the house*. Three floors of the Capitol: loaded down with enough catered gourmet *island cuisine* to feed an army of, let's see, look at Hayashi way over on the opposite balcony chatting with Michael Prescott…how would he put it?

An army of fat fucking pigs, was what it probably looked like to Hayashi. Russ had to agree, his own ample gut notwithstanding. Sure, the odd Keep the Country Country faded green T-shirt hung on the bony shoulders of the odd emaciated vegan, my God someone *get that guy a frikken sandwich!* Here and there you did have a few hot and slender office candy hotties prancing around this crowd of *approving* freeloaders, a lot like the ones you always saw strutting their Honolulu Pulse Party Pix stuff across Bishop Square every morning on the way to their seek-a-lawyer-husband jobs. (Although many of them were probably lawyers themselves, Russ had to admit.) And sure: the Honolulu Club gym crowd, the I-Paddle-For-Lanikai crowd, the Look-At-Me-On-My-Stand-Up-Paddle-Board crowd were all well represented. But the rest of them? Jesus Christ, no wonder health care costs had skyrocketed so much in the last decade! Every third person you saw was a walking heart-attack time bomb!

Oh god, here comes one of the green shirts. Two of them. Three. A second-wife looking woman with high-cut shorts meant to show off her *terrific legs* even though she was forty, a typical Serial Protester UH Professor with little wires of hair poking out of his ears, and some skinny long-haired hippie-looking guy with a traditional Hawaiian fishing hook for a necklace.

They were bee-lining it over with the deep crevices in their (haole) faces already announcing that they weren't going to have any of this Dolphin Bay development nonsense going on up in God's country, each one clutching a fistful of bright green flyers.

So what do you do?

You turn on the *charm!* Russ just about ignited his own grin, and held out a put-'er-there hand, and greeted them all like long-lost relatives who'd survived a shipwreck, and let me take a look at your flyer, and boy, we're interested in *sustainability*, and why don't you come inside and *make yourself a plate.*

And with each of the buzzwords—*sustainability, pristine country, spiritual place,* etc.—he watched their faces melt, right before his eyes. True, none of it would have worked on its own, but Russ was a twenty-year veteran of this *charm* business. It was a delicate mix of pace and warmth and physical contact of the understanding-hand-on-your-forearm variety, and Russ had it *down.* Before any of them knew what had happened, they were nodding their heads and commenting on all the wonderful aromas emanating from within.

"Eh Cliff," Russ called. "Could you show these folks inside? Have them make plate, show them where the drinks are in the refrigerator. In fact, why don't you seat them at the table we set up in the inner office." He could almost hear their thoughts: *Inner office! State Senate President Lee! Well, the squeaky wheel gets the grease, doesn't it!*

"That way they can take their time with the food, and even enjoy the view." He turned to them: "Please, folks. Step inside! I'll be in to join you in *just a few minutes!*" *Smile!* They took him at his word (of course they did) and headed for the trough before the popovers ran out.

Handshake, pat, handshake, pat, and on it went. And finally, a good hour into the whole thing—it wasn't exactly a thank-you, but Russ would take it: "Nice spread, Senator!"

Ah yes, the food! Russ wondered how he'd ever forgotten what Opening Day used to be like back in those *prosperous* times. As he looked out across the rotunda to the crowded balconies all around, again he couldn't help but wonder if people in general had just been getting bigger and bigger since the last proper Opening Day party. And maybe that was why Ikaika was so hard to spot in here: just about everyone was the size of a former potential NFL linebacker. Admittedly Russ himself wasn't all that far behind in the fat department, and tomorrow, yes, tomorrow would be the day he'd start up at the gym—

There he was: across the rotunda on the opposite balcony, nodding his head as he listened to this animated haole banker-looking guy standing next to him. So Russ leaned in to alert Cliff to hold down the fort, and then turned to start making his way through this…sea of asses, was what it felt like…of asses and giant bellies, all belonging to people shamelessly standing in line in front of nearly every office…you had to lift both arms and pivot this way and that just to make any headway…

"Nice speech, Senator!"

And on Russ went, excuse-me-ing through, squeeze here, suck in the gut there, until at last the crowd thinned a bit in front of…Tom Reed's office, as it turned out…and there was Reed, talking with a short Filipino guy in one of those red Jesus T-shirts…a whole cluster of red over there, several of them scarfing down plates they held straight up to their mouths so they could just go ahead and shovel it all in. As Russ got closer he could see that they'd all gotten that food from elsewhere, Senator Reed's office bare of even the expected chips and salsa or cheese and crackers the haoles always put out, and not even a single flower in sight other than Reed's own lei, and of course!

Russ had to give credit where credit was due: Hayashi had asked Cliff to draw up a list of legislators whose support they had no hope of winning for the gambling bill, a list he'd handed to the people in charge of the *festivities* and instructed them to leave a few select offices bare of both food and flowers. Russ had only gone along with it as a kind of practical joke, but look how it was working! These guys were looking like a bunch of party poopers! Is this what "fiscal conservative" was supposed to mean? Worse! They looked like…outsiders! And the lei—that was part of the joke, too: Reed and Arthur Tafai and the handful of others on the list had indeed been given leis just like everyone else, but they were those cheap purple-and-white ones that either marked you as cattle on a package group tour, or a visiting guest speaker in a UH classroom.

Classic!

Here was Senator Tom Reed, probably at this very moment strategizing on ways to kill Russ's bill, with nothing at all to offer to the vast legions of partygoers—no Panang curry, no Yanagi sushi, and none of those famous popovers you were always hearing about from that restaurant in Neiman Marcus. And these people expected to go up against the likes of Bradley Zao?

Just past Reed's office the crowd thickened again, squeeze here, squeeze there, asses, asses, everywhere, and wouldn't you know it: Bradley Zao himself, right over by the rail, about twenty yards past Ikaika-them, right near where Hayashi and Prescott were standing, plus that woman who'd met them at the plane back in Macau, the one from Alan Ho's Pauahi Tower meeting. Centering a cluster of bulky public-worker-union-boss-men, Zao was holding a little cocktail plate of chicken skewers, smiling and nodding along. A couple of his own wired-up security goons lurking behind. The union guys were obviously trying to shake him down in some kind of local lay-down-the-rules, jovial don't-fuck-with-us we're-joking-but-we're-not-really-joking way, but come on.

While there must've been some version of meet-and-greet gladhanding back in Macau, this little us-guys strong-arm attempt was going to be about as effective as…the college marching band down there blaring out the theme from the old Hawai'i Five-0 again and again.

Russ would have loved to have known what the little billionaire thought of the whole circus—of a statehouse packed with grown men and women parading around like pre-teen star-worshipers hoping for their dreams to come true in the form of a scrawled signature from a hope-against-all-hope-they-keep-me-on-as-a-"graduate-assistant"-so-I-have-a-foot-in-the-door-towards-an-assistant-coach's-position-because-I-have-no-hope-of-ever-making-the-NFL-or-even-playing-in-Europe, headed-for-the-scrap-heap-of-college-sports-plantation slave.

Or all these freeloaders shamelessly wandering around with heaping plates of food, and not one of them even coming up to acknowledge Zao even though the entire day, a tab that stood in the hundreds of thousands of dollars, was on his dime.

Or Kainoa Long over there—what did Zao think of that tall and hapa-handsome television spokesmodel in the cheap gray suit not ten feet away, a microphone in his hand and a bulky TV camera pointed at him as he "interviewed" people for the nightly "news" segment on Opening Day? Zao was probably expecting to be interviewed himself, and possibly to be asked to do a more extensive profile piece for some magazine edition of the news. But no. There was Kainoa Long beaming a bright smile at Chef Nom for what you just *knew* was going to amount to a mere two-minute report that would be all smiles and football, focusing entirely on the ceremonies retiring Tapusoa's number, and on…the food. If the casino gambling issue was mentioned at all, it would come in a long list of easily forgotten "proposals" and "plans" for the next legislative session, whatever that was.

What, indeed, did Bradley Zao think of all this? If Russ could take a guess, looking over at the man so comfortably absorbing whatever nonsense was then spilling from the mouths of the union bosses between their own chomps and swallows of chicken skewers and whatever else it was they were slobbering over, he would guess that Zao was thinking that everything was going *smooth*, going according to plan, going nicely.

For indeed it was: now that you dropped the casino bomb, you wanted to keep things on the low-pro, right up until the final week of the session. Sure, you had that delicate mix of PR for the jobs-creation aspect of the five-tower construction project—you'd make all the noise you could about that one: slick TV ad blitzes, Twitter and Facebook, and even print ads for the old folks who still read the Sunday newspaper. *Imua*. But here at the Lege you'd keep the casino thing under the radar right to the end of the session, whereupon you'd be able to slip it in at the last minute in a moment of "crisis."

Crisis? Did someone say crisis?

No sooner had the word formed in Russ's head than did the recognition that—holy fuck—that Chinese woman, Mae Ling Cheng, her name was, Russ now recalled, right there blazing out in her bright yellow skirt-suit combo…Prescott is pointing…the woman is turning and excusing herself from the group…she's making her way…coming from the other direction towards…Ikaika…and fuck, somehow Russ could feel it down to his bones that this wasn't going to be good, and fuck, he had to get there first.

Squeeze, squeeze, excuse me, pardon me.

"Nice speech, senator!"

All Russ could do was launch into that excuse-me twist-and-weave-with-the-arms-up gait to try and get through all these frikken *fat people*, all over the place, and if he could just get past the conference room, squeeze his way through this—it was like a line of homeless people at a soup kitchen waiting for a plate of *free food!* courtesy of some lobbyist, and I'll be sure to pay attention to who, but right now I just can't wait to *stuff my face*, even right here, standing up, just like that woman right here: look at those *shanks!* You could *sit* on one of her shanks and talk story with your friend if he sat on the other one, so far out did that giant ass of hers jut. And she probably wouldn't even *notice*. She's got one, two, *three* pieces of cake, of *cheese*cake, and she's labbering away at it right here in front of everyone. And just *get the fuck out of the way* so I can…intercept…intercept this Chinese woman, this Macau fucking dragon, she's *closing in fast!*

Squeeze, squeeze some more, and there he was, right over there: Ikaika. Just ten yards away in a cluster of followers, hair slicked back neatly, thick arms folded in front of him. Not even *charm*—all Russ had to do was get there first and envelop the big man in a hug, lean in, and tell him, eh Ikaika, let's just sit down over this thing next week, just me and you, just let me say my piece and—

"Well look at this!" a voice called out over the mid-party roar, a woman's voice, and although Russ couldn't recognize it, it stood out to him because it didn't seem to be referring to some scrumptious offering from any of the nearby buffet lines. It sounded like a voice that was about to throw what Cliff always referred to as *a Hawaiian hissy fit*.

Another voice: "See, Kanoe: it's just like Ikaika said. They think you going take the cheese!"

Ikaika: that smirk on his face as he looked down upon…who was that? Russ had been introduced to her at some point…yes, she was one of Brushette and Hyde's "senior staff"—although she couldn't have been a day over 29, and a real looker, hapa herself, tall and tan and willowy—Tanya Moore was her name, Russ now recalled—there she was, withering away under Ikaika's smirk, right next to…fuck. Next to a hot fucking Chinese woman in a blazing yellow power suit. Fuck.

A glance told Russ why this Tanya Moore had skipped the newscaster rung of the PR career ladder and gone straight to Brushette and Hyde: she didn't have much *charm*—at least not enough to command that *presence* on TV, to get viewers to *trust* you even though you had no idea what you were "reporting" on. What charm she did possess was wrapped entirely in her model's good looks, so forget about *that* ever getting you anywhere with Ikaika Nāʻimipono, or this Kanoe woman, who was waving a little piece of white paper around in the air. Kanoe here looked like she could smell a full range of bullshit from fifty miles away. And here was this Fashion-Design/Communications double-major thinking she could match up somehow right here at the State Capitol? Look at the two of them: *surrounded*.

Surrounded by Ikaika and four of his followers: a skinny guy with a goatee, Aunty Maile, the haole banker-looking guy, the young woman about to throw her *Hawaiian hissy fit*. Thanks to the drums of the UH band blasting up from the rotunda floor below, the voice hadn't carried very far. And yet the woman wasn't twenty yards from Kainoa Long's microphone and that TV camera, holding that piece of paper in the air, waving it around.

"Look at this!" she said again. "Look what this nice lady just gave me!"

Russ briefly considered squeezing his way over to interrupt with the big public Football Brother hug he'd had planned anyway, but then he feared such a move would draw Kainoa Long's attention, and well, something told him things were about to go very, very wrong.

"Look at this!" Kanoe said again. "For 'whatever I want it for,' huh?"

And didn't these PR people ever learn? Hayashi had told Russ all about that disastrous meeting at WCC where they'd openly tried to buy Ikaika-them off. And here they were handing over a *check*—Russ was dying to know how much it was for—and was this some Chinese thing, this handing out money right out in the open?—this Mae Ling woman was about to hand a check to what any idiot would pick as the most stubborn target among these activists. Right here on Opening Day!

All Russ could do was hope that the young Hawaiian woman was calculating the number of Hawaiian drug addicts, the number of Hawaiian homeless people, the number of ambitious Hawaiian high school kids who couldn't afford college—whatever it was, he was hoping that she was calculating how many of them she would be able to save if only she were to accept the check. She kept waving it around in the air, while Ikaika's smirk deepened, and Aunty Maile glared, and Tanya Moore and the Chinese woman looked at each other more and more uncomfortably.

"Who are you?" Kanoe demanded. "Where are you from? Because I've only ever heard of this kind of money from three places: Department of Defense, Department of Transportation, or the Department of Energy, and that was with the Thirty Meter Telescope, and that was a fifty billion dollar project. So, which one are *you*? Or is TsengUSA really worth so much that it can compete on the same level as the U.S. Department of Defense? Is that it? Wait—you're from TsengUSA!"

Department of Defense. DOT. Thirty Meter Telescope. Russ figured the check had to be in the high six figures, at least. Maybe even a million. And look at Aunty Maile over there: forget about a hissy fit—the woman looked about to explode. Mae Ling Cheng opened her mouth to eject some kind of platitude or empty phrase—anything—but nothing came out.

Then the young woman, Kanoe, addressed her comrades: "Look!" she said again. "This nice lady has presented me with *this*."

Ikaika's thick fingers grabbed the paper and he held it up to his face. "How interesting!" he said. He turned to the haole banker: "Eh Makana, this lady just gave Kanoe a *blank check*."

A blank check! On Opening Day! What the fuck was she *thinking*?

"Look," Kanoe said. "This is what I need to tell you both. And I'll tell you once, yeah? There are some things in the world that cannot be exchanged for monetary value. And so I, before these witnesses, have to give this back to you." She then proceeded to rip the check two, three, four times and then sprinkle its little white remains on the front of Mae Ling Cheng's yellow power suit, where it stuck like little white flakes of confetti.

And right at the moment this whole thing was ready to devolve even further into the kind of attention-commanding performance that might pull Kainoa Long away from his food-fest and into the…issues… or otherwise grab the attention of Bradley Zao and start him wondering when the man whose campaign for governor he was bankrolling was ever going to deliver on his promise of taking care of Ikaika Nāʻimipono, the final hurdle toward his billion-dollar development's official approval…

Right then and there, another state agency lifer secretary-type waddled by, yet another let's-just-give-up-and-pull-a-sweater-over-this-here-gut-of-mine porker. She was carrying her own heaping plate of food out in front of her like some kind of religious offering, and calling out to anyone and everyone within earshot: "Ooooh! Popovers! You gotta try these popovers!"

What a relief!

The Bottom Feeder

All those dark-tinted Escalades and Tahoes with the double-D chrome rims filling the little parking lots along Kapiʻolani Boulevard after dark…Club Rose…Evergreen Lounge…New Office…Club Bye Me—maybe they usually belonged not to some tribe of linked up *bangers*, but to castrated construction workers, delivery drivers, Hawaiian Electric Apprentices, stevedores, and other young local guys who just wanted to *look* and *act* like bangers, out looking for some kind of *action*, if only a story to bring to work about "catching polish" from a Korean woman from LA older than Aunty Beth who dressed like Julia Roberts on the red carpet.

But not tonight, not at Susie's Penthouse—"penthouse" meaning way up on the second floor of this prefab concrete warehouse-of-a-no-windowed Keʻeaumoku building midway between Wal-Mart and Ala Moana Center. Because tonight Susie's was crawling with the real thing, must've been forty-fifty boyz packed in here, half of them your usual fortress-looking NFL linemen-types, all of them shouting to be heard above the laughter and the volume blaring on the karaoke, four guys trying to slur out Prince's 7 at the same time, four girls laughing along like it's the most entertaining thing they'd seen since Prince himself played the Blaisdell like…fifteen years ago…when most of them were still in frikken elementary.

Girls!

Forget about FOB Korean hostesses and "oriental relaxation" massage workers—here at Susie's, that meant local girls, which these days meant Kapolei and Mililani and Makakilo, because the moment

Kekoa had lugged his ski boot in through the door, the rest of his army marching in behind him, Susie herself—she must be what, fifty by now?—she'd hung the "closed" sign and started making calls. Just like that, an equivalent army…materialized…an army of girls, none more than two or three years out of high school.

All were dressed, if that's what you could call it, in low-cut this and high-cut that, miles and miles of fresh young tanned tattooed smooth taught *flesh*, all of it there for the taking, every one of them eager to get *out in the world*, most of all to get out into *this* world, so distant and exotic was it when compared to the daddy's-little-girl suburbia where they all still lived, so removed from even the same I-married-a-dentist-or-attorney world where many of them were headed, cashing in on that *flesh* right around age 28 while it was still worth something in the Ewa Plantation Villages homeowner-and-two-kids-at-'Iolani range.

Before surrendering to that humdrum destiny, they had work to do, and look at them go! Look at those two over there! They're *standing on the bar*, and giggling it up the whole time while a whole O-line of mountain-thick braddas waves their fists in the air and rhythmically chants out above the music, chants out like rabid dogs, *Woof! Ooof! Ooof! Ooof!* And watch them spin and bend right over and send a mighty cheer rippling out all around, watch them turn and pull each other's tops all the way up to *there*, yes, we all see the tattooed snake wrapped around your waist and flicking his evil tongue right *there*!

Watch them grab and start feeling each other's tits and hear another cheer rise up, and what, they going start *making out* right there on the bar? Fuck yeah they are! Woof!

Look at Nalu in that booth over there, that fat ugly fuck, look at him with that local-Japanee downtown office girl, hadda be, the one with those tan lines reaching down to…yep, right here in the bar, she's got them both out, too, and letting Nalu just do what he likes right here in front of everybody, even her—a Niu Valley 'Iolani girl all the way, JPO in elementary, but much older than all these other bouncy me-and-my-friends bitches just dying to get thrown around in the back room by a real live *playa*, like Kimo over there. Look at her, pulling at Nalu's frikken zipper right *there*.

Kekoa wondered if she was the one Nalu was talking about back at the baby luau, the one he met at church. Marisa? The one that did live in

Niu Valley, just wanted to *fuck*, to fuck like a Jay-Z groupie. That's what all these frikken girls were: groupies. Kekoa and all his boyz, wheneva they walked into Susie's Penthouse, they were rock stars. Mounds-of-white-powder-on-the-table, I'm-gonna-fuck-your-girlfriend rock stars.

And the girls?

You could tell they weren't your typical throw-it-around skanks, either. Sure, they'd come *here* specifically to throw it around, but there was a reason for that, and that reason, if you boiled it all down and got past the Tap Out black T-shirts and the diamond stud earrings and even the thick wads of cash every one of Kekoa's boyz had packed into his pocket—none of these girls were even frikken *pros*, they were doing all this for *free*—the reason these otherwise, like, *conservative* and even *chaste* girls were suddenly stripping each other down and making out in a roomful of a hundred-something people—it could all be boiled down to the most potent aphrodisiac known to woman:

Sway.

Kekoa Meyer, and every man in the room by extension, now had it in greater abundance than at any point in their careers. Sway: that lethal combination of a man's notoriety and his *power*—the kind of power that, if he had it, even a fifty-year-old college football coach could throw it around and bed down long-legged hotties from the volleyball team.

Even a fat rich land trustee could use it to fuck his married secretary in a hotel lobby bathroom, and get caught, and get away with it.

Sway!

Because everyone knew about the Lāʻie shooting by now—it hadn't exactly been *front page*, pushed as it had been by Tapusoa's funeral to some deep-in-the-paper police blotter section. But the coconut wireless had been quick to pick up the slack, heating up island wide with one rumor after the next. Javen had told Kekoa it was all over Maui, too, how Kekoa Meyer-them wen' wipe out three frikken *solés* not a quarter mile from Ufi Tapusoa's funeral, and then just *driven away*. How no one could pin it on him.

They had *nothing*.

The story had picked up the usual embellishments along the way, too—stuff about Salanoa-them shooting back, about a video-game-like chase through the narrow streets of Lāʻie, about plenny people wen' *see it happen*, look how linked up Kekoa-them is wit' da cops, I wonda who he wen' pay off, fucka get *powa*, Kekoa Meyer get the *connects!* Don't fuck wit Kekoa Meyer!

As for the cops, that part kind of surprised Kekoa. A platoon of them did spend their off-duty hours working "security" for him at Aloha Protectors of Honolulu, but not nearly enough to be able to bury this thing on their own. And yes, Crime Stoppers had put out that phone number and a plea for "information," but it seemed about as half-hearted as the HPD investigation. All Kekoa could think was that the cops had wanted Salanoa-them dead too and were too lazy to go any further with it. Plus, the cops had to be thinking that the whole nature of Kekoa Meyer's current bump in fame had to do with *conjecture*.

That is, things could not have worked out more closely to how he'd planned them: let everyone see me at the funeral, then hit these guys, and then let everyone fill in the rest—j'like like Tapusoa getting killed, except this time no doubt about who did it. A prosecutor wouldn't be able to do a thing with it, which the cops knew, an' on toppa that Kekoa going start keeping the rest of the guys we gotta deal with in line, easier for us when only one guy get the powa.

The powa! If the cops *were* in fact *grateful* to have a single enforcer like Kekoa in charge—then here he was. He'd done it. *Sonny Bulger*. It almost didn't seem real, like you had to say it out loud: Sonny Bulger. Just look around the bar: forty-fifty guys doing whateva they like, no one going say nothing, not even their wives at home with the kids and they *know* what's happening right here. And here comes The Parade, all night long, everyone coming up to Kekoa's table with pledges of loyalty and big-slap handshakes, looks of reverence and "You know we love you, brah!" and on and on.

Yes, he'd done it: fucken *solés* try make me look stupid, an' look: I wen' Machiavellian alla you mothafuckas.

All the way back to Aloha Stadium. All the way back to a distant phone call from Maui, his cousin Javen laying it all out for him, the one true way for put this place on the frikken map. Six-seven rounds through the windshield of a blinged-up black Tahoe, and once again everything was falling right into place.

Except....Kekoa wasn't quite sure what it meant yet, being the next Sonny Bulger. Yeah, he ran the this, the that, he taxed the strip clubs, the gamerooms—plus now Salanoa-them's Koreamoku gameroom. But every time you walked into the place, you were lucky to see two aging Chinese men over in the corner on the video slots, probably the only two gambling addicts left in town who hadn't fled to the internet—even football bets through a house in Vegas, could do 'um all on your phone now. Chinatown, Koreamoku—fuck, his own place in Pearl City was hardly worth the hassle anymore.

The gambling, from what Kekoa understood, had been a major source of capital for the Sonny Bulger empire. And now? Fucken penny-ante, cuz. And wait till frikken Russell Lee gets it legalized. Watch then what happens to the gamerooms, the football lines, the chicken fights.

Russell Fucking Lee.

"Kekoa, you know you always going be the man, cuz!"

Another *slap* of a local-boy handshake.

"Top shape, cuz!"

Slap!

"Automatic!"

Slap!

"Owe-raaht!"

Slap!

Here at his own table everyone kept re-telling the whole thing, too, the latest addition to the Kekoa Meyer legend, like it was some kind of spectacular play in the Super Bowl, you shouldda seen it! Shouldda seen how we all wen' walk right up on the stage and we even *greet the mom!* Almos' like they was happy to see us! An' everybody else wen' see us all up there too—brah, they was trippin'!

"They was trippin', ah, Kekoa!" Rodney Gomes was the one running his frikken mouth down the end of the table, one of Nalu's cousins, a young guy still in his twenties, real gangsta'd up with tats covering even the side of his face and spilling out from the sleeves of his…Raider jersey. On and on he went, everyone *listening* even though they'd all heard ten different versions of the story by now.

Kekoa wondered why he suddenly wished the guy would just shut the fuck up—something about how undisciplined blabbering on like that seemed, something unseemly about it, like it was just too close to bragging. Or maybe Kekoa was just tired of hearing it all again. But then he recalled that the Lāʻie thing had been Rodney's first hit, and well, let the kid go on—he probably can't help it, and who wouldn't be excited to finally *really* be a playa, a don't-fuck-with-me, I'll-fucken-*shoot*-choo playa.

So Kekoa blessed the remark with a look of approval, and then he took a long pull off his Heineken and hoped that no one had noticed how half-hearted that look had been, and that word—yeah, it just sat there lingering in his brain: *undisciplined*.

"Ho, you seen those two Mormon girls, the ones in the long dresses!" Now Jay Bolsom was joining in, going on about how Sister Mills and Sister Wang—"...I wanted for pound her on the spot, brah—you know she hadda be one virgin!"—how the two girls had seated them in front of that Mormon video and some old haole man with three chins had started going on about "sealing" his marriage, which got Jay wondering if they had some kind of supernatural epoxy up there in the Mormon temple.

"An' then we seen them fuckas, Salanoa-them, had t'ree of them, right in front of us on the stage!" Rodney went on. "Ho, I was ready for start blazing right there cuz!"

Jay explained for the third time how Kekoa had led everyone to keep cool head, main t'ing, him and his six other bangers packing heat at...a funeral...and all Kekoa could think was how he'd handpicked the only six boyz he knew he could bring who wouldn't fuck things up somehow, an' here was frikken Rodney and Jay both going on about how they almost *did* fuck it all up just because they couldn't keep cool head, blabbering on like it was some kind of great accomplishment.

The funeral. Plus Kekoa had been surprised that the next day it wasn't the bullets flying or screams emanating from all over an abandoned cane field that mattered. Yeah, the hit had gone down, sure, but then you just added it to the list and moved on. No, the image that kept coming back was...the traffic. A couple thousand cars descending on little Lāʻie, and the frikken Mormons had been ready—parking, shuttle busses, station after station of orange-vested teams of Mormon boys, along with the tents to shield those boys from the sun or the rain, water to keep them cool, walkie-talkies to coordinate and keep the whole operation running smoothly, while fucken Nolan Kahaiue couldn't even get them fucken seats.

Had Kekoa not been so locked in on gunning down a bunch of *solés* at the time he would have been...impressed. He may have been able to fix a UH football game, may have run the entire East side, may have been able to get a platoon of his most loyal foot soldiers together to risk pretty much everything right in the middle of enemy territory, but none of that came even remotely close to the airtight *organization* he'd seen up in Lāʻie.

"You shouldda seen how both our trucks pull up, all calm, cool, collec'," Rodney was saying, "an' how Kekoa wen' step out an' pull outtiz nine and jus' start *pumping* bullets into that fucken Tahoe they was all in: Pa! Pa! Pa!" He kept going, too, about how you could see the frikken sparks from the bullets tearing it up, ripping straight through the metal, crashing through the windshield, how bullets was flying everywhere, how those frikken *solé* bitches inside just start screaming like fucken little girls.

Except...well, was that...all? Was it...enough? Should Kekoa have been doing something....more? And let's be honest: he'd felt that way right from the start—put the whole thing off for so many weeks because somewhere deep down in some rational internal compartment separate from where his adrenaline-fueled *masculinity* dwelt, he knew that wiping out three or four *solés* with Glocks and Rugers wasn't much different from t'rowing hands at a baby luau. Hitting Salanoa-them was just the latest step since the hit he and Javen had made two years ago outside Club Green Lime, or the hit he and Nalu had made a year before on Kauaʻi, or any number of other hits, and that he was getting too old for *this*, too, *already* looking over his shoulder for whoeva like challenge him next.

Fuck, he had frikken three *daughters* at home to raise—what, they going come visit him in fucken Hālawa? Had he really risked *that* much on...this?

"You wen' send one message, ah Kekoa," Rodney said. "You wen' put some blood on the table!"

Kekoa blessed that one with a nod, too, but his mind drifted right back to...the Mormons? The Mormons. He didn't know much about the Mormons other than that they didn't drink and that they had huge families and that pockets of them somewhere in Utah still had four or five wives or whatever. But what he'd seen all over the place up there was a kind of *discipline*. It was hard to pin down, but it had something to do with more than just how they ran the parking, or how they'd set up those huge tents, or how they managed the reception line, or how pressed and clean they all looked in their Sunday Best clothing with their impeccable grooming habits and those *smiles!* of theirs—although the smiles, now that Kekoa thought about it, they put you in that... group...they marked you as a "worthy member" of that...gang—better than someone's *USO Family* tattoo linked you to one of the most fearsome gangs on the island, the United Samoans Organization.

Plus it went much further than just Lā'ie. What had Nolan said? *These fuckas linked up.* From Sister Mills and Sister Hong in their long-sleeved dresses, all the way up to the older members, and then on up further still to some church leadership and even some king pin all the way in Utah. Kekoa had since heard that these poor fuckas had to pay ten percent of their annual income to the church—the church that owned the whole town of Lā'ie. Talk about protection money—no wonder they owned all that land up there, what, six-seven *thousand* acres?

No wonder that temple sparkled like some kind of palace. Every Monday, nationwide: *a hundred million fucken dollars.* These fuckas was getting taxed like no one else on the island, more than the game rooms, more than the massage parlors, more than Nolan-them. And they *smiling* about it. An' no wonda they always trying for convert everybody—more Mormons means more *money.* Talk about gangsta. You in, brah, you *in.* You Mormon an' that's it. You *in.*

"Fuck you you fucka!" Now Kimo was shouting across the room through that slobbering smile plastered on his face, his arms wrapped around a pair of topless Mililani cheerleaders, they looked like. "We do one shot! Right now, you!" Kekoa wondered if Kimo was even talking to anyone directly. "Mudslides!"

Mudslides? Where the fuck had he come up with that one? But then Kekoa had to admit that Mudslides, a drink of the *eighties*—they were good for getting the girls drunk, and so that's what they all used to pound, even Kekoa's frikken *college* friends, even well after the eighties, way back...deep into...the nineties. Mudslides and Lemon Drops and Kamikazes. Slippery Nipples. And here was Kimo shouting out for a round of Mudslides, these two girls looking at him like he'd just ordered like a gin and tonic or a scotch and soda, a *highball.*

And this call for a Mudslide—rather than fill Kekoa with any sense of party-on reverie, or even jus'-like-back-in-the-day nostalgia—it made him feel *old*. It made him feel older than that stupid cast on his foot did. And with that thought, a troubling notion began to take shape, the notion that—could it be?—that becoming the next Sonny Bulger…was this it? Did it mean that—

"Ho *nah!*" Rodney shouted it out, his eyes wide with drunken surprised anger, like he was ready to pounce on whoever it was he'd spotted over there across the room. Right here in the middle of a celebration, and fuck, of course someone's gotta get so amped up that he wants to *t'row hands?* Fuck. So much for fucken discipline. Always somebody gotta ac' stupid, gotta cement his own place in the order of things, even among his boyz, gotta prove he not one punk, gotta prove he not one bottom feeder.

"No fucken *way*, cuz," Rodney said, half out of his seat now, so enraged that Kekoa had to turn and take a look.

And yeah: *Ho nah!* Who the fuck this guy t'ink he is walking straight in here, right into the fucken lion's den, especially after all that jus' wen' happen? Who the fuck he t'ink he *is?* Like what, not enough for laugh off one solid kick to the jaw right in front of everybody in Waimānalo? Now you fucken dare walk right in here, on this night of all nights, me an' my boyz, alla my boyz, my whole frikken *army*, we out celebrating, an' you going walk right in here? Fuck, you lucky I don't just stand up an' rip you in half myself, cuz. You like some more a *this?*

But in the next instant another thought raced across Kekoa's brain: Fuck, what the fuck am I thinking, right away the fucken anger starts up, the hands get fast, right here, me even, all ready for start…acting stupid. Right away I thinking of the four fastest ways to take this steroid mothafucka down.

Again. Even me. Fuck.

And here comes the guy walking straight towards their table, all six-foot-six of him, all 280 pounds of him, dressed in that vintage BJ PENN.COM T-shirt, those black denim shorts reaching below his knees, those…slippers? Fuck, this betta be good.

You'd have thought the whole place would have gone silent at the sight of the guy too, but no. Everyone was just too far gone into full-on party mode that beyond Rodney over here, and now Jay, no one even noticed. Onward he came, a bee-line right to the table at the back corner, a man on some kind of mission, until at last he stood right over

Kekoa, a look of...what was this? Of humility: his head tilted downward, avoiding eye contact out of deep respect.

Half the boys sitting around the table: stunned. The other half ready to pull out their nines and start firing, never mind the other hundred people in the place. But even Rodney waited, waited for Kekoa himself to react.

Kekoa waited too, like the high school principal waits after he's summoned you into his office and made you stand there while he attends to more important things first. And despite everything, Kekoa was surprised to find that the thought then entering his mind was: Fuck, you gotta give this bitch *credit*.

Still, he waited some more, until the guy began to shift back and forth on his heels, until his eyes began to shift this way and that out of...fear...that someone else might recognize him, might come up and false him right here at Susie's. And as the fear set in—you could see it in the guy's face—Kekoa waited some more, waited while the beat of one song ended and another began, waited through the joyous drunken shouts of ambient party noise until finally he said, "You get some *alas*, ah boy, coming in here like this."

The guy glanced around and then at Kekoa before locking his eyes back on the floor, and you could tell he was worried about how whatever he'd come to say would come out, like he trying for figure out how for put 'um. "I no like make trouble," he finally said. "I no like interrupt you guys's party. I jus' came for apologize to you Mista Meyer."

He was raising his voice a bit to be heard above the karaoke, the shouts and laughter coming from the bar, his voice clear and loud. "I sorry about alla da trouble I wen' cause you."

Now he was looking Kekoa in the eye, pleading. "I know you probly like kill me too, an' I don't blame you. But I telling you, I wen' make one big mistake. I taking responsibility. I ratha make everyt'ing right. I sorry, Mista Meyer. I sorry about your foot, I sorry about mout'ing off. I sorry I end up acting stupid. I neva going do notting like that again, I telling you. I sorry."

He took out a thick envelope, stuffed not with hundreds, as it would have been coming from a guy way up near the load, a guy like Nolan Kahaiue, but with twenties. It was a real purse-snatcher kind of tax the guy had scraped together, real bottom feeder, and Kekoa was impressed less by the money than with the resourcefulness that must have gone into collecting such a wad of *twenties*—of twenty-thirty grand worth of twenties. Like, how many street-level chronics did you have to shake down to come up with so many twenties? Resourcefulness. Motivated by *fear*, fear that was now turning into *obligation*. This Jus' Scrap tower of lightning quick muscle, this mouth-off show-off bragger, here he was, now scared enough to *eat it*, and now that Kekoa thought about it, it wasn't exactly *alas* that had led this kid straight into the lion's den—it was just the opposite.

The guy was so frikken scared he thought that the only chance he had was to punk himself right here in front of as many of Kekoa's boyz as possible, just so they all knew. And now if Kekoa didn't bury the guy in a cane field somewhere (like you could even find one without going to a neighbor island anymore), then he basically owned this GNC mothafucka.

So he looked up and said, "The only way I going kill you is you keep calling me 'Mister Meyer.' I not that old, you know." He'd tried to say it with a smile, but the guy looked ready to jump under the table. So Kekoa said, "You welcome to join us, brah. My cousin just ordered a round of Mudslides. You know what a Mudslide is?"

A look swept over the kid's face like Kekoa had shown up on his doorstep with his long-lost puppy or something. He grabbed Kekoa's hand with both of his and kept on going with it: thank you, thank you brah, I not eva going let you down, Kekoa, I promise you that brah, till the day I die, I do anything, "I doing 'um for help Kekoa Meyer." He then respectfully declined the invitation, saying, "I don't know, I know this your 'ohana here tonight, everybody celebrating, I no like bring no bad blood into dis place, you know what I mean? But thank you anyway, Kekoa," thank you thank you thank you.

The guy finally turned and started making his way through the thick wall of bodies and toward the door, Kekoa Meyer's new recruit, loyal foot soldier, his new…*convert*. A new worthy member of the Church of Sonny Bulger, a—what did they call it? Tithing. The guy was a full-fledged tithing member. A worthy payer of his taxes. And a disciplined one at that, in some ways anyway—the guy may have acted stupid at the baby luau, but there was no forgetting that sculpted frame of his, product of endless daily *disciplined* workouts. You just get him to learn his lesson about acting stupid…a lesson he already appeared to be absorbing. Worthy. And scared, too. Still! Scared of the power emanating all the way from the top, from Kekoa Meyer.

Again Kekoa thought of that…hierarchy. The Mormon sway. How *linked up* things had immediately looked up in Lā'ie, all those "volunteers" up at the funeral, most of them frail looking FOB Utah haoles with no idea even who Ufi Tapusoa was, they ordering big die-hard UH football fan knuckleheads around with nothing but the authority of their precise politeness, with that *smile!*, with that…connection…to the Mormon church. An' the big die-hard UH football knuckleheads? For the first time in their Kill Haole Day lives, they *listening*.

And how different was this? This one fucka who wanted to punk him not two weeks ago, here he was ready to do whatever Kekoa Meyer said, ready to keep cool head and stop acting stupid. And if you could get even this amped up mothafucka to maintain cool head, then maybe there was hope for the rest of them. Maybe you wouldn't have to carefully screen out the knuckleheads whenever you had an important mission. Maybe you could just go on cultivating that reputation, just keep putting fear into everyone. Maybe you could—

"Whoa! Whoa! Whoa! Whoa! Whoa!" the shouts *exploded*, fifty voices strong, exploded over the karaoke even, some poor bastid trying to blast out a Bon Jovi song and the whole thing is drowned out by the kind of collective roar that could only be announcing one thing: a fight. A frikken fight, right here in Susie's Penthouse. For real.

Rodney and Jay and three other guys jumped from the table, leaping over the high-backed booths like they were climbing fences, dashing toward the action, everyone else charging from all angles, the screams from some of the girls beginning to pierce the din, the whole room now bathed in bright light, and all Kekoa could do was shake his head.

Right in the middle of their celebration. Somebody acting stupid, even though we all supposed to be brothers up here, but no: listen to the shouting, half these guys in their forties already and shouting out like they on the high school playground, and now he could make out Susie's voice above the whole thing.

Kekoa finally turned and stood on his own seat and he could see her there, charging up behind a man four times her size, a man winding up and throwing punch after punch after punch into the face of whoever it was he'd thrown to the table in front of him, and there was Susie, pounding on his back and screaming, pounding on the mighty back of…Javen? Of frikken *Javen?*

"Javen! Stop! Stop Javen stop! You going *kill* him! You going *kill* him Javen!"

With the help of three human-wall-looking braddas, she finally got him to stop swinging. He stood over his prey, breathing heavily and bathed now in sweat, his thick shoulders rising up and down with each gulp for oxygen. He wiped the sweat from his eyes with a tattooed forearm and then appeared to…come to his senses. He reached down and lifted his victim by the armpits—oh, Jesus fuckin' Christ, Javen, what the fuck were you *thinking?* Barely conscious, the guy was, badly bruised, his right eye now swollen completely shut, you could hardly recognize him, looked like he just rolled his tricked out Honda all the way down the H-1 an' somebody used the Jaws of Life to get him out. And here was Javen now dragging 280 pounds of solid muscle across the beer-stained carpet, his own eyes a raging red mix of anger and coked up drunkenness.

When he finally reached Kekoa's table he leaned down and started screaming in the guy's ear: "Kiss his feet, boy! Kissiz fucken *feet!* Now! How *dare* you fuckin show your fuckin ugly ass fuckin face in dis place! I *shouldda* fuckin killed you. I *still* should fuckin kill you. But here's your fuckin' chance, boy. Now *do it!*"

The guy struggled to his knees, utterly dazed, and again, despite everything, the thought that flashed through Kekoa's brain was, fuck, you gotta give this bitch *credit,* look at him getting up like that after taking the worst kind of beating, you gotta give him *credit.*

And do you call *Javen* out for being the one that was acting fuckin stupid, when all he thought was that he was doing you one favor in taking out the kid who fuckin punked you in front of everyone in Waimānalo, your own frikken home town? Do you really let Javen know how much he just fucked up, right here in front of everybody?

While that battle raged inside Kekoa's head, the kid on the floor was…fuck, give him credit for that, too—he was fucking doing as he was told! No explaining. No *I paid my frikken tax already, you stupid mothafucka,* no *I already wen' apologize.* No pleas for Kekoa to intervene. It was like the kid frikken *knew* the dilemma now facing Kekoa, and he'd decided to play along, if only out of respect for his new boss. There he was, manning right up by doing what looked like the complete opposite: punking himself, frikken *castrating* himself, frikken kissing Kekoa's *feet* just like he was told. *Eating* it. The sight of him there grabbing that ski boot and planting a kiss on it—it nearly moved Kekoa to tears.

So he stood, and he helped the guy up, and he spoke right into the guy's ear—the good one—and let him know that he would make this right, no worry, I seen how you wen' handle this cuz, I going take care. He ordered Rodney and Jay to escort the guy to his car, and the hospital if he needed it, and then he shouted it out: "Nobody touch this fucka. Javen wen' take care. 'Nuff already. Pau."

Then Susie dimmed the lights and *just like that* the whole place was roaring again, *fueled* by the excitement of what had just gone down. Everyone was retelling the whole thing and acting it out, couple guys drunk enough to start kissing Javen's feet in jest and then dissolving into high-pitched giggles, Javen slurring it out: "Get the fuck away from me, you fuckin' faggots with you fuckin' faggot foot fetish! Beat it!"

For a second Kekoa was surprised there had basically been no lingering reaction to a man nearly being killed right here at Susie's—although now that he thought about it, any response straying from the matter-of-fact would have fallen dangerously close to being…gay. What you had to do instead was use the beating as fodder for more exciting who-wen'-lick-who and who-wen'-back-down stories dating all the way back to playground legend.

Playground legend.

That was really it. And not just the little barroom brawl Javen had started for no good reason. No, it was the whole thing, the whole *life*. Even back at the funeral as Kekoa had half-heartedly followed through with the hit on these *solé* bangers, that's all he really was: just some kind of glorified playground legend. From the moment he and Javen had turned north onto Kahekili Highway, when he'd found himself looking for Salanoa-them in the black Hummer or the lifted Titan or Tacoma or whatever, when Javen right away started *working him up for scrap*—from that moment right to when he'd found himself locked in his death stare with Lave Salanoa, the two of them exactly like a couple of junior high school kids coming to an understanding…an agreement…on meeting outside later for a *schoolyard fight*—fuck, when did it ever end?

"Mudslides!" someone shouted out over the now-blaring karaoke, another slurred-out version of what was that, Nirvana? Some teen-angst anthem from...the nineties? Twenty something years ago? "Mudslides!" In full rage, the party was now, half-naked women everywhere, straddling guys at their seats, a laughing riot of bare titties, of beer and coke and whatever else you wanted, loud music from back in the day, everyone partying on like...rock stars...the whole room now a roar of solid good fun, roaring on and on until suddenly it occurred to Kekoa that Sonny Bulger was dead.

Dead.

Yeah Kekoa knew that already, but never in the way it was hitting him at this very moment as he watched a godfather's dream unfold all around, a dream that was suddenly doing nothing but remind him of how...old...how *old* he was...how forty-two years *old* he was, how father-of-three he was. Too frikken old to be t'rowing hands, sure, but too old to be pulling out a nine mil and shooting people, too. Linked up? Just look at the Parade, look at what that hit up in Lā'ie had done, Kekoa wen' *send one message*, he wen' *put some blood on the table*, he was fucken *linked up* all right, linked up jus' like Sonny Fucken Bulger.

But how linked up was that? Yeah, you control the this, the that, you get one judge in your pocket, okay, you linked up. But then you dead. At the age of 53, you dead, dead from wasting away in a prison in *Kentucky*, seven thousand miles from home, strung out on the very same heroin you used to smuggle into Hawai'i. Dead. Dead because it never ends, does it, always going be some young punk mouthing off at one party, always going be someone you gotta *send one message* to.

"Mudslides!"

Fuck, fuckin' Mudslides. And here was Kekoa Meyer, a 42-year-old man, which in real life meant he was about two weeks away from his 53rd birthday.

Mudslides.

EXHAUSTION

So here they all were in the office of WCC's Interim Associate Vice Chancellor for Student Success for yet another Team Building meeting: Makana, Curtis Kam, Barbara Dietz, Sandra Green, Henry Carson, and Owen Funai himself. Owen liked to try to hide his utter incompetence at doing whatever it is that Interim Associate VCSS's do (Makana had yet to figure that one out) by projecting a "bottom-up" leadership style. He was always shifting back and forth in his seat and peppering his pronouncements with such phrases as "so basically it's going to be up to the faculty," and "I need to hear from the department chairs before I make any decisions."

Complete bullshit, every word, because whatever the decision was, it had long since been made, and Owen had been strong-armed into providing admin with the most important weapon in their arsenal, namely the phrase, "The faculty were consulted." Once everyone around the table had had their chance to two-cents and blabber and personal-anecdote the thing to death, Owen would pretend to have listened, do what had been ordered anyway, and then say, "Next time I'll need the department chairs to give me a better argument to persuade the Vice Chancellor."

Today's "issue" had come all the way down from the System level, where some pinhead wanted to tie each campus's funding directly to its graduation rates. Owen had already dispensed with his usual clumsy extended metaphor to try to illustrate the severity of the latest financial crisis ("Let me put it this way: the college is like a big tire, but that tire has run over a spike in the road, and now it's gushing out air, and pretty soon if someone doesn't do something to plug that hole, we're going to have a flat tire, and that means the car is going to come to a stop, and someone's going to have to call a *tow truck*, and that means…"). Now he was asking for "input" on how "the chairs" would best like to implement this new funding formula "on a department level."

This obviously meant that Mitch Barnes had already decided to fund each department solely on the number of *majors* it graduated regardless of the service courses and electives it offered to the rest of the college, and then punt the problem down to his department chairs, and here was Owen foisting it upon them in the spirit of "collaboration" while he and Barnes each cashed paychecks three times the size of those they were tasking with the work. Again.

That was when Curtis Kam, Chair of Anthropology, looked across the table and fixed Owen in a death stare and said, "Great idea, Owen. Why don't we all go back to our faculty and order them to stop giving D's and F's. You know, just shovel everyone on through."

Whereupon the skinny man began bobbing and weaving and back peddling in the form of offering some kind of fantasy of "more effective advising" and "better coordination of courses" and "there are better ways to meet that goal than just passing people through."

So Barbara Dietz, Chair of English, started going on and on about how hard it would be to get students to do anything in English 100 once word got out that they'd stopped failing anyone for fear of being cut off financially, and why can't the Interim VCSS stand up for the faculty, and on and on and on.

Makana was long past wondering when the fuck Barbara would ever retire—she had to be about 75 by now and had yet to publish anything at all. Curtis Kam, their union rep, could have told you exactly how much *less* she was making by working than if she'd started collecting her pension and Social Security. But of course the answer came in two words: Makana had heard Barbara had access to some kind of $3 million travel fund for "assessment study" that she dipped into two and three times a month to go visit her grandchildren in Chicago. So never mind that UH Mānoa had already credentialed a stadium full of M.A.'s and Ph.D.'s over the last ten years who were all now working piecemeal at some online "university" instead of very capably taking her place—

she had to feel *needed*, had to *make a difference*, even now at 4:34 on a Friday afternoon.

Sandra Green, who chaired the Art Department and coordinated the Women's Studies Certificate Program, chimed in with the observation that "We'll have an open door on both sides! Let anybody in, let anybody out! Just another diploma factory!" She dutifully wore no makeup of any kind, and (you couldn't help but notice, although anyone would rather have not) no bra, her sixty-year-old teats pointing straight down into that faded Bart Simpson T-shirt.

Henry Carson, Chair of Communications—well, Henry just sat there in a kind of smug silence. Whether it was because he was too dim (or too old—Henry had just turned 70) to be able to imagine the immediate consequences of such an ass-backwards policy, or because he stood to gain the most by it, no one could tell. Communications already had an open door at both ends, and in the middle all you had to do was attend class once in a while and talk about your feelings, or watch a movie and then "reflect" on it in your journal. Already far and away the most popular major on campus, Communications now looked set up for a giant windfall.

Makana thought to bring all this up, but right now he had neither the heart, nor the interest, nor, above all, the *energy*, because he hadn't slept in three—was it four?—he hadn't slept a wink in over four days. Sure, he'd drift off for a few minutes into that tease of blissful rest. But then the car alarm would go off. The one in his head. At first it had only sounded once in a while—he'd see a white Ram 2500 in the parking lot at Long's, and the sirens and bells would go off, and his head would whirl this way and that, and his pace would quicken towards his own truck, all of it without a shred of prior consultation with his *will*. Or some random gang of big banger-looking playas would be waiting for a table in front of him at Koa's Pancakes, and *Whrrr! whirr! whirr! whrrr! A-h! a-h! a-h! a-h! Oooh-wEE! ooh-wEE! ooh-wEE!*—before he knew it his feet were heading out the door.

After a while his own *thoughts* began triggering the alarm. A simple What if? As in, what if someone *saw* me? What if they'd sent someone back to check all the parked cars in the area? Should I get rid of my truck? Should I make up some story and tell Helen I need to take her Honda to work for a couple of weeks instead? A month? Longer? And what if they do get arrested somehow, and it comes up that I never came forward? Does that make me…an *accessory?* And what if that's exactly what they're afraid of: the cops coming and asking around? Are they going to come and…*assassinate* me? *Whrrr! whirr! whirr! whrrr! A-h! a-h! a-h! a-h! Oooh-wEE! ooh-wEE! ooh-wEE!*

Helen. No, he hadn't even told Helen about it. He hadn't told *anybody* about it. Not a word about the *clack* of bullet after bullet onto the hardtop bed cover of a white Ram. Not a word about a Hawaiian thug with a broken foot. Or about how different a cannon of a handgun sounds from what you hear in the movies when they put a silencer on it, the thing still has to deliver a tremendous amount of force of metal upon metal just to create the explosion of the bullet, and the explosion itself turns out to be the only thing that really is "silenced."

Not a word about the screams.

Makana had no trouble admitting it: he hadn't said a word because he was *scared*. The guy had *seen* him. Sure, he was squinting, and yeah, he'd been mightily distracted at the time, but the guy had turned and looked straight down that narrow road at Makana, not more than fifty yards away, and…*made* him. He'd had to have seen Makana from inside the tent, too, and hadn't they locked eyes when the guy was up there in the reception line? Why he hadn't lifted that cannon and taken one more shot right then and there, no one could say. Either way, the guy had driven off behind the other two trucks and disappeared down the highway. Maybe they turned back towards town. Maybe they turned up towards the North Shore. For all Makana knew, they'd headed straight for the Kahuku cop shop because they had the whole place on their payroll to help cover up their mess.

Cover-up? Hadda be. Worse even than the hit on Ufi Tapusoa. You would have thought the cops would have been out combing the island to rid the streets of whoever it was who'd been bold enough to blaze away right there in broad daylight, and even asking for the help of the area's vulnerable citizenry. But no.

Maybe the killers had counted on the funeral contributing to a perfect storm of just plain…*laziness*…laziness on the part of not just the cops, but the "journalists" sent to cover the star-studded event. While everyone had so busied themselves at Tapusoa's funeral with getting video interviews with Coach Brock and snapping pictures of Tapusoa's grieving teammates, a wild-west shootout had been underway a quarter mile away. Did some enterprising investigative reporter jump all over the story and follow every possible lead into the ground? Hard enough as it was to believe, when the dust had settled, the whole rain of bullets merited nothing more on the *Sentinel*'s website than a three-line mention in the police blotter section. "Unattended death" was what they'd called it, asking anyone with "information" (a complete physical description? a white Ram 2500? the makings of a license plate number?) to contact police.

For all anyone knew, it could have been a bunch of FOB *solés* from San Francisco arguing over a drug deal. Front page? The front page was all Tapusoa, all the time. And forget about the TV "news"—they were too busy talking about some mining accident in New Zealand or somewhere, and profiling some Hawai'i Kai doctor who took his dog out on his stand-up paddle board after work every evening.

In truth Makana could only be grateful, because the call for "information" had surely gotten buried along with everything else.

Or not. Because what if it hadn't?—and that was the thought that had Makana irrationally checking the *Sentinel* website every three minutes since the day after the funeral. What if some "information" arose about a man emerging from the cane grass beside the road and rifling through a nearby parked truck and running off with a stack of paper? What then?

Or the bangers themselves? Were they *after him?* Both the bangers *and* the cops?

And who on earth could Makana *talk to* about all this?

"Look, everyone, what we've got to understand is that going forward in these difficult times, it's just not going to be business as usual at WCC." Owen went on filling the air with the usual platitudes, and another metaphor—this time it was a patient on life support waiting for a blood transfusion, but the patient had some kind of rare blood type, and on top of that the blood was failing to "coalesce," so the patient was bleeding to death and it needed much more than "the usual band-aid solution" because that's not what a good vascular surgeon would do, and we have to start thinking like vascular surgeons around here, etc.

Makana took one look around the table at what had, for the last seven years anyway, amounted to his comrades in arms in this perpetual fight against administrative incompetence—a fight he himself had always taken so deathly seriously, but that now seemed so ridiculously inconsequential—and all he could do was sigh. Curtis Kam went on making fun of Owen's usual platitudes. Barbra Dietz went on arguing for the "integrity" of her "curriculum." Sandra Green added something about some kind of community survey on the effectiveness of WCC graduates. Henry Carson went off on a long monologue about the time his wife needed a blood transfusion. On and on and on, even at 4:41 on a Friday afternoon.

The words were all gelling into a kind of abstract sound Makana imagined you'd hear in a factory (as Owen Funai might have put it) when gears start grinding and metal starts snapping. Normally he'd have his sleeves rolled up and be leaning in towards Owen, delighting in the man's discomfort. But really, what difference did any of it make? This graduation rate formula thing had to have come from some haole University of California reject they'd hired at the system level for three hundred thousand a year (after contracting a mainland headhunting firm to conduct a $100,000 national search) to run UH more "like a business" that defined college degrees as the university's "product," so therefore the campuses in the ten-campus system that "produced" the highest number of degrees should be rewarded based on the number of degrees they "sold" to their "customers"—regardless of each campus's demographics or unique individual missions or anything else—like how obviously WCC was *succeeding* if students transferred out to a four-year campus before graduating with a useless AA degree.

Yet another gem of…outside advice.

Even mired in the current fog of his walking-dead sleep deprivation, it occurred to Makana how more and more of what happened at UH was done from the outside, even above and beyond this particular little incident. It had all started years ago (Curtis had explained it to him once) when UH asked for, and won, "autonomy" from the State Legislature. No longer under protection from the local boys downtown, within a heartbeat the whole system had been overrun by California carpetbaggers who immediately added layer upon layer of administration positions for their carpetbagger friends. The whole thing became so top-heavy they had to create a legal counsel division of outside lawyers *for each campus* to deal with the corresponding flood of faculty grievances instead of going through the attorney general's office for free. And just look at how NASA (with the help of UCAL) was able to plant a stadium-sized telescope atop Mauna Kea, at the rental cost of a *dollar* per year, on ceded land once belonging to the Hawaiian monarchy now "managed" by UH.

Makana had even heard of a scheme where some (imported) professors who were paid so much that they didn't even have to live on a deserted back-country outpost like the Big Island—they could trade their valuable telescope time (the oft-cited justification for the dollar-a-year-deal) to mainland colleagues in exchange for a byline on a "co-authored" peer-reviewed publication, and thus pad their resumes without lifting a finger, all while collecting a six-figure salary from local taxpayers and getting vested in the state pension system.

"What do you think about all this, Makana?"

Huh? Oh. And shit—this didn't look good, not paying attention in a department chairs meeting, even a bullshit one like this. Had to be on your *game*…couldn't give them any *reasons*. Heated disagreement and even outright ridicule of the Interim VCSS were one thing, but not paying attention while seated around the very altar of academic identity construction, the conference table, was another thing entirely.

It wasn't even like I was concentrating on *work*, like I was preoccupied with that *PacAsia* article I've been working on, just that I simply wasn't *paying attention*. Didn't want anyone to think *that*, couldn't give anyone any *excuses* to trash you at the next All Campus Council meeting in front of…President Varner…or anyone else involved in the UH West O'ahu deal. Couldn't give them any ammunition, any…did someone say "ammunition"?

Whrrr! whirr! whirr! whrrr! A-h! a-h! a-h! a-h! Oooh-wEE! ooh-wEE! ooh-wEE!

And there was Owen waiting for an answer, and for Chrissakes, I've gotta at least *tell* someone about this…*murder*. Maybe that way I'd at least be able to start getting some frikken *sleep*. But who the fuck can I tell? If I did tell Helen, she'd make me go straight to the police, probably even call them herself, and that would just make things worse, especially if these guys had some…connection…who could tell them Makana Irving-Kekumu had *ratted them out*. What about Tom Watada? Anyone here on campus?

My god, I've been working here for nearly ten years and I hardly *know* any of these people, we just pass each other in the hallways and gossip about *this* coming down from admin, and *that* coming down from the system, and have you ever had to deal with so-and-so in your class, and wow, is your kid already *seven?* Weren't you just on maternity leave? And besides, talking about it would require me to admit something far worse than being an accessory to a murder: I'm a *football fan.* A *UH* football fan. And there's no way I'm going to admit that, not with the likes of Curtis Kam running around to remind me how many *millions of dollars* were *flushed down the toilet* of UH athletics *every year!* And even if I could confide in Curtis, just bringing it up would reveal a…weakness…and worse, it would provide Curtis with fuel for pointless time wasting spontaneous I-sure-don't-want-to-be-*working* hallway gossip sessions for weeks to come: Hey, did you hear what *Makana* is going through? He's got some *issues!*

So who the hell can I *talk to*?

Thankfully and without too much of a pause, the Interim VCSS repeated his question: "We haven't heard from Hawaiian Studies on this."

And the words Makana heard spilling from his own mouth were these: "I don't think it matters, Owen."

Everyone looked on with mild surprise, waiting for Makana to go on, for the other foot to drop. But he said nothing. And around the room, eyebrows began to rise, as if to say, "What's gotten into Makana? He usually *leads* these rants. Owen tries to *defer* to him as much as possible, just like everyone else on campus, if only as a way to try to convey that he's sensitive to 'Hawaiian issues,' to show that he's not one of those outsiders who doesn't respect our 'host culture.' And here's Makana Irving-Kekumu, with nothing at all to say on an obviously bone-headed policy that will most certainly do great damage to his people. Nothing. What, did Owen manufacture some kind of bogus workplace violence complaint in order to silence him?"

Even under the circumstances Makana himself was a bit surprised, but there it was: he did indeed have nothing more to say. Because the only thought now whirling around his head was: who the fuck can I *talk to*? And that was followed by an even sadder admission—pathetic, even, given the way Makana had patterned his life around the general concept of *aloha*—and not the colonized commodified version, but the feel-it-in-the-*na'au* honest-to-goodness real thing. Most especially given his understanding of such cultural realities as *local boy loyalty*, the admission was tragic: Makana had…no friends. Just a couple of loose social commitments to a couple of his neighbors to sit in the carport and watch the football game over a few beers, and now that he thought about it, pretty much every single conversation under those circumstances had focused on the minutia of sports trivia and fantasy football speculation, so he really couldn't tell you the first thing about any of those guys either even though he'd known them all for seven-eight-nine years.

Beyond that, there were no *braddas*, no boyz from *hana-butta-dayz*. Beyond Helen—and now that he thought about that, too, most of his social calendar revolved around engagements with *her* friends—beyond Helen, there had been no one at all with whom he'd had even a single conversation approaching any level of intimacy since…

"Doesn't matter, Makana?" Owen was saying. "Isn't there a way you'd like Hawaiian Studies to be viewed by the rest of the college in light of this proposal?"

There went Owen again with his power-point-speak, which must have meant that Makana's silence was making him nervous. The *in light of* and the *viewed by*, and under other circumstances, the *in terms of* or the *with regard to* and so on—it wasn't like Owen Funai ever actually spoke this way in real life. When Owen was nervous, it would kick in like someone had flipped the Empty Phrase switch—a trick the guy must have learned from Mitch Barnes, king of the space-filling Empty Phrase.

That's how Ikaika had put it, anyway, after Owen had tried to buy them out with a few token "scholarships" at that hilarious meeting with the Dolphin Bay developers.

Ikaika. And right then Makana knew he should have spoken with Ikaika days ago, if not directly after the harrowing incident. Ikaika Nā'imipono. It wasn't like they were *hana-butta-dayz* braddas or anything, but given all that they'd *been through* together, given their link in *the struggle*, the way they'd fought together and analyzed together, prayed together after each meeting, of course Ikaika would understand. And while you didn't exactly want to reveal such a…weakness… in front of the man on whom you tried to pattern much of your behavior as a teacher, your big brother in the fight for Hawaiian rights.…

"No, Owen," Makana finally answered, "as I said, it doesn't really matter what Hawaiian studies or anyone else has to say about it. Whatever this is, it was likely decided weeks ago, and everyone here knows that." Was that a gasp he heard from the other end of the table? A snide *sotto-vox* comment from Sandra Green? It didn't matter. What mattered was that the mere thought of finding Ikaika and finally spilling what had been pent up inside him seemed to release little drips of…energy… from some reserve up there in his brain, dripping down into his chest, a wave of hope.

"You're going to do whatever you want Owen," he went on calmly, "and then announce your gratitude for faculty buy-in on this issue when there obviously is nothing but strong logic-based opposition. So I'm afraid I don't really have much to say. And it's nearly five o'clock on a Friday afternoon. So if you'll excuse me."

With that Makana found himself standing to leave. Faintly through the metal-snapping factory-grind in his head he could hear some words of earnest protestation coming from Owen's direction, and what might have been a sarcastic round of applause from Barbara Dietz, but his own mouth wouldn't open to acknowledge any of it, and his feet were taking him out of the room and toward his truck, and god he hoped Ikaika would say something, anything, that would at least allow him to get some fucking sleep tonight.

Within minutes the F-350 was chugging its way up Waiāhole Valley Road toward a three-acre patch of kuleana land where Ikaika planted taro. Normally, Makana would have been filled with nostalgic pride as he slowed for a gaggle of chickens and drove past the little farm houses—the ones still owned and occupied by the very people whom Tom Watada had helped organize years ago in the land struggles that had first defined "local" as an us-guys fight for three thousand unspoiled acres of what the 1961 general plan had slated for massive suburban development.

Many of the yards lining the road were still cluttered with hand-lettered protest signs: "No Fake Farms!" and "Ag Land is for Ag!" and "We Will Fight Greedy Developers To The End!"—all warnings to anyone with their eyes on the hundreds of privately owned acres stretching back towards the distant curtain of mountains, all of it green to this day, all thanks to activists like Tom Watada. That old maroon-painted house with the sagging front porch and the giant billboard out front—"Keep Your Eyes On The Crooked Guys!"—that one might have even belonged to Aunty Maile.

But instead of being *fired up* at the sight of the signs, reminders of a powerful ongoing local history that he himself was now a part of, all Makana could think was, God, I hope he's home. Ikaika might even know who the guy was, might even know the family in some kind of mother's-cousin's-aunty's-sista's way. Sure, it would seem like a hell of a coincidence, but not if you really thought about it, what with how all these Windward Hawaiians seemed to know each other, because, really, there were...so few of them...so few of *us* left. Maybe he'd be able to at least reassure the guy that Makana wasn't going to rat him out, that out of pure fear, if nothing else, his lips were sealed.

When he reached the fork in Waiāhole Valley Road about halfway up the valley, Makana was reminded that in all the time he'd known Ikaika, he'd never actually visited his home. Everyone knew Ikaika was a taro farmer and that his mother's family had been one of only four of the area's original thirty five Hawaiian families that had managed to hang onto a sliver of what had once been the sprawling spread of their kuleana land. But all anyone except maybe Tom Watada really knew about Ikaika's land was that it was "at the back of Waiāhole" somewhere, and that it was Ikaika's dream to pull everyone together to someday cultivate as much of the fertile valley as possible.

The fork Makana took brought him along a weary field of papayas—a few rows of six-foot trees hung with fist-sized green bulbs that stretched out feebly for an acre or so before dissipating into a sea of invasive shrubs. After a few more bends the road sloped downward into a low-lying swampy area. The canopy of leaves thickened overhead, as did the pungent moist smell of the encroaching jungle. A bit farther down he saw a red-lettered "kapu" sign in front of a muddy driveway and tried his luck, half-hoping, at the very least, to emerge with a few vine scratches that would announce that he did indeed take his big truck off road once in a while.

The thick leaves soon opened up to an area three or four times the size of Makana's Ahuimanu house lot, filled with what could only be called the disheveled mess of a racing-to-just-*keep-up* life of...poverty.

The typical not-one-but-*two* spent VW Beetles up on blocks under a frayed grey tent-roof...an old metal swing set rusting away next to the tendons of a banyan tree that had been carved all around with names and symbols Makana couldn't make out. You couldn't tell whether or not the swing set was just part of the adjoining pile of rims and bent bed frames and crushed air conditioning vents that made up what looked like a collection of scrap metal someone was gathering in hopes of a couple-hundred-dollar payout from the Sand Island recycler. More frayed grey tents covered the cars—a real beater of a blue Chrysler Aerostar family van with a length of gray duct tape running up the side, a couple of lowered and hand-sprayed Honda Civics parked at odd angles—friends of Ikaika's sons?—he didn't see Meg's old 1999 Maxima anywhere. But over there under another gray canopy in front of the house sat Ikaika's original model once-black F-150.

Farther on, a carport had been thrown together with what looked like scrap lumber—different sized support beams holding up oddly cut pieces of T-111 and flooring boards, the whole thing draped in royal blue tarp. Two boys were leaning over the engine of yet another Honda Civic, this one up on blocks, two more pairs of legs sticking out from underneath. Over on the side someone had taken apart a rusted washing machine but never gotten around to changing its belt or whatever the problem was. An old refrigerator sat next to the washer, which sat next to a long home-made work bench—two Home Depot saw horses supporting another length of T-111 covered with all manner of wrenches and sockets and spare parts Makana had no hope of recognizing.

The only thing in sight that wasn't at least ten years old appeared to be the gleaming black leather heavy bag hanging from the thick tree branch that served as the carport's middle support beam.

Makana stepped down from his truck, the slam of his door drawing the curious stares of two pit bulls chained to the carport's support posts. Over the sound of a gas generator he could hear the clink of a wrench dropping on the cracked concrete slab of the carport's foundation.

"Uncle Makana!" one of the kids turned and greeted him—Kaleo, the younger one—though they'd only met a handful of times over the years. With that, the kid's brother Kalani unfurled himself from under the car and stood to the height of his father, wiping his hands on a pair of board shorts, and the first thought that struck Makana was: black heavy bag notwithstanding, both big boys lacked the athletic build Ikaika would have had at their age just a couple of years removed from his St. Martin's football days, flabby midsections hanging over each of their waistbands.

"You guys work on trucks, too?" he asked. "I need a tune-up."

"Sure, jus' leave 'um on the side, Uncle," Kalani said. Swirls of calligraphy and life-like faces that looked nothing like Makana's own triangular patterns covered the thick arms of both kids. "We'll take the whole thing apart for you and put it back togetha in no time." He turned towards the carport: "You know how the F-350 works, ah Shane."

Shane, a short skinny kid with a stud pierced in his lower lip, started comically scratching his head. "Yeah, jus' leave the keys inside, Uncle, we'll take care!"

"Nah!" Kaleo said with a laugh. "No let these guys touch your truck, Uncle Makana—they don't know what they doing, I telling you. This the third car they wen' try fix, an' look at the odda two!" He pointed to the two VWs, and then approached to give Makana a hug before stopping himself. "I almos' forgot—I stay covered in grease."

Makana gave him a local-boy handshake anyway. "Your dad around?"

"I t'ink he inside—you can jus' knock on the door."

Past another stretch of jungle Makana came upon…the house… Ikaika Nāʻimipono's house. And try as he might to jam the sight into some concept of "rustic" or "back to da kine" or "off the grid," he was surprised to find himself fighting off a sense of embarrassment at the way his hero must have been living. Sure, the whole thing stood high on a solid row of hollow tile blocks to avoid what must have been constant flooding during the wet season, and here and there throughout you could see brand-new planks of scrap lumber hammered on in a way that fell short of what a lot of the haoles were doing lately with their "recycled" and "sustainably constructed" homes.

But with its sagging roofline, with the roped-off half of its rotted lanai—the half not covered with more scrap T-111—with its worn-out clapboard façade (if that's what you wanted to call the front of a structure that essentially looked like a double-wide trailer up on concrete blocks), and yes, with its long sections of blue tarp tied down to cover not just the roof, but a couple of sections of wall-and-window, too—

with all that, the word you had to keep from charging to the front of your brain was *dilapidated*. Here was Ikaika Nā'imipono, one of the very faces of the Hawaiian rights movement, a man as recognizable as any of the Sons of Hilo, not to mention one of the smarter and stronger and more generally capable people anyone would ever meet, here he was shoving so much of himself into the *fight*, day after day, year after year, that he could barely even maintain his own house.

Makana climbed five wooden steps to find the front door open, and not like he wanted to just peer in, but somehow the surprise of the whole broken-down scene had made him forget all protocol in favor of curiosity. Before he knew it he was staring at the slumped and worn shoulders, the back of the nearly bald head of what must have been Ikaika's father, who was seated at a kitchen table set up in…the living room?…his arms resting on the table in front of him, his feet…his blackened dark purple feet…you couldn't help but notice it…a toe missing?…his blackened feet with the cracked dry soles resting on another brand-new scrap of plywood.

And now a woman, Ikaika's mother, she was walking in from another room, a small-ish plump old woman in white sweat pants and a pull-over hooded sweatshirt, silver hair up in a tight bun, she was carrying…a needle?…a needle with a syringe.

Makana could hear her: "Okay Dad, it's time for your insulin," which the man answered with a grunt, and just like that she stuck the needle in his shoulder and then wrapped its tip in cotton as she extracted it, all with the practiced ease of a nurse who had performed this little ritual hundreds of times.

"Oh, hello!" she said, startled at Makana's presence.

Makana found himself at a loss, like he'd just gotten caught looking in on the most intimate private act. "I'm…I'm sorry…I'm a friend of Ikaika's. I'm…Is he here?"

The woman's face lit up with a warm smile, and she made no effort to hide the needle, though Makana couldn't have put into words exactly why he thought she might have wanted to. It seemed no different than if she'd just brought her husband his lunch, this insulin shot thing. "You must be the one from the college!" she said. Makana had never met Ikaika's parents before, but he was instantly flattered by the recognition, blissfully unaware that it was his khaki pants and his Sears aloha shirt that had given him away. "The professa!" she went on. "Come, let me get you something to drink. You like soda? Some juice? Dad!" she turned to her husband, raising her voice a bit. "It's Ikaika's friend—the one from the college!"

Makana stepped into the small room—a TV blaring over in the corner, the walls lined with homemade bookshelves stuffed with texty-looking paperbacks. He leaned down to kiss Ikaika's mother and shook the weary hand of his father, who smiled up at him proudly.

"You hungry?" the mother said. "Let me fix you some stew—I just made a new pot. Come."

Makana waved off the invitation as graciously as he could. He didn't want to seem impolite, or worse, *haole* in his rush to get down to the business of his sudden visit, but still, where *was* Ikaika anyway?

"Ikaika's out back, working the farm," his mother said, as if answering. But before Makana could run, she snared him in what was sure to be a long stoppin'-by-for-a-visit-out-in-the-country anecdote: "That boy—I don't know where he gets the energy from. Like back in the olden days, you know my father used to get up when it was still dark, and he'd tell all of us, me, my sisters, my four brothers, he'd tell us we had to—" and on she went, way back into some bygone era when her family sold vegetables by the side of the highway, how they used to play way back in the valley, how she and her sisters had come across live bombs left by the U.S. military who used the area for live fire practice, all of it spilling out as though Makana's entrance had turned on a faucet of some kind.

But Makana himself heard nothing beyond *Ikaika's out back*. He did his best to hold back from interrupting her—this was Ikaika's *madda*, after all—and as the faucet ran and ran, he tried to keep his eyes from drifting around the room…an old Kim Taylor Reece hula poster tacked on the back wall…a rather new looking fluffy maroon sofa set that clashed violently with its worn surroundings…the bookshelves…you could see all the usual titles at a glance: *Aloha Betrayed* and *Broken Trust* and *Dismembering Lāhui* and *From a Native Daughter* and *The Tattoo*, along with *How the Land was Lost* and one frayed text after the other on land use issues and Hawaiian history, *Land and Power in Hawai'i* and *Who Stole the Crown Lands*, the odd paper or fluorescent post-it sticking out from the pages.

In an instant Makana could picture Meg pouring over them as an eager young UH student on the way to her environmental studies degree, and then later scouring them for background on one or another of Ikaika's battles. In another instant he could picture her working late into the night serving Heinekens and Bud Lights to the pau hana construction workers and WCC janitorial staff at Ohana's for all those years, counting out the fistful of ones that made up her night's tips. And despite everything then crowding his mind, Makana's heart welled a bit at how…selfless… how full of personal sacrifice this haole woman's life had turned out to be, what with its delicate balance of trying to make ends meet—and for once that little nugget of homespun economic analysis could actually be taken literally: *make ends meet*—of pouring literally everything into her husband's fight for social justice, of giving up whatever bright suburban future had otherwise awaited her and trading it for this struggling blue-tarp house.

"So every day he's out there farming his taro," Ikaika's mother was saying, and with any luck, she was nearing the end of her far-reaching historical monologue. "Just like my fadda used to have us do as little kids. But then the whole thing was covered with weeds and *honohono* grass and thick scrub bushes, nobody use 'um for years and years, and Ikaika, hard head, my son, one day he insist on clearing it all by himself, t'ree acres, it take him a month jus' to clean it all out, another month to rebuild the rock walls, alladat. Anyway, you find him out back."

Makana stood there a bit startled until it finally registered that yes, he was now free to go. So he thanked her and headed out, back to where the opened area narrowed into a muddy road cut with tire ruts. The deep jungle on either side felt like some kind of wet leafy tunnel, and once again it occurred to Makana that he had no idea what on earth he was going to *say*.

Was there some way to contextualize it? Or was it as simple as some group of Hawaiian thugs with guns was after him? And would it sound like he was overreacting, frightened like a…well, *fag* was too homophobic, not to mention a term a sophisticated liberal professor would normally avoid for fear of being branded a Neanderthal anti-civil-rights bigot. But in the current milieu of how *gendered* his situation appeared, maybe that was exactly the term Ikaika himself would use upon hearing his frantic story.

And yet, on the other hand, the story did involve guns, and the role Makana had played in the whole thing was about as man-up bradda-bradda as it got here on the Windward side: he was *eating it*. He wasn't *ratting anyone out*. He was *taking it like a man*.

The dilemma was pushed from his head—indeed his whole reason for seeking Ikaika in the first place was pushed away, at least for a moment—as soon as the thick layered canopy gave way to open blue sky and bright, bright sunshine, and the most breathtakingly beautiful sight Makana Irving-Kekumu had ever laid eyes upon, was the only way he could even begin to describe it. Rising up from the valley floor in front of him was a sea of waist-high green leaves almost *glowing* in their brightness, and extending far, far back, two, three, four stepped rows, rising all the way to the wall of scrub trees and more thick jungle some fifty yards distant. Taro leaves! *Kalo*! Tens of thousands of them, three feet high, sacred and beautiful, symbols of life!

In each one of them, from the smallest hand of a green spade all the way up to its blanket-sized parent, Makana could see Haloa-naka, the son of Papa and Wakea, earth mother and sky father, from whose body, as Hawaiian creation chants explained, had sprung the very first *kalo* root. More: hours and hours of back-breaking work, work that drew directly upon ancient Hawaiian ingenuity. Just look at the terraced *loʻi* patches, walled off with stone to maximize the use of flowing water! Just think of the centuries of cross-pollination that led to the highest standards of taste and nutrition! Just think of the multiple uses of the entire plant, from root to stalk to green leaf! *Kalo*! The very symbol of living breathing Hawaiian culture! A metaphor for life itself!

This was it: Ikaika Nāʻimipono's masterpiece!

Of course Makana had seen taro patches before, with those service learning classes where he'd taken his students to trudge through the mud in Kahaluʻu, and the cultural restoration projects in places like Makiki and Waiʻanae, where he'd helped to uncover a few rows of ancient existing rock walls and restore them to working order. But compared to this, those little projects were mere…museum pieces! This was a *farm*!

True, a good football field-sized hunk of what Ikaika looked to have long ago cleared and restored with such ambition and hope was now choked with chest-high weeds, and the weed whacker there at Makana's feet, caked with wet grass, with an engine the size of a small outboard motor—it indicated a thankless ongoing fight to beat back the relentless jungle.

But look at the rest of it! Maybe a third of Ikaika's planned taro field was this...*sea* of green spades. You could feed a whole family on that single acre alone! You couldn't look at what Ikaika had done, basically single-handedly, and not wonder why the whole valley wasn't covered with taro, or why the back of Mānoa, or Makiki or Palolo or Kalama or Waiʻanae or any number of valleys all over the state, why they weren't completely covered with *kalo*, and why on earth we were so dependent on imports that Hawaiʻi basically had less than *five days* of food at any given moment, why so many young men were unemployed, or worse, imprisoned, when they could be *working the land*, doing what Ikaika was doing, as their ancestors had done, raising a plant with as much cultural significance as the Hawaiian language itself. And right then Makana made a note to ask Ikaika for a few stalks of the godly root to plant in that four foot section of his Ahuimanu yard, right next to the patio.

If he'd been at all focused on the moment instead of swept off into Hawaiian Studies Preacher mode at the startling sight of all those leaves waving in the afternoon breeze, not to mention how re-amped the other side of his brain was now starting to get by the news he was about to break, news of a *shootout*, for god's sake—if not for all that, any romantic notion of *working the land* would likely have evaporated the moment Makana saw how hard even the ripped and thick Ikaika was now struggling just to keep his balance, up to his knees in water and mud way off in the far corner harvesting fistfuls of taro into a rusty wheelbarrow.

A white bandana shielded the big man's head from the now-blazing sun, and his shirt was off. His taught skin—free of tattoos, Makana couldn't help but notice—was covered in a sheen of sweat. Down he would bend, all six-eight of him, down over that belly of his, and reach deep into the murky water, and then grab, and pull, and toss his catch in the general direction of the wheelbarrow some ten or twenty feet away, all the while trying to steady himself.

The closer Makana got, the louder he could hear the man's grunts and moans of effort, and if you could judge by the forty yard row of black watery mud Ikaika had left in his wake, he'd been at this single assembly-line task for some six or seven hours straight.

Any such thoughts registered faintly if at all, though, because the closer Makana got to Ikaika, the more anxious he began to feel, a particular type of anxious he wouldn't have been able to define beyond citing some combination of excitement at the idea that he had…a story!…a story to share!…a story with guns and everything! Excitement, and hope: that the big Hawaiian toiling away in the mud over there represented some kind of solution.

Now right upon the man, Makana found himself afraid to interrupt, so focused was Ikaika on whatever thoughts were filling his head as he performed the repetitive motion with a…troubled…a troubled look on his face. But interrupt he did, as politely as possible, with this: "Eh, I'm getting hungry just looking at this place!"

Ikaika stopped what he was doing and turned, and suddenly that struggling face was overtaken by the warmest of let's-just-pull-up-a-chair-and-talk-story-for-as-long-as-you-like smiles.

"Professa!" he said. "Welcome to my office!"

And exactly: you do this assembly-line work all day and your head's got nothing else to do but zone out and turn the events of the previous meeting or whatever over and over and over again until you've figured out exactly what everyone was up to, what got accomplished, what didn't, and so on. Right at this moment, right here in his "office," Ikaika was likely working out the strategy for the upcoming Burial Council meeting—either that, or some way to line up his contacts at the Lege to roadblock this gambling bill Russell Lee had introduced back on Opening Day.

"You need a hand?"

Ikaika gave him a chuckle and said, "You wouldn't want to get those clothes all muddy, but thanks for the offer."

For a second Makana thought Ikaika had just called him a haole. But then again, could you blame him? Although there was nothing like a dress code at WCC—for god sakes, Curtis Kam was always walking around in these tight shorts that revealed the little gray wires of hair sticking out all over his broomstick legs, and some kind of old white T-shirt cut, purposefully it seemed, to form around his little man-boobs in the front and his two blobs of kidney fat behind—Makana had always chosen the typical banker's aloha wear as a way to lend a veneer of professionalism to the proceedings when he stood in front of his classes.

Right now he felt like he was dressed like the man who comes to take away your land.

Anyway, Makana still felt it would be wrong to just jump right into the whole story of the shootout, as though, well, how would you put it? It felt a lot like walking into a church back here, like you were supposed to keep your voice down. "I can't believe no one's seen this," he said. A wave of the hand indicated the sea of fluttering green spades. "Talk about *back to the 'āina*! You've got a living, breathing argument right here for everything we've been fighting to preserve."

Ikaika looked down. "It's just what I do, work the *lo'i*," he said. "It gets into the blood, you know." He appeared to think about that for a second and then said, "But that's a kind of, well, romantic idea for most people." He lifted his thick forearm to wipe his brow.

"What about your boys?" Makana asked.

Ikaika gave him a half-amused look. "They're at that age, you know? All I can do is…advise. All I can do is try for set an example. It's not like when they were little kids and just did whatever I said. Now it's just, 'Here's what I think, and afta that you on your own.'" He shook his head, kids-these-days. "Cannot force them out here. You get them out here now, all you going hear is a lot of grumbling: 'Dad, this stone age-kine work,' and 'Dad, betta we go Foodland.'"

Makana offered a smile and recounted those service learning excursions he'd always taken his intro classes on, how so many of his inked-up *Ainokea* soon-to-be WCC dropouts would react to the prospect of a day-long work project that consisted mainly of walking through the mud of someone's Kahalu'u taro patch, bending at the waist and pulling weeds, and generally expending more energy than they'd ever been asked to expend in their lives, all without that all-important college-age-kid's motivation factor: *instant gratification*.

He and Ikaika had spoken at length about the relationship between the typical local-boy need to *make hard*, to *roll*, to *roll wit' one big truck, gotta have rims, too, dubs, double-D's*, the whole fascination with even drugs and dealing as the tragic final stab at *asserting some autonomy*. And no, it didn't match up well with taro farming.

"It looks like they're pretty good with cars," he offered.

That drew a don't-I-know-it look. "Oh, it's not like they're that afraid of work," Ikaika said. "But it's gotta be you eitha working on your car, or you working on your flying kicks or whateva they are, getting ready for the octagon!" This rhymed with *wasting your life*. "Hawai'i Tough Man Competition!"—pronounced *Castrated Local Boy Prostitution*—"But slaving away out on a *kalo* field, not too glamorous." Ikaika paused for a moment and tilted his head away, as if searching for some kind of answer. And then he suddenly seemed lost in thought, somewhere else, perhaps off in that place he'd been when Makana'd first walked into his…church…and wherever it was, you didn't have to be all that perceptive to tell that it wasn't a happy place where his mind had traveled to. Ikaika hadn't been *figuring things out*. He'd been…grieving? That was certainly what it looked like, what with that tired and resigned look on his face. But over what?

Finally Ikaika turned back to Makana: "But like I said," he went on, "at this point I'm just a guide. Alla the tattoos and the cars and alla that…" He shook his head. "I'm just glad they not out there bangin'."

Bangin'! He'd said it. *Bangin'*. Was this the opening for Makana to bring up the whole reason he'd hiked all the way out here to talk to Ikaika in the first place? Normally he would've jumped at it, out with it, for Chrissakes, just *tell him*. But for some reason it still didn't seem appropriate—something about that look, that *tired* look of Ikaika's.

So instead he decided to keep the subject on Ikaika's boys, saying, "Well I guess at some point it's gonna be their land—you'd think they'd be interested in preserving it."

"Preserve!" Ikaika lifted a thick hand to his brow and wiped the sweat and the little flecks of mud, and now there could be no doubt about it, that look: that combination of fatigue and…sadness…now it was registering as clearly as if the big man had been standing in front of a good friend's casket at Hawaiian Memorial.

Makana waited for him to go on, but Ikaika just looked up with a sigh and surveyed the cleared muddy path behind him. And that image—it wasn't one Makana had ever seen before. It stood in stark contrast to the last time the two men were together at the Capitol on Opening Day and Ikaika and Kanoe shut down those two air-headed servants of TsengUSA. They'd all agreed to attend Opening Day ostensibly to begin their public show of support for James Hendrick's run at the governor's seat—Aunty Maile and Uncle Paul, Josh Gibson, Ray Boy Thomas. But when Russell Lee had made his big food announcement, they figured they might as well go upstairs and touch base with a few of the legislators. No one had ever imagined that Mae Ling Cheng would show up out of the woodwork with a *blank check*, and well, neither had Mae Ling Cheng ever imagined how hard she was going to get showered with bits of white confetti, Kanoe and Ikaika both at their don't-fuck-with-out-*aloha* strongest. Now he just looked…exhausted.

At last Ikaika turned to him and said "Ray Boy." That was it. Then he had to turn away, choking out the name again: "Ray Boy."

Makana was stunned. Those two words alone covered, in an instant, pages worth of explanation that boiled down to a single tragic conclusion: Ray Boy had taken the cheese. They'd gotten him. They'd found his cracks. They'd offered his kid a scholarship, or whatever it was, even if was another *blank check* or even a fistful of cash at the right time and under the right circumstances, just as Ikaika had warned back at the Kahuku meeting, and again and again after that. Ray Boy. They'd taken him out.

For a brief second Makana worried that the news would make the murder-mayhem story he'd come to deliver seem trivial by comparison. But he caught himself, and worked to stoke some anger over what Ikaika was telling him. Ray Boy! Ray Boy had watched them dig up his great aunty's *bones*, he'd seen them *sticking out of the ground!* And who had it been, anyway? Was it Mae Ling Cheng, or had she learned her lesson and simply sent that dimwit from Brushette and Hyde? Who could *do* such a thing? Who, exactly, had been the one to put Ray Boy in that place, offer him those options, thrust that decision in his face? And if you're gonna go to such lengths to make a man eat his principles, why not do it—and Makana surprised himself with his next thought: why not man up and take out your cannon of a gun and shoot the guy, whoever the fuck you were. Shoot him!

"That. Is. Fucked. Up," Makana said.

"I telling you, it was like one *circus*," Ikaika said. "Last night. Koʻolauloa Neighborhood Board."

My God, Makana thought, have I been wandering around in such a sleepless daze that I forgot about the neighborhood board meeting? (It register barely that no one had called to remind him either, but anyway.)

"It was the most embarrassing thing I've ever seen," Ikaika went on, "to see our brother, standing up there on the stage, talking for these union guys, like a *clown*. In a *circus*. I had to *leave*." He turned away again, lifting that thick hand to wipe...a tear?

Union guys. The phrase cut through everything Ikaika was saying, *union guys.* The Union of Builders had been trying to get its members organized around supporting those hotel towers at Dolphin Bay, even paying for TV propaganda, local-boy members talking about "I love to bring my family fishing out there on the beach," and how the hotel will mean not only jobs in this bad economy, but more access to the isolated spots "where my grandfather used to take me fishing."

And now Ray Boy. At the neighborhood board meeting. Speaking in favor of the project. *Like one circus.*

"You gotta promise me one t'ing, Makana," Ikaika said, looking him in the eye now. "You get one good job, you one professa, you comfortable, right? You an' Helen, you comfortable. You get whatchoo need. You gotta promise me one t'ing: you neva going take the cheese. *Neva.* We cannot let these guys divide us, you know what I mean."

"Not going happen," Makana said.

He didn't know how to put it into words, the tremendous sense of honor he was feeling at this moment as Ikaika Nāʻimipono himself stared up at him from knee-deep in his taro patch at the back of Waiāhole Valley, and frankly, against all instinct, he didn't want to cheapen the moment with words.

It was Ikaika who finally broke the silence. After a deep breath and another wipe of the brow, he turned to Makana in let's-just-try-to-move-on fashion and said, "And how about the professa? There's gotta be a reason why you came all the way out here into the jungle. What can we do for you?"

"I don't know, somehow it doesn't seem all that important anymore" was what came out, although if Makana was being perfectly honest, he would have admitted that the car alarm blaring in his head was of far deeper concern than the fact that one more castrated fool had taken the cheese.

"C'mon, professa," Ikaika said. "Out with it." He even managed a little bradda-bradda smile, like he wanted to put this Ray Boy thing behind them now that he'd addressed it. "You get one a your students pregnant? Helen kick you out? You need a place to stay? We get one extra room, you know."

"Nah nah nah, it's nothing like that." And then, let's go—out with it: "It's, well…I witnessed a murder."

All at once Ikaika turned serious again. With some visible effort, he lifted one leg and then the other out of the deep mud and made his way over to the wheelbarrow, where he grabbed an old towel hanging from one of the handles and wiped his face and his hands, plopped himself down for a seat on the grass, and then turned and lifted his eyebrows as if to say, "Go on."

It was as though all concern with Ray Boy and anyone taking the cheese and TsengUSA and the whole thing had vanished into thin air, because Ikaika Nāʻimiponoʻs friend, his *bradda in the fight*, was in trouble.

Makana just launched right into it: his reason for missing the breakfast meeting with the LG that day, the big crowd up in Lāʻie, the friend of Tom Watada's where they parked the truck, the bangers he'd seen up on the stage, and maybe they saw him too.

The more he spilled, the easier it came, and as the words poured out of him he started to feel…lighter…a palpable, physical sense of *relief*, just to have Ikaika sit there and listen in silent understanding, with that look…that look that said everything would be okay, you're making too much of a big deal of this.

"And he put down the gun and looked right at me, just like he did when he was on the stage, *right at me*, and then he got into the truck and drove off. And then the paper says they're looking for anyone with 'information,' but that's basically it, like someone's trying to cover it up, and well, if there's some kind of, I don't know, *connection* where something this huge could get covered up, I don't know, they wouldn't want anything leaking out, is I guess how you'd put it. So I just don't know."

Ikaika's thick arms were folded over that belly of his, that same relaxed look on his face he always had at meetings when someone from the other side dropped some kind of so-the-project-is-going-to-move-forward-anyway bomb.

"Sounds like you ran into the next Sonny Bulger," he said. Makana didn't have the faintest idea who he was talking about, and his expression must have registered as much, because after curling his lips into another brief smile, Ikaika went on: "Sonny Bulger. You know. Seventies-eighties banger, had some cops and a judge in his pocket. He ran the whole island. Guy was a *legend*. He used to—" and on Ikaika went, apparently not realizing that he was actually filling Makana with even more fear and anxiety than what he'd brought on his own: "…they cut these guys into little pieces" and "this one guy, they buried him in the sand at Makapuʻu, he was still alive," and "vicious, the guy. My dad met him a few times, back when he was driving truck out on that side of the island. He always said guys would just walk out of the room when Sonny Bulger walked in, and everyone who stayed just sat there in fear, like you were around a wild Rottweiler or something, like the guy was just *off*."

Maybe it was the calm way Ikaika was going about explaining all this terrible shit, like he already had some solution in mind, but Makana thought this might be a good place to ask his big question. "Any chance you'd know who they were?"

Ikaika gave him another smile and said, "No, that's one whole different world, cuz. But I bet that's what they're trying to do—be the next Sonny Bulger. And looks like they've got some cover, too—I can't believe none of this was on the news, three-four people gunned down."

Three-four people gunned down. Once again Makana was frozen. Witness to a murder! A multiple homicide! Witness to a murder planned and executed by…the next Sonny Bulger!…*off*, the guy was *off*, like one Rottweiler!…cut you into little pieces!…bury you alive in the sand!

Ikaika must've detected the alarm going off in his head, because he said, "Eh, you cannot worry about that, Makana. Like I said—that's one whole different world. Think about it: you live on an island. Don't you think they would have found you by now if they really wanted to?"

Ikaika had a point. Two weeks had passed since the shooting. Two whole weeks. Surely they would have found him by now. Ikaika was right. Nothing to worry about, was there. Nope. Nothing at all.

"What would *you* do?" he asked.

"Me?" Ikaika turned and looked out over the sea of green leaves, the waist-high choking weeds beyond. Makana couldn't tell if he was trying to figure out a way to put it, or if he was suddenly preoccupied with some other concern—his sons, or Meg, or the farm, or even if he'd drifted back into grieving over Ray Boy. Whatever it was, that must have been the reason why Ikaika didn't seem to be taking Makana's concern all that seriously.

Finally the big man said, "They'd betta think twice before coming up here for me, 'cause it's not just me they going have to face."

"What do you mean?"

"Defend Hawai'i," he said. "They come down here, an' it's welcome to my farm, welcome to my land, and welcome to my semi-automatic assault rifle."

Ikaika gave him a smile, but now it was ringing louder than ever—because how on earth would Makana ever explain an automatic assault rifle to Helen? And let's face it: he wasn't built to even lay hands on one, let alone *shoot* someone with it even if he did own one—louder than ever, louder than ever: *Whrrr! whirr! whirr! whrrr! A-h! a-h! a-h! a-h! Oooh-wEE! ooh-wEE! ooh-wEE!*

Sunday Fellowship

Though they may have called this little feel-good arms-swaying music festival now blasting away inside the darkened Joseph Rider Farrington Memorial Auditorium "church," all Sean Hayashi could think was: you could get *laid* in here! *Hot*, many of these women—and dressed that way too: lacy pink bras poking out of little tank tops...bare shoulders everywhere...tight pants!...a black cocktail dress all the way up! To! *There!* Too bad he hadn't discovered this place a couple of years ago, before he'd met Marisa.

But then the reason for all the Take Me clothing hit him: with most of these women here in Kalihi only blocks away from the state's highest concentration of public housing, at a "church" meeting held at a school where nearly two-thirds of the 3,000-or-so students qualified for lunch assistance, there wasn't going to be much to choose from in their closets beyond what they used to wear to go out clubbing. Forget about a nice "work dress." If any of them actually worked, it was in a uniform with a name tag. So all through the crowd of like a thousand-something "worshipers," Sunday Best meant Check Me Out!

Which was easy enough to do, what with everyone standing, and *swaying* to the steady beat of that key-change-on-the-final-chorus *uplifting anthem* the band was pumping out of those towering stacks of Marshall amps on either side of the stage. *Swaying*, just like the "singers" draped in that blue-tint-foot-lighted fog machine mist: four local-Japanese former Pearl City High drama club geeks, it looked like, plus a couple of fat middle-aged out-of-my-shell state-worker lifers, all of them flanking the *beaming* figure of a you-can-see-my-powerful-lats-even-beneath-this-comic-pineapple-print-banker's-aloha-shirt forty-ish-looking tanned Asian-Portagee-haole-Filipino, a man known far and wide as "Pastor Randy."

All seven of them were clutching cordless microphones in one hand and lifting the other open palm skyward, faces clenched in *earnest* concentration, singing out along the same melody line (with no attempt at harmony), singing out in...praise!

> *My Lord, You are awesome!*
> *You have helped me overcome*
> *The rising river of the flood.*
>
> *My Lord, You are awesome!*
> *You have the keys to the Kingdom.*
> *You are eternally good!*
>
> *My Lord, You are awesome!*
> *I'll sing Your praise to everyone*
> *In this entire whole wide world!*

Feeling it, everyone, eyes closed, or clapping along. Even Marisa, who was practically belting out the...not exactly a *hymn*—it was more like one of those old Freddy Mercury songs a stocky little Filipino bus boy named Benny Aquino always used to sing when the Lehua's waiter mafia went out to karaoke after a busy shift. And now that Sean thought about it, "karaoke" was truly what was going on here. Someone had even typed the song's words into PowerPoint and projected them onto the two huge jumbo-trons flanking the stage, and all seven singers up there were giving it their high school musical best, shower-singing in astoundingly amateurish fashion.

Especially compared to what that long-haired haole drummer was doing perched on that riser, his ten-piece drum kit protected by one of those plexiglas sound-blockers that bands like U2 used to better control the sound mix. With the rest of the band following more tightly than a stable of LA pro session musicians, between verses the drummer would stick in a power-ballad drum fill that reminded Sean of those Journey anthems you were always hearing on oldies radio that the grandpa-of-a-baby-boomer DJ would call "lighter songs." Sean took a look around half-expecting to see some candle-like flames dotting this crowd—goodness knows, there had been enough tattooed smokers outside puffing away in that roped off area they'd passed on the way in—but apparently lighter-waving wasn't part of the sacred ritual of the particular religious ceremony to which they were currently bearing witness.

What he did see was nothing like the church he remembered from back in fourth grade, when his mother had made an aborted attempt to "stay in the will," as she'd put it, appeasing grandma's religious sensibilities by dragging him to St. Patrick's in Kaimuki. More of a medieval Catholic fortress than a church, St. Patrick's was crowned with this bell tower whose pointed spires cried out for the appearance of a mad hunchback, a midnight strike of lightning illuminating the *wrath of an angry God.*

Even on beautifully clear January Sundays much like this one, Sean had had to sit on a hardwood bench under the plaintive glare of a twenty-foot emaciated Messiah stabbed with a crown of thorns, His hands and feet nailed to the cross with giant spikes. For an interminable hour He looked down upon your privileged, worthless, guilty being from above the altar—and from the flanking walls, too, which someone had lined with bleeding life-like renderings of all fourteen stations of the cross. And just in case that wasn't enough, then they surrounded you with a battalion of aging aunties armed with dour expressions commanding you to *behave!*

Sean had to wonder why, here inside the Joseph Rider Farrington Auditorium, you didn't actually *see* a Jesus anywhere. It was just the band, a couple of bare crosses spotlit on either side of the stage, and, when the lights came up, a few giant banners adorned with sun-breaking-through-golden clouds images and bumper-sticker and-He-shalt-raise-thou-soul -up-on-the-wings-of-eagles inspirational quotes from scripture. And as far as the "behavior" codes went, let's just say the dour-looking aunties would not have approved.

People were coming and going from their seats and waving across long distances to familiar faces. That older local-Japanese guy over there—was he wearing a baseball hat? Right here in church? The woman holding hands with that skinny pony-tailed ex-con-chronic-looking Hawaiian: sipping on a half-full tub of Starbucks frappuccino. Two teenage girls over there had their phones out and their thumbs working a text. A young woman a few feet away whose mighty breasts were bubbling over some kind of tight-fitting black straps-over-the-bare-linebacker-shoulders bustier-top-thing was snapping away on a wad of gum. Like most of the women in the room, the long rope of permed hair spilling out over the swirl of tattoos stretching across her thick upper back was still wet from her morning's shower.

And yeah: you could get *laid* in here!

Except that not one of these put-it-on-display hotties could even come close to…Marisa Horiguchi. Hotter than any of them. Look at her clapping away in that flower-print sundress of hers, even without her own perky breasts half-exposed like theirs—though *getting laid* was hardly the term anyone would use with a woman as pure and chaste as Marisa.

In due time—for regardless of how Sean was ready to *explode*, he was in this one for the long haul, and in just a few more months, just after their June wedding…forget about *getting laid*—he and Marisa would *make love* in the most intimate and touching way possible. Marisa: his sweet, loving, beautiful, and well-connected *fiancé*. That six-karat rock there on her dainty little finger, the one she waved around to draw *oohs* and *ahhhs* from all of her girlfriends when they went out for lunch at Ballena—it was an icy piece of proof that at long last, she was *his*.

That ring—it also turned out to be the reason Sean now found himself clapping along to the next '80s rock-anthem power ballad for Jesus, "King of Kings," because the moment he'd slipped it onto her finger, Marisa had charged full speed into planning the wedding.

He may have told himself that this whole little Sunday excursion was nothing more than a reconnaissance mission into enemy territory for some *intel* to satisfy Russell Lee's increasingly paranoid ramblings about "the religious right" killing his gaming bills. But the truth was a bit more mundane: like many a prospective groom before him, Sean had immediately been relegated to the role of *hanging on for the ride*, a ride which would include weekly trips to this feel-good carnival.

He could hardly begrudge Marisa that part of the deal. However tempted one was to make fun of all these hand waving idiots, it was something she believed in, and something that, no matter how cynical you wanted to be, was just so damned *positive!* She'd told him a friend from work had brought her along one day, a woman named Amy Ogata, whose lawyer husband of fifteen years had traded her in for a 27-year-old Stanford-grad paralegal just after they'd both turned forty, sending her into a deep depression that "the Lord" and "His fellowship" had pulled her out of.

Now Amy was on the Worship Squad, and volunteering in the Divorce Workshops, and leading a Wednesday prayer group, and getting on with her life. Though Marisa had only gone along out of curiosity, she'd been astounded by the *feeling* of it all, how *blessed* she had suddenly felt to have God back in her life.

With this hula halau now filing onstage mid-anthem, it occurred to Sean that if Marisa had ever felt oppressed by the Episcopalian doctrine they'd spoon-fed her over at 'Iolani—a free-love party compared to the hardwood Catholic guilt they peddled at St. Patrick's—then a hula-for-the-Lord-and-Savior to the rising climax of Purple Rain (was what this song sounded like) would have been just the ticket to get your Jesus on again.

So so what if she'd insisted on having Pastor Randy here officiate their wedding. So what if Sean had to endure a few Sundays of rockin' with the Lord for such an event to come to pass. I mean, just look at her! Can you even *begin* to believe it?

The day after he'd walked off the floor for good at the Lehua, Sean had invited her out to that little hole-in-the-wall Japanese place on Kapahulu, just as he'd planned it, breaking out that oh-so-familiar pale blue box, the Tiffany's box cradling an ice cube of a diamond big enough to announce: *I belong.* I belong with an 'Iolani grad. I belong in Pauahi Tower.

The moment may have stretched long enough for Sean to begin to worry, as in: someone as hot as Marisa Horiguchi is *really* going to say "yes" to a former lunch money shakedown target, near-forty-year-old near-virgin like Sean Hayashi? But hey—you drop in enough references to private jets, to *governor* this, *governor* that…

Best of all, Sean had done it all *by himself.* Sure, there had been that lucky break with Alan Ho, but really, if he hadn't run into Alan, one way or another…a phone call to the governor…or to Senator Russell Lee or someone. Yes, his whole plan was falling into place. And this was no little apartment flip in Makiki. Against all possible odds, and in the face of all conventional wisdom, here was Sean Hayashi at the center of the biggest development deal ever to go down in the history of the state, all on his own, all the way from…yes! Let me shout it out now! No shame about it now, not with Marisa Horiguchi on your arm: all the way from Kaimuki High School! Praise His Name!

And could it be? Did Sean now find himself…swaying? Was Sean *Hayashi* of all people, was he *clapping along?* Well, why not? Really, why on earth not? To tell the truth, the music actually wasn't so bad if you let yourself get swept up in it. I mean, with all this hand clapping and singing along, how could you *not* be…feeling it?

When the song's soaring finale dissolved into a round of applause, Sean couldn't help but join in with real enthusiasm, even with some of the *whoop*s and hollers now flying around the room like they actually were watching U2 perform.

Only after a good long ovation did the hula dancers file off the stage, and then an anticipatory the-movie's-about-to-begin silence fell over the big hall. The drama geeks and the out-of-my-shell state workers moved off to the side, and the band sat idle, all except for the guitarist, who went on playing soft arpeggios of the Purple Rain song's chord pattern. Pastor Randy strutted back and forth up there under white stage lights that competed in *brightness* with his own *positive* expression, all fifteen hundred worshipers now hanging on what he was about to share, which was this:

"Aloha kakahiaka everyone! Good morning to our Farrington 'ohana! Let's put our hands together one time for our King of kings, our Lord and Savior, Jesus Christ!"

With that he led them in a round of applause. It had sounded like he was about to ask everyone to give it up for the band again. "And you know, I don't think enough of us realize it's okay to just cheer for our Lord," he went on. "We cheer for our UH Warrior football team. We cheer for our favorite singers. But we kind of hold back when it comes to cheering for our magnificent Creator." Sean could actually hear the capital letters. "So let's all give Him one more big round of applause, and this time let's make it a *standing ovation!*" He motioned for everyone to stand, a thick-banded gold watch on his hairless forearm glinting reflected light in all directions. "A standing ovation for our Lord of lords, our King of kings."

The place erupted like the Warriors had in fact just scored a touchdown. And when things finally settled down, Sean expected the guy to go on preaching, but…that was it. Instead the band started right up again, perhaps to run through an encore verse of the Purple Rain song? No—on they went for another fifteen minutes of soaring and rising and lifting *up*. Three more songs! And was that all it was? Music?

When this one ended—a screaming Christina Aguilera number about Jesus "on mercy's seat" in heaven—Pastor Randy stepped forward onto…a catwalk…and made his way further into the crowd, completely at ease. "Let's have a show of hands. Who among you would say you're sure that an all-powerful mighty Creator is looking down over us all and protecting us at this very moment?" Hands shot up all around, and suddenly it was utterly inappropriate to not have identified yourself as one of the believers—and what was this? Almost against his will, Sean felt his own hand begin to rise.

"You know, he is," Pastor Randy went on. There was something about his tone that was so familiar, but Sean couldn't quite place it. It was certainly *motivational*, but that word didn't quite nail the way you wanted to describe it. In any case, it wasn't at all the hysterical stereotypical evangelical tone he'd been expecting. "Folks, you can be comforted," Pastor Randy said. "Whatever challenges you may be facing in this lifetime, you need not worry, because He is protecting you, and when all is said and done, at the end of the day, he will take you *home*. Let us pray now as one big 'ohana."

Suddenly Pastor Randy bowed his head and closed his eyes and began, well, a conver*sation* with his Lord and Savior, eyes closed the whole time, pacing back and forth in front of his backup singers, whose own heads were bowed as they swayed back and forth to another soft chord progression, this time from the electric piano: "Heavenly Father, we are eternally grateful for Your everlasting love, Lord, Your protection, Lord, and we thank You for walking on the path with us this morning Lord, and sitting among us, and guiding us with Your Word so that we may better understand Your *purpose* for us, Lord, that we may better understand that You are our magnificent and awesome all-powerful God, Lord, that you are a *real* God, Lord, one who has supernatural powers that can transform our lives, and we praise you in Jesus' name as we uplift our hearts to You. And we all say?"

Fifteen hundred strong: "Amen."

"Now I want you to go ahead and give someone you don't know a big hug, a hug from the Lord, and welcome them here to our family this morning."

A hug! And why not? Hugs, everyone! Hugs! Hugs to the sound of joyful murmuring above this new yet-again uplifting instrumental. Sean hugged the ex-con welcome-my-brother, I'm-rebuilding-my-life, mahalo-for-not-judging-me JTB Trolley driver standing next to him. He turned around and hugged a roly-poly five-foot Joyce Yamashita clone with waves of graying hair spilling out around the rim of her Sony Open golf visor. Of course he turned to hug Marisa. And yes, why not? He hugged the gum-chewing tita, boobs and all. Ah, fellowship!

"How about all the love in here this morning!" Pastor Randy said. "I'd say the Lord is already at work in here, wouldn't you?" A few people up front called out affirmations, and then Pastor Randy went on some more about *purpose* and about the Lord taking us "home." And, just like that, the word "communion" came out, and how it made us "one with the Lord." Then he whipped out his bible and opened it up and read a single line: "for as the Lord sayeth, in the gospel of Luke, verse 22, 'This is my body, which is given for you: this do in remembrance of me.'" The band started up again, and Pastor Randy's back-up singers returned to their wing formation, and off everyone went on another musical journey, this one sounding a bit softer, penned not by Freddy Mercury or Prince, but by George Harrison.

Sean couldn't believe it. Back at St. Patrick's, communion was what they'd *built up towards*—it was the climactic moment of an elaborate ritual, with line after line of call and response you had to memorize beforehand and then dutifully recite as the priest basically reenacted the entire Last Supper over the final twenty minutes of the mass.

Sean's grandma had once told him that they used to have to memorize the responses in *Latin* when she was a little girl. But Luke: 22, that one little line of scripture, had just about covered all Pastor Randy needed to say about communion, which was now being distributed not by a group of church ministers ordained for that specific purpose after years of study and yet another elaborate and detailed initiation ceremony, but by a collection of Worship Squad volunteers dressed in jeans and sneakers and identical blue polo shirts who were passing through the aisles two trays that looked like the 22-inch chrome rims from someone's lifted Tacoma out in the parking lot, one piled high with communion wafer bread, the other drilled with inch-wide holes to hold these little plastic medicine cups of *juice* in place as it made its way down the aisle.

And let's get on with the music!

Which, after a quick communal gobble of the bread and sip of the juice, and another minute of "prayer," and another eight-or-nine-word quote from scripture, Pastor Randy was happy to do, grabbing his mic and launching right into another Praise His Name number.

Sean looked around wondering if this would be the pattern for the rest of the morning: seven or eight minutes of singing, and then three minutes of talking, followed by seven or eight minutes of singing. If that was going to be the case, then this pre-wedding "church" assignment of his wasn't going to be so bad after all. A nicely dressed aunty in her fifties over there was waving both hands in the air, her eyes shut tight and her head tilted towards the heavens. In another life, Sean figured, that face might have been fixed in *behave!* mode on some poor squirming little kid getting tortured by a Catholic priest's endless monotone of a fire-and-brimstone Sermon from the Mount.

Here, it was joyfully rockin' for the Lord. And this wasn't some just-out-of-prison, help-me-rebuild-my-life, tattooed give-me-some-*hope* uneducated Hawaiian. This woman was an older version of Marisa. She was East Honolulu, Hawai'i Loa Ridge, downtown Executive Center parking all the way.

And Farrington or not, Kalihi or not, there were different versions of this affluent Christian everywhere, male and female, *professionals* clapping along to the everything's-gonna-be-*fine* Lord and Savior Jesus Christ. It was hard to see them at first among the swirl of tattoos and black long-sleeved T-shirts emblazoned with a nail into a hand and the words, "His Pain Your Gain," but they were all over the place, these downtown white Toyota Camry commuter drones.

For a second Sean thought, you could make *deals* in here—though just as quickly it occurred to him that what he was looking at was more likely a collection of HGEA union-protected Department of Transportation and Department of Health state-worker paper-pushers than anyone on the level of, like, say, all the hundreds and hundreds of millions of I-banker *hedge fund manager* money stacked up inside the

Makani Kai Tower, a staggering collective *outside money* amount Sean was still having a hard time getting a handle on. But still—here were people with decent houses and decent incomes and good family lives, here at Farrington High School on a beautiful Sunday morning looking for some kind of…reassurance.

Or maybe they were just looking for *something to do*. If so, they'd come to the right place, the stage now filled with a whole troupe of Pearl City High Class of 2003 drama geek rejects. Dressed like hip-hop stars. In sideways gangsta baseball caps and baggy black homey jeans and blinding white high-top sneakers. And they were…break dancing!

Bring on the fog machine! Now *that's* entertainment!

And of course. They were all here because this was so damned *easy!* My God, we've already gotten communion out of the way! What's next? The announcements and let's go home?

Sean looked at his watch: in and out of here in under an hour. Ah, fellowship!

Another blast of music, another earnestly-sung tear-jerking demonstration of karaoke, another round of thundering applause, and then a woman emerged from the dissipating pinkish fog, a fifties-ish Portagee mix of a Kam School Hawaiian, her narrow face wrinkled from years under the sun. Her own pants-blouse-high-heels Sunday Best suggested she'd come straight from her job as an elementary school assistant principal—though the jumbo-trons were introducing her as Executive Pastor Christine Medieros.

And now that Sean thought about it, maybe this giant operation actually needed an *Executive* Pastor. He was astounded at the level of corporate organization to which he'd already…borne witness…right down to a band so tight they must have rehearsed nightly. Communion for over a thousand people. The orange-vested parking attendants outside, the overflow parking shuttles to HCC. All those activities for the kids—on the way in he and Marisa had passed a bank of classrooms draped in colorful posters delineating the appropriate age group ("Lil' Shepherds," "TeamKeiki," "TeenSpirit") where you just dropped your kids off for the day's fun and instruction.

They even had a computerized kid-identifier security system so no one would kidnap your little ones while you were inside worshiping. The jumping castles. The food tents out in the school yard. The step van selling shave ice. The logo shop tent with the inspirational books and pamphlets and T-shirts and hats. The Aloha-Stadium-sized jumbotron out on the lawn broadcasting Pastor Randy out to the overflow crowd of five hundred-something people in the folding chairs outside. And not just here at Farrington—this whole Broadway carnival was also happening in smaller versions all over the island at upwards of fifty different locations, including Kapiʻolani Theater, where Sean was awakened every Sunday morning by the equally loud but less polished Jesus anthems emitting from the Ala Wai School down below.

Right then as Executive Pastor Medieros went through her in-His-awesome-name greeting, suddenly all of this...organization—it began to make Sean Hayashi feel a bit...uneasy. Maybe Russ was right. Maybe they all were, his exploratory committee. The whole time Sean had been working with Tony Levine and Darryl Kawamoto-guys they'd been talking about this. Levine, who among other brilliant ideas had come up with the scheme to get a couple of college "interns" to plant comments referring directly to Russ on the local blogs whenever a story arose on either TsengUSA or the gambling bill ("And they'll do it for free!"), had also explained that over the twenty years he'd been involved in lobbying for legalized gambling, his most formidable opponent had been "the churches."

Only now was Sean beginning to see why. The Executive Pastor started laying it out about "membership" and "service" and "blessings" and so on—not in the usual cliché stereotypical Baptist evangelical show-me-the-money! way Sean would have expected, but rather directly, as though this was just the way things ran around here—*here* meaning not the greedy and accusatory *in this church*, but rather the more general *in God's world among the blessed and the true believers.*

By the time she came out and said "tithing," it didn't even come off as though she'd been trying to soften them up—it was just...assumed...just like the communion on the chrome rims, the clapping of the hands, the fog machine. Someone had paid for that fog machine, just as someone had paid for what looked to be a ground-to-roof renovation of a crumbling *public school* auditorium, right down to the air conditioning and the wiring for this incredible video-sound-lighting system. "So if you're new or if you're just visiting us today and you're ready to take a step further along on your walk with the Lord," she went on, "please make sure to visit us at the membership table after worship service so that we can talk with you about partnering with us so we can partner with God and do His work in this community." *Partner with God!* What double-your-income Hawaiʻi Convention Center $600 motivational seminar had *she* attended? Partner with God! The whole pitch had taken, let's see…two minutes.

Pastor Randy then headed into what looked like The Day's Activity, saying, "I'm going to ask you to take a look at this short video, and I'd like you to imagine what part *you* might play in such a video. And then we'll regroup and dive right into it." The room darkened and everyone stared intently into the jumbo-trons, where some Pixar-looking cartoon appeared depicting a group of storks carrying their packages through God's sun-beamy clouds.

Whenever the stork unloaded a new puppy or a kitty or whatever it was on a happy new animal parent, a wave of *Awww!* swept through the whole place. Then the stork would return to some kind of cuddly animated cloud up in the heavens and be given another baby animal to bring back to Earth, every little exchange bringing a stream of giggles from the moonfaced retired first-grade teacher Joyce Yamashita clone sitting behind Sean. Oh, she was enjoying this! As was that silver-haired mail carrier-guy three rows up, as was pretty much everyone, practically hypnotized like a roomful of second graders when the teachers plop them in the library to watch "Free Willy" for the third time instead of teaching them to write. This, too, made Sean a bit…uneasy…the way everyone was just sitting there, rapt, like they'd do *whatever Pastor Randy told them*, including even contacting their representatives about some evil gambling bill.

"Cute, chya?" Marisa said to him.

Sean dutifully smiled and gave her arm a squeeze, and then they both turned back to the screen, where a dispute had arisen, brought on when the cuddly cloud began to produce less-cute animals like sharks and electric eels and porcupines. The point of this whole thing, if there was a point, appeared to be that they could wind up *working it out*.

After a final *Awww!* the lights came up, and the pattern for The Day's Activity quickly formed: Pastor Randy would refer everyone to their "notes"—meaning, the glossy-printed program they'd each been handed on the way in, which was emblazoned with a hip-hop image of two sneakers on a pitted asphalt street pointing up at the graffiti-sprayed word, "Faith." Printed on the inside was a schedule of upcoming events and a detachable "survey" designed to extract contact information from first-time visitors. A separate sheet included two fill-in-the-blanks questions—*two*—each followed by four random quotes from scripture that seemed tenuously built around the vague theme of *purpose*.

Pastor Randy offered a string of three witty examples of what he meant by "purpose." Next he stumbled over an attempt at a stand-up riff on each example ("Baby wipes have a purpose! And moms, I don't know how you do it! You only need like *two baby wipes!*" Eyes wide. "You're so efficient! *I use like nine!*"). Then he opened his bible and read some random quote from "Ephesians, chapter 2, verse ten or eleven," which he used as "evidence," taking care to call out each chapter and verse citation in the way an academic would have cited peer reviewed research, or a prosecutor would have cited a string of precedent-setting legal cases.

All anyone heard were a bunch of funny names floating around in a pool of numbers, which, on its own, delivered as it was in Pastor Randy's *beaming* and *earnest* and *encouraging* and *passionate* and *positive* way, was enough to make them go, "Wow—this man knows what he's talking about!"

The whole thing struck Sean as, again, *easy!* It reminded him of Sara Watanabe, one of Marisa's friends from Niu Valley who was also living with mommy and daddy while she piled up the necessary UH education classes for her teaching license. (Her Master's in Biology from Penn State and her education minor weren't enough for DOE certification, which required her to complete an *additional* two-year undergrad program.) Sara had once complained about the stupid pattern her classmates were always falling into when it was their turn to do a demo lesson on, say, metamorphosis. They were always beginning with some kind of "activity" that would include construction paper and crayons, or some "skit" the students would "role play." Then there would be some show-and-tell of the finished products, where the teacher would try to drop the word "metamorphosis" into the conversation in some spur-of-the-moment poorly constructed attempt at a Socratic dialogue. The demos would all end the same way: "And then I'd have the students go back to their desks and write in their journals." No mention of any education psychologist or theorist ever came up in later discussion of these "lesson plans"—it all just fell under the vague headings of "accommodating different learning styles" and "hands-on learning."

"Let's refer to our notes again," Pastor Randy went on. Sean kept waiting for him to refer back to the cuddly cloud video, but that part of the "activity" already seemed buried in the distant past.

Instead Pastor Randy was riffing on the idea of *discovering God's purpose for you*, further linking everyone to baby wipes, and then reading a three-line quote from Exodus in which God calls out to Moses, and Moses says, "Here I am."

"Now let's think about that for a moment," Pastor Randy said, bringing a hand up to rub his chin. "Moses, you know, he had kind of a rough upbringing. You know when he was a baby his mother put him into a basket, and she put the basket in the river, and she floated the basket down the river!"

His eyes were wide again. Unable to readily find some kind of connection, he decided to repeat himself: "So Moses had a rough upbringing. Moses made mistakes! He even killed a man!" Big dramatic pause, eyes wide, a flash of light off the gleaming gold watch. "He made a *big* mistake." Pause.

Where was this going? The strategy didn't seem to extend beyond *keep it moving, keep it moving!*

"But he never gave up." Pastor Randy retreated to the polished wooden podium his roadie had brought onstage, a finely grained koa cross glued to the front. He held on for support before going on: "Moses never gave up. And when God needed someone to lead His children out of Egypt, He called upon Moses, and Moses said—remember?"

"Here I am!" another Joyce Yamashita clone up near the front called out.

Pastor Randy gave the whole congregation a proud smile and said, "'Here I am.' That's right! And God is calling out to all of us, he's telling us our purpose. Whether we're a grandma or a cashier or a lawyer or a truck driver, a husband or a wife, a son or a daughter, He's telling us what our *purpose* is! He's telling us to *be* the best grandma we can be, to *be* the best cashier we can be, to *be* the best husband or wife or daughter or son we can be. If we wear that orange apron at Home Depot"—this drew a small chorus of understanding laughter—"or the blue one at

Wal-Mart"—more laughter—"we wear that orange and blue with pride! Just like Moses led God's children out of Egypt!"

Sean was at a loss as to how any of this related to Moses, but that didn't seem to be the point. The point was that Moses *had a kind of a rough upbringing*, and that he *made mistakes*, meaning, as that chronic over there must have been thinking, and the one covered in jailhouse tats just in front of him must have been thinking: I had a rough upbringing too! And I made some mistakes too! I'm *just like Moses!* So I'm going to be the best cashier I can be! (Pastor Randy kept using "cashier" as his prole job example.) All over the place, people were nodding their heads and writing things down in their "notes"—they knew the drill, they'd all come equipped with pens. (It fleetingly occurred to Sean that "activities" were probably also a big part of prison outreach programs.) Pastor Randy *had* them! They were *swept up!*

And holy fuck!

Because if it hadn't been clear from the start that all these sheep were going to do *whatever the fuck Pastor Randy said*, then for fuck's sake, it was now.

Right in that moment, Sean figured out why Pastor Randy's tone had seemed so familiar at first. Like a revelation from on high, it hit him: Pastor Randy wasn't talking like some kind of evangelist. Here he was up on stage in front of over a thousand *Sunday worshipers* delivering...it wasn't a *sermon*. Be the best you can be! No wonder all of these ex-con bangers scattered throughout the crowd were nodding their heads so emphatically! Pastor Randy could *relate* to them! He spoke in the voice of the only male authority figure to which any of these thugs had ever listened in their lives!

He spoke in the only voice that could come close to the voice of God here on Earth! He spoke in the voice of the magnificent, the truly awesome and all-knowing and all powerful...delivering a half-time *locker-room pep talk*...forget about frikken *uneasy*—these people are indeed being led by the Lord of Lords, the King of Kings: they're being led by the fucking *Football Coach!*

And fuck paranoia—Russ was right! All on his own Pastor Coach Randy could kill the whole thing!

"Now we're going to do our exercises," Pastor Randy said, and everyone dutifully pulled out the inlay with the fill-in-the-blanks problems, whereupon both answers were immediately displayed on the jumbo-trons: "In the first blank, go ahead and write 'I under*stand*.' 'I under*stand* I have a purpose,' just like Moses understood he had a purpose." The gum-snapping fat woman in front of Sean with the enormous breasts was looking up at the jumbo-tron and adjusting the answer she'd written in her blank for Number 1. "In the second blank," Pastor Randy went on, "you want to write, 'Dis*cover*.' 'Discover God's purpose for me.'" Sean waited for more, but that seemed to be it—never mind that Number 2 was a sentence fragment.

Damn, this was easy! Sean could picture Pastor Randy downloading the "purpose" flyer from some church master website—either some pre-ordained common corporate schedule to keep all fifty-odd branches on the same page, or some clearinghouse of inspirational sermons, it didn't matter, as long as it was *easy*—and then rifling through his bible for some random quotes, and then half-planning a few of the witty baby-wipes anecdotes about his newborn grandson on the drive over. (His *grand*son! The guy couldn't have been much older than 40!) And then he goes ahead and gives them the "answers."

And what was this? What was this little logo printed on the back of Pastor Randy's flyer? "A Full Circle Church"? An address for Houston, Texas? Was this whole operation *that* organized? Out of Houston? A Coca-Cola franchise of a McChurch all blue-printed out, right down to the day's sermon? If you put in on a national scale, you weren't talking about a mere fifty thousand people. You were talking about *hedge fund manager*-level money! You were indeed talking about what Eric Busey's predictable rants had helped Sean begin to see: the wave of outside money now sweeping over Hawai'i (and indeed if Sean had gotten any real intel from his final stint carrying a tray, it hadn't been from Michael Prescott—it had come from, of all places, Eric). Full Circle? Houston? Tony Levine had no *idea*.

"Now let us bow our heads and pray," Pastor Randy was saying. "Heavenly Father…" and he went on with a plea for "guiding" us all to "find our purpose" and so on. When it was all over, it occurred to Sean that Pastor Randy had never actually gotten around to telling anyone what that purpose was supposed to be—no "Go forth to help your fellow man," no Hail Marys, not even a plug for donations. "Purpose" was enough. You were already *doing* what God intended. You just have to *keep doing* it with the faith that such is God's plan. If your husband is beating you, you need to work on being a better wife, and perhaps go to the church website's Prayer Board and submit a request for your fellow true believers to pray for your marriage. If you're a miserable state-worker drone, then you should *continue* to be a miserable state-worker drone and understand that such is God's purpose for you. Wear the orange? A cashier? Well, we need cashiers. You're just like Moses.

Another revelation: a skies-parting, speaking-in-tongues, somebody-*catch*-me-I'm-about-to-pass-out-in-*rapture* revelation: *We are in trouble!* No, *uneasy* was no longer the word. If "the churches" wanted to oppose Russ's gambling bill, that meant tens of thousands of people in lock-step opposition—enough to frighten the shit out of any career-climbing low-ranking legislator, any entrenched wouldn't-know-how-to-even-*find*-a-real-job-if-I-didn't-get-reelected old-timer.

Sure, Marx may have talked about religion as "the opiate of the masses," something that blinds the proletariat into thinking a better life awaits them up above in the clouds somewhere just so they go on being faithful cogs in bourgeois machinery. But this? This was the crack, the meth (and it occurred to Sean that the feel-good nature of this whole affair might have had something to do with the preponderance of obvious addicts in here), the acid, the ecstasy, and the pure jack *heroin* of the masses. Three times on a Sunday, every Sunday! Twice on Saturdays! All over Hawai'i! Do the math—that's more like over a *hundred* thousand people, all brainwashing themselves into thinking *everything is okay the way it is!* Get me some shave ice! I'm just like Moses!

Maybe you could go and build your five towers at Dolphin Bay and none of the purpose-filled opiated masses would even notice. (Environmental destruction? No, it's *God's will!* Cultural destruction? Should I get involved? Well, look—I'm just going to focus on being a good cashier, and let God handle that little dispute over the bones of my ancestors.) But how on earth could you get them to stop and think about…the arguments…about Tony Levine's arguments…that gambling wasn't *evil*…that gambling was necessary…that you had fourteen *billion dollars* in unfunded pension liability hanging over your heads (Tony was saving that one) that was going to wipe out all of *your* social services, your EBT and public housing, and all of *your* union pension and health care if we don't *do* something about it. How could you get any of these it's-God's-will worshipers of the Easy Jesus to ever *do* such a thing: to *think* about it?

Worse: if rallying the Jesus troops right here in Hawaiʻi turned out not to be enough to kill Russ's bill, then there was an army tens of millions strong, a Full Circle army that you could tap into, one that stretched from coast to coast, and probably all the way across the South Pacific and to the Philippines beyond, if you could guess from the looks of the organization in this one hall alone. Full Circle!

If there in fact *was* a God, Sean would have begun praying to him right this minute, because all he could see right now, like it was blaring down at him from both jumbo-trons, was the epitaph of Russell Lee's casino gambling bill, and thus Bradley Zao's involvement in Dolphin Bay, and thus Russell Lee's campaign for governor, and thus—could it be?—Sean Hayashi's white-picket-fence future with Marisa Horiguchi? God help us all!

But just as Sean Hayashi was running out of…faith…just as he was starting to no longer…believe…another fat out-of-my-shell state worker-looking guy stepped forward, the "Assistant Administrative Pastor," a guy who introduced himself as "Pastor Rick," to give the announcements. After a rousing "Good morning!" of his own, and another call for a round of applause to "thank our mighty and all powerful and all loving God for walking amongst us this morning," Pastor Rick set in to remind us about the upcoming Prison Ministry Luau. He invited "visitors" to take a free bible from the table in the lobby on their way home to "accompany you in your walk with the Lord." He solicited "volunteers" for the Divorce Ministry so they could "help" children caught in the middle of messy divorces "heal." The image of one of these tattooed chronics, or even one of these drama geeks counseling a traumatized and very impressionable little kid faintly struck Sean as odd, if not dangerous or even illegal—but only faintly, because the next announcement simply bowled him over:

Here's Pastor Rick with a big smile and a rolling-the-dice hand gesture, and he's speaking directly to Sean Hayashi, telling him that yes, Sean, there *is indeed* a God, and he's answering your prayers at this very moment, because everything *is indeed* going to be *all right*. But Pastor Rick, he's using different words to communicate his message to Sean. He's speaking in *parables*, just like Jesus. He's saying: "And don't forget to buy your raffle tickets! As part of our 'Re-ignite Your Marriage Month,' we're giving away pairs of Las Vegas packages to three lucky worshiping couples!"

Halleluiah!

I mean, Halle-fucking-*lu*iah!

Vegas? Rolling the dice? Gambling? The wink-and-a-nod "reignite" discussion of sex in church—apparently a month-long discussion, no less—that was one thing. But Gambling? Weren't these people supposed to be part of that Christian Coalition of Hawaiʻi thing? Itself a part of the Hawaiʻi Coalition Against Legalized Gambling? Or did it only matter *here* but not in Vegas? Jesus—*Jesus!* Were they kidding?

Or were there *other* churches lined up against gambling? The Catholics. What was left of the Protestant missionaries. Sean had heard of some Mormons living up on the Windward side, but you never saw Mormons *protesting* anything. Minor, it was! Nothing when compared to *this*! Praise His name! This place wasn't *obstructing* Russell Lee's gambling bill! It was *paving the way!*

Halleluiah!

Another soaring hands-in-the-air anthem began to rock the house, signaling everyone to start streaming towards the exits, yammering away on their phones as they did now that the painless—*painless!*—ceremony had reached its joyous finale, which Sean himself was more than happy to get wrapped up in: Can I get an Amen! Yes! *Do* praise His name!

Swaying, Sean Hayashi was! And voluntarily this time! Both hands waving in the air! And as he and Marisa made their way back up the aisle, he felt one of those manly fraternal slaps on his back, must've been that beaming chronic with the ponytail from two rows up spreading his fellowship around, and yeah, brother, I'll give you a hug right here.

But when he turned to smile it back to the guy, he was surprised to be looking into first the forehead and then the eyes, narrowed into an emphatic smile, a smile on the face of...

Grant Nishikawa.

"Eh, I neva know you was one true believa, cuz!" Grant said, offering up a hand for one of those local-boy soul handshakes. Sean reached for the hand and, and of course Grant grabbed on with a real bone-crusher and did his best through the brotherly warm grab, right here in church, to communicate that he could *kick Sean's ass.*

But fuck it—I'm *feeling* it so much, I'll even give fucking Grant Nishikawa a fellowship hug.

Because ever since the Pauahi Tower meeting Grant had basically become Sean's puppy dog. While the guy never gave up on this physical manhood thing, unable to see that it didn't ever amount to much if you were some typical got-handed-a-job-through-daddy's-connections, always-protecting-what-I've-got-to-lose *pussy* who did *give a fuck*, Sean could now clearly see that it was even worse than that. Fucking Grant had a *purpose*, an order from God to just follow along and do no more than what is asked on the safest, *easiest* path you can find.

"I guess we all see the light at some point!" Sean shouted over the music.

"Having God in your life, it's an awesome thing!" Grant said, shamelessly eyeing Marisa up and down from head to toe and back again. Grant's own girlfriend or wife or whatever it was had a cute face, but she was as *daikon*ed out as Grant was, and you could tell that a few too many of those Ballena popovers had swelled her ass into something that was probably noticeably bigger than when Grant had first met her, and that he'd never have the balls to tell her so, or to ditch her for someone who took better care of herself.

So before everyone could be introduced, Grant moved on to "touch bases" with someone else he seemed to know further up the aisle, that emphatic smile blazing a trail in front of him.

Sean and Marisa followed the long line of worshipers out into the blinding bright light of a beautiful sun-drenched...*recess* seemed the word for what they'd walked into...this boisterous sea of kids darting around the jumping castle and the bounce house and the surrounding dirt-pocked field, overseen by a collection of high-school aged "mentors" in cross-emblazoned bright blue T-shirts with nametags on them.

Recess, out here among this typical prison yard of a crumbling pre-war DOE campus whose main building's façade may have been designed by the architect of the Halekulani Hotel, but whose collection of ancient cell blocks—too old to be fitted with air conditioning that would allow their banks of jalousie window covers to be closed against an adjoining freeway traffic roar so loud the teachers had to wear handsfree microphones just to make themselves heard—it was all concrete hollow-tile...iron gates...caged open windows.

Looming over the whole twenty-six acres of hopelessness, from up above the steep slopes of the mountain on the other side of the freeway, was the sprawling billion-dollar campus of Kamehameha Schools, and with just a glimpse of its green-roofed halls and dorms, and its baseball field and football field and even an in-ground Olympic-sized pool, all carved into the side of a mountain, the thought blipped through Sean's mind of how *brilliant* it had all worked out—this idea of committing a bottomless supply of money and resources to just a select few Hawaiians, and then positioning them in all ways, figurative and literal, to *look down* upon the vast multitudes of their ethnic brothers and sisters wasting away down here at Farrington, *looking up* at that mountain every single day in a state of utter envy and resentment. Brilliant!

Almost as brilliant as this church here, aiming its sights at people most in need of "hope" and "purpose"—drama club punching bags, redundant state workers, retired Sony Open Visor Joyce Yamashitas, prisoners, drug addicts, and divorced mothers, and most especially their traumatized children, who were all busy running up to Mom and Uncle and thrusting coloring book page images of shepherds and doves into their faces.

Many of the tattooed uncles were digging into the pockets of their Sunday Best jeans and handing out shave ice money. These kids here were already being conditioned, right from the Lil' Shepherds age of two, that you just had to put your faith in Jesus, and life would be one giant carnival where they served shave ice all day long.

Except wasn't it, after all, turning out to be just that for Sean?

"Admit it—you feel good!" Marisa said to him, her own beaming smile spread across that tanned geisha face of hers.

Sean fought against the usual impulse to bathe his reply in irony—and it wasn't easy with all of these *happy* people all over the place, even considering his own admittedly *uplifted* mood—and said, "All right, I'll admit it. How could you not be? I mean, that band was tight."

She gave his hand a squeeze and then said, "Oh look! It's Lokelani—that woman from the prison I was telling you about. Wait here—I've just gotta double check something about the meeting on Wednesday."

Marisa ran to catch up with a skinny dark-skinned Hawaiian woman in one of those purple muʻumuʻus the hula halau onstage had been wearing. She had told him how she'd gone up to Lokelani at a Prison

Ministry meeting, having recognized her as one of the former prisoners she'd seen performing at that Hokulani Treatment Center fundraiser a couple of months ago—the one Russell Lee kept bringing up. Now they were standing in a gaggle of beaming dancers so beautiful you'd have thought they'd just stepped right off of some hotel stage.

His own commitment to his (hot!) fiancé notwithstanding, yet again the thought crossed Sean's mind that *you could get laid here*, so packed was the schoolyard with not just these hula girls, but a whole crowd of check-me-out dressed-for-the-club women, from that UH-dancer-looking tied-my-Jesus-T-shirt-in-the-back-to-show-off-my-belly Chinese-Hawaiian girl over there with the shoulder-length black hair that cried for you to run your fingers through it, all the way on up to that milfy forty-year-old in the red tube-top and denim short-shorts by the fenced-in cratered remains of the condemned swimming pool over there *ooh*-ing and *ahh*-ing over her daughter's stick-figure drawing of Moses or whatever it was.

And just then it hit Sean that maybe you couldn't exactly *get laid here*—that *I'm Hot!* more than likely also meant *I'm in here trying to hook my third husband*, and *my keiki need a father*, and that *getting laid* probably wouldn't have been much of an option without some kind of feigned commitment combined with an airtight exit strategy. And just as suddenly he felt a twinge of…appreciation…appreciation for Marisa Horiguchi, for his *fiancé*, who had rescued him from that sad and frustrating and ultimately unfulfilling and generally just *inconvenient* life of *trying to get laid* (for eventually they *would* make love, and regularly, too). The only men he did see among the schoolyard throng were all these thank-you-for-not-judging-me uncles—and it was here that Sean finally did see an image of Jesus—in fact, they were everywhere, not just on the men but on many of the women, too: that bearded Paul McCartney Jesus face expertly tattooed onto biceps and the backs of shoulders all over the—

Wait a minute. At Farrington High School? At a Sunday worship service? Here? Was that…Kanoe Silva? Indeed it was! Standing next to that towering dark King Kamehameha statue-looking Hawaiian in the red Praise His Name T-shirt (her brother? her boyfriend?), there she was. Her nearly-dry hair was a bit matted down, and she was smiling brightly—Sean had never seen Kanoe Silva smile before—but there was no mistaking that stocky second-row-Merry-Monarch-dancer's frame of hers, even in that billowy green sundress she had on.

When she caught sight of him, the smile vanished for a moment, confirming that it really was her. And maybe you didn't have to be a complete Grant Nishikawa airhead to want to get your Jesus on and listen to some good uplifting music once in a while—goodness knows, even as hot as Marisa did look in a micro bikini at Kaimana Beach, she and all of her downtown 'Iolani connections would hardly have been worth the trouble if this I'm-just-like-Moses! easy-street "religion" was all she had going in her life. But Kanoe Silva?

Oh shit! Now she was walking towards him. Fuck. What was he supposed to *say?* They weren't very well going to get into some discussion over *purpose* and the opiate-crack-ice-ecstasy-acid-pure-jack-*heroin* of the masses now, were they? Or talk about the negotiations? Not here! Maybe it was just going to be one of those *local* greetings, one of those small-town things where you both know exactly what you'd *like* to be talking about, but you avoid the subject and *be pleasant*, avoid it in such a way that it's *clear* you're avoiding it, so it does wind up being the subject—you're just using different words to talk about it.

"Hi Sean!" she said with a bright smile, a *pleasant* smile.

"Kanoe!" He put on a smile of his own.

"Eh, don't look so shocked," she said. "We're not all right-wing homophobe Jesus-freaks around here, you know." To his surprise, she lifted her arms to…give him a hug! And then she said, "But I think I'm the one who should be shocked. I neva expected to see a wheeler-dealer big-shot like you here at church!" She was still smiling. And that little touch of we're-on-the-same-wavelenth pidgin—Sean had never heard that from her before either.

"Well, it's not a bad place to network," he said, and she laughed.

"What, you looking for advice on where to get a good Jesus tattoo?"

Sean had to laugh at that one. Jesus tattoo! He tried to keep up: "Actually I'm in the market for a wife and her three kids—I've seen about twenty or thirty potential candidates so far."

"Eh, you betta watch out," she said. "Most of them, their husbands stay at home—they all watching football."

Of course! That explained the extreme ratio around here, didn't it! Sunday morning at 10:00—this was prime time for that other, more important god, the NFL. Especially here in January, if Sean wasn't mistaken: playoff time.

"I don't know why I hadn't thought of that," Sean said. "I thought they were all single moms hunting for their third husbands."

"I think you'd make a good candidate for that, Japanee boy!" She said it with real affection, too, and truth be told, Sean had to admit it: he *liked* Kanoe Silva. He'd liked her the whole time.

She was passionate, but she was always respectful, and damn, she was smart. It really was a shame that they were always sitting on opposite sides of the table, especially since they really weren't that far apart on what they ultimately wanted, at least on a general level, which was to lift the living standards of the Hawaiian people in and around the development area. Maybe one day they *would* be able to find some common ground.

All wrapped up in the…in the *fellowship* of the feel-good day, of the soaring and uplifting music, the laughing children everywhere, right then and there Sean decided to take a stab at it: at bringing up what they were trying to avoid, and maybe advance things a little, come to some better common understanding here bathed in the sun and the cool breeze under these clear blue skies instead of around some conference table somewhere.

So he just came out and said, "Look Kanoe, I just want to thank you for all you've been doing to try to help us, and help Prescott and Mae Ling and everybody really understand your concerns. I know we're pretty far from agreeing on anything, but still."

Kanoe kept smiling at him, and then she said, "That's really nice of you to say, Sean," and hey, maybe this was working. And then: "But you need to be thanking us a little bit more."

Uh-oh. "Well, you know, I'm kind of *trying* to thank you."

"No, no," she said, her warm smile having melted away. "Because if we didn't exist, if we weren't taking a position, you wouldn't be getting your *kinikini*. And we know that Sean."

And there went *pleasant*. Right along with *avoiding the subject*. Couldn't just leave it alone, could you Sean.

"So you tell 'em to pay you and pay you good," she went on calmly, "and pay you now, and you *cash 'em*. You cash those checks. Because if we win in court— "

"Whoa, whoa, what are you talking about Kanoe?"

"Just cash your check, Sean, cash your check, because we're not going anywhere, and you'll want to get paid before they finally realize that." She leaned in and kissed him on the cheek and turned and walked away.

So much for *fellowship*.

TEAM CAPTAIN

Dream Team. Someone over at the *Sentinel* had actually done a bit of old-fashioned reporting to figure out exactly who TsengUSA had hired for *influence* over at the Lege, and that was the term they'd come up with for the heavy-hitting deep-pocketed lobbyists currently splayed back in various too-manly-to-sit-properly positions all around Russ's office.

There was Tony Levine of Insider Communications—the old guy had just gotten a proposal to re-open a Big Island prison killed in committee, much to the satisfaction of his client, a mainland private prison franchise called Homeland Corrections which housed most of the state's felons in Arizona and Kentucky. Hank Martin of Pacific Rim Relations, whose long list of clients included both the Construction Workers Union and the still-powerful hotel workers union.

Darryl Kawamoto—back in the '80s he'd managed to wipe from the books a state law requiring 2/3 majority legislative approval to develop ag land by coordinating "contributions" from some Japanese billionaire to more than 200 Hawaiʻi politicians, drawing a swarm of FBI agents who "never got a goddamned thing on him!" was how Tony Levine always liked to retell it. Nearly a century of intuitional knowledge between the three of them, plus connections reaching into every office in this building, into the judiciary, across the street at city hall, and onto more boards-of-directors than a modern-day Walter Dillingham.

Along with Cliff Yoshida and Sean Hayashi here, right now they were all waiting for their latest target, Senator Jayden Kaneshiro from District 4, to arrive for a meeting that Russ, unfortunately, had had to call himself.

Which was why "Dream Team" wasn't exactly what Russ would have called them at the moment. Never mind that he himself had pulled the whole group together weeks ago, or that Darryl Kawamoto was doubling as the chair of the Russ for Governor exploratory committee.

Already Russ was getting a bit irritated at how nonchalantly they all seemed to be taking the whole thing about the casino bill, like you could just stir up this complete circus of an Opening Day performance, mount a relentless PR campaign, and then just...*sit back*...was what they were all doing, and for fuck sakes they were talking about *legalized gambling*. And not some watered down bullshit multi-state powerball lottery, either, or scratch tickets for the tourists in Waikiki. Legalized *casino* gambling.

Listen to them, bantering back and forth like they completely forgot that gambling proposals had been landing with thud after thud on the floors of both houses for the past thirty years, sometimes twenty or more at a shot: a horse track in Hilo. Video poker in the airport. The Employees Retirement System had once even looked into *purchasing* a casino in Vegas to "enhance" funding of state worker pensions. Just name it. Between 1990 and 2010 alone (Cliff had told him all of this) 213 gambling-related bills had been introduced. *213!*

Didn't they know that if there was any hope at all of shoveling it through this time, even with Russ and Charles Uchida in charge of the relevant committee chair appointments and referrals and so on, that it was going to be an uphill battle all the way to the end of the session?

Nevermind that Uchida had already locked up all the necessary house votes, or that all this *Dream Team* really had to do was round up just thirteen senate votes. All that small number did was put that much more pressure on securing every single vote, which basically meant getting thirteen career politicians to grab onto the most scalding political hot potato the state has ever seen. Even so, though you'd never know it from the tone in here, so far these guys weren't even *close* to the magic number.

"Talk about deer in the headlights!" was what that lanky little masters-division-marathon-runner-of-a-haole Tony Levine was saying. "Kaneshiro's not gonna know what the fuck hit him!"

"He's gonna get eaten *for lunch*," Hank Martin chimed in from the arm of the little sofa against the back wall. "For *fucking lunch*." Hank's stumpy hands were tossing a football up and down in neat little spirals. He'd grabbed it off Russ's display shelf, where it normally sat next to Russ's old Rainbows helmet. Never mind that it was a WAC Championship game ball, or that Hank, a *prosperous* looking guy in his sixties with a good-sized tube of fat stretching that red-print Reyn's aloha shirt out over his khaki pants—even standing at 6'4" he had to have been your typical bench boy way, way back in high school.

"Welcome to the big city, Hilo boy!" Darryl Kawamoto said from an arm chair over by the big room's wall of a window, his legs spread wide, his arms folded behind his head. "That kid," he said and shook his head. "*Hooo!*"

When Tony sent another volley of *har-har-har*-ing around the room by asking if anyone thought Jayden Kaneshiro even knew how to shave yet, Russ tried to tell himself they were all just masking their scathing intelligence with that purposefully informal way of speaking to try to exude some *manly strength*. Because, legislative history notwithstanding, the task at hand wasn't in fact all that complex: after the big Opening Day splash, you quietly steered your two identical casino bills through the Ways and Means house committee, and Tourism, Judicial, and Finance in the senate. And for the next couple of months, from now until the end of April, all you talked about out loud was the budget: *Gotta pass the budget!* You stoked general anxiety by predicting a shortfall in the hundreds of millions of dollars. You put specific social programs on the chopping block to pit the 22 senate Democrats against each other. (Forget about the three Republicans.)

Then when the final-day proceedings became so rushed and hectic that no one had a moment to properly consider your casino bill, all you had to do was convince enough fence-sitters that it meant *anticipated future revenue*, which technically counted toward balancing the *budget*, thus saving all their pet projects included therein.

Russ tried to remind himself of all these things. After all, no less than Alan Ho had once told him that simply sitting in a room with these very men was "like getting a Ph.D. in the workings of politics and influence." *Getting a Ph.D.*

Right now, well, you couldn't help but *miss* Alan.

That was when Sean Hayashi spoke up: "You're making a huge mistake taking Kaneshiro lightly. And you should also be concerned about people like Marcia Kim. Nathan Fremier. Rudy Santiago." Then he let out a sigh.

Everyone turned to see the young man rubbing both temples and staring ahead, and sitting properly, *not* splayed back in locker-room man-cave mode. Hayashi went on to explain Marcia Kim's record of supporting prior gambling bills in committee and turning around and voting them down on the floor. He detailed Fremier's blanket opposition to development, and suggested that the Kauaʻi haole would view the gambling bill as a prelude to more of it. And with every measured word Russ began to wonder why he was ever even astounded anymore by how capable and professional and *connected* Sean Hayashi had turned out to be. The memory flashed into his brain of that private waiting room on Lagoon Drive, Hayashi waiting for the governor, the house speaker, and the president of the senate, no less. And inviting Russ along—anyone could now see that, chair of his exploratory committee or not, Darryl Kawamoto had had nothing to do with it. That one had been all Hayashi.

To Russ's relief, this Dream Team responded by nodding along to everything Hayashi was laying out. Hank Martin had stopped tossing the football, and Darryl and Tony were both now leaning forward, listening intently and sprinkling Sean's monologue with the odd "That's true!" and "Good point!" So yeah, maybe there was actually some hope—just had to wake these veterans up a bit and put this thing on track.

But then Hank looked straight at Hayashi and said, evenly, "We've already got Marcia Kim's vote. We met with her this morning." It couldn't have been more obvious that the big haole had suddenly felt the need to, not so much as put Hayashi *in his place*, but at least reassert his own sacred *insider* status, his long years of *experience*. On he went, succinctly expanding on Hayashi's point about Kim's voting record, how she always personally believed in legalized gambling, but that all these *crime statistics*…

Tony backed him up: "She thought some group of elderly white ladies from Nuʻuanu were gonna storm her office because they saw *Casino* about four hundred times and they're convinced that Joe Pesci is gonna come and live in the room upstairs."

"We told her the expected 1.62 percent rise in crime would be more than offset," Hank said, "by an increase in dollars into the community of approximately sixteen thousand percent," an overall figure that would trickle down to social services, county-level police presence, and so on. And then he started in again with the football: *toss-spin-catch, toss-spin-catch.*

Tony: "She started crying about the Hawai'i Coalition Against Legalized Gambling, how they'd come back with"—a real girly-man voice now—"'You know as well as I do Senator, that this sort of thing is gonna destroy our economy, and it's gonna destroy our state. And I've got the chief of police here with me, I've got the deputy director of the attorney general's office, I've got the chief prosecutor for the City and County of Honolulu, and I've got untold number of people in between saying exactly that: we don't want this sort of thing happening in our community because it *will* increase crime. I don't care what your academic has to say about 1.6 percent. It's going to be *massive.*'"

"Those damned Chicken Littles always go all anecdotal on you too," Darryl said.

Tony laughed, and then put on the voice again: "'What about the case of Harry the bum, whose kids are clogging up the CPS system, he used to work for the City, and he stole 2.4 million dollars, and then we had to totally transform his entire department, that was a terrible black eye, we *never* want that to happen again!'"

When the laughter died Hank explained how they'd basically just worked out a deal with Senator Kim to drown out the crime noise and *Vili* her to some neighborhood watch thing at the same time.

Vili.

The term reminded Russ that TsengUSA's PR had helped him close the huge gap James Hendrick had opened with his helicopter rescue stunt by ten percentage points, leaving the haole with a mere eight-point lead in Brushette and Hyde's latest polling numbers that would evaporate the moment Nakayama singed the gambling bill into law. (How Darryl had allowed the gap to get so big in the first place was something they'd have to…talk over.) But that thought hardly lightened his mood, because Hank here was treating *Vili*-ing like some kind of magic pill you could use to get all twenty-two democratic votes, never mind thirteen.

"So she's already ours," Hank said, *toss-spin-catch, toss-spin-catch,* and enough with the fucking football already, bench boy.

"That's all well and good," Russ said. "But you really think that's gonna work with Kaneshiro?"

Hank just shrugged his shoulders and said, "He's a legacy." Everyone knew Kaneshiro had only run in the first place because his father Miles Kaneshiro, who'd taken the seat of his own father, had decided not to run for a ninth term. After that, if your name was Kaneshiro all you had to do was get a crowd of people to hold signs and wave shakas at twenty minutes of Hilo rush hour traffic a few times and you were in. On top of everything, the guy was still only in his twenties, was what Hank's little shrug had communicated.

All Russ could do was shake his head. From what he recalled, the father had always been the sort of "leader" who would take a look around the room to gauge how everyone else was voting before ever raising his own hand, and forget about something as politically risky as a gambling bill. Come to think of it, old Miles had to have seen piles of gambling bills land on his desk over the years, and what had Cliff said about that this morning?

But before Russ could ask his clerk, Hank changed the subject, *toss-spin-catch, toss-spin-catch*: "And I'm afraid we'd be wasting our time with Santiago." He looked right at Hayashi again: "Lost Cause."

Despite the clumsy paternalistic way Hank had gone about putting it, Santiago's district did include the heavily Catholic Ewa Beach, and even Russ knew that the Catholics made up a significant part of the Hawaiʻi Coalition Against Legalized Gambling.

"They're just gonna put the full-court press on," Tony said. "They'll bring down ten, dozens, hundreds of people, and they scare the livin' shit outta Santiago is what they'll do."

"A shakedown," Darryl said with a smile.

"Absolute extortion," Hank said, with real admiration. "'Jesus wants it that way, and that's the way it's gonna be.'"

Now Hayashi looked about as irritated as Russ was getting with all this locker-room posturing. And then *he* looked straight at *Hank* and said: "I'm afraid you're just *throwing away a vote* if you don't go after Santiago."

Silence. Looks darting back and forth between all three Dream Teamers, raised eyebrows all around. Hayashi may as well have punctuated his sentence with the word *asshole*.

The young man cleared his throat and began detailing how Santiago, a six-term senator in his seventies, had for the past thirty years been introducing the same bill asking for a zoning change and a state appropriation to build a film studio on what had since turned out to be the last piece of state-owned ag land on the Ewa plain, where a few affluent haoles were boarding their horses in an old stable for fifty bucks a month. It had been the guy's dream for his entire legislative career: a vital economic boost, not to mention a way to give the families in his district a sense of hope that some future existed for their children beyond the service industry, and that such a sense of hope could keep these kids in school and off drugs and all the rest of it.

Paternalistic looks overtook the faces of all three Dream Team veterans: first surprise, then skepticism, and then…Hayashi keeps spelling it out…is Darryl's whole face registering an oh-isn't-this-*fun* grin brighter than it had at any point since the fabulous '80? Is Hayashi bringing back memories of the old shakedown years? Except that this Santiago thing was *even better* than "shakedown" in the old sense of extorting a film studio out of a huge foreign conglomerate in the way Darryl used to scrape millions off the Japanese, because from the casual way Hayashi was explaining it all, TsengUSA must have factored all kinds of payoffs into their budget as *costs of doing business.* $15 million for a film studio? No problem!

And are those looks of…admission? That this young gun is exposing the Dream Team as a bunch of…could it be? Has-beens?

"The guy is *ripe*," Hayashi said.

"But what are you gonna do about the money?" Tony said. Hank probably had the same question in mind, but understood that simply asking it was an admission that he *hadn't even bothered to consider* any of what Hayashi had been able to unearth about Santiago. "Getting that appropriation through—that's a whole nother project."

"We won't need the appropriation," Hayashi said evenly. "We just need the zoning change. Your client is going to fund the film studio."

Silence. Again. Not even the tap of fingers on football. And this time you could hear the punctuation as clearly as if Hayashi had come out and said it: Your client is going to fund the film studio, *you arrogant dumb fuck of a complacent baby-boomer.* Russ turned to see if Cliff had some line of statistical evidence on Catholic opposition to gambling in

Santiago's district or whatever that would further back up what Hayashi had just laid out—then again, little Cliff hardly spoke during these sort of testosterone-soaked meetings to begin with, let alone jump in at a moment like this one, where it looks like Hank is about ready to heave the frikken football right at Hayashi's smug face, and fuck, Hank, what the fuck are we *paying* you for anyway, was what Russ was about to say.

What stopped him was this palpable cloud of—you couldn't mistake it—of *charm* now drifting into the room, a cloud followed by the bright beam of the grin radiating out from District 4 freshman Senator Jayden Kaneshiro's entire tall and powerful *being*…young and handsome…hadda be Japanee-haole mix. They'd all met the guy before, and yet he was so filled with charisma that all heads turned to him immediately, looking up into a face that had been your *friend* since *hana butta dayz!* All arms reached up to shake the hand of a former all-state thick-enough-to-have-played-tight-end 'Iolani state champ wide receiver who, above all else, reminded Russ of a much younger version of… himself.

Introductions all around, and then an invitation to sit, and okay, let's just see what the Dream Team has in mind for racking up one of our precious thirteen votes. These little strong-arm meetings have always been their forte, so let's *see*.

A grinning Hank Martin indicated a place on the sofa that caused Kaneshiro to sink far down below the big man's gaze, and even that of lithe little Tony, who sat on the sofa's arm—so far down, in fact, that he was eye-level with Hayashi across the room. And okay, right away you could tell that on top of wedging a vote out of Kaneshiro, Hank was going to use this whole little exercise to try to school Sean Hayashi in the ways of *influence*, to indeed put little Japanee-boy back in his place.

And fuck, let's just see if it works, Hank.

The obligatory small talk didn't last two minutes before Tony jumped in with, "So let's get down to business here, Senator. We are fast and faster becoming a service society which services the rich. We service the old rich. We service the *nouveau riche*. We service all kinds of *rich* people!" Over a hundred private jets in the Kona airport this, Maui time shares that, billionaires the other. "The kind of people that when they're building their sixty million dollar fourth home in Kona, they can compete for local construction workers with the Department of Defense, even-Steven, and *win*. The Department of *Defense!* On and on. Hawai'i's middle class pushed back to Vegas. Seattle. Oregon.

Hayashi looked like he was holding back—like he already had Kaneshiro figured out, but that he, too, wanted to see how the Dream Team planned to approach things. That exasperated look of his was directed more at the twenty-nine-year-old *state senator* now nodding along to some fat-cat lobbyist's Everyman speech about reviving the middle class in a 21st-century Hawai'i whose unions had been rendered pretty much obsolete, whose police officers and nurses and teachers—thanks to the mainland speculators who'd turned every residential area into an enclave of illegal vacation rentals, and to a housing crisis on all 26 military bases that provided an army of military renters with $2100 monthly housing stipends as they flooded an already bursting housing market—even Hawai'i's *professionals* were lucky to find a two-"room" converted garage in Makiki to call "home." Meanwhile, this eternally-cashing-in-on-the-boot-straps-caché-earned-three-generations-ago-by-my-grandfather 'Iolani pretty boy here split his time between his waterfront condo and a ten-acre Big Island cliffside spread, because while Daddy may not have been able to compete with the DOD, the man pretty much owned Hilo and much of the Hamakua coast.

"I couldn't agree with you more, Tony!" Kaneshrio said. *Tony*. "And what we need to really work on is diversifying the economy. That's why I'm eager to start work with the Agriculture Committee to create some initiatives for farming. You've got Waiāhole and Waikāne, much of the North Shore, part of the Ewa plain. And that's not even considering the Big Island."

Now it was Kaneshiro's turn to go on and on: "luxury crop items" this, and "sustainability" that, plus "ethanol plants" and "energy independence," along with as many references as possible to the environmental studies courses he'd taken "back at Yale," and the environmental law concentration he'd done "before passing the bar."

All the while Tony sat there with his spindly arms folded, openly shaking his head back and forth, while Hank twisted his face into a smirk that announced, "You've gotta be kidding me with this 'sustainability' shit."

Then Darryl Kawamoto leaned forward and said, "We're not gonna make it in Hawai'i on subsistence agriculture, okay? We're not. People are not gonna become truck farmers. They're not. It's hard frikken work. I did that kind of work. I know."

Kaneshiro seemed surprised, but he somehow regrouped and launched into a Plantation Days nostalgia trip that Russ figured had been ingrained since the moment the guy popped out of mama's womb in Hilo Medical Center.

When he was through Hayashi said, "Look, Jayden, you're— "

Hank cut him off: "That's nice," he told Kaneshiro, "except that the only way we've been able to figure out economically how to do what you just said is to use slave labor. The moment the ILWU unionized the sugar plantation workers, the whole operation was done for. As soon as you had to pay field hands a living wage, everyone started planning on how to pick up stakes and move to the Philippines." He then cut a smug glance at Hayashi, as if to let him know he was digging right into Kaneshiro on purpose with that "ILWU" comment, knowing full well that the union's middle-class-proletariat narrative basically ran through Kaneshiro's veins.

But Kaneshiro…somehow he worked the muscles of his face in just the right way to create that I'm Your Buddy smile, pulling it off as well as Russell himself ever had. Despite how his greatest political ambition had just been ground under the heel of fat little Hank, the freshman was somehow still pulling off that…aura…like his whole being had been forced into projecting a single message: Just a group of guys talking story! Just looking for the right solutions to the world's problems!

Which was exactly what Kaneshiro went on to say: "So what do you propose as a solution Tony?" *Interested* face! He's a *listener!* He's *listening!*

"I believe that a casino can help bring back the middle class."

Kaneshiro locked his lips and darted his eyes from face, to face, to face. He must not have taken Russ's Opening Day bomb all that seriously, because you could tell it was only just sinking in now, the whole reason he'd gotten called into the senate president's office in the first place.

Hayashi: "Look, Jayde—"

Tony interrupted: "I can make the argument specifically. We now have a billion after-tax dollars leaving here every year. Tens of thousands of local people *per month* are going to Vegas to spend their Hawai'i money. We don't get any additional income over that money. It isn't spent here, it doesn't multiply in the economy, it doesn't do a damn thing. It's gone. Way over there. Okay?" Tony opened his eyes wide and pounded his fist into his open palm in rhythm with each word: "All. That. Money. Goes. Away. From. Hawai'i."

Big Hank: "That's not all." Kaneshiro had to swing his head all the way around to look up at Hank, *interested*. "Our tourist industry is already quote-unquote 'mature', and what that means is, *old*. If you go down to Waikiki tonight, you will see tourists down there walking around like they're the Night of the Living Dead. They've got no place to go, they've got nothing to do, so they're walking around, just lookin' at shit. They can't go to a movie. There aren't very many shows. You wanna go and have a drink with your spouse or your girlfriend or your boyfriend or somebody? Put your twenty dollars down on the bar and the bartender's gonna look at you like: 'Where the hell's the rest of the money?' It is no longer a place where you can enjoy yourself very much."

"That's certainly true, Hank!" Kaneshiro said. "And that's really what motivated me to seek this office—working to diversify our economy, to put an end to our dependence on tourism."

Charm.

Right there Russ could see it. It wasn't *charm* in the Russell Lee sense at all, the ingratiate-yourself-so-you-can-get-things-done sense. No, it was the Miles Kaneshiro brand: the *safe* brand, the kind you used to make people *like* you—not because you wanted to persuade them to action, but simply because you needed to be *liked*—the kind of charm you used, above all else, to *avoid making waves*.

Kaneshiro's father had perfected that brand of charm, which was probably why he'd lasted for eight safely unremarkable terms as a state senator. A *pussy*. One who'd voted against every gambling bill he'd ever come across, was what Cliff had told Russ only this morning.

And here was Miles's son, all-state footballer, a no-fear, run-across-the-middle wide receiver, but sadly, just as much of a pussy, which meant that if these guys were trying to *educate* Kaneshiro, they didn't have a prayer of getting anything more than what he was currently offering: a *smile*, and a bunch of head-nodding, and some spirited glad-handing, followed by a "reluctant" *nay* when the floor vote came up in April. And surely the Dream Team had more in mind than…educating people. Right?

"We're all with you on diversifying the economy, Senator," Darryl said, leaning back. "But we need to do more than just exchange one piece of the pie for another. We've gotta make a *bigger pie*." He explained how social services and the UH and the DOE and everything always gobbled up existing revenue, "but really, the eight-hundred-pound gorilla is going to be our unfunded pension liability. We've got hundreds of millions of dollars leaking away year after year for that alone, and with the number of in-service workers about to equal the number of retirees, it's only going to get worse. We're talking *fourteen billion dollars*." Then he went on about other revenue-generating ideas that had been floated in the past, like legalizing marijuana. "I'm all for that! You just need a bigger pie!"

And was this all Russ could expect from here on out? More *educating*? He had to jump in and save things somehow, *throw* something to Kaneshiro. Except that he didn't have the faintest clue where to begin to find the guy's…cracks…in the way Hayashi had found Santiago's. Maybe he should put Hayashi on it, because Tony here seems content to just lay down the *facts*. Hank: the statistics. As if *that* will be enough to just *change Kaneshiro's mind*.

Darryl too, over there by the window…that window looking directly out onto Washington Place, the residence of…the governor of Hawaiʻi. From the moment Russ had been assigned this plum office more than fifteen years ago—and what measure of status could be more important in the senate pecking order than the view you commanded?—he'd begun seeing that Victorian mansion outside as the ultimate prize. And since then the historic building had gone from just another version of football-glory *winning*, to meaning so much more in Russ's mind in the way of *doing good*, of *helping his people*, and—

His heart rate jumped.

This little meeting with Kaneshiro—it wasn't the only one upon which Russ's chances at occupying Washington Place rested. For fuck's sake, they still had 21 more to go, and if this one was any indication, the Dream Team was basically pulling the whole thing out of thin air, relying on nothing more than their reputations as connected men of *influence*, and their years of *experience*, and was that how *all in* Russ had become? Had he really laid it all on the prospect of pulling off the most unlikely legislative accomplishment in state history?

And yeah, he knew the rest. Lately it had been creeping up and then flashing straight through his brain like some kind of horror-show mantra: *No gambling bill, no Dolphin Bay. No Dolphin Bay, no run for governor. No run for governor, no…Portlock home! No wife! No nothing! Forget about helping my people! Nothing but…shame! The shame of standing penniless in front of my own son!* Only right now was it hitting him that all of this, above all his exploratory committee in this stealth run for governor, lay in the hands of a guy like Darryl, who always joked about this *all in* thing by shrugging his shoulders and saying, "You either win, or you go bankrupt, or you go to jail."

Go to jail! Had Russ really put…his life?…in the hands of Darryl Kawamoto?

"One casino would raise about a half a billion dollars a year," Tony was saying. "Half a *billion*." *Educating* Kaneshrio. *Explaining*. "Additionally, it would employ at least 14,000 people directly, and then ancillary would be even more. Think about it. Sure, it's still tourism. But it's diversified tourism. Anything we could do that is vaguely legal that would get the attention of people where they'd say, 'You know I went to Hawai'i with my wife twenty years ago for our honeymoon, and that was great, but now they've got *other* stuff I can do!'"

And there was the old Kaneshiro *charm*, reincarnated in this fabulously charismatic young man. *Listening*, yes. But more: Kaneshiro was *humoring* the entire Dream Team. *Humoring* them! Like he had some deep religious convictions against gambling, or an uncle in gambling addiction rehab somewhere. Or some connection to a string of chicken fighting rings over on the Big Island.

No. It was far simpler than that. Russ had been to the freshman's office—he'd even arranged for the kid to get his dad's old corner office—and there he'd seen nothing but pure vanity: diplomas, framed in *koa*, an 'Iolani pennant more important than Yale or any law degree… the office itself a mere stepping stone to a run at Lieutenant Governor, and who knows? Hawai'i's other U.S. Senate seat was also octogenarianly occupied, and a few years from now, the timing might be just right. So for someone as *ambitious* as Jayden Kaneshiro, a gambling bill was far too much of a political risk. Whereas some cockamamie "progressive" idea like "sustainable agriculture" was a winner all around, even if it never went anywhere. (Everyone's gotta eat, right?)

No, all that mattered was how to get to the next level.

Right in the middle of another Tony Levine jaunt through Revenue Pie Territory, now it was Russ's turn to interrupt, and though he didn't exactly know what he was going to say, fuck, enough with all this *explaining*: "Look, Jayden,"—Tony kept going, but Russ plowed in anyway—"I've known your father for—"

Hayashi cut him off: "Hey Jayden."

Russ: "…more than twenty years now—"

Hayashi, raising his voice: "Hey *Jayden*."

Russ paused. Heads turned.

And then Hayashi looked the freshman in the eye and said: "We need your fucking *vote* on this."

Silence.

Then Hayashi just turned to look out the window, as if to make some kind of point. Russ wondered if he'd follow it up with some kind of grad power gesture, like Alan Ho would have done, but then Hayashi was hardly built like his powerful mentor had been. All he did was give Russ a nod. And of course. Of course. Hayashi had been to Kaneshiro's office and seen it too: flat-out student-body-president vanity that said *Look at me, I went to 'Iolani*.

"You really have a nice view from up here, Senator Lee," Hayashi said.

And of course.

"Yeah," Russ said. "You know, back when I was a freshman, the senate president put me in this, well, it looked like some kind of *broom closet*." He turned and looked straight at Kaneshiro.

And then the Dream Team, they fell into line too. Hank Martin: "Yeah, must be nice to have a corner office." Then Darryl: "I bet people are really impressed with that, Senator." Tony: "I bet everyone likes all that natural light. Su*stainable*." Big smile!

Now the muscles in that pretty-boy face were working mightily to hold up some sort of a *reasonable* and *professional* and *I'm listening* posture, while the eyes could only register flashing mixes of *contempt-charm-contempt-charm-contempt-charm*. If it hadn't looked so comical, Russ would've been worried the poor guy's head was about to explode.

Finally Russ decided to put Senator Kaneshrio out of his misery: "Look, we know this is a tough decision, and we don't expect you to make it right here on the spot." Then he looked at his watch and stood, reaching out for a put-'er-*there*-pal handshake. "Just think about it."

Though it couldn't have been clearer that Kaneshiro's vote had been bagged, the little gesture allowed the freshman to charm right back up again as though he were leaving on his own terms—and Russ didn't envy Sean Hayashi the bone crusher of a handshake Kaneshiro was now laying on him—as though he were indeed being allowed to "think it over" instead of being threatened with removal to a windowless office and some meaningless career-sinking committee appointment on Military Affairs, or whatever else Russ felt like doing with him, now and forever.

That was just how you did it—not that this was any kind of great revelation to a roomful of men who had built decades-long careers on their understanding of the nuances of *influence*. More like a… reminder…that you didn't just sit back and rely on your *experience*, or even your relationships. You had to throw them something. More: you had to know *what* to throw. A $15 million film studio. A corner office. Maybe sometimes it *was* a blank check—but never with a great and principled (though certainly misdirected) man like Ikaika Nāʻimipono.

And yeah, now that that whole Opening Day fiasco had had a chance to cool off a bit, Russ would give his old football brother a call, too. Right after this meeting. Lay it out. Help him justify it. Throw him something: really, Ikaika, what *has* your lifetime of activism won for flesh-and-blood Hawaiians compared to what this one single project will give them? How many of them have you brought back from Vegas? Watch: someday you're going to thank me, Ikaika.

Kaneshiro made his way out of the office. And one day this little pussy of an ambitious career climber would have to thank Russ too, when this huge political risk he was about to take paid off, when he could take *credit* for all the jobs and ancillary income and the rest of it Tony was talking about. Shit, the guy would even have to thank Hayashi, because without Hayashi, Russ might not have figured out how to…persuade him. That much was obvious even to Hank Martin, and Darryl Kawamoto, and Tony Levine, who were all now taking turns glad-handing Alan Ho's prodigy like he'd just made the team.

For whatever that was worth, was the thought that suddenly registered in Russ's head. Sure, Tony Levine, obviously one of the most highly respected lobbyists in town, was already working the casino bill from all angles, his main client, Homeland Corrections, having long since lined up in anticipation of the future "product" the projected rise in crime promised. But hadn't Tony's Insider Communications been raking in tens of thousands of dollars from the gambling lobby for decades? Yeah, Hank Martin and Darryl Kawamoto had gotten a *special legislative session* called to draft the law allowing an interisland ferry the size of an aircraft carrier to operate without an EIS. But didn't the courts wind up striking that law down? And look: all three of them had just tried to rely on reputation alone to *educate* Jayden Kaneshiro into a legislative position. Was that really where you wanted to put literally all of your chips?

Or did you slide them across the table and place them on someone as capable, and connected, and hungry as Alan Ho had once been—especially compared to this whole segment of state *power* he'd just exposed as...quote-unquote "mature"—meaning *old*: stagnant, inbred, and complacently *lazy*. And not just in how Hayashi had known it was time to simply lean on Kaneshiro. All on his own he'd studied up on Santiago too, asking around, finding the cracks, while these *old men*, these *paternalistic baby boomers* sat wallowing in good-old-days glory, buoyed by the thought that here in Hawai'i your age and *experience* counted for something—a quaint thought, Russ could now see, that belonged somewhere back in the '80s. Hayashi had crept right up on them and pounced before they'd known what was happening.

So as the men began filing into the outer office, Russ put his arm around Sean's shoulder and told him: "You know, Alan would have been impressed."

Hayashi thought for a moment. "Alan?"

Russ raised an eyebrow. "Yeah, Alan. Alan Ho."

"Right! Right!" Hayashi said. "I guess I was just focused on 'Iolani boy here."

Okay, Russ figured. Hayashi had in fact just been a bit...distracted. "How's he doing, anyway?"

"Alan. Of course. Yeah. He's just been at home...you know, taking it easy I guess."

I guess?

"Well if you talk to him, send him our aloha."

Russ may have taken a moment to wonder whether Alan had even heard of the trip to Macau and the meetings with Bradley Zao at all, but when they all walked into the outer office, he found himself facing a more urgent concern—one that caused him to save the news he had been about to share with Hayashi for some other time—and one he was thankful the entire Dream Team and even Cliff Yoshida overlooked as they all offered goodbyes to Sandy Izawa, Russ's office manager, and headed out into the hallway.

There in the two seats right across from Sandy, like a couple of lobbyists themselves, sat two arms-folded Hawaiians who may as well have been wearing signs that read *gangsta*. The big one had his hair cut so short he looked almost bald, and wore a blaring yellow Lakers jersey over a white T-shirt that shone out even louder than the two rocks pierced into his ears. Next to him: a slender character with a thin gold chain hanging out over his black sweater, one leg of his baggy jeans stuffed into a blinding white basketball sneaker, the other pulled over the kind of soft cast Russ had worn years ago after breaking his ankle in a game against Boise State his junior year.

"Senator, this is Kekoa Meyer," Sandy said. She gave the other guy's name, too, Javen something. Then she went on about how they claimed to be his constituents, how they didn't have an appointment, that they were willing to wait, that you would know what it was about. But beyond *Kekoa Meyer*, Russ didn't hear a word.

Hello, Kitty!

If someone wasn't going to tap him on the shoulder now, then Sean could be sure it would never happen at all, because how much frikken *better* could life even *get?* Like, shoot him now, because from where he lay at this very moment, right here in the lair of every one of his boyhood fantasies, the rest of it could only be a downhill ride. Pauahi Tower, sure. The State Capitol, fine. But how much higher could one man climb than all the way up to here, into the white four-post bed of Marisa Horiguchi?

When Sean had called to tell her that, wedding or not, it was *time*, not only had she eagerly agreed—she'd insisted she'd only feel comfortable in her own bedroom. Just look at her, snuggled right up next to him, her naked skin as soft as velvet, soft as *puppy fur*. In all his 34 years he'd never touched anything so soft, and yet there it was, right there for him to freely run his hands *all over it*. For the *rest of his life!*

To think that only moments earlier he'd finally been *making love* to her too, right here in the very same bed where she'd slept peacefully, innocently, since her JPO-Girl-Scout-Little-Mermaid-for-Halloween childhood. Made love! Twice! True, the first time had been a bit of a fumbling disaster that had pretty much ended before it began.

But the second time! You could have filmed it for a porn video! Sean had surprised himself with what a sexual athlete he could be even though up until tonight you could have counted a lifetime's worth of encounters on one hand (two if you included the rub-and-tugs he'd paid for in some Keʻeaumoku hostess bar, but did those even count?). Maybe it had been all those hours upon hours he'd spent…*studying* was what he'd liked to call it…studying the art night and day on his favorite internet porn sites. But once he'd gotten through that first awkward explosion of nerves and settled down a bit, it had all just come so… naturally.

Even for Marisa. She'd been pretty relaxed about the false start, giggling it away and then teasing him just a little before making a joke about how flattered it made her feel. Then she calmed him down with a nice long massage from her loving hands, from toes to shoulders, one that ended with her—he still couldn't believe it—with her taking him in her mouth! It was so erotic and—surprisingly—so damned *intimate* at the same time! That Marisa Horiguchi would even think to do such a thing must have meant that she was *in love* with him, really and truly *in love!* Right away Sean had been ready to go again. And *go* he had, pulling out moves he'd never known existed—naturally!

And *oh* how she'd responded! Like they were just…meant to be together!

Add in the high contrast of the setting, and it just got all the more erotic, if not a little, well, *dirty*, although of course in such an innocent way: the gleaming white dresser adorned with ceramic bows for drawer handles. The shelves over on the wall: little clusters of Precious Moments figurines—a set of winged angels, the characters from the Wizard of Oz—a pair of My Little Pony dolls, purple and pink hair combed out. A giant stuffed Snoopy dressed in an official infant-sized UH Warrior jersey, his feet jutting out from the top shelf, and cute little Woodstock in his lap. The bottom shelf, eye level, cluttered with framed photos dating back to an innocent little girl time: an adorably tutu-ed and tiara-ed six-year-old; a pigtailed tweenager hugging a puppy at the Humane Society. Though some of the photos stretched out through high school—Marisa and a couple of guys from her history class or whatever waving shakas in front of the Eiffel Tower, a happily drunken Marisa holding up the little plastic container of a Jello shot at some UH dorm party, all the girls from work smiling over a tableful of popovers at Ballena's—the rest of it was frozen in time, right down to the platoon of stuffed animals lined up against the opposite wall—the very very *pink* wall—led by, yes, the Queen of Adorable herself, three feet tall if she stood an inch, *Hello Kitty.*

Hello kitty indeed! Because this shrine to the very type of cute and popular high school girl who would have laughed out loud at the thought of taking…Sean Hayashi?…To my *room?*…Are you *serious?*…all of it clashed with the mountain of makeup cases and hair brushes and the yet-unfolded pile of lacy Victoria Secret lingerie lying there on the vanity, which together formed an image that screamed out: *Woman!* And what was that over there next to that red heart of a valentine's candy box she'd gotten from work last week? A brand new box of condoms?

Had Marisa really been preparing for this moment all along? Had she been *waiting* all these weeks, just properly waiting even though she'd wanted to rip his clothes off right from the start, but you know, that's just not what a proper girl would do. Was that the reason—that he'd gotten her so *pent up* by delaying the moment until this very night—was that the reason she'd started *slapping his ass?* It must have been! And even the screaming, screaming just like the passionate couples escaping the sorrows of their working poor lives in Kapiʻolani Theater, *Oh yeah! Oh baby! Oh baby! FUCK ME! FUCK ME!* Marisa Horiguchi!

It was almost as if she'd been studying as much internet porn as he had just to get ready for this one spectacular moment! Oh, happy endings!

And good thing her parents weren't home!

Her parents weren't home. What a magical phrase that was, if only in how it added to the whole passionate throw-back nature of their…you could even call it a *courtship*, so long had he and Marisa patiently waited, was what Sean had been thinking when he'd bee-lined it over to Niu Valley straight from the State Capitol. It was then that he'd also finally admitted to himself that the real reason he'd ever agreed to "wait" in the first place had had less to do with moral convictions than with the outright *fear* of standing naked in front of…shit, in front of a damn *calendar girl* who should rightly have been marrying some volleyball stud a foot taller and fifty pounds thicker than Sean Hayashi. Having just destroyed that frat-boy pussy Jayden Kaneshiro—not to mention a roomful of over-the-hill lobbyist legends—Sean had suddenly felt a foot taller himself, if not a few inches…longer.

As if that weren't enough, Russell Lee had called less than an hour later, squashing such *fear* for good, and leaving Sean suddenly…*ready*…more so than he'd ever been in his life. Russ was making some "changes" to his exploratory committee, he'd explained, and since Sean had basically been doing the heavy lifting all along, it was time for him to take over as chair. Sean had hardly been able to believe the words as they'd spilled out of his phone, because it was such a short step to imagine that Exploratory Committee Chair would equal out to Campaign Chair, and then Transition Team Head, and finally a cabinet position—if Sean actually wanted one of those instead of the more lucrative consulting work he'd be able to pile up (And should he start hiring his own staff of bean counters and attorneys?) once he had unlimited access to the sitting governor of Hawaiʻi.

After all that, I mean, who *wouldn't* have exploded within seconds of entering the Hello Kitty shrine of Marisa Horiguchi?

"What's funny, babe?" Marisa asked. And was she really inviting him to share the entire career-defining victory in all its detail? As blissfully delirious as Sean had become thanks to…making love!…this was almost even better.

"I was just thinking of something," he said.

"What, hon?" she said, turning to face him, and damn, how the fuck were you supposed to *focus* with that…work of art!…that perfect naked body right there in front of you?

"This guy Jayden Kaneshiro, this pretty-boy frikken *legacy*, he basically—"

"Jayden Kaneshiro?" she said. "Oh my god, you know Jayden?" And then she lay back and started giggling. "*Jay*den?"

More giggles.

It had indeed crossed Sean's mind that Marisa might have known the guy at ʻIolani. They were the same age, after all, and frikken Kaneshiro looked just like your typical glad-handing student body president—and not the nerdy kind, either, but the kind who would have had "friends" on the football team and the drama club both, who'd probably soundly defeated his nerdy-geeky opponent in the election, the first of many elections leading up to the state senate and beyond.

"So you knew him?" he asked.

"*Knew* him?" she said. "Who didn't know him? That boy was such a man-whore! Even in high school he had his own apartment right across from campus."

His own apartment! Tony Levine had imagined as much when he'd launched into that diatribe out in the hallway about how there were "two kinds" of neighbor islanders: the stuck-in-the-seventies provincial country bumpkins who got on a plane once or twice a year—if that—for someone's wedding or baby luau, and the ones like Kaneshiro, who'd been flying to Honolulu weekly since they were in elementary, and who hadn't needed to dorm at 'Iolani because they'd had their own condo in that glass tower right across the street—Kapi'olani Theater, Sean knew—as fifteen-year-olds. Tony had been spot-on.

Sean could imagine the stories Marisa had heard of such a place. And good. So the guy had been even more "popular" than Sean had even guessed—a real rock star of a high school stud, one of those tall pretty-boy muscled-up hapa boys with product in their hair that gaggles of daddy's-little-girl types would swoon over, then tell Sean what a good "friend" he was to them…just like a brother, such a good listener. Sean had just *slain* the King Bull of all those vain motherfuckers. *Slain!* So once again he recounted the whole thing, from the dust-up with Hank Martin, to how Tony Levine's little lecture on the disappearance of the middle class had like, zero effect on Kaneshiro.

And yeah, just like Alan Ho had said so long, long ago.

"What's funny now?" she asked.

"I was just thinking, it's just like Alan told me that time, this thing about Kaneshiro." The thought brought back the flickering memory of an old man, stuck with all manner of wires and tubes, pathetically flirting with his hot young nurse. And then another memory: Russell Lee asking about Alan, and Sean…drawing a blank. Alan had in fact texted him a few times over the past couple of weeks, but Sean had just never been able to find the time to get back to him.

"Alan Ho," she said. "Is he all right?"

"You know, I really don't know exactly," he said. The last he'd heard, they'd sent him back to his Mariner's Ridge estate under orders to "take it slow" for the next "several months," if not retire altogether. "But it doesn't really matter. Anyway, he was always telling me about how these Punahou-'Iolani-Yale guys, they've all got—"

"Something to lose," they both said at the same time, both of them smiling, and damn, that little anecdote may as well have been part of Alan's name, he'd recited it to so many people.

"But sometimes it's true," Sean went on. "That's exactly what happened with Kaneshiro today. He knows how important this gambling bill is, but he was too weak to commit his vote."

"Yeah, he's got a lot to lose all right," Marisa said, rolling her eyes.

Sean explained how he and Russ and the rest of them had successfully threatened to end the guy's career in the Lege right then and there with a simple not-so-subtle reference to his daddy's corner office.

"We need your fucking vote on this!" Marisa repeated, breaking into a real endearing cackle now, her body—my God! she's *not wearing any clothes!*—her naked body bouncing up and down on the bed. "That's just *so* perfect!" She kept right on looking at him, staring into his eyes, intimate. You could hear a car whiz by outside, the sound of a TV laugh track from the house next door.

And then she said it: "You know, that's why I love you, Sean. You're smart and all, and handsome too, in that samurai way, handsome like my dad. But it's more. You *get things done*. You have a plan, and you figure it out, and you just *do* it. You don't worry about failing. How many guys do you meet downtown, or guys from 'Iolani like Jayden Kaneshiro, everyone with big dreams? And look at you: you've practically got a cabinet position because you just *do* things."

Normally Sean wouldn't have heard a word beyond *I love you*, but come on: how could you not but focus in on every last word of such praise for the bootstraps don't-give-a-fuck all-the-way-from-public-school Sean Fucking Hayashi? How could you not just drink it all in? And she was right, too. With every word of it.

"Me too," she went on. "I had big dreams too you know."

Sean waited for her to go on with something about becoming the first female president, or curing cancer or whatever. She looked embarrassed to share her little secret.

"Since I was little—my god, it sounds so cliché—I just loved animals." She gave this little embarrassed smirk. "So yeah, I always wanted to be a veterinarian." Another smirk to wipe away how stupid-cliché-girly the whole dream sounded. "I really did though. And my mom and dad would even feed me all the usual parental bullshit, too: 'You're our special little girl! You can be whatever you want to be! You have it in you!' Right!"

Sean surprised himself by asking, "What happened?"

"O-chem," she said. "All the prereqs for the pre-med program. Even with all the science at 'Iolani, I couldn't pass O-chem. It was just too hard." She looked right at him. "Doesn't that sound so weak? 'It's too hard! I give up! Daddy, come help me!'" she laughed. "But that's what happened. I was going to double major in agriculture, maybe work on one of those ranches on the Big Island where they breed horses. But after that...you know I've never even *ridden* a horse?"

God, she was just so *cute*, this young woman. Cute like a Hello Kitty little girl, so eternally cute. And so in need of Sean Hayashi's fatherly protection.

"And look at you," she went on. "You'd never give up on anything. Look at all you've done already," she said again. "It's like you don't even need Alan Ho anymore."

And okay, yes, hearing such talk, all of it taken together, it was indeed better than the moaning and the slapping that had basically just christened this pure white bed after all these years. She was right, too, about Alan.

Now that Sean thought about it, he could hardly have been any happier that the old man was no longer even remotely involved. Even the casual observer would have been able to tell that Sean Hayashi was basically pulling off this whole deal on his own just fine. How could anyone have concluded that the guy would have done anything other than...gotten in the way?

"I bet you'll even shut down those Vegas guys, no problem," she said. "Even all the local underground gambling guys."

Sean had to laugh at that one. Underground!

"What."

"Illegal game rooms," he said, "that's kind of a relic of like the '80s, Sonny Bulger years."

"Oh, they still have, you know," she said, with real little-girl innocence, too, like she was reciting some kind of urban legend filled with blinged-up tattooed banger-thugs—and for a second the image of those two shady characters waiting in Russ's outside office blipped through Sean's brain—filled with bangers who break your kneecaps for an unpaid football bet...and come to think of it, nothing at all had yet come of frikken Ufi Tapusoa, Mister UH Game Fixer. Gunshot wound!

So he just said, "Yeah, maybe for a handful of old-man retired stateworker gambling addicts who like to feed the slots, they've got a couple of gutted apartments in Ke'eaumoku or Chinatown, maybe an old warehouse in Pearl City or someplace. Except that the internet dried up most of that business years ago." He could have gone on, too, but just *look* at her! Look how damned impressed she is!

"What about Vegas?" she asked. "Aren't those the main lobbyists against the casino bill? You know, the whole 'ninth island' thing? Seriously, every dumb local who's ever picked up a thirty-pack of Bud Light at Foodland goes to Vegas like three times a year. That's a lot of money those guys stand to lose."

Poor Marisa! So smart, and yet she could be so naïve at times.

"Nah, that whole thing's a myth," Sean said with a dismissive wave. "The players in Vegas—even people like the Boyds who cater almost exclusively to Hawai'i gamblers—they'd be fully behind legalized casino gambling here, because they already know how to cater to that market, and they'd just want a piece of it. No, any problems with a Vegas anti-gambling lobby could be worked out immediately."

Were those stars in her eyes? Look at the way she's looking up at him! Never mind that he's simply reciting a bunch of Tony Levine jargon—and now that Sean thought about it, it was probably better to go ahead and blame the anti-gambling argument squarely on Marisa's imagined Vegas lobby just so you could keep casting it as an us-guys-versus-outsiders issue—but just look at her: stars!

So he went right on stealing from Tony: "Their position is, 'We're doing great in having Hawai'i's gamblers all come over to our spot in Vegas, but if these idiots want to have gambling in Hawai'i, we wanna run it.' Or at least part of it. I'm not sure if it will come to that, but Bradley Zao isn't stupid. He's got five towers to work with. I wouldn't be surprised to see him lease one out to someone from Vegas."

"Fuck!" she said, sitting bolt upright. (Still *naked!* And look at those tan lines!) And right when he was about to get deeper into his analysis of the gambling lobby's more nuanced view, too. "Fuck!"

"What."

"Fuck fuck fuck fuck fuck!" she said some more. "That car. Didn't you hear that car pulling in? It's my parents. They'll freak. We have to get you out of here." Despite the urgency of it all, the words had come out calmly, just as every single movement that followed as Marisa mobilized: jump out of bed, throw on a robe, throw him some boxers ("Quick: just put these on and grab your clothes—you can get dressed later."), out into the hallway, left through the kitchen, right through the screen door out onto the little patio, a hedged alleyway leading to the street, and suddenly Sean was *living* it, living the fantasy of a world he'd imagined night after night alone in his own room back in high school, and just make sure you're out before the parents get home!

"When you hear the front door close, just go right down this path," Marisa said—again, calmly. She turned to head back inside, and then stopped: "Sean Hayashi, I love you!" She planted a kiss on him and then left him standing there, now in complete rock-solid knowledge that she did indeed love him, because just look at how *ready* she'd been for just such an emergency, like she'd been lying in her own bed night after night and *planning* it: what would I do with Sean Hayashi if Mom and Dad came home early? It was almost like she'd rehearsed the whole thing, like she'd been practicing.

For him!

NATIVE INTELLIGENCE

"Fuck!" Javen shouted out. "Turn, you fucka! Turn!" He was leaning over to his right and trying to direct the flight of a little white ball with his outstretched arms, his back to Kekoa and the other four men looking on from the Dolphin Bay Resort's wind-swept third tee box. For good measure he waved the long Big Bertha driver held aloft in his right hand. "Turn!"

"What—that's the first one you hit straight all day," Kekoa said.

Javen's ball rocketed out against the backdrop of giant spinning white wind turbines and soft green mountains, going…going…except that the fairway curved to the right, bordered on one side by a thin line of trees and then Kam Highway, and on the other by a long brackish pond running nearly all the way from tee to green. Javen had been playing his slice—that and the wind, which was howling in off the ocean about a half mile away—only to have nailed his drive as sharply as Jack Nicklaus himself. On it sailed, dropping now, and landing with a distant white splash that was immediately erased by the stiff breeze.

"Fuck!" he said again. He slammed the Big Bertha's softball-sized head into the immaculate green carpet of grass. "I wen' *crack* dat fucka. Fuck."

But right then Javen caught himself. He raised a hand to his mouth like there were little kids around and said, "Ho, sorry, ah, Governor! I t'ink I getting carried away!"

"Yeah Governor, you'll have to excuse my cousin for talking like one *thug*," Kekoa said, glaring back at Javen on the last word. "You know, it's the rough upbringing." He cracked a smile. "Plus he's never actually played on a course where they had a dress code and expected you to pay attention to golf etiquette."

Although Javen didn't look all that out of place in that white-collared aqua DB logo shirt he'd just dropped $85 on in the pro shop—Kekoa had had to point out that they were in the *governor's* group, and look: you didn't see anyone else in Raider's jerseys and ever-the-banger gold chains. Though Javen had put up a good fight about *dressing like one fag*, he'd seen the point. But realistically there wasn't going to be much you could do about the language, so all you could really do was hope that Javen could control himself enough not to mess the whole day up.

Luckily Governor Nakayama let it all go with a laugh, and bent down to tee up his own ball. He didn't have to bend far over that pot-bellied midsection, and good thing, too—the guy looked old enough to break a hip. His spindly old arms swung the driver back and forth a couple of times as if to stretch out, and he said "Eh, like I always say: dis the game where you probably going say 'fuck' more times in one hour than you usually do in one week!"

The gallery, all five of them, broke up laughing like it was the funniest piece of comedy ever uttered, and the old man let loose with another big loping swing that hit the ball with a metallic *crack*, sending it along the same trajectory as Javen's ball—though not nearly as high or as long. Nakayama followed up with a shout of his own: "C'mon, wind!" And when his ball disappeared into the murky water with another wind-blown splash, he turned to Javen and said "Fuck!" Then he smiled and said, "See, I think that's just the technical term for it: fuck!"

Everyone broke up again, and that pretty much said it all. Sure, Kekoa knew all about The Parade, about being surrounded by a bunch of hangers-on whose every move was governed by a combination of respect and fear that weighed more heavily on the latter the further you moved outside the immediate circle. He knew all about everyone falling all over themselves to laugh at every one of your lame-ass jokes, or dying in expectation for your blessing of whatever comment they'd thrown out into the conversation. But here was an old man you could break in half with the twitch of a finger, and even Kekoa, even *Javen*—they were breaking up right along with the rest of them.

Kekoa still couldn't believe it. Glenn Nakayama, the two-term Governor of the State of Hawai'i, right here yucking it up over a flubbed golf shot with the likes of Kekoa Meyer and Javen Campbell. In frikken pidgin, no less. And the rest of their six-some, too: Tony Levine, the little bone rack of a heavy-hitter lobbyist from way back, the guy who got the *SeaHighway* ferry passed through. (Javen had Googled him on the drive over this morning.) Plus Senate President Russell Lee. *Senate President.* And this other little Japanee, Sean Hayashi.

Hayashi was some kind of point-man on this whole multi-billion-dollar deal, was what Russell Lee had told Kekoa and Javen back in his office the other day. Maybe like five-eight, the guy. On toppa that he looked like this wind was about to blow him away, the poster child for some Kaimuki High lunch money target. He'd topped all three of his drives so far too, all of them dribbling just past the ladies tee. Hayashi looked maybe like thirty, yet here he was, calling the shots on the biggest frikken game room this state had ever seen. Hadda give him credit.

"At least we playing Best Ball," the Governor said. "Go get 'em, Tony!"

Best Ball. Though Kekoa wasn't much of a golfer—not any more than Javen, who was more of a dust-off-the-clubs-on-someone's-birthday, grab-the-cooler-of-Heinekens hacker—he did know what Best Ball was. Before this morning, Russ here probably hadn't, even though the senator was the whole reason why they were even out here. Along with Nakayama, the booster club had invited Russ—more as a former player than a state senator—to attract rich donors to their annual Prince Kuhio Day Warrior Fundraiser Best Ball Competition.

Kekoa had been sitting in Russ's office when the phone call came from Levine, who'd bought the spots in both men's threesomes with two five grand donations. Russ had then told Levine to fill out the group with Hayashi, and two more "important guests," was how he'd put it.

"Whooo!" Levine was now watching his own ball land far down the fairway and bounce and bounce again and roll to a stop over on the right edge, where a pair of Filipino groundskeepers dressed to clean up a nuclear melt-down were standing off to the side waiting for the group to play through. "Guess all those lessons are finally paying off!" he said, heading back to his cart. The guy's driver shaft was almost as tall as he was. "Are we playing longest drive today, too?" he asked.

"We can play longest drive if you want," Russ said. "But my money's on Kekoa."

Longest drive. Greenies. Closest to the pin. Plus these instant bets on holing the ball in two shots from just off the green ("murphies"), or on putts longer than the length of the flag stick ("pole-ies"). Plus bets for lowest stroke count per team on each hole, along with the overall score for the sanctioned part of the tournament, where you could walk home with all kinds of sponsor-donated prizes: replica helmets, logo gear, a weekend stay here at Dolphin Bay, or dinner with big fat pink Coach Brock himself. Dingle Ford was even putting up a brand new Warrior-green Expedition for anyone who sank a hole-in-one on the final par-3 out by the ocean.

And frikken Russ: by the second hole he was calling "Murphy!" from like twenty yards out, putting five bucks on his own chances of sinking the ball in two shots even though you could tell he was a worse hacker than even Javen. In the first two holes alone he'd bet on himself like four times.

"You sure, Russ?" Levine said. "I'm feeling pretty good, you know. I just cracked that thing like...like, well, like it was Jayden Kaneshiro!" Levine broke up at his own joke. He turned to Kekoa: "You should've seen what Sean here did to the poor guy. We're trying to lean on him, and he's going on about this *sustainable ag* bullshit, and I'm trying to tell him, 'No son, the casino will bring far more jobs, and no one wants to work on a farm, and yada yada yada.' That's when Sean here just jumps in and says, 'Hey Jayden! We need your fucking vote on this.' *We need your fucking vote on this!* Classic!" He stuffed his club into his bag. "So now we've got his fucking vote!"

Kekoa tried to picture little Japanee boy calling out Kaneshiro. *We need your fucking vote on this*. To a state senator. And fuck, sounded like Russ was right about the guy. Plus they bring it up and he's not even reacting. Hayashi.

Russ was swaying into a couple of unsteady practice swings and saying, "Maybe I ought to say 'Fuck' before I even hit." He wound up and let rip, and out came three sounds with an even rhythm: swing! *Crack!* "Fuck!"

But Russell Lee, he didn't try to direct his ball. He just dropped his club and raised both hands to his head, crouching at the knees as he watched it sail off to the right and over the trees toward...the highway...you could read it in Russ's face: *the highway!*...a stream of non-stop traffic, even on a Saturday morning…a rocketing white projectile…the roar of a tour bus…painted on the side with two young brown Polynesian lovers staring into one another's eyes against a dark backdrop, a light emanating from around their heads like two glowing halos. And then another loud metallic *crack* as Russ's ball nailed the side of the rumbling bus.

The moment stretched, everybody waiting for the sounds of some horrific pile-up.

"That's it—my money's on Russ for the rest of the day!" Tony Levine shouted out.

"After a shot like that?" the Governor said. "He could've killed fifty, a hundred people right there. Russ! Put dat thing away!"

"That's what I'm talking about!" Levine said. "You slice one out into the highway without drawing the sound of a squadron of ambulances? It's your lucky day! That's it: I've got twenty bucks on Russ for closest to the pin on every hole. I say Russ takes them all!"

"Eh Seneta!" Javen shouted out. "You almos' wen' nail one driva witchoa driva!"

Kekoa shot him a look but was relieved to find the governor cackling out a laugh: *HEE-hee-hee-hee!*

Russ was making an exaggerated tip-toe walk back to his cart and saying, "Eh Tony, that might have been dog-shit lucky, but I wouldn't throw my money away if I was you—I think I used up *all* the luck on that one! In fact I think I'll put a C-note on Kekoa right now."

"You're not gonna find any takers here!" Levine said. With that Levine and the governor's cart zipped up the fairway, Hayashi and the senator following behind.

"Fucken Russ," Javen said. "That fucka chasing again."

Chasing. Again. For years they'd watched the guy trying to wear down retired DOE assistant principals deep into the night at their Pearl City gameroom just to win back whatever he'd blown in his first ten minutes. He'd definitely been chasing that night a few weeks back when Nalu spotted him the fifty grand, chasing what he'd lost on the UH game. So after weeks of waiting, all calm, cool, collec', Kekoa had finally come to cash in, and cash in he had.

Right in the State Capitol, him and Javen sitting right across from the State Senate President in his own office, Kekoa starting in all cold:

you don't just owe us fifty grand, Seneta. You on the hook for whatever you owed those *solés* who took you down on the UH game. Whatever you owed them, now you owe *us*, cause we've taken over their…enterprise. And here's how you settle up: this casino thing? Fine. Even though it shuts down our most lucrative tax base, long as you put us in charge of security—and no, we not talking about "security" in the usual "protection" sense. We talking about the real deal. And yeah we know what a complex operation casino security is. We already got people lined up, Senator, people in Vegas been doing this for years.

Right away the guy had looked like there was this…house of cards, and Kekoa had been tugging on the one that would bring the whole thing down. He'd tried to play it off, asking if these people in Vegas were *local*, and yes Senator, these people aren't just local, they're Hawaiians, we talking about my cousin, and not in some hire-my-cousin-cause-he's-my-cousin way—the guy coordinated the MGM *Grand*, the frikken *Bellagio*, he knows what he's *doing*.

That had been the clincher, more than the hundred large even—except you could tell that the hundred large had turned Russ here into like some crackhead looking for the next fix. Even though any idiot could tell that all kinds of risk went along with Senator Russell Lee associating himself with the likes of Kekoa Meyer, that one word—*Hawaiians*—it was like Kekoa had somehow tapped into one of the man's great political ambitions. The next thing you knew, Russell Lee was reaching across the desk to shake hands, and trying to justify it in his head at the same time—like, how could anyone trot out that old "legalized gambling will attract a criminal element" argument if we had the criminal element… under our control? Just like that Kekoa Meyer's *domain* had expanded to one whole new level. Forget about fucken Mudslides—here he was in the most powerful six-some ever to tee it up at Dolphin Bay.

Here he was, at long last, bringing Boy Ching and his family home.

He found his ball sitting up high on the smoothly cut fairway carpet about twenty yards ahead of Levine's, and by the time he and Javen pulled up, the other four men were already loosening up with more practice swings, Russell Lee repeating Hayashi's line again with a smile: "*We need your fucking vote on this!*"

Hayashi just dropped his ball next to where Kekoa's drive had ended up, still some 200 yards away from the little red flag sticking straight out way up ahead. Jayden Kaneshiro—Kekoa remembered the guy as a tall 'Iolani wide receiver who wasn't afraid to go across the middle. And here everyone was laughing about how little Kaimuki boy here had strong-armed him for his vote.

Fuckin' Hayashi. Kekoa never would have picked it the first time he'd seen him walking out of Russ's office that day at the Capitol—he'd thought the guy was some kind of college intern or something. A first-class nerd—you could tell from that little I'm-using-my-brains-to-get-even-with-a-world-obsessed-by-physical-manly-strength smirk he'd thrown at Kekoa and Javen when he'd walked past.

"It's pretty simple," Hayashi said. "The guy likes his window." He topped another dribbler down the fairway, put his club back into his bag, and stood to watch the governor's shot. No "Fuck!", no slam of the club, no excuse, no nothing. Just a little shrug of the shoulders, and let's get on with this silly exercise.

"*We need your fucking vote on this*." Now Nakayama was chiming in, standing over his own ball. "That's almost as good as what Russ did up in Macau. *We need your fucking vote*."

Macau. Kekoa figured it had something to do with that Chinese investor Russ had mentioned, the guy backing this whole thing.

"No, Governor," Hayashi said. "It wasn't even close to that. Jayden Kaneshiro—he's pretty easy to read. You just have to appeal to that pretty-boy 'Iolani vanity of his and basically you can get him to do whatever you want." Everyone laughed. "What Russ did in Macau—that was just plain shakedown."

Javen shot Kekoa a look: Listen to this fucka! And again Kekoa had to give the guy credit. Not only did Hayashi not give a fuck—it was starting to look like he had it on all these old men somehow, like he noticed all kinds of shit that just flew right over their heads, and that he catalogued it all in his brain and put it to work somehow. Shakedown! Fuckin' Sean Hayashi. Fuckin' *gangsta*, this fucka.

Kekoa thought to say so, but for maybe like the first time in his life, he was worried how it might come out. Like, what must all these power brokers been thinking, anyway? That he and Javen were Russ's nephews? Had Russ even explained their part in his casino plans yet? What did they think of the white Ram 2500 with the chrome double-D's out in the parking lot, Javen's where'd-you-ever-get-the-money-for-*those* gold chains and diamond studs? The *Turn, you fucka, turn!* What did they make of it? And would saying something *confirm* what they'd made of it? Would it sound…cliché local-boy *thug?* Would it sound…stupid?

Nakayama took a smooth swing that swept his ball off the green and sent it flying through the wind. It seemed to float for a moment before falling just in front of the green, everybody shouting congratulations.

"Shakedown, huh?" Levine asked. "What'd you do, Russ? Stand over the poor guy and glare at him?"

"C'mon, Tony," Russ said. "You know that's what I've staked my entire political career on. You guys—you and Kawamoto, and Sean here too, and even the governor—you guys all use your short stature to fool people into feeling superior, and then *Pa!*" he punched a fist into his open hand. "You pounce all over them."

Levine shouted out a laugh.

"Me, yeah," Russ said. "I stand over them and glare."

"That's what he did too you know," the governor said. "And that poor little Chinese guy, he may own half of Southeast Asia, but he gave in to every single demand Russ made."

Kekoa could picture the whole thing: this Chinese kingpin had probably tried to impress the local power triangle with a ride in his private jet, a stay at his sparkling casino, and then here comes Russell Lee: chasing.

"With respect, Governor," Hayashi said, "I think you're all selling Russ, well, *short*." This drew big laughs that everyone eventually worked to quiet in time for Levine to send his shot up near where Nakayama's had landed.

"Selling him short!" Levine said. "Selling him short!"

"What I mean is, yeah, he may have activated some kind subconscious of short-guy fear in Bradley Zao, but what he really did was out-smart him," Hayashi said. "Zao had to go along with the whole thing—the revenue sharing, the state partnership, the state control over hiring. He had no other choice. It was that kind of shakedown."

Kekoa stepped up and swept the grass a couple of times with his five-wood, again thinking: you had to give Hayashi credit. All of them. *Bangers*, these fuckas. Sonny Bulger? Forget about frikken Sonny Bulger. Forget about scraping the *yakuza* ice importers, taxing the fucking clubs. Forget about even cutting up some tattooed thug and burying him up in the valley just for *send one message*. What was that compared to staring down the kingpin of kingpins, was what it sounded like, getting him to put up like five billion dollars and then taxing the poor fucka like no one's ever been taxed before, was what this "revenue sharing" bullshit sounded like. Fuckin' Russ. State Senator Russell Lee, bringing it to the billionaire and walking away with the guy's frikken wallet. How's *that*? Frikken' *gangsta*.

Me an' Javen, we going fit right in with these guys. No problem.

The wind howled in his ears as he stood over the ball, sitting up there like someone had come out here and teed it up for him, and yeah, Kekoa was starting to like it, this Best Ball thing. You could just swing away and not worry about anything—if you fucked up your drive, you could just drop and hit your second shot from someone else's ball. So far he'd roped every one of his drives into the middle of the fairway. Easy.

His foot was feeling good too, only a week out of that ski boot cast. So he leaned into a slow backswing to wind up the spring, and then he let it go, sweeping the club head down and following through, his eyes still on the green spot where his ball had been sitting, until at last he looked up and found the little white dot in the sky rocketing towards the green more than two football fields away, and then drifting back right with the wind, dropping down only feet from the tiny red flag and rolling to a stop.

"Ho!" Javen's shout rang out above those of everyone else. "Shotta da *day*, cuz! Shotta da *day*!"

"That's my *pahtna*!" Russ shouted. "My teammate! My bradda! I *know* that guy!"

Levine: "Hey Governor, I've changed my mind! Forget about Russ—I'm betting on Kekoa!"

"And shake *me* down?" Nakayama said. "I don't think so, brah!"

On they went, "Taiga Woods!" this, and "You need to give Russ some lessons!" that. Russ went on about how he himself didn't even have to hit now—they could just play Kekoa's ball again. And no one was more surprised than Kekoa himself, who stifled a *Yeah!* and calmly stuffed his five-wood back into his bag as though he hit such shots all the time, shooting Javen a look that said: "I wen' *school* dese fuckas."

Up on the green Kekoa let Russ sink what turned out to be a three footer for eagle, and that basically set the tone for the next couple of hours: some flubbed shots, some unlikely spectacular shots, shouts of congratulations, groans at missed opportunities, and lots of laughter back and forth among The Power. Tony Levine flagged down the cart lady like a little kid who'd spotted the ice cream man, in this case a modified golf cart the size of a Toyota Tacoma filled with all kinds of gourmet sandwiches, sushi rolls, barbecued chicken and shrimp and crab, and beer. Cases and cases of beer, all of it iced up and free. So things soon became relaxed enough that Kekoa began throwing a few good-natured digs at Javen's shirt right in front of everyone. Even Nakayama caught on, aiming a "Nice, dat shirt!" in such a one-a-da-boyz way that Javen could only laugh along.

As the holes went by, Kekoa couldn't tell if it was the beer or the wind or just the general lack of combined golf skill, but more and more everyone's shots were finding…water. And it wasn't just the big brackish pond that had swallowed Javen's ball on 3—there was water pretty much everywhere. Up there surrounding the back right side of the green on 6. Cutting right across the fairway on 7. Hidden by a grove of ironwoods running the length of the right side of the fairway on 11. Hardly a hole passed without someone dropping another F-bomb in the direction of the water.

"Fuck, this place looks like a fuckin' shrimp farm," Javen told him. "I'd be shooting like 80 today if it wasn't for all these fucken water penalties. Fuck."

Shrimp farm. And yeah, just look up the road: not a mile away you had all this brackish swampy land that someone had long ago squared off into shrimp farms, like back when they'd dumped the fill for all these fairways, must've been one hell of a job, no way anyone could get away with it today, just pouring millions of cubic yards of gravel and sand into these wetlands all so a bunch of rich haoles and Japanese and now Chinese could chase a little white ball around and make ten-dollar bets on murphies and pole-ies and sandies, rich haoles like…

Like right here: look these full-a-themselves fuckas right here, walking up the five-six steps carved into the side of the 16th tee box, you can just tell by how they frikken walk, each one of them get more money than the governor, Russ, Tony Levine-Hayashi-guys *combined* ever going see in their life, that easy *assumed* gait of theirs, those crisp relaxed practice swings, and who the fuck is *that* anyway, and wasn't he on TV somewhere a few weeks back? Or was it at the funeral, at fucken Tapusoa's Mormon funeral?

Irritated *on sight* Kekoa was—though there was no rationalization for it. More like it was some kind of reflex, a sixth sense. And fuck rationalization. Just plain fucken irri*tated*.

"Well, if it isn't the Governor himself!" that banker-looking-guy said as they all pulled up.

"And the President!" Nakayama said. "How're you hitting it today, Mr. President?"

President? Kekoa wondered. First Pacific Trust?

"Not too bad," the President said. "I think Hunter finally fixed my slice."

Kekoa looked around for this guy Hunter, but no one spoke up, an' what, Mr. President? You talking about your own personal swing coach, ah? That's how you roll. An' the governor here knows who you talking about, because alla you rich fuckas, plus Tony Levine and Nakayama and all six a these guys ahead of you, and probably the six guys ahead of *them*—what, you probably all play together every weekend at Waialae or Oʻahu Country Club?

Fuck you an' your little man-servant Hunter. I'll mop you up right here, alla you fuckas.

A soft rhythmic thumping: Javen's heel kept hitting the floor of their cart, his knee pumping up and down. His face, too, hardened, for no reason, into a look that said *who these fuckas t'ink they are?* Back and forth this in-the-club banter went, greenie this, birdie-par-par-birdie that, along with a few in-good-fun jibes at Russ's golf game. One guy had this *accent*—the one wearing the...designer aloha shirt? On a golf course? And while they all had a haole accent of one breed or another— that thick-looking younger guy over there must've come straight off the Bayou, and he punctuated pretty much everything with a real *Haw haw!* of a country boy laugh—but the guy in the aloha shirt sounded like frikken Austin Powers or someone. Javen: his foot bouncing, he just waiting for one a dese fuckas for say somet'ing about his shirt.

Kekoa called Hayashi over to find out who all these fucken haoles were, bantering away like they owned the whole fucken golf course.

"They're all big downtown donors to the UH athletics program, even those guys up ahead." Hayashi pointed way up towards the green by the ocean, where another six-some was putting out, the CEO of a local solar company, a couple of connected bankruptcy lawyers, he said. Three muscled up male Warrior cheerleaders stood off to this side protecting a brand new Expedition from errant shots, a giant placard of a Warrior "H" roped down in front of it to hold it down in the gale blowing through that wall of ironwood pines that grew at an angle, and now that you noticed, the entire back nine had been covered with a pine forest—otherwise this whole tranquil place would be one long wind blasted plain where you probably wouldn't even be able to grow grass for fucken Varner, the UH President, was who this fucken Mister President was.

"It's a pretty tight circle," Hayashi was saying. "Except maybe for Bubba over there—I don't know who he is, but I bet he's got a poster of Dale Ernheart Junior hanging in his garage next to the black Mustang he likes to polish on Sundays while he blasts Hank Williams Jr."

"The Running Back's Coach," Javen said. "Topher Hyde."

"Oh," Hayashi said. *Oh.* "The rest of them—the one with that red golf shirt he wears to announce he's an anointed member of the Outrigger Canoe Club, probably works out at the gym there to keep up with his younger-than-some-of-my-grandkids third wife who volunteers to stop domestic violence, and after the workout with his personal trainer he cracks racist frat boy jokes to his buddies over a vodka gimlet that it's really the Out-*nigger* club and then tries to play it off like he's being ironic? He's the President of Pacific International Bank, old money kama'āina Punahou-Yale trust fund baby, never lifted a finger in his life. An old friend of that kingpin U.S. Senator that just died, too. Sidney Rogers."

Right through Kekoa's building resentment cut this thought: so *that's* what you do, Sean Hayashi, sitting around the edges like you bored. You not bored—you trying for nail everybody. You *watching*. Calling out the rest of them as you nail them, too: nail those other two banker CEO wrinkled-up haoles. Nail Prescott, the rep for Zao's company, that Austin Powers motherfucker.

Javen: "The British guy already linked up with the downtown power, ah."

"I'm not so sure anymore," Hayashi said, walking back to his cart. "If I was those guys, I'd be thinking the other way around."

The other way around. Hayashi saw it too: alla the frikken *money* up there, a good eight feet above the height of the little turn-around area where all of the carts were parked, had these six fucken haoles way up there when Varner shanked his drive into the trees, an' when the governor cracked a joke, how he shouldda used his "t'ree wood," everyone up there standing above him started laughing. But that laughter—it wasn't the I-better-laugh-or-*else* kind. No—it was…surprised…they're *surprised* that the dumb local has any…wit. Hayashi saw that too.

An' then this fucka Prescott, he *looked down* at the governor of the State of Hawai'i an' he said, "That was a very funny joke, Glenn!" Then Russ said something, and Rogers said something, and Varner said something, and now the man-banter wound up again. And not one of them picked up on how the governor of the State of Hawai'i just gotten *mopped up* by some fuckhead Brit dressed for the Merry Monarch here on the 16th tee box of Dolphin Bay's Jack Nicklaus Championship Course. Not one.

Except Javen saw it right away. And he said something too: "So let's see you put it on the green, cuz." He said it with a smile, but from the reaction up there you would have thought he'd just pulled out his .45 and started blazing. Look the ancient banker and the dusty old fucken lawyer shooting those who-invited-this-*local-thug* glances at each other, everyone else sucking in a breath and waiting for someone else to react first, alla you fucken *pussies*. You all…uncomfortable…just being around guys like us unless we pouring concrete.

When someone finally did say something, it was the governor: "I've got twenty bucks that says he can." And just like that people started taking bets back and forth. A couple of them even tried out their own sports repartee with Javen. The fucken Texas Running Backs Coach, on that get-in-with-the-locals train he must have ridden with his players and probably their parents, he threw in a haole pidgin "Mo' bettah!" in his fucken NASCAR accent.

Except when these guys finally did step up to tee off, right away you could tell it wasn't like anyone had needed the governor to cut the tension—any tension would have been drowned right away by all that *money*. You could see generations and generations of *money* in those picture perfect, smooth and graceful practice swings, perfect not because of hours at the practice range with man-servant Hunter, and not even from a lifetime on $200-a-round championship courses, but from *confidence*. Not the I-can-fuck-you-up confidence of Kekoa Meyer's world—this confidence was rooted in private clubs, private jets, Aspen-ski- vacations-since-age-ten, and of course private school. Fuck-up-at-Yale-and-they-just-buy-you-into-Harvard confidence. Fuck up on the field and we'll buy you a personal trainer, and the body flexes in just the right spots, and the right arm stays locked through the back-swing, the knees bend just so, and the club head comes through the zone crisply and without any violence, in so doing making the governor of the state of Hawai'i twenty bucks richer, because yeah, of course fucken Prescott lands it on the green.

They all do. Wind and all.

A couple of them even grumble about their shots, too far from the pin. Clubs are stuffed into bags and bets are settled amid another round of country club man-banter, Varner and Prescott and Sidney Rogers and the fucken Running Back's Coach and everybody driving up to the green…and wait…fuck, not one mention of Russ's casino.

Nobody had even brought up this multi-billion-dollar development every one of them had to have their hands in somehow. Or the fucken Chinese investor. Or Russ running for governor. Nothing. It was like the whole thing was some kind of…like, oh yeah, that? Those four new hotel towers? The legalization of gambling in Hawai'i for the first time? Yeah yeah yeah—that's a done deal, so let's just focus on our golf game, because we came here to win, and well, you can tell a lot about a man by how he pays attention to the particulars of his golf game…

So when everyone stepped out of their carts Kekoa said, "Eh Russ! One of your towers going up up by that green?"

"Not if the SHPD has anything to say about it," Hayashi said.

Kekoa shot a look at Japanee-boy, but he was already walking up the steps to the tee box.

And what was that fucken smirk Kekoa was starting to hear in Hayashi's voice?

"The SHPD!" Levine chimed in. "The SHPD was decimated ten years ago by the Republican governor. It's a joke."

Russ leaned over and told Kekoa they were talking about the State Historic Preservation Division—words that did little to cool the rising furnace of Kekoa's anger, because now he was starting to see what

Hayashi was doing, just like when he *nailing* everybody in his mind, he not just sitting off on the side.

An' what, Hayashi? You been nailing me too, me an' Javen? You thinking we stupid. You thinking: Russ, what the fuck you bring these guys along for? They don't fucken belong, Russ. That's whatchoo thinking boy? Fuck, keep on thinking that. You lucky I'm smart enough I don't just give you The Bump right here, give you that little shoulder-to-shoulder push, that *announcement* that unless you bump back and we start t'rowin' hands, I already wen' mop you up in front of everybody.

"But they already recommended that 150 meter setback back when they did have some power," Hayashi said. He took a lazy practice swing. "And the County permitters had to go along with their recommendation. So I don't think anyone will be building up by that green—it's like fifty yards from the ocean."

Another smirk. Fucka. I telling you.

"I'll grant you that," Levine said, taking a couple of practice swings of his own. "And they do have the Burial Council. Talk about a graveyard for worthy development projects."

"Graveyard!" Nakayama said. "You heard what he said, Russ? Graveyard! The Burial Council! Hoo, I gotta rememba that one, Tony!"

Hayashi rolled his eyes.

"We shouldn't have to worry about the Burial Council if Russ here ever talks to his old football brother," Levine said.

When the group up ahead finally started walking off the green, Russ teed up his ball and said, "Don't worry about that. Ikaika will understand. Especially now. And we're gonna meet for lunch next week."

Ikaika. Ikaika Nā'imipono. You could picture the big man standing to hug Russell Lee at a Waimānalo baby luau, just like you could picture the guy opposing this whole thing, sticking to his core beliefs about the 'āina, and what, was Russ going to meet with Ikaika to tell him he'd already hired a few Hawaiians for…security?

Hayashi: "Just throw him a couple of trinkets."

Javen shot Kekoa a look like he ready to wrap his seven iron around Hayashi's neck, like sure, you gotta reason with someone like Ikaika Nā'imipono, butchoo not going treat him like you can just fucken buy him off. Ikaika Nā'imipono! The guy frikken *righteous!* Who dis fucka think he dealing with?

"Trinkets," Levine was saying. "I *love* that! Trinkets!"

When Russ yanked his tee shot into a thick jungle of trees, Hayashi walked up and *patted him on the back*. Sean Hayashi, the only one with less game than Russell Lee.

"Eh, I just showing Kekoa where we really gonna put that tower!" Everyone was laughing now. Russ looking back at Kekoa. "It's going right behind all those trees up there, right next to the 17th fairway." More laughter.

Hayashi: "Yep, like I said: past the 150 meter setback." He teed up to dribble another shot up near the ladies' tee, was what Kekoa figured, an' look at that girl swing of his, he swaying his hips like one hula dancer, the ball just going—

Except somehow this time Hayashi connected, his club head sweeping through the zone with the same *crack!* as President Varner's, his ball rocketing up towards the green into the teeth of the howling wind up ahead and floating and then dropping...dropping...can you fucking believe this?...dropping right next to the fucking pin.

The shouts erupted all around, high fives everywhere, and Hayashi looked bored by it all, which pissed Kekoa off even more, and look at Javen here too, ready for fucken mob fucken arrogant little Kaimuki boy.

When everyone finally settled down, Javen teed up his ball and took a practice swing and turned to Russ: "That building going up next to the 17th fairway you said?"

"Right over there," Russ said.

"The fairway," he said again.

"SHPD-sanctified," Hayashi said. "It's the state agency that—"

"I know what the frikken SHPD is, cuz," Javen said, waving him off. "I been working construction almos' twenty years." Which was true. Javen owned his own trucking company on Maui—still had his CDL, too, just because he liked driving big dump trucks.

Russ went on about where exactly the tower would rise, the road that would service it, the landscaping features that would ease its fit into the surrounding golf course, all like he'd spent plenty time studying all the development plans.

And then Javen said "I bet you going find bones in any one a these fairways, you start digging up alla dis fill."

Silence.

"You know, they hadda get this fill from somewhere," he said. "When did they build this place, anyway?"

More silence.

Javen just shook his head and stood over his ball, he probably thinking: fuckas neva listen.

Mad now too, he took a big swing so hard that he couldn't connect—he just topped his ball about halfway to the green. And this time there was no "Fuck!" and no slam of the club—he just stood off to the side, one blank sullen look on his face.

Except fucken Hayashi, he wouldn't let it rest. Right after Levine sent his shot up into a greenside sand trap, the guy started in on 1971 for this course, and 1977 for the other one, all like he schooling Javen. Nakayama teed off and then added something about some haole bankrolling the hotel back in the sixties. And fuck, how the fuck not one of these four power players, every one of them with huge interests in the casino, all the way up to Russ, who had chased it so far he was basing his whole frikken campaign for governor on it—not one of them had ever even *considered* what Javen just said, that all of this…fill…had to have come from someplace…in the sixties…years before anyone had even thought of some agency like the SHPD to catalogue and protect… ancient Hawaiian burial sites.

"But I doubt there's anything to worry about," Hayashi was saying. "The reports are pretty comprehensive."

And right there Kekoa got it.

He got this Sean Hayashi fucka.

Here was Javen Campbell, here among the power elite just because he had State Senate President Russell Lee *in his pocket*. Here was Javen: just another ignorant banger from Maui, and he stepping all over Sean Hayashi's *kuleana*, and fuckin' Hayashi, he *worried*, worried that Javen might just be…right.

Just listen to Hayashi: he talking down to Javen like he some castrated dumb fuck *moke*: The reports are pretty comprehensive *you stupid fuck*, was what he just said.

Nothing to worry about?

All you had to do was look around at this place to see that there were hundreds of acres these guys not even considering. Almost every hole, lined with water. Right up the road? Acres and acres of squared off prawn farms, probably the only stretch of land on the whole island that would always be farmland, because if you ever wanted to develop it, first you'd have to find hundreds of thousands of cubic yards of fill.

And nobody listening to Javen. Nobody.

Look at you Hayashi, I can hear you think: *Don't listen to the drug dealer, the security goon, the local thug! The criminal element! Listen to me!* Okay, you may be the kind of short don't-give-a-fuck Japanee who'd been a high school outcast, but all day you been dismissing your own sorry excuse for a golf game by defining golf itself as a waste of time, money, and mental energy, so if anyone happened to be any good at golf, it was because he was a fool.

You been categorizing everybody's clothes, brain power, their this, their that, alla the privileges anyone got to reach their high positions, all so you can make yourself think you on top.

And why you so worried about being on top?

Is it because you *seen* it? You seen what I seen looking down on *all of us* from up here—not just me an' Javen, but *alla us guys*? That Russ, Levine, fucken Nakayama, fucken governor of the State of Hawai'i, and especially you—you not gangsta, brah, you just barely pulling this off with alla your bullshit—not *one of us* belongs on this frikken golf course wit' Sidney fucken Rogers, with Prescott and even fucken Varner. You *see* that, ah Sean Hayashi. That's why you dogging us, you looking down to the next step on the ladder, looking down because you think we fucken stupid, you think the only reason we even here is cause me an' Javen, we the fucken *trinkets* Russell Lee going offer his righteous friend Ikaika.

Trinkets.

Yeah, I fucken caught that too, Japanee boy.

Kekoa leaned over and used the shiny white ball to push his tee into the soft carpet of grass, and somehow all of a sudden it did matter. Fuck, it was fucken *vital* to at least get inside this fucka.

Then Levine said, "This is a big one, son."

"That's right!" Russ said. "All four greenies are riding on this—that's like what? Thousand-somet'ing!"

"$1,200," Hayashi said.

Greenies: everyone puts up fifty bucks a hole for the four par-3 holes, the guy who hits his tee shot closest to the pin gets everyone's fifty bucks. Since no one had even come close to the green at any of the three prior par-3 holes, all the greenies had piled up. And by some miracle fucken Hayashi had just managed to land on the green up ahead. Sean Hayashi, fucka neva even contribute one single shot to their Best Ball team's efforts all day. Sean The Reports Are Pretty Comprehensive *You Dumb Fuck* Hayashi was about to *beat* everyone.

"Hoo! Presha!" the governor said.

A couple of practice swings—perfect, just sweeping the grass, nice and smooth—a gauge of the wind, and at last Kekoa stepped up, concentrating, gotta swing straight through, up-and-down, don't yank the shoulders, up-and-down, just get it up in that wind and let it drop, play it left-to-right, slow backswing, just a *little* extra, and *THUNK!*

"Fuck!"

Nothing. The whistling sound of the wind whispering through the pines—that was all you could hear—nobody saying nothing.

Couldn't tell which was worse: the ugly earth-colored gouge in the green carpet where Kekoa's ball had been sitting, or that silence, sounded like…fear…like this-guy-is-*off!* fear…silence that understood Kekoa Meyer was now *mad*, and not just in a frustrated this-game-will-drive-you-crazy way, but *mad* because it fucken *did* matter to him, that Sean Hayashi had gotten into his head, had punked his ass right here in front of everybody.

It was the governor who finally made the attempt to lighten things up: "Like I been telling alla you: dis the game where you going say 'Fuck' more than any other time in your life!"

Russell Lee picked up on it, and set off on a jokey monologue about how at least your ball's in the fairway and not off in the jungle somewhere—which it was, though a good fifty yards from the green. Then Levine chimed in with how he should have had laid odds on Hayashi, what a dog-shit lucky shot he came up with. And then out came the wallets, and out came Hayashi's hand, each man counting out ten twenties, including Javen, who was standing there *eating it* before heading down the steps to the cart.

And now Kekoa stood before Hayashi, thinking, just fucken say something about the divot went farther than the ball, you fucka. Just fucken say something. Just fucken say something about how fucken comprehensive the fucken burial reports are.

But as Kekoa counted out his money, Hayashi said nothing. He just stood there with that…smirk. And the smirk all alone said, "What a stupid exercise this competitive bullshit with a little white ball is, and how ironic that even I could wind up beating all you wanna-be locker-room heroes."

As Kekoa walked past Hayashi, who was busy stuffing all that loot into his own wallet, he suddenly found himself…leaning in—was this really happening?—and…stepping forward…like the tee box was so crowded with people he had no choice but to…dig his shoulder into Hayashi's chest, spinning the little pussy a good ninety degrees as he did. Then he kept right on walking, down the steps into his cart.

That was it.

Except here comes fucken Hayashi walking down those same steps, and Kekoa can't fucken believe what he's seeing: the guy jus' wen' get The Bump, an' he *still* get that fucken smirk on his face! An' how the fuck? How the fuck he doing it? For the first time in world history somebody wen' *take* The Bump, he wen' take the bump like he shaking off one open-hand to the head…one kick to the jaw…he shaking it off! Somehow he taking The Bump so *Kekoa* look like the one just got mopped up. He smiling! Yeah, nobody saying nothing, butchoo know they know you know: mopped up!

Which was nothing compared to the next thought—the one that hit him when he sat down next to Javen: The fucking *Bump?* Did I just *do* that? In front of the fucking *governor?*

That sound—that *thump thump thump thump*, the sound of the heel bouncing against the cart floor—it made Kekoa looked down to check, and yeah, there was no getting around that one either: the knee madly bouncing up and down? It was his own.

Hawaiian at Heart

"I've read your work, Professor. You've really been able to articulate some important connections between land use and the concrete manifestations of colonization." Martini glass in hand, the guy went on a bit more about *defeated native population* this, and *menial service jobs* that, but Makana didn't really hear much beyond *I've read your work, Professor.* All he could think was, maybe these people aren't so bad after all. Sure, we're standing poolside on flagstone imported all the way from Oregon for the singularly vainglorious purpose of completing the finishing touches on a "green" $40 million dollar seven-acre North Shore property for *one man* to use for maybe *two weeks* out of a given year, standing among a good seventy or eighty of Honolulu's Progressive Elite out here generating enough mid-party buzz to compete with that Iz version of "Somewhere Over the Rainbow" that trio is pumping out over there. But listen: I've *read your work, Professor!*

As if that weren't enough, The Producer chimed in, too, Adam Sondheim himself, the evening's host, a scruffy-looking Hollywood-type if Makana had ever seen one (which he in fact hadn't). His hairy arms folded over a prosperous little belly that protruded out against his polo shirt's black fabric about as far as Helen's swelling womb, Sondheim scratched his graying beard and told Makana, "I heard your interview on NPR last year—the one about the export of Hawaiian prisoners to private mainland jails. Really fantastic stuff. Someone should do a documentary on that, you know? I bet we could get the funding for something like that easy." Then he turned to the guy next to him, some B-list actor Makana had been trying to place for the past ten minutes: "Whaddaya think, Robbie?"

Robbie. That's who it was: Robbie McClain. He'd starred as the bumbling sidekick in a couple of buddy movies filmed on the North Shore before "buying some property" up here and taking an interest in "Hawaiian issues". Makana had seen him on some local news program surfing in Waikiki, where he'd explained how he wanted to "produce" a documentary on the history of Hawaiian surfing. Just like that. Which was why his face had stuck in Makana's mind: here was this Hollywood-type who thought he could just waltz right in and present himself as some kind of expert on a topic whose depth he hadn't the slightest hope of comprehending. *Hawai'i Chic* personified, the guy was.

The whole damned evening was *Hawai'i Chic* on steroids, just like Makana had predicted from the moment he and Helen had driven past the little guard house outside Sondheim's compound, and then down the meandering hibiscus-lined driveway, right past the sign that Helen had read out loud with a laugh: "*Hale Nani*"—because who on earth *names* a house? And while we're at it, why did these haoles always have to give their dogs names like "Leilani" and their blonde kids names like "Malia" and "Makua" and their yachts names like *Moana Luna*, if not to place them *above* less…enlightened…haoles?

Hale Nani. For fuck's sake, it was worse than the seventies, when the Park Avenue (white) elite, the limousine liberals, perfected the art of making progressive causes look ridiculous by growing afros and hosting Black Panther parties in their million-dollar duplexes, thus allowing someone to coin the term *Radical Chic*.

Nowadays if you were someone like Adam Sondheim, you didn't just host a party—you went all out. You bought and cleared your North Shore spread. You paved your driveway with crunchy Big Island volcanic pebbles, and walled your yard in with more volcanic rock, eight feet high, even if it meant you could no longer see the ocean, because *Hawai'i Chic* or not, haoles liked their privacy. You hired your California architect to roof your "main" house, your six "guest cottages," your pool house, and your stable next to the tennis court in that unmistakable "Hawaiian Sense of Place" green pitched-roof style (to separate you from the surrounding tasteless Taco Bell haciendas), and then crown it with skylights and two lengths of made-in-China photovoltaic solar panels. Inside two thick koa front doors you darkened the foyer and centered it with a man-sized turtle sculpture spotlit with pin lights so you could tell your guests the Hawaiian word for turtle was *honu* before they "emerged from beneath the sea" out into your naturally lit living room with the vaulted ceiling. Log-shaped pillars, sliding glass, open-air spaces wherever you looked. Then, especially out here by the requisite infinity pool, you landscaped everything to make it look like a natural part of the usual grove of swaying palms growing up through a rolling lap of immaculate lawn.

Only then did you show off your real sincere interest in all things Ha-vai-ee by hosting fundraisers, where you cluttered up the silent auction table with koa canoe paddles that would be hung on walls rather than used to propel an outrigger canoe, vintage ukes none of these people could possibly know how to play, antique Hawaiiana, polished koa sculptures and bowls, petroglyph hot plates and coaster sets. All to raise a few grand for some Windward hula *halau*'s April trip to Hilo for the Merrie Monarch hula festival. For Keep the Country Country (now that *I've* built my house—a *weekend retreat*, really, not even my real *home*, I only ever set *foot* in it five or six times a year). And of course, to rake in the Moveon.org money for Hawaiian-at-Heart, anti-development, friend to the *'āina* James Hendrick's run at the governor's seat.

Now Hendrick himself was rattling off the list of prison-related statistics he'd long since canned for his stump speech. Robbie McLain managed to wedge in a prisoners-as-economic-product joke aimed at "the private sector" that owned the facilities in Arizona where Hawaiians were being shipped. And thankfully, Helen cackled out a laugh that made Makana happy she'd come along, if only so he wouldn't be taking the whole thing so…seriously. A good couple of months along now, she was prominently showing, especially in that tight red off-the-shoulder dress. And yeah, she *glowed*.

Right then she gave his hand a little squeeze, too, as if to remind him of what they'd discussed in the car on the way up here: *Let it go! It's just a little show-face cocktail event. It'll raise a lot of money for the campaign!*

Makana had to admit that sometimes he did waste far too much energy on…little things…things he indeed should have just *let go*. Like, for one, that business about the Mormon funeral, which had only popped into his head this evening when they'd driven past that big "H" outside the Dolphin Bay advertising the booster club's Prince Kuhio

Day golf tournament. (Makana could see no relationship between golf and Prince Kuhio other than that his "day" allowed all the Chevron middle managers in the booster club a Friday off in March, but anyway.) Ikaika had been right about that one, as usual. *Weeks* had passed with no sign whatsoever of anybody coming after him for witnessing their wide-open execution. Nothing.

So what did it matter if Chip Gillis here—an entertainment lawyer who "owned property" in Mokuleia, and the man who'd started this whole thing with his *I've read your work, Professor* comment—what did it matter if he was quoting Makana *again*, or that doing so was (let's admit it) nothing more than another form of *Hawai'i Chic*? What did it matter if Lori Hendrick was beaming an *interested* look at Gillis that matched her red hibiscus muʻumuʻu in wattage?

If this was all in the name of getting her husband elected, Makana could deal with Lori here, even if she was one of the tens of thousands of middle-aged Punahou grads claiming to have been "Obama's classmate," even if she did nail the Dutiful Asian Wife role that helped to local-ize her husband for potential downtown voters, just as it provided a vicarious fantasy for the Mānoa Valley local-Japanese grandmas who'd always wondered what it might have been like to be with a chivalrous and attentive haole man. Her interest—in Makana's *work!*—at least hers seemed to be sincere.

Not that she could get a word in edgewise—nor could Helen, or Sondheim's (third?) wife, a mid-thirties boobed-up looker named McKenzie—not with McClain, Sondheim, Gillis, and Hendrick all prattling on and on about this Hawaiian prisoners thing. It wasn't long before they were comparing it to every Hollywood trope from Andrew Jackson's Trail of Tears all the way up to the Japanese internment camps—faint connections at best, but that was how Hollywood worked: you took a uniquely located story and did your best to strip away all the important context and turn it into something "universal," meaning, something with a redemptive Disneyfied struggle/resolution scenario that you imagined fat white Midwestern popcorn chompers identifying with, not because it necessarily represented them any better, but because it fit your utterly narrow concept of what they thought an acceptable storyline entailed. If you really wanted to score, you gave the popcorn chomper safe entrance into some exotic setting, and you let them walk away with…a message…that helped assuage their collective latent white guilt. Dances With Wolves. The Last Samurai. Eat, Drink, Pray, Love. Robbie McClain brought up Once Were Warriors, but that gritty epic, made not in Hollywood but in New Zealand, was far too "in your face," as Gillis put it, for an American audience.

Once in a while Sondheim or Gillis would turn to Makana as they completed a thought, nodding with eyebrows raised, as though they were seeking his "expert" approval on a sensitive subject. But mostly you had four men trying to out-do each other with the best "idea" in some kind of pseudo-intellectual circle-jerk. Sondheim waved one of the waiters over to get a local micro-brew for Makana, but then he went right ahead trying to steer the conversation back to the kind of "big picture" observations only a producer could see, just as Gillis kept trying to throw in semi-comparative anecdotes to, in fact, Dances With Wolves, just as Hendrick kept chiming in about Hawai'i's film tax credit, just as Robbie McClain kept bringing up all the former pro surfers he'd encountered in his "research" who'd wound up as mainland inmates.

Well, at least Makana wouldn't have to stand up and deliver any remarks for this crowd and likely face an equally look-at-me question period from, say, that group of designer-mu'umu'u'd second wives over there admiring how the bases of the palm trees are all landscaped with thick bushels of spade-shaped authentic Hawaiian taro leaves. And was that Aunty Maile surrounded by Punahou reunion down-towners over by the bar? He could see Ikaika, too, taking refuge behind the stage talking story with the sound guy, while the three big braddas onstage harmonized into the chorus for Olomana's *Ku'u Home O Kahalu'u*.

And then a voice: "For goodness sake, you could feel the *mana!*"

It may have come from the next cluster over, but you could hear it as loud as if it had been spoken into one of the mics on stage. Two baby-boomer frat boys in opposite colored Reyn's aloha shirts holding identical glasses of Mehana Red beer brought over from Hilo—they were trying to out-status each other worse than even Sondheim and Gillis and McClain here. But instead of some speculative masturbating about a never-to-be-made movie capturing *the real Hawai'i*, these guys were exchanging tales of having sailed upon…the *Hōkūlea*.

The *Hōkūlea*! The doubled-hulled Polynesian voyaging canoe that had launched the Hawaiian Renaissance back in 1974, sailing all the way to Tahiti using nothing but traditional native navigation techniques, the first of what would turn out to be more than a hundred similar trips all over the Pacific. It was as important a 21st-century living symbol of a thriving and advancing scientific and artistic culture as the Merrie Monarch hula festival, as the outrigger canoe race from Molokaʻi to Oʻahu, as…as….as the UH Hawaiian Studies program. The difference was, at least as Makana had thought up to now, that participants in these trans-Pacific journeys were carefully selected as much for their adherence and respect for the culture as for their nautical ability. And here were Harry and Stan from some executive suite in Pauahi Tower trying to one-up each other with tales of the *"mana"*—that was what they kept saying—the *mana* they'd felt emanating from that sacred ship's wooden rails.

"….and he was explaining how the lines carved into the rails coincided with different stars," you could hear Harry just about shouting, "and how basically the canoe itself, the entire thing, was a kind of navigation tool, a giant Polynesian sextant."

So that was it: although Harry here had only been taken out as far as Waikiki on what amounted to a kind of sunset cruise, the legendary Nainoa Thompson had been onboard. An almost other-worldly figure of the Hawaiian Renaissance, the master navigator had long since become a wizened and respected leader that Makana himself looked up to with tremendous respect. Nainoa Thompson! To Harry here, Thompson's presence just *had* to trump the fact that Stan had squeezed his way onto an *interisland* trip, across *open ocean*, all the way to Kauaʻi. But Stan wasn't giving an inch, and as the debate raged on—and to their credit, especially for haoles, the little game resembled more of a name-dropper contest ("Nainoa" *this* versus "Big Blue" and "360-degree horizon" *that*) than a back-and-forth argument—it all started to make sense: Polynesian Voyaging Society.

The whole enterprise—the permanent base at Sand Island, rigging and maintaining not just the *Hōkūlea*, but the *Hōkūʻalakai* and the various escort boats that accompanied them on longer voyages, not to mention the voyages themselves—it all had to cost a small fortune. One of the most important components of Native Hawaiian cultural reclamation and advancement (for as Makana himself knew well, even just the initial voyage had once and for all squashed the long-standing racist notion that the first Hawaiians had found these islands out of sheer dumb luck), one of the very *pillars* of contemporary Hawaiian pride in a time where such pride was pretty much the only weapon left in the fight against the Bradley Zaos and Sean Hayashis of the world—it was dependent for its very existence upon handouts from the likes of Harry and Stan here, who'd listed their names high enough on that particular clipboard at the Polynesian Voyaging Society's silent auction to have been invited out for a little sail.

Another voice, this time from within his own cluster, coming from Hendrick: "And what something like that could also do is bring some positive attention to the Islands."

Positive attention to the Islands? Weren't they talking about a prison movie?

Hendrick went on: "This privatized incarceration thing has turned into a big business all around the country. Hawai'i could act as the model for a more humane and rehabilitive prison system. There's the end of your movie: we *bring the prisoners home*."

Nodding heads all around. They'd done it. Here it was, all over again for the 21st century audience: Dances With Wolves and Once Were Warriors all wrapped up into one. It had "blockbuster" written all over it.

Inside it was Taro, taro, and more taro. The cavernous open living room may have had all the finishing touches of a professional decorator aiming for all things "Native"—solid koa pillars carved with lauʻae fern reliefs, koa sofas and chairs pushed up against the walls to make way for the banquet chairs—but above all else, the image that assaulted the senses was the living god itself, *kalo*. Everything in sight was upholstered in taro-leaf prints. And you could hardly even see the ceramic pots that matched the various bronze Wyland dolphins and turtles in aqua-green, so overflowing were they with real-life billowing bushels of those unmistakable spade-shaped leaves.

It didn't stop with the décor. If it wasn't Waimānalo baby greens *this* or Maui onions *that*, whatever anyone was shoving into their mouths had been concocted from that authentically Native Hawaiian staple. All around the room Chef Nom had set up little buffet stations with little folded cards that announced it in flowing script: Taro chips with guava-chutney dip. Miniature Big Island free-range beef burgers on little purplish taro rolls. Seared ʻahi with mango-jelly-poi salsa. Lau-lau tako poke. Lau-lau chicken skewers marinated in yellow curry and lemon grass. If Nom could have caught a taro fish, he would have served it up in his famous green curry sauce.

Makana and Helen found a couple of seats in the third of around ten rows of chairs set out as though someone had rented Sondheim's house for an oceanside wedding. But instead of an altar, the silent auction table presided, cluttered with koa this and koa that, and more Wyland turtles. Next to a 50s-era hula doll Makana could see a clear plastic box filled with a blizzard of checks written out to Hendrick's campaign, doubtlessly to the full amount allowed by law, and, now that he thought about it, signed mostly by people who were not even registered to vote in the State of Hawaiʻi.

Off to stage-left, on a big easel spot-lit from above, sat a detailed color-coded map of Kahuku point running from Sunset Beach all the way to the municipal golf course. An artist must have colored the map, its swaths of red and yellow and green and blue indicating where a new tower would stand, where the existing hotel stood, where the fairways of the current golf courses stretched themselves out, and so on, because the Dolphin Bay property stood out from the surrounding gentle soft green like some kind of prehistoric monster. One look at it, and even Makana had to admit that the symbolic value of holding the fundraiser at *Hale Nani* started to make a little bit of sense: Sondheim's property lay at the very tip of the beast's nose, only half a football field from two of the proposed new towers.

"Makana, we'd really be honored if you'd begin things with a chant."

A chant. For *these* people?

Makana turned to see McKenzie Sondheim clutching a cordless microphone, an eager look on her face. Somewhere in his brain a switch was flipped. Should he stand up and prostitute himself, his culture, and his beliefs for these people, and thus buy in completely to the Hawaiʻi Chic *performance* aspect of this ridiculous evening? Should he *sell out... justify* it as a necessary means to the desired end of more money for Hendrick's campaign?

He *had* already crossed that bridge by simply being here tonight— and somewhere down deep, he had to admit that the queasy feeling of just standing among all these shallow socialites in the first place was what had ramped his status-detector mode enough to *despise* a well-meaning nice lady like McKenzie Sondheim *on sight*. From the moment he'd taken that numbered card from the California valet out in the driveway, now that he thought about it, Makana had been scared to death at even the chance of being lumped in with the rest of these *haoles*, and so the natural defensive response had been to *rip them to shreds*.

On the other hand, if getting Hendrick into office was your only hope for saving this final stretch of pristine coastline, and if these were the people you needed to tap for enough campaign contributions to give him a fighting chance, then why not? It would be an honor—not to mention a little lesson for all these Hollywood-types about *authenticity*.

That's it: he wasn't selling out at all. He wasn't *performing*. This was no taro chip dipped in mango chutney jelly. These people needed to experience *the real thing*, if only to see the difference between that and what Sondheim had constructed here behind his rock wall.

So before you knew it, there was Makana Irving-Kekumu, standing before a roaring surf of crowd noise sixty voices strong. Aunty Maile was sitting right up front in a soft red muʻumuʻu, a lovely crown of a haku lei on her silver hair, tied in the back with a bun, Kanoe right next to her.

Ikaika stood off to the side in the foyer's Wyland gallery dark, his thick arms folded over his stomach. Stan and Harry sat over by the lanai side, both talking at the same time even as they each worked their thumbs texting someone. Sondheim and Hendrick were up front opposite Aunty Maile, next to Sondheim's wife, whose face still held that eager look. And the rest of this big, cavernous room was packed with food-chomping, personal-anecdote delivering, white-guilt assuaging *Me Me Me* haoles who just *would not shut up*.

No matter, though—he'd get their attention: a deep breath, eyes closed, another deep breath, and Makana reached down, down to the *naʻau*, and let loose with a deep guttural "*I-I-I-I komo I ka ula hala-a-a!*"

Startled, they all were—even deep in concentration on the *mele*, Makana could tell that much—startled out of mid-chew, mid-brag, mid-name-drop, until all you heard was the sound of the chant rising up to the taro ceiling fans, over the rows of heads, back to the breaching whale painted on the opposite wall: "*Ulu hīnano o Pō ʻohalulu-u-u-u.*"

Some of them were burning in envy at how the haole-looking man's ability to chant out like an ancient *kahuna* stomped all over their own insertions of the odd *akamai-opala-puka* Hawaiian words into their conversations. Others had clearly never heard such a sound before, but took their cue after spotting the *intense* faces dotting the crowd: *that's* how you were supposed to react to a chant such as this one, even when you had no hope whatsoever of understanding its meaning: like you're in church. Even Harry over there had put his texting thumbs to rest.

"*'O ia nahele hala ma kai o Kahuku*," Makana went on, drawing a few understanding nods here and there at the mention of Kahuku (I know *that* word!). McKenzie Sondheim was holding her phone up to capture the moment to post on Facebook, her own head dutifully bowed in deep reverence.

"*He aha ka hala*," went the chant—What is my offense?—"*I kapuhia ai 'o ka leo ē*"—that you refuse to listen to my plea? And then the powerful finish: "*E hea mai ka leo ē!*"—Respond with your voice! (Implied: respond *to what was just spoken to you. Respond*.)

Except, of course, that once the last faint echo of Makana's chant had made its way to the skylights, the room, packed as it was, wall-to-wall with E*xactly!*-Now-it's-*my*-turn-to-talk haoles, remained silent.

At last Sondheim himself graciously took the mic from Makana with a put-er-there pat on the shoulder and said, "Wow!" Though it hardly seemed appropriate, Sondheim led the room in a spirited round of applause, saying it again: "I mean, *wow!* Chicken skin! That was a chicken skin moment if I ever felt one. Really, people."

And then, as if to stay completely in character, Sondheim went on to talk about…*Me!* "Let me tell you, I really *felt* that chant that Makana here was kind enough to deliver for us. I *felt* it!" The little man paced around a few steps, searching for the right way to continue, even though it was immediately clear that no one cared to listen to a word the Hollywood Producer had to say—they were all primed for the real deal: the Native Hawaiians.

But Sondheim had a mic in his hand. "Because while I may not be a Hawaiian myself," he went on, "I can identify with these people. I know all about persecution and dispossession. Let me tell you. My grandparents came to this country with *nothing*." Blank looks, all around. Makana could see people begin to dig into their appetizer plates again, if only to pass the time while Sondheim here blabbers on and on about some bootstraps fantasy ancestors clawing their way to the American

Dream. "To make a long story short, not only was their homeland robbed from them—their very *lives* were nearly taken. Taken by the Nazis. World War Two. So I know. I come from dispossession."

A long pause. For a second you thought he might be wrapping up, but no: "And what I've learned in my years in these islands is that I also come from *aloha*. Some of you may not be aware of this fact, but the Hebrew concept of 'shalom' encompasses the very same values as 'aloha'. No kidding. The words are interchangeable. You can actually say them together: *shaloha*. Go ahead. Say it with me," he said, lifting his hands like a preacher eliciting a response: "Shaloha!"

His congregation offered a half-hearted, all-in-good-fun response, as though they weren't sure if he was kidding or not with this "shaloha" bullshit.

"And like I said," Sondheim went on, "while I may not be Hawaiian myself, I am Hawaiian at heart. That's something you *feel*. And when Makana here was delivering that tremendous chant, I think we all couldn't help but *feel* those words, here, and *here*, in the nah-ow. Right Makaner?"

Now all eyes were on Makana, who found himself standing off next to Ikaika nodding and grinning along, while half of the rest of the room silently looked down upon the other half for being unable to place the Hawaiian word, *naʻau* (just as that half silently critiqued the first half for that little bit of local-knowledge snobbery).

"As you all know," Sondheim went on, "we've gathered here tonight for an important reason, and that reason wasn't to hear me go on and on about my own experiences, however germane they may be to these proceedings." Relief! "We are here to show our support for a great man, a leader. And perhaps at no other time in the history of these islands have we been in need of a great leader than *right now*, in these dark times of land grabbing and profiteering and unchecked development. But before I introduce you to that man, who, like me, is as Hawaiian at heart as any man you'll ever have the pleasure of casting your vote for, we have a few very important people who have shown us the courtesy, the generosity, the *aloha* of joining us this evening to speak to these issues of wanton destruction of what we can all agree is…God's country."

More silence. Though clearly meant as an applause line, it was met with a much different kind of crickets-chirping silence than what had greeted the end of Makana's spectacularly moving chant. This silence said "Get on with it. Give us the Hawaiians."

Despite himself, Sondheim eventually did oblige, this time in a heartfelt and surprisingly detailed introduction of Kanoe Silva, an "expert on land use issues in general, and on the biography of this area in particular," he said, pointing to the monster on the map.

Kanoe stood to polite applause. And when she thanked the crowd for having taken an interest in issues relevant to Hawaiians, and then thanked Sondheim and his wife by name for "opening up" their home, and Hendrick and his wife by name for "all that you've done to help our cause over the years," Makana felt a little better about having performed his chant. She began with a brief romp through some of the highlights of history that had brought us to "what we are facing today," stopping to underline that taking any historical event out of context would cause you to miss the larger point about colonization.

"The thing to remember is that they're always well meaning," she said. "Even the missionaries. They thought they were helping. They thought they were saving our souls." This drew a murmur of in-the-know laughter: *Those silly missionaries!* "Then they thought they were teaching us the ropes of capitalism. The schools thought they were preparing us for life on the plantations. The military thought they were protecting us. The hotel developers thought they were providing jobs. The Thirty Meter Telescope people thought they were going to help our children all become scientists. And now these nice people from China are saying the same thing: jobs, money, education. But what I always ask them is, what kind of jobs? And education at what cost? Because these things they do, they can't be undone."

The room filled with knowing righteous nods, and Makana couldn't help but think: these people never had it so good. Is that Julia Roberts over there up near the front, the ridge above her nose creviced into a look of deep concern, like she's trying to dig into some vicarious well of Kanoe's resentment at how history has treated the Natives? She looks like everyone here, munching away on their hundred-dollar plates from NomFusion, sipping on their Dom Perignon, clutching onto the hope that their bid for the polished koa salad bowl will be the winner, writing their five thousand dollar checks, all a couple of hours away from stepping into the Lexus and driving off to fourth homes of their own, their bellies full and their consciences bolstered by their selfless acts of having given to the cause.

"Over here you can trace it all the way back to the Great Mahele, the mid-19th century," Kanoe was saying, "when Hawai'i went from a place where land was commonly used, to a place where land was owned." On she went into the biography of the surrounding area, which even included the very land upon which volcanic rock had been blasted to make way for *Hale Nani*. But rather than make that uncomfortable connection, everyone focused their resentment on…Charles Gordon Hopkins, a man who, as Kanoe explained, had taken advantage of the Great Mahele by purchasing enough land from Kamehameha III to plant a cattle and sheep ranch that covered more than 3000 North Shore hectares. Hopkins' cows and sheep immediately began running rampant over the area's traditional Hawaiian farms, destroying every plant in sight. When the Hawaiian neighbors complained, they were told to put up fences. Within twenty years, the area's local population had dropped by over a quarter, simply because Hopkins had moved in.

Charles Gordon Hopkins, that insensitive brainless fool! Nevermind that Kanoe here had just drawn a very clear line back into history that equated nearly everyone in the room with the likes of Walter Dillingham, of Lincoln McCandless, of…Charles Gordon Hopkins. Really, what were you supposed to do? Exchange glances with one another, and take a look in the mirror, and say those words out loud? *I just built my forty million dollar dream home on vacant land that I purchased without hurting anyone, and it doesn't contribute any reef-damaging runoff or even leave much of a carbon footprint, but well, my neighbor's tax assessment then skyrocketed and now they have to sell their ancestral land and move to Vegas, simply because I moved in.* Did you come out and *say* such a thing? Or would that…spoil the party? What *was* the fashionable way to respond to such a thinly veiled accusation?

Apparently it was to pretend that no such accusation had ever been made, that you were on their *side*, that you were here to *help* the Hawaiians—though of course not in that same *missionary* sense that so many well-meaning-but-ignorant haoles had been guilty of before. No, *you* were *empowering* them, which was the thing you loved about James Hendrick—he was going to staff his entire cabinet with Native Hawaiians. He was going to put them in positions of responsibility, and he could only do it with *your help*. That's what Julia Roberts (it sure looked like her, anyway) was thinking as she nodded along. That's what Harry and Stan were thinking—no doubt about that—because that's what Harry and Stan were always thinking—especially when they set foot on the sacred decks of the *Hōkūlea*: these Hawaiians, they need our *help*.

All of this became clear the moment Kanoe concluded in time for "a few questions." Some guy from the half-shaven-on-purpose tribe in the back began with this: "I guess I have more of a comment," and then proceeded to go on for a good five minutes about the gentrification of… Harlem…in New York…seven thousand miles away. "So I guess we see this happening everywhere."

Then a woman in the front chimed in with, "Kanoe, I think that's just terrible, everything you've described, I mean you people have been *dispossessed*, and in so many tragic ways." Someone else jumped in with a rambling look-at-me question that began by lecturing back to Kanoe the details of what she'd just presented, and then came up against a wall before heading into, "So is there really any hope?"—which was answered not by Kanoe, but by a voice somewhere in the back. Someone over on the left then responded to Mr. Back row, and in no time you had people two-cents-ing it back and forth all over the room to the point where Kanoe Silva basically vanished into thin air.

Mercifully, McKenzie Sondheim began ringing a cocktail fork against her crystal champagne flute loudly enough to silence the room. She took the mic and thanked Kanoe profusely for sharing her mahna-ow, encouraging a rather spirited amount of applause. And then Sondheim's wife went into a brief intro that suggested she'd spent the morning googling Ikaika Nāʻimipono. With broad strokes she began painting a moving picture of a "taro farmer," milking Ikaika's Hollywood moments like a movie trailer voiceover: his decision to give up football, his work fighting H-3, his role in stopping the SeaHighway ferry. All around faces grew rapt—even the people who'd used the between-speeches interlude to work their thumbs out on their smartphones began looking up, the wheels turning, perhaps, rifling through the mental list as to where one could get the money together to film such a courageous story, and you could probably get someone like The Rock to play the leading role, and maybe get Sean Penn or George Clooney involved somehow.

When Ikaika was finally handed the microphone, yet another kind of silence fell over the room—this one of the sit-and-stare variety that had *celebrity worship* written all over it. Seriously. That was all it had taken: a few highlights from Ikaika's (admittedly) moving backstory, and then the big noble Hawaiian himself, a man who certainly fit the part, and in a powerful, charismatic, and physical *projection* kind of way that only a Hollywood-type could fully appreciate. (Although Makana couldn't help but notice right then how Ikaika looked to have somehow aged a few years over the past couple of months.)

"Aloha everybody," he said, which was greeted with a hushed choral response.

And then, as always, he began with, "You know I'm not much of a public speaker, but what I have to say comes from the heart." Some nodding heads around the room, and then Ikaika went on, just as Makana had seen him do at so many neighborhood board meetings and city council meetings and DLNR and Burial Council meetings for the past—had Makana really been watching this same speech for…twenty years now? And after twenty years, Ikaika had it down, rifling the details off in monotone like he was reading off a teleprompter, pausing on each of the lines meant to tap into *angst*, and into *anger*, and turning up a few drips on *pity*, but only to the point of softening everyone up for the big blows that got them shaking their heads in disgust, as these people were all doing already, and murmuring to their neighbors. "And I want to tell you about one of our brothers in this fight."

Brothers? This was something new. Was Ikaika going to talk about Makana, right here in front of everyone? Go into detail about how he devoted his life to this cause, pouring over volumes and volumes of primary texts to get to the heart of the real story? Just the thought of it made Makana swell with pride, and even turn to Helen with a little knowing smile.

"I won't tell you his name," Ikaika went on, and Makana's spirits dropped a bit, but, well, once Ikaika got into the details, people would know, right? Chip Gillis would know. "Because stories like these can get unintentionally twisted around in the re-telling." Twisted around? "Anyway, this brother of ours, he was put in that…position." And Makana's spirits dropped further, because now it was clear that Ikaika hadn't been talking about him at all. He was talking about Ray Boy.

"This brother of ours, he stood by our side for sixteen years. Sixteen *years*. He sacrificed everything. Football games with his kids. Camping trips to teach them fishing. Maybe could've bought a house—at least on homestead land or Big Island. But no. Brother put every waking moment he wasn't working into this same fight James Hendrick is fighting with us today. Brother saw bulldozers—and this was years ago—he saw bulldozers dig up his own family's burial ground. He saw his *own aunty's bones* sticking up outta the ground." Murmurs, heads turning this way and that, can-you-*believe*-that!

"Let me ask you folks a question," Ikaika went on. "What do you think it would take for a man like that to all of a sudden…switch sides?" Puzzled looks. "You know, get up there and alla sudden start speaking out in favor of 'creating jobs' and 'economic opportunity' and 'a future for our young people' an' alla dat, 'we need to build this thing now.'" More murmurs, louder now. A couple of women in the fourth row raised their hands, ready to interrupt with some kind of amen "comment"—the fact that the question had been rhetorical in nature was clearly lost on them—but Ikaika ignored them.

"Now, I know what your reaction probably is," he said. "That was my reaction too: 'Ho, brother sold out on us! He betrayed us! He's a Judas! Stabbed us all in the back!'" A few nodding heads. "But I don't want you to judge our brother. What I want you to do is think about how they got him into that…position. I want you to imagine that, like you were going put it in one of your movies. I want you to imagine the bills or the bounced check or the hungry kids, *again*. The little flare-ups between a loving husband and wife living paycheck to paycheck your entire life. *Again*. An' alla sudden they turn around and say it: 'Am I really going up against a multi-billion-dolla corporation? Me?' That's what I want you to imagine. I want you to imagine what it means to *lose hope*."

The woman next to Makana had her eyes shut in concentration.

"You got it? Good. Now here's what I want you to imagine next. I want you to imagine that…position…that position where they come looking for our brother, they *hunt him down*, they box him in. They say, 'Hey, brother, you struggling, ah? You an' your wife an' your two kids living in that two-bedroom fourth-floor walk-up in Makiki, they jus' raised your rent again, ah? Tough times. What? Now you not going be able to send your boys to college? You banking on football scholarships to get them educated? Well, we got a simple solution. An' we going help you *justify it*, too.'"

He *had* them. *Locked in*. Double crevices forming on every nose bridge in the room, heads shaking in how-*could*-they disgust. And the corners of Ikaika's mouth creased up into a little smile, the smile of the approving teacher. He went on to point out that these people, the ones who had put Ray Boy in that…position…were the very people James Hendrick had spent a career fighting against as a dedicated public servant, and that he needed—*we* needed—we needed everyone to dig deep and support him in this fight with all we had. We needed him to fight for all the rest of the people in that…position.

"Because that's the position we all in," he said. "That's the position we been in for the past, thirty, fifty, hundred-something years. Mahalo."

Silence. No mine-is-more-of-a-comment. No look-at-me questions. No two-cents-ing. Silence. And it wasn't the celebrity-worship kind, either, at least not entirely. Ikaika handed the mic off to McKenzie Sondheim, who was wiping away tears.

After a few moments she somehow managed to move into an introduction of Aunty Maile without a "Wow!" or more Hawaiian-at-heart bullshit. Instead she began depicting Aunty as "one of our *kupuna*" and among the first who had "stood up for the rights of her people" and had indeed played an important role in "rescuing Hawaiian culture" at a time when it was "most in danger of being lost" just before the Hawaiian Renaissance. Makana was forced to hand it to McKenzie Sondheim: she knew what she was talking about.

Finally the great woman faced the crowd with her usual stout self-assuredness, the mic held low around her stomach in a way that indicated she intended to speak loudly, and yes, from the *na'au*.

"Aloha everybody," she began, a gracious smile on her face. "My name is Maile Nanaikaponoko'olauloa Chang. I was born in 1954 at Queen's Hospital. I grew up working my fadda's store in Kahalu'u. We sold staples delivered from town, and produce we grew with my fadda's brothers on their *kuleana* land in Waiāhole. Sometimes we sold fish that my brothers would catch. During the plantation strike of 1958, I remba my fadda offering lines of credit to the striking workers so that they could feed their families. Sometimes he just gave the food away—that's just how he was—and my madda would get mad at him. She'd tell him, 'Henry, if you wasn't so generous, you would be a good businessman, and we could all be rich!'"

Of course McKenzie Sondheim was capturing the whole thing on her phone—though still nodding along to show that she was also here in the moment along with everyone else, fixated, never having seen the likes of this *wise old woman*, who was *so full of mana*.

"Seven acres, my uncles had," Aunty said. "And we used to have more, on my madda's side too, not two football fields from where we're all standing at this very moment. But somehow we lost that land. You can go downtown to the Bureau of Conveyances, right on Punchbowl, and you can trace my madda's name all the way back to that parcel. My madda would tell me stories of that land, of her father, my grandfather, catching fish right there where they have the golf course now. I rememba when they were building that hotel back in the sixties, she would tell me how her father, my grandfather, had even won a Land Court Award to protect his land before she was born. Exactly how my family lost that land, no one can remember. But to this day I take my moʻopunas out to that place, and that's where I tell them the stories of their ancestors. We are *of* that land, and we always will be."

Nodding heads everywhere.

"I could go on, but you already know what happened next. Kanoe just told you that story. Ikaika just told you that story. An' we're *tired* of that story." Serious looks now. *Concern.* "Eventually they finished the Dolphin Bay Hotel and Resort. They promised jobs for the local community. People said they were going to turn it into a casino. Stimulate the economy. Alla that. An' now we hearing the same thing. *Jobs for the local community.*" Murmur, nod, murmur, nod. "As Kanoe said, what *kind* of jobs?" Still more nods. "And you know, 'jobs' is fine. Our young people need jobs. But what all of these nice people will neva understand is our spiritual connection to the land." Her face scanned the room. "Towa Numba Four. These nice Chinese investors, they plan to build Towa Numba Four right on top my grandfather's land. What am I supposed to tell my moʻopunas then? What they going tell *their* kids?" Rapt attention. "I tell you right now: we're *tired of it.*"

A round of applause, spirited enough that no one would have caught Ikaika stifling a yawn.

"So I want to thank you folks for showing your support, thank you folks for taking the time to learn something about this place. An' I want to thank you folks for giving a good man a chance." Here she turned to a blushing James Hendrick. "James Hendrick is one good man," she said again. "He has been fighting for these causes for many years. And now he is up against an entrenched old-boy network, in his *own party*, financed by a billion-dolla corporation, and we need his help. Governor Hendrick—and I'll be the first to say it, I no care, I'm Aunty Maile." This drew some church laughter. "I'll call him 'governor' right now, that's how much I believe in your support."

Aunty let that sit for a moment. And then she turned to Hendrick, suddenly all business: "Governor Hendrick, you gotta put one stop to this. Help my people."

She walked over to wrap the tall man in a hug and the room erupted in cheers, everyone on their feet now. Aunty lifted Hendrick's hand high.

The LG made a show of humbly thanking her, bringing his hands together in a kind of pyramid in front of him and bowing, for some reason, as though Aunty Maile had just gotten off the boat from Thailand. He then made another show of having been tremendously moved by the whole thing, and as he stood there between the Wyland whale and the koa framed Pan Am "paradise" poster (and hadn't these movie people *thought* of what a ridiculous image that would make?), Hendrick wiped away a tear.

"Aloha kākou," he began, and right from the start Makana had a hard time listening to "sustainability" this and "host culture" that and "Hawaiian at heart" the other, mentioning the Dolphin Bay development as something "foreign" and alien to "our local values" while everyone nodded along. *Hawaiian at Heart*. That was all you could really hear among the brand-new-day message of *hope* that was pilfering the righteous indignation of all four of the Native Hawaiians who had just spoken, and right then it finally crystallized in Makana's brain, exactly what he'd been finding so…distasteful…about this whole affair from the moment the tires on Helen's Prius had crunched across the stones of Sondheim's winding driveway. It wasn't so much that James Hendrick was cashing in on his association with the most roots-righteous Hawaiians in the state. It was more that he was *standing in* for the rest of these haoles. Hendrick was *in with the Hawaiians*, and that meant that *they too* were *in with the Hawaiians*. He was their bridge to all things just and righteous about Hawai'i, and *that*, rather than any of the particular point he was now elaborating on, was why they were all so eager to throw their money at him. Everyone in the room: Hawaiian at Heart.

That much became clear when *Hōkūlea* Stan sidled up—his actual name was Ned Devine—and in a lowered voice told Makana and Ikaika, "Listen, I'm having a little get-together in Lanikai next weekend, and I'd really be honored if you'd attend."

Makana deferred to Ikaika, mostly because he had no idea how to respond to such an invitation, delivered as it was right in the middle of what was supposed to be the evening's main event. He watched as the great Hawaiian's face morphed from respectful concentration (aimed at Hendrick's speech), to courteous *listening*, to, well, was that a smile creeping around the corners of Ikaika's mouth? Of course it was, but it was being read in very opposite ways: Ned Devine had to have been seeing *gratitude* at his generous gesture, while Makana saw nothing but: You stupid fucking predictable Hawai'i Chic moneyed-up *haole*—do you really think we're a bunch of *party ornaments?*

Makana couldn't take it anymore. How could the guy be so fucking *oblivious?* And did Makana have to finally *say something?* Did he have to *translate* what Ikaika's smile was actually trying to announce in flashing neon? Fundraiser for the future governor was one thing. A chicken-skin chant in the name of saving the 'āina? Okay. A winning bid for a sunset cruise aboard the *Hōkūlea?* Fine. But *party entertainment?*

"Listen, I know you don't mean anything—" was all Makana could manage to get out before he felt that mighty hand on his shoulder.

Ikaika took a step forward to put his giant frame between the two of them, nodding graciously and grabbing the business card from Devine. Up onstage Hendrick was building up to an applause line about *the values we hold dear*, and when the requisite clapping began, the big man gave Makana a look and then led him out through the Wyland gallery foyer in unspoken understanding that the Professa needed a break from all this before he blew the whole evening.

When they found the old F-150 over by the hibiscus wall outside, parked next to someone's bright red Viper, Ikaika dropped the tailgate and took a seat, the whole rear of the bed lowering under his weight with a squeak of the springs. He handed Makana a Heineken out of that duct-taped cooler in the back of his truck and then cracked one open for himself. Makana leaned on the bed wall and took a sip, still angry—not just at this Ned Devine character, because what, really, was the difference between what they'd done tonight "for the campaign" and in what Ned Devine had asked them to do?

"What." Ikaika was looking at him, reading his mind again.

"You know what," Makana said.

"Ah, no worry, cuz. We knew dis was going be one long road, right from the start."

Ikaika took a long swig of his beer and tossed it with a metallic *clink* in the bed of the truck. He grabbed another from the cooler almost in the same motion and popped it open, another long sip.

And then, right out of nowhere, he shook his head and said, "My frikken wife neva come home until late last night."

Makana had a hard time grasping that one. Sure, Curtis Kam complained about his wife all the time. Makana's football buddies across the street treated Wife Complaining like another kind of status measure, each one trying to out-do the other, before turning around to look at Makana with envy because he had a wife who derived vicarious pleasure from the good times he had without her, instead of one who wanted to "get even" whenever he drank with the boyz. But Ikaika? Never in twenty years had Makana heard anything but praise for Meg.

"She's got that new job, right? That green builder start-up thing downtown?"

Ikaika took another sip and looked up at the palm trees whipping in the wind, like he was thinking about whether to go on. "Yeah, and I know it's commission and all, an' she striving, doing something she likes. But lately it's starting to go past that. Pau hana drinks, going in on the weekends. Fuck, she neva see her kids anymore." More: she was always coming home after dark, and then up in the morning and out of the house before light. Her boys at those critical teenage years too, especially the younger one, all they seem to want is the instant gratification of a fast car, or the empty dream of getting recognized by some MMA scout when they compete in some amateur Fight Night thrown together by some scrub local "promoter." Another empty green bottle, clinking around the bed of the F-150.

And then a deep breath. "No mattah," he said. "Afta we beat this one, should be all right. Afta that we fix everything. See, this is the big one right here, Makana. We stop this one, other people going start getting involved, we can step back and maybe advise next time." A smile. "How's that? Advise!" A bigger smile now.

Makana had to say it: "You really think we can win? These people are a bunch of self-interested fashionable fucking clowns."

"You mean win the election?"

"If that's all we've got left to stop the expansion, we've gotta get Hendrick elected, and if it's six more months of this bullshit, and if these are the kinds of people we've gotta count on…." He tossed his empty in with Ikaika's, another ringing roll of glass on metal.

"You know," Ikaika said, popping open another and handing it over, "even if Hendrick doesn't get elected, we still get chance."

"How? I looked at the mitigation report. Either Russell Lee's gambling bill doesn't pass, or Hendrick gets elected—that's all we've got. And from what Tom Watada's found out at the Lege, the gambling thing looks like a done deal already."

Ikaika shifted his weight a bit, drawing another groan from the old truck's springs.

"You saw that map in there," he said.

"I have that map tattooed on my brain."

"Okay then. Five towers, and that 'service road'—that access road that's supposed to wind through the golf course from like, just past Sondheim's wall over there, all the way to the Kahuku side, yeah?"

"They've scaled it down to four towers to make it look like they're 'compromising' with us, but yeah."

"Scaled it down!" Ikaika said with a laugh. "Anyway, at least three of those towers, they can't build them. Better yet: that 'service road' thing? What, two miles long? They can't build that either."

Makana didn't get it. He'd stared holes into the plans for hours and come up empty every time. Whoever it was—Sean Hayashi, that pompous Brit Prescott, Russell Lee himself—they'd dotted all their i's and crossed all their t's, and legally speaking, there was no longer anything anyone could do.

"You don't know, do you," Ikaika said. "Well, don't worry about it Professa. See, that's the clincha. Nobody knows."

Makana waited for him to go on.

Ikaika let out a yawn, and then a sigh, staring again up at the tops of Sondheim's palms in the wind above. At last he took a breath and said, "You know my dad, he used to drive dump truck. Years ago, way back in the sixties." Makana nodded along dutifully. "If you drive dump truck, chances are you going be working with some guys that's linked up. An' my dad, well, he neva got involved with that world, but you know, you drive dump truck, you going see some things. Let's put it that way."

"Okay…"

Ikaika gave him a smile. "So anyway, my dad, he was driving dump truck when they built this place, the original Dolphin Bay, plus the golf courses. They contracted to do all the fill one time—and was one *big job*. Try ask my dad about it next time you see him. Had the big dump trucks, the tractor-trailer-kine. Fifty sixty of them dumping their fill, all rotating in and out, seven, eight, ten times a day. For weeks. You know this whole place used to look like the Kahuku prawn farms?"

Makana nodded again.

"Anyway, you listen to my dad: right from the beginning they started losing trucks."

Losing trucks?

"That's what he said," Ikaika went on. "'Losing trucks.' The trucks would come in here with their fill, roll into the swamp, and *flip ova*. Ten-fifteen-ton dump trucks, all full load. An' had trucks flipping ova *every couple days*."

Makana thought about it, astoundingly, for the very first time. He'd driven past that demarcation between the acres of pond-like prawn farms and the golf course hundreds of times and never once had it occurred to him how the resort area had been filled in. Now he went through a quick calculation on how long it might take to load one of those big tractor-trailers, how many loads they'd carried in a day—even if the number had gotten a bit inflated over time in Ikaika's dad's memory—and settled on a driving distance of what couldn't possibly have been more than a few miles, meaning they had to have gotten the fill from somewhere nearby. Kahuku had long since been developed with plantations back in the sixties. Same with the ranch toward Lāʻie. The Waialua plantation in the other direction. That left…right across Kam Highway? Millions of cubic yards of fill? Long before the creation of the

SHPD? From what, topographically anyway, looked like a valley that would have at one time housed an *ahupua'a* of perhaps ten thousand people? Had they just gone into that valley with excavators and dug?

"You know where they got it all, now that you think about it, don't you." Ikaika asked.

"Right across the street."

Ikaika gave him another smile. "Very good, professa. You get an A." He took another sip. "You just neva thought about it before. Now think about this: why would alla those dump trucks start flipping ova?"

Makana had already put that one together. Sure, they had been in a hurry, and the short driving distance may have caused them to overlook a few safety concerns as far as load weight and height limits were concerned—the company was 'linked up' after all. Ten-ton trucks, flipping over. You never wanted to say it out loud for fear of sounding like some kind of the-spirits-*cursed*-them believer in some kind of occult. But what other reason could there have been? And even if that wasn't the reason, the theory suggested *anyway* that if you did a little…digging… in the right places, not the usual places where the private archeological consultant would normally think to dig—which is to say, if you dug straight down into the middle of the sixteenth fairway, or the fourth fairway, or the eleventh fairway, or anywhere along the planned path for the 'service road'—you would find them.

"Bones."

Part Four

God's Country

Marisa's little ponytail bounce-bounce-bounced, until she turned to call back from her perch on the horse up ahead: "I never thought I'd ever see this! You look like a real paniolo cowboy, babe!" She had that mischievous smile spread across her face, too, her whole body bouncing up and down on that chestnut mare or filly or whatever the hell you called it. Bouncing seemed to be how it worked way up on one of these beasts, even at such a slow gait. What Sean still hadn't been able to get over, even after a mile or two up from the flats of the ranch down by Kam highway, was how *high* you were way up here in the saddle. Yeah, his horse—a stallion or bronco or whatever you called it named Wakea—though its back must have only been like five feet up, it felt like looking down the face of a twenty foot wave (or at least what Sean Hayashi imagined the face of a twenty foot wave to look like).

"I reckon he'll get the hang of it, little lady!" That was their guide, an Idaho (?) cowboy named Johnny, on his own big horse up there next to Marisa. Whether it was just an act for the tour company or not, Sean couldn't tell, but the guy seemed like a real Marlboro Man of a comfortable-with-everything-from-power-tools-to-ropes-and-livestock man's man, right down to the *spurs* on his worn frikken cowboy boots, spurs that did indeed jingle-jangle-jingle. And while the cowboy-from-the-movies talk was indeed an act, Johnny here had only begun busting it out after Marisa had set the ball rolling with a "Howdy, pahdna!" down at the stables. Since then the two of them had been trying to outdo each other with rustlin'-the-doe-gees home-on-the-range banter all the way up the trail.

Yep. Cowboy Johnny was clearly smitten with Marisa. And Sean didn't really mind that, either. I mean, who wouldn't be? Those smooth tanned legs running all the way up to her tight little jeans shorts…the red shirt tied across her bare waist…that endearing bubbly smile of hers—any man would have to be blind or a fool not to notice. Although *notice* wasn't exactly the word. Sean had caught the guy, who looked to be about his own age and who'd even mentioned a wife and four kids, *ogling*—though unlike a lot of local guys who would have false-cracked dis fucka right off his frikken horse by now, Sean looked at it as a point of pride, having a girlfriend so hot everyone clearly *wanted* her on sight.

Girlfriend? How about *wife*. Just two more months from now they'd be married at last. Right up the road at Dolphin Bay, which was what had led to the improbable image of Sean Hayashi on horseback in the first place. *Along for the ride*, he'd agreed to take Marisa up to the North Shore for the weekend to finalize the rooms and the food and the party favors and the frikken *centerpieces* and all the rest of what you apparently *absolutely had to have* so as not to embarrass yourself while hosting a June wedding for a crowd of 'Iolani grads.

Over mai tais by the windswept pool their love-talk had turned to trading childhood stories, which got Sean thinking how sad it was that someone who'd grown up wanting to breed horses had never even gotten to ride one. The concierge told him about a "ranch" not three miles from the hotel, and well, why not admit it? He'd decided that a ride on horseback, through the Koʻolaus, with the woman of his dreams, would be…*romantic*…a memory they'd joyfully recall at their fiftieth anniversary…and had Sean Frikken Hayashi really fallen that far…in *love?* Ah, happy endings!

"I reckon so!" Marisa said with a laugh.

The gap between them was widening as their horses crossed an open field towards the mountains, thanks to how immediately comfortable Marisa seemed on hers, and to the hard time Sean himself was having with old Wakea here.

"Eh, by the time we get back I'll have this thing galloping," he called ahead.

Except he couldn't figure out how to get the wheezing animal to even walk any faster. He let out one of those clucking noises he'd heard Johnny using and then dug his heels against the big animal's belly—

he wanted to say *into*, but the thing proved to be rock-solid—and the beast responded by turning its head to the side and coming to a complete stop. He tried urging it with a "C'mon, Wakea!" Another pair of kicks seemed to finally do the trick (unless the thing had simply decided to start moving on its own), and now Wakea resumed that rumbling clump-clump of a leisurely walk, causing Sean to have to adjust into rocking along to that…bounce…and try not to fall off this thing *all the way down* to the ground way down there.

It hardly helped matters that Cowboy Johnny was steering his own horse around with pinpoint control, aided by nothing more than those little clucking noises and maybe the *threat* of those spurs, which never did seem to make contact with the animal's flesh. Neither did it help that Johnny's horse—a stallion (or whatever) named Lono—had come straight out of one of those comic books where the superheroes and the dinosaurs or whatever are all drawn like they spend more time pumping steroids than they do eating.

Maybe Sean's usual instinct was to start mentally tearing down everything else about Johnny so as to compensate for the man's blatant physical advantages, perhaps settling on how out-of-place such an Idaho country fuck seemed on the North Shore, even nowadays. The four kids, the wife studying for some bullshit pharm tech certificate at BYUH, was what Johnny had said—the whole of it made for an endless supply of good comic status rip-down material. But Sean didn't have it in him to be ripping on Johnny for any reason.

The guy was just so *nice*.

Indeed Johnny had been far more *considerate* than anything else about Sean's inability to keep up, and right now, up ahead where the open field ended at a thick wall of jungle, he and Marisa sat waiting at the trailhead, and my God, just *look* at her! I mean, *look!*—and why was Sean even surprised anymore?—his pulse sped up just to see Marisa there, her lithe little body way up on her own mare or whatever. On top of that, there she was: *waiting!* For him! Marisa…dare he think it? Marisa *Hayashi*. True, the name had a bit of a DOE second-grade teacher ring to it. But it fit the daddy's-little-girl way Marisa had been born for a more…domesticated life.

And dare Sean even entertain the next thought? That they would soon have…kids? A son, perhaps? And what a different father Sean would be than poor little Milton Hayashi had been to him! Sean would provide an *example*. He would give his son *confidence*, teach him to *not give a fuck*, and look what you get, boy: you get to the *top*. You get to where they put you on the future governor's exploratory campaign committee, and then you'll *kill* it, raking in donations numbering now in the millions of dollars and kicking off a "stealth" advertising campaign that wins your candidate a 78% approval rating, was how Russell Lee had just fared in Brushette and Hyde's latest *Sentinel* poll. You'll kill it so hard they'll make you *chair*.

And when they ask you to help work the halls in the State Capitol, you'll do like the great and connected Sean Hayashi did when he won certain passage—yes, *certain passage*—of Russ's bill creating the state agency that would control the TsengUSA property, a bill whose upcoming floor vote had become a mere formality. You'll get to the *top*, boy! Like when your dad made *history* by helping gather, for the first time in like *forty years of trying*—holy shit!—had Sean actually *done* it?

Had he really managed to collect all thirteen senate votes for the gambling bill? Was he actually going to be the one to finally *open the door* to legalized casino gambling in Hawaiʻi? True, Tony Levine had warned that since you never knew for sure how some of these younger senators were at following through, from here on out they'd have to keep working for more votes, and then delay the floor vote until sometime before midnight on the final day of the session when maximum chaos reigned, and yada yada yada. But there they were: thirteen votes! Talk about being *on top!* The very top of the world!

"Don't worry about giving ol' Wakea a couple of good strong kicks!" Cowboy Johnny was telling him, turning his own beast up the jungle trail. "Especially up this little rise just up ahead."

Rise? Sean didn't like the sound of it, or the look of it when he did come upon the muddy incline. A bit steeper than a flight of stairs, and hardly twice as long, to Sean it may as well have been a sheer rock cliff, never mind that the Mighty Super Lono had just taken it in about four steps. When Marisa followed right behind, leaning forward into her animal's neck like some kind of *jockey*, was what she looked like, Sean's heart jumped with…concern…even though the little obstacle clearly *excited* Marisa—she even let out a little *whoop!* on the way up, high-fiving Cowboy Johnny at the top.

That left Sean with little choice but to dig his heals in again—or, more accurately, rub them *against* his animal's belly—but he'd be damned if he was ready to wind up and actually *kick* the thing. The thought alone sent all kinds of terrifying bucking-bronco shoulder-in-a-sling embarrassing images into his head, maybe even an air ambulance touching down in the field behind them.

"He's a gentle old man, but once in a while he needs a little reminder that he's on the job," Johnny called down. "If you don't kick hard enough, he won't even feel it." A smile. "And in the whole six months I've been here I've never once seen him throw anybody." Another understanding smile, without a hint of the sort of tour guide condescension one might have expected a Cowboy Johnny to show someone like Sean (if only in an I'm-kidding-but-not-really sort of way), particularly in front of someone as hot as Marisa. No, that was really it: Johnny here was just sincerely…nice…and now that you thought about it, the guy may not have exactly been *smitten* with Marisa after all. You could just as easily picture him giving the same amount of attention to some Crispy-Cream used up fat woman from Wisconsin. Or Utah.

Utah. And why hadn't Sean seen it before? The wife at BYUH…from Idaho…the *four* kids, for God's sakes. And so damned *nice*. Maybe you just couldn't picture Cowboy Johnny here in the black-pants-white-shirt-black-tie-bike-helmet missionary uniform walking door-to-door under a blazing hot sun—at least not any more than you could imagine such a stand-up Marlboro Man worshipping a blond Jesus who was born in North America like, two hundred and fifty years ago, who looked like Charlton Heston. But that *smile* of his was as good as the uniform. No doubt about it: Cowboy Johnny was Mormon.

Though admittedly *scared*, Sean gave out a few more clucks and then finally did wind up with a couple of heel kicks into old Wakea, who let out a snuffle before lumbering forward again and then digging his hind legs into a solid thrust up the slope. Sean's left hand swung around and grabbed that little saddle horn and hung on for dear life, the weedy thick tunnel of leaves passing frighteningly close on either side until at last old Wakea emerged in a grassy open flat area, Cowboy Johnny pulling up right beside with the look of…a proud father…that warm, warm ingratiating *smile*.

"You did it!"

Sean's inclination may have been to try to mask his heaving breaths and then respond with the kind of shrug that eloquently communicated the true silliness of the entire endeavor of torturing an old beast of burden day after day with kicks, and with pulls on that metal bar they'd jammed between his teeth, but he couldn't help but, well, *smile back*. I mean, the guy was *beaming*. With true sincerity! Even as Johnny turned Lono up what looked like a much wider trail and—wow, it really opened up back here, didn't it, just look at how far back the valley goes, the soft green peaks of all these mountains way off in the far distance, half of them capped by misty clouds—even as they turned up the trail and Cowboy Johnny launched into his little tour-guide bio of the land they were traversing, that was the word: *nice*.

It wasn't even a word you used that often anymore, and maybe the only reason it bubbled up into Sean's head was because of the way Johnny was reminding him of all the really *nice* folks he'd seen just this past Wednesday crowding the Kahuku High School Cafetorium, where the word first reemerged into his working vocabulary. Sean had come to speak in favor of a Koʻolauloa Sustainable Communities plan that had been back-doored through the Office of Planning and Permitting, a plan that would allow TsengUSA's four new hotel towers to be built by "limiting" them to "the current resort-zoned area." But for once it had been hard to even see any of the Green Shirts in the crowded hall, *drowned out* as they'd been by a sea of…blue…a couple of hundred (mostly haole) people in powder blue T-shirts emblazoned with the words, "Stand Up for Sustainability!" A unified regiment they were, many of them *flown in from Utah*, mostly retired baby boomers who wore their T-shirts over their button-down oxford shirts, their Edith Bunker house dresses, not one of them full of the usual haole anger, each one taking a second to offer a sincere *smile* if your eyes met. Among them Sean had been surprised to see Senator Arthur Tafai, who'd spent his two minutes at the mic delivering what had sounded like a campaign stump speech.

Sean had learned that all these Mormons had been mobilized to create the illusion of "community support" for a scheme that would fill God's Country with a Mormon-backed "commercial center at Malaekahana," expansion of "both BYUH and the Polynesian Cultural Center," and more than twelve hundred new suburban homes the developers had brilliantly labeled "workforce housing"—meaning, as Sean understood it, you'd only be eligible to buy one if you worked for one of a handful of companies that all wound up being owned by the Church of Jesus Christ of the Latter Day Saints. *Twelve hundred homes.* Built right here, too, no doubt, on the very land they were riding across today.

"Originally this was all sugar back here," Johnny was saying, his hand waving in a gesture meant to encompass what looked like thousands of acres of rugged jungle. Sean had to chuckle at the thought of how someone like that haole professor guy the other night would have reacted to how Johnny here had basically dismissed hundreds of years of pre-contact history with that wave of the hand. On he went about how "the church" had bought up five thousand acres, how the old refinery in Kahuku had processed the sugarcane, how the agribusiness had basically built two whole new communities out of nothing. "But once they unionized all the plantation workers," Johnny was saying, "it just wasn't sustainable anymore."

He turned Lono to charge up another little rise and waited at the top, and all Sean could think now was, there it is again: *sustainable.* The word had been tossed around the meeting the other night like a football. "Sustain" means *this.* No, "sustain" means *that.* "Sustainability" means we need to be able to *feed* ourselves, and we only have *five days' worth of food on this island!* I know, because I'm a farmer!

No, it means that since Hawai'i's most popular paid visitor attraction since 1976 has become a "mature destination," in order to attract the all-important "repeat visitor," the Polynesian Cultural Center needs to be expanded to include "Polynesian themed rides," but without compromising the "cultural integrity" of the PCC's island villages. I'm an executive at the PCC, and we've *studied* these things.

Cultural integrity? How about my family's *kuleana* land? You want to call that a "cultural resource?" Well guess what: we're not museum pieces. You will not display us for your tourists. That is *not* how you sustain a culture. Do you want to be responsible for the *end* of our culture?

But I'm Hawaiian too, born and raised, and this is the *best* plan anyone has come up with yet to bring my daughter back from where she'd had to move to in Oregon. We need affordable housing.

Sustainable! Like a *football,* from haole Green Shirt to brown Blue Shirt. (Except for the BYUH president, who'd been "delighted" to address everyone, and a couple of extra-creditors from some BYU communications class, the Mormons had sent a long line of Samoans and Maoris and yes, Hawaiians to the mic in favor of all the dorky white folks in the crowd.) By the end of the night all the usual suspects—Tom Watada with his bible-speak about the struggles of the common man, Kanoe Silva and Ikaika Nāʻimipono with their lectures on colonization, and even Aunty Maile, who'd begun her two minutes with a loud guttural chant that shook the walls, and ended it with an accusation of *murder* of our *very identity*, after we've *welcomed your people for generations*, and you *keep taking more, and more, and more!*—despite the overwhelming logic of their arguments, they'd all been chewed up and spat out simply because "sustainable" had come to mean whatever all the sheep planted by the Mormon-run bank behind all this development wanted it to.

Marisa charged up the little rise with another *whoop!*, and this time Sean dug his heels in hard—apparently much harder than before, because now the old beast took it as some kind of signal to start charging ahead, up the rise and past Marisa's *concerned* face and Johnny's *astonished* face and on up the trail, bouncing up and down the whole time. Though he couldn't have been going all that fast, suddenly the scrub trees lining the trail seemed to fly by like Sean was driving a motorcycle on H-3, the trail's edges dropping off steeply on either side into what looked like…piles of rocks. He gripped the reigns harder, and he might have fallen off had his next reflex not been to pull back. Thankfully old Wakea slowed right down like someone had stepped on the brakes, stopping so quickly Sean's hand again grabbed for the little horn on the saddle as he slid forward into the back of the thing's neck.

"Ride 'em cowboy!" Johnny called out.

"Yee-ha!" Marisa said, her shoulders bobbing up and down as she laughed.

"I told you he'd get the hang of it," Cowboy Johnny said, bouncing past him and on up the trail, further upwards and into the mountains. "We'll have you in the rodeo before long there, my friend!"

Getting the hang of it was hardly how Sean himself would have put it. Now he was trying to mask the fact that he was gasping for breath, his heart having jumped to like two hundred (although he had at least figured out how to stop this damned animal if he had to), so before he could get too far behind again, he managed to get his horse moving along, his own breathing now settling down to something a bit less than frantic.

This time Marisa stayed back with him, the trail wide enough for the two of their horses to walk side-by-side. It wasn't exactly the romantic image Sean had had in mind, what with her, like, coming to his *rescue*. But he had to admit, it was nice to have her next to him, his… future wife…and yeah, in spite of how all his don't-give-a-fuck confidence had ballooned up from all the recent good news coming from the Lege, sometimes he still couldn't believe it. For years he was certain he'd someday have to…settle, just like little Milton had when he'd married a Joyce Yamashita clone named Aimee Koyama. (And had the Great Sean Hayashi really emerged from such a shallow gene pool?) But there was Marisa: bouncing up and down right there next to him.

"Look," she said, pointing off to the side of the trail, which, the more he thought about it, seemed a bit wide for some kind of hiking trail. There was that line of rocks again way down there where she was pointing, trying to fight its way through the onslaught of weeds. "Didn't the Hawaiians used to grow taro up here?" She went on about a school trip she'd taken years ago into Makiki Valley in town where some kupuna had restored a quarter acre of the terraced rock wall taro patches with some state cultural reclamation grant, and how *sacred* the whole experience had seemed.

Sean followed her gaze, and…of course. The rocks, lining the trail evenly and caked with crumbled cement, you could now see, it hadn't been a taro patch at all—this was the old irrigation system for a sugar plantation. And the trail itself?

"No way," he said. Once again, you just had to tip your hat.

"What?" Marisa asked.

"The road," he said. "The bypass road."

"Bypass road?"

"Yeah. That Mormon town I was telling you about? The twelve hundred homes? 'Workforce housing'? They threw this bypass road into the plans to ease the traffic impacts that would show up in the EIS."

"That must have added what, ten or fifteen million to their costs, depending on how long it was supposed to be," she said. "Where was it supposed to run?"

"We're *riding* on it," he said as they clumped along. "This is an old cane road. I bet it runs all the way from Hauʻula to the other side of Kahuku, just like the road on the Planning Commission's map. You just run a grader over it and lay down some pavement, and you're done."

Up ahead Johnny called out: "We've got some company up here."

Marisa: "OhmyGOD!"

And there they were: a little herd of six wild foals and their mother, feeding freely in a little grass clearing off to the side of the trail.

While Johnny went on about how these and other young horses had the run of the entire valley, along with enough wild boar to feed Kahuku for a year, all Sean could really think about was the "bypass" road. Though the Mormons could build another Salt Lake City up here for all he cared—if anything, they were providing cover for TsengUSA—something else at the meeting the other night had been, well, *pecking* at his thoughts ever since: the little exchange he'd had with Kanoe Silva as the crowd filed out into the parking lot. "You'd better watch out for those guys," she'd told him. "You know how you're always saying that you and I aren't that far apart? That we're both really on the same side? Well this time you might be right." She'd been pulled away by an earnest Green Shirt before she'd had a chance to explain too much more. And here were her words again: pecking, pecking, pecking.

So Sean sidled right up next to Johnny and Lono, and shit, FOB cowboy that he was, people probably just babbled away right in front of the guy like he too was some kind of…invisible waiter.

"Eh Johnny, does the church own the ranch down there, too?" he asked as they headed onward.

"The ranch? Well, they lease it to a guy named Roger Ferguson." He went on about how many head of cattle the guy raised, how he was able to sell it locally and even make a bit of money on it, how he sub-leased a portion where a Filipino family grew papayas.

"Is he really making a go of it?" Sean asked.

"I can't imagine," Johnny said. "Like I was saying, after they unionized the plantations way back, agriculture just wasn't sustainable anymore. If you want to make money on ag, you've basically got to have someone willing to toil away for hours in the hot sun for pennies an hour. Believe me, I've tried it up in Idaho. I grew up on a farm. It's hard work."

"I bet you can get pretty good terms from a church."

"I'm afraid Roger's lease ends next year," Johnny said.

Next year?

"They're not gonna kick you folks out of here, are they?" Sean dug his heels into old Wakea a bit to keep pace with Lono. Sure enough, he did seem to be…getting the hang of it.

"From what I understand, they've got some developments planned," Johnny went on. "I don't know the details, but they're not kicking us straight off. I suspect there'll be some kind of gradual reduction of the ranch's size that goes along with the pace of the development. I couldn't say why, but the ranch is still important to them."

It was so simple Sean wondered why he hadn't thought of it himself. The word *ranch* was so hot with wide-open-spaces connotations that any developer would want to hang onto it for dear life. The twenty-thirty acres fronting the highway would remain "ranch" land, and the little operation run by Johnny's boss would be *sustained* in its drastically scaled down version so the whole thing could be labeled and sold as "preservation" of the rural landscape.

Nice.

"What do you think of all that development?" Sean asked.

Cowboy Johnny lit into an excited account of how he and his wife had always dreamed of living in paradise, how they'd come here specifically to get themselves on the list for the workforce housing.

"It's kind of far from Idaho, isn't it?" Sean asked. "You know, your family and all?"

"Mom and Dad are set to retire this year," he said, "and so are Rachel's parents. They're already on the list." On the list.

"For workforce housing?"

Johnny gave him a look of wonder for asking something so obvious.

"They all worked for the corporation," Johnny said.

Sean just left it at that, and anyway, the trail had narrowed into a little switch-back section that seemed to lead to the top of the foothill they'd been gradually climbing, so Johnny pulled Lono ahead to lead the way. Though he kept his coach-like banter going through each switch-back all the way to the top, the words that remained stuck in Sean's head were "workforce housing"—a term that was now obviously about fifteen times as brilliant as he'd initially thought, because while it did indeed limit those able to buy into the "affordable housing" that Senator Tafai had been arguing for the other night, according to Johnny here, every church-employed Mormon from California to Idaho to Utah—current *or retired*—fell within those limits.

"Oh. My. God!" Marisa shouted out. She was stopped up ahead on a grassy plateau, her black hair swept back in the wind, and when Sean rode up next to her—

Wow.

Spread out in all directions as far as the eye could see, a vast blanket of pure blue, from the faint line of the distant horizon where its royal shade lightened, all the way back to the reefy coast, from Kaena Point all the way down past the sweeping ironwoods straight below, and then on past the rocky cliffs of Crouching Lion, miles onward in the other direction, all the way to Mokapu peninsula, a hazy black shadow on the horizon, the mighty ocean sent its brilliant slow-motion angel-wing sprays high in the air, its crashing waves joining with that jagged verdant curtain of mountains, a curtain cut with valley after deep hidden valley, the thin white line of a distant waterfall cutting another right before his very eyes. Alive!

You heard it all the time: *it took my breath away*. But right here Sean actually felt it happen, and then felt his lungs—*felt* them—involuntarily suck in another breath, *felt* his pulse quicken, felt himself swallow, all physical reactions to what he was *seeing*, finally seeing, after 34 years living in the one place in the whole world that people spent their entire lives saving to visit *just once*, on a *dream* vacation, to *paradise*, the one place in the world where a multi-millionaire, a celebrity, an I-banker or a trust-fundie or even a worthy self-mader just *had* to have a second or third home, had to *own property* right here in—say it—right here in God's Country.

Paradise! Such a cheap word it was for what was now pouring into Sean Hayashi's eyes! And only now was he finally seeing it!

For minutes, it must have been, the two of them just sat there in silence, Cowboy Johnny having moved off to a respectful distance to let them share a moment he got to enjoy two or three times a day—and look at Johnny over there, too: even him. You'd think he'd be tired of it by now, but he looks just like a Minnesota tourist seeing it for the first time, the way his gaze keeps sweeping over the same incredible vista. A full-on uninterrupted chance to *ogle*, no less, and it's like Marisa isn't even here. God's Country! And look: there's the Dolphin Bay Hotel itself, a—how had Prescott put it?—a *spaceship* of a building right on the rocky point, surrounded by a few condo cottages, yeah, but mostly by acres and acres, nearly 900 acres of sweeping ironwoods and marshy grass and the green carpeted strips of the Jack Nicklaus golf course.

And what a stupid waste of time *that* little activity was, was the next thought that began to pierce Sean's immediate feeling of awe at the tremendous view. Golf! With State Senate President Russell Lee making five-dollar bets with a couple of frikken thug bangers, and what the fuck was Russ even *thinking*? Sure, Kekoa Meyer and his moke cousin both had *years of experience* running doors at illegal game rooms, and if anyone could keep the "criminal element" out it was the criminals themselves, and yeah, Meyer's other cousin was indeed a legit security coordinator in Vegas.

But come on. They must have…*had something* on Russ for him to simply ignore all the risks…just like…just like he'd done with Sean himself, really, gambling on him to take the place of Alan Ho, and then Darryl Kawamoto—and look how *that* little bet had paid off, was what Russ must have been thinking, from Macau all the way to *thirteen votes*, to legalized casino gambling after decades of failed attempts. So why not double down on Kekoa Meyer? Against all odds Russ had gone all in on Sean Hayashi, and he'd won. So why not Meyer?

"I love you Sean Hayashi."

And again he could feel it: his lungs sucking in a breath, and just *look* at her there with the breeze blowing through her hair! Marisa… Hayashi! The perfect and devoted woman in every way. If he'd ever had the confidence to angle his way into a meeting in Pauahi Tower, to quit his hotel job, to strong-arm Jayden Kaneshiro for his vote, on and on and on, it had only been because he had known he would be able to recount the tale to a woman far better than what little Milton Hayashi's son ever had any right to expect, and she would gush in admiration.

Don't give a fuck?

The confidence had come straight from his *wife* there on horseback, set off against the curtain of mountains—even the ones off to the left over there, capped as they were with a wind farm's platoon of towering white fans, a hundred feet tall, spinning, spinning, generating enough power for…twelve hundred homes, was what one of the blue-shirts had said at the meeting the other—

The map. Sean was looking at the map! The very same view that had, yes, *taken his breath away*—it had all been depicted on the Sustainable Communities map projected up on the screen the other night. Now it was right upon them in three windy dimensions of real life. There's Dolphin Bay, the golf course, the shrimp farms, Kahuku town just off to the left. Just below them: the scrub trees and weeds of the abandoned cane field—all of it colored "urban" yellow on the map—rolling out towards the flat pastures of the highway-side ranch, the swaying ironwood pines of Malaekahana State Park across the road (a "commercial center"), all of it running into the homes to the right in Lā'ie town. And then beyond: the new tower of the (Mormon-owned) Marriot Hotel; the PCC and the BYUH campus, both set to expand into the open spaces behind on their way to turning into the "Polynesian" version of Universal Studios on one side, the Hawai'i clone of BYU's vast Provo campus on the other, all the way back to the base of the Ko'olaus, all of it coded yellow.

Except for one thing: on the map the Planning Director had projected up on the screen, the coastline had run across the top of the page from west to east under a thin stripe of blue ocean, above about eight feet of *empty white space* drawn purposefully to include thousands of acres of rugged mountains—a little trick of proportions designed to make the Mormon development of *twelve hundred suburban homes* and their commercial center and the rest of it all look like a mere sliver of yellow. It hadn't at all looked like what Sean was now seeing, which was a wide block of urban sprawl that would connect Lā'ie, all the way from the blinding white Taj Mahal of the Mormon Temple that presided over the whole operation, with…TsengUSA's casino, less than five miles up the road at Dolphin Bay.

"You can just see forever up here, yeah?" Marisa was saying.

Sean could feel his hand reaching for his phone, and God he hoped you could get reception way the fuck up here, and look this way, at that spaceship of a hotel: the godfather of Southeast Asia dropping multiple billions on the first casino in the state's history.

Now look that way at the bright white tower of the temple: one of the more linked-up corporations in the world, ruthlessly efficient thanks to the…mission…the belief that we are working for God, which in turn leads to the complete absence of the usual infighting and backstabbing found in corporations staffed by ambitious career climbers. And you think *money* was washing over these islands back in the 1980s? A few connected Japanese "investors" snapping up every hotel and golf course in sight? First Hawaiian Center? You think that was *money?*

"Hon?"

Fuck, turn your head from Dolphin Bay all the way to the Mormon temple, and understand that if the '80s Japanese yen washed up on this island like a wave, the Chinese (and do you really think Bradley Zao will be the only one?) and Mormon, and yes, the Makani Kai I-banker money too—it's *already* covering this place like a frikken tsunami, a tsunami of planning map yellow. You can close your eyes and watch it roll in, right over those ironwoods across Kamehameha Highway and up to the foot of this very mountain, from Dolphin Bay all the way to the Mormon temp—

Kanoe. He could *hear* her voice, like she was sitting right behind him on a horse of her own: *Watch out for those guys.* Powerful, the memory of what she'd said out in the parking lot that night: "You know, there's only two states in the whole country with no form of legalized gambling—Hawai'i and Utah. Think about it." Of course she'd been talking about the usual theory of a Mormon conspiracy against gambling, and at the time Sean had been happy to dismiss her warning as so much far-fetched paranoid bullshit.

Until it kept pecking at him. He'd looked it up when he got home, too, how the Mormons had used various front groups to dump millions into defeating a Hawai'i referendum allowing same-sex marriage way back in the '90s (so they must've been fighting gambling the same way all along, right?), and how the reason *why* the Mormons opposed gambling and drugs and pornography, and even alcohol and coffee wasn't just moral. It was practical: these things robbed a human being of their God-given *agency*—and that was the word, too—their agency over their own decisions, enslaving them not to God's will or even their own, but to desires and addictions beyond their control.

"Look! You can see the little white gazebo where we're getting married!"

Bars, bars, give me bars!...and yes, the faintest little dot of a remaining bar on the screen of his phone offered the slimmest hope he could frikken *call* someone, call Russ or Tony or Darryl or *anyone*, Michael fucking Prescott even, because how much of a step was it from this Mormon concept of *agency*—and the cold efficiency of that particular religious tenet was really beginning to creep Sean out—from *agency* to the "social ills" arguments Tony Levine was always making such fun of?

Look at that temple down there, a hundred years old and gleaming like it opened yesterday, a beacon of hope to millions of Mormons from around the world, people who *believed*—not simply Tony's usual NIMBY old white ladies frightened of Joe Pesci, but people who'd actually convinced themselves that their families could be "sealed" for all eternity simply by visiting a shining white room somewhere upstairs—*believed*, also, in the simplest most logical terms, that gambling was simply bad for us. All of us.

Now look down at all that abandoned sugar land, a thousand acres of cane grass waving in the wind. Florida, Arizona, southern California all boasted mild climates and beautiful scenery and more established retirement communities in much closer proximity to the grandkids than way the hell out here in the middle of the Pacific. But look again: a truly *Mormon* community stretching out in all directions, all the way even to Waikiki, where plans to simply sell scratch lottery cards to the tourists had been defeated year after year after year. To a retired Mormon from frozen white Utah, a true believer, a "worthy member," this was indeed, in the most important sense of the word, *paradise*.

A ring, a ring, a call out to Russ, it's ringing...but then that double-beep cut-off and then silence...and retry...I need frikken *bars*!...and turn your head further left: *this* is where gubernatorial candidate Russell Lee wants to build his four-tower Vegas-style casino. The one he hopes to staff almost entirely with...local people. With the very *poster boyz* for the argument the Mormons were likely to start pounding any moment now, and especially throughout the campaign, likely to the tune of millions of dollars funneled through the coffers of...State Senator Arthur Tafai. You could picture one of Tafai's ads being filmed from right up here on this windswept mountain: "Folks, let me tell you about a good friend of my opponent, a man he's already hired for his big casino plans, a man named...Kekoa Meyer."

That was it: they had to get rid of fucking Meyer. They had to find a way. Find...the cracks...and guaranteed, it would be much easier with a thug like Meyer than with a man of principle and integrity like Ikaika Nāʻimipono—and yeah, that was the only good news with Russ's little gambles lately—that he'd finally made concrete plans to sit down with Ikaika. But fucking Meyer: still had to find the cracks. Which didn't mean Sean had to talk with Russ or Tony or Hank or even Darryl. He had to talk to Prescott. Like, right fucking *now*.

If only you could get some fucking *bars* up here.

What the fuck: service unavailable.

A Hawaiian Sense of Place

Kekoa's dad would have been proud—as proud as he'd ever been of that space-age architectural wonder, Aloha Stadium. For the first time in its twenty-plus-year history, the building dubbed the "jewel in the crown" of the Waikiki skyline was finally measuring up to its promise, envisioned long ago by designers so relentlessly committed to a *Hawaiian Sense of Place* that they'd etched the concrete mold they used to make its hundred-foot walls with a traditional *kapa*-patterned relief. The spectacular and lovingly floodlit structure, crowned with a fleet of rooftop sails evoking Hawai'i's proud open-ocean voyaging roots—it may have always given off the phosphorescent white glow of a Washington monument…a Spanish cathedral…a Mormon temple…one with a radiant four-story glass foyer that supposedly beamed its bright beacon out from Singapore to San Diego, signaling that this, here, was the *Crossroads of the Pacific*.

But it had taken tonight's line of trucks and SUVs being waved away from the jam-packed parking garage's entrance to make the Hawai'i Convention Center finally look like the kind of mega-multipurpose exhibition hall that could host the sixty annual events they'd projected before it opened back in the '90s (instead of the twenty-or-so they'd averaged since), that could in fact draw a half a million visitors a year. It had taken these thick streams of people now flooding in from all angles to confirm that one of the acts it managed to book could actually draw the promised seven thousand attendees (rather than the usual few hundred per flower-show event). Or that its construction had really "created" three hundred and fifty (and not a hundred-something) jobs. Or that it did generate $2 billion in annual visitor expenditures (instead of like, $100 *million* that didn't even cover the juice on what Hawai'i taxpayers still owed to some mainland bank).

Proud. Just as Dad would have been if he'd ever gotten to see the building's double-pitched roof, its "green" construction, its state-of-the-art technology, its open-air spaces, all that glass providing so much natural light for the pre-function spaces during the day, the occasional glimpse of the stars above at night. Or the breathtaking fourth floor roof garden's acre of bi-color concrete, sculpted in lava-like "waves" and garnished with spade-shaped taro leaves, waving *lau'ae* ferns, glossy green *noni* leaves and Big Island *hapu'u*. Even the "grand staircase" out back that led conventioneers down to the river-front Ala Wai promenade. Had he lived to see any of it, George Meyer would have been proud, because tonight the Convention Center wasn't just another linked-up politician's crumbling rusting corroded boondoggle.

Tonight it was *pumping*. That much Kekoa could plainly see after he and Javen had parked across the street at Club Mix Ja and made their way through the crowds past the statue out front: a ten-foot parade balloon of a half-kneeling Hawaiian with a snake in his hands. Tonight the giant glowing white money pit at the edge of Waikiki was as loud as it was bright, buzzing with the roar of hadda-be-a-thousand tap-out jus'-scrappers on hand for Fight Night, which in this case meant the fourth annual Kombat in the 'Ki. A whole sea of them were milling around the grove of live palm trees inside the soaring lobby, itself thundering with a hip-hop beat booming out so strong from inside the Kamehameha Exhibition Hall that you could hear the singer's voice—a West Coast rapper named B-Dolla T—like it was coming through earphones:

> *I got a billion DOLLas!*
> *I said a billion DOLLas!*
> *An' you think YOU a heavy hitta?*
> *Then why you follow me on TWITta?*

Fight Night! The big event! The Kombat in the 'Ki! All of it explained why the parking garage, whose limited size understood that conventioneers would be bussed in from their Waikiki hotels (no way they'd actually *walk* along the Ala Wai and run the gauntlet of homeless camped out in the bushes landscaping the back of this place)—it was stuffed with the chromed-out big boy king cab trucks owned by a stream of tattooed braddas and sistas flowing in and out of the giant exhibition hall doors, hundreds of t'ick-looking high school kids in the latest BJ Penn gear, the usual old-school black "Jus' Scrap" T-shirts, "FBI" Big Island logo wear, "Maui Built", "Defend Hawai'i" written over the silhouette of an AK-47, every T-shirt brand-new and still creased in the sleeves like some kind of low-brow evening wear.

Inked up moms and dads much younger than Kekoa and Javen, some of the dads still obviously hitting the heaving bag, others who just thought they were, the moms with gold heritage bracelets running up and down each arm, fifty-inch strings of thong panties wrapped around pockets of kidney fat and visible above the backs their "good" jeans, everyone surrounded by herds of running…kids…little kids, nine- and ten-year-olds, hair buzzed on the sides and bleached to a flaming orange-tinted white on top, blingged up with zarchonian rocks pierced into each ear (*I got a billion DOLLas!*), with fake gold chains, look at those two seven-year-olds over there throwing practice spin-kicks at each other and then breaking away with joyous little-kid laughter.

The first thing Kekoa did was start a mental calculation of how much scrip was flowing in through the doors, and the second was to look around and wonder who among these gangsta-boys in the stiffened black 808 baseball caps with the gold sticker on the brim was the "promoter" so he could send somebody over to collect the tax. These little fast-talkers, who all used to direct their energy at setting up concerts at Aloha Tower and Pipeline Café, or "theme parties" at the downtown yuppie bars, or on the ultimate prize: a "battle of the bands" at the Waikiki Shell—nowadays it was either a freestyle rap contest or a series of kickboxing fights, and to hold an MMA night at the Hawai'i Convention Center was big-time stuff for—

Hold on. More than the indoor palm trees, more than that waterfall cascading three stories down the rock wall over there, that's what Kekoa's dad would have been proud of: that there was no need to tax any of it anymore. Not even Club Mix Ja across the street. No, Kekoa had risen to one different…level. *Don't end up like me, Kekoa—you gotta do good in school, you gotta try your best.* Kekoa had taken what he'd seen as the best path toward *pushing back*, toward living up to his father's tremendous pride for Hawai'i, because *Don't end up like me*—even *with* the education Kekoa would have wound up ten-dollar-whoring his way through life had he not thrown in with Javen all those years ago.

And now? Forget about taxing frikken Nolan Kahaiue and his little army of bottom-feeder drug dealers. *This* was more like what Dad had had in mind. Shot-caller fear-and-intimidation street cred *blood on the table* Sonny Bulger presence? Fuck, it didn't even matter anymore whether the next up-and-coming GNC steroid mothafucka wanted to take down Kekoa Meyer. And look at alla these bottom-feeder braddas roaming around in their *Ainokea* shirts anyway: it's like they *know*, like Kekoa Meyer's power now reaches so high, well, don't fuck wit' Kekoa Meyer, cuz—he not only *off*, brah, he *linked up*, all the way to the frikken *top* cuz. Kekoa, he playing *golf* with the governor of the State of Hawai'i.

"Cuz!" Nalu's voice shouted over B-Dolla-T's booming beat. There was the big ugly bradda walking up with Kimo and a couple of the younger boyz, Randy and Kevin, and this other short stocky boy Kekoa didn't recognize dressed in a—damn, is that a *Russell Lee* jersey?—yep: a throwback UH Russell Lee jersey, and what, did this new power connection flow both ways? Russell Lee getting some banger street cred from being linked up with Kekoa Meyer?

Only when Nalu threw out his huge local-boy handshake with its mighty *slap!* did Kekoa remember how he'd *burned his fucking finger* this morning, and *FUCK* did that fucking *hurt*. He hoped no one saw the wince, because no way was he about to explain how it had happened—while he was frikken cooking breakfast—one giant blister rising up right at the *exact point of impact* for a hearty how-you-brah handshake. Fuck, even with the thick band-aide Dawn had wrapped around it, felt like fucking Nalu had just fucking stabbed his fucking finger wit' one fucking pencil.

Plus now they were only getting started:

"Dis my cousin Jesse," Nalu said.

Slap!

"How you Uncle."

And then all the way down the line:

Slap!

"Top shape, Bradda Kekoa!"
Slap!
"Automatic!"
Slap!
"Owe-raaht!"
Slap!
Half a dozen fucking slaps, and fuck, was that water welling up in his eyes? Like it does, against your will, if somebody false-cracks you hard enough? Welling over into fucken tears—and how the fuck would *that* look? Kekoa fucken Meyer frikken crying because of one fucking blister on his finger…

Somehow this kid Jesse hadn't noticed, or at least he wasn't saying anything, and neither were the rest of the boyz, every one of them wearing matching black T-shirts emblazoned with a photo image of Nalu's cousin, fists up in a fighter's pose under the words Brandon "The Hawaiian Supa Man" Camacho, the words "His Pain, My Gain" and a Jesus hand with a nail through it stretched across the back. And then Kekoa finally recognized the Jesse kid: Nalu had been talking about him, another cousin, just got out of Hālawa prison.

"Cannot find parking anywhere!" Nalu shouted out over the noise. "Hadda leave my truck over wit' Joe-dem, else I neva wouldda made it." Joe Tripp, that big sumo mothafucka, he ran the door at Mix Ja. He couldda made some extra money tonight selling parking.

"Your family-guys save seats?" Javen shouted.

"Nah, I already wen' text the promoter, dis guy Kyle!" Nalu said. "He know we coming. But then I texted my aunty for tell her about the parking, she said get plenny room inside anyway, only like three-four hundred people."

Three-four hundred people? Hadda be that many crowding among the palm trees out here in the foyer alone. And yeah, probably no one even taxing this Kyle whoever-it-was, the promoter, because except those two cops leaning against the wall over there talking story, rented for the night to fill some kind of event code requirement, you hardly needed "security" in here. Instead of all the bangers and their arm candy, the old-man Japanee gamblers, all the cigar-chomping shady characters you'd expected an event named "The Kombat in the 'Ki" to attract, you had…a family reunion… and fuck, should've brought Dawn and the girls, probably even had some of their classmates darting around in here among these folks, all of them falling into joyous hugs and deep sincere local-boy handshakes because half of them had flown in from neighbor islands to support their son or cousin trying to escape some Kona or Kahului or Waiʻanae ghetto. KPT housing. Some Army recruiting officer or whatever. To become the next BJ Penn.

But yeah, when you looked a little closer, you could see…downtown aloha shirts…formal dinner attire that hadn't been bought at Ross Dress for Less…and that yeah, half these people in here were dressed more for some 1950s version of a Vegas title fight than for some last-minute thrown-together collection of amateur brawls like the Kombat in the ʻKi. Snaking their way through the Zippy's tailgater crowd, Kekoa now wondered how he could have missed any of them, these people, all done up more for a wedding—and not a country wedding, but the kind you held under a chandelier in some ballroom, or outdoors under the stars…in the roof garden.

Look: a line of men in designer aloha wear and even dinner jackets, their "dates" wrapped in five hundred dollar cocktail dresses, rising the length of that long escalator climbing all the way up to what looked like a third floor balcony, where another escalator met it to take everyone up to the roof.

Mixed in with the Hawaiian mommies and daddies whose soft bulbous shoulders protruded from Tap-out tank tops—so we can see that photo-perfect tattooed image of your baby daughter, or the Chinese character for "strength," or the map of the Hawaiian islands—had the same crowd of folks you'd expect to see at…the opera. The same *white people* you might find teeing it off on the Jack Nicklaus Championship Golf Course. Throwing their five grand around to gain whatever *local* influence they still might have needed well into the millennium—or was it that politicians and football coaches were the closest things you'd find to a celebrity here in Honolulu? Someone who provided the kind of star power that denoted a certain…status…if you were blessed enough to be invited, like Kekoa Meyer had been, to their golf tournaments. That long line of wealth—it rose up and away from the brown, unwashed masses *down here*, up towards that glass ceiling high above.

The only truly well-dressed *local* people in sight were the thick boyz in the gray suits with the soft purple dress shirts, those flex cords crawling out of their ears, the…security…and security was in fact needed tonight…but not for the Jus' Scrap family affair down here in the bowels of the glowing jewel of Waikiki. No, these were top-of-the-line, ex-Navy Seal-kine, *secret service professionals*, so much on their game that you couldn't even call them the more thuggish "bodyguards"—the security detail for a *single guest* of whatever that affair was *up there*.

The governor of the State of Hawai'i.

And how's *that?*—little Sean Hayashi?

Three thoughts at once: what the fuck is Sean Hayashi doing here and should I just make like I neva seen him; I like rip that fucka's throat out right here in front of everybody; an' look atchoo in your black long sleeve shirt buttoned all the way to the top, your gray *slacks*, those black leather shoes hugging your feet like a second skin, I betchoa fucken girlfriend wen' dress you in all that faggot metrosexual shit, you even get *product* in your hair Sean Hayashi.

Next: Hayashi's girlfriend! His fucken' girlfriend! Better yet: a sparkle of light coming from her finger, must be four karats, that diamond, she not his girlfriend—she's his fiancé! One and the very same, no mistake about it: it's fucken Nalu's Niu Valley bedroom ninja! Look that stricken look on her face like she praying nobody going say nothing, she the same one Nalu wen' use as his naked personal serving tray for body shots back at Susie's Penthouse. Look! At her arm looped through Sean Hayashi's, the two of them buckling under the weight of that thick diamond rock.

And no fucking way: that cynical cold punk, the same one Kekoa watched shrugging his way through a round of golf? No way: Hayashi, he *in love* with the girl. Her frikken puppy dog. Her Yes Dear fuckin' *bitch*. In love! White-picket-fences love, let's-make-a-happy-family love, an' ho, you not so fucken smart after all, ah Sean Hayashi.

Until he looks up at Kekoa and just for a split-split second, *irritation* crosses his face, lips shut tight, and then right away it's pushed away wit' that same calm look the fucka gave when he was trying for lecture Javen about bones, about the SHPD or whatever it was. An' look now: Hayashi of all people, here he comes with one real roots-Hawaiian bradda-bradda how-you-cuz *slap!* of a local-boy handshake, and *FUCK* that *hurt*—especially afta all these otha boyz just wen light up Kekoa's hand, an' what, Hayashi doing 'um *on purpose*, like he *know*.

Fuck!

"Wow, you okay Kekoa?" Hayashi asked. "I'm sorry—I didn't see the band-aide. What happened to your finger?"

Kekoa narrowed his eyes, at the same time praying they weren't welling up with water again. But he ate it, and instead of ring Hayashi's fucken neck, or even let him know he'd gotten in his head, he changed the subject, moving the introductions along, an' *let me show you how well everyone here already knows your future wife, cuz.*

He leaned down and kissed the girl on the cheek—Marisa—who looked like she wanted to close her eyes and disappear. But the girl, she wen' eat 'um too, at least enough to make like she brightening up enough to throw around some social kisses.

"You should have seen this guy taking everybody's money the other day," Kekoa said to her. He held the gaze just long enough to make her wonder whether he was going say something about…body shots.

"I got lucky," Hayashi said with a shrug. And good: he feeling *uncomfortable*, a little bit *scared*, however hard he trying hide it—an' watch him when Marisa here introduces everybody as her "friends from church."

Now it was Hayashi's turn to change the subject: "So there's some kind of boxing match going on here tonight?" he asked, eyeing Kekoa from head to toe. You could almost hear him thinking, *that's quite a gold chain around your neck, Kekoa, and those D-Rose 9.8 Adidas you've stuffed your baggy black jeans into look* just like *the ones B-Dolla T wears in that video—real nice get-up for a guy in his forties who pretends he's some kind of executive!*

Along with all that, Hayashi was announcing in a glance that he and his smoking hot fiancé were certainly *not* here at the Hawaiʻi Convention Center for the same reason they were, just as you could tell he knew all about MMA and kickboxing and how they differed from boxing, but was feigning ignorance to confirm how low-brow and thuggish something as stupid as the "Kombat in the ʻKi" really was.

"My cousin from Maui fighting tonight," Nalu said. "You folks should come watch." And then he took a look at Marisa. Took a *look*.

"We'd really love to," was what she said, looking around. "It looks like there's a lot of people from church here, too." Then she squeezed Hayashi's arm a little tighter and said, "But they'd probably miss us upstairs." And god, get me out of here before my Sean starts suspecting anything, was what Kekoa could hear her thinking.

You could also tell Hayashi wanted someone to ask about "upstairs," but nobody took the bait.

"It's kind of important," he finally said. "It's a fundraiser for Russell Lee's campaign, although no one's supposed to come out and say that out loud. So we've gotta go up there and schmooze with all the rich haole donors." This came out as, "It's too bad you weren't invited, ah Kekoa! You cliché banger brainless thug!"

Kekoa thought of saying something, something about fat fucking Nalu, he the one been ripping your wife's clothes off brah, pounding that shit like one porn star. But even saying something—it would have been so fucken feeble that he just kept his mouth shut and started simmering.

The Kamehameha Exhibition Hall had in fact turned out to be an overly optimistic venue for the sad excuse of a crowd now making its way over to the far corner of what looked like a darkened airplane hangar. Way over there, The Octagon!, a boxing ring enclosed on all sides not by ropes, but by a black chain link fence, had been set up under blazing white lights and surrounded by twenty rows of folding metal chairs that were in turn boxed in on three sides by the kind of aluminum bleachers you'd find in a high school gym. On the fourth side a short catwalk ran from The Octagon! to the hall's velvet-curtain stage, where a huge movie screen projected the ring's action in in-your-face detail.

And the thought then running through Kekoa's head was: What the fuck is going on upstairs?

Down here all these little kids had a good acre to zoom back and forth on, throwing spin-kicks at each other, playing chase, weaving their way around aunty in her wheelchair or uncle hobbling slowly with his cane, his ankles swelled to the size of his calves. Other kids were working their way into that flag football game over there, one of the skinny shirtless boys having thought to bring a nerf along.

A gaggle of teenage girls balancing on high heels, dressed more for a night's work at Club Mix Ja than a family reunion, were Oh-my-*god*-ing and *se*riously-*NO*-comment!-ing over a text one of them had just gotten. A three-year-old girl, it looked like, was hoisting her infant sister all the way to the top row of the aluminum bleachers—you wondered if you were supposed to run over there and *do something* before the two of them tumbled ten feet down, headlong into polished concrete—until a hefty mom who looked like a tank-topped bulldog in a baseball cap with two broomsticks for legs and a phone stuck to her ear began yammering away at the top of her lungs for little Crystal to get da fuck down hea right now befo' I rip outchoa fuckin' *arms!*

And all Kekoa could think was, *why the fuck Russ leave me off the guest list?*

Way down here, a platoon of uncles and aunties were hustling away behind that long row of banquet tables, hand-lettered signs pushing kalua pork plates and hot dogs and sodas and shave ice, an' yeah, listen to Nalu shouting over the pounding rap music to see if anyone was hungry, he knows everybody over behind the tables, they made good pig, not the kind where you get a boxful of watery cabbage and a few stringy strands of tasteless meat, they do this every week at that luau of a church service over at Farrington.

Upstairs? They eating out of *styrofoam boxes* upstairs? They sitting in folding metal chairs?

Yeah, *luau* down here, everybody sharing food, shouting out across the rows, greeting each other with big hugs. An' yeah, here comes The Parade, starting with the promoter—this little Kyle Wong boy, he all smiles and handshakes and rapid-fire ass kissing—an' here come the usual line of you-know-we-love-you-Kekoa, the usual respect, the silent eyes-down nervous hand-slaps from the younger boyz. An' *bring on* the hand slaps, cuz, the pencil stabs into that blister, the fucken *pain*—bring that shit on, cause yeah, right now alla that searing pain starting for feel good, starting for create energy, starting for mix with…anger… and what the fuck going *on* upstairs? I like go up an' mafia that whole fucken party—an' here come that one loyal-to-the-core fucka I wen' crack my foot on his head, *slap!*, an' you competing tonight boy?

Not tonight Mista Meyer—I mean, Kekoa—but thank you for coming anyway an' maybe you could cheer for my little brother, he fighting in the 13th fight outta the blue corner right afta Camacho, his name Josh.

No worry, brah, we get his back over here.

Thank you bradda Kekoa.

Slap!

Pain! Searing hot stabs of pain. An' what, I been fooling myself the whole fucken time? Been getting played? A *trinket*? Only fucken sway I eva really get not with Russell Lee—it's with the kind people cover their ten-year-old kid in tattoos and then bleach his hair so he can run around looking like a lit match? Cannot be. But how my Parade any different from all these other meet-and-greets going on all over the place in here, little kids kissing their grandmas—none of the grandmas much older than Kekoa Meyer—and then going down the line of aunties and uncles before running off to join the nerf football game or whatever, women hugging each other over rows of metal chairs, the usual gossip flying this way and that, proud dads trading stories about their sons in Pop Warner—

"Ho!" a collective roar sent all heads spinning towards The Octagon!, where the fighter from the blue corner was unleashing a flurry of blows on his opponent's head, many of them catching the thick pads of the kid's red headgear, but many of them getting through…and now the crowd was *quiet*, everyone locked in, because right now it was *on*. An aunty up in the bleachers was on her feet and throwing air punches of her own, and *screaming*: "Hit 'im, Kayden! *Hit* 'im!" And the other guy, the guy in the red, his shoulders even tattooed red in a Spider Man pattern—he was game, this kid, he wasn't backing down. His face right up in that blender of punches, he started throwing roundhouses of his own, snapping his opponent's blue headgear from side to side.

On they went, for several minutes, these lithe fighting machines, so tireless that Kekoa found the typical old man's thought filling his head, the one that was appearing lately just about every time he saw a six-year-old—a *six-year-old*—in high gear: where do they get all that *energy*? The final bell just rang, and these two rug rats now flanking the ref could've kept going at it for another ten minutes. Here's the ref on his knees holding each by the hand awaiting the decision, and their little chests are hardly even rising up and down.

And is this how it works? Instead of sipping champagne with the future governor of Hawai'i, I stay down here. Worse: I just watched a sanctioned kickboxing event, in The Octagon!, in the Hawai'i Convention Center, between two second graders.

"And the winner in the junior novice division," Kyle Wong was belting it out in his best announcer's voice, "is Kayden Gomez!" The two little boys dissolved into hugs and handshakes announcing that the whole brawl had been designed to teach the concepts of good sportsmanship. Then they were replaced by two taller and more elaborately tattooed versions of themselves—a ritual all on its own involving a minute-long recorded promotional video up on the movie screen ("I don't know much about my opponent, but I know I trained really hahd fo' dis fight, an' I going do whatever it takes to win, I'd like to thank my coaches, my maddah, my fiancé, my son R.J., my sparring pahtas…" etc.), then the thumping beat of B-Dolla T or whatever the guy picked for his ring music, and finally a spotlight on the velvet curtain and the emergence of a bouncing fighter, followed by a posse of at least twenty gold-chained and black-creased-T-shirted boyz all making hahd, and finally the actual brawl.

The trend continued throughout the night, interrupted only by the appearance of a rotating line of heavily made-up and inked up high-heeled ring girls, each one a former Roosevelt High beauty who'd apparently struck out at Mix Ja, the strings on their bikinis straining against a rising tide of cellulite as they waddled around to the blaring soundtrack of some castrated West Coast rapper bragging about his bitches and his crib and his whip in some synthed-up mechanical robot voice.

All the while, stragglers from The Parade kept walking up for Kekoa's blessing (*slap!*). Nalu kept shouting out commentary on what was going on in The Octagon! and letting it hang there for his approval. Kimo, Randy, Kevin, same thing. The new kid, Jesse, kept trying to impress him with this or that three-word comment about how much he'd had to man-up inside at Hālawa, not like before, not like back when his dad stay lock-up back in the eighties.

But the whole time Kekoa was hardly listening, still wondering what the fuck was going on upstairs, *up there* in the roof garden or wherever it was. And more—except he had no idea why it was bothering him so much—why he hadn't been invited.

An hour passed before Nalu's cousin finally stepped up into The Octagon! and ripped off his Velcro-ed sweats and did a couple of skipping laps, throwing two or three combos into the air along the way to a version of Bob Marley's "Get Up Stand Up!" layered with a pounding beat to make it sound like gangsta rap. Kyle Wong shouted out a big "Ladieeeees and Gentlemen! In the Blue Corner! Fighting out of Kahului, Maui! Let's give it up for Brandon 'The Hawaiian Supa Man' Camacho!" Nalu and his boyz were on their feet and shouting, so Kekoa stood too, a shout of encouragement to the chunky kid in the blue trunks—or, more like board shorts—now rolling his shoulders over there. Kekoa had never met Brandon Camacho, but "Supa Man" wasn't the ring name that would have come to mind.

His pale thick arms were covered in triangular Hawaiian warrior tats, and an even paler stomach hung out over his waistband, his flabby boobs jiggling up and down as he bounced on his heels. Though Javen had told Kekoa the guy could fight, that he never backed down, Kekoa couldn't help but hope that some cut and roided monster hadn't been pitted against the poor fucka.

Nevermind that: when Brandon's opponent emerged from behind the curtain to the sound of the Iz sovereignty song, "E Ala E"—also overlaid with a pounding gangsta rap beat—and ripped off his sweats with let's-*do*-this finality, you saw a red-trunked mirror image of Brandon, the same fat pale stomach and handles and backblubber hanging over his waistband, the same tree-trunk arms—though his were covered in swirling calligraphy and not warrior triangles—and the same jiggly boobs. And when he bounded around The Octagon!—with surprising grace for such a big bradda—his *whole body* shook like a bowl full of jelly.

"Ladieeeees and Gentlemen!" Kyle Wong brayed out again. "In the red corner! Fighting out of Waiāhole on the Windward side! Let's give it up for Kalani 'Da Hamma' Nā'imipono!"

Nā'imipono. Nā'imipono. From Waiāhole? Hard as it was to picture a son of the great activist wrapped up in this living video game, a look around confirmed it: there sat the big man over in the second row of the seats to the right, just behind Fiji's wheelchair. Ikaika Nā'imipono. All by himself, it looked like. He may as well have been one of Russell Lee's haole bankers having mistakenly shown up at the wrong party, so out of place did he look here. But that's how Ikaika was: one devoted dad, going support his son no matta how he himself feels about what a dreamer's event some fucken bottom feeder had spent some time naming the "Kombat in the 'Ki". No matta what, he going support his son in his moment of kickboxing glory.

The flabby Kalani "Da Hamma!" touched gloves with Nalu's flabby cousin, and one of the high-heeled ring girls waddled around The Octagon! holding up a placard announcing Round 1. And Ikaika Nāʻimipono. Look at him: arms folded and resting on that big stomach of his. Look at his face: that I've-seen-it-all-before look. You almost had to feel sorry for him, sorry that such a great natural leader had wasted so much talent and charisma and...*sway*...on such an impossible life-long struggle, when all along he could have been shaking these fuckas down like Russell Lee, like Kekoa himself.

Russell Lee. Russell Fucking Lee.

And now the fight—not the main event, but the moment Nalu-them, and Ikaika Nāʻimipono too, that they had all been waiting for—this fight was already following along in the very same sorry pattern they'd been watching all night long. The Hawaiian Supa Man had already charged out of his corner, and Da Hamma had fearlessly charged to meet him, and the two of them had already traded their seconds-long series of upper-cuts and roundhouses and jabs and leads worthy of the climactic scene in a Rocky movie. Now they were already in the clutch, leaning upon one another like a couple of drunken frat brothers searching for a lost contact lens, their backs heaving up and down as they gulped for air while a puddle of sweat collected beneath them on the canvass...*drip, drip, drip*...*heave, heave, heave*...*drip, drip, drip*, another minute passes.

Another.

The entire round, two big blalas hanging onto each other for dear life. Second round: same story, except this time the Supa Man, leaning with all his own weight, has all the blubbery bulk of Da Hamma waffled out through the holes in the chain link fence right in front of Kekoa, you can hear them both heaving for breath. Third round: again. Waddling ring girls in between, testing the engineering of a four-inch heel as they make their way around all eight sides of The Octa—

Hold on. One, two, three, four...had it really taken this long? Had it taken Kekoa Meyer over an *hour* to even notice? Or was it just because Kyle Wong had been drilling it into everyone's head all night: "The Octagon!" this, and "Settle this thing in The Octagon!" that, plus all around everyone kept saying it, too, like it was some kind of sacred altar: The Octagon! Kekoa himself had even started calling it that. And now he felt stupid.

Still, he had to count again, and point with his finger just to make sure he hadn't missed anything. He counted a third time as the ref lifted the gloved hand—and there was some suspense, no way to really tell which man had "won" this scrum, each of them with one eye swollen shut, the fat Hamma with a stream of blood dripping down from the cut on his forehead—as the ref lifted the gloved hand of a dripping Brandon Camacho up there, yes, up there in the…one two three, four five…*six*. No, there was no getting around it, no matter how many times you counted. It was a fucking *hexagon*.

When Kekoa arrived alone on the crowded fourth floor balcony, right away you could see why they left him off the guest list—never mind the thing had to be pages and pages thick. A pullover black Nike warm-up hanging out over black jeans stuffed into blazing white B Dolla Ts, not so *threatening*. No ink. No bling. No more even too much muscle or intimidating size—at least compared to someone like Kimo or even young Rod. Man enough already, cuz. By reputation alone. But up here, even if none of these haoles wandering over to the smoking area or the restroom had the slightest clue who Kekoa was, still they all giving him a berth wide enough for a couple of thugs like Javen and Nalu combined.

Good. One hard stare and one head-pump and that dot-com fucka over there with his hair sculpted into the Koʻolau ridge would probably just leap over the railing in pure fright. Or that fifty-year-old blonde woman, looks like someone stuck a couple of softballs to her chest, and did you ever think you'd find people trying not to stare at the cleavage of someone so *old*? She takes one look at the Hawaiian—not a *roots* Hawaiian like Ikaika Nāʻimipono or an academic Hawaiian or a famous musician Hawaiian or a Kam School Downtown Hawaiian (and even a few loyal soldiers from that army dotted the white crowd up here), one look at the local…*local* rhyming with *ignorant inarticulate racist who once yelled 'Fuckin' Haole!' at me in the parking lot at Neiman Marcus for no reason*…one look at this *local*, and this lady's face scrunched up like she'd just swallowed that lime on the rim of her pink designer martini.

Good.

Except…except…well…she didn't seem the least bit uncomfortable with openly *having* such a reaction at the sight of an actual Hawaiian because, well, I'm here to *support the Hawaiian people*, I'm here to *contribute to the cause* of electing the first *Hawaiian governor* since 1994, and without my *help* he doesn't stand a chance.

Now Kekoa was surprised to find he wasn't getting frikken *irritated* at the sight of this woman and all the rest of the privileged and clueless haole money floating around up here, surprised to find his natural urge to just heave this bitch over the railing too—you couldn't explain why—it just wasn't there.

Maybe he finally saw the point of the whole thing, of why Russ or that little jellyfish of a side-kick of his, what's his name, Yoshida, or whoever it was that had decided to not include Kekoa Meyer—the very symbol of Russell Lee's pledge to create real jobs for real Hawaiians—in what was clearly a gala celebration kicking off his (as yet unofficial) run for governor—whoever made that decision was *thinking*. Whoever it was *knew*. They knew that tonight was only the first of many chances ahead to shake these people down, and that just the sight of someone like Kekoa Meyer would have scared away all the *money*.

One look past those two skirted banquet tables guarding the roof garden entrance was enough to tell you what that meant. Just do the math. The crowd: three or four times bigger than that ragged and tattooed bunch downstairs. If this was one of those thousand-dollar-a-plate things, then you had what, like six hundred grand coming in. Russ's hook-ups must have brought down the facility cost too. You had the usual three blalas in the matching aloha shirts playing hotel music, but how much could that have run? Altogether, Russ's campaign had to be walking away with like half a million dollars from this one fundraiser. Half a million dollars from, isn't that the UH President over there, Varner? And those downtown country club fucks from the UH football golf tournament, Sidney Rogers? That Austin Powers mothafucka, whatshisname, Prescott? The whole place looked like a red-carpet event right out of the front section of *Honolulu* magazine, except with like ten times as many money haoles from who knew where else.

There he was, too: Russell Lee, the Governor-to-Be, talking to Hayashi and Prescott right behind those banquet tables, like Hayashi had stationed him there to greet this incoming parade of money, to let them in on how his father had raised him in a house with a kerosene powered refrigerator and instilled in him a need to lift his people out of the throes of *Ainokea*—all the same bullshit he'd told Kekoa and Javen that first day in his office. And they were all eating it up, too, these people, like Russ was some kind of televangelist who'd tapped into a need that dug and twisted at their insides: *guilt*. Russ alone could assuage their guilt. A thousand dollars, and you were no longer part of the problem, part of the squeeze that pushed half the Hawaiians out to Vegas and the other half through Hālawa prison and on to Arizona. No, a thousand dollars, and you were *helping*.

And now yeah, the sight finally did start digging at Kekoa, irritating him, sending that knee bouncing up and down, because he could see what Russ was up to…and he wanted in. Russ needed him. Needed his help recognizing the lines of power that he seemed so oblivious of… needed him to let that aging 'Iolani Bishop Square motherfucker over there try out his haole pidgin on him, ask him about football, talk about way back when he played on the line with the one non-Kam-school Hawaiian he'd ever exchanged words with in his life, all so he could out-*local* that aging hapa Punahou frat boy next to him—the one with the shriveling Euro-wife he met in Tokyo after his daddy's connects got him both the Stanford law degree and the outpost multinational sport's agent position representing unknown Korean soccer players or whatever.

The three of them could *local* down right here, trade stories about inhaling two-three mixed plates at Gracie's Drive Inn between summer two-a-day practices back in the day, while Kekoa reached into their trust-fund-lined pockets to help Russell Lee shake these mothafuckas down.

"Aloha!"

Kekoa turned to see a stocky blond-ish haole woman in a black-business-skirt-white-blouse get-up clutching a clipboard to her chest, her face a beaming smile. She had one of those two-name gold colored name tags pinned to a black-and-white print suit jacket, marking her as someone living on a plane far above the front-line first-name wage slaves. You didn't need to read its fine print to know she was some kind of assistant general manager—no, you could hear all that in the reams of

Hawaiian-Sense-of-Place she'd packed into the word *aloha*, like she rehearsed it in front of the mirror every morning before coming to work. Kekoa wondered if anyone had seen the irony of having such a person run the coming out party of a man who planned to put an end to the usual practice of rotating California haoles in and out of all the executive positions every couple of years, the irony of having someone like… Ellen Doran, her nametag read…conducting "customer service" orientations for their back-of-the-house Hawaiians to teach them all the true meaning of *the aloha spirit*.

"Can I help you?"

Can I help you. Dripping with sincerity, the words came right out of a segregated coffee counter in 1950 South Carolina or someplace.

A wave of anger. And good thing this was a woman and not that skinny blonde motherfucker over there with his spindly arms jutting out of that PJ-top of an aloha shirt, cause yeah, that fucka would have gotten the head-pump and the hard stare, or maybe Kekoa *would* have just lifted him up and heaved him right off the fucken fourth-floor balcony, which was exactly what he felt like doing to Ellen fucking Doran right fucking now.

Except…except…except now the wave of anger was falling on the sands of a need to…justify…to justify his presence way up here in the roof garden to this weeks-off-the-boat haole woman. And why the fuck was it important at all that Ellen Doran here know that Kekoa…belonged? That he was a personal friend of the guest of honor, who was looking right at them this very moment not fifty feet away, exchanging words with Hayashi and Prescott right now, looking at Ellen Doran, a piece-of-shit *assistant* general manager of a perpetually failing convention facility, and for sure Russ will give a little wave, or maybe send over one of those boyz in the suits flanking the entrance. Or maybe he'll send Hayashi, and look: Hayashi sees him too, and then he says something to Russ—he's like, in Russ's *face* for some reason, yapping away, and now Russ starts giving a little nod—then Prescott pulls something out and starts…writing?

Just like that, Russ's charm-filled face *turned away*, focusing its attention hard on the aging boob lady, throwing itself back in laughter, shifting so that when it looked up again it would be facing *somewhere else*. Facing somewhere a little less…awkward, somewhere where things were *simple*: I do *this*, and you do *that*, and we'll all pretend that *everything's okay*. You can go on thinking that your thousand dollars makes up for the fact that you've displaced my brothers and sisters from their ancestral land (or forced them into menial service jobs, or toward the military, or into the employ of some local gangster, or into the deep spiral of addiction to crystal meth), and I'll go on thinking that I'm *shaking you down* so that I can go on to bigger and better things, to a real position of power, and *then* I'll *truly* help my people.

Now here comes fucken Hayashi and Prescott both, Prescott's wearing a suit jacket over his designer aloha shirt, except it doesn't look like they're on their way to clear up this little misunderstanding and escort Kekoa Meyer into the party. An' what's that Prescott's got in his hand?

And that guest list. Hayashi wasn't just on the guest list—he *wrote* the frikken guest list. Hayashi, the Chair of the Russell Lee for Governor Exploratory Committee. Hayashi, who knew all about Russ's dreams of doing something new with this casino, of bringing Hawaiians home from Vegas, Hawaiians like Boy Ching and his whole family. Hayashi, who would have seen clearer than anyone how Kekoa Meyer could have been used as the concrete example that those dreams were already being put into action.

Hayashi, who could nail allathese motherfuckers on how they trying for out-*local* each other, he could've figured out a way to get them past their initial fear, a way to *use* that fear to make the point about how important it was what Russ was trying to do. But no. Hayashi left him off the guest list. On purpose. An' it wasn't like it mattered all that much to Kekoa that he wasn't *invited*. Anyone could see the point, and the point wasn't that Russell Lee was playing Kekoa. It was that fucken Sean Hayashi here was playing everybody, Russell Lee above all. *Playing* him.

Here's fucken Ellen Doran with her *clipboard*, her eyes starting to shift this way and that, she looking for...security.

"No thank you," Kekoa finally told her. "It's just that there was this long line downstairs and, well, I really had to use the restroom."

All she could do was give him that professional service industry smile of hers and point the way.

Hayashi, here he is with another *slap!* to the hand, big smile on his face, fucka knows how much it hurts, the slap, except he get no idea how *good* it feels at the same time. What, Sean, finally one playa now, all the way to the top, ah? An' what, you scared of me too, you gotta bring along this fat pink rugby mothafucka, gotta alert the governor's security in case Kekoa Meyer go *off*, in case he rip this fucka Prescott's face right off right here in front of everybody, starts splattering fucking trust fund bodies all over the fucking lobby floor way down there. Good you worried about that. I like do 'um, too, I like damage alla you. Ten years ago, who knows? Ten years ago, send me to Hālawa, I no care the place all run by Mexicans and neo-Nazi haoles, was what that kid Jesse was saying, Bloods and Crips, USO Family West Coast *solés*, I no care, I take down alla you fucken punks. Watch.

"You remember Michael Prescott from the golf tournament?" Hayashi was saying.

Kekoa reached out his hand.

"Whoa, careful," Hayashi said to Prescott. "Kekoa hurt his finger—don't squeeze to hard."

"Eh, no worry cuz," Kekoa said to Prescott, hadda look up into his haole blue eyes, "squeeze as hard as you like."

"The golf course," Prescott said. "I'm afraid that's what we're here to talk about, Kekoa."

Fucka neva waste time. Neva even shake his hand.

"You see, it's still a very delicate situation, this business of drumming up support for legalized gambling in this state. I'm sure you understand." That clipped fucken accent of his—was he making this shit up? An' the whole time Hayashi's standing there with that fucken smile on his face.

"Not to be indelicate," he went on, "but I'm afraid I have to point out that your…aggressive behaviour…made some of our supporters a bit…uncomfortable." A resigned pink look, like it pained him to even have to bring it up: aggressive behaviour. What the fuck?

"There was a meeting about the guest list," Hayashi said.

And right there Kekoa could picture it: little whining Hayashi *telling on him*, fucken ratting him out, making up all kine bullshit about gangsta this, murderer that, about the frikken Bump, turning the frikken Bump into a hit on his frikken sorry ass little Japanee boy life.

"Look, TsengUSA is fully committed to Senator Lee's plans to create jobs for local people." *Accent!* He putting us on! "And we fully intend to honor that commitment. Especially with Ernest Ching."

Ernest Ching. Boy Ching. You bringing my cousin Boy into this, you British fucken cocksucker.

"But we're afraid that for any of this to succeed, we're going to have to distance Senator Lee from—and you'll have to excuse me—from the criminal element that the opposition so often holds up in its arguments against gambling."

Prescott handed it over, the check that was in his hand. It was a normal Pacific Savings check, from what looked like a normal Pacific Savings checking account. And yet it was written out—in pen, just as it was signed, in pen, by Prescott—for $120,000.

"This should settle all accounts between you and Senator Lee," Prescott said. Behind him the two door guards from the governor's security detail were inching closer, one of them whispering into his microphone. "Including whatever juice you had running on it. Look, we're very sorry Kekoa, but we've been left with no other option." He held up his pink frikken palms.

Real sorry.

Numb. Not even the usual anger could penetrate the wall of Kekoa's skull and inject some emotion, much less set a train of thoughts on its way to the usual violent conclusions. Numb. Fucken Prescott: the guy just whips out his checkbook and *writes a check* for $120 large, no problem. Who the fuck writes a personal check for *a hundred and twenty thousand dollars?* Plus then he drops Boy Ching into it, like a *threat*, like you take this shit any further an' you can forget about your cousin's dream of bringing his family home.

Fucka probably would have brought up the girls, too, if he'd known about them, an' yeah, as if Kekoa needed the still-throbbing finger to remind him, the finger now clutching on to that fucken $120,000 personal check, on toppa everything it was the girls. He could maybe live with being away from Dawn for ten-twenty years, plus she'd understand, and she could fly over to Arizona to see him. But nobody like their daughters see them all buss-up, let alone sitting behind bars like…Sonny Bulger…and that's exactly what would happen. Cause I no care how linked up you are, you t'row some arrogant haole checkbook motherfucker off the fourth floor balcony right in front of thousand-somet'ing people, plus the governor's security, you going Hālawa. Arizona. Pennsylvania. Kentucky. Mandatory.

Hayashi and Prescott turned, leaving Kekoa standing there clutching his check, punked yet again. Only as he watched them walk away did the drips of anger start leaking into all of that numbness, an' fuck, he had to at least *say* something. Say something about eh, congratulations on getting engaged to frikken Marisa, she *hot*, cuz, you marrying *up*, brah, an' I can tell you in love, too—I know, I get one marriage just like that. So I like you rememba somet'ing: appreciate the moments, Sean. Appreciate them. Especially next time you giving her that kiss, you know, that *ten minute* kiss. Next time you giving her that kiss, all *intimate*, well you seen that big fat fucka downstairs, Nalu? Ugly bradda wit' the capped tooth and the tomato nose and that frikken Frankenstein hairy mole on his neck? Next time you getchoa tongue deep inside sweet Marisa's mouth, you getting all passionate like I said, all *intimate*, jus' rememba that my boy Nalu: he had his fucken *cock* inside that same mouth. He wen' *blow his load* inside that same mouth. I *seen* 'um. Marisa—she not going *church*, brah, she polishing him right there in the bar in front of like two hundred people. An' she get *skills*, I telling you, like one *porn star*.

And who the fuck writes a fucken *personal check* for $120 large? Who the fuck?

Plus maybe it would have felt great to tear down Hayashi's marriage right here, but Kekoa also knew that on top of everything else, he wasn't going rat somebody out, not even Marisa Horiguchi. Was enough to be castrated by one simple piece of paper, which he crumpled up and stuffed into the front pocket of his pressed black diesel jeans, that piece of fucken paper. For da boyz. For his daughters. For bring back Boy Ching. Fuck.

But he did at least have to say *something*. So they *knew*. So they knew he wasn't one fucken punk. Kekoa Meyer not one punk. Had to *say* something.

"Eh Sean!" he let out a shout that startled about fifty people, causing Hayashi to spin around like someone had just fired a gun. "My hand," he said, loud enough for them to hear from across the balcony. Hayashi and Prescott exchanged confused looks. "You asked about my hand." He held it up, and then Hayashi gave him a nod from all the way over there. "Was making pancakes with the girls this morning, I spilled some hot scalding fucking cooking oil on my hand. Fucka wen' swell right up. *Sore.* Pancakes." Now they were looking right at him. "Wit' my girls. I get t'ree daughters you know. I jus' letting you know: I get *daughters*."

Before Hayashi and Prescott could give him their condescending nods of pity, Kekoa turned and stepped back onto that long, long escalator, the whole thing so clear in his head now he couldn't believe he hadn't seen it earlier. Russell Lee didn't need Kekoa Meyer to help shake these people down, because this wasn't one *shakedown* up here. Russell Lee? Mista *All In*, king of staring down multi-billionaire Chinese investors, the man who would help Kekoa *push back*? Just as Kekoa had dreamed way back one rainy night at Aloha Stadium? That bucket of rust, surrounded by military housing and Pearl Harbor, the only place you going find any Hawaiians was north, up in Hālawa prison, a whole frikken *army* of Hawaiians, young and strong and *ready*, ready for push back, just talk to the Bull of Hālawa. Well guess what: the Bull of Hālawa lives in Arizona. Even frikken Hālawa run from the outside now, just ask that boy Jesse, Nalu's boy. Only Hawaiians you had left in Hālawa was all fucken bottom feeders.

Bottom feeders! Down, down, down Kekoa went, down the escalator through the palm leaves to the bottom of that fishbowl, and through the glass you could see that statue out there on the sidewalk holding that frikken snake, the final touch on this $350 million monument to all things Ha-vai-ee, that towering god-like bronze statue: the Hawaiian himself, his face the classic expression of the *noble savage*…clearer now as you descended down, down…ten feet tall and cut with a UH linebacker's muscles, naked except for his *malo*, on bended knee, suppliantly cupping in both of his thick but gentle hands not a snake at all, but the offering of flowing, life giving water, a *gift*, a symbol of his generosity, of his *aloha*, an invitation from East to West, from Sydney to San Diego, from LA to Macau: Come! Come to Ha-va-ee! And *take*!

Take all you can buy up. Then watch the bottom feeders fight each other for your scraps, fight to the sound of some Californian rapper's pounding version of Iz's "E Ala E," again now blasting forth from the Kamehameha Exhibition Hall, blasting out across the street onto… Club Mix Ja? And had they done it on *purpose*? Just to *get it right*? Projected their whole million-watt message not from Tokyo to San Francisco, but across eight lanes of urban traffic right onto Club Mix Ja over there: the *actual* Crossroads of the Pacific, if anyplace was, where a rotation of women from San Diego to Singapore, from Burbank to Bangkok had been parading it all in front of Japanese and Australians and mainland haoles since long before the first politician was paid off. Since long before the first shovel was sunk into the swampy ground to squash this dazzling *global meeting place* onto a street corner *behind* the Waikiki hotels and way, way off to the side to die its miserable lonely death—less from its seedy location than because someone had once invented a thing called "jet air travel," so if you lived in Singapore and you wanted to meet with someone in San Diego, you could fly straight there without even looking out the window at that little collection of dots on the map far, far below, where even now another inked-up blubbery blala was on his way into the…hexagon…his hopes set on administering *dirty lickings* for the benefit of a sparse crowd of *bottom feeders*. And their kids. Kids raising kids. Because we're all bottom feeders. All of us.

And future Governor Russell Lee: he was the biggest bottom feeder of them all—he should be riding this escalator all the way down too, and hadn't they gotten it right in the end. *Perfect.* At least for this one night, they couldn't have gotten it any better. *This* was what they'd been aiming for the whole time, with their indoor palm trees and their taro and water features and portraits of *Pele*-shaped volcanoes with lava-dripping hair on the walls of every hallway and meeting room, portraits of Kalākaua, Liliʻoukalani, Kamehameha, Duke Kahanamoku, their whole frikken two-million-dollar "native" art collection. This! Tonight! From that parade-balloon statue out front, to the swap meet tents up on the roof, was what those "sails" really looked like, and all the way back down again. From roof-garden top to cave-like bottom, from a ten-thousand-dollar boob job to a young mother's jailhouse tattoo. This!

A Hawaiian Sense of Place!

A Done Deal

There it was again: the Conference Table—this time in a big second-floor meeting room at the Department of Land and Natural Resources, a bank of windows looking right out on the State Capitol. People would laugh if they only stopped to think about what actually happened all across the state around these slabs of synthetic wood. The whole set-up was supposed to ensure a good back-and-forth, an Aristotelian search for the best possible solution. But all you had to do was attend a UH Faculty Senate meeting and watch the non-tenured members shift their eyes this way and that as they tried to gauge who around that table might wind up on their tenure review committee before saying a word to find the perfect set-up for the over-confident blowhard to push his agenda and the nervous babbler to go on and on, both ignoring that neither has the slightest clue *what the fuck he's talking about.*

Meanwhile the more timid/humble/soft spoken person (likely the best informed about the matter at hand) dies in silence from lack of oxygen.

This morning, however, those were the precise sorts of reasons why Makana Irving-Kekumu was just fine with the Conference Table—though not necessarily this particular one *per se*. It was more like the sight of the table evoked the meeting he'd been imagining non-stop since the moment he'd picked up the phone in his little cell of an office yesterday to hear Peter Varner himself, the UH president, going to great pains to *flatter* him: Dr. Irving-Kekumu, may I call you Makana? How shall I put this? An anonymous donor has come forward for the new UHWO Center for Hawaiian Studies, more than $40 million, and while the donor can't exactly put such conditions on a gift, they've identified you as their…preference…and I might add that, having heard much of your extensive work helping our host culture in my short time here in the Islands, it would also be an honor for me personally should you decide to apply.

The mere memory sent yet another physical wave of pleasure sweeping through Makana's body, right here in the DLNR's State Historic Preservation Division meeting room, which was now filling with people to watch or perhaps testify before the soon-to-arrive nine-member Oʻahu Island Burial Council. That wave crested and crashed right upon the Conference Table, causing Makana to close his eyes and imagine it peopled not with the Burial Council, but with Varner's hiring committee, a group of hand-picked administrators (and one token faculty member) gathered to select (and was it really happening?) UH West Oʻahu's new Hawaiian Studies Director.

Two of them would think it was a legitimate search, and diligently read through and rank all the applications. For their token faculty member they would have picked someone needing to fill out her tenure dossier with university service who would thus simply follow along with the chair's vote. The chair: some stooge from the business college, sights set on having his interim admin appointment made permanent. A milk crate—no, make that *two*…no, *three* milk crates full of application files—would sit on the table between them all, a good hundred hopeful applicants who had *no chance*. (Though of course Makana's own CV would have trumped all of theirs anyway in a straight-up competition.)

Decided. Long in advance.

Just like today—although half these people filing in may have thought this was just another dog-and-pony show designed to let a couple of Green Shirts rant, and to allow a couple of Hawaiian rights activists to shed tears.

Look around: some twenty people now packed into the little room, and Makana knew right away that the only ones who could know what really was about to happen were himself, Ikaika (although the big man himself had yet to arrive), of course Ikaika's dad (if the old man was up to making an appearance). Plus Aunty Maile and Kanoe Silva up there in the front row, and Tom Watada, over there nodding his head under a conversational assault from, looked like that retired California lawyer who lived a couple of compounds down from Adam Sondheim.

Everyone else? No clue. Not the Green Shirts. Not the extra-crediters from the Mānoa Hawaiian Studies grad program. Not...Lieutenant Governor James Hendrick, now walking in with a back-slap to Tom Watada and a radiant *charming* smile. Not his lovely wife Lori, the two of them no doubt here for the photo-op chance to further portray themselves as "fighters" against "rampant" development, as champions of "sustainability." And certainly not...was that really him over there? It was. Hayashi. With that usual self-assured look on his face, too—the one he must have learned from that smug condescending racist haole with the British accent sitting there at his side. Prescott.

Now here came The Deciders themselves, the Oʻahu Island Burial Council—all one-two-three-four-five...all nine of them, which in and of itself was unusual, since the volunteer council often had trouble simply coming up with a quorum at their monthly meetings. Makana recognized Craig Knox, the earnest head of SHPD whom Governor Nakayama had, to his credit, brought in to try to hold the sinking ship together in the face of what amounted to an annual slash in its operating budget. That local-Japanese late-forties Mid-Pac grad trailing Knox must have been the secretary. Some other suit-and-tie-from-Sears guy followed her, probably from the AG's office. And as they all began to take their seats with a shuffle of papers, Makana had to admit that even among those with the most cynical opinions of The Conference Table, the OIBC meetings did contain some modicum of spontaneous unscriptedness (and where on earth was Ikaika?), mainly because the council's membership, by law, was stacked 3 to 1—community members to developers—in favor of the community representatives from each of the island's six districts.

The key member at today's meeting, if Makana was reading things correctly, was a Hawaiian-Japanese woman named Sandra Ota, the Koʻolauloa district representative who had been appointed on the strength of her UH anthropology degree and her record as a "cultural consultant."

As Makana saw it, Ota was a sell-out of the worst kind: a credentialed-up Hawaiian who made herself feel good by scrubbing out a developer's (or a movie maker's, or a restaurant designer's, etc.) Brady Bunch Hawaiʻi tiki-torch coconut-shell-bra howlers and replacing them with "authentic" cultural symbols. In reality Ota merely made it *"pono"* for companies like Disney (although Makana wasn't sure if she'd worked on that project) to turn twenty pristine Leeward acres into a Lilo and Stitch theme park for California haoles and the recent influx of Chinese, complete with a fake erupting volcano right out of the Flintstones and ten-dollar jobs for mainland college drop-outs eager for the chance to live in "paradise." Makana had her vote pegged for shutting down the application Ikaika was set to bring, and if you added up the votes, like that representative from the Mormon bank over there, and the guy from Hawaiian Pacific, it looked like a 5-4 decision in favor of, at best, a deferment. *Looked like.*

Makana could tell Sean Hayashi over there thought as much. He was already double-thumbing some text into his phone, as though the mere entrance of the Council were already enough to make this thing look like a *done deal.*

Except that after Ikaika testified—and especially if his dad could make it down to deliver his own testimony in person—Makana was counting on 6-3 or even 7-2 going in the *other* direction, including even Sandra Ota. Nevermind that she must already be angling for some kind of "consulting" contract with TsengUSA—even Sandra'd have no choice but to put the brakes on this thing—either that, or resign from the Council completely, and well, that would leave an opening for next year, wouldn't it, an opening for—of course somebody would ask him—for Makana Irving-Kekumu, Director of the UHWO Center for Hawaiian Studies. A center he helped develop *from the ground up.* Literally!

And yes, he would certainly have a say in the building's design. Surely he could convince Adam Sondheim—anonymous or not, the $40 million had *Sondheim* written all over it, and thank God Makana had wound up attending the party at the great man's home—surely he could convince Sondheim to move away from that sad cliché of a *Hawaiian Sense of Place* design he more than likely had in mind and aim for something more…meta-classical…an ironically *un*-Hawaiian design, with Greek columns and grand marble staircases, as if to say *we are colonizing your* architecture, elevating your discarded designs so that when you enter our hallowed halls, you will be overcome by the feeling that Hawaiians have stopped *laying down,* have stopped playing your part of *living symbol of generosity,* and if you want our *aloha,* you have to earn it. We are no longer your servants!

Just then the current Chair—another Kam school development consultant named Henry Kanahele, a (mere) Richardson's law school grad in his early thirties draped in a crisp rust colored lauʻae fern print designer aloha shirt—he called the meeting to order. One of the other district members began leading everyone in a *pule*, and Tom Watada took the seat next to Makana. The two of them exchanged whispered greetings while the Council approved the minutes from last month's meeting, and then Tom said, "You know, this meeting could actually have some bearing on the outcome of the vote on Russell Lee's bill."

This was news to Makana, and good news at that. You kill the gambling bill *and* delay the construction? How many more nails in the coffin did you need?

In his hushed don't-wanna-disturb-the-meeting voice, Tom went on to have Makana understand he'd learned through his contacts at the Lege that the bill had made it through all of its referrals and was ready for floor votes in the house (slam-dunk, courtesy of Charles Uchida), and the senate, where, apparently, three senators were holding back their commitments until they were absolutely sure the TsengUSA project wasn't going to be hung up on some technicality over at SHPD.

"What they're saying is that if they're going to have to absorb that kind of political damage," Tom went on, "they need to be able to tell their constituencies right away that there was at least *some* benefit to voting against one of their core values. They need to be able to make that 'job creation' argument right away, because many of the first construction workers will be coming from their districts. Until they can make that argument, they don't want to waste any political capital—especially in an election year."

That left Russell Lee, Tom had learned, with only eleven out of the thirteen votes he needed to send his bill upstairs for the governor's signature. "And frankly," he went on, "especially considering the validity of Ikaika's claim, I think they've been very smart to wait." He discreetly pointed out the three clerks the senators in question had sent over today, all of them sitting together up near the front.

Henry Kanahele read out today's agenda and then explained the procedures of hearing testimony, and the purpose of such testimony in relation to the power and function of the council. He introduced the first agenda item, something called "The Recognition of Lineal/Cultural descendants Burial Treatment Plan for Paradise Garden Terrace, Waikīkī Ahupuaʻa, Kona District." Kanahele looked up and explained, "This is a discussion to determine recognition of lineal and/or cultural descendants of the previously identified burials located at the proposed Garden Terrace assisted living tower on Date Street, and a determination of whether to remove or to preserve in place those previously identified burials." And then, with a wry and knowing smile he asked, "Is the applicant present?"

This drew more knowing smiles from around the table, and even a chuckle from Sandra Ota. A skinny, silver haired Hawaiian man sitting up there next to Kanoe, also dressed in a Sears suit and tie, raised his hand. His stern look suggested he was already taking offense to Kanahele's treatment of what were supposed to be proceedings of the utmost seriousness. Craig Knox then read into the record the particulars of the application brought today by Albert Apao, was the guy's name, how he wanted to claim himself as a lineal descendent of bones found during the initial construction of the Garden Terrace tower.

Approval of such an application, as Makana was aware, was an extremely big deal. It could put the developer more or less at Apao's mercy, as the testimony of a "lineal descendent" had far more leverage with the Burial Council in determining whether a "previously identified" burial could be removed, or whether it had to be "preserved in place"—itself a process where the lineal descendant's input regarding project alterations would trump those of both the developer and the SHPD.

"It is my recommendation," Knox was saying, "that Mr. Apao be recognized as a cultural descendent." *Cultural descendent.* It meant something, but it didn't mean much. Makana himself, with his three percent Hawaiian blood having *more than likely* originated somewhere between Diamond Head and downtown—that is, within the ahupuaʻa where these particular remains were interred—could just as easily be named a "cultural descendent" of Garden Terrace.

From his seat in the front row, Albert Apao piped up: "That would be a slap in the face to me and to my family and to all of our kupuna buried in that location. We are not just 'cultural descendants'. We trace our line all the way back to that area."

Knox went on to patiently explain the documentation required to prove lineal descendant status, and from the knowing looks shooting around the table, it seemed pretty clear that they had a professional claimant on their hands—a shakedown artist who'd familiarized himself with the workings of the Burial Council and the laws related to *iwi kupuna*, a man who'd made such a career off the spoils of a successful claim here, a successful claim there, that he probably had more institutional knowledge of the Council than the members themselves, who were each limited to two four-year terms. (Apao, too, may even have had a degree from Richardson's.) Right now they all seemed to be doing their best to dispatch old Uncle Albert and get on to the more important matter at hand.

Sandra Ota explained that "more information" was required, and when she went on with examples of what might constitute solid evidence, Makana couldn't help but look down at the folder in his hands, which contained all the information Ikaika would need for his own claim.

First you had the simple news about the existence of bones in the fill into which TsengUSA planned to sink the foundations of their four new towers. Ikaika's testimony, recorded in the minutes of an official Burial Council meeting, meant that when the burial was found either through an archeological dig or during construction, it would henceforth be referred to as "previously identified" rather than an "inadvertent discovery." An "inadvertent discovery," which the Council technically had no jurisdiction over, had an "Oops!" quality to it that allowed the developer to feel bad about upsetting anyone, but claim he'd done his due diligence in trying to avoid all the other bones he *knew* were there, and well, it was an *accident*, and hey, we actually *found* your bones for you, but, you know, our project is already in motion, and we'll re-inter your great-great-great grandma in a nice place under the parking lot and landscape the area with some native plants.

But "previously identified" remains were a whole different story—particularly if you managed to win recognition as a "lineal descendent." As the law read, the "proposed reburial site location" of previously identified remains "must be *mutually agreed upon* by the land owner *and* any recognized lineal descendants." The simple task today, then, was for Ikaika to first prove where the bones-in-fill had in fact originated, and then prove his lineal descendancy not to the golf course, but to that area. Since reaching "mutual agreement" on relocation of the remains could conceivably drag out indefinitely until the end of time, this was it: the very technicality upon which this multi-tower, multi-billion-dollar project would be *hung up*.

Ikaika's proof started with the moving testimony of Stanley Nāʻimipono, which Makana had recorded and transcribed himself in case the fragile old man was unable to make the trip into town this morning and deliver it in person. Even the written version was sure to bring tears to the entire Council, job-creation justifiers included.

Makana had sat with the old man for a couple hours in Ikaika's kitchen, and in a voice as broken down as the house itself, Ikaika's dad had told a tale far more tragic than even today's usual jump-into-the-octagon castrated local-boy narrative. The trucking company had indeed gotten their fill from, not *directly* across Kam highway, but very nearby. Uncle Stanley could still identify the place because, through stories from his Uncle Harold and his Grandma Rose, he'd known that until sometime after the turn of the century, *his own family* had belonged to that land.

He'd known even as he watched the bones of hundreds and hundreds of his own peacefully interred ancestors lain bare by the teeth of excavators and carelessly thrown into the clanking bed of his truck. "But was different back in those days," he'd explained. "You, Makana, they pay you for teach people the Hawaiian language today up at the college. Me, my own parents—they told me neva speak Hawaiian. 'You not going get anyplace in this world you talk like one dumb kanak.' Back then, you know, I wasn't educated enough for understand these things. I agreed with my parents. We thought the world was moving forward, an' we neva like get lef' behind."

And though Ikaika's dad didn't bring it up, it wasn't hard to imagine that if he had indeed said something about the bones (never mind the usual fears that must have gone along with working for a company that was indeed "linked up"), Stanley Nāʻimipono, all of twenty-six years old at the time and trying to support a wife and three kids—he could forget about ever working again in construction. "But even though we was moving forward, even I had one good job," he'd gone on, "even though I thought I was one young bull, all fast an' loose, get money in my pocket…you know I neva *feel right* about what we was doing." One look at Ikaika's dad leaning on that folding table trying to hold himself up as they spoke—you didn't need to be a master observer to see how it had eaten at the man ever since.

The rest of what Makana needed had been easily found in the room right beneath the one where they were now sitting. Among the stacks of dusty ledgers in the Bureau of Conveyances records room, he'd traced the biography not of the Dolphin Bay land, but of the area just inland that Ikaika's father had pointed out on the map. The list of potential "cultural descendants" for that particular area had turned out to be so small that, at least in this case, "cultural" and "lineal" had to be one and the same. There was no ambiguity. Best of all, the list included the name of Ikaika's great-grandma Rose.

Poor Albert Apao here didn't seem to have such an open-and-shut case, and now that Makana thought about it, normally he would have been disgusted with the likes of Albert Apao. Guys like him did *damage* to what was perhaps the only bright light in a collection of corrupt state regulatory agencies. Indeed, the SHPD's formation had been one of the major victories stemming from the Hawaiian Renaissance, when people finally began to realize that around a million *kanaka maʻoli* had lived in these islands prior to Western contact, and that over the years a rotating amount of that number died and were buried, usually in locations that later became prime targets for resort development. For decades the bulldozers had pushed on anyway, until a single Maui hotel project that had promised to unearth nearly a thousand remains finally sent people into outrage.

Ever since—except during the years under the millennial governor, who'd nearly decimated the SHPD—the Burial Council had been speaking out for the protection of Hawaiian burials all over the island, and here was old Albert Apao making a joke of the whole process.

And thank God for Uncle Albert, was all Makana could think today. Let the old guy bumble and grumble—those emotional outbursts and that utter lack of preparedness are going to make Ikaika's case even more air-tight than it already is.

Right now someone was explaining to Apao that they could defer his application for "lineal" but offer him the "legal protection" of "cultural descendant" status, and Apao wasn't buying it. He went off on a well-worn lecture about his responsibility to protect his *iwi kupuna* so that his ancestors would be free to "move between worlds" and "mingle with their descendants"—all true and accurate representations of the unique cultural claims Hawaiians had on the treatment of burials, as Makana well knew, but Apao couldn't possibly have made them sound more parroted and opportunistic.

He turned to make this observation to Tom Watada, only to see that Ikaika had finally entered, somehow without his having noticed. Old Stanley Nāʻimipono was nowhere to be seen—but given the man's condition, his absence was hardly surprising. And good thing Makana had indeed taken the time to transcribe his testimony, now right there in that folder in his hands.

Perhaps more surprising, particularly in light of the morning hour, was that Meg had come along too, apparently having taken the day off. The sight of them there together brought a smile to Makana's face, for it recalled the old days, even all the way back to when the two of them had first met during the H-3 protests, at how Ikaika may have been the natural leader, but that Meg was always at his side. And she'd stood beside him for so long, sacrificing everything, working in that bar all those years, living in that…house…and of course such circumstances would lead to friction in a relationship now and then. Plus there was that new job of hers—an admission, now that Makana thought about it, that it was *her turn*, that her proud husband had…failed. And yet in the end here she was once again at Ikaika's side in the crowning moment of what he'd been fighting for for so many years.

Makana tried to give Meg a smile that might welcome her back to the fold, but she was focused on the goings-on up front. He did catch Ikaika's eye though, and he held up the folder as if to say, "I've done it, Ikaika—I've got everything we need right here." Ikaika, perhaps a bit nervous, and uncharacteristically so, gave him a nod. Then he, too, looked back to what was going on around the table up front.

"I move to defer recommendation until such time as the applicant can return with more information proving lineal connection," was what the Mormon banker was saying.

Under a stubborn glare from Alfred Apao, the motion was seconded and carried unanimously, freeing Henry Kanahele to move on to the next agenda item: "Recognition of Lineal/Cultural descendants Burial Treatment Plan for the TsengUSA Expansion Project, Hanakaʻoe Ahupuaʻa, Koʻulauloa District."

"I see that the applicant is present," he said with a smile, looking Ikaika in the eye, and all Makana could think was, Of course you recognize one of the most important and righteous fighters for what really is *pono*, a man who gave up a multi-million-dollar football career, a man who *grows his own taro* so that he may *feed his own family*, a fighter for the last twenty-thirty years, the polar opposite of Sandra Ota up there, that coconut sell-out driving back to her Kahala home every evening to sip a martini and admire the hibiscus trimmed by her Filipino yardman. Ikaika Nāʻimipono. And just wait till you see what he's about to do. What *we're* about to do—and not just here in this room, either: now that we're on our way to the top, I bet there's a way I can start to credential up Ikaika, college credit for life experience, a cultural consultant, a guest lecturer, teaching a course intersecting language, culture, and agriculture. Ikaika Nāʻimipono, Hawaiian Studies Professor. It could be done.

Again Craig Knox summarized the particulars of the application, and when he got to the part about Ikaika applying for status as a lineal descendent, all around the table looks were exchanged and eyebrows raised, half of them curious about what new information Ikaika had unearthed regarding an area whose mitigation plan had been done and then re-done three times in the past twenty years, the other half probably wondering how such a man had stooped to the level of an Albert Apao, because how the hell could a new lineal descendent for such a thoroughly documented property suddenly emerge? Knox went into some detail on the property's history, and Makana took more delight in that smug look on the face of Sean Hayashi over there, his little arms folded in front of him.

At last Ikaika stood, and the room, already silent to begin with, now *felt* silent, its only sound the faint *whrrr* of a siren passing outside on Punchbowl, the muted roar of a motorcycle, a cough into the hand of someone up front. With an open palm and arched eyebrows Henry Kanahele indicated a seat at the table, but Ikaika waved him off and stared at the floor, letting a few more seconds tick away.

And finally, without looking up, he began: "I jus' want to apologize for taking up you folks's time this morning." Up front Aunty Maile, Kanoe, even Albert Apao were all turned in their seats in rapt attention. Meg was staring up at her husband with pure love in her eyes, her hand reaching up and squeezing his as the big man went on, eyes still on the floor: "And I want to thank all you folks who came here for support us, for alla the work you been doing. And again, I don't want to cause you folks too much trouble. And I didn't really have to be here today, but I woke up this morning and I knew I at least had to look you folks all in the eye an' do this thing right."

Do this thing right? What was he talking about?

At last Ikaika looked up, fixing in his gaze first Aunty Maile, and then Kanoe, the grad students, the cluster of Green Shirts behind him. He turned his head to look at Tom, and then Makana himself, and finally, back up at the Council, his eyes now glassy with water. A deep breath, and finally, in strange legalese, "With deep respect to the Council members for all of their hard work and due diligence, I hereby withdraw my application in its entirety. I am truly sorry for having wasted you folks' time. Mahalo."

Silence.

With that Ikaika turned to leave, Meg shuffling out beside him with her narrow arm draped around his mighty back, a chorus of murmurs and shaking heads, a smile…a *smile*…exchanged between Sean Hayashi and the racist Britt. Over there Kanoe: leaning on her knees, head in her hands.

Aunty Maile: on her feet! You half-expected her to break into some kind of chant, from deep, deep in the *na'au*, cursing her betraying nephew for all eternity. Except that all she could do was stand there stricken, mouth open wide, at last a slow turn of her head back and forth, and finally, "Boy…" Just that: her head turning back and forth, speechless.

Makana stared down at the folder in his hands. For the briefest flicker of an instant he thought to stand, to shout and wave that folder around and make sure everyone knew what it contained, so that at the very least the Council might recognize the *possibility* of the bones, a recognition that on its own might be enough to define the burials as "previously identified" and thus cause the delay they'd been looking for.

Maybe.

But the moment passed, Ikaika gone now, and Makana was forced to just sit there and open his eyes at long last to the reality that he was not the kind of man who would have even quit the high school team, let alone give up an NFL career. And neither would he risk his hard-won directorship at UH West Oʻahu (was there a connection?...there might have been...Varner never said where the money was coming from... better to be *safe*). He had to stare it all right in the face: that he was not even the kind of man who would call the police with an anonymous tip upon witnessing a multiple homicide, that he would instead wander around for weeks consumed by an anxious and unjustified irrational fear.

He had to swallow it, that bitter pill of recognition: that when he drove his F-350 and worshipped UH football, it was without irony, and not because he was as castrated as the next inked up pit-bull Defend Hawaiʻi thug, but because he had never really been much of a man in the first place, and it was not even worth pretending that he ever would have done anything more than stare at the folder in his shaking hands, and sit there in silence, and do nothing.

OUR OWN TRUE SONS

It all began and ended in Hilo, that tiny little excuse of a dead former sugar town way out on the Big Island, drowned in the rain shadows of two cloud-catching mountains that reached up nearly fourteen thousand feet. So dead, so rainy, that even the recent wave of Chinese investment sweeping the state had fallen far short of its rocky shores.

The tourists had figured it out, too. Direct flights from LA may have brought a brigade of haole real estate agents to peddle cookie-cutter spec homes to a handful of retired California schoolteachers and firefighters—people who could never afford a place on Oʻahu. But it never took long for anyone visiting to tire of the two blocks of trinket shops that constituted, in its entirety, the "quaint" and "sleepy" clapboarded downtown area, and point their rental car towards sunny Kona. Even most of UH Hilo's academic tourists were quick to go home after failing to find a single beach, umbrella drink, or smiling Hawaiian showing them *aloha*, or even a few consecutive days of sunshine, let alone a worthwhile class at that sorry excuse of a glorified community college.

That left a surrounding population of state workers, third-generation hippies, and welfare locals who couldn't make it on the Waiʻanae Coast. Even the town's elite power center, the Hilo Yacht Club, was peopled mainly by mediocre divorced alcoholic Baby Boomer UHH and Hilo Medical Center administrators with no political connections whatsoever, good for little more than comparing notes on the travel money they'd scammed to go visit the grandkids on the mainland. (Forget about parking your yacht—stuck out on a lava bluff and smothered on three sides by a deafening coqui-frog-infested jungle, you couldn't even launch one of those hard plastic sea kayaks from the place.)

Still, if you were a member of the Democratic Party of Hawaiʻi and you were running for the highest office in the land, you made sure to visit Hilo repeatedly. You met with the ILWU. You photo-opped the Farmer's Market. You ate samples at Big Island Candies and bought The Big Box to bring home. You did the talks at UHH in front of twenty or thirty stoners and a couple of graying haole "returning" students so self-conscious about still being in college that they had to two-cents on every utterance that occurred, just to prove that their "life lessons" had brought them priceless wisdom rather than just an endless mental file of missed opportunities and nervous breakdown triggers. You sign-waved in front of the King Kamehameha statue. Got your picture on the wall of fame at Ken's House of Pancakes. Rallied the troops at your downtown headquarters—a former dance studio or Thai restaurant gone bust you were able to rent for pennies per square foot. You addressed the hongwanji meeting groups up and down the Hamakua coast. You packed the Civic for five-dollar fundraisers, plate lunch included.

On the night before the primary, you took back the downtown Moʻoheau Bandstand from the handful of chronics who used it as their shelter, and you met in big-tent fashion to shake hands with James Hendrick, if only to "bring the party together" after a rough-and-tumble primary and focus on the real objective: putting another Democrat on the fifth floor.

Of course all of that was months away. Right now Russell Lee was just getting started. And like all Hawaiʻi Democrats (and some Republicans, lately), Russ knew that here at the end of April, long before any kiss-and-make-up with Hendrick, you kicked off the whole months-long performance with the most important photo-op of all: Hilo's Merrie Monarch hula festival.

"I can't believe we're here!" Cathy said. She wasn't talking about the run for governor, either, which she'd been treating all along as Russ's "little project." She was talking about the decades-old hula contest born in the rebellious-roots years of the Hawaiian Renaissance and named for Kalākaua himself, the 19th-century Hawaiian ruler responsible for rescuing hula from death-by-missionary. Though Cathy had been gluing herself to the TV for these three nights for as far back as Russ could remember, it had taken until now for her to finally make the trek all the way to Hilo's Edith Kanakaʻole Municipal Tennis Stadium. Armed as she'd been with the excuse of Russ's (unofficial) campaign appearance, Cathy had flown over on Wednesday all by herself. She'd been getting deep into the spirit of things ever since, and Russ couldn't complain: just look at that beautiful rust-colored form-fitting muʻumuʻu running so tight over the swell of her breasts—he practically had to hold himself back, even after all these years...look at her *glow!*

Again it occurred to Russ how wonderfully things had heated up recently with Cathy, and well, you probably just had to chalk up the old tingle...the old *feeling*—the only thing that explained it was that Russ was *winning*. Yes, winning. Not only was his gambling debt (hadn't he said he'd *figure it out?*) a long-gone thing of the past (although it sure was a shame that Kekoa Meyer hadn't been smart enough to see the chance Russ had offered him). On top of all that, the fundraising machine had gathered close to the million dollars he'd need for the primary. That Convention Center event alone had grossed half that amount.

Tony Levine had shaken down the three public worker unions he represented. Darryl Kawamoto had tapped his circle of business interests, cheap fucks that they all were. Even Alan Ho had resurfaced to drop off his own five thousand dollar check in person. *Old*, the guy had looked, and surprised to find himself, as he told Russ, enjoying his time with the grandkids, what's truly important in life, etc., and that he didn't miss the game one bit. All that, plus the network of hopeful volunteers that had sprung up out of the ready-made UH football booster club, and the money had basically poured in from so many angles that beyond Opening Day and a few other expenditures, they had yet to even tap Bradley Zao.

Winning.

Winning with money, winning with the legislation that would set up the state partnership for Dolphin Bay, winning with—come on, whose wife still looks this incredibly...voluptuous? After 25 years!—winning with *life itself.* Even Joel looked like he was going to finish the semester on a high note. The kid had fallen for a hot little local-Korean girl from his glass-blowing class at ʻIolani who'd managed to talk more sense into him in a week than Russ could have in a lifetime. That anyone had something so 20th-century as a *girlfriend* these days instead of perpetually indulging in handshake sex, let alone the fact that it was Joel Lee, Mr. Instant Gratification personified, was beyond rational belief. She even had him going to *church*—a source of endless delight for Cathy, who lovingly tore into her son at every opportunity about his "conversion," and there really must be a God if you managed to finish the semester with—oh my…God!—a B average!

Talk about *divine intervention!*

"I guess we had to wait for the stars to align," Russ told her. "This must be our year!"

They followed a flood of Japanese grandmas through the chain link fence of a gated entrance, maybe ten yards behind…isn't that James Hendrick over there headed into the tunnel, with his lovely (Asian) wife Lori? Hard to tell in the bustle of this pressing crowd…yes it is! It's them!

Anyway: "But you know, usually I can never get away—Merrie Monarch always happens at the end of the session." Just as it did tonight. At this very moment, in fact, Russ's casino bill was sitting in a long line of bills up for a final floor vote in the senate, where discussion promised to run past midnight. That's how much Russ was *winning*.

"Are you sure it's all right?" Cathy asked, looking up at him.

"What."

"Well, that you're here and not back at the Lege."

Before Russ could answer, they were greeted by the *beaming* smile of Eddy Akiona, the 40-ish bull of an up-and-coming star for the party who was filling out his second term as Big Island mayor. No doubt Akiona, too, would resign in a month or two to cash in on his father's (and grandfather's) ILWU union cred and put it together with the *roots* neighbor-island *local* persona he had long since crafted to trounce the handful of lifers from the Lege throwing their hats in the ring for the two U.S Congress seats, both vacated so their current occupants (they had to be in here somewhere) could duke it out for the up-for-grabs U.S. Senate seat. Short, but stocky in the shoulders and carrying a gut that announced he liked to enjoy himself, the guy was leaking all over with *charm*. Russ could easily picture a future where Eddy and Russ's new protégé, Senator Jayden Kaneshiro, wound up as half of Hawai'i's congressional delegation in Washington.

Right now Russ was less surprised with the beaming grins and the slaps on the back, the utterly sincere how-come-you-folks-left-Joel-at-home kiss on the cheek to Cathy (never mind that he'd never laid eyes on Joel), or with the fact that James Hendrick had just walked by earning nary a glance, let alone this type of welcome, than he was with what happened next:

"An' you know Aunty Noelani, ah Russ?" With an open palm Akiona pointed down to the worn but equally *beaming* face of Noelani Makaʻawa, a seven-time judge of the Merrie Monarch (even Russ knew this—Cathy had pointed her out repeatedly on the TV over the years and gone into long digressions on the debt the world owed this woman's work at reclaiming the best of Hawaiian culture, etc.,), the sister of one of the festival's original founders, and the *de facto* reigning queen over these proceedings annually. *Aunty Noelani.*

That was it, wasn't it—that's what Russ had put on the table by skipping out early on the final night of the legislative session. Everything was in the bag, after all. Sure, a couple of noisemakers would try in vain to sneak in their outrageous tax cut bill (or gun ownership bill, or land conservation bill, or whatever). But the casino bill? Russ had had those votes locked up since eleven a.m. last Wednesday, with room to spare. The numbers were so strong that his own vote wasn't even necessary, and if you're all in, well, you're all in, right? Cliff Yoshida had even considered it a good idea, this Merrie Monarch appearance, and once Eddy Akiona had called with the personal invitation to ride aboard his float in tomorrow's parade, there was no holding old Cliff back.

Cliff! At the time, Russ hadn't been able to believe it. The little data machine himself had been the one to explain that however "irrational" the trip may have appeared "on the surface," finding an event with the political payoff of the Merrie Monarch was "an impossibility." The Merrie Monarch wasn't the traveling Chicago symphony at the Blaisdell Concert Hall, and it wasn't the Sons of Hilo at Nom's, and it wasn't an aging Janet Jackson at Aloha Stadium. It was the very *essence* of what everyone from Niʻihau to Puna and from Waiʻanae to Waimānalo liked to think of as their Ha-vai-ee. It was *sacred*. Chicken skin!

Those two well-worn words reminded Russ of all the stories Cathy had sprinkled through the years whenever he'd taken a few minutes to sit with her and watch on TV. Like most of the politicians around here set to use the event to launch their own campaigns, Russ had never counted himself much of a hula enthusiast. But Cathy would always try to get him to sit for one more performance, pointing out how what happened on that stage could incite the elements, connect land and sea and sky in earth-shaking ways, and that it indeed *had*, sometimes with swirling winds and huge claps of thunder. "Really!" People said it was as close as you could ever get to a holy Hawaiian temple, this fortress of a municipal tennis court surrounded by a cement bowl of metal bleachers. Because when bare feet pounded into the plywood stage, Cathy had explained, Edith Kanaka'ole Stadium rivaled the greatest cathedrals of Europe. *It came alive!*

Russ himself had a hard time believing in the idea of supernatural forces choosing a dance contest that appeared to double as a package tour for little groups of Japanese aunties as a portal between two worlds—and in *Hilo*, of all places—but Cliff and Cathy had combined to convince him that yes, this was how everyone *saw* the Merrie Monarch. A dance contest? No. It was a real living symbol of a sentiment that, in these drop-the-kids-off-at-two-different-schools-on-the-way-to-your-slow-crawl-into-a-downtown-parking-garage, just-scraping-by-on-two-six-figure-incomes times, was, every day, getting more elusive. *Lucky we live Hawai'i!* was what you could call that sentiment, and one of the few places you could still find it, devoid of any irony, was in front of your TV during the last weekend in April.

Above all else, Cliff had explained, even in the age of hand-held computers that gave you instant internet access to all kinds of sports and concert and theater tickets, there was no way on Earth to *buy* your way into the Merrie Monarch. Sure, outside you had a handful of people hoping to score an extra ticket and be a part of the magic, but the price was never much more than face value, the ticket available only because someone's aunty or cousin had been too sick to attend. And forget about eBay—a few years back, someone had been caught putting their twenty-dollar tickets up for bid (good for all three nights), only to be *banned for life* from ever buying tickets again.

And to get floor tickets like the ones Eddy's staff had sent to Russ? Within the first ten rows? It meant that you had something far more valuable than money—particularly in the eyes of the typical Hawai'i Democratic voter, the local-Japanese grandma and the rest of the *local values* voters spread out over every island, and perhaps especially back home on O'ahu, where folks were more self-conscious about such values because they hardly existed there anymore. A floor seat at the Merrie

Monarch meant you held sway among an old-style web of *local* family connections so deep that you could have this whole event patrolled, as it was, not by professional security or the police, but by a motorcycle gang, uniformed not in faux-cop gear, but in jeans and T-shirts and black leather vests. And you just knew that at the top of this pyramid you would find not some Don Corleone Godfather figure making deals in a darkened back room. You'd find...Aunty.

Not necessarily Aunty Noelani here, who had to be approaching 90 and appeared to be more of a figurehead who warranted only two of these leather-and-denim-clad bodyguards herself. But aunties none-the-less, some collection of powerful matriarchs with steel-trap minds and long memories for things like the name of the poor fool who put his tickets up on eBay ten years ago.

You got floor seats at the Merrie Monarch? Forget about money. It meant you were *somebody*.

When Russ and Cathy emerged from the entrance tunnel onto the stadium floor, now soft-lit from the sun-reflected clouds that back-dropped the stage on the stadium's open side ahead, right away all the *somebodies* began to register: Peter Varner over there with the UH Hilo provost, in front of all those back-country county council hopefuls, everyone dressed in brand new Eve Yuen lehua blossom aloha wear. The Hilo Yacht Club set. The UH Hilo crowd, Dr. this and Professor that. The old-boy local-Japanese from the Hilo Chamber of Commerce. The "rancher" crowd down from Waimea. That whole section over there: kama'āina haole baby boomers, every one of them, the Outrigger and Pacific Club crowd, like you'd helicoptered over an entire Lanikai side street, and that one on the end in the Reyn's aloha shirt (Hadn't anyone *told* him about Eve Yuen?) is the owner of Legacy Candies, the guy who paid to put up that huge billboard behind the stage. And look: Chase Stone over there, Maxine Honda not twenty feet away. *Somebody*, both of them, set to fight it out for the open U.S. senate seat. Somebody, somebody, and somebody. And was that James Hendrick all the way up there—was it *true?* it couldn't *be!* this was *not fair!*—right in the front row, standing up (the better to be *seen*) and talking animatedly with... Nom Souphanvong, the celebrity chef?

Well, never mind, mister Lieutenant Governor, Russ thought. I've got you. Sure, maybe you're basking in the envious glare of these three thousand-or-so faces, all of them bowled up around you on three sides of bleacher sections like they'd come here to see *you* glad-handing it up there with the *elite*. But here's what they're all really thinking:

Here comes Russell *Lee!*

Russell *Lee!*

Because while Russ may have eventually been headed for the eighth row over on the right somewhere, nothing could dull his feeling of... victory...of elation...of pure adrenaline of the sort he only used to feel way back when he'd come charging through a different tunnel onto the flood-lit Aloha Stadium turf. Heads turned from all directions as he made his way up the center aisle, a murmur rising as though Kimo Kahoano's booming baritone had just announced his entrance, rising not because Russ was any more of a Somebody than anyone else at what looked more like a Democratic Party of Hawai'i Convention than a hula contest. But because, well, how did you ever manage *that* one, Russ? Look at him down there: Russell Lee doesn't just *know* someone! He's *pushing Aunty Noelani's wheelchair!*

What with all the glad-handing and back slapping accompanying such an entrance, the meet-and-greets up near the front where he parked Aunty Noelani, a kiss here, a handshake there, a let-the-best-man-win greeting from Hendrick (who was clearly trying to shoe-horn his way into Russ's Aunty Noelani cred), and a mighty local-boy hug from a beaming Eddy Akiona, and finally a can-I-get-you-some-water-or-anything to Aunty and then a kiss on the cheek before he turned to leave, it was a good twenty minutes before Russ made it (all the way) back to his own seat (all the way) back there with Cathy.

But before Russ could complain about the seats (way back here) she said, "Look! Isn't that Eve Yuen up there in the second row?"

Sure enough, there stood the humble designer herself, decked out in some kind of Chinese jumpsuit, yellow background outlined with a red lehua blossom print. She was smiling, and bowing her head politely while some middle-aged local woman introduced her to...My God! It's Arthur Tafai! Senator Arthur Tafai! Russ had heard that the pubescent head of the Hawai'i Republican Party was from Hilo—the guy must have scored a couple of tickets for Tafai. And there he was, Senator Tafai, standing right up there trading banter with the great Eve Yuen. In the fucking *second row*.

A stab of envy. Anger. And then no small amount of concern about the general election—that Tafai might actually present something of a challenge once Russ dispatched Hendrick over there. And then—

Russ could *feel* it, and there was a name for it, a neurochemical name for it, this feeling: it was a wave, a huge crashing wave of *dopamine*, like none he'd ever experienced, either on the football field, or at the tables, or on the floor of the senate chambers. Because now it was certain. Now it was no longer a gamble, skipping out on the floor vote for his own casino bill.

Because Arthur Tafai: *he'd skipped out too.* He knew Russ's bill was a...slam dunk!...so why not fly over and kick off his own gubernatorial campaign here at the Merrie Monarch. Tafai—he'd *given up!* You could say it out loud if you wanted to: Russell Lee had just made history! He'd gotten casino gambling passed through the Hawai'i State Legislature! Talk about *winning!*

That wave, that *dopamine tsunami*—it was so powerful Russ wanted to stand up and hug everyone around him, take Cathy back to their room at the Naniloa Hotel and *rip* that beautiful new Eve Yuen mu'umu'u right off of her shoulders. The Naniloa, built back in the '70s with enough "restaurant" and "banquet" space for a hotel four times the size—you don't think they had *casino* in mind for that one? Shit, years ago they'd even built a *horse track* right here in Hilo. And where *they'd* failed every time for decades...Russ almost wanted to have Kimo Kahoano make an announcement, invite him on stage! Senator Russell Lee! A true leader!

"Good evening ladies and gentlemen!" And there it was: Kimo Kahoano's famous baritone, echoing out all around, hushing the roaring surf of meet-and-greet crowd noise. Kimo was more subdued than usual, Russ couldn't help but note—though the content of his announcement, you could now see, indicated a solemn moment deserving of restraint and respect: the Merrie Monarch could not commence until the Royal Court of King David Kalākaua himself was properly seated.

Russ turned around and looked behind to what his eyes had only fleetingly caught during his own entrance: a row of gold-fringed thrones that looked to have come straight out of a children's picture book, set up in the roped-off area of the floor section's back corner. He turned back to see four (Kam) schoolboys clamber onstage from the rear, each dressed in formal 19th-century white-with-black-sash mode. They paused to blow their conch shells in all directions, and then proceeded diagonally across the stage toward the catwalk to Russ's right. They paused again to repeat their tonal announcements, while the procession mounted the stage behind them: a small collection of what must have been state workers and their kids flown over from Papakolea or Waimānalo or somewhere, centered by the "king" himself, a middle-class work-a-daddy, Russ figured, which, let's face it, in Hawai'i meant paycheck-to-paycheck (even if that paycheck ran to the mid-four-figures), some lucky Kam school grad who'd let his sideburns grow out and dressed in the 19th-century-general's outfit of the sort the Merrie Monarch himself used to wear.

The reactions to this little show among those seated around Russ were mixed. The two haole women in front of him, Merrie Monarch vets both (you could tell by those seat cushions they'd brought along that they'd be in for the long haul on these folding metal chairs) simply kept their conversation going in stage whispers. The older couple behind them faced the procession with their heads bowed, like that really *was* Kalākaua walking down the aisle over there. The UH Hilo provost over there was scrolling through his email. Hendrick up front: also in exaggerated head-bowed pose, phony, Russ wanted to think, although you never knew with Hendrick, who was known for dropping so much Ha-vai-ee into his speeches that it came off as a verbal punctuation mark.

Russ himself couldn't help but think right along in those Ha-vai-ee terms, because to him, Kalākaua was a badass. He'd done the *possible*. He'd shaken down the haole sugar barons for 'Iolani Palace and a trip around the world. And yeah, reviving the hula—it wasn't simply because he liked to be *entertained*. No, it was a way to stoke the fires of pride in a people he saw in danger of caving to a shrinking world converging on these islands, a man so astute and charismatic and…winning…even when he'd stepped up to hang onto the Hawaiian Kingdom in the face of missionary conglomerates so moneyed and powerful that they could get away with having him killed, but not before he'd done… *this*…not before he created this timeless lasting reminder that Hawaiians were *Hawaiians!* And as the procession made it down the ramped catwalk to Russ's right and then down the side aisle to the throne area, it was no struggle at all to push past all the ironic baggage that came with watching a homestead Hawaiian playing dress-up in a municipal tennis stadium, because Russ had the feeling that there was something... pure?...no, that sounded stupid...putting any word to it made it sound stupid. But nonetheless it was there.

"And now ladies and gentlemen," Kimo boomed out, "to honor America, let us give a warm Merrie Monarch welcome to the Hilo High School Chorus!"

You had to raise an eyebrow at that one, even if you did have your sights set on the highest office in one of America's fifty states. The "Star Spangled Banner"? Here? But then, from the spirited sound of a couple of thousand people joining in in time with the waving arms of the Hilo High music teacher up there onstage—all around you actually felt far more sincere participation in this little ceremony than in the last one. The bomb-dropping lyrics celebrating what someone like Ikaika Nāʻimipono would have called "the occupying forces" hardly seemed out of place.

Ikaika. Ikaika would have probably pointed out that a lot of these Hawaiians probably had civilian jobs on one of the 26 military bases (26!) spread out across more than twenty percent of Hawaiʻi's limited amount of land, or that they were in fact military themselves, that they'd had this flag-waving stuff drilled into them, that *putting on that uniform* and getting stationed in Texas or Colorado or Guam or somewhere, maybe even getting sent to fight in the Middle East, or even just at Schofield or PTA—they'd all tell you it made them feel *a part of something bigger*, because they suffered from the worst kind of colonization, was what Ikaika would say: colonization of the mind.

Ikaika. In spite of such sentiments, Russ had somehow managed to win that one, too: the talk with his old football brother. They'd finally met for lunch in Kāneʻohe, a rare break in Ikaika's rotating schedule of fighting morning traffic to drop his younger son off at—yes, the minor celebrity he'd crafted over the years had won Ikaika the connections to get the boy into Kam School—and then toiling on his taro farm all day, fighting afternoon traffic to pick the boy up after practice, feeding both his sons and his parents (since lately his wife was usually stuck downtown "finishing up" one project or another at her new job—either that or catching a bite to eat and a couple of pau hana drinks at Aloha Tower with her new friends from work, was what Ikaika had kept telling him), and then sitting through a neighborhood board meeting, or at least talking on the phone about an upcoming meeting before falling into bed, more and more often, alone.

This and more Ikaika had poured out to Russell Lee, of all people, in a matter-of-fact way that was surprising in its open honesty, and above all, its exhaustion. Between bites the big man spoke in a tone that suggested he'd been thinking about it all for a long time but just didn't have anyone else to talk about it with—a void, Russ figured, that had up until recently been filled by his wife, who had just (let's be honest here) *unmanned* him, struck out on a career of her own as if to say, "I've tried giving up my life for your causes, and look where that's gotten us." The job itself seemed to have been crafted for what had been a string of nearly useless Environmental Studies classes back when the wife had taken them. Now you had these little "green" industry start-ups popping up all over downtown, solar this, bio-fuel that, renovate your home in an eco-friendly way, save the planet, do some good. Though she worked almost entirely on commission, in a month she'd brought home more than Ikaika's taro generated in ten years.

Russ hadn't had the heart to tell his old football brother that despite all the fashionable-status bullshit that surrounded it, his wife's "green building" company had also probably indeed done more actual "good" for Hawai'i than all of Ikaika's efforts over the years combined—but he had a feeling the big man knew this, too. His wife had basically abandoned her own kids, Ikaika had explained, *An' my youngest, he right on that...edge, that adolescent edge—the boy needs his madda, an' right now she not around.*

All Russ could hear in the rest of what spilled out was *regret*. It was the closest Ikaika could come to saying that if his sons had turned out to be more interested in flying MMA kicks, in fighting in the octagon like a couple of tattooed blubbery castration clichés, it wasn't because the mom wasn't around. It was because, for all these years of putting himself into the causes of his people, Ikaika himself had never really been around to teach his own boys how to be men.

That was when Russ had pounced:
Brah, they out there helping you farm your taro?
Even in the bustle of the little restaurant the question had stung so hard you didn't know whether even the big and peaceful Ikaika was

going to take a swing at Russ. There it was: H-3, the Thirty Meter Telescope, the bones in Kakaʻako, the Molokaʻi wind farms. Dolphin Bay. Russ hadn't even had to elaborate. It was all right there in the question. Here's what you *sacrificed* by devoting your life to all of those impossible battles: your own sons. You could have had them both right by your side the whole time, doing the one thing that will *always* be most important, even when this entire island is covered with timeshares. You could have had them knee-deep in *loʻi*, could've had your entire spread cultivated by now, could've been really and truly perpetuating the culture *in your own family*, for generations to come.

Russ hadn't even had to say what he'd planned next: I'm not trying to buy you off, railroad this t'ing through, collect my check, ride this to the governor's office, and so on. Also left unspoken: the sales pitch about how inevitable it all was: if not this time, then next time, if not these Chinese guys, then some other Chinese guys, or haoles, or maybe the Japanese make a comeback, if not now, if not five years from now, then ten years from now. He hadn't even had to detail how he was bringing local people back from Vegas.

Ikaika had just taken a deep breath. And let out a sigh. And slowly turned his head from side to side, resigned. *The possible, ah Russ?* was all he'd said, looking down at the table with another turn of the head. *That's whatchoo always saying: 'The possible.'*

Russ would never forget how that moment had stretched (and to be honest, he would rather have not considered the…position…he'd just put Ikaika in)—not because there was any suspense, but more because of how easy it had been to imagine how even the great Ikaika Nāʻimipono, after a lifetime of taking nothing but utterly *principled* political stances, was working to *justify* what you knew he was going to do in the end. It had only taken a look at the big man's face, covered in wrinkled lines marking years of fruitless struggle, to know that Ikaika would, yes, reach across that table and clasp the hand of his old brother, State Senate President Russell Lee, in a strong local-boy handshake.

Braddas!

Russ had *done it*.

Except…except…

And the home…

Of the…brave!

A rain of applause, and then when the sound faded, before Russ could dwell any further on what he had in fact caused Ikaika to give up, a good third of the stadium began carrying everyone along through "Hawai'i Pono'i," written by the Merrie Monarch himself, written for Hawai'i's *own true sons*, for men like Ikaika—yes, Ikaika (and someday Ikaika would thank him, Russ decided)—men like Russ, written as a call for loyalty to Kamehameha the Great. These powerful singers carried folks like the woman seated behind Russ, who mumbled along until reaching the *Makua lani e* refrain, which she then belted out like an opera star. They carried James Hendrick, who you just *knew* was trying to mouth along to a song he'd heard hundreds of times but never quite got those Hawaiian words to stick. They carried Russ himself.

Yes, that familiar refrain—it was enough to wash out the memory of the (manipulative?) way Russ had gotten Ikaika to *compromise his principles for the greater good*. All alone, the words of the great Kalākaua, a man who, if nothing else, had done *the possible*—they were enough to re-start those drips of dopamine flowing through Russ's body again.

"*Ma-ku-a la-ni e!*" Russ belted it out, too, oh Royal Father, Kamehameha! "*Kameha-me-ha e!*" before dissolving into soft mumbles and then simply moving his mouth along, but no matter: they were there to carry him, that reliable stadium-wide…*chorus*…it sounded as though these people sang this song for a living…you could hear people *harmonizing*…it sounded like the Kam School *Song* Contest.

The Kam School Song Contest. Russ had had a feeling just walking into this place he hadn't been able to put a name on: that feeling you get when you eat at NomFusion, or when you catch a Concert on the Lawn at Bishop Museum, or make an appearance at an HPD Foundation fundraiser at the Sheraton Waikiki or a funeral at Kawai'ahao Church. As if to confirm the conclusion Russ was now drawing, "Hawai'i Pono'i" was followed immediately by an interminable benediction, and then the Hawaiian protestant hymn that may as well have been the Kam School *alma mater*, and give me an *aah-men-ay!* And of course! Maybe the bleacher section bowling up at the back of the stadium was packed with true Hawaiian roots hula aficionados, with pockets among them of those aging haku-lei-crowned housewives all the way from Japan, hundreds of them. But the rest of these people? You had to be sitting among them to pick up on it: this whole thing was just one giant Kam

School reunion. Years of catching glimpses of it on TV, and it had never occurred to Russ. In fact, no one at home likely had any idea what they were really watching unfold.

On TV.

Just like that, Russ's seat, way way back here in Row 8—suddenly it was the best seat in the house. Suddenly Row 8 was *perfect*. Row 8 was just *fine*. Sure, James Hendrick looked *hooked up* whenever he stood to show everyone he was sitting right up front with his lovely (Asian) wife Lori, as did Tafai up there with Eve Yuen, the Lady of the Hour, whose little bay front shop was, in this one week, grossing enough to pay the rent for years to come.

But if you were in the eighth row? On the aisle? Well, that staff member in Eddy's office had been thinking. Or maybe Cliff had alerted them after calculating an algorithm correlating passive TV exposure minutes with votes in the Democratic primary over the last thirty years and then drawing a grid of the Edith Kanaka'ole Stadium seating layout. Because when you sat in the eighth row at the Merrie Monarch, on the aisle, you were right in line with the primary television camera facing the stage. On every TV across the entire state. Almost without interruption. For more than *six straight hours.*

Yes, it was the *back* of his head (a thought that got Russ wondering if it might not have been better to have Hendrick back here, giving everyone that extended look at how ridiculous a graying ponytail looked on a fifty-year-old haole). But all you had to do was turn around once in a while to remind them all that you, Russell Lee, the only Hawaiian even in this race, were steeped in the most important traditions of the Hawaiian people. You, Russell Lee—even at this very moment you were fighting for *a place at the table* for your people, for including Hawaiians at all levels, not merely as "aloha" front-line slaves who had to eat their pride in front of fit-for-life retired investment bankers whose own wealth was founded on trust funds and frat-boy connections forged at wealthy private colleges. Not just as security guards. As executives in charge of the entire security program. People with a stake in the company! You, Russell Lee, our bootstraps Hawaiian!

For the greater good.

"Ladies and gentlemen!" Now *that* was the Kimo Kahoano Russ had been expecting! Boom it out with en*thusiasm*, Kimo! "From Kāne'ohe, on the island of Oʻahu"—you could *hear* Kimo's okinas: *Kāne*-O*he*, and *Oh*-A*hu*—"under the direction of Kumu Hula John Kahaʻomanu Lloyd, please put your hands together for the men of Nā Kāne Nā Lani o Lono!"

With that Kumu John, a heavyset man around Russ's age sitting on the stage to the far left, a reddish robe draped over his big stomach, eyes glaring out from the wreath of *maile* ringing his bald head—he began a thump-slap-slap rhythm by pounding the hardened gourd into the hollow stage's plywood and then hitting it twice with his thick open hand. The sound summoned a line of men five, six, seven, sixteen long onto the stage in front of him, each one naked except for a reddish puffed-out *malo* around the waist and the same ring of *maile* as Kumu John, all twisting nearly ninety degrees at each step in perfect symmetry as their eyes scanned the path before them. They fanned out into a formation of two lines, and then four, the entire stage covered now. Every one of these guys: ripped. *Jacked.* Bricks, they had, running up their stomachs, ballooned-out pecs and bulbous shoulders, and the thick biceps to match.

Kumu John began chanting into the microphone set up close to the floor in front of him, words Russ had no hope of understanding (and he wished he could somehow hear that woman on TV who explains the chants), words that the rest of the men replied to in chorus, just as a collective foot-stomp into the plywood would fall right on the beat, all the men chanting along, and now smoothly lowering themselves to their knees, *thump-slap, thump-slap-slap*, the kumu's chant hypnotic, the men swaying left as one, back right, and then a full pivot from the right that had them *laying down* at the back before they lifted themselves on the left, a move that instantly explained those *bricks*, and that drew a cascade of knowing "Whoop!"s from twenty or thirty people up back in the bleachers, a sound that tripled in volume with the slow rise to a squatting position and a four-step duck-walk forward that ended with the men back on their knees and repeating the pivot motion.

A beaming smile from Cathy, and even Russ himself couldn't help but join in with a "Whoop!" of his own.

On they went, with angry looks that must have reflected the proud nature of Kumu John's chant, and as the hypnotic beat drove on, the next thought to cross Russ's mind was that except for that one guy over on the left with the traditional Hawaiian warrior triangles ringing his shoulder, these young men, all in their twenties and all blessed with the kind of physique a young man would want to display at all times, were completely free of tattoos. He had to look carefully at each one as they all turned and planted a foot, turned and planted, even the cloth of their swaying *malo* rising and falling in unison, and *no ink*. Forget about *Ainokea*—this band of brothers on stage could not possibly have cared *more*. Look at that *precision!*

Sure, for all Russ knew, the five judges at those desks up front spaced the width of the stage—they could've been dinging these guys left and right on points for who-knows-what. Russ did know that an error of any kind in hula at one time had been treated as sacrilege, thought to invite tremendous bad luck. But as far as he could see, this performance was flawless. *Flawless*, reflecting not just talent, but *commitment*, and *hard work*, and *pride* and all the rest of what Russ's father had always preached to him in his back-country folksy way.

How many hours had these guys put into this one ten-minute stretch of their lives? How many scoldings from Kumu John had they eaten over the past year? How many social engagements had they given up? How many mornings had they awakened too sore to move, just look at those rocks of muscle stuck to their legs, watch them *rise* from their knees again, and yeah, I'll join in: "Whoop!"

With two lines of eight men strung down each ramp of a catwalk on either side of the stage, Kumu John ended abruptly, pulling the plug on his *thump-slap-slap*, and as the men shouted out the chant's conclusion, turning their heads this way and that in a kind of purposeful *lack* of symmetry that suggested they were shouting it out to all the world, near and far, the crackling of applause and the *whoop*s and screams began to drown them out, everyone on their feet now and cheering wildly. The deafening sound sustained itself for a good two or three minutes as the two rows converged now on the floor in front of center stage, all sixteen men (boys, really, they seemed to Russ, now that they were so close), fists at their waists and elbows bowed out, their faces still serious, locked in character, they filed down the center aisle *right past* Russ and out through the same tunnel where he'd entered earlier.

Only once they were out of sight did the applause die down, whereupon Russ turned to Cathy, who was wiping away tears.

"Chicken skin, yeah?" she said.

And yes, he had to agree. Chicken skin it was.

As Kimo Kahoano introduced the next *halau*, though—a group of women from Maui—Russ couldn't help but wonder how this was supposed to go on for more than five more hours. How could anyone improve upon what those guys just did? Was this like Fight Night, where you had a series of undercards before the main event? Or was it like tennis, where different *halau* were seeded or ranked in some way? Or could they very well have just seen the eventual winner, meaning that from here on out, for *sixteen* more performances, it wasn't going to measure up?

As if to answer the last question, the women now onstage were, to Russ's utter astonishment, making the initial men's group look like rank amateurs. *Thump-slap, thump-slap-slap*. Even Russ could see it now that he had a basis of comparison. *Ti* leaf skirts, rich untamed hair spilling out over their backs and bare shoulders and their billowing light blue fabric tops—they'd been growing it out for *months*, just for *these ten minutes*—these women even more *locked in*, more *serious*, more in tune with what they were *saying* than the men had been, chanting along with their kumu, not simply *performing* here at the Merrie Monarch in Hilo, but retreating deep into the *mele*, the story of this particular chant (and again Russ wished he'd bothered to learn Hawaiian).

No, they weren't just dancing. Right before Russ's eyes, these women were *becoming the words*, just as with some incredible concert pianist, the piano itself is *beside the point*, a mere vehicle through which you communicated the *spirit* of whatever it was you were playing, that was what these women were doing, they now *were* the *mele*, even Russ could see that—

Wouldn't you know it: right in the middle of this hypnotizing performance Russ began to feel the vibration of his phone against his leg. By reflex he pulled it out and nearly even held it up to his ear before being compelled by, well, the *aura* surrounding him, was what it really felt like…by being compelled by the aura enough to understand that even in a world where people routinely pulled out their phones in movie theaters and meetings and legislative sessions and even in churches at funerals and weddings, doing so right here would amount to some kind of blasphemy.

He did however take a look at the screen: Sean Hayashi was trying to reach him from the Lege. When Russ had told him to *text* with occasional updates, Hayashi had given him this exaggerated look of surprise aimed at making fun of his well-known case of technophobia—*Text? You Russ? Really?* Even though he'd agreed to do so anyway, here he was *calling*. Before Russ could get very far into speculating why, his phone vibrated again, this time with a text: CALL NOW.

For the life of him Russ couldn't figure out what all the urgency could possibly be about, and either way, you couldn't very well walk out right in the middle of one these performances like it *was* Fight Night or something. For one thing, you'd have to face that motorcycle gang of ushers, who were also in charge of strictly controlling everyone's entrance and exit to coincide with breaks between performances. For another, a good two-thirds of the stadium, not to mention the *halau* onstage that had spent the better part of a year preparing for this singular moment—they'd all *see* him walking out on them.

Another text: WALK OUTSIDE AND CALL!!

Walk outside? How did he know—? Of course! Hayashi must have been watching the TV in Russ's office. He could see Russ sitting right there in Row 8. All the more reason *not* to stand up—it would only beam his wholly inappropriate exit out to hundreds of thousands of other televisions statewide, a full frontal shot of Russell Lee completely obscuring the action on stage.

He fumbled with the options on his touch screen—who the hell types with their *thumbs?*—but got nowhere. He had to hold back from just turning his head to stare straight into the camera and mouth out a *What?* Had Tafai's tax cut bill actually gained some support? No, that couldn't have been it—why then would Tafai himself be sitting up there in the second row? Something else? Had someone had a heart attack on the floor or something, putting the casino bill vote in danger? Nah—that whole thing had been locked up for days with votes to spare. Must be, Russ finally decided, that it had already come up for a vote, and Hayashi wanted to be the first to give Russ the good news. Hadda be. Look at alla those exclamation points. From Sean Hayashi of all people.

So okay, let's just sit here and *revel*, revel in the *anticipation* of finally hearing those sweet words spoken aloud, just as soon as this chant is through and I can get out to the foyer.

Another text. This time Russ ignored it, savoring his moment of victory, letting it stretch. No, he didn't want it spoiled with a two-word blip on a three-inch phone screen—he wanted to hear Hayashi live, going on about how the whole thing had gone down just as they'd all foreseen it.

Another text.

So when the chant finally did end and the rain of applause began to die down, Russ took his time. He excused himself from Cathy, who was trading evaluations with the woman next to her, and slowly made his way up the aisle, and through the tunnel, and into the dusk of the bustling foyer. He didn't even have to call Hayashi, because by the time he reached a spot near the fence away from the crowd, his phone was already heating up again.

"What."

"Russ, you've gotta get back here. Now."

Get back here? What the fuck was this? "Sean, you realize I'm in Hilo, right?" An old uncle in a forest green Merrie Monarch lei T-shirt smiled with a shaka and a *Eh Russ!* on his way to the restroom. Russ threw him a nod.

"The whole state realizes you're in Hilo, Russ. You got great seats. I'm sure it's great for your campaign, but you gotta get back. Sam was able to push our stuff to the back of the agenda, but I'm telling you, you've gotta get back here. I already booked you on the last flight—8:56. That would get you in just before 10:00. That might be just in time."

Just in time?

More *Russ's*, and a couple of *Govna Lee's*, too, Russ trying to beam out *charm* in response and still concentrate on what Hayashi was saying, which was that Jayden Kaneshiro, that sniveling little legacy fucktard, had chased him down the hallway during one of the breaks, begging to be put in touch with "Senator Lee" so that he could explain why, at the last minute, he wasn't going to be able to offer his vote for the casino bill after all, and "the senator" would just have to understand how Jayden no longer had the political cover to get away with it in his district—right here in South Hilo, as Russ was well aware—and surely Senator Lee would understand, and he wanted to at least let him know ahead of time just in case they could pass the bill without his vote. "He was practically sucking my cock right there in the hallway," Hayashi concluded.

"Doesn't have the cover," Russ said. What the fuck was that supposed to mean? "Did he say who'd gotten to him?"

"Nope. You know it had to be the Mormons, like I've been telling you."

Like I've been telling you. Shit, Hayashi hadn't shut up about the Mormons since the Convention Center fundraiser, when he'd just about gotten in Russ's *face* about getting rid of Kekoa Meyer.

"I asked him about that, too," he went on. "But Kaneshiro—he just shook his head and said he couldn't do it. Look Russ, you've gotta get back here."

Russ could see that people were beginning to stream back into the stadium, which immediately evoked the image of his own empty seat on TV. His watch told him it was only just after 7:30. "All right," he said. "At least he told us, I'll give him that. Let's think about this for a few minutes. Even without Kaneshiro, and without me, after what happened at the Burial Council we're still up what, two votes? We're still good, right?"

"Not quite," Hayashi said. "Without you, we're tied at 12-12. I'm telling you, we need you Russ."

"You mean Kaneshiro's voting *against* it?"

"That's what he said. Fucking pussy, the guy."

And all along Russ had thought it was a two-vote cushion. Shit, he never would have come up here if he'd thought they were only up by one. Why hadn't Cliff said anything?

"Look, we've still got some time to think about it," he said. "Tafai is over here, too. That makes it 12-11, so right now we're still good. Look, I've gotta get back inside. I'll call you back."

Russ just managed to take his seat the moment Kimo boomed out his intro: "Ladies and gentlemen! From Las Vegas, Nevada…"

Cathy leaned in: "Is everything okay?"

"Fine," he said. "It's just Sean Hayashi checking in. Everything's fine."

She gave his hand a squeeze, and turned back to the stage.

Her reaction kind of put Russ at ease, too. Really, as long as no more surprises came up, they did still have the votes. The fact that Hayashi was getting so worked up, well, that just showed you how much the guy had yet to learn about the Lege.

"Isn't it wonderful how hula is spreading across the mainland?" Cathy whispered.

Russ nodded with a smile. He thought to point out that all the *halau* from LA and Oakland and Texas and of course Vegas told you more about how Hawaiians were getting displaced to the mainland, but, well, he didn't want to do anything to remove that…glow…from Cathy's smile.

The kumu hula up there had probably studied under one of the greats, Aunty Emma DeFries or Aunty Maiki or Sonny Ching or someone. He kneeled at the stage's edge, head crowned in *maile*, the pound-slap-slap rhythm of his *ipu* amplified by the pounding steps of his charges, as he chanted out the tale of Waiʻaleʻale, the rain-quenched mountain on Kauaʻi to where he could no doubt trace his own roots (even Russ could figure that one out).

Jump, these men did, into every step of the hula, all eight of them moving as one, their pale tone of their stomachs hanging out over their *malo*, and of their naked legs, combining to speak of long days at some job over there in Vegas that paid a mortgage they could afford while still leaving them the hours to prepare for *this*, to embody the *mele* before not just the collection of photo-op politicians and wannabe local status climbers scattered about the floor seats, but for the folks seated around the bowl, the folks in the bleachers, comprised, it was now clear to Russ, of the most sophisticated aficionados of this art form on the entire planet, the folks who could see *mana* in a dance step, a strong arm thrust, a look of fierce anger, and finally, at the very end—this time Russ could hear it clearly: *Hey!*

—a collective shout of "*He inoa no!*"—which is to say, this is not just a song about Waiʻaleʻale. One does not just throw together an *inoa mele*, any more than one simply calls a song or a chant an *inoa mele*, was how the lady on the TV had explained it last year. No, those words, as Russ was now recalling—maybe it was his father who'd taught him?— the words were hard to translate, but at the very least they meant, when you appended them to your song or your chant, that what you just said could not possibly have been more serious or sincere, this story, this chant: "*He inoa no, Waiʻaleʻale!*" Those words, they made you *listen*.

Down came the rain of applause, up went the cries of *Whoo!* and the screams of the odd names, up and down and up and down went the now-heaving chests of the proud men, now glistening with sweat, those looks of...*strength*...not having left their faces. Strength!

Another text. A look at his watch: 7:36. If Russ left his seat now he could be on the plane in half an hour, nearly an hour to spare—this was Hilo: no lines and no waiting and certainly no traffic, the airport just two minutes away. He could leave right this minute.

But at what cost? For a second he thought about calling Hayashi back right from here—it looked to be a TV break rather than just a pause between two performances, five or six black-shirted guys on stage now sweeping it clean of *maile* leaves—to try to figure things out, and well, maybe this Row 8 thing and all the free TV exposure it offered hadn't been such a good idea after all.

But then just as he pulled out his phone he was interrupted: "Senator Lee, I'd like you to meet Provost Foster!"

He looked up to see a woman he'd never met before, haku-lei'd, Eve Yuen'd, and smiling because of course she, some sort of unofficial hostess of the event, knew who *he* was, and well, since you're in town you probably want to meet the new UH Hilo provost, newly hired from...Arizona...rail thin, not a hair on his gleaming head...and right then Russ could pick the guy, inept to the core on sight despite the Firm Handshake and the grin he was now trying to lay on Russell Lee, charmer of all charmers—right away he could pick the guy as Varner's puppy dog, perhaps a frat brother, although you'd have a hard time picturing such a...*pussy* in a frat to begin with...and didn't you just love how all these UH administrators always hired the *worst* person for the job *on purpose*, so as never to be questioned from their ever-growing cabal of non-instructional minions?

Still, the guy was kissing up, which felt good. It reminded Russ of the real value of his being here: let's turn on the *charm* too, and yes, it's a such a pleasure to meet you, too, Provost, and Mrs. Provost, and I've heard all about that volunteer literacy program you're working on at de Silva Elementary, and we hope to have you both here with us for a long, long time. And it's a pleasure to meet you, too, Mr. Lance Yamaguchi, and we certainly appreciate the support of the Hilo Kiwanis Club. And you, Dr. Hughes. From the University of California, you say? Yes, that telescope up on the summit of Mauna Kea represents a great partnership between our states, and it's really helping to diversify the economy and create jobs, and again, we really, really appreciate your support! No, I haven't had the chance to meet Eve Yuen yet, but I sure hope to!

And from the other direction? Nothing but pure flattery. Waves and waves of it. So much of it you couldn't tell the difference between the players who were looking for some kind of payback down the road, and the celebrity worshipers who merely wanted to *be seen* talking not with Eve Yuen or Nom or the UH President, but with Senator Russell Lee! Senator Lee! I doubt anyone else can move this state forward in the ways you can! We need someone like you with the foresight to bridge the gap between public and private. And I'm really impressed with how you've gotten the state to partner with private interests—I think that's a fantastic idea. Senator Lee! You're really doing it, aren't you! For decades now, one gambling bill after another has been dead on arrival down at the Lege, and look at what Hawai'i's been missing out on because of it, I mean, Singapore generates more than twelve billion dollars annually in gaming revenues, and you're right: it's *about time* Hawai'i started claiming its fair share. It takes real leadership to bring people together to get that kind of stuff done—just imagine what you'll be able to accomplish from the fifth floor! And I don't mind saying it: what a lovely First Lady Mrs. Lee would make! Senator Lee! Senator Lee! Senator Lee!

Another wave of *dopamine*, and never mind Sean Hayashi's texts, and is that Arthur Tafai marching past down the aisle, phone stuck to his ear as everyone else takes their seats? He's only getting the news just now? And look at Cathy, too—did you ever think a mu'umu'u could make your wife look so *sexy*, even after all these years? I can't just *leave* her here. If I *did* that would mean, let's see, two-three hours of my empty seat right there on TV. We could think up some damage control thing to say in the morning about that, but well. 7:50. Time for one more performance anyway, so let's just try to figure it out, just wait a minute.

And wait they did. Everyone. The kumu for the next *halau*, flanked by two attendants in full *hula kahiko* regalia, all sitting on the stage over towards the right, *ipu* at the ready in front of the mic: not moving. A group of women were already standing center-rear in two lines down the steps at the rear of the stage behind their two leaders, all of them stock-still, fists on the hips of their *ti* leaf skirts, their own untamed hair wrapped in thick strands of *maile* and spilling over their own bare shoulders, their puffed red fabric tops, eyes straight ahead, locked in.

And they waited, waited for Kimo Kahoano, who was apparently waiting for some signal from the TV gods. The moment stretched, and stretched, getting awkward now as the crowd worked to maintain its silence, and while the precious seconds dripped away Russ grew more and more anxious that if the chant didn't begin soon, then, well, any decision about catching that last flight to Honolulu might just be made for him, and by the way, where the hell was Tafai? Had he returned to his seat yet? It's hard to tell from here, and sure, he could have gotten caught outside the ropes at the tunnel entrance, but what if he didn't? What if *State Senator* Arthur Tafai is on his way to the airport?

"Cathy, that call? Look, it looks like I'm going to have to— "

"Ladies and gentlemen!" And there at last was Kimo. "From Kahalu'u, on the island of O'ahu, under the direction of kumu hula Darlene Wright, would you please welcome, Nā Wahine o Halau Pu'u Ō'Hulehule!"

Shit, Russ could still make it anyway, and in any case, the startling *shouts* exploding out of the mouths of these twenty women riveted him to his seat. They wandered in purposefully haphazard form, *ti* leaf skirts and earthy untamed hair swishing out towards the four corners of the stage, heads nodding left to right as if to say *All* of you *listen* to us! The shouts: they burst out almost spontaneously, without the *thump-slap-slap* direction of the kumu's *ipu*, just the *acapela* rough chant, almost *un-*rehearsed, truly from the *na'au*, the voices not quite lined up with one another. One of the women, a skinny one lifting a bony hand, she seemed to be looking *right at Russ*, her *maile-*shaded eyes ablaze, each new line of her chant begun with a new explosion, angry, directed, it felt like, at Russell Lee, her eyes locked into his. Even as this little intro chant came to a close, leaving all twenty women somehow in a perfect and tight configuration of four rows spread as evenly apart as though someone had drawn dots on the stage floor, as if the wind itself had blown them there, every one of them, their chests now heaving, and this skinny one, yes she was: *looking right at him.*

The applause rained down harder, the cheers and *whoops* rose louder than at any point so far in the evening, and damn, they hadn't even *started*. Now the *thump-slap, thump-slap-slap*, and a *dive* into the dance's first move, a dive with *authority*, a dive that brought another *Whoop* from the crowd a thousand voices strong, a *whoop* that grew louder with every move, with every spin-plant-stomp, with every shouted response to the kumu's chant, and even Russ could tell—and how could you not? How could anyone not?—even Russ could tell that this wasn't just *precision* and *practice* and the recited tale of yet another creation myth.

More: not just a mere *embodiment of the mele*, a pianist's journey into the heart of his concerto. No, these women were not *forgetting* the lights and the crowd—they were building energy in the crowd, tapping into the surrounding wealth of collective *mana*, and *taking the crowd along with them* for their celebration of Kalākaua, and yes, throughout the chant all twenty of them would spin directly toward the stadium's rear corner just behind Russ and then pull back into a deep bow to their king before stepping into the next move, their whole bodies, their whole *beings* thrust into *saying* it: Kalākaua!

More still: they were *possessed*, these women. There was no other word for it. And just putting the thought into words only cheapened it, made you sound like some kind of crystal-worshipping Puna hippie freak, but yes, the explanation was indeed that they were *possessed by the spirits*, the spirits their own *mele* had called to this sacred stage, and yes, I'll say it out loud: *sacred. Sacred!*

The whole moment, so sacred an entire stadium full of look-at-me status climbers couldn't trendify the purity out of it. As sacred as... *deep guttural chants*... as sacred as the image of a humble artist toiling away in the loft of her Hilo bayfront designer aloha clothing shop, a good woman, bemused if anything by her local celebrity....sacred as a twenty-dollar ticket for three days...*ti* leaves grown and watered and fed and finally picked for *this night*, sacred as...the buried remains of someone's ancestors...

...as someone's convictions...

...sacred as an old football brother's convictions...

...convictions left un-compromised...even for *the greater good.*

And here they come, right into the crowd now, not at all finished yet, not merely filing down the two catwalk ramps under polite job-well-done applause, but *dancing*, each rhythmic step catlike and electric, their own two lines converging at the center, swaying *ti* leaves and untamed hair, each of them, their skin covered in a sheen of sweat, so *young* now as they approach, so young as the first two, three of them move right past Russ, *girls* they are, except for...they stop...turn...heads turned toward the stadium's back corner…their king! All so young except for this one, the skinny one, standing right in front of Russ now, inches away…she's older…perhaps thirty, perhaps more…her shoulder, ringed not with traditional Hawaiian warrior triangles, no—these are jailhouse tats, hand-scrawled Chinese characters, a date, somebody's birthday. The shoulder is covered in ink and sweat, both shoulders, the bony chest heaving up and down and she's glaring right at Russ, so close he could touch her, teeth bared and yes, two of them missing.

An instant of silence.

The beat of the *ipu* unplugged, three thousand people frozen in that single moment before the final shout—*hey!*—the *inoa*, all twenty of these women…girls, really, except for *this one*…all of them, as one they draw in a final deep breath, and she lifts an open palm toward her king, so close now her hand is in Russ's face.

Right away the *Shout!*—it comes as an explosion, an *accusation*, pointed at Russell Lee with an aim so true it knocks him back to his seat like bullets, *Eh Russ!*, loud and clear, this time as a single voice, a voice, yes: from the gods:

"*He inoa no, Kalākaua!*"

Russ cannot hear the applause.

There is some sense that the women, heaving for breath, have filed past him on their way down the aisle. There is some sense, even, that another performance has already begun, and ended. Maybe another.

He only knows he's been sitting there for some time when he feels Cathy shaking him by the shoulder, and he finally lifts his head, and his gaze meets the night sky, where the two red-dot taillights are making their way back to Honolulu.

Epilogue

Game Day

For the 6:00 pm kickoff, TV coverage started at noon. The dusty Lower Hālawa parking lot a quarter mile from Aloha Stadium was packed by 1:00, thousands of Warrior faithful finally gearing up, for the first time in eight interminable off-season months, out there in the frying pan high heat of Hālawa's blazing hot sun, as only the Warrior faithful knew how: pound some Jawaiian tunes through your subwoofer as you pull the drum-sized gas grill from the back of the king cab Titan or Ram or Tacoma. Set out the green and black Craftsman Camping Chairs (with drink holders) under your made-in-China NCCA College Canopy Tailgate Tent emblazoned with the green and black Warrior "H" that you got from Wal-Mart. Crack open a Heineken. Start texting everyone you know and asking why they haven't shown up yet. Grab the Fred Flintstone slab of Costco steak out of the cooler and throw it on the grill. Then post a few photos on Facebook so all your "friends" still stuck at work can envy you.

All the while you engaged in hopeful, this-is-the-*year* Opening Day banter with the guy who pulled his F-150 into the neighboring parking space. Never mind that the entire season is a pre-ordained failure full of flashes of false hope against a few WAC pushovers and the odd D-2 teams the in-over-his-head AD threw in to fill out the schedule because, let's face it, if you were a big-time team, what would be the point in coming all the way to Hawai'i mid- season and tiring out your boys with jet lag for a game that would be decided in the first quarter? As for the D-2 blowouts: any joy they brought was always quickly stomped out by the bone-jarring reality of a typical lop-sided loss on the road, or to one of the stronger conference opponents like Boise State.

This being Opening Day, though, the AD had somehow managed to score a real marquee opponent—the defending national champs, no less: the University of Southern California. So for a few delicious hours anyway, Warrior Nation could throw back the greenies and *pretend*. Look at us! We're big time! We're playing the National Champions! Sure, they're deeper than us, they've got scholarships going six players deep at every position. And sure, they're more talented than us, they've got the Heisman trophy winner from last year returning at quarterback, and the hands-down favorite for this year at running back, plus the NCAA's most crushing front line on defense. But if we can just get a few stops…if Grady can get free on the outside couple times…if Rice can get open across the middle…if the line can give Lewis enough time in the pocket…if, if, if, if. If we can pull off an upset of the defending National Champions, then who knows? A BCS bowl appearance, more scholarship money, more attention from the next recruiting class—no more of this scraping around for junior college charity cases—more respect from the NFL—no more sending out players to Europe and Canada, if only someone would just give them an honest *look* in the NFL, Hawaiʻi just doesn't get enough *attention*, enough *respect*…

USC. By 3:00 the USC alumni booster tent is wall-to-wall with rust-colored polo shirts and baby boomer silicone and just-graduated midriffs and yards and yards of blonde hair. Big as a circus tent, it covers the entire Kamehameha parking lot less than a hundred yards from the stadium. And not just the tent—soon they're everywhere, the USC crowd, outnumbering Warrior Nation on their own home ground, most of the Hawaiʻi fans still at work on this Thursday afternoon, and let's just get it on pay-per-view and invite a few of the boyz over, forget about trying to get through that parking lot known as the H-1 freeway to frikken Aloha Stadium right in the middle of rush hour, lucky if you leave work and get there by the second quarter.

No, other than way out there across Hālawa stream (stream? it's a *dust*bowl), where the I-wen'-take-vacation-today state workers and the this-is-my-weekend service industry slaves are busy drawing up Coach Brock's plays for the first three quarters and arguing the best way to contain the explosive Trojan offense—other than them, it's all Barbie Baywatch breasts and muscle shirts, Greek brush-head helmets and white off-the-bare-shoulder replica jerseys. It's all, Hey Bro! and Oh-my-God!, Seth-and-Ashley all speaking in i-*talics*: the game starts at *six*, okay? And there's already so many *people* here, and they're all people you *know*, ohmyGod this place is so-o-o-o *Orange County*.

Sure, the odd pockets of local went-to-UH-anyway-trust-fundies toss their green footballs within legitimate walking distance of the stadium, plus that long line of Nā Koa third-tier power brokers and their families, Hawaiian Tel and Oceanic Cable and Chevron middle administrators, along with a few retired DOE principals and Assistant Superintendents of this-or-that, and other season ticket holders lined up along the stadium's coveted shady freeway side, plus the roped-off corporate sponsor areas flanking the main entrance: a live Jawaiian band, hot-looking Pearlridge beer girls in short shorts, catered food, full bar.

But even there within the ropes, *that* crowd is half Trojan too, transplanted *local* Trojan, Kam School went-to-USC-and-never-came-back Hawaiians-in-exile, taking advantage of the game for a rare trip home *junket*.

A junket. From Wednesday to Sunday, if not the entire week, more Hawai'i Chic California haoles parade up and down the sidewalks and clog the beach at Waikiki than that weekend years back when the Pearl Jam concert coincided with the Honolulu Marathon. Hey bro, we're going to *Hawai'i*. We got ourselves a room at the Makani Kai To*wer*, we are *so* gonna park ourselves next to the infinity pool and sip on an *umbrella drink*, dude. *Shaka*, my friend. I'm *so* looking forward to this? We're gonna make a long weekend out of it, *fly* over to Hawai'i, catch a few waves in Waikiki, take in a Trojans game.

And that's just the players.

In fact, the only reason USC agreed to the non-conference matchup in the first place was because it fell on the schedule's opening week, so hey, why not reward ourselves for all the hard work we put into training camp? Why not take a little vacation, recharge the batteries before the grind of the real season begins, and throw up an easy win in the process? And what a great opportunity for the alumni, too, for the rest of the fans. It'll be like a home game in paradise. And no, in all honesty it won't entirely be fun in the sun. We'll make sure to work out a few of the remaining kinks in our timing while we're over there. Plus Hawai'i always gives your pass defense a decent workout. And then we'll give the freshmen a taste of the spotlight. It'll be good experience for them.

Hawai'i will get a nationally televised game—free exposure for their tourist industry. Everybody wins.

At 5:00 p.m. Tom Watada sat down to watch the nightly news, broadcast directly from Aloha Stadium, which was how someone like the Reverend would have any idea whatsoever that all of this had been going on for the past five hours. Weary from packing all day, Tom had earlier turned on the TV for background noise while he made his last few trips around the house, and there it was—Game Day! On all four local channels. KHAW even had a helicopter shot of the whole scene that they cut to before each break.

Right now a young-looking Trina Hyde was interviewing a crowd of green-painted local-Japanese frat boys beer-bonging it up out in the afternoon sun, *whoop*s and shouts and waving shakas in the background drowning her out until she signed off with a giggling *back to you*. And wait, that wasn't Trina Hyde. Tom now remembered Trina Hyde had retired from KHAW two or three years ago. Apparently they'd simply rotated in the next telegenic hapa UH communications major to take her place, and damned if you could tell the difference.

The camera cut to other man-in-the-streeters giggling it up with other reveling fans, serious predictions for Warrior success spoken in pidgin-inflected ESPN-ese. And there was the future governor, Arthur Tafai, draped in Ufi Tapusoa's 58 and waving shakas all over the place, a double-digit lead over James Hendrick more than two months ahead of the election. Both would run unopposed in their upcoming primaries, but Hendrick, you could tell, was just going through the motions. From what Tom could tell, he hadn't even shown up for the game, let alone hired one of those 18-wheelers with his name emblazoned on the trailer in eight-foot block letters to circle the stadium like Tafai had done.

Arthur Tafai. He'd sure come a long way since his neighborhood board days only what, three or four years ago. Tom had to give him that much. Astonishing, how quickly the young man had been able to rise. Not even forty yet, set to become only the second youngest governor in Hawai'i history. It would have been strange if it hadn't seemed so… preordained…like he was *anointed*—though not by the old Democratic Machine.

Tom had to smile at that thought. *Democratic Machine.* Ever since the patriarch of the party passed away last year—the old U.S. Senator whom Tom had come up against more than once in his various anti-development crusades—once they lost him, the whole party had basically gone into chaos. Tom had seen it happen before his eyes. He'd walk through the atrium at the State Capitol and suddenly realize how utterly vulnerable Hawai'i was way out here in the Pacific, with its power flowing through the kind of wide-open democratic institutions where waving a shaka and a sign could get anyone elected, where lobbyists and other special interests could basically have their way. He'd even begun to think that maybe Hawai'i would have been better off as a dictatorship, with some benevolent despot in charge to keep the troops in line, put up a united front. Up until a year ago, now that he thought about it, the senior U.S. senator had been that despot.

Not that Tom was so naïve as to forget that yes, there was larceny in every heart—or at least some self-interest—and that in such a small state, in the world's largest small town, where everyone wen' grad with somebody else's cousin, Hawai'i had seen (or more accurately, *not* seen) more than its fair share of unsavory compromises as the whole thing inched forward over the years. He knew the idea of a dictatorship was completely antithetical to his own value system. But even when there was out-and-out corruption, at least it had been *our* corruption. That is, the money had stayed here regardless.

And when you looked at it from the standpoint that the senator—despite how he'd let the military run rampant, or sold out the summit of Mauna Kea, or destroyed UH by perpetually staffing its executive offices (behind the scenes, of course) with a parade of dim mainland rejects so utterly mediocre that they were guaranteed to say "yes" to whatever he asked—when you thought of the alternative had he *not* been there, you could almost argue that in many ways he had *protected* the islands from being totally overrun by outsiders.

Ah, well. If you knew what to look for, a glance at the TV would tell you that the alternative had arrived. How else could you explain how someone like Arthur Tafai could wind up in that Tapusoa jersey, being interviewed by some Trina Hyde clone as though his election were a foregone conclusion? Ex-military himself. Born and raised in Lā'ie. BYUH, and then a law degree from Provo. A two-year mission in China. Then he goes straight from the neighborhood board to the state senate before resigning to run for governor? It sounded like a miracle.

But Tom knew better. He had known since the late 1990s, back when the social cause that had filled most of his calendar was the referendum on legalizing same-sex marriage. 1998. Hawaiʻi had been all set to become the most progressive state in the country, more than a decade before other states began to see that withholding basic rights from homosexuals equated with the racist Jim Crow laws of America's dark and shameful past. But then something happened: a "coalition" of religious groups banded together, the airwaves were flooded with "traditional family" messages to "protect" marriage, the streets filled with sign wavers—the whole shebang.

Combined with the voting-for-the-first-time-in-my-life local-boy homophobe brigade that charged the polls that year, they'd been able to defeat the referendum soundly. It later came out—documented through emails and other correspondence—that the religious "coalition" was nothing more than a front group for…the Church of Jesus Christ of Latter Day Saints…in Utah.

So there you had Arthur Tafai. And there you had Russell Lee's legalized gambling bill going down in flames at the last minute, trounced by a vote of fifteen to nine, as it turned out, leaving only two states in the entire country free of any sort of gambling: Hawaiʻi, and…Utah. Tom had heard the theories about "payoffs" this, and "Mormon conspiracy" that, how ruthlessly the LDS church could operate. He'd seen the evidence.

One story floating around was that the Lāʻie development's main selling point to its intended customer base—retired middle-class Provo baby boomers—was that Hawaiʻi was just like Provo Utah in the most important moral and spiritual ways, and that to even have scratch-ticket lottery cards for sale in Waikiki, let alone a world-class resort casino only a couple of miles away, would destroy all of Hawaiʻi's Mormon-friendly purity. In other words, just like the tax-exempt Polynesian Cultural Center and a number of other things, the economic concern was being cast in moral terms.

But rather than some kind of sinister conspiracy, to Tom's way of thinking, the death of Russell Lee's gambling bill really looked more like old-fashioned political lobbying. Lobbying of *Democrats*, no less, all of whom in past years would have been right on board with whatever they'd been told from above. And while Tom had been surprised to learn how deeply what one scholar called *The Mormon Corporate Empire* extended into everyday American life—really, these smiling delighted-to-be-here folks projected a wholesome image that was about as street-smart as Ward and June Cleaver—to him it seemed to come down to how well the Mormons had been able to work what was essentially a leaderless, rudderless State Capitol, thanks to their own…benevolent dictatorship. From the tithing on down to the family mealtimes, from the Sunday services all the way into work the next day, when you were Mormon, you were *Mormon*, a creature of a common belief system, a soldier for the cause. The result appeared to be one of the more disciplined and tightly organized top-down *corporate* and *political* structures Tom had ever encountered. Just look at Tapusoa's funeral. The Mormons got things right.

It wasn't that Tom wanted to judge anyone for the nature of their relationship with God, either—particularly when there in fact *was* a relationship with God, when the object of worship wasn't…football… wasn't the gospel spilling forth from that fan-favorite quarterback there on the screen, the one who'd graduated from St. Martin's decades ago and set a couple of NCAA passing records and then lasted just three minutes at an NFL training camp.

No, the larger point about the Mormons was that a well-financed major legislative initiative—presumably one with all the votes lined up and then some, otherwise Russell Lee would never have missed the vote himself—was that the gambling bill could be so soundly defeated, at the last minute, all the way from…Utah.

Even more to the point: unlike the same-sex marriage issue of the '90s, the losing player in this particular battle had been fighting all the way from…China. Russell Lee, Charles Uchida, Sean Hayashi or Alan Ho or whoever it was, even Nakayama—Tom had to wonder if those little pawns had any idea how little power they actually had anymore.

Certainly Russell Lee must have come to see it by now. It had smacked him like a two-by-four, killing his unofficial run for governor in the process. After the floor vote Russell had immediately disappeared from the radar. Finished before he started. Some thoughtful investigative reporter might have tracked him down to ask him about it all, but no one had—and here they were blabbering away the first half of the evening news on the story of a football game whose result had long since been decided. The last Tom had heard, Russ and his family had moved back to Kahaluʻu, something about his father's land, which his sister had been on the verge of selling before moving to Seattle for her new husband's work.

Now twenty minutes into the usual half-hour newscast, and they finally cut back to the studio to dispatch with the non-football items. The cheerful good-boy hapa face of Kai Milquetoast filled the screen, his sleeves rolled up in Hard Working Journalist mode. He was holding down the fort back at KHAW, seated in front of a faux-newsroom set-up.

After some wish-I-could-be-there-too banter with the anchors at the stadium, he quickly recited the police blotter: another break-in in Portlock, a pedestrian traffic fatality in Kaimuki, four San Francisco residents with suspected gang ties arrested in the fatal shooting of a 42-year-old Waimānalo man at a Keʻeaumoku hostess bar, an abandoned infant's body found under a freeway overpass in Waikele, another break-in in Mililani Mauka. And then the court roll: a retired Maui pharmacist found guilty of identity theft, a UH Hilo professor guilty of marijuana possession with intent to distribute, a DOE teacher guilty of marijuana possession, four men from LA acquitted in the Hotel Street shooting of a Kalihi man, a Waiʻanae man convicted of manslaughter resulting from another altercation with a young military family outside the Kapolei Jamba Juice.

The news: a two-minute shot of the groundbreaking ceremony for the new UH West Oʻahu Bradley Zao Center for Hawaiian Studies, the excerpt of a heartfelt chant from the center's newly-hired haole director, Makana Irving-Kekumu, a shot of a short Chinese man in a five thousand dollar suit plunging a polished chrome shovel into a pile of dusty reddish dirt, a brief sound bite from UH President Peter Varner at a podium *first-class-institution*-ing it on what preserving our host culture means for the children of Ha-vai-ee, a gaggle of aging California haole UH administrators looking on solemnly. A cut to an artist's rendering of the building: surprisingly, for some reason it's neo-classical in design, fronted by a wide staircase guarded by four Greek columns. Then the shot of the dog on the standup paddleboard. The weather: sunny, with a chance of Windward and mauka showers.

We'll take you back to the game, right after this!

A slew of ads: the Outback Steakhouse, Ford trucks climbing up rocky mountain cliffs, Budweiser grimy-faced blue-collar *guys*, and another campaign spot for Arthur Tafai. Here's former Staff Sergeant Tafai, saluting the flag in support of military families. There's Family Man Tafai, dropping off all five of his keiki at Lāʻie Elementary and promising to focus on reforming the Department of Education for Hawaiʻi's future. Here's Foreman Tafai in his yellow hard hat touring the construction site for a thousand homes at Malaekahana, grateful his children (and yours, my *local* bradda) will never have to leave their birthplace. A big local-boy handshake with a smiling working man Tom recognizes right away: Bud Souza, from Hauʻula.

There's Problem Solver Tafai, seated at the head of a conference table earnestly overseeing…looked like the BYUH president, and a couple of the others from the Mormon bank and the Polynesian Cultural Center, they're deep into what's supposed to look like some kind of win-win with…the Chinese…and the voiceover speaks of *international partnerships*. Finally the fade-out shot: Tafai stands with his wife and five kids in soft-tinted dusk before a tinted green mountain backdrop, a pinkish-purple sky and fluffy clouds creating a halo-like glow behind him, *Tafai: for a stronger Hawaiʻi*.

When the broadcast finally returned to Aloha Stadium, the happy banter and the speculation continued, the man-on-the-streets interviews out in Lower Hālawa having increased in their *whoop!-whoop!-au-riight!* Volume. The interviews nearer to the stadium had begun to search out all the B-list Hollywooders milling around near the drop-off area out front, taxis, polished black hired SUVs, and even a line of tour busses now arriving from Waikiki. Noise, noise, and more noise, and thank God for the *mute* button, and let's see—have I forgotten anything?

Tom had never been all that organized, both his house and the church office filled with the boxes and boxes of scattered papers that, now that he thought about it, defined his whole life: copies of the EIS for Dolphin Bay…statements from the banana farmers in the path of H-3… old *Hawaiʻi Observer* clippings chronicling the Waiāhole/Waikāne Valley housing development fight…conservation reports for the planned golf courses in Waikāne…the Master Plan detailing the golf course plans and the planned hotel fronting Waiāhole Beach Park… gallons-per-minute measures and statistics from the fight to bring the water back to the Windward side...the fight for the homeless...the fight against the crystal meth problem. It was all in there somewhere, jammed now into all those cardboard boxes against the back wall: the whole story of what a man could accomplish in one lifetime, all the little victories he'd been able to notch along the way, every one of them against an opponent ten times his size. "Gideon," was how one of the older silver-haired local-Japanese ladies in Tom's church had once referred to him. Gideon, one of those brave champions called by God to raise an army against the Philistines.

Oh, but those boxes, stacked all the way to the ceiling—just looking at them exhausted him. At one time not too long ago, Tom had thought he'd keep going forever, facing the next challenge, fighting the next fight, raising the next army.

But now?

Well, it wasn't just that he was tired—he was tired of *being* tired. Already halfway into that blink-of-an-eye decade of his seventies, he had finally begun to understand what Moses, what Martin Luther King, were saying in their mountaintop speeches: Believe in the indefinite future, because *that* much is assured. As for the current struggle, I may not get there *with* you, but I have done *my part* in preserving things in *my lifetime*. God will have to raise up others to continue the fight.

And sure, the Dolphin Bay expansion was on hold again, but what did that mean? The fight would go on anyway. The fight against the Mormon church in Utah. Against the Chinese, now arriving in wave after wave, following in the wake of Bradley Zao, who surprisingly hadn't pulled up stakes after the initial defeat of Russell Lee's gambling bill. The days of the shakedown were long gone—payoffs like Makana's building, well...it didn't take a genius to see that someone like that Sean Hayashi character had probably engineered that entire deal, and had likely taken a nice healthy cut out of it. But who was Hayashi kidding? The money for that building amounted to about half the cost of the corporate jet that had flown Bradley Zao in for the ceremony. And then here's Zao "falling in love" with Hawai'i, here for the "long term." The place, Zao had learned, was much more than just an investment opportunity—so much more that he'd recently purchased the Diamond Head estate once belonging to Akio Morita, the founder of Sony.

Yes, someone else would have to fight them...someone else...

And those boxes—the sight of them also reminded Tom that he had indeed forgotten something. None of it would do him any good up in Sacramento, where he had finally decided to live out his retirement near his sister and her family. So the folks at the new Waiāhole Learning Center had agreed to come and cart all the boxes off before the movers came on Monday.

They were going to set up some kind of summer program for WCC students to start archiving what essentially amounted to this history of Hawai'i's anti-development struggle. And while Tom had been honored by the request—and what a great way not just to preserve the historical record, but also to start immersing these local kids in the history of their community—with all the loose ends he'd had to tie up in the past couple of weeks, he'd just never gotten around to stopping by and dropping off a key to the house.

He looked at his watch: plenty of time to drive over there. Plus it would be a good chance to take care of something else Tom had been putting off since…since back at the end of April, really. Over four months ago, when he'd made his final decision to move. It would be a good chance to say goodbye to Ikaika.

He went out to his car and started it up, fumbling to silence the blare of the radio, where some announcer was talking about a 7-0 "hole" for the Warriors to "dig themselves out of" just fourteen seconds into the game.

Down toward Kāne'ohe Bay, north on the highway, left on Waiāhole Valley road, which, as always, was a passage back through time. In an instant Tom could recall the protests of the '70s, the golf course battles, then the fear that someone would cover the valley with McMansions just at the turn of the millennium. Many of the weathered signs from that campaign still hung proudly in the yards of the graying veterans of all of those battles: *We will fight greedy developers to the end!* Old, the signs were, and for a moment Tom wondered if any of the kids at the Learning Center really had any idea what these valley residents had *done* back in the '70s, that stopping such tremendously moneyed forces amounted to far more than T-shirts and bumper stickers, Facebook and Twitter, that people had risked their *very lives* for these valleys when they'd burned their eviction notices, or stood in the way of the Child Protective Services workers there to haul their children into foster care.

Maybe after they began sifting through Tom's boxes, Ikaika's students would be able to tell the rest of Hawai'i that *protest* was far more than just some kind of fashion, and oh what a lousy job our generation has done raising our children, Tom thought in that moment, sending them to Punahou and 'Iolani to get the best educations, so they could go to Yale, so they could get the best jobs, so that they could take care of…themselves. The Puritans actually had an important truth, Tom decided: affluence is not good for human values.

There was Aunty Maile's old house, sagging on its foundation, a fading *No Fake Farms!* sign out front. Tom wondered if at some point in the past four months—and had it really been that long?— if Aunty Maile had bothered to speak to Ikaika at all. Given what had happened, he wouldn't have been surprised to have seen her chant out a curse upon him right there at the Burial Council meeting—and yet the shattered look of disappointment covering her face that day had probably done more to hurt the man than any curse could have. Maybe she'd never be able to let it go.

On up past what was left of the withering papaya fields, left at the fork and down into thickening jungle, Tom's tires splashed in the wet mud as he turned down the familiar road to Ikaika's. The jungle thickened, almost dark now in the soft evening twilight.

Whenever he drove up here it was always hard to imagine that someone had once hoped to cover it all with suburban homes jammed together on tiny postage-stamp lots, especially when you came upon Ikaika's rough-looking camp…except today…this wasn't exactly rough-looking….and had he turned up the wrong driveway?

For just a second he thought so, when the drive opened up into a generous parking area newly paved with reddish volcanic cinder, where a brand new black F-150 sat alone. And up ahead…the house.

It was indeed a house, there in the place of the perpetually-under-repair dwelling Tom had visited so many times over the years. One wall looked to be neatly constructed entirely of…discarded hotel room doors? Another was made of…intricately fit-together hotel room headboards. But instead of that thrown-together look of Ikaika's old place, it looked *polished*, even the wall of doors, cut with brand new energy-saver windows. A skylight peeked through the brand new roof. And of course. Meg's company must have renovated the entire place. Probably did the inside, too. Probably gave it all the nice touches. From the concrete pillars up to the shining black solar panels, it was all green technology and conspicuously recycled wood. That barbecue pit over there and the patio that surrounded it were probably made from old fire bricks rescued from some abandoned sugar factory, too. All together the whole job had to have cost a fortune.

Finding no one home, Tom scattered a little flock of clucking chickens and walked out along the narrow road through another green jungle tunnel thick with vegetation, his feet crunching on the bright new cinder stones. Soon the canopy opened out to that vast green sea of spade-shaped leaves, of Ikaika's reason for living, was the only way to put it. Thousands of leaves, tens of thousands of them swaying gently in the evening breeze. An uninterrupted green apron stretched back into the valley, much farther back than Tom remembered, one, two, three acres. Though the light was fading fast, he could pick out a little bobcat bulldozer parked in thick vegetation way in the back, as if preparing to clear even more of the ancient *loʻi* patches back there next to…the Learning Center…Waiāhole *Halau*.

Just the sight of it all brought home the fact that Tom had neither seen nor spoken to Ikaika in…four months?…because a lot could be accomplished in four months. All this, for instance, had been built, as Tom had heard, with a grant that had suddenly appeared from the Office of Hawaiian Affairs. A traditional thatch-roofed open-walled Hawaiian *hale* the size of a small church, the structure reached up nearly to the height of the surrounding trees. It centered what was looking like a little compound of traditional Hawaiian dwellings back here, three, four, five smaller versions of the same design bordering the waving taro field's edges. Was it dorm space for week-long service learning projects? Or maybe classrooms for the fourth graders from schools up and down the Windward coast. A retreat for visiting anthropology students in the summer.

The whole compound—it had all the makings of a real living, learning laboratory, not to mention a small commercial enterprise: Tom had also heard that Ikaika had contracts to sell his taro to NomFusion and Alfred Hudson's.

No sign of Ikaika out here either—even after a couple of Tom's shouts had echoed out against the wall of jungle—so he headed back and gave the house another try. Another knock at the door went unanswered. So Tom tried the knob, thinking maybe he'd just drop the key off and give Ikaika a call from the airport.

To his surprise, it opened, but right away Tom was hit with a powerful rank stench, a hot human stench that registered all too quickly, a mix of urine and stale beer and—could it be?—a fecal smell straight out of an outhouse.

He called out: "Ikaika?"

Silence.

He reached around and found a bank of light switches and lit up the driveway, and then the living room, the sudden brightness sending two cats mad-dashing past his feet and out the door. There was the polished koa coffee table, the leather sofa, the koa book case, the area rug. But the walls...bare of pictures or hangings of any kind, and...the *smell*...and look at the polished hardwood floor gleaming all around with bits of broken glass, green and brown and clear glass everywhere, trails of it leading this way and that, and oh, God, the *smell*, piles of excrement on that polished hardwood floor, a fresh puddle, a...sound?

He could hear a shuffling coming from the second floor, and now a figure gingerly making its way down the stairs.

"Ikaika? Ikaika, is that you?"

Coming closer, though hardly with the bounding weight of such a big man as Ikaika Nāʻimipono.

"Who are you?" Tom called. "Where is Ikaika?"

Down each step, the legs, pale and thin and hung with folds of skin...an open sore...the man completely naked...dangling genitalia in a forest of gray...more and more folds of pale empty skin sagging out around the midsection, hanging from the deflated gray arms...and now his face...the graying hair...a long and untamed beard reaching his shriveled chest. The eyes: sunken behind a face so swollen and aged, Tom could now look straight into them as the man stepped down onto the hardwood floor, not crazed or angry or unstable eyes, but pleading eyes.

Ikaika Nāʻimipono's eyes.

And finally a voice, ancient and labored, it was all the man could do to wind up his remaining strength and croak it out in a tired rasp:

"Reverend."

Pleading, Ikaika Nāʻimipono's eyes. Sure, Tom had not looked into those eyes for months now, and yes, he'd hear whisperings that "Ikaika, he not doing too good," Kanoe Silva having called at one point, Tom was now recalling, to ask him to check on him. And where was Meg? Where were the boys? And had those been *weeds* growing up around the edges of the bobcat tractor out there in Ikaika's taro field?

With much effort Ikaika—indeed it was Ikaika—still laboring to breathe from simply walking down the stairs, he placed a bony hand upon Tom's shoulder.

"Help my people," he said. A deep breath. "You've got to *help my people.*"

Help my people.

In an instant the images again flashed in front of Tom: H-3, the fights for water access, against the golf courses, the withering protest signs nailed to the trees on Waiāhole Valley Road. Tom had *poured his life* into helping Ikaika's people, into helping all local people, into keeping them here, into protecting what was rightfully theirs.

And what had it done? What had it done except to preserve Hawaiʻi as a beautiful place for rich people to come to live.

"Okay, Ikaika," he said. "Okay."

About the Author

Mark Panek was born in New York City. A graduate of Colby College, he has travelled widely, having lived in Maine, New York, Sydney, Honolulu, and Tokyo. This is his third book.